PRAISE FOR
DRACULA OF TRANSYLVA

"Stunning artwork and unforgettable prose. Delgado's book is a must-have for every horror and vampire fan. Its images are seared forever in my head."

—Gary D. Rhodes, Ph.D.,
author of *The Birth of The American Horror Film* and writer-director of *Lugosi: Hollywood's Dracula*

"If you thought Ricardo Delgado was a great dinosaur artist... well, you're right—he is! But with his Dracula *book, Ricardo has outdone himself. He has dramatically risen to a new artistic plateau in a genre and territory previously unassociated with him.* Dracula *will long be remembered as a major marker in Delgado's impressive body of work as a graphic storytelling artist. Bravo, my friend!"*

—William Stout

"Ricardo Delgado breathes new life into the prince of the undead like he has done with every genre he has worked in!"

—Geof Darrow,
creator of *Shaolin Cowboy* and conceptual designer for the *Matrix* films

"Delgado takes us on wild ride in a style reminiscent of the original Dracula *novel!"*

—Dacre Stoker,
co-author of *Dracula the Undead* and *Dracul,* and great-grandnephew of Bram Stoker

DRACULA
OF
TRANSYLVANIA

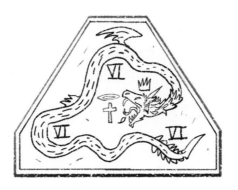

Written and Illustrated by
Ricardo Delgado

Based on the Original Bram Stoker Novel

Writer and Illustrator
Ricardo Delgado

Editor and Book Designer
Robbie Robbins

Publisher
Hank Kanalz

Proofreader
Leslie Manes

Clover Press offices: 8820 Kenamar Dr. #501, San Diego, Ca. 92121

ISBN: 978-1-951038-61-8

First Printing September 2023

4 3 2 1   23 24 25 26

Printed in China

Clover Press:
Matt Ruzicka, President
Robbie Robbins, Vice President/Art Director
Hank Kanalz, Publisher
Ted Adams, Factotum
Mike Ford, Shipping Manager

Clover Press Founders:
Ted Adams, Elaine LaRosa, Nate Murray, Robbie Robbins

www.CloverPress.us

DRACULA
OF
TRANSYLVANIA

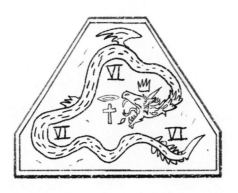

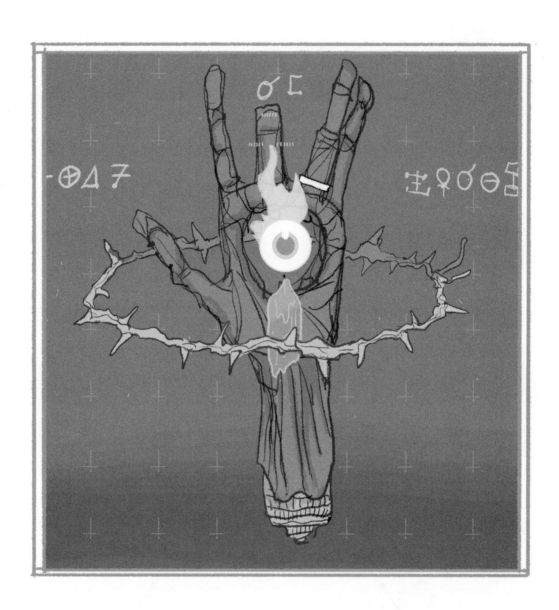

ACKNOWLEDGMENTS

My life is rich with family and love, so this dedication is long, with good intentions.

To my parents, Ricardo and Ana, immigrants to the United States from Costa Rica, who changed the lives of their children and grandchildren. They were the first people to make me believe that this was a worthwhile pursuit. I also thank them for understanding my fascination/obsession with monsters at a very young age. They never told me I had limits in life, and I am forever grateful to them for that.

To my siblings, Vivian, Bob, John and Ralph, who I thank for not getting annoyed with me when I used all of the family haircut clippings to glue to my face one Halloween to fulfill my strange yet prophetic Wolfman makeup wish. I'm glad we're all friends as well as family. For my cousins Minor, Sandra and Willie, much love to you always.

To my nieces and nephews, Christian, Stefanie, Junior, Rebeca, Eric, Soraya, Monica, Karla, Lily, Isabella and Juanito, so that you may all take into your futures the fact that anyone can accomplish anything.

To my siblings-in-law Becky, Alba and Martin. Wish you nothing but the best in life always.

To my extended families both here and in Costa Rica, with much love and appreciation for each and every one of you.

To my amazing, wonderful, incredible kids, Rebeca and Ricky, who make me feel like I have done one thing right in life by having children that are far better human beings than I could ever be. I can never express the depth of my love for you both.

And last but far from least, for my wife Frances, the love of my life, who sank her teeth into my heart in 7th grade, put me under her spell and I have never been the same since, for better or worse. I love you deeply.

May you all live forever.

FOREWORD
by Donald F. Glut

Sherlock Holmes, Tarzan and Count Dracula—what do these names share in common? Yes, they all belong to bigger-than-life characters created by various authors on the printed page. But they are far more than just fictional persons whose lives were limited to novels and short stories.

Since their introduction to literature well over a century ago, the World's Greatest Detective, Lord of the Jungle and King Vampire have all transcended the original stories in which they existed courtesy of authors Arthur Conan Doyle, Edgar Rice Burroughs and Bram Stoker, respectively. They have, in a way, taken on lives of their own; in Dracula's case, a life beyond even undeath, attaining iconic status.

During the decades succeeding the passing of Messrs. Doyle, Burroughs and Stoker, Dracula et al. have provided source material for a seemingly endless parade of new novels, short stories, stage plays, motion pictures, radio and television shows, comic books, music, toys and other merchandise. These characters now belong to the world and, to the present day, remain fair game to new interpretations and presentations concocted by other authors and artists.

Enter Ricardo Delgado, a well-known concept designer for major motion pictures and television shows, but also the author-artist of the present work.

Ricardo and Philip José Farmer also have something in common. The late Farmer was a famous and prolific author, mostly of science fiction stories. Not only did Farmer pen original pastiches not-so-loosely based upon Tarzan and Doc Savage, he also recognized and wrote about the iconic natures of characters like the Ape Man, The Shadow, Scarlet Pimpernel, Clark Savage, Jr., and many others, explaining in detail how their histories interconnected and involved much more than their creators revealed—indeed, even knew themselves—in their canon tales. Farmer enjoyed authoring meticulously researched tomes (e.g., *Tarzan Alive*) explaining how such famous and infamous literary characters as the Spider, Dr. Fu Manchu, Professors Moriarty and Challenger, and myriad other colorful heroes and villains coexisted over time in the same universe and related to one another, oftentimes by blood lineage.

Farmer's contemporary successor may very well be Ricardo Delgado.

Ricardo and I have been good friends since about 1993. I met Ricardo for the first time shortly after Dark Horse Comics began publication that year of his *Age of Reptiles*, an epic graphic series, set during the Mesozoic era, that he both wrote and illustrated. I knew from those comic books that Ricardo was a masterful artist and that, although the series was primarily a visual work, he knew how to tell a good and rousing story.

Age of Reptiles would evolve into what was, or so it seemed at the time, destined to become Ricardo's best-known popular work—his magnum opus, perhaps even becoming his legacy. However, that status was to change, thanks to an evil, sanguinary immortal from Transylvania, whom Bram Stoker loosely based upon the historical 15th century tyrant, warrior and sadist Vlad Tepes... aka Vlad the Impaler... aka Vlad Drakula or Dracula.

Meeting Ricardo, I learned that the two of us had much in common. Besides things prehistoric, we both loved classic monsters, sharing a particular fondness for the old *Dracula* and *Frankenstein* movies made years ago by Universal Pictures and Hammer Films, but also upon their literary inspirations, the original novels penned by Bram Stoker and Mary Wollstonecraft Shelley. Regarding the subject of this book, there have been numerous portrayals of the Lord of Vampires over the years, but Ricardo and I were partial to both the elegance and urbanity of Bela Lugosi's interpretation, also the physical strength and ferocity of Christopher Lee's (especially in his debut outing *The Horror of Dracula*). We were both also impressed by the personified-evil interpretation of the character in

Marvel's long-running *Tomb of Dracula* comic book series, as scripted by Marv Wolfman and illustrated by Gene Colan.

Ricardo Delgado has been fascinated by Dracula since early childhood. Like Farmer with Tarzan, et al., he long suspected that there was a bigger—a far richer, more expansive and encompassing—history of the Count than revealed by Stoker in his 1897 novel. That greater story was one that Ricardo long wanted to invent and tell—in his own way, reimagining characters (e.g., Renfield, Jonathan Harker, but mostly Dracula himself), their motivations and relationships to each other, and also the events as described by the original novel's author. Although based on Stoker's character and narrative, Ricardo wanted to tell the "full" and "true" story of the King Vampire, a tale that, until now, only he knew, being locked inside his mind.

According to Ricardo's thesis, Stoker just scratched the surface with his novel, leaving the basic theme and storyline wide open and just waiting for some successor to embellish, expand upon and reinterpret. Similar liberties had only recently been taken by the BBC, in its well-received Dracula television mini-series; but Ricardo's reinvention would be far more challenging and on a much larger, even global canvas. Not just injecting Stoker's tale with new blood, so to speak, Ricardo's version would, in a sense, reinvent Dracula, giving the character a massive literary transfusion.

Dracula of Transylvania, as Ricardo Delgado would title his vastly more ambitious story, would span not only continents, but cover one and a half millennia (337 to 1899), and include an enormous cast of characters, certainly those from Stoker's work, yet some of them historical (e.g., Emperor Constantine, Jack the Ripper, and of course, Vlad). Attributing Dracula's vampirism as more than merely an evil human being dying and subsequently returning from the grave as an undead blood-sucker, Ricardo, a fan of the movie *The Exorcist*, devised a new demonic origin to the character involving both Constantine and Lilith, an evil female character of Biblical legend. Ricardo would also refine and expand upon Dracula's array of supernatural abilities, such as transforming into a far more formidable version of a vampire bat.

One thing I'd realized from *Age of Reptiles* and getting to know Ricardo personally is that he wasn't a lazy writer or artist; he did his homework and did not "cut corners." Ricardo was adamant at getting details correct. Even when creating fictional scenarios with long-extinct Mesozoic animals, he did his due diligence, getting his facts as accurate as his research materials permitted. Sticking to historical accuracy would also be the case with his Dracula retelling.

Here now, after five years of arduous research, writing, drawing and editing—all in his spare time, when not busy designing some character, vehicle, building or prop for a movie or TV show—is the final product, a passionate story that was inside him and needed to escape, a true labor of love, which to be proud.

In 1950, Bela Lugosi was in England, having just finished starring in the movie *Vampire Over London*. Bela, on board a ship discussing Dracula with British interviewer, stated. "Dracula never ends." How correct Lugosi was—as the Count has turned up in myriad media ever since that Hungarian actor first donned the vampire's black tuxedo and cloak on the New York stage in 1927, four years before starring as the character in the Universal film.

But in the case of this book, Dracula of Transylvania, Ricardo Delgado has accomplished this non-ending on a grand scale. Not only does he not let the King Vampire character "end," Ricardo—in this, a work that promises to supplant *Age of Reptiles* as his magnum opus, indeed even becoming his legacy—has made the story and legend of Dracula an epic.

Donald F. Glut, author, The Dracula Book, True Vampires of History, Frankenstein Meets Dracula *and* Frankenstein and the Evil of Dracula.

I bid you welcome.
—*Bela Lugosi*
Dracula (1931)

So many evils by Satan's prince
will be committed
that almost the entire world
will find itself undone and desolated.
—*Nostrodamus*

Now is the time of night
That the graves, all gaping wide,
Everyone lets forth his sprite
in the church-way paths to glide.
—*William Shakespeare*
A Midsummer Night's Dream

Of all ghosts,
the ghosts of our old loves are the worst.
—*Sir Arthur Conan Doyle*
The Memoirs of Sherlock Holmes

In the struggle for survival,
the fittest win out at the expense of their rivals
because they succeed in adapting themselves best to their environment.
—*Charles Darwin*
The Origin of the Species

The world is a dangerous place to live,
not because of the people who are evil,
but because of the people who don't do anything about it.
—*Albert Einstein*

CONTENTS

PART ONE : THE ANCIENT WORLD

PART TWO : THE MODERN WORLD

EPILOGUES

CODA

PART ONE:
THE ANCIENT WORLD

THE HOLY LAND
32 A.D.

Mark 5

1 And they came over unto the other side of the sea, into the country of the Gadarenes.

2 And when he was come out of the ship, immediately there met him out of the tombs a man with an unclean spirit,

3 Who had his dwelling among the tombs; and no man could bind him, no, not with chains:

4 Because that he had been often bound with fetters and chains, and the chains had been plucked asunder by him, and the fetters broken in pieces: neither could any man tame him.

5 And always, night and day, he was in the mountains, and in the tombs, crying, and cutting himself with stones.

6 But when he saw Jesus afar off, he ran and worshipped him,

7 And cried with a loud voice, and said, What have I to do with thee, Jesus, thou Son of the most high God? I adjure thee by God, that thou torment me not.

8 For he said unto him, Come out of the man, thou unclean spirit.

9 And he asked him, What is thy name? And he answered, saying, My name is Legion: for we are many.

NICOMEDIA[1],
ANCIENT TURKEY
LATE MAY, 333 A.D.

"Has Death come for me at last?"

After a snort and a laugh at his own joke, the tall, barrel-chested, bearded old man settled back into his expansive Roman settee and let his gaze drift to his right, to the west. Beyond the horizon, sprawled between the cleaving Bosphoros Channel, knew the old emperor, lay the city that was given the gift of his name. He smiled as he thought of all those golden sunsets that caressed the city he had helped build, a city where the resplendent Hagia Sophia would not be gifted to the world for another two hundred years[2]. The once-virile conqueror's creased mouth managed a worn, crinkled grin, knowing that he was being provincial but that Constantinopolis sounded much better than Byzantium, Augusta Antonia or New Rome. The name sat well the first time he'd heard it, and even better now at the end of all things.

Outside the elaborate Roman villa, sunrise had begun to glow in the east, like a long, lone watercolor wash of tangerine. A saturated glaze of orange framed Nicomedia, near the eastern corner of the Sea of Marmara. Warm aromas of oils, spices and incense from the city intertwined with the citrus wash in the sky to form the most artistic of ambiances. A few lonely dogs barked in the distance, as if they knew what moved among them. The expansive antique of a metropolis sat in silent anticipation, as if it knew that the moment which the empire would lose its emperor had arrived.

A soft zephyr teased through ornate, violet drapes and brought a coughing fit from the old man. He was dying and knew it, gasping like a fish that had no water pumping through its gills. Running away from the frigid bluster, maroon flower petals danced through the night air and into an open patio. The petals fluttered a bit more to avoid the bed, preferring to end their spirals on spectacular tile floor tile mosaics that depicted an enormous battle and a map of the Ancient World, instead of landing on the body of a dying royal.

The emperor chuckled at the irony, then became angry with himself for stirring his failing lungs. Another violent coughing fit followed, this one like the organs themselves wanted nothing more to do than to leap from of his mouth. Blood and bile actually found open air, and the old man's breath ran ragged until he managed to control the attack on his breathing system. Warm bile streamed over his once-proud beard.

Knowing death was before him, the emperor had tried to make his way back to the eastern

---

[1] Modern day city of Izmit.

[2] One of the most extraordinary places in the world, Hagia Sophia's construction would be completed in 537 AD upon order of Eastern Roman Emperor Justinian. From 537 to 1204, Hagia Sophia served as an Eastern Orthodox place of worship. As a result of the Fourth Crusade (1202-1204) the structure was a Roman Catholic cathedral, before then being turned into a mosque after the Fall of Constantinople in May of 1453. Hagia Sophia is presently a museum.

capital of the Roman Empire, but his body had gradually failed him. Nothing helped Flavius Valerius Aurelius Constintinus Augustus, not the hot baths near Helenopolis[3], nor the elaborate baptism for the man who had helped assemble the Bible and made Christianity in Rome a faith not punishable by death.

The villa was exquisite, with vines like bubbling spring streams that flowed over and along Corinthian columns. Frescoes depicting the romance and violence of Roman conquests lined the walls. The patio's view revealed that the entire city that was at his feet, far enough away to fill a guest with its spectacle yet close enough so that a ruler's gesture could crush it. A plate of figs, olives and grapes sat untouched at his side on a beautiful ceramic plate, itself decorated with painted Roman legions in battle. The emperor was alone on the last night of his life, with the eager whispers of the slaves inside the villa beckoning the embittered royal, knowing they would come to their master's whim at a moment's notice, yet preferring not to be around him. Preferring to let him die. Constantine looked around, eyesight fading like embers of a dying fire. Something stirred in front of him, in the gloom.

Constantine sensed he was not alone.

A shadow writhed against one of the columns, a foreboding sliver of smoke that mingled with the vines. The sliver became a creamy thigh that softened, hardened, then faded away. The sliver moved toward him.

"Non sum morte," hissed the shadow, which became feminine as it neared the old man. *I am not Death.*

The shadow giggled like a woman of the world and continued, each phrase spoken with calculation and interest. "Sed hic erit propter vos ante solis petala florent. Ut foras eius plenissima vita vestra vitae tuae? Nonne omnibus, qui stabat contra te conteret te, stultus vetus?" *But it will be here for you before the sun's petals blossom. Have you lived out your life to its fullest? Did you crush everyone that stood before you, old fool?*

"Ποιος μιλάει για μένα σαν να ήμουν αγρότης ή πόρνη;" said the old man, covered with robes, jewelry and solitude. *Who speaks to me as if I were peasant or prostitute?* He squinted and searched. Before him, a blurred feminine haze of an outline, nothing more.

The smoky shadow glided even closer, into focus, at its own leisure, as if to hypnotize, and the emperor no longer had to squint. Fear rippled over him. The woman was indigo and hypnotic, with cat eyes that glowed of crimson and hate. Bat-like wings twitched behind her obsidian shoulders and a robe that never seemed to end. Short, black, dagger-like horns grew among long, cold locks. Over her skin, hellish tattooed figures undulated, ever-flowing, ever-writhing. Her vicious grin would have made a crocodile shiver.

She was sensual but not human.

Fruit lips parted over rows of shark-like teeth. "Lamia nomine dabatur. Ωστόσο, άλλοι έχουν ψιθύρισε Λεγεώνας στο σκοτάδι της καρδιάς τους." *I was given the name of Lilith. Yet others have whispered Legion in the darkness of their hearts*

"Animam malam!" shouted the man who had strangled nations. *Demoness!* He picked up a primitive, gold crucifix and held it out in front of the intruder with a brittle, trembling hand that used to wield swords and shape continents. "Quid venistis ad me audes, baptizatus Christianum me transiens hora! Dico Oct! Dimitte me in salútem occurram meo pacem!" *How dare you come to me, a baptized Christian, in my hour of passing! Out I say! Let me meet my Deliverer in peace!*

Lilith arched her right eyebrow with contempt and hissed, "Σίγουρα δεν πιστεύω ότι μια τέτοια τέλη του βαπτίσματος θα επηρεάσει την απόφαση για μια ζωή γεμάτη από κακία, κρεοπωλείο

---

[3] Helenopolis was an ancient Greco-Roman/Byzantine town in Asia Minor.

και αιματοχυσία; Δεν έχουν κατακτώντας την τιμή του; Δεν ήταν οι πόλεις παραδοθεί σε εσάς πριν από τις πολιορκητικές μηχανές και πολιορκητικές ήταν στη θέση του?" *Surely you do not think such a late baptismal would sway judgment on a life full of malice, butchery and bloodletting? Does not conquering have its price? Did not the cities surrender to you before the siege engines and battering rams were in place?"*

"Ego sum Imperium Romanum!" roared Constantine, lungs aflame. *I am the Roman Empire!*

"Ego ædificavi civitates, formetur ecclesias, et omnis exercitus velle meo mihi! Fui in concilio Nicaeno expulsi sunt, cum in Arianos, et veritate verbum Dei et in unum document—" *I have built cities, formed churches, had entire armies at my call! I was at the Council of Nicea when the Arians were expelled and the true word of God was formed into one document—*

"Και όμως," snarled Lilith, "εσείς στοίχημα Κατά εδώ να πεθαίνουν μέσα στη μιζέρια και τη μοναξιά! Ούτε καν οι δούλοι θέλουν να είναι κοντά στην εξαιρετική Κωνσταντίνος. καρδιά του καθενός είναι γεμάτο με τίποτα, αλλά κακεντρέχεια για σας!" *And yet you lay here dying in misery and solitude! Not even the slaves want to be near the great Constantine. Everyone's heart is filled with nothing but malice for you!*

Constantine shook his worn, noble head. "Legimus apud occursu cum Sanctissima Trinitate Filius Gergesenorum. Vos dont seducat mecum, siren." *I read of your encounter with the Son of the Holy Trinity in Gadarenes[4]. You do not fool me, temptress.*

Lilith shook her sharp-featured head and laughed. Her words were laced with acidic irony. "Et quid de Crispus et Fausta? Filius tuus et uxorem quid fecit opust? Forsitan misericordia? Executionem!" *And what of Crispus and Fausta? What did your son and wife need? Mercy perhaps? Certainly not execution!*

Her words stung Constantine like a wasp. He put the cross down. "Έχουν βλασφημείται! αμαρτίες τους ήσαν ασυγχώρητο!" *They blasphemed! Their sins were unforgivable!*

"Περισσότερα Χαριστικό από ό έχοντας τους σκότωναν?" Lilith's giggle was a scythe, and it cleaved his heart. *More forgivable than having them killed?*

She slid ever closer.

Constantine held the cross in his fist like a broken toy. "Et-et nihil postulo ex te—" *I-I need nothing from you—*

"At vero dissentio, imperatori," danced Lilith's forked tongue. The Babylonian robe fluttered in the breeze, covering her like a jealous lover. "Χρειάζεστε εμένα πάρα πολύ." *Oh, but I disagree, my Emperor, you need me very much.*

"Να φύγει ζωύφια!" he gurgled, full of conviction that was laced with regret. "Ας θάνατό μου να είναι ένα ειρηνική." *Be gone, vermin! Let my death be a peaceful one.*

"Constantinus, Imperatore Romae Magna," Lilith's eyes burned with the happiness of evil, "Instrue te pro incidunt in magno hiatu portae Inferorum, quibus Lucifer dominatur maritum caderent habuisse angelos peccatores." *Constantine, Great Emperor of Rome[5], prepare yourself for the fall into the great, yawning gates of Hell, where Lucifer, my husband, rules over the fallen angels.*

All around the demoness, the morning stretched wider. The hour of magic, those innocent, sinful moments at dusk and dawn where anything was possible made the air fertile with anticipation and dread. Closer still, Lilith plucked a grape and popped it into her mouth in a playful, feminine, powerful way. She giggled at Constantine the way women laugh when they have humiliated a man.

---

[4] Biblical gospels Mark 5:1-9, and Luke 8:26-39.

[5] Constantine the Great 272-337 AD was a Roman Emperor primarily known for introducing Christianity to Rome and helping to arrange the Council of Nicea, which then assembled the known contents of the Christian Bible.

Constantine's eyes shut in fear and denial. The gnarled emperor looked away, covering his face. He squeezed the cross under his bony knuckles like a last hope, gathering himself until the old man could at last look back at her and shout, "Serpente Evae iacet! Ego Imperet tibi, res vilissima de nocte! Ego baptismum recepit tempore ab Eusebio Nicomediae se!" *Lies from the serpent of Eve! I rebuke you, vile thing of the night! I have received baptism by Eusebius of Nicomedia[6] himself!*

"Dei est per stultum. Sed etiam Eius reus corde nec ignoscet a vita de sanguine peccati, et homicidium." Lilith's words were lances into Constantine's soul. *God is a fool, but even His guilty heart will not forgive a life of blood, and sin, and murder.*

She saved her sharpest lance for last. "Η καρδιά σας δεν ήταν εξαρτά από τα δάκρυα Crispus! Έκανε ο γιος σας δεν επαιτούν για έλεος?" *Your heart was not swayed by Crispus' tears! Did your son not beg you for mercy?*

The Emperor was silent in front of the truth.

His firm grip on the cross began to melt.

She froze, a predator girding to pounce.

The air throbbed with tension and the golden beauty of the oncoming dawn.

"Ego potest moram tuus inevitabilitatis." Lilith's purr was full of venom. *I can delay your inevitability.*

"Silentium a tuum furcatum lingua!" shouted Constantine, trying to gather his strength in the face of liquid sin. *Silence from your forked tongue!*

Then Constantine's throat closed around him, as if an invisible force was strangling him, but it was merely his life slowly draining away. After a long fit of coughs, his eyes begged for an answer.

"Offero solum veritatem et vitam," she leaned back and laughed. *I offer only the truth, and the life[7].*

"Nullus enim tuorum Daemonum dolis!" spat the Emperor, but she could hear the waver in his voice. *None of your demon's tricks!*

Constantine gasped for air, convulsed, nearly vomited, then went on. "Legi scriptis Apostolorum. Tua impius dominus posuit extra civitates et thesauris ante Sanctus filius et expecta eum ut tentaretur—" *I read the words of the Apostles. Your vile master laid out cities and treasures before the Holy Son and expected him to be tempted[8]—"*

"Ego potest auxilium vobis vivet innumeris dies et noctes," Lilith mused, eyes glinting with seduction, "Si solum te dicere verbo, Et ecce sanavi te.' Θα κάνατε για άλλη μια φορά γίνομαι μεγαλείου αυτό κάθε αυτό, Κωνσταντίνο Κωνσταντινουπόλεως."

I can help you live for countless days and nights. If only you say the word, I will heal you[9]. You would once more be greatness itself, Constantine of Constantinople.

"Vos praedetur in animam meam, blasphemus," said Constantine. *You prey on my soul, blasphemer.*

"Vos interemistis tua filius et tua uxorem." *You executed your son and wife.*

His head turned in shame, eyes shut with guilt, Constantine the Great wept in silence.

"Ego servabo vos ab inferno," she cooed. *I can keep you from Hell.*

In the distance, somewhere in the city, a child's morning cry for the comfort of his mother reverberated throughout the worn streets and sacred temples.

Constantine lay there, with the weight of a thousand conquests and sins on his brow, which was

---

[6] Eusebius of Nicomedia (died aprox 341 AD) was the bishop who baptized Emperor Constantine.

[7] Lilith is mocking the biblical words of Jesus, from John 14:6, "I am the way, the truth, and the life."

[8] A reference to the Temptation of Jesus, as described in the biblical Gospels of Mark, Matthew and Luke.

[9] Another biblical quotation, Mathew 8.8: "But just say the word, and my servant shall be healed."

cradled by old, soft hands that held shields but never worked a day in their life. His eyes at last found their conclusion, and then sought hers.

He released the cross, and it fell, clattering against the mosaic that depicted his victory at the Battle of the Milvian Bridge[10].

"Quo modo?" he whispered at last. *How?*

Lilith chuckled before she struck like a viper, leaping in a blur onto the fragile old tyrant. They tumbled off the settee like bricks off a sagging wall. Lilith pinned the old man under her like a lioness upon a gazelle, her mouth clamped over Constantine's aging, ragged neck. Her languid, muscular leg kicked the cross away, into the recess of the night.

She snarled like a tiger before she gulped, drinking in his blood.

"Micericordia," he whispered. *Mercy.*

A hiss of a woman's giggle, amid the drinking.

Silence.

A series of deep, long, quenching swallows.

Constantine's fragile old arm, frozen with fingers reaching for the skies, twitched.

Wafting in the distance, a single church bell rang out over the ancient city.

And she sucked from his neck even more.

A ribbon of blood serpentined out of Lilith's mouth as she supped, and the Emperor of the Ancient World grew paler and paler. Constantine trembled, the coldness of death dancing through him. She writhed over him, in heat. Night moved again, pushed by day, eager to see. The demoness' complexion darkened, swollen with blood like the engorged abdomen of a mosquito.

Moments staggered by.

He kicked like a dying goat, and she pressed against the old man like a constricting python. More petals danced over them, blessing and condemning his unholy choice.

At last, satiated, she slid off of Constantine, who lay there in a silent, open-mouthed scream that could have held the collective morning prayers of Christendom. Lilith beamed in triumph as she took one of the long fingernails of her right hand and slid it over her left palm. She slit herself, then raised her left hand in a fist, and let the blood from her open wound drip down into Constantine's silent agony.

As the dawn reached out to embrace them, the crocodile grin returned as Lilith whispered, "*In nomine dei nostri pater Satanas.*"

"Vos sunt mea," leered Lilith to the corpse of Flavius Valerius Aurelius Constantinus Augustus. *You are mine.*

Stillness.

Dawn, drinking of the night, sun rays supping of the stars and the planets.

Children, satiated.

Dogs, barking.

Prayers, answered.

Then the corpse of Constantine snapped back to life like a fish that had been thrown back into the sea. As if in a seizure, the old man swung his withered arms around and knocked over the plate of grapes, shattering it on the mosaic of the conquering army. Constantine coughed, then realized his lungs no longer held pain that seared him, just air and a reprieve.

---

[10] The Battle of the Milvian Bridge, between the forces of rival Roman Emperors Constantine I and Maxentius occurred in Rome in October 312 AD. According to chroniclers, Constantine witnessed a cross of light in the sky. That victory was the beginning of Constantine's conversion to Christianity, and the Arch of Constantine in Rome was subsequently built and dedicated in honor of that victory. Maxentius died during the battle. His body was found and beheaded.

Sounds, stirrings from inside the villa.

Moments passed, weighted with petals.

Flavius Valerius Aurelius Constintinus Augustus trembled to his feet. He was no longer dead.

No longer a corpse.

Yet not alive.

He was *undead*.

Hearing the clatter, slaves charged out from the other rooms, full of concern that their emperor was dead and fear that they might be put to death for their neglect. They found nothing but a broken plate littered with grapes, an empty reclining couch and a small golden cross hiding in a corner of the patio like a lost child. The painted Roman legion, broken into pieces.

Another bitter breeze blew by, then left them. The servants looked out into the widening dawn.

Two shapes moved.

One was a shadow that swept toward the city.

The other, flying away from the dawn, was a man-sized bat.

WALLACHIA,
EASTERN EUROPE
DECEMBER 999 A.D.

Dark things danced in the night.

They writhed around a huge, roaring bonfire to a deep, resonating drumbeat. Some of them had goat heads on human bodies, others looked like medieval gargoyles with knobby heads, ape-like torsos and lizard tails. Some had hooves and padded paws like deer and wolves, while others had clawed feet like birds of prey or lizards. A few had horns on their head and bat wings on their shoulders. Yet others had evil runes carved all over their animal-like bodies. They all howled, mewled, screamed, roared and bellowed in unholy celebration and insanity.

Evening air was ripe with sin.

Some of the demons were nearly human, looking like characters out of a Renaissance painting with pale bodies and darkened wings. Among the undulation of these imps, goblins, fiends and evil spirits stood the demoness Lilith, unchanged after six hundred and sixty years.

Among the unholy celebration, she watched the enormous bonfire, hypnotized, glowing eyes aflame with intensity and anticipation. She was a nubile, feminine figure in a torrent of hideous frenzy, as if she knew her moment of fate had arrived, watching the dancers with distant interest. The others undulated and frothed maniacally around the expanse of wood and flame, which cast gigantic shadows into the impenetrable, towering trees in the deep, black forest that tried to reach up and snatch the last moon of the millennium right out of the night sky.

Outside the ring of demons were ravens, rats, snakes, owls, roosters, goats, horses, dogs and cats that fluttered, slithered, jumped, flitted, hopped, pranced, and flew in a perverse, exuberant *bacchanal* in a scene right out of a medieval wood-cut. The screams, wails, barks, roars and shrieks of the creatures, both natural and supernatural, pierced the cloak of the night like swords through wool. The air reeked of sulfur, defecation and burnt flesh. Rotting, deformed human skeletons, animated in movement yet without soul, pounded on hollowed-out logs in perverse synchronicity, producing an ear-shattering, orgiastic rhythm.

Massive logs encompassed the mound of wood, and the pile of dead, burning trees yawned forty feet tall as the firestorm roared through it. Huge, deformed black candles smoldered in five different corners that radiated from the bonfire, with burning fat on the ground forming a flaming pentagram for anyone in Heaven to dare witness. Tiny bones of human infants drifted inside the candlewax. Sparks ran from the bonfire's frenzy, tiny incandescent flowers in the black, bleak night that drifted among the supernatural celebrants like wicked blessings.

In front of the bonfire was an enormous rock slab, black and evil, and tied to it with ropes made of thorny branches and animal skins, was a terrified human being. A young, raven-haired woman from a nearby village, the victim wailed in terror at the density of evil around her. In front of the victim was a lone figure draped in a black shroud. The thing stood very still, twitching occasionally like a corpse.

Clawed, wrinkled, pale hands reached up like they had all of the time in the world and pulled back the hood of the shroud, revealing the pale, taunt face of Flavius Valerius Aurelius Constintinus Augustus, all these centuries later. Time had taken its tribute from the old emperor, sagging his face even further into a hideous, desiccated visage. Eyes that had seen the fall of Rome were milky white with vigor and hate, except for piercing ebony pupils. Lips that had once contorted with deception were now black and framed yellow, razor-sharp canines. Constantine's beard now stretched out like a sea of thorns. Horrid patches of skin of different shades of grey and textures wrapped him like a piece of rotted, cadaverous fruit. He wore an ornate robe of pure ebony silk with intricate patterns that somehow morbidly combined medieval Spain with Ancient Rome.

The fallen emperor's clawed right hand extended over the perverse celebrants as he shouted, "Benedic nos Pater Satanas, tuis fidelis servus!" *Bless us Father Satan, your most loyal servants*!

An insane roar bellowed forth from animal and demon alike. The chanting grew in its depth and chorus. The forest bled evil.

"Ave Satanas!" screamed the demons. *Hail Satan*!

"Ave Satanas," shrieked the things of the night.

"Oramus," roared Constantine. *We pray.*

Silence slammed over the ceremony. After a moment engorged with insane stillness, the emperor then raised his arms and shouted, "Scelesti patri sic fiat sacrificium de hoc pura animam dignus vos!" *Unholy father may the sacrifice of this pure soul be worthy of you!*

In Constantine's gnarled, bony hand was a jagged, diabolical knife that looked like it could cleave open the heart of an angel. The young woman took in the blade and burst into deep, sobbing wails of terror. Around the slab of rock, the candles of the pentagram burned with hate. Then, the bonfire, roaring like a wounded beast, went out like in an instant, like a cry for mercy.

Then, from the fire, something grew.

Venomous clouds of blackness materialized and were sucked into the clearing like air into a set of lungs. Three ferocious eyes, glowing in the shape of an isosceles triangle, the top eye right in the middle of the forehead, blinked to life from within the arcane cloud and surveyed all of the evil that had gathered, then looked to the smoking pile of logs. Then in a moment of rage, the ground shook as if it were going to split open, and an otherworldly wind swept around the clearing with a howl that came from the end of the world. The inferno then exploded back to life in sound and fury, knocking all of the wicked celebrants back with a powerful shockwave. The skeletons, those closest to the blast, were instantly incinerated. The fire boiled into a vast conflagration that threatened to burn the bulbous, rotting moon out of the ancient night sky.

Out of the heatwaves, among the flames, rose two twin hooks, which were attached to two wings longer than pine trees. The gargantuan wings rose out of the unholy fire, slowly spreading and stretching out farther than half a football field. The stench of sulfur and rotting garbage streamed out from the wings, and some of the animals vomited, their sense of smell overwhelmed. Trembling like a newborn calf, the sacrificial victim passed out, emotionally overwhelmed.

A massive, jagged head, the size of two confession booths, with three sets of horns that changed shape from goat to antelope to bull to kudu and back to goat hoisted itself out of the fire. Three eyes blinked independently, like a chameleon, as the head pivoted slowly, yet frothing with hate as they moved from demon to animal to skeleton. Ragged breath raced in and out of a half-dozen tiny nostrils like smoke out of a blast furnace. A mouth filled with shark-like teeth and glowing, dripping lava-like blood snarled at the worshippers and they all cowered like beaten dogs. It took deep, ragged breaths.

Nothing dared move.

"Ego sum filius perditonis," purred the voice at last, with the resonance of a thousand lions. *I am the Son of Perdition.*

The crowd of demons and animals and skeletons and all things of the night gasped in awe and plunged to their feet, hooves or claws. Everyone trembled, worshipped and cheered, prostrate in blasphemous reverence. A colossal torso covered in scars and open wounds was hauled out of the fire by muscle-covered arms longer than ladders, arms that ended in six barbed talons. A foot with four cloven hooves stepped out from the fire, and all of the grass around it burned, withered and died in a heartbeat.

Constantine chanted, "Pater Satanas, qui tibi offerunt hoc sacrificium—" *Father Satan, we offer you this sacrifice—*

Satan pivoted and as he roared, shot melted fire out of his maw and engulfed the body of the poor woman. She startled awake and *was burned while she was still alive.* Constantine had to leap out of the way to keep himself from being incinerated. Her screams of pain and suffering gradually faded away under the column of fire that was being breathed onto her. Satan turned to the demons and animals, roared like a hundred beasts and shouted, "Ego sum pater mendacii, Abaddon, Behemoth, Leviathan, Enma-O, Set et veteris Aegypti!" *I am the Father of Lies, Abaddon, Behemoth, Leviathan, Enma-O and Set of Old Egypt!"*

Lucifer's taloned hand pulled a whip out from a belt made of skulls and stretched-out human skin, and when the whip unfurled it had a hundred tails, and the hundred tails lashed out over the prostrate worshippers like a new tiller over virgin soil. The zealots screamed with both agonized joy and intense pain. Some of the animals were simply cut in half by the searing blows and were ravenously consumed by the others.

"Ego Samnu!" frothed the mouth as it raked its whip again and again over the backs of its worshippers. They wailed in pain and rolled over in sheer agony, and those that revealed their pain received another lashing. "Cultus nihil aliud!" *I am Samnu! Worship no other!*

Trees fell, cut in half by the raging lashes of the Hundred Tails, some of the minor demons cleaved in pieces in the process and vanishing in clouds of sulfur. Animals brayed and squealed but did not dare run away. After it had cut open the backs of everyone around it, the dark figure bellowed, "Ego sum Marodach Babylonis, primus angelus cecidit, Moloch, de Graecia in infernum, de Christo tentator, accusatus est et tuaimmisericordes Mephistophilis!" *I am Marduk of Babylon, the first fallen angel, Moloch, Hades of Greece, Tempter of the Christ, the Accused One and your unmerciful Mephistopheles!*

Sobs and wails were suppressed.

Satan's bellowing laughter shook the trees and the souls of everyone around him. He whirled to Constantine and snarled, "Non expectabat ut vocant ultimum dies mensis huius primi millennii. Non semper est causa in mea coetus? Loquar, Constantinus vetus Byzantium, primus vampirum, et renuntiavit Hypocrita christianae vomitu Lilit! Quare ergo non invocant meam ocius?" *You waited to beckon me to the last day of this first millennium. There is always a purpose in my gatherings! Speak, Constantine of old Byzantium, First Vampire, renounced Hypocrite of Christianity and Vomit of Lilith! Why did you not heed my call sooner?*

Constantine nearly gagged, his throat empty of bile but full of fear. He took in the hideous, massive form in front of him and gathered the vigor and belief to say, "Rupere Pater foedus, non est meus intentio—" *Unholy Father, it was not my intention—*

"Recordare ego sum primus mendax, Constantinus," snarled the great shadow. *Remember I am the First Liar, Constantine.*

"Etiam, dominus meus," whispered the fallen Emperor. *Yes, my master.*

After a long growl full of suspicion, Satan said, "Confitentur supercrescit fides vestra, et acolythi sycophantarum meum. "Profiteri vestra fides, meum sycophantae et acolythi." *Profess your faith, my sycophants and acolytes.*

The demons all chanted, eyes glowing eerily in the darkness, their words in unison rippling through the dark, black forest:

> "Cupimus et nam caligavit de stellam de Bethlehem, nos volo quod sigillum septimum comestum disrumperentur. Et nos volueris nam capita septem et cornua draco decem et septem diademata at conterat Michaël et maledicte angeli. Spero nos perditionem de Agnus Dei magnum, et et corruptionem omne quod est sanctus in hoc mundo."
>
> *We wish for the dimming of the Star of Bethlehem. We desire that the Seventh Seal to be torn asunder. And we wish for the seven-headed dragon with ten horns and seven crowns to crush Michael and his accursed angels. We hope for the destruction of the Great Lamb, and the corruption of all that is holy in this world.*

"Mei servi et supponitur eunuchi didicistis lectiones bene," rumbled Satan. "Et vocavi te omnium circumstantium pro ratione. Quo est Lilit, mea fornicariam de uxorem?" *My slaves and supposed eunuchs have learned their lessons well. I have summoned you all here for a reason. Where is Lilith, my whore of a wife?*

The blasphemous congregation trembled. It took every ounce of will inside of Lilith to not glance in any way toward Constantine. Somehow the demoness found her voice and in the midst of the teeming, infernal crowd, Lilith gasped, "Expectans mandatum meus dominus." *Awaiting the command of my Master.*

Satan took in the she-demon, who slipped onto the sacrificial rock, standing tall and proud. The First Liar snarled in silent disgust. He looked to a groveling Constantine, who simply bowed his quivering head in unspoken, revealed shame. She and Constantine both withered with fear, past conspiracies rippling over both of them.

Satan of Hell stood, watching them both for a moment, his anger rippling like heat waves over the unholy congregation. Larger than a house, the monstrous entity swung an oak-sized right arm around, and as its shadow passed over the imps, skeletons, demons and animals, all of them could only chant collectively, "Ave Satanas."

The arm settled in Lilith's direction and she knew she was doomed, but it was now a matter of how much her punishment would be, and that hope held her stout in the face of white-hot eternal punishment.

"Profanum altare meum," purred Satan as he reached down for her with his barbed taloned hand, a hand that was wider than a door was tall. *My Unholy Altar.*

Lilith suppressed the urge to run, and simply closed her eyes to accept her fate. "Tuus sum, profanum patrem et mariti." *I am yours, Unholy Father and Husband.*

"Semper," said Satan, casting his trio of eyes toward Constantine as his claws slowly enveloped Lilith, like the petals of a Venus flytrap around a helpless insect. *Always.*

Constantine, no stranger to the theater of politics, before his mortal death and afterward, had managed to unbow his head and stand straight. For the moment, he had been spared.

In one movement, Satan picked her up and crushed the demoness like an insect. The crowd gasped and fell silent. Lilith's screams clawed at the stars, her glowing blood dripping and squirting out from between his talons. Bones crunched like dry tinder under a sandal. He tossed her broken body into his jagged, cruel mouth and swallowed. Satan turned to his worshippers and bellowed, "Ego dabo, vobis nongenti sexaginta sex annis post interfectionem pendan Christi, meum corpus et meus sanguis, ipsum unitas impaenitens animam malam et me! Ego nunc genuit semen meum et semen sanctum anima mea!" *I give you, nine hundred and sixty-six years after the death of the Christ, my body and my blood, the unity of the unrepentant demoness and myself! I now birth my seed, the seed of my unholy soul!*

Lucifer then savagely thrust his right hand into his own chest, punching into his own sternum with his talons, blood squirting everywhere, to be lapped up from the ground by the hysterical acolytes around him. Out of the chest came his hand, bleeding lava, fire and holding a flaming, crying, beating heart. Satan roared as he threw the heart onto the woodpile, and the violent column of fiery bile incinerated and obliterated the pile of logs. A vicious explosion of fire and hate filled the night.

Animal and demon alike wailed with terror.

Another swirling gale struck down the celebrants, cowering in terror as the tempest of wind, ember and fire swarmed over them. Satan let the wind and the fire envelop him, a maelstrom of all that was wrong with the world, and as he faded away into the fiery cauldron, he threw the piece of heart into the firestorm at his feet and the crowd heard the First Liar's deep, animal-like voice rumble, "Meis vocavi servis meis, martyribus et amisit animarum sunt huc per noctem praesentare omnem ira mea furoris corporis et sanguinis. Es genua ei flectere iurare fidem ad eum, mortem tuam et mei subsequentem ira. Ille arbitrium crescet ad adultam et impleas quod est apud omne apocalypsis. et relinquam eum titulis Servus autem Draconis, consorte autem Sancta Mater, Interfector de Apostolis et Devorantem Christianae Leonis. Vobis enim dico nunc quod nomen filii mei est Dracula." *I summoned my slaves, martyrs and lost souls here tonight to present to you all the body and blood of my wrath and fury. You are to kneel before him and swear your loyalty to him, to your death and my subsequent wrath. He will grow to adulthood and fulfill all that is found in Revelations. I bequeath him the titles Servant of the Dragon, Consort of the Holy Mother, Slayer of Apostles and Devourer of the Christian Lion. For I say now that the name of my son is Dracula.*

"Ave, Dracula!" shouted Constantine. *Hail Dracula!*

"Ave, Dracula!" shouted the crowd. "Ave, Satanus!"

The wreckage of the bonfire frothed like a forest inferno, with logs jutting out like enormous daggers. Out of the embers in the middle of the firestorm stirred a shape. It pushed aside some of the huge, burnt logs with a black, jagged wing. The evil crowd gasped.

A bat.

An infant bat.

A baby, a cub, but a bat nonetheless.

It was the size of a human child, with clawed wings reaching out wide yet strong, and glowing, intelligent eyes that took in everything.

It stirred slowly, looking over the crowd of unholy zealots and animals like a royal, and it blinked its all-seeing eyes, as if knowing that they all served him. Large, triangular ears pivoted and heard the terrified whispers of the worshippers.

Then it hissed.

And began to change.

Metamorphosis.

Transformation.

Anatomy melted, then reformed.

After another moment the bat rose, and when it did stand was no longer a bat, but a young human, or near human.

An undead human infant.

His eyes glowed with malice.

A child.

The boy leered at the zealots like it wanted to eat them all alive.

Demons cowered and knelt.

Animals prostrated along the ground.

Constantine knelt and plotted.

Night trembled.

The son of Satan was born.

PART TWO:
THE MODERN WORLD

DEPARTURE

TRANSYLVANIA
MAY 1ST, 1899

ONE

"Why are you *afară*[11] so late in such a terrible place?" said the Romanian woman to Jonathan Harker.

They shared a carriage that rattled, bounced, swerved, shuddered and shrieked along a dark country road. They had bounced around inside the horse-drawn carriage for the entire journey in silence until this moment. The horses that pulled the carriage neighed nervously, more scared than their driver, who hurried them onward, and for good reason.

"I'm sorry?" said Jonathan, lonely, alone in a strange country and not the faintest inkling that his life was about to be changed forever. "This might be the roughest coach ride I've ever been on."

He was being jostled around in the haggard coach like a rag doll. Twenty-one years old, with dark hair and aqua eyes that made women smile, he fidgeted in discomfort. Harker wore a nice, sharp, brown suit that seemed to gather more and more wrinkles and creases with each passing bump, shiver and bounce of the coach. He rapped a gentleman's cane against the carriage wall in impatience. In contrast to Harker's solidarity of ochre, the woman wore humble yet colorful traditional clothing that covered her from head to toe. She held an infant bundled in peasant cloth. They sat in the dark, rim-lit by moonlight that drifted in past curtained windows.

The vehicle that held them was two generations removed from being fashionable, had an axle that squeaked with pain and a back wheel that creaked from exhaustion. The horses neighed as they exerted themselves, racing up the prodigious climb. It was night outside and the passengers could only see moonlit slivers of half of their faces.

"This route is a strange and dangerous place," said the woman, "full of evil *spiritele*[12], young sir. Why a gentleman out so late tonight?"

"I was given this timetable by the landowner client I'm meeting tonight," said Jonathan. "Must admit it's a strange place to finalize a transaction. What brings you and your child out here?"

"My father is near *moarte*[13]," she said, "and he lives on the other side of this pass, in Vatra Dornei[14]. This was the last coach tonight, and I must see my father before he leaves this world of

---

[11] Romanian, meaning outside.

[12] Romanian, for spirits.

[13] Romanian, for death.

[14] Vatra Dornei is a small city in Northeastern Romania, on the Eastern side of the Tihuta, or Borgo Pass in Transylvania.

the living behind. My husband is away at work, so there is no one to care for my baby, so we must both go. The driver say you pay him more to go overnight, so I am grateful. Maybe I see my *tată* before he passes."

"I am sorry for you and your father," said Jonathan with sympathy. He closed his eyes, feeling a hundred years old at the moment. "I miss New York. And Whitby."

"Are you well, *domnişor*[15]?" said the woman, with a heavy accent, as she gave her infant the end of her right pinkie to suck on.

Jonathan nodded and half-shouted over the din of the carriage, "Yes, thanks, I'm fine. I'm just tired from a long trip on a miserable errand. As I said, I've been sent here to complete a purchase of land, but I also have to find the head of my company. He's missing. I've never traveled through this part of the world before, and I miss a comfortable bed. I miss the food at Delmonico's[16]. I miss my fiancée."

"I hear your accent," said the woman as she cradled her baby. "Is it American?"

She read his nod and said, "I have never been to the West."

"I am sure your fiancée misses you as well," continued the woman, her accent lush and beautiful. "She also is from New York?"

"No, English. From England. My parents are English as well."

"My country is *simplu* and strange," she nodded, looking beyond Harker and into the darkness.

"No, it's beautiful, what I've seen of it," said Harker with a weary smile, "The mountain ranges are amazing. I'd love to retire to a place like this someday. Climb some of these mountains. And the people are charming."

She gave Harker a smile worth gold. "You are very kind."

Outside, the vast Carpathians sped by, shrouded in might and mystery. The carriage kept rising, heading up a ribbon of a road hewn out of what the mountains would allow.

Harker beamed at the child. "How old is she?"

"My Nadya is seven months," said the woman proudly. "She will travel to New York one day. I am Catina."

"Please have her come visit me," said Harker with a grin of kindness and sincerity, which the mother reciprocated. "I am Jonathan Harker, at your service."

Just when Jonathan thought the trip would indeed be endless, the vehicle reached a crest then skidded to a hurried stop. A hard gale swept into the carriage, and cold became colder.

"This is Borgo Pass[17], Young Master, and hurry for please," announced the coachman from atop the carriage, through a thick, regional accent. Fear and haste lined his words. No sounds of weight shifting from atop the driver's seat, so it was clear to Jonathan that the coachman was not getting down to help with the luggage.

Harker had snapped up his hat and cane when Catina reached out and snatched him by the arm, terror splashed across her face. "No, not here, Young Sir! *Periculos*[18]! I did not know you were going to stop here! *Vrăjitorie*[19]!"

"Please," said Jonathan, gently but firmly pulling Catina's hand off his arm. "This is where I have my business."

---

[15] Vatra Dornei is a small city in Northeastern Romania, on the Eastern side of the Tihuta, or Borgo Pass in Transylvania.

[16] Delmonico's is a series of quality restaurants in New York, originally established in 1827.

[17] Borgo Pass (Pasul Tihuta in Romanian) is in the Bârgău Mountains and connects Transylvania and Moldavia.

[18] Romanian; danger, dangerous

[19] Romanian; sorcery

"Let him be, *femeie*[20]! It is his concern. Hurry, good Sir!" shouted the coachman from above and outside, and Harker opened the door of the cab and slipped out into the night. Cold slapped him like a curse. The hard soil crunched under Harker's shoes, as if it did not want him there. He looked back at Catina, and she shook her head repeatedly at him in fear, her eyes begging him to step back inside the cab. She held Nadya as if she did not want her baby to get anywhere near the door, much less outside.

"It'll be all right, Miss," said Jonathan to reassure her. Clearly the local superstition was getting the better of her, he thought. Harker shut the door as she shouted, nearly hysterical, "Come back inside! Don't let him leave you! *Teren profan!* This is unholy ground!"

The coachman, a native Slav covered in a blanket, coat, scarves and hat backlit by a single lantern atop the carriage, hurriedly launched two bags down from atop the carriage that landed on the ground next to Harker. He seemed to be ready to leave as fast as possible. The four horses were whinnying and stomping with alarm.

"You are armed, Young Master?" said the coachman with a shiver and a quick look around. Harker nodded.

"Then God be with you. *Domnul fie cu tine*[21]. Do not speak to the ghosts. Run from everything else."

The woman reached out a hand to grab his cane and pull him back inside, but Harker stepped back and said, "Do not worry for me, Miss Catina. The master of this place comes for me. I will meet your Nadya in Manhattan soon enough."

He gave her that smile, but she burst into tears as the coachman shouted at the four-in-hand team of horses to start, and they did. The carriage swerved to the left and headed down into the road and the other side of the pass. Even the dust clouds evaporated quickly, as if they were afraid to be seen. Jonathan realized that the lantern atop the carriage was taking the only source of illumination with it.

Jonathan heard Catina cry in Romanian, "Nu-l poți lăsa!" *You cannot leave him!*

"Taci din gură sau te va lăsa, de asemenea!" shouted the driver, his voice disappearing as fast as the carriage did. *Shut your mouth or I shall leave you as well!*

Jonathan Harker, Englishman from New York, was alone and was enveloped by darkness.

Harker took a deep breath, then saw it exhale, and knew his eyes were merely adjusting to the night, which after a few seconds, they did. The road had crested at the top of the pass, and he stood in the middle of it. Surrounded by elaborate silhouettes of tree lines on either side, with a smaller dirt road leading off the right. A bulbous moon drew what light it could from the terrified sun and cast it down over a large bank of mist, which moved toward Jonathan faster than a man could run.

Then, stranger still.

To his left, three swollen corpses hung by rope to several large hanging posts, rotting out in the open air.

Their skeletal hands were at their throats, still trying to pull the nooses off their necks. Their bodies were covered with welts *that were in the shape of upside-down crucifixes*. The ropes made a dull, creaking sound as the wind swayed the corpses back and forth. Five graves lay to his right, with simple wooden crosses in various stages of decay and exposure pushed into each one. One of the graves, recently dug, swelled with unknown horror, while the four others sagged. What he thought were barren tree trunks were actually three large, ancient stone monoliths, covered with runes. They sat among the other trees, visible from the road.

Instinctively, Jonathan turned around, sensing that this was a place to be alert. A lone shrine stood next to the road. Jonathan looked closer. A small statue of the Virgin Mary stood inside it,

---

[20] Romanian; woman

[21] Romanian; 'God be with you.'

defiant, as if it had been there for centuries. Half of her head had been cleaved off. The entire shrine was covered with hundreds of tiny crucifixes. Blood had recently been poured over the statue. Birds and animals had defecated all over the crumpled roof. The base of the statue reeked of urine.

It was a terrible place.

Mist, silence and fear embraced Jonathan Harker.

In the distance, the sounds of the carriage faded, and Jonathan now understood the urgency of the driver and Catina's fear.

He reached into his coat pocket and found his Webley revolver. His dear friend Quincy Morris would be upset that he did not carry an American Colt, provincial as Morris was, but this was Jonathan's favorite pistol, and the Texan was far too precious about his firearms anyway. Harker found it strange that no sound had been made, either by beast or bird, nor even tree creaking, since the carriage had left. The hard, bitter soil crunched under his shoes, sounding like thunder.

Mist cleared, then deepened again.

Cold began to seep over him.

His breath came faster, and Jonathan Harker had to fight the feeling that he was being watched. His right hand found the Webley again, for comfort. His left hand held the cane. Chiding himself for being silly, Jonathan began to steady himself when another strange thing happened.

A lone light came through the mist, toward him, and in an instant the boundaries of reality began to crumble around Jonathan Harker, who staggered backwards, terrified.

Toward him shambled an apparition.

A spectre.

A spirit.

The ghost of a soldier, wearing the armor of a 16th century *Cuirassier*[22], his chest and front of his legs covered in metal, holding a lamp in one hand and a sword in the other. His head held up a helmet. The ghost was that of a man in his 30s, and Jonathan realized he could see *right through* the apparition. The ghost looked like he'd fought in a hundred battles and survived ninety-nine of them. The soldier was haggard, bleeding spiritual blood from wounds and rat bites along his neck, right arm and leg. Scars old and new scribbled over his face, the ghost looked at Jonathan with the thousand-yard stare of an aged man-at-arms.

"Be ye aware," moaned the ghost with an antiquated British accent, nodding as he spoke. "All the kyngs and realms rose again' him! But to no avail! Gutted us lyke pigs! The Hellspawn ys vulnerable when he transforms! But we could never take the byre[23], and t'was was our decree of death. That, and hys accursed rats. It need not be yr fate. Only ours."

Jonathan nodded back, his eyes larger than the moon, heart in his mouth. He trembled as the ghost staggered past him, toward whatever path a ghost takes during his or her nightly haunting.

The mist began to clear.

"He comes, even now, our conqueror, your nemesis," said the ghostly man-at-arms as he faded into nothingness. "Heed my words, boy."

Faster than the ghost had arrived, it evaporated, the light lingering for but a moment longer than the apparition.

Harker was once again alone.

A quick dip into his coat to check the pistol gave him miniscule comfort.

A sound of old metal parts moving together came from the smaller worn road, and a carriage

---

[22] Cuirassiers were European armored cavalry. A Cuirass is a two-piece, front and back metal breastplate.
[23] Byre: Old English word for opportunity

came out of the mist and at Jonathan Harker, who at that very moment, forgot all about Delmonico's or any other of the great eateries of the world.

A low growl behind him whirled Harker around yet again, wondering what he would see next. Weaving their way out of the mist and forest, a half-dozen wolves moved silently, spreading to Harker's left and right. Behind him, the carriage clanged closer. They seemed larger, darker and more ferocious than any he had seen at the Zoological Society of London.

Jonathan had his cane in his left hand, and his right dove into his coat for the Webley.

The wolves began to snarl viciously, slathering spit, baring canines and tongues as they advanced.

Three corpses twitched in the wind, interested in the outcome of this unexpected joust.

The horrifying, swollen grave was curious as well.

Behind Harker, the coach kept coming.

"Sir!" shouted Jonathan over his shoulder as he backed up, "If you be my host, I surely hope you have a weapon!"

Harker was surprised the horses had not advanced. The wolves drew nearer, backs arching, lips back, teeth exposed and barking ferociously now. Their eyes blazed desperation and hunger. Jonathan's patience for his silent host ran out, and he shouted without looking back, "Are you blind as well as deaf? Can you not see the wolves!"

In frustration Jonathan turned around to scold the driver when he saw that *the carriage had no horses and was moving right at him, of its own will.*

There was no coachman, no driver, no passengers. The carriage was a silhouette, knifing through the mist and towards him. Stunned, Jonathan tried to swallow but shock and terror clamped his mouth shut. The carriage skidded to a sharp stop upon its own, scattering soil at Jonathan's feet, and with a long, single creak, the passenger door opened like a coffin. Harker was stunned beyond comprehension.

Then, a grand shadow draped itself over the carriage, a blur of complete darkness, before an enormous, black shape swept down from the macabre night and landed with tremendous force on the driver's bench. It crouched sharp and still as a tombstone, as wings with a twenty-foot wingspan extended themselves into the mist and the night.

The wings of a bat.

Twin eyes of fire, surrounded by a massive head with two triangular ears that folded back in anger glared down at Jonathan Harker, unblinking with fury and malice. A mouth full of opalescent fangs, canines and incisors parted and snarled at him. Jonathan sucked in air, terrified at this new menacing presence.

Then Jonathan remembered he was armed.

In a heartbeat Harker raised the Webley and opened fire.

TWO

In Harker's hand, the Webley barked.

Again and again, shattering the eerie silence of the night, Harker emptied the revolver into the huge bat. Jonathan could feel the hammer slam against the back of the pistol after he'd pulled on the trigger, yet the thing still stood alive and stout behind the smoke of Harker's firearm, lowering its ears ever further and squinting its crimson eyes in fury at the young man. Its snarl was like metal being torn to pieces. Realizing that the rounds had done nothing to harm the beast, Harker turned and ran.

Right into the leap of one of the wolves.

It was as if the young man had been hit in the chest with a mallet. Jonathan had the air ripped out if his lungs with incredible violence as he fell. The back of Jonathan's skull slammed against the cold, unholy ground of Borgo pass, the largest wolf's eyes and canines flashing inches from his face. Saliva splattered over Harker's face in an absurd baptism of nature. Jonathan's cane had wedged itself between himself and the wolf, and he used the cane and all of his strength to keep the snarling animal off him, if barely. The weight on Jonathan's chest felt like it was about to snap his ribcage like dry branches. He realized that through the madness and intensity, he had regained his breath and was screaming like a madman even as he tried to fight off the wolf. With snapping canines just inches from his face, Harker saw that the other members of the pack were charging in from either side with the intent of tearing him to pieces. He thought of Mina, his parents, friends and everyone back in Whitby and New York.

The weight of the wolf was then ripped from his chest with a tremendous blow. A horrific yelp, like the largest fingernail in the world screeching across a vast chalkboard, threatened to tear Jonathan's eardrums to shreds. An agonized howl of deep pain followed, then a dreadful silence. When he looked along the ground to where his feet lay, Harker saw the massive bat crouching, facing away from Harker, holding the inert body of the attacking wolf in its huge, canine-lined mouth, in front of the rest of the pack, which had already begun to back away. The bat's proportions and construction were very similar to that of a normal-sized bat, but with much longer legs, with nearly human anatomy on those fur-covered, satyr-shaped legs that ended in jagged, horrific claws.

The huge bat spat the wolf's body out of its mouth like a discarded puppet before it snarled like a hundred serpents at the pack, which cowered in fear, whining and yelping, their confidence torn out of them in an instant. The bat then turned to look at Harker with its malice-red eyes, then at the bleak, black carriage. It blinked, and the coach moved *as if upon silent command*, bringing the open passenger door nearer to Harker. The bat then reached out with its huge right wing and enveloped Jonathan with it. Harker felt long, vice-like 'fingers' underneath him, wrapping themselves around him like he was a limp doll, scraping the New Yorker off the ground like he was roadkill. In one powerful, fluid motion the bat picked Harker bodily off the ground, then whirled and threw the young man through the open air, past the passenger door and into the carriage with savage force.

Jonathan crashed hard against the far door, then collapsed in an upside-down heap to an old wooden floor. For a few moments Jonathan Harker was stunned into unconsciousness. The first thing he smelled when he came to inside the carriage was death, as if a thousand corpses had been stored inside the compartment for centuries. Jonathan's two pieces of luggage were then slingshot into the carriage and slammed against his stomach, knocking the wind out of him again. The cane followed, clanging against Harker's skull before rattling to a still.

Terror, astonishment and loathing rushed through Jonathan as he looked back through the door to see the bat. The thing gestured at the door with its wing and the carriage slammed shut, as if obeying the animal's unspoken whim. Jonathan then felt the front axle underneath the carriage pivot, as if invisible horses had just moved, and the entire vehicle began to slowly creak forward, circling the open area, gathering momentum and speed, moving back in the direction it had come from. Still upside-down in body as well as mind, Harker heard the frustrated barks, yelps and snarls of the beaten wolfpack recede into the distance. The carriage picked up speed. Jonathan crawled up into the back seat of the rattling coach and looked out the left door window.

Harker could see that his carriage was driving at breakneck speed along a tiny, precarious mountain path, each wheel clattering along the parched, angry road like it would fly apart at any moment. To the left was a spectacular, yawning view of the Carpathian mountain range, flying by as the carriage gathered even more momentum and recklessness. Just outside of the right-hand carriage window was a canyon wall blurring by at terrific speed, rocky protrusions that yearned to knock the carriage out into a thousand-foot fall into a ribbon of river far below. A backward glance revealed the remaining five wolves, yelping and howling as they gave up the chase in frustration and distance. But none of this alarmed Jonathan more than the gigantic bat with the thirty-foot wingspan that soared down and alongside the left side of carriage, glaring at Harker with its menacing, fiery eyes. It caught Jonathan's stare and snarled at him in fury, spittle caught in the wind.

Jonathan clung onto the inside of the carriage as the coach skidded around a broken-leg bend in the road, scattering debris as it turned and leaving the rear left wheel spinning over the precipice for a heart-stopping second. The discomfort of the previous carriage was a merry-go-round compared to the violence with which Harker was thrown about in this coach. He had expected to be sent bouncing down along the walls of the gorge on the way to a watery grave at any moment, but instead he was hurtling along a crease of a road in a ghost carriage, chaperoned by a monstrous bat. The road and carriage pivoted to the right, away from the path at the edge of the world.

He sat back up and looked around the interior of the carriage. Unlike the used worn and out-of-fashion carriage that had brought Jonathan Harker to Borgo pass, this coach was luxurious, with inlaid wood, plush carpeting and embroidered cloth along the ceiling. Even the drapes were beautiful, along with windows that were etched with filligree associated with the great houses and courts of the continent. And yet, everything in the coach was dead black. No other color was allowed to exist within the coach, even the upholstery in the seat across from Jonathan looked comfortable, luxurious and even suitable for a king, but Harker could not shake a sense of eeriness, of unease, of forboding from this beautiful but dark carriage.

He then looked outside, and Jonathan's mind reeled yet again.

A vast, dead, ashen plain lay ahead.

Silence blanketed the plain, along with a thin but strong mist that drifted just above the countless clumps of dead brush and thousands of corpses that lay as far as the eye could see under a malevolent, clouded night sky.

Skeletal remnants of soldiers from the 17th century, covered with armor and representing the regions and city-states of the continent. Yet they did not lay sword to stomach or pike to rib cage.

They sprawled everywhere, having died in battle together, but *not fighting against each other*. Some of the bodies looked like they had been torn to pieces or eaten alive. Shredded bits of *cuirass* lay everywhere. Horse skeletons lay side by side with their riders, in death throes, legs up in the air as if kicking away at unseen attackers. All of the countless bones on both humans and horses were covered with millions of tiny bite marks, as if *the meat had been shaven off the bone*. Broken and battered cannons lay on their sides, groaning from hundreds of years of exposure, rust and rot. Broken pikes protruded out of the parched earth like morbid blades of grass. Shields littered the ground, covered with thorny grey vines that had begun to envelop the entire tableau like a titanic spider pulling its prey into the recess of its vast cobweb. There were ravens everywhere, and above all that soared the great black bat from Borgo Pass, ever-vigilant of the carriage from above.

Wearing the ornate armor of the Turkish Empire were staked corpses, with the jagged posts cleaved through their torsos in every possible and horrible angle. Some bodies were piled five high on the same piece of wood, while others had the stake put through their skulls. Other corpses lay sideways, with horrible, thinner stakes that ran through the belt, chest plate and out of the helmets' face masks. One unfortunate soul hung upside-down, the stake hammered in *through his mouth*. Camel and elephant skeletons, in full armor, were also impaled, lying next to their human military kindred in open-mouthed rants of insanity. Siege towers lay among the elephant corpses and stake labyrinths, splintered and cast aside with incredible violence.

Harker's carriage bounded furiously across the plain and through the night, threatening to fly apart at its old, worn edges, passing all of the silent testaments to so many lost lives. The carriage's pace refused to reduce by even an increment as it bolted past the hundreds of large, ten-foot-tall stakes facing outwards and radiating away from a massive, ominous stronghold that loomed before Jonathan. He gasped at a fortress and castle that defied conventional architectural description while evoking the simple, stark impression of malevolence. The carriage roared past colossal battlements and fortifications that, to Harker's amazement, were held up by enormous columns from ancient Egypt, Rome, Greece, Constantinople and China. The columns seemed planted in a non-sequential, haphazard way, as if they actually predated the construction of the fortress itself. Jonathan was further entranced by the realization that there were actually *two* walls surrounding the fortress, the outer wall about twenty feet tall, stout and lined with primitive battlements and arrow slits in the shape of inverted crucifixes. The interior wall was thirty feet high and wide, made of gargantuan grey bricks that were individually bigger than the carriage itself and would have dwarfed the most imposing of the Crusader castles in the Holy Land. Both walls were covered with thousands of protruding arrows from different cultures, fired hundreds of years ago and lodged into the crevices and cracks of this mammoth, imposing place.

Harker was agog as he saw, outside and in between the outer and inner walls, two parched moats that framed the entire length of the monstrous outer walls, both twenty feet deep and filled with more demolished remains of siege towers, trebuchets, ladders, lances, swords and corpses, all broken, battered and blackened with the mother of all fires. Along with caked mud, the moat bottoms were lined with the remnants of bile, blood, vomit and excrement from the victims of the untold atrocities committed along these fortress walls so many years ago. The carriage then clattered and skidded violently across a burnt-but-intact wooden drawbridge so large that it could have held legions, then through a massive, corroded castle outer gate that yawned open like Leviathan[24] itself.

Through the side window of the carriage, Jonathan could see the massive drawbridge close without a sound, cutting him off from the rest of the world. As if it had a mind of its own, the black

---

[24] Leviathan is an enormous creature from Biblical Old Testament.

carriage swept into an open area between the outer wall and the keep[25], which was an enormous building complex that defied architectural categorization. The ambiance inside the outer wall was no less grisly. Thorny vines grew and spread out from each corner of the inner wall like absurd, behemoth tarantulas. More columns of antiquity and conquest lay in ruin along the ground or supporting the main structure, with sagging turrets covered with blood spilled generations ago. There were remnants of severed limbs scattered at will and whim, with piles of human skeletons clothed in peasant garb thrown to each corner, and conversely stacks of human skulls piled neatly in another, representing both adult and child. Broken, aged guillotines stood as solemn sentinels full of rage, hate and destruction. Legions of vultures roosted atop the inner and outer walls, battling each other over space, and chasing the vermin, rodent and arachnid alike, that scuttled from crevice to recess.

Everything reeked of rot, mold and death.

A lone, cold stone slab sat solemnly in the middle of the open area, the same slab that had borne witness to the creation of a child-sized bat nearly a thousand years ago. Carved all over the rock now were mysterious, indecipherable runes, hieroglyphics and petroglyphs. Yet the most prominent of all the indentations were three separate Roman numerals, scrawled repeatedly over the slab:

VI

VI   VI

The carriage side-skidded to a stop in front of what remained of the keep, which had been attached to the main part of the castle at some point in history. Massive, foreboding, the main building seemed just as impenetrable as the two walls, but with stouter columns and towers, all lined with the inverted crucifix arrow slits and battlements from different eras. If the outer walls were grey, the keep was midnight-black itself, with a colossal metal door looming in front. On the door was a magnificent depiction of an elaborate dragon of different styles from different periods in time, its long body, perhaps that of a dragon depicted in ancient Asia, and the face of the creature seemingly European but not really European. This dragon had in its mouth a winged lion, the symbol of a crown and rays emanating from atop the lion's mane as it valiantly but fruitlessly fought off the dragon's forged, jagged maw. Intertwined between the two characters were the same three sets of Roman numerals as on the slab of rock:

VI

VI   VI

The momentum of the skid threw a terrified Harker to the bottom of the cab. As if on cue, the right passenger side door whipped open, and Jonathan heard and felt the bat land atop the carriage like a bull colliding against a wall. The bat's left arm reached in to grab at him.

"No!" he screamed. "Leave me alone!"

Jonathan went into a terrified frenzy as he tried to push and kick the arm away, at last remembering he had his cane with him. He took the hilt, turned it counter-clockwise ninety degrees, and slid out a short sword.

"Get the hell away from me!" spat Harker as he struck out at the vast, webbed arm and hand. He pierced a 'finger' of the left wing with the sword. The bat emitted a grunt as the sword did its work,

---

[25] A keep is traditionally a fortified tower built within castles during the Middle Ages.

but it was a grunt of impatient annoyance, not pain. The wing withdrew outside of the carriage, and in horror Jonathan watched as the wound healed itself in seconds, even as the arm retracted from view. Weight shifted atop the carriage, and the sharp head of the bat came into view, upside down, followed by a deep, angry growl, blood-stained saliva dripping down onto the step and into the carriage. Fast as a cobra strike, the right wing shot in and grabbed Harker by the throat, raising the young man and pinning him to the ceiling of the carriage. The pressure was enormous, the bat incredibly strong. Jonathan tried to yell, but his esophagus was clamped shut. The claws were cold and dead yet they flowed with power.

The demonic bat snarled at Harker in anger as it then pounded him against the carriage roof with terrific force. Jonathan felt the vertebrae in his neck throb as his head was continually slammed against the roof. He tried to breathe again but could not. He flailed with the sword and cane, but the pressure was tremendous, and the weapons clattered to the carriage floor like broken playthings. His esophagus and windpipe completely shut off, Jonathan stopped fighting and began to black out. It was then that the bat released him and he fell to the floor. Semi-conscious, Jonathan heard the metallic scream of the dragon doors opening, then felt a single claw slip around the back of his collar before he was forcibly yanked out of the carriage, the door of which closed upon another silent command. Harker hit the ground like a freshly butchered pig and was dragged along a battered stone path that seemed to gnaw at him with its sharp edges. Jonathan found his breath again, and he grabbed hold of the clawed wing that pulled him along to be able to soak fresh air into his lungs.

Harker could hear the bat breathe raggedly as it bounded up some stone steps, each one punching Harker in the kidneys and lower spine. Jonathan was pulled through the open, yawning doors and into a vast room that had partially collapsed, leaving open air above. As he was pulled into blackness, Jonathan looked up at the boiling clouds of the dark night sky and wondered if he would live to see another sunrise.

The massive doors closed silently behind them.

THREE

The taloned finger that held Jonathan by the collar suddenly released him, and he collapsed onto the stone floor, stunned at the incredible turn of events. He lay on his stomach as his eyes scanned the darkness, letting air fill his lungs with ragged, desperate intakes. The ground was cold, hard, wet, made of uneven brickwork and covered with generations of dust. Harker could hear his breath echoing around in the open, expansive chamber. Because his eyes still could see nothing but the velvet, dangerous night. Jonathan's heart rate was frantic as he tried to size up the terrifying situation he had placed himself in. The gigantic bat gestured at the titanic doors with a wave of his enormous left wing, and they closed by themselves with screeches and groans.

Harker squinted up and saw that he was at the center of what was a vast, crumbling hall where the roof of the keep had partially collapsed onto the floor. The open area reflected the malevolence that Jonathan had already seen outside. Collapsed columns and beams made the stone floor look like a broken jigsaw puzzle. Dilapidated staircases, collapsed archways and fallen sections of ceiling made the vast room look like a realistic version of the most absurd of Piranesi's[26] renderings. All of the semi-collapsed doorways led to tunnels of foreboding blackness. Enormous cobwebs choked corners and stretched *everywhere*. Jonathan sensed that the open area in the keep connected to the hallways and passages of the main castle building. Above, there were only more brooding night clouds. A single lantern, left in the middle of the floor, illuminated the entire room.

Everything reeked of mold, candles, dust, crumbling parchment and ancient carnage.

With horrifying speed and power, the gigantic bat then turned and bolted away from Harker, pounding along the ground, moving like a bat ordinarily did, with the knuckles of its wings on the ground, yet with the agility and energy of a charging lion or bounding gorilla. It screeched in deafening fashion as it leaped onto one of the pillars, its claws latching onto and raking the stone easily. As quickly as a cat, the mammalian behemoth scrambled effortlessly up along the wall. And as it did so, every nook, recess and hole of the room surged to life with strange, disgusting motion. Dozens, hundreds, thousands of large grey rats poured out of the darkness and streamed toward the menacing shadow. The great beast moved like a leopard in a tree along the chamber walls, screeching and calling out to the night while frothing waves of rodents poured out from within the nooks and crags of the dilapidated stonework.

Above, motion came from the remaining beams and hanging roof tiles, and thousands of black blurs became a storm of bats that swarmed toward their master. The winged streaks gathered around the bat and became a violent, cyclonic wind tunnel around the enormous creature, which launched itself from the ceiling and into the air, its expansive wings stretching out to their maximum reach, and landed with a profound thump on the ground next to the lantern. The brickwork around Jonathan shuddered like it was about to shatter. In a deep crouch, the thing raised its malevolent, black head

---

[26] Giovanni Battista Piranesi (1720-1778) was an Italian artist most known for his etchings of Rome as well as fantastical depictions of vast, impossible prison chambers.

to Jonathan, and as it stood, amidst the swirling vermin in the air and on the ground, began to transform. In seconds, mammal physiology metamorphized into human anatomy, fur became skin and cloth, snout became nostril and wings became arms, as the cyclone of bats swirled around him faster and faster.

A tempest of fur, bone, canines, wing and blood.

Jonathan lay on the ground, astonished beyond any reaction other than sheer terror. The man beckoned the lantern with a soft opening and closing of the fingers of his right hand, and it complied, skidding along the stonework until it reached him. With the maelstrom of vermin swarming around him, the mysterious shapeshifter in human form picked up the lantern and as he did so, the vermin scattered, as if fearful of the shapeshifter's every move. In seconds, both cloud of bat and flood of rat had surged and collected behind the shapeshifter, either fluttering onto him or lying on the ground and staring intently at Harker, and Jonathan could finally get a clear look at his host.

He was dressed completely in black, with dead, pale skin, black hair and a sharp, fearsome countenance. There was an indescribable sense of power emanating from the man. His face was dramatic, with protruding cheekbones, a short but jagged hawk nose with a long, sharpened chin. A strong forehead covered sunken eye sockets that held eyes of unrelenting strength, a gaze that could have cut Jonathan Harker in half. The shapeshifter's eyes were white, even the irises, except for a pronounced rim of piercing, savage black around the edge of the pupils. It was as if an eagle or owl glowered at Harker, blinking like a predator examining a potential meal. His clothes looked like they were out of different periods in history, but without a definitive description, save the billowing cloak, which flowed and formed around him, giving the massive, powerful figure a strong, shifting silhouette. The man had the presence of a king but the embodiment of complete and utter evil. He projected the capability of incredible violence. Lion, leopard or tiger would have withered under the shapeshifter's glare. Stray bats crawled over him like tarantulas. His hands were powerful, bone white and looked strong enough to tear anything apart. Thick, talon-like fingernails ended the hands like claws on an eagle's feet. What Jonathan had realized instantly was that the shapeshifter was not a living human, but a supernatural being of incredible presence. The shapeshifter smiled like a secret sin, and Jonathan trembled, for the man's mouth was full of wicked canines and incisors.

He was dark majesty.

"I am *Dracula*," he said in a clipped English reserved for royals, "Master of this stronghold. May your Lord and Savior have more mercy upon your soul than I ever will."

Jonathan was so terrified all he could do was gape.

"Master Harker, I am everything you have seen me to be this night," Dracula said as he gestured around the room, as if to acknowledge the foreboding circumstances around him. "My titles of Count, Cardinal and Royal Heir were granted to me by three significant beings: Vlad Tepes[27], then Voivode of Wallachia, the most disgusting Rodrigo Borgia when he was Pope Alexander VI[28], and of course my Most hateful Father. Even the Khans and Draculs knelt before me. You look upon history itself."

Overwhelmed, Jonathan could gather no words. Dracula took Harker's terror in and was amused. "I presume that all of my correspondences have reached you and led you here well. This humble abode can provide you with any form of hospitality you require, other than kindness and love."

---

[27] Vlad Tepes (1428-1477?) was a Viovode (prince) of Wallachia, second son of Vlad Dracul (?-1447), and older brother to Radu Bey (1437-1475), another future Viovode. Vlad Dracul was also referred to as Vlad the Dragon or Vlad II.

[28] Rodrigo Borgia (1431-1503) was Pope Alexander VI from 1492 to his death. The first marriage of his daughter, Lucrezia Borgia, was held in Rome in 1493.

Cowering on the stonework, Harker could muster nothing but silence.

"Many rooms are available to you, mortal child, should you choose," continued Dracula as he gestured toward the two doorways to the rear of the cavernous hall. "Save those of myself and my concubines."

The vampire then pointed to the front doors of the keep and said, "The stone outside is very important to me, Master Harker. I am particularly proud of the two outer walls that surround us, inspired by the famous Walls of Constantinople[29], I must admit. The fortress and castle surrounding you were built around this stone. I was actually born next to that rock, if one can believe it."

Bats crawled eerily over the vampire's shoulder, face and head as he continued, "Life, if we can call it that, never ceases to bring ironies. Well then, to matters at hand. You have brought the documents that I require?"

"M-Mister Hawkins, Sir," was all Harker could manage. "My uncle. Has he arrived—"

"You will address me as Count!" roared the vampire, the reverberations of a lion's bellow in his throat. Vermin scattered everywhere. In a blink Dracula was upon Harker, shifting the lantern to his left hand and savagely wrenching Jonathan's throat before raising him bodily off the ground. "Compositoque![30] Do not disrespect me in my own home, child! Have you the documents, Master Harker?"

"Ah," said Dracula with sudden illumination, his burst of fury evaporated. "They must surely be with your luggage in the coach."

Dracula threw Harker aside, Jonathan landing hard among the swarming rats and bats. Dracula looked to the colossal, broken doors between them and the carriage. He gestured with his taloned right hand, and the magnificent, imperial doors creaked back open on their own. The vermin surged voraciously at Jonathan, eager to tear into the traveler's bones, flesh and blood until the vampire hissed, "Tu nu esti la-l atingă fără acordul meu." *You are not to touch him without my consent.*

Vermin scattered instantly, the bats pirouetting back up to the groaning beams and recesses of the open hall, while the rats retreated into the darkness that the lantern could not reach, their vermillion eyes ravenously focused on Harker. The vampire gestured again, and in the distance, framed by the massive doorway of the keep, the carriage door opened once again, with the luggage bouncing out and sliding along the ground, up the stairs, past the enormous broken doorway and toward the vampire, scattering rats as it did so.

Harker was nearly done coughing and retching his throat back open when the luggage stopped in from of Dracula. With a flick of his wrist Dracula opened the first bag, and a bound, officially sealed stack of documents rose out. The vampire snatched the document out of the air with his right hand, turned to Harker and hissed, "You will follow me to my library, boy."

This was a command, not a request.

This most mysterious host pointed the lantern to the left, to one of the half-crumpled stone archways. Harker was still too terrified to move, so as Dracula walked away, the vampire waved with his right hand. The rats to Jonathan's right surged forward, a million tiny red eyes twinkling at Harker in the gloom, a half-million tiny appetites eager to gnaw at Harker's fingers, throat and eyeballs.

Jonathan realized the rats were moving toward him, pouring over each other in ravenous anticipation, so he scrambled backwards and to his feet, repulsed and terrified. He moved tepidly in the direction of Dracula's indication. The vampire saw this and chuckled, "As if you had any choice in the matter."

---

[29] Two stone defensive walls that surrounded the ancient city of Constantinople, modern-day Istanbul.

[30] Latin; mongrel. A dog of mixed breeding.

As Dracula bounded to the archway, Jonathan could see the light from the lantern cast gigantic, arcane shadows along the walls of the room as the direction of the light changed. He could see his own trembling silhouette stagger along the granulating, fungi-ridden walls, mingling with the jagged, malevolent shadow of the vampire.

"Adso," said the vampire, apparently to no one, "Aduce bagajele." *Bring the luggage.*

In the deep gloom, amid the catacombs, something rumbled, "Da, stăpânul meu," in a voice that chilled Jonathan's bones. *Yes, my Master.*

Jonathan heard and felt the subtle, macabre rustling of another, unseen presence in the gloom and shuddered.

As Dracula moved to the hallway, he gestured behind him. The colossal dragon-consuming-lion doors creaked to a close.

Twisted like a broken box, the forlorn corridor ahead of them was an orifice of both neglect and decay. Dracula and Jonathan made their way along, with the vampire's lantern casting spider-like shadows everywhere.

"Trophies of conquest," chuckled Dracula as he pointed to impossibly old Chinese stone columns that shored up one side of the deteriorating hallway. They passed various decomposing wooden doors, some looking like the combination of rust and rot would prevent the door from ever being opened again. The architecture of the hallway was perhaps Romanesque, appearing to have been built, torn down, and built up again over the centuries. An overwhelming stench of death swam over Harker's senses, and he had to suppress the urge to gag as a dark spot on the hallway floor revealed itself upon a longer glance to be blood that had not dried up. The legions of infernal rats poured over the reddened brickwork, pausing to lap up the blood and mixed pieces of viscera while in silent pursuit of their master. Dracula glanced back and enjoyed seeing their slavering mouths so eager to tear the young man to pieces, their red eyes dancing in the lantern's light. Jonathan Harker staggered along in a state of shock. He nervously watched the vampire glide along the corridor and felt nothing but revulsion and fear from this most malevolent figure.

"Eu vărsare de sânge," chuckled his host. *I adore bloodshed.*

They came upon an enormous, ornate mirror[31] hanging on the left side of the crumbling hallway. The mirror was Chinese, bronze, old, scratched and badly polished, but as Jonathan looked to his left he was astonished to see himself as a terrified, discheveled young man. Then a wave of quiet horror overwhelmed him as a hair-raising realization came upon him. The reflection of the lantern and document in Dracula's hands *drifted of their own accord*, as if suspended by invisible wires, and when Jonathan recovered from the shock of what he initially thought to be an old magic trick, he realised that *the vampire had cast no reflection of his own.*

The document and lantern drifted idly past the mirror's reflection, and Harker's angle was such that he could take in both the vampire to his left, and the impossibly suspended lantern and document in the mirror itself.

Dracula looked sideways, soaked in Jonthan's surprised expression, and gave out another delighted, dark chuckle of satisfaction.

They walked on, through the blanketing gloom.

Jonathan was too terrified to even ask for an explanation. He spied paintings, old and framed in gold-encrusted frames, in different, familiar and famous styles along this exhausted yet resolute hallway. Then, despite all this, one piece of hanging artwork kept his attention. Harker gaped at a

---

[31] Mirrors go back thousands of years, to the beginings of Civilization. The process of making the modern mirror began in Germany and by Venetian glass-blowers during the Renaisance. The Silver-glass mirror was perfected in 1835 by German chemist Justus von Leibig, though the process of metallurgy in mirrors goes back to 500AD in China. Mirrors were part of Arabic culture as far back as the 10th century, and part of Mulsim Spain.

lush portrait of the vampire, hundreds of years old. Dracula was younger, virile and full of classic *chiaroscuro*[32] sepias and blacks that tried to engulf the sharper, crueler features of the vampire. In the painting, Dracula sat facing the viewer with the unblinking, piercing gaze of a bird of prey. He reclined in a chair, both hands clasped before him. A painted candle burned brightly to one side, the crackle of the oil-stroked hearth flickering on the other. In front and behind the subject was the painter's most fascinating subject: the infinite darkness.

The painting technique was worthy of a master, and the vampire's jagged glare overwhelmed the piece, his inherent menace perfectly captured by the artist.

Through his fear Jonathan managed, "Is that portrait painted by—"

"Do not speak the Dutchman's[33] name," growled Dracula as he moved, half annoyed and half impressed at the young man's knowledge. "*Ingrato*. He and I ended on poor terms. It is not often that I commission a piece of art, whether it be a painting, poetry or music. Yet when I do, the work must be fulfilled to the satisfaction of the *patron*. It was the rule that the Castilian[34] Cervantes and the Austrian Mozart both readily accepted, but the Dutchman did not. 'Pearls before Swine'. Below this fortress, amid the glorious dungeons of my lower *Bibliotheca*, you would find an unpublished manuscript by Cervantes, his continuation of *La Galatea*[35]. Somewhere there is also a minor, uncompleted composition by *Herr* Mozart. I must share them with you sometime."

They reached the end of the dilapidated corridor, which then branched off into entrances to two rooms. Both doors were open, the room to the right was unlit, and Dracula's lantern revealed the stone-lined chamber to be crammed with musical instruments. Horns, flutes, musettes, violins, lutes, guitars mandolins, cymbals, drums harpsicords, and pianos, all enveloped by gigantic, multilayered cobwebs. Scrolls, piles and portfolios of sheet music were stacked further back into the gloom of the chamber.

To the left was where the Transylvanian drifted, and the young man followed, terrified yet spellbound. The sounds, shadows and silhouettes of the rat horde followed, like a blanket of starvation, disease and malice.

Another sight to behold, a gargantuan room awaited them through the corbel arch. Centuries-old shelves lined the walls of the massive, three-story, octagonal-shaped room, which was crammed with aged folios, disintegrating scrolls and molding papers. In shelves closer to the brick-lined floor lay stacks of dust-ridden medieval books. The scent of countless pages and scrolls from every corner of the world gave respite to the odors of decay and death from the hallway. A table that looked like it was used as a door to keep out invading Christians many lifetimes ago, complete with the sword-cuts to prove it, now adorned the middle of the room and was garnished with chairs that were hewn just this side of the Dark Ages.

A large jeweled, gold-lined goblet sat in solitude on the table.

"My humble collection," sighed the vampire with pride. "Alexandria and her scrolls, the archives of Ugarit[36], the Villa of the Papyri[37], even the Imperial Library of Constantinople[38], rest

---

[32] Chiaroscuro, Italian for *light-dark*, is a painting technique in classical art that produced strong light and shadow.

[33] Dracula refers to Rembrandt van Rijn (1606-1669), one of the great artists in the history of art.

[34] A large, prosperous region in Medeival Spain, the name coming from the abundance of castles (*Castillos*) in the area.

[35] *La Galatea* was a pastoral romance written by Miguel de Cervantes and originally published in 1585. Its sequel was promised to be written by Cervantes but never published and presumed unwritten.

[36] A port city in Ancient Syria. The civilization at Ugarit was at its height around 1300 BC. Archives containted pre-Bronze Age tablets of legal documents, land transfers, and poetry.

[37] A private villa in Ancient Herculaneum (Southern Italy) covered in volcanic ash during the eruption of Vesuvious in AD 79 and excavated in 1750 by Karl Weber, a Swiss architect and engineer. Over 1,800 papyrus scrolls were discovered at the site, the so-called Herculaneum Papyri.

[38] One of the great libraries of the Ancient World, which despite being the capital of the Byzantine Empire, held many Greek and Roman texts for nearly a thousand years. A series of fires and the raid of Constantinople during the Fourth Crusade crippled the library, which was done in completely during the conquest of the city in 1453.

their collective literary souls, would be envious of my series of documents. This treasure trove though, is not my complete library. I was forced to move the more valuable works to one of the dungeons below this fortress. I own the only known manuscript of *Divina Commedia*[39], bestowed upon me by the author."

Harker took in the crammed bookshelves with awe.

"Even the envious and cursed medieval libraries of the Christian monasteries would attempt to catalogue my collection, much to their collective disappointment. Their curiosity would overwhelm any kind of displeasure they would discover upon examination of certain titles here," sighed the vampire with a sense of foreboding that would make rosary beads melt.

Dracula let the lantern float out of his clawed hand and settle gently down onto the table. He tossed the documents down onto the table as if they were uneaten food. Dracula pointed to one of the chairs and said, "Sit."

At that moment, Jonathan Harker somehow found himself; his resolve, his inner strength, his anger, in the midst of all this evil. He moved over to where the chair was, but remained standing, a defiant sparrow in a storm of malice. Dracula glared at him like a leopard at a gazelle. With another gesture the vampire brought the heavy chair skidding under Harker's knees and he fell into the seat. Squinting his eyes and shaking his head, the vampire growled "Child, if you only knew whose patience you test."

Creaking, scraping noises wafted in from the corridor, and out of the endless shadows clambered in yet another supernatural apparition in this night reeking of evil: an animate skeleton, also the source of the noises heard from the gloom in the keep. A motley aggregate of moving bones, the skeleton staggered into the library carrying Harker's luggage.

Jonathan's mind reeled. When would these horrors end? A gangly fungus-ridden thing, bones grinding against each other like pieces of kindling, limping with the weight of the luggage, the macabre skeleton placed the bags on the table and groaned, "Quod puer sarcinas. Estne quicquam vos requirere, Dominus?" *The boy's luggage. Is there anything else you require, Master?*

"Nuntiare quod alii ad manseritis parare," grumbled Dracula, still busy burning a hole through Jonathan's skull with his glare. "Tum vos sunt conplevit nam vesperum, Adso." *Inform the others to prepare. Then you are free for the evening, Adso.*

"Da Maestru," said Adso. As the skeleton bowed with supreme courtesy, a beautiful black spider curled up inside Adso's right eye socket as he turned away.

Shadows then engulfed Adso.

As the echoes of the skeleton shambling away through the darkness faded, Dracula abruptly beamed at Jonathan, "A good solicitor is nothing without his quill, inkwell and seal," and again opened the terrified young lawyer's luggage with a flick of his hand. Of their own accord, neatly folded clothes fluttered out and above the bag, and as Dracula glanced among them, he said, "Of course. Your accoutrements would be with your business ware," when among the clothing he spied a tiny frame.

The vampire beckoned the small frame, and it floated to him.

Inside the frame was the photograph of a beautiful, serious young woman. Dracula took the frame into his taloned fingers, looking deeply into it, transfixed. "I have never seen anything like this! This is an image that has been captured somehow and reproduced onto paper and framed. How can such an image be re-created? Astonishing."

---

[39] *The Divine Comedy*, or simply, *Divina Comedia*, is an epic poem completed by Dante Alighieri in 1320 and among the great works of literature in the world. Divided into three parts, *Inferno*, *Purgatorio* and *Paradiso*, no known original manuscript of Inferno or Alighieri's signature is known to have survived into modern times.

He looked pointedly at Harker and gestured to the frame. "Your fiancée, Miss Wilhelmina Murray, correct?"

"How do you know her name?" gasped Jonathan, with enough territoriality in his voice that the vampire perceived it. "Or that I have a fiancée?"

"Are you too young to know death when it stands before you?" Dracula's sharp head swung to face Harker with the burst of intensity of a wild animal.

Again, the Transylvanian's owl eyes burned with anger. "Along a similar subject, if you ever raise a weapon to me again such as you did at Borgo Pass, I will surely kill you where you stand. Truly, kings have tested me less, child!"

"Y-yes, Count," said Jonathan, bowing politely in his chair. "My sincerest apologies."

"Accepted," purred Dracula as he turned his focus back to the picture of Mina. The vampire was entranced, examining every corner of the photo, as if simultaneously consumed by its beauty and the technological advancement which made the image possible. Harker watched the lantern's light flicker as it played over the vampire. Jonathan felt extremely uncomfortable watching this menacing man's eyes take in his fiancée's photograph. Just when it seemed the vampire's concentration was at its apex, his sharp-featured head jerked up toward the shadowy ceiling, having heard something that had escaped Jonathan's hearing. Dracula smiled at Harker like a schoolgirl strangling a kitten and said, "They have arrived! I am interested to see your reaction."

Jonathan fought the urge to look up, certain that it would bring a new abomination in a night overflowing with the macabre. Then, as if to deepen the overwhelming dread, ambient sounds of shrieks and wails forced Harker to shift his gaze to the rafters of the library, an odd, octagonal-shaped wooden construction that contrasted with so much of the other stonework in this labyrinth of a castle. As Harker looked up, Dracula pocketed the photograph. Jonathan's arms blossomed with goose pimples as he realized he recognized the voices behind the shrieks.

Among the beams and posts, three evil masses slithered in from horizontal windows just below the roofline, around the beams and posts of the roof before beginning a descent along the creaking shelves and piles of scrolls. To Jonathan's horror, he realized the shadows were three more huge bats, brown not black, and they carried the driver of the carriage, as well as Catina and the baby Nadya.

"They were my travel companions!" shot out of Jonathan, panic growing within him.

Dracula's burst of laughter delighted in Harker's distress. As the bats moved down between the third and second story, Jonathan could see that the first bat held the carriage driver with a firm right hand wrapped around his neck while using the free left wing to lower itself. Nearby, the second massive bat held tiny, helpless Nadya in its mouth, carrying the infant by the neck like a lioness carries her cubs.

Lastly, the third bat held Catina, who was screaming and writhing in terror, her horrified eyes locked onto her infant, "Do not drop my little girl! Have mercy! Vă rog[40]!"

The trio of huge bats all leaped off the second-floor railing and landed on the moldy stone flooring, just behind Dracula, who barely turned to acknowledge their presence. As they rose, the three bats transformed as quickly as Dracula had, becoming three very pale and very beautiful vampire women. All three wore elegant and aristocratic black gowns. Their eyes glowed in the darkness like leopardesses. All three looked over Jonathan Harker like they wanted to devour him, in every manner of speaking.

"These," cooed Dracula, ignoring Jonathan's horrified expression, "are my concubines."

Jonathan could see that the women bristled at the word 'concubine'.

Harker could also see that Dracula delighted in the bristles.

---

[40] The Romanian word for please.

"Firstly, this is Petra Ali," said Dracula as he pointed to the tall, lithe, dusky Egyptian woman in a midnight-black dress that elegantly combined Georgian Era[41] couture[42] with the textures and whispers of Ancient Egypt. She had long, flowing raven hair, a regal countenance and the cast-iron gaze of a cobra. Her eyes were elegant, catlike and beautiful. Her lips ripened fruit of sensuality framed by strength, courage and ferocity. Petra held the terrified driver by the scruff of the neck. The poor cab driver tried to squirm away but she shook him so violently the man stayed still, clear that the next thrashing would snap his spinal column.

"Andromeda Philaras, our youngest, holds the human infant," said the vampire, pointing to a younger-looking nubile woman with dead, soft, pale skin and elegant Greek features that could have adorned a Hellenist vase. Beautiful almond-shaped eyes were filled with a fearsome power and malice that sought to tear Jonathan to pieces with just a blink of her sumptuous gaze. Andromeda had curled, dark hair fancily done up with bows and ribbons. Her locks draped over the vampiress' extraordinary ebony gown that made one think of sumptuous Greek mosaics as well as middle of the century fashion. Her skin had somehow been drenched in Mediterranean sun as well as bathed in pale moonlight. Andromeda's bird of prey eyes bored a hole through Harker's head.

"And this is Venus de' Medici, our abbess, *mater superior*," growled Dracula. Venus was the most resplendent of the brides, a formidable presence. Voluptuous, courteous, ferocious, beautiful and lethal, all at one glance. Her hair was brown, not black, and her spectacular Italian gown was sewn of different textures, shades and patterns of black. Her large, perfect eyes took in everything in around her, and looked over Jonathan Harker with murderous intent. Venus was a tigress in human form. Her smile would have been beautiful if it were not laced with menace and jagged canines; her ripe, full lips would have been irresistible if not curled with ravenous hunger for human blood. She emanated power and confidence. Venus held the crying gypsy woman in a vice grip with her bare hands.

All three women were stunningly beautiful, and incredibly deadly.

As if he was showing off three thoroughbred mares, Dracula of Transylvania stood proud.

Catina was beside herself trying to reach out to her infant.

"Copilul meu!" she wailed. *My baby!*

"Concubines, may I present to you all Master Jonathan Harker, the young, eager solicitor from England I informed you would be arriving."

The brides said nothing, all of them taking in Jonathan as if they wanted to butcher and sell him by the pound. Courtesy seemed absurd at the moment. The Egyptian vampiress turned to Dracula, the driver firmly in her iron grip.

"نحن وليمة الليلة، والماجستير," said Petra to Dracula, somehow combining the air of aristocracy grace and animalistic ferocity.

"English, Petra," said Dracula with a horrible laugh. "For the benefit of our guest. We as the ruling class must remain courteous to commoners."

"We feast tonight, Master," translated Petra, to the collective chill of Jonathan, the driver and the gypsy, who began to wail.

"A nostra volta presente per la nostra scoperta, maestro," snarled Venus, ignoring Dracula's request. *We in turn present to you our find, Master.*

---

[41] The Georgian Era is the period in British history between approximately 1714 to 1837AD.

[42] High quality, fashionable clothing tailored to the specific measurements of the wearer, made by hand using the finest materials. From the French phrase 'haute (high) couture', which originated in Paris in the mid 1800s. Englishman fashion designer Charles Fredrick Worth took the revolutionary step in having his clients select colors, patterns and fabrics before the design process began, and was the first designer to sew brand labels into his clothing.

Jonathan sensed a moment of tension pass between Venus and Dracula, a history of resentment bottled up into a second of time. After another such measurement of time, Dracula decided to ignore the tension.

"Which is to be your pleasure, Master?" said Andromeda in perfect, clipped English, which drew a nod from the Transylvanian for her courtesy. Petra and Venus exchanged not-so-discreet glances laced with the layers of a complex relationship between them all, yet with a palpable sense of envy and resentment toward Andromeda, who failed to suppress her smirk of satisfaction.

Dracula then smiled coyly, walked over to tenderly take the baby from Andromeda and sighed, "κάνει ό, τι θέλετε με τους άλλους." *Do what you will with the others.*

Catina understood the inference if not the language, and wailed in mortal pain, "NO!! *She is my child*! Take me and bleed me dry but spare her! "Ea este copilul meu!" *She is but an infant!*

"Count, please release them!" begged Jonathan, close to tears. "I beg of you."

Harker moved to intervene, but Dracula reached out, and with a mere flick of his right hand slammed the chair behind Harker against his legs. The chair shot in and locked against the table, Jonathan Harker trapped within it. Jonathan attempted to wrest himself free, but Dracula's telepathic hold was iron-clad.

Andromeda rounded and crouched at Harker, livid at his daring attempt to interfere. The sound of a ravenous wolf surged from her pursed lips, but Dracula waved her off as he said, "δεν πρόκειται να αγγίξει." *He is not to be touched.*

The infant began to shriek in Dracula's hands, as if Nadja sensed what held her. Dracula chuckled like a sword stroke in the darkness as he turned back to a horrified Jonathan. "Would you deny a carcass to a pack of jackals?"

Petra instantly and powerfully threw the driver to the ground, leaped on top of him like a panther, and dove for his jugular. He managed a succumbing yelp, gurgling as his throat was invaded and severed. Kicks and punches were fended off, then faded into an uninterrupted feeding. The sounds of canines clicking against neck and jaw bones began.

"Spare my daughter!" continued Catina, now being forced to the ground by Andromeda and Venus. Despite the vampires' collective strength, the woman's terror spurred her. She bawled as she said, "Nu ai nici o milă?" *Have you no mercy?*

Dracula pivoted to face her, cradling Nadya with tender care. "There is more mercy in my rats."

Andromeda and Venus enveloped Catina. Venus bit into her neck and ripped her jugular right out of her neck, spraying blood in an arc, while Andromeda pulled out Catina's voice box with her canines, mid-scream. Catina fell over, and the women began to devour her.

As they fed, the eerie sounds like the growls and snarls of jackals competing for meat in the aftermath of a killing wafted over to Jonathan, who turned his head in disgust and horror.

Then the only sounds were that of the women drinking, biting and digesting.

And the baby Nadya crying.

As he approached Jonathan and the table, Dracula giggled at the little baby and said, "Shhhh. Do not cry, Little One. Let me help you sleep."

Jonathan again tried to rise out of his chair in defense of the child, but with another wave of his hand, Dracula kept a struggling Harker seated against the knobbed, massive table. Dracula gave Jonathan an impatient look, then saw the goblet on the table and drew it toward him with a beckon from his talons. The goblet hissed as it glided toward the vampire and stopped. Dracula then raised his taloned left index finger to the wailing Nadya's neck.

"NO!" roared Jonathan, struggling in his chair, veins in his neck and temple exposed with his fury. "Don't touch her!"

Dracula gently, tenderly slit the neck of the baby.

Nadya continued to cry as her own blood ran along her tiny neck before it began to pour down into the goblet. Jonathan agonized as he watched, tears streaming down his face, trying to wrench himself free, thinking he could still somehow save the child.

As life ebbed from Nadya, Dracula sang sweetly:

Du-te la culcare copilul meu minuscul,
până în zori alb rupe ziua.
Du-te la culcare copilul meu minuscul,
niciodată se tem de spiritele forestiere,
până când noul zori.
Apoi, mama ta te va săruta delicat.

Go to sleep my tiny child,
until white dawn breaks the day.
Go to sleep my tiny child,
never fear the forest spirits,
until the new dawn.
Then your mother will gently kiss you.

In her death throes, the baby Nadya stirred one last time. Dracula saw this and glanced up at Jonathan, who was horrified beyond words. The vampire chuckled, still in a whisper, before he continued with a dreadful hiss:

Niciodată se tem de Dragonul în castel,
el niciodată nu va ucide leul Crestin,
iar mama ta te va proteja pentru totdeauna.

Never fear the dragon in the castle,
he will never slay the Christian lion,
and your mother will forever protect you.[43]

Then the baby Nadya moved no more.

Jonathan was overwhelmed, furious and did not care whether his tantrum would cost him his life. Harker locked his tear-filled eyes with the Transylvanian and snarled, "You are no king! You are a coward, a fiend, and a vile monster of the night! God damn you! Damn you to Hell! You are a *demon*, Count."

"*Now*," hissed Dracula with a leer of appreciation, "you understand, Master Harker."

Behind the vampire and amid the gloom, the brides giggled their agreement, sending a cavernous chill down Jonathan's spine.

Dracula's lantern flickered as it sat on the table, continuing to cast macabre, soft shadows everywhere.

Jonathan slumped back in his chair, overwhelmed with sadness, defeat and fatigue.

Dracula stood straight up and coldly tossed Nadya's limp body to the side, where it landed with a wet, tragic slap against the brickwork and was overwhelmed instantly by the starving horde of

---

[43] Adapted from the Romanian folk lullaby Culcă-te, puiuț micuț, or Go to Sleep, My Tiny Baby.

rats, even as her corpse rolled horribly along the irregular, misshapen flooring. Harker was yanked from his sorrow and tried to look away but could not as the baby's torso was ripped to shreds by the ravenous tide of rodents. Rat after rat poured into the child's windpipe, consuming flesh along the way. A few made it into Nadya's skull through her mouth and throat, even as others began to chew away at her eyes and nostrils. Dracula swept up the goblet and drank like he'd just come out of the Sahara. For a few moments there was only the sound of Dracula drinking, as well as the cascading sound of rats tearing at Nadya's flesh. Dracula of Transylvania put the goblet back down on the table with a huge, satisfied sigh.

Meanwhile, Petra, Andromeda and Venus continued to feed. Sounds of soft ripping of the flesh mixed with lapping of fluids and the occasional snap of bone. The driver was already dead and drained, ashen with the loss of blood and flesh, while Petra was reinvigorated with energy and color. An occasional animal growl, lathered with blood, slipped out. The gypsy mother gurgled one last time before she joined her daughter in eternal lullabies.

Dracula's blood-filled leer infuriated Jonathan, yet the vampire ignored Harker's seething and continued, "So, boy, to the work at hand. I do not know how long I will need the properties in question, but one should prepare for any possible eventuality. Let us find your seal, Solicitor[44]."

"I'm not going to help you, vermin," hissed a livid Harker, despite being still pinned to the table and the precarious situation he was in. "You disgust me."

Surprisingly, Dracula took no offense, already satisfied with Jonathan's agony. He merely shrugged and said, "We shall observe the amount of assistance you need supply."

Jonathan's second travel bag opened at the vampire's invisible whim. More folded clothes and objects of toiletry[45] began to float out and settle down upon the table. While this was happening, Dracula opened the document package with a flick of his clawed fingers. He scanned the document briefly but with deep concentration while he took another long, deep drink from the goblet. As the objects of Jonathan's privacy continued to float next to him, the vampire took notice of one in particular.

"Ah," said Dracula with a strange disappointed tone in his voice, "there it is."

Dracula put the goblet down on the table, then dipped his right fingertip into the blood-lined goblet. The documents opened before him like rose petals in the spring, and he signed each page with the blood of the infant. The seal opened in front of the vampire and dipped itself into the goblet before raising itself up and out and pressing against the last page of the document.

"I have not ventured a transaction of property in a great deal of time," said Dracula, "but I do understand that it is both bad form and good fortune for you to have signed these documents beforehand. Bad form because that behavior is an indication of sloth, but good fortune because I do not need to torture you to achieve it. This disappoints me. I was relishing and anticipating a gallant lack of cooperation on your part, but your novice or laziness as a solicitor deprives me of that delight."

Dracula took a small stack of travel tags out of the luggage.

"And now we have completed our transaction," said Dracula, now in a cheerful mood as he slipped the tags into his own pants pocket. He then handed back the blood-soaked solicitor's seal to Harker, who was too repulsed to take it. Dracula waited until he realized that Harker was indeed not going to touch the seal before pointing to Jonathan's left coat pocket. A handkerchief fluttered out from within the coat. Dracula snatched it in mid-air and used it to clean off the seal. He then

---

[44] A legal practitioner of the time, yet not always a lawyer.

[45] Soap, washcloths, toothpaste, toothbrush, shaving kit, etc. Soap was present as far back as ancient Babylon, bristle toothbrushes date back to 7th century China, though many cultures had used chewsticks, toothpicks and other variants much earlier.

wrapped the handkerchief around the seal, then with another gesture, led the articles back into the bag. It snapped shut tightly, and this business finished, the fearsome vampire turned his penetrating owl eyes right back at Harker.

"Count," said Jonathan, at this point too outraged and nauseated to even speak to the vampire out of anything other than necessity. "Mr. Hawkins, the head of my firm, you called him to this castle ahead of me to complete the purchase of the property, and we have not been given word from him in some time so I was sent to follow—"

"Ah, yes!" grinned Dracula like a tax collector, pointing his right index finger into the air in delighted surprise as he did so. "In all of this activity, I had forgotten about Mister Peter Hawkins. What a jolly chap, as the British would say. Quite the classic English gentleman, I must say. He preceded you out here, in good faith, thinking these matters were solely about a lease. In a further irony, he is the reason you are alive at all, child. Let me take you to him."

He waved to the chair, and it released Harker. The vampire turned to the brides, all three rising with mouths full of blood and engorged, satiated looks over their mouths, and said, "Sequi me, humano cautum, et affer ad luminis." *Follow me, guard the human and bring the lantern.*

The brides glided into positions that herded Harker toward Dracula, who glided toward another doorway, this one at the other end of the library. Andromeda was to Harker's right and Venus on his left. As Dracula walked, skin darkened, fur grew like weeds, cloth melted, bones stretched and repositioned themselves. In seconds, Dracula had transformed into a huge wolf, or a wolf-*thing*, with massive jaws lined with huge, bone-breaking molars and steak knife canines. Larger than a lion or bear, the wolf bounded along on four massive legs, covered in fur from nose to tail. The formidable beast loped ahead, huge claws clicking on the worn, tiled floor. A tail switched at the end of the body, the wolf seemed more than a wolf, something out of the Pleistocene era, a species that primitive man would have shuddered to encounter.

Jonathan staggered back away from the transformation, shocked at yet another one of the vampire's metamorphoses, when he backed right up to a firm, cold hand pressed against his spinal column. Jonathan turned into the lithe, dangerous beauty of Petra. Her cobra eyes penetrated into Jonathan's soul. Petra leered at Harker past her jagged, blood-caked canines, then blew him a kiss with supple, ripe lips that had just torn flesh from a human being. Jonathan took a step back from her, terrified that this being of such beauty could project such a menacing countenance. The Egyptian's hand then melted into the clawed wing of a bat as it pushed against Harker's chest, and she sneered at him as she began to transform into bat form. Unsure of what would happen next in this endless series of surprises, Jonathan whirled around to see that the other brides had also started to metamorphose.

As she began to transform, Andromeda looked Harker over and purred, "He *is* handsome."

"I would cover him with kisses, then devour him," snarled Venus without batting an eye. He jolted at Venus' words and looked at her. The intensity of her stare as Venus' human physiology became that of a bat told Harker that the vampiress meant every word.

Andromeda merely giggled, throwing a lurid glance at Harker that chilled him to the bone as she too began to melt into the dark brown form of a bat.

In their wake, the leftover carcasses of the driver and gypsy were being swarmed over by the horde of horrible, voracious rodents. Bones broke, muscles ripped and intestines popped horribly, a horrific symphony to accompany the ghastly feast.

Jonathan gulped and said a quick prayer for the souls of the victims, then looked back again at Petra, who now held the lantern in a mouth full of jagged incisors. She hissed at Harker and pushed him with her fur-lined forehead, not-so-gently headbutting him forward. Jonathan stumbled forward in the direction of the Dracula wolf's loping exit, with the three bride bats as his macabre escorts, with the living wave of rats in tow, millions of tiny claws creating a harmonic sound as they clicked, clattered and writhed along the motley aggregate of bricks and tiles.

As they walked, Jonathan noticed the musculature of the Andromeda and Venus bats' huge shoulders as they moved along the mottled stone floor. Their wings, curled up along the bats' respective forearms, were huge. Jonathan estimated that their wingspan might be twenty feet. He noticed that Andromeda's shade of brown fur was lighter than Venus', but when he turned back to confirm that Petra's fur was the darkest, the Petra bat merely snarled at him, the lantern still firmly in her maw.

They moved out from the library and into another expansive corridor that led to a wide, sweeping staircase. Architecturally, the marble, iron and wood stairs had no place in the castle, because the railings were hewn of carved wood and forged metal and were less than a century old, but there it was, in this jigsaw puzzle of a stronghold, time standing still and blurred at the same time. There seemed to be no end to the dark menace of the place. Generations of gargantuan cobwebs spread like absurd tapestries over the delicate staircase railing, which seemed based on the flamboyant Rococo style of a hundred years past. Something bright drifted from behind and just by Jonathan's head, and the young man jerked sideways, bursting with fear. It was the lantern, which had floated out of the Petra bat's mouth and by Harker's head. The bride bats, walking on their knuckles like gigantic parodies of their tiny counterparts, noticed Harker's reaction and, if huge bats could do such a thing, chuckled collectively and darkly at the terrified solicitor. The lantern glided up and along the staircase in front of them, toward Dracula, casting a strange, eerie countenance to the scene, shadows ominously stretching and yawning over the architecture.

With disgust, Harker noticed bulbous, opalescent spiders the size of a man's hand moving strangely in and out of the cobwebs that hung over the railing like vast sheets of linen, pretend ghosts in a house crammed with evil spirits. The spiders chased each other in and around the web labyrinths, cannibalizing each other at every opportunity in a perverse contest of survival. Behind him, the Petra bat unleashed a sharp, deep chirp, which Andromeda answered with one of her own, added upon by a series of chirping responses from Venus, which became a cacophony of conversation between the she-bats. Ahead, entangled in the flickering incandescence of the lantern, the Dracula wolf heard all of this and snorted a growl in annoyance. The lantern hung in the air next to the Dracula wolf, clearly under the mental control of the great beast.

Amid all this death, gloom and morbidity, everything seemed possible for this horrific man.

This *undead* man.

They reached the landing at the top of the stairs, where wood and metal of the past century gave way to stone from half a millennium ago, rococo staircase transitioning into medieval hallway. The second story floor continued to be wood, but the walls were lined with strange bricks, some well placed, others haphazardly so, and bulged out, swelling grotesquely. Along this strange, oblong brickwork, a few wall gargoyles protruded, garnishing their clay compatriots. Stone demons, major and minor, greeted anyone foolish enough to make their way this far into this bizarre and dark place. Clay satyrs flayed angels, demons ravaged knights, and imps devoured the remains.

To their right was an atrium, open aired, but with a strange wooden-beamed roof constructed along the top, a fascinating combination of Moorish and Chinese, something perhaps out of the Himalayas if it not were for the definite Near East influence, a mish-mash of cultural architectural styles. Everything was caked in layers of dust and sacrilege. Doors of various ages, materials and styles, leading to unspeakable horrors lined both floors. The ground of this strange atrium or courtyard was lined with lush, ancient red-stoned flooring, with another grand representation of the ornate dragon consuming the Christian lion, with the following entwined within:

VI

VI   VI

Atop the dragons, rising up from the brick floor were twenty stout wooden stakes six inches wide and ten feet high, and atop the stakes, or rather around the stakes, were long-dead human carcasses, human remains in their original armor, representing different regions of Europe, the Holy Land, the Byzantine Empire as well as the great civilizations of Asia. Generations of caked blood textured the crimson bricks. Large, bizarre, scarlet candles, hundreds of them, all filled with the bones of small children and animals, sat on the floor, licking at the remains and flickering an unholy illumination over the courtyard of the dead.

Back along the hallways in this morbid atrium, the Dracula wolf stopped for a moment to make sure they were all following him before the lupine figure loped down the hallway and toward a craggy wooden door that looked as if it had been hung during the Dark Ages. Jonathan hesitated at the top step as the Dracula wolf stopped in front of the doorway and began his transformation back to human form. To Jonathan's left, Venus continued to chirp as she started to transform back to her human form, then from behind, Petra's animalistic chirps and hisses became human spoken words: "—عندما فتحت الباب للقن، أرماة كان جرذ زرع كانه أن عم مع يصرخ، شيء فظيع في ذراعيها."
—*when I opened the carriage door, the gypsy woman was just lying there with that screaming, horrible thing in her arms.*

"ο οδηγός ήταν ένας δειλός," scoffed the now human-form Andromeda, "αφήνοντας τη γυναίκα με το παιδί και τρέχει να σώσει τον εαυτό του." *The driver was a coward, leaving the woman there with the child and running to save himself.*

"Questi auriga sono solitamente armati," said Venus, her transformation complete. "Avrebbe potuto cercato di aiutarla." *Those drivers are usually armed. He could have tried to help her.*

"وهذا وه السبب في أنني أصر على تناول الطعام. لهذا الرجال الجبان يغيظني.," hissed Petra. She sneered at Harker before she shoved him forward. *That is why I insisted on eating him. Cowardly men infuriate and disgust me.*

"Poi ci sono l'altro tipo," hissed Venus full of meaning, near a whisper, glancing with intent toward Dracula. *Then there are the other kind.*

Dracula waited at the door, his patience clearly fleeting, the lantern floating next to his sharp, wicked head.

"Αγροτικό αίμα είναι σαν το κρασί της χαμηλότερης ποιότητας," sneered Andromeda. *Peasant blood is like wine of the lowest quality.*

"تتذكر ما النبيذ الأذواق مثل؟" teased Petra as she gave Jonathan another shove. *You remember what wine tastes like?*

Venus giggled, and the hairs on the back of Harker's neck stood up straight.

They were in front of the door.

"Silete," growled Dracula. *Be silent.*

He beamed at Harker, and Jonathan realized that the only reason Dracula had shown patience was the relish of seeing his guest's reaction to whatever was behind this door, which Jonathan realized was covered with carved, tiny roman numeral sixes. "Follow me. There is no reason for dread."

Dracula pointed to the door's primeval, corroded lock, which turned of its own accord, metal grinding on metal as it did.

The door creaked open as if begging Jonathan not to come through. He felt a profound helplessness, a fly covered with webbing in a cobweb filled with deadly arachnids. It was only a matter of time before he himself was devoured, Jonathan realized. *Tonight, or worse, tomorrow night.*

They passed though the moldy doorway, which led to a stone staircase, spiraling upward into more darkness.

The lantern led the way.

Harker followed, his dread building, followed by Dracula, who did not have the courtesy to wave the ladies of his home through first, such was his eagerness to see the reaction of his guest and future victim.

As he ascended the staircase, Jonathan took note of the worn and broken tibias, fibulas and ribs lying along the steps, trying to hide from the monstrous shadow that followed Harker. He thought that if a window presented itself, he could dive through and either escape if there were a hand-hold, or if not, have a fall to his death spare him the experience of being devoured. He thought of Mina, and of his parents, and his friends back home, and gulped back tears. But there was no window, just more stairs illuminated by the glowing lantern floating ahead. He sensed Dracula behind him, and Jonathan knew that at least he would make it up to the top of the stairs and see what the vampires wanted him to see. Then, out of the darkness above him, appeared another door, old, metal, and covered with the now-familiar dragon-consuming-lion motif, entwined with the trio of roman numeral sixes.

It opened, manipulated by the evil behind Jonathan's right shoulder.

"At last, we are here," said Dracula, just behind Harker.

He could hear the brides giggling in eager, schoolgirl anticipation.

The metal door led into another dark, dank chamber, yet this one clearly at the apex of one of the castle's towers. Into this tower room walked Jonathan Harker, solicitor. A section of the ceiling above had collapsed into the chamber, revealing nothing but night's wickedness above. A bleak set of windows sat across from them in this round room, which was a veritable museum of instruments of torture through the ages and continents, with brazen bulls, thumbscrews, racks, wheels, pillories, scavenger's daughters and iron maidens lining the walls. All these wicked devices were caked with rust and dried blood. Corpses old and new, all in positions and gestures of agony filled the devices, crumbling bones in the corners a silent history of pain. But Jonathan did not notice the macabre collection as much as he took in the lit candles around a pentagram on the ground, with a cross that hung perversely upside down, built into the roofing beams of the ceiling that remained intact.

Crucified upside-down on the inverted symbol of Christ, dangled an aged British gentleman who had become elderly not just through his time on Earth, but what been done to him in the last few weeks. Covered with clothes that had been torn to shreds, bleeding from his mouth and multiple wounds along his quivering body, dripping with sweat, urine and filth was one of the sweetest, kindliest older men anyone could ever know.

"Dear God, *Uncle Peter*!" bellowed Jonathan, his soul ripped out of his body in one heartbeat. He sprinted over to the cross, thinking he would undo whatever bounds were holding his uncle to the beams, when he realized that Peter Hawkins' hands, feet and torso had been nailed through the body and directly into the wood.

FOUR

"I thought it ironic for your sow[46] of an uncle to be crucified as his biblical namesake," bubbled Dracula, relishing Jonathan's anguish. He and the brides stood watch, eyes aflame with both supernatural glow and malicious glee. Dracula's smirk twisted with sadism as he giggled, "Though it has not been actually proven that the accursed apostle died on the cross[47]."

"Uncle Peter!" whispered Jonathan, voice cracking amid his weeping, cradling the old man's blood-soaked head with the deep affection reserved for a beloved family member. Hawkins was unconscious, but at the mention of his name, the crucified man stirred. Blood, teeth and bits of flesh slogged out from the old man's mouth. Deep ragged breaths shot out of Peter Hawkins, who was in terrible agony. They both then knew the wounds were fatal.

"What have they done to you?" gasped Harker, full of tears and regret.

"Jonny, my boy," whispered Uncle Peter, smiling like Christmas morning despite the savagery afflicted upon him. Then his eyes shot open with realization. "Why are you here?"

"Came to bring you down from there so we can football together on the Seward's back lawn like the old days," said Jonathan, holding onto a shred of composure, shuddering with the effort. "Ian always picked you first, didn't he?"

"My dear boy," sighed Uncle Peter, bursting into deep convulsions of weeping, sorrow and pain, as he shook his head in mourning, "there is nothing you can do for me. Save yourself."

Dracula looked like he had just plucked a flower. "Hawkins has been awake since I had him crucified, waiting for you so he could die like a pus-filled dog in a filthy gutter. Stronger than I had considered. I hoped he would pass in agony while mustering the strength to see you. I had told him you were coming, you know. Usually the crucified die rather quickly, their lungs simply collapse from exertion. That has been my experience with the many who have tasted my attention."

Uncle Peter looked past Jonathan at Dracula and gasped, "*Vampire!* Let not our old sins taint his innocence! You are a royal; let your sense of justice prevail upon you here. You've taken your pound of flesh!"

"Hawkins," chuckled Dracula, "surely you have come to know me better than that? As I explained to someone mere moments ago, my rats have more mercy."

"What I said was," growled Jonathan, giving his back to the Transylvanian, "that you are no better than the vermin you live with."

Dracula ignored Jonathan's statement and smirked with malevolent irony. "Master Harker, how may your parents be faring in these days of dark clouds and ominous horizons? William and Cynthia, I believe?"

Still in his crouch and holding Uncle Peter's head in his hands, Jonathan turned to Dracula with a

---

[46] Fully grown female pig.

[47] Dracula is referring to Saint Peter, one of the Twelve Apostles of Jesus Christ, who according to Catholic faith was the first Pope. Peter was supposedly crucified upside down in Rome under Roman Emperor Nero.

combination of shock and revulsion as he said, "Why do you speak of my parents as if you knew them? What have *any of us* done to you all the way from England to deserve your torture and murder?"

Dracula looked away from Jonathan, bored. He stalked over to a corner of the room the way a captive lion walks across a large cage, exuding impatience. The lantern followed. Amid the candlelight were hand-drawn property maps nailed to one of the racks, and Jonathan could barely make out the outline of the eastern English coast on one map. Another had the township of Whitby, with circles drawn around various estates and Carfax Monastery. Without looking at Jonathan, the vampire said, "Your uncle drew these for me in good faith to explain who my new neighbors would be. How charming and ironic. What your family has done to deserve my wrath is completely without question, Master Harker."

Jonathan stood, livid with rage, kicking over one of the pentagram's corner candles. Harker did not care if he died this night, only that he had been infuriated by all of the evil around him. He pointed to the dying Peter Hawkins and shouted, "I'll kill you for what you've done to him!"

Petra, Andromeda and Venus took a step forward, anticipating a leap from Jonathan at Dracula, yet the boy did not care, staring at the four sets of owl eyes glaring incandescently in the gloom, daring him to charge and be torn to pieces.

"Volo iecur eius," said Venus after a wolf's snarl. *I would have his liver.*

Enjoying Harker's anger and trembling fury as the youth confronted the vampires, Dracula waved the brides back while giving Jonathan a sincere smirk, as if to patiently dare the boy to charge.

"Did the faded British infantryman Peter Hawkins not regale his young nephew with the tales of his youthful misdeeds? His glories of war?" Dracula glared at Jonathan and growled, "I believe I quote the damnable New Testament correctly, since I cannot touch the perverse document myself, but I shall do my best: 'But one of the soldiers with a spear pierced his side, and forthwith came there out blood and water.'[48]"

In one motion Dracula gestured to one of the lances mounted up along the wall. It leaped, as if summoned, into his clawed hand. The vampire grasped the lance and threw it with incredible violence and force. Flying past Jonathan, the lance skewered Hawkins' torso before imbedding itself into the back beam of the crucifix.

Jonathan screamed in mortal torment at seeing the blow his uncle had suffered, his voice intertwining with Peter's explosion of a singular, silent scream. At last Peter Hawkins' soundless wail passed, and he trembled and looked at Harker, blood running out of his upside-down mouth.

"Run, Jonny," groaned Hawkins, as his tear-filled eyes closed.

His face filled with waves of torture, a livid Jonathan Harker pivoted to confront the vampire but stepped right into Dracula's right hand, which found Jonathan's throat and clamped it shut. The vampire's breath reeked of blood and hate as he snarled, "I shall drink of your Mina and sup of your mother when I am in Whitby."

Dracula bounded across the room, holding Jonathan aloft. He gestured to the ancient set of window shutters, and the shutters tore open as if they knew better than to defy the master of the castle. Jonathan struggled futilely in the iron-forged grip and panicked. He looked out the window and saw the yawning drop into the depths of the Carpathians before him.

"Die, Young Harker," seethed Dracula, full of venom and malice.

Without another word, the vampire threw Jonathan out of the window.

Harker plunged into the cold, dark night, and out of sight. And as he fell, Jonathan was not as afraid of his impending death as much as he was at the thought that everyone he loved in the world would soon be murdered.

---

[48] John 19:34.

FIVE

Jonathan Harker was gone, thrown to the destiny in his next life.

Inside the tower torture chamber, the shutters fluttered and banged against their wood and stone frames in the wake of Jonathan's fall. Dracula stood with his head down, arms clasped behind him and head lowered, with a satiated grin. He listened as Harker's scream melted into the gales whipping around Castle Dracula.

There was only the howl and hiss of wind, much to the Transylvanian's satisfaction. "Acum, cu privire către alte chestiuni," he said. *Now, on to other matters.*

Petra and Andromeda knelt before the pentagram, hissing *Ave Satanas* in repeated, hushed tones. Venus was on her feet, taking in Dracula. With a hint of question in her voice the vampiress said, "Avremmo potuto nutriti su di lui durante il viaggio." *We could have fed upon him during the journey.*

"Vor fi susținerea de-a lungul călătoriei," said Dracula as he gestured for the windows to close. "Nemo et rerum omnium abundantia quia sanguinem." *There will be sustenance along the voyage. No one will lack for blood.*

A moan crept from the impaled corpse of Hawkins, or rather the still-living, impaled body of Uncle Peter. He stirred, the blood from his impalement running over his chest, neck and head. Petra and Andromeda bolted upright, both gasping in surprise.

The five candles at each of the pentagram's corners ebbed, surprised as well.

Taken aback, Dracula turned to his victim, raised his arms in a gesture of exasperation and gasped, "Did my lance not yet finish you, Hawkins? Does the everlasting slumber elude you yet, old dog? Die, you stupid fool!"

"I still live, if only to spite you." Peter laughed as more blood seeped out of his mouth. "You are no monarch, your *goat of a father* no king. Your women are beasts suited for cages in the zoological gardens, not souls to share a life with. I am glad for our past deeds, regardless of your wrath. And Jonny's right, you are nothing but a filthy rodent fit for a Roman sewer."

The brides gasped, both at the insult hurtled at them and the audacity of the man. This time, the vampire took deep insult. A slit of a sneer covered his jagged incisors. His eyes blazed with hate.

"Where's my Jonny?" gagged Hawkins, blind as his own blood poured over his face and life ran out of him. "Run, boy!"

Gliding over to Peter, Dracula bent over to speak to the crucified man. The vampire's eyes danced with fury as he whispered, "Hawkins, I have just murdered your nephew. I threw him out that window from this tower. And before I rip out your heart and feed it to my women, I want you to know that I am going to travel to England and kill everyone that has ever meant anything to you."

"I do not fear death, nor you," smiled Peter past his sheer agony. Blood coughed out of his mouth and into his nostrils and eyes. "And I thank you for killing Jonny quickly and sparing him the torture you've given me. And I'd rather Jonny and anyone else I love be dead and in gracious hands than at the mercy of a toilet rat."

The brides blinked in shock at the completeness of the insult.

Dracula's face twisted with rage as he roared, "If you won't die as the accursed apostle[49], then you will die as did the damnable Baptist![50]"

Dracula pointed to an axe that protruded out of the rib cage of one of the tortured corpses. It flew out of the bloated, infected body, across the room and into his hand. The vampire raised the weapon over his head with enough energy to cleave the world in two, but he stopped.

Hawkins had given his ghost, but with a sly, peaceful grin over his face.

Disappointed that his fury had gone unfulfilled, Dracula dropped the axe with a disgusted, unsatisfied look. He growled, "Ut suam animus et perpetuum cruciaris." *May his soul be forever in agony.*

"Ave Satanas," whispered the brides, their eyes dancing with hateful joy.

"Devorandum eum," said Dracula to the rats. *Devour him.*

The slithering, rabid mass of rodents, which had lingered and frothed along the staircase behind them, surged forward to overwhelm the corpse of Peter Hawkins. The supernatural vermin encountered delicacies in Peter Hawkins' sleeves, pants, mouth, cheeks, tongue and eyes as the vampires left the torture chamber. Pieces of flesh and bone quickly began to fall off the inverted cross in the process, consumed even as they landed on the stone floor by the smaller yet no less ferocious members of the legion. Such was the rat horde's collective mass that even the candled pentagram became covered with sinewy fur in the process.

In the aftermath of Peter Hawkins' death, the tower's circular stairs were descended in contemplative silence by the vampires. As he sauntered down the extravagant, crumbling rococo staircase, Dracula realized that a familiar sense of tension had begun to eminate from the brides yet he decided to ignore whatever was simmering or boiling inside them. The brides were complicated, intelligent, strong women, and Dracula a powerful, impatient man, and that combination was a completely combustible formula. The only thing that kept the explosion from happening was Dracula's penchant for violence. His malevolence ruled them all with an iron fist. Yet even with that hold of fear over them, these three women, who represented all that was beautiful and learned and exotic and evil from the Ancient World, were restless.

Dracula sensed their mood like incoming gales that heralded a storm off the coast. His current satisfaction after the eradication of both Jonathan Harker and Peter Hawkins allowed him to permit whatever feminine gloom was being silently concocted behind him.

Behind him, three leopardesses stalked.

All around the walking undead, the freshly nourished legion of rats cascaded down the stairs in a morbid parody of a frothing waterfall. The lonely lantern floated with the vampire as Dracula took the tiny photograph of Wilhelmina Murray out of his coat pocket, the murders of two human beings now the farthest thing from his mind. The brides took turns exchanging conspiratorial glances as their shadows spread and bloated over the walls, covering the rats with a cloak of moving blackness that comforted the supernatural pestilence.

"Tale res mirabile, hoc facultatem capere imaginibus et custodiat eorum praeteritis nobiscum. Mundus movet deinceps, nos in circum," muttered Dracula, mesmerized by the woman's image. *Such an amazing thing, this ability to capture images and keep their past with us in the present. The world moves forward, all around us.*

Petra, Andromeda and Venus moved in agitated silence, filled with unspoken jealousies, fears

---

[49] Another reference to Saint Peter, the first Apostle.

[50] Dracula is referring to John the Baptist, who was beheaded at the order of King Herod Antipas. John was the cousin of Jesus of Nazareth, who himself would be crucified six months later.

and envies, garnished by secretive and not-so-secret glances between them. The women had spent generations rivaling for the attention and affection from their master, only to discover that he had none, save for himself. Dracula, who was many things but not a fool, sensed this, his patience ebbed, and without halting his long stride, half turned and said, "Sentio tua sermones. Loquuntur." *I sense your gossip. Speak.*

Petra was to Dracula's right, Andromeda to his left, with Venus in tow, lingering behind them, soaked with unresolved resentment. The vampiresses all shot more apprehensive glances at each other before Petra said, slowly but full of meaning, "Virum, apud respectu, quid veteris hominum locutus est erat veridicus. Vos adnuntiet nos sicut sponsæ ad aliqua, et concubinae ad adii. Voz nondum habebitis ad accipere ulla dei nos tamquam uxorem." *Husband, with respect, what the old human spoke of was truthful. You present us as brides to some, concubines to others. You have yet to take any of us as a wife.*

Dracula did not miss a step, still entranced with Mina's photo, yet he said matter-of-factly, "Aegyptiae, vos faciet oratio mihi sicut dominum uel ego faciet habere tua lingua scissa exire." *Egyptian, you will address me as master or I will have your tongue torn out.*

"يديس معن," said Petra, suppressing a resentful growl as they moved once again past the massive pillars of ancient, conquered China. *Yes, my Master.*

"ول مل كذخأي كذوزج، اذام يف كلذك؟" hissed the vampire without hesitation. *If I never take you as a wife, what of it?*

Dracula slipped the photo back into his coat as he continued to move, his voice echoing around them. "Quid est negoti tua? Tua doluistis est iussa egressum et introitum meum apud silentio." *What business is it of yours? Your concern is to carry out my bidding in silence.*

Behind Dracula, as they entered the library where the carriage driver, Catina and Nadya had been murdered, Venus bristled with anger.

Almost as if she had anticipated Dracula's response, Andromeda in turn replied, her voice laced with frustration. "Έχουμε κάνει πάντα ρύθμιση προσφορών σας, adhuc numquam habebitis adduxistis nos honoris." *We have ever done your bidding, yet you have never brought us honor.*

A vision of classical beauty and antiquated ferocity, Andromeda added, "ο κόσμος μας θεωρεί ως παλλακίδες, non haberet uxores." *The world sees us as concubines, not wives.*

Dracula's laugh was bloated with irony and sarcasm. "Δεν έχετε καμία τιμή να σας δώσει." *You have no honor to give.*

Waves of insult and revulsion swept through the brides. Their eyes glowed in the morbid gloom of the library, but Dracula's eyes were also aflame with a barely-contained fury. Petra fought to suppress both the snarl of a wolf and the urge to attack. Dracula heard the suppressed snarl and was satisfied that his verbal lance had done its work.

Dracula continued, enjoying the ferocity he was stirring, "Hawkins est verum vos quod nobiles carnivores, non feminae, non uxores. Turba canum. Femina canibus. Letalis instrumenta, nihil diversis quam mea Sagittæ, Lanceae et scipiones magnas." *Hawkins was correct that you are aristocratic carnivores, not women, nor wives. Pack dogs, bitches. Lethal instruments, no different than my arrows, lances or maces.*

Fury lit the women up like torches.

He turned to a simmering Petra and snarled, "Sunt in Romani antiqui, vos bestias tres esset scissa seorsum Christianus et leo aeque apud Colosseum. Tigres untinam habet non certamen pro ulla vos." *In Roman antiquity, you three beasts would have torn apart Christian and lion alike in the Colosseum. The tigers would have been no match for any of you.*

The three female *nosferatu*[51] followed the vampire into the next hallway, each hating the Transylvanian more with each step.

تسل انن أ امبو ، ,ةلحرلا هذه ىعسن نيعتي ال," hissed Petra, "ءاطعإل فرش انيدل سيل اذإ" مستحقا مارفقة سيدنا." *If we have no honor to give, we should not endeavor this journey, since we are not worthy of accompanying our master.*

"E dobbiamo anche non dimenticare quanto il mio maestro mi ha disonorato a Roma," spat Venus from behind him as they passed the bloodstain that the rats had tried so hard to lick clean from the grimy stone floors. *And let us also not forget how my master dishonored me in Rome.*

"Για να μην πούμε τίποτα για την απαγωγή μου στην Αθήνα," rumbled Andromeda as they neared the end of the hallway. *To say nothing of my abduction in Athens.*

"Εσείς δεν μπήκε καν στον κόπο να πληρώσει προίκα μου," she continued, nearly at a whisper. *You did not even bother to pay my dowry.*

Petra and Venus felt Andromeda's sorrow. Dracula cared more about the rats that were retching at his feet. They moved in silence, the lantern still floating around them, haunting one of the most haunted places in the world.

"Tu m-ai necazuri ca și cum corbii de peste un cadavru," said Dracula as he reached the wide, ceilingless hall, pivoted at the slab and headed for what remained of the massive, dragon-consuming-lion front doors. *You trouble me like ravens over a corpse.*

"Inima unei femeie trebuie să vorbească sentimentele sale, Maestru," said Venus, her sarcasm garnished lightly. "Forse noi donne dovrebbero stare e proteggere il castello del maestro, mentre lui è via." *A woman's heart must speak its feelings, Master. Perhaps we women should stay and protect the castle of the master while he is away.*

The women all sensed that Dracula was reaching his boiling point but did not care, such was their collective resentment. Dracula gave them an impatient snarl that combined wolf, lion and bear before he said, "Voi puttane mi accompagneranno in questo viaggio e continuare a fare come si sono ordinato, o avrò tutti picchettati fuori davanti alla mio castello a turbare gli avvoltoi con le vostre preoccupazioni!" *You whores will accompany me on this voyage and continue to do as you are instructed, or I will have you all staked out in front of my castle to trouble the vultures with your concerns!*

They reached the keep, where a rusted dragon consumed a corroded Christian lion in this macabre, colossal castle. With a gesture, Dracula made doors that weighed tons creak open, flakes of crimson rust littered the stone flooring as they let the cold, dark air pour into the castle foyer. The lantern flickered with the sinister whispers of the gusts that blew the secrets of the fortress walls for all to hear if they listened carefully enough, legend becoming fact, fact birthing myth, and myth mating with legend. Rats poured out around Dracula's feet, and hordes of the bats within the great hall flew outward from crevasse to night skies, creating a malevolent torrent that would terrify an army and rip valor from any soldier.

Yet the brides were unimpressed, their dark souls ripe with dissent and accrued, simmering resentment.

Outside, the night had stretched further out its macabre arms.

In front of the gigantic doors and beside the carriage that had brought the late Jonathan Harker to the house of the Son of Satan was yet another, surreal tableau. Dozens of skeletons were using wooden hoists that looked like they had been built during the Fourth Crusade[52] to lift coffins from

---

[51] *Nosferatu* is the antiquated Hungarian-Romanian word for vampire.

[52] The Fourth Crusade (1202-1204), ordered by Pope Innocent III, culminated with the conquest and sacking of Constantinople, the capitol of the Byzantine Empire. This event began the great divide between the Roman Catholic and the Eastern Orthdox Churches.

within the castle onto a large, ragged wagon. Others were finishing filling a black dagger of a coffin with dark, fresh soil. Dracula's bleak carriage, the same that had carried the late Jonathan Harker to this hellish place stood next to the wagon.

As they worked in morbid silence, some of the skeletons had their bones colored with an odd, almost clay-like red, others a moldy olive hue, while others were covered with different splatterings of coloring all over their anatomy. The walking anatomical lessons were of smaller stature but lithe, many with the wound that felled them still visible, a broken sternum with the hole the size of a spearhead visible, or a partially collapsed cranium. One still had a Roman axe embedded in the back of his skull. Another featured a broken sword that had been thrust cleanly through his rib cage. Yet another worked eagerly despite the dagger that he been placed through his left eye socket and into his dust-filled brain cavity.

On they worked.

A torrent of motion sloshed around Dracula's feet as the rats poured by him, down the steps then up and into one of the coffins, the rats squirming, biting, spitting and still drooling blood-soaked saliva from their feast of human flesh. Their last conversation still in their thoughts, the brides burned with anger all around the Transylvanian.

"مارتحالا قح أ ىلع نكن مل اذإ ةصاخلا انتايح روث علاو امور ىلإ اديعب ريطي نأ ةطاسبب انن كمي," said Petra, not bothering to add 'Master' this time. *We could simply fly away to Rome and find our own lives if we are not deserving of respect.*

In a blur, the Transylvanian rounded on her.

"سدقملا ءاملا لخاد ىلغملا كل مكل نوكي نأ دوأ تنكو" snarled Dracula as he leaned his face closely into Petra's and roared, "ءالشأ ىلإ عطقت نأ وأ لقنلا يف لصحت!" *And I would have you all boiled in Holy Water! Get in the carriage or be torn to pieces!*

Dracula's shouts reverberated over the courtyard like a storm over a meadow.

The skeletons all stopped their work to watch. The brides, despite being every ounce the carnivores that the vampire said they were, were nonetheless humiliated, but as women, not beasts. His words were laced with violence, and the women knew all too well that at that point whatever discussion they were having was over.

One of the skeletons, a large brutish set of bones covered in shoulder plates and body armor from Ancient Rome was supervising the lowering of Dracula's coffin, a sleek obsidian thing, onto the wagon when he heard Dracula's shouts. He pivoted instantly and stalked over to the vampire. The skeleton ignored the women, kneeled at the feet of Dracula and, with fossil jaws grinding said, "Quomodo potest ego serviturus sum vos, Magistri?" *How may I serve you, Master?*

Dracula nodded with satisfaction as he looked at the skeleton, then back toward the brides before he said, "Primus! Hoc proprie servus fidelis rex salutat." *Primus! This is how a loyal servant properly greets his king.*

Petra, Andromeda and Venus all threw Dracula sizzling daggers of hate.

The vampire chuckled as he patted the armor-plated right shoulder of Primus and said, "Tu servis Satanas bene." *You serve Satan well.*

"Existo servire magistro meo," followed the skeleton, speaking in the straightforward manner of a veteran soldier. "Tuis cogitationes factum praeparatus." *I exist to serve, my Master. Your plans have been made ready.*

Primus had long ago discerned the dynamics between his master and these women, leaving the complexities of their relationships between the four of them. The soldier took this all in and never shared it with anyone, preferring to have whatever occurred between husband and brides, master and queens, to play out around him and without his participation.

Which is not to say that Primus the skeleton did not have his opinions, but as a servant of old Rome, having seen so many Roman Emperors assassinated or executed[53], he simply knew his place and stayed there, firmly out of the way.

As the brides simmered, the vampire nodded with approval at Primus and said, "Debemus transite proximam villam meridie, et noctu ad Pontum Euxinum. Vester unus legiones comes peregrinationis nostrae. Cetera manere excubabunt in castri praefecto Adso." *We must pass the nearest village by mid-day, then be at the Black Sea by nightfall. One of your legions will travel with us. The rest will stay and guard the castle, under the command of Adso.*

"Sicut velis, dominus meus," rumbled Primus as he bowed deeply. *As you wish, my master.*

At Primus' nod in accepting his marching orders, the skeletons worked the complex, ancient pully-and-winch system to open the gigantic drawbridge, which groaned in protest like a dying elephant. As he pointed at Primus to punctuate his instructions, Dracula continued, "Aici veți purta o giulgiu și conduce transportul pe zi, in timp ce dorm, și noaptea după concubinele și mă hrănesc. Unul dintre oamenii tăi pot conduce vagonul. În cazul intervine cineva, chiar și după ce a luat în Fețele voastre colective, măcelăresc-le." *You will wear a shroud and drive the carriage by day while I sleep, and by night after the concubines and I feed. One of your men can drive the wagon. If anyone interferes, even after taking in your collective countenances, butcher them.*

"Da, Maestrul meu. Ordinele tale sunt lege," said the skeleton, turning to pointedly look at Petra. "اذإ ناك هناك يأ تأخري إضافي، ونحن قد كرت." *Yes, my Master. Your orders shall be law. If there are no further delays, we may depart.*

Petra hissed at the skeleton, "أي وقت تضى المتملق الذليل، بريموس" *Ever the sycophant, Primus.*

"Ego servite dominum meum," answered Primus in a cold, even tone, before he added, "Et suis uxoribus." *I serve my master, and his wives.*

Hordes of bats swirled above them in the night sky.

Dracula nodded in the closest way that a selfish, uncaring being such as the Transylvanian could express satisfaction and pride. He reached out and patted the crumbling sienna skull of the skeleton with some semblance of respect as he purred, "Primus meus fidelis canis. Romanus Centurionis et Gladiatore mortalia diebus, nunc servi nobilis in interitum." *My loyal dog Primus. Roman gladiator in your mortal days, now a noble servant in your afterlife.*

"ويجوز له أبدا أن ننسى الذين أخذوا حياته البشرية،" sneered Petra with a vicious grin. *And may he never forget who took his mortal life.*

"تمق بقص عميق، سيدتي،" replied Primus with a slow, courteous bow that successfully mingled respect, courtesy and contempt. He was too old and too smart to become entangled in their politics yet he knew how to respond with curt diplomacy when it mattered. *You cut deep, Milady.*

"Και η καρδιά του, αν θυμάμαι καλά," gushed the Greek. *And his heart, if I remember correctly.*

Primus then turned and gave Andromeda the same bow, ever courteous, whatever feelings were buried far within his dusty rib cage.

"Μέσα σε κλουβί σας, σαρκοβόρα ζώα," laughed Dracula at the brides. *Inside your cage, carnivores.*

Resigned to their participation, Petra and Andromeda melted into two grey/white figures made of spectral mist that drifted down from the doors and toward the closed carriage door, the twin banks of mist seeping in between the cracks of the doorframe. Once inside, they both rematerialized and

---

[53] At least thirty Roman Emperors were executed or assassinated between 41 and 474 AD, by either their own Praetorian Guard, another Roman Emperor, or by the Byzantine Emperor. Emperor Claudius was poisoned by his wife Agrippina in 54 AD. Agrippina was the granddaughter of Emperor Augustus, sister of the Emperor Caligula, and mother of Claudius' successor, Emperor Nero.

solidified, seated and awaiting the journey. Petra gave an exasperated, angry hiss, just low enough to respect the master, but loud enough to be heard. Venus stayed in her human form and with her chin up, gracefully slid past Dracula and Primus, giving them her back as she pulled open the door handle of the carriage. Venus did not bother to turn and acknowledge Dracula before she slid inside, leaving the carriage door open in a petty, symbolic gesture of lingering resentment. She sat next to Petra, across from Andromeda. Venus and Petra instantly clasped hands in silent support.

"تلظ قووة, أختي," whispered Petra to Venus. *Remain strong, my sister.*

Outside, Dracula chuckled and pointed to the carriage door, which swiveled to a close, locking the vampiresses in.

"Είναι ένα τέτοιο μπάσταρδο," snarled Andromeda as she looked out the far window, taking in the enormous fortress walls. "μου απήγαγε και πήρε τη ζωή μας μακριά από όλους μας." *He kidnapped me and took our lives away from all of us. He is such a bastard.*

Venus looked at Petra with a sense of understanding and sympathy before she said, "Saremo forte per a vicenda." *We will be strong for each other.*

"Il nostro momento arriverà." *Our moment will arrive.*

Moving as one, the colossal swarm of bats soared over the open area, as did the legions of ravenous rats that searched the courtyard for any signs of consumable life forms. The fungi-ridden Adso made his way out to stand inside the open doorway, framed by the metal dragon descending upon the rusted lion, watching the skeletons retract the hoists, preparing to leave. Atop the two coffins on the wagon, some skeletons stepped inside and *disassembled themselves into piles of bones*, one after the other, until the coffin was lined with femurs, tibias and skulls with empty, angry eye sockets.

Primus sauntered over to the wagon, which like the carriage, was horseless. Standing on the driver's seat, he saluted Dracula with a fist to his chest, which the Transylvanian acknowledged with a single, satisfied nod. Primus sat and took the reins, an odd action given the lack of horses. A dozen skeletons surrounded the vehicles, as the other skeletons lined up in military rank and file in the courtyard. The creaking sounds of their bones and the wheels grinding against ancient axles chilled even the cold, clouded night.

Primus pivoted his skull to await Dracula's command, and with a flick of the vampire's hand, Dracula gave the wagon and carriage their invisible impetus.

Wheels groaned.

Bones scratched against each other.

Wind gasped.

Bats screeched.

Dracula of Transylvania watched the macabre caravan begin to move forward, with the wagon in front, followed by the carriage with the brides. Clouds parted, revealing the bulbous, loathing moon. He smiled, looked to the west, and quoted, "'Ego sum poena ex Deus.'" *'I am the punishment of God.'*

"'Si non operatus magna peccata,'" continued the vampire as he began to transform, "'Бурхан хэлэхгүй байсан биз байгаа илгээсэн нь авах ял над шиг та нарын дээр'" *'If you had not committed great sins, God would not have sent a punishment like me upon you'.*[54]

The gigantic black Dracula bat threw open its massive wings, swept up into the air and glided down away from the keep, landing with a thump atop the carriage. Inside, the brides were in human form, lounging in their seats in silence, their hate-filled eyes were searing irons into the night. Dracula then gestured with his massive black left wing at the keep door, and the huge tableau of the dragon attacking the lion began to form itself as the door inexorably closed with a pronounced *clang* while the fungi-ridden Adso slipped into the recesses and darkness of Castle Dracula.

---

[54] Quote from Genghis Khan (1162?-1227) founder of the Mongol Empire.

With only the sound of the wheels turning, the caravan of darkness moved out into the night, a morbid procession of skeletons marching alongside a horseless wagon full of coffins, and a carriage driven by the whim and thought of a vampire. Pouring out of the castle gates behind them were thousands of rats and bats, confetti for the unholiest of parades. After the carriage passed the wreckage-laced moat, Dracula turned back and gestured with his right wing and the drawbridge closed shut, as if cutting off the world from Hell itself.

Outside, the great walls of the massive fortress that housed a keep, a castle and a labyrinth of dungeons, a cloud of ravens lifted off the dreaded landscape and began to accompany the caravan as it wound down along the lone road, a symphony of calls raining down upon the gigantic bat as it stood alone atop the carriage, driving it toward the village, the coast of the Black Sea, and their fate.

Upon the whim of their master, the gigantic horde of bats circled around and headed back to their home, where Satanic dragons ate Christian lions, where blasphemy reigned and where the head of a pope lay in dreadful, destined unrest.

Castle Dracula was left behind, dark and full of secrets of hate, death and love.

EUROPE, EGYPT, AND THE MEDITERRANEAN MAY-JUNE 1899

By the pricking of my thumbs,
Something wicked this way comes.

—William Shakespeare
Macbeth act IV, scene I

In 1899, interesting, sad, glorious and horrible things had either happened, were about to happen, or were still to come.

The Coca Cola Company had been in business for over a decade in America. The telephone had been invented by various people, Thomas Edison and Alexander Graham Bell the most prominent among them. Even though the history of the camera dates back to Ancient China, George Eastman had offered his 'Kodak' camera for sale in 1888. Each camera came with 100 exposures and had to be sent back to the company to have the film, which Eastman also had invented, developed. Flush toilets were popularized by Thomas Crapper & Co in London, with the chain-pull indoor toilet having been invented a decade before. Postage stamps had come into use in the 1840s. Japan had ended its policy of isolationism, known as sakoku, which had been in effect for over two centuries, in the mid 1850s. In England, wars in both Russia and India would take their toll on Her Majesty's Armed Forces. The Pony Express rode back and forth across America in the early 1860s, helping forge the relationship between California and the rest of the United States. The Civil War and the assassination of Abraham Lincoln at the hand of famous actor John Wilkes Booth had happened less than thirty years before 1899. The Winchester repeating rifle, known as The Gun that Won the West, made its debut in 1866. Alfred Nobel had invented dynamite in 1867. Amidst its unification, Italy had moved its capital from Florence to Rome in 1871, the same year that Lucy Walker became the first woman to ascend the Matterhorn. Steel had begun to be used in the framing of buildings instead of iron. Wagonways in England had yielded to steam-powered locomotives, a product of the Industrial Revolution, and train tracks exploded outward across Europe and the Americas. In 1882 the Married Women's Property Act in England assured that upon marriage, a woman would not lose the right to own her own property and could divorce without fear of poverty. 1885 had yielded petrol-powered three-wheeled, one-cylinder motorcars invented by Karl Benz. In Paris, the Eiffel Tower had been erected in 1889 as the entrance to the World's Fair. The Statue of

Liberty had been erected three years before. In 1890, the first electric underground train ran along a London public railway. Inventor Guglielmo Marconi worked on long-distance radio transmissions in 1899, for which he would share the Nobel Prize for Physics a decade later. The Lumiere brothers had invented moving pictures five years before, in 1894. The speed limit for motorcars in 1896 was 20 miles an hour. Queen Victoria herself, for which this era had been named, also known as the Empress of India, would live another two years before being succeeded by her son Edward. William McKinley had taken the office of the president of the United States just two years before and would be assassinated in 1901. Theodore Roosevelt would succeed him. Congress would then instruct the United States Secret Service to begin to provide security for the president a year later. Walt Disney would be born in Illinois that December. Composer Maurice Ravel would compose Bolero thirty years later. Artist Claude Monet, who made water lilies eternal, played with sound and light, respectively, in 1899. Ragtime music was popular in the United States. Americans Wilbur and Orville Wright were four years away from flying less than a minute but making flight possible for humankind. Mexico was in the midst of a dictatorship by Porfirio Diaz that would last for thirty-five years and end in 1911. World War I was fifteen years away. Charlie Chaplin was an impoverished ten-year-old in England, a decade away from stardom in Hollywood. Jim Crow laws that suppressed former slaves for generations were firmly entrenched throughout the United States and would remain so for another six and a half decades. Women would not be able to vote in a general election in either England or the United States for another two decades. As the American educational system began, it was not uncommon in the days before Child Labor laws for young children to work a ten-hour workday, six days a week. The debate over Child Labor laws in America would continue into the 1930s. In 1882 President Chester A. Arthur signed the Chinese Exclusion Act, prohibiting the further immigration of Chinese laborers, which would not be repealed until 1943. United States expansion further eliminated, and in many instances eradicated, Native American cultures from the landscape of America, which would start to end with the Indian Civil Rights Act passed nearly seventy years later. The top three causes of death in 1900 were influenza, tuberculosis and gastrointestinal infections, while all along, the gap between the rich and poor was enormous...

ONE

"Mina Murray, I'm flat-out callin' you a cheater!" roared Quincy Morris with an intermingled laugh that only enhanced his thick Texas drawl, and far too loudly for the customary Victorian era social setting. Tall, lean and not too bright, Quincy cut an unabashed Western figure with his dark, wide-rim Stetson[55] cowboy hat, boots, Western bow tie and twin holstered Colt 1871-72 Open Top revolvers[56], yet he bore the customary Victorian era coat, vest and pants worn by the sons of wealthy men of his time. The Texan also wore a perpetual smirk on his face that was somehow charming; he was smart enough to know when someone was trying to make a fool out of him, but just dumb enough to think he could accomplish any fool thing he wanted to.

"Sticks and stones, Morris!" shouted Wilhelmina Murray right back at the Texan. A beautiful, strong woman with raven hair and almond eyes that could bore their way into anyone's soul, she held the rifle like a grandmother held a newborn. Her warm smile could light up a dark room. A powerful personality that carried that power elegantly and easily, Mina snarled as she giggled, "Learn to fire a weapon like an Englishman, and you won't have to slander a woman to win at shooting!"

A group of gregarious young people enjoyed the early afternoon on the grassy, flower-littered foothill while watching the two contestants. Around them was a hilly, wide meadow of velvet green, dry-brushed with petals and buds that swayed gently in a supple ocean breeze that ran a soft hand over the entire estate. A cerulean sky yawned over them, drenching the flowers and emerald velvet in sunshine. In the distance, snuggled in the hills behind them was a sprawling estate covered in lush, manicured ivy. The manor stood next to an adjacent, more severe building with multiple floors, barred windows and more ivy. Spread out in front of them, to the east, was the English coastal town of Whitby. Beyond that frothed the North Sea, with Scandinavia tucked behind the horizon.

"Y'all took my turn, Missy!" wailed Quincy, quicker with his mouth than he was with his trigger, and damn sure of himself. "I was up to fire, and ya shot my glass ball right out the air!"

Everyone around Mina and Quincy were either smiling politely or openly laughing at their conversation. Loudest among them was Dr. Henry Seward, an older, normally more reserved gentleman with distinctive Piccadilly weepers[57] whose violent laugh was the most ridiculous thing anyone had ever experienced. Next to Dr. Seward was his wife Lillian, a tall, thin woman of similar age and a more even-keeled, genteel nature. They sat resplendently in graceful wooden chairs, with a picnic lunch spread out on a small but ornate table. A tablecloth on the table blew like skirts amidst the breezes. The servants among them smiled warmly, like people who were treated well and fairly by their employers. They all had to snicker at what they secretly referred to as Quincy's Americanness as they moved plates of roasted duck, cheese, fruit and wine around for everyone to

---

[55] The John B. Stetson Company was founded in 1865, and is still in business. The original hat model was called "The Boss of the Plains."

[56] The Colt 1871-72 Open Top, or simply Colt Open Top, was a rear-loading .44 caliber revolver manufactured by the Colt Patent Fire Arms Company, founded in 1855 by Samuel Colt.

[57] Piccadilly weepers were long, manicured sideburns of the time, worn without a full beard.

dine from as they took in the contest.

"It was my mistake, Morris," bantered Mina as a few gusts whipped around and threatened to undo her long, pinned-up hair. Every bit the portrait that currently resided in Dracula's coat pocket, she wore a black Victorian dress and an expression that mixed humor with confidence as she looked at the Texan past an arched eyebrow. "I hereby apologize to you for taking your turn and shooting your little Christmas ornament out of the air."

Lucy Westenra was a charismatic, staggeringly beautiful redheaded young woman wearing a day dress that was a bit too stylish for outdoor activity. To add to Lucy's abundance of style, velvet and silk ribbons were woven into her perfectly coiffed hair. With blue eyes that sparkled like the distant ocean, Lucy lounged with grace and refinement in a seat at the table while she tried to contain her vicious giggle like a proper English lady. The victim of double-dimples since childhood, that had made her the interest of the schoolboys around her, Lucy watched Mina and Quincy with piqued curiosity as she nibbled on some cheese and fruit with complete understanding to the effect that she had on the men around her.

Quincy, who never met a pitcher of beer he did not like and preferred to not sip tea with a raised pinkie finger, heard Mina's sarcasm and smirked as he looked over his rifle in mock indignation. "I appreciate the apology, Mina, but y'all know I hate shootin' with an English hunka metal!"

"Those were the terms, Morris!" interjected Arthur Holmwood, a stocky, cherubic yet handsome young man sitting at the far end of the table while finishing off a plate of duck and fruit himself as he alternated between watching the match and taking in the zephyrs that wafted through Lucy's scarlet locks. A British version of Theodore Roosevelt, Arthur sported a thin mustache and grey-brown tweed coat and trousers, which were tucked into high hunting boots. Arthur enjoyed mountaineering and the football pitch. He preferred a rough and tumble in a dingy pub to many of the formalities that his social status required of him. Done with his meal, Holmwood pushed his plate away and lit up a dark-and-light wood pipe as he added, "The weapons are part of the wager. Mina shoots with the whatever that so-called representation of American firearms is—"

"I'll have you refer to the product of the Winchester Repeating Arms Company[58] with respect, Artie!" shouted Morris in a mock-huff. "That there is a Winchester 1873[59]—"

"—and you'll use the Martini Enfield[60]," finished Ian Seward, son of the elder couple, a very thin, pale young man, dressed in a sleek off-white waistcoat/vest/pants combination with shiny brown boots. In contrast to Arthur's virility, young Seward was a bookish, nervous fellow as he sat next to Holmwood. Ian was clean-shaven while on his way to becoming prematurely bald. He was also done with his meal and was in the midst of both taking a sip of wine and adjusting his glasses. Incredibly well read while eternally socially awkward, Young Seward found that he could be himself among these treasured friends and let loose his secret: a cracking sense of wit, sarcasm and humor. Ian alternately watched the shooting match and also taking in as much of Lucy Westenra's movements as possible.

Seward and Holmwood both watched Lucy gracefully pull back a loose lock of her scarlet hair and tuck it up into her contemporarily fashionable yet completely outrageous bonnet. Lucy realized both men were observing her in the way most beautiful women sensed when they were being taken in, and secretly relished the attention. This game between the three of them had been going on for some time, much to the secret delight of Lucy and annoyed eye-rolling from Mina. Quincy and

---

[58] The Winchester Repeating Arms Company, an American weapons manufacturer, was founded in 1866.

[59] The Winchester Model 1873 was a repeating rifle and was nicknamed "The Gun that Won the West."

[60] From 1878 to 1903, the Martini Enfield was the standard British service carbine, and thereafter used in places like India and New Zealand into the Second World War.

Jonathan, two peas in a pod from across the pond, had decided months ago to simply let this theater play out between their two kindred spirits of social revelry and the idiotic bliss of newfound manhood.

"The Enfield is a rifle befitting a *gentleman*," shouted Lucy, full of the tone that she knew would get under the Texan's skin. "More refined than the Hank, or whatever the American piece of metal tubery is called."

"Y'all keep out of this, Red!" spat Morris, holding his rifle like it was a rotting fish. He pointed the butt-end of the rifle at Lucy's bonnet and said, "Are you wearing a hat or a flower field? I'm used to my Henry rifle. My momma, rest her powerful soul, taught me how to shoot with that there gun. Along with my Uncle Billy."

"Aunt Tracy was half-Comanche[61], if I recall," mused Lucy.

Genuinely touched, Quincy took his Stetson off and bowed politely at Lucy. "Indeed she was, Red, God bless ya for rememberin' that! Consider yourself somewhat redeemed in my eyes."

Mina could not help but react, such was her competitive nature. She pursed her lips, looked over her Henry rifle with respect intended to annoy Quincy and said, "Then I shall truly prize my late Aunt Tracy's Henry above all my weapons when I have beaten you, Quincy Morris of England!"

"*Texas*, woman!"

"Is that Uncle Andrew's rifle?" said Ian to both of them as he nudged Arthur. Seward's eyes were alight with mischief, which Arthur understood instantly. Despite their romantic rivalry for Lucy, Ian and Arthur were like brothers, and placed mischief above nearly all else. Their problem was that they both placed Lucy Westenra above causing trouble. Holmwood readied for Ian's impending joke to fall, and his jokes were always best delivered at Mina's expense, who could not help but react to their off-color humor.

"No, she purchased it in London a few months ago," said Lucy, in complete innocence, unwittingly helping Ian set up the crack of his comedic wit.

"Are women even allowed to own pistols and rifles?" came Ian's punchline, to which Arthur clasped his hands in delight while they both chortled with laughter.

Mina's glare could have withered a flower field.

Quincy's laugh came sharply before it was cut off completely the moment he took in Mina, who chose to let the ferocity in her eyes speak for her.

"If you continue to take offence, I will be forced to walk over and hug you to death," said Ian with a warm yet wicked grin, and that broke Mina's icy glare, and she settled for sticking her tongue out at Seward in response.

Mina squinted her eyes at Ian and Arthur and said, "You two are nothing but trouble!"

"Godamit, let's get this shootin' match goin'!" huffed an impatient Morris.

"Quincy!" shouted Lillian Seward, startling her husband as he reached for the last of the grapes. "What have I told you about using the Lord's name in vain!"

"Aw hell, Aunt Lillian, I'm sorry," said Quincy in an 'aw-shucks' kind of way as he kicked a clump of dirt, a little embarrassed as a young adult to be scolded by his aunt.

Lillian Seward threw up her arms in frustration, shaking her head at the charming Texan, who blew her a kiss to receive a warm smile in return.

"Hurry and fire Her Majesty's weapon, then, Texan!" shouted Arthur Holmwood after a hurried puff of his pipe.

"I'm afraid this pea-shooter's gonna blow up in my hands like a Mexican firecracker! What do they use to put these things together, tin foil?"

---

[61] Comanche is a Native American tribe from the Great Plains whose historic territory once spread from New Mexico to Oklahoma, and Northern Texas to Chihuahua, Mexico.

"I'm afraid," giggled Mina, "that the only Mexican firecracker in this family is the one you are about to marry, Mister Morris."

There were very few things that could stifle the gregarious Quincy Morris, and the mention of his fiancée was one of them. Everyone knew this and exploded in cackles at Mina's quip. Dr. Seward chortled so hard he began to cough. Ian clapped his father in the back and said, "All right, Father?"

Henry tugged at his starched collar and smiled through his throat-clearing cough before he tenderly pinched his son's cheek with affection, which drew embarrassment from Ian, as well as a chuckle from Arthur that included secret fodder for a free round of beer at Ian's expense at a future date.

"I'm fine, my boy, just fine, though the Texan's humor will be the end of me one day," finished elder Seward with a laugh.

Quincy planted his hands on his hip, feigning disgust. "Uncle Henry, stop pinchin' Sewie's cheeks like he's in diapers and pay attention! How can I concentrate with all this talkin' goin' on around me?"

"Shut up and shoot, Quincy!" squealed Mina through her fit of giggles.

"I'll fire when I'm good and ready, woman!" roared Morris, and they all roared with him.

"Come on, Texan," joked Ian past tear-filled eyes. "Don't let our gender down, mate."

Morris raised his weapon, had a thought come to his Texan's mind and turned to Lucy. "And Miss Westenra, I'm surprised at your provincialism. You have spoken highly of the—"

"—colonies" chimed Arthur between puffs of his pipe.

"—the colonies," blurted on Morris, and at everyone's peals of amusement, he had to correct himself and blather, "I mean the godamned *United Stated of America*!"

"Quincy, you know I don't like your cursing!" corrected Lillian.

Quincy bowed his head humbly. "My apologies *again*, Aunt Lillian. I am drawn to the devil's words by the cherubic and Imperial rapscallions around me."

Everyone was crying of laughter at Quincy's gaff, but the Texan knew he had his audience by the horns. He wasted no time in pointing at Holmwood and shouting, "I knew you'd tell a good joke one fine day, Artie! And that was the one! Nevertheless, yours truly, the gentleman from the great state of *Texas* will prevail."

"Or die complaining," said Ian after a quick sip of wine and another tweak of his glasses.

"I heard that, Sewie! And I'm still waitin' for *your* first attempt at humor!"

"I didn't mind Boston or New York, Quincy," interjected Lucy as she held her flower field bonnet in place while a breeze tried to knock it from her head, "but the heat in Austin was simply overwhelming."

"I must agree with you, Lucy," said Lillian, clasping hands with Henry. Quincy saw the hand-clasping, and while he was happy for the Sewards, a split-second of melancholy for his late parents flashed through Morris. Everyone noticed his nostalgia, a small shadow passing among friends, and their love for the Texan grew ever more. They had all helped raise the boy from mid-teens through his transition to young adulthood after the passing of his parents, and though Quincy Morris had many extended family members throughout Texas, the boisterous American considered the people around him at the moment his true family.

"We've somehow ended up with most of Austin's hot air here in Whitby," teased Ian, drawing a sideways glance and wink from Quincy. Ian coolly winked back.

"You keep to the doctorin' Sewie, and I'll handle the shootin'!" boasted Morris, recovered from his flash of memories dear, near and far. "And I'll remind you that an American Henry rifle is what's winnin' this contest right now—"

"—held by a powerful schoolmistress from Whitby!" said a giggling Lucy. Her retort received a mock-frown from Mina, which was healed in a heartbeat by a wink of conspiratorial humor from Lucy.

"—who is gonna marry Jonathan Harker, an *American*, Miss Westenra!" said Morris, winking and pointing a finger at the laughing redhead. "Don't you forget that."

"Morris, you *idiot*! Harker's an Englishman by birth!" shouted Arthur to another round of cackles. "Also, if you win, then by logic you are admitting that The Crown's weapon is superior."

Quincy, without an ounce of shame in his body, rolled his eyes at Holmwood and said, "Now see, that's where 'The Crown', with all due respect to everyone here unfortunate enough to not be from Texas, is mistaken, because by American law, Jonathan Harker was born in New York, and by so doing is an *American citizen*!"

Morris then added a quite stupid and impromptu, "*Yee*-hoo!"

"He sounds like a cow," quipped Arthur.

"A flatulent one," finished Ian, which nearly made Lillian Seward snort out her wine in laughter.

"Shut up and lose, Quincy!" spat Mina, beside herself in laughter.

Quincy sighed and looked away from the table and toward the target-launching mechanism that held a glass ball. "I see that it's up to me to represent the integrity of the American institution of the repeating rifle. But either way, a colonial's gonna win this thing!"

"All right then, so does Mina's shot count or not?" guffawed Henry as he stroked his sideburns. Lillian was in a mid-giggle fit.

"Well," sighed Morris, "I would not be a gentleman if I waved off a lady's shot."

Modest applause laced with caustic English sarcasm brought a guffaw from an unimpressed Morris. "Oh, I have a nose for what tickles the British fancy, ladies and gentlemen. Your misshapen version of what constitutes humor does not pass under my watch undetected. Give me a rodeo clown any day of the week! And I shall remember who stood for me today, and who did not."

"I wager that Wilhelmina wins," shouted Henry, through a wry smile. He gave a grinning Mina a hand wave of support and said. "Go on, dear. Beat the lad. He needs a measure of humility."

"Thank you, Uncle Henry," beamed Mina. She'd always loved Uncle Henry, though Uncle Abraham was her definitive favorite. Of the others, only Jonathan Harker, off on business in the Orient at the moment, knew this.

"Appreciate the faith, Doc," sneered Quincy, giving Henry a belly-laugh of enormous proportions.

"You show him, dear," said Lillian in a quiet show of support for the Texan. She nodded her support to Quincy, who took it in like a sponge takes in water. He snapped his fingers in exultation at Mina, who stuck her tongue out at Morris before she turned her head away from the Texan to pointedly ignore him.

"I'll take that wager, Uncle Henry," said Arthur with a straight face. He whispered so Quincy would not hear him. "Remember that shooting contest with Buffalo Bill[62] and Annie Oakley[63]. He was a bloody *child*."

Arthur and Ian, two bookends of friendship, looked at each other in silent like-mindedness as they had a million times previous. The two could order for each other in most of London's pubs and restaurants and could share a mutual admiration for the same woman without having it affect their relationship. So far. They differed deeply when it came to football, Arthur preferring the Newton Heath LYR Football Club[64], while Ian always let his adoration for Dial Square[65] be known to

---

[62] William Fredrick "Buffalo Bill" Cody, (1846-1917) was an American scout, hunter and showman.

[63] Annie Oakley (1860-1926) was an expert markswoman in the American Old West.

[64] Founded in 1878, Newton Heath would come to be known as Manchester United.

everyone. They would take the train into London together to see their teams, and while they would sit alongside each other when one of their teams played another club, they resigned to never sit together when the two teams played each other. Wilhelmina Murray ferociously preferred the local team, Whitby Town Football Club[66], Lucy's fanaticism was comparably tepid, much to Mina's consternation, as she often derided both Arthur and Ian for their support of the 'foreign clubs'. Quincy steadfastly 'didn't give a crap' about football.

"Morris still *is* a child," said Ian with a nod of agreement to Arthur. "I'll take that wager as well, Father. Ten pounds?"

"Done, both of you," nodded Henry. "If memory serves me well, our Wilhelmina was reprimanded for putting a round in the rectory bell tower? What was she, eleven?"

"Ten," said Mina with a sideways look at Quincy, whose eyebrows shot up in a mock, sarcastic surprise. "And I also aspired to shoot through the eye of the Pantheon that summer we spent in Rome!"

"Ha! I remember!" bellowed Henry. "You wanted to knock on the Holy Door as well, Mina! Might as well give me my winnings now, boys. Go on, dear lass! Prove the boys wrong yet again."

Morris closed his eyes, thumbed his thin nose up in the air and looked away from the others in a comedic gesture of anger. "Maybe I don't wanna shoot no more then, if my friends are all linin' up against me like this!"

Another collective expression of the British wit, this one of false sympathy laced with sarcasm, rose from the crowd in the form of polite applause, and a collective and completely sarcastic, "Awwwwww."

"You are such a baby, Quincy!" shouted Mina.

"Sticks and stones, Mina," shot back Quincy.

"I'll pay you ten pounds *not* to shoot, Morris!" shouted Ian to another round of roaring laughter that was followed by a genuinely sarcastic round of applause.

Quincy glared at Ian with mock anger as the others brayed with joy. The Texan's eyes became mischievous slits as he sneered, "I've got ten pounds that says Cambridge beats Oxford *again* in next year's Boat Race[67], Sewie! Waddaya think of them apples?"

"Steady, my Lad," said Henry. "Surely such a horrible event could not happen in my lifetime."

"Unless one hails from Cambridge, Doctor Seward," said Holmwood with a wide, Cheshire cat grin. The others applauded with knowing hilarity.

"Let's not get this one started again," snipped Ian with an impish grin. "We can finish this ahem, *'row'* before we begin another."

A bloated and collective groan seeped from everyone, including the servants.

"Lordy, your puns get worse every year, Sewie," sniffed Quincy.

"Quincy's just trying to distract us from our favorite sporting event, which is Watching Quincy Lose at Shooting," teased Lucy with a brow arched at an indignant Texan's direction.

His courage questioned, Quincy shot Lucy a sideways glance as he cocked his rifle and roared, "Cue it up for me, Archie!"

Fervent applause from the crowd, dear friends all. Archibald Swayles, a grizzled older servant who stood next to a small stack of glass balls and the launching mechanism, loaded up a ball.

"All right there, Swayles?" said Henry. "Should I run and fetch more globes?"

---

[65] In 1886, the Dial Square football club was founded by munitions workers in East London and later renamed as Arsenal FC.

[66] Founded in 1880 and known as both The Blues and The Seasiders throughout their history.

[67] Cambridge would indeed defeat Oxford for the second consecutive year in 1900. The so-called 'Boat Race' is a series of annual rowing races between the storied British Universities' boat clubs, which began in 1829 and continues to present day.

"We're fine, Sir. Many thanks regardless."

"Cued, Mister Quincy," said Swayles with a crisp nod. "No disrespect to our Miss Wilhelmina, but you are my champion, Sir."

"I'm glad to know," mused Morris as he simultaneously nodded at Swayles and cradled his rifle, "that there's one Englishman among y'all with good taste."

The American was peppered with boos from the others. Quincy feigned offence as he lowered the rifle and said, "Y'all know how tender I am to criticism from my loved ones."

Before anyone could react, Morris said, "Pull," loud and crisp.

Swayles jerked the mechanism and the globe launched into the air, into the distance and toward the East.

"Made outta copper," said Quincy with a dirty glance at his weapon.

Onward, the globe sailed.

Then, in one liquid, cobra-like movement, Quincy raised his rifle, gave a quick glance at the target, then *casually looked back toward the crowd* as he fired. As it tried to disappear over the hill, the globe exploded like a dandelion under a sneeze.

"I still say this thing fires funny," sniffed Quincy, bloated with false modesty.

Everyone was silent, breath held.

Lillian Seward then gasped with astonishment.

Ian and Arthur looked at each other, smiled and thought, *Uncle Henry's paying for the first pint.*

"*Sir*," was all an awed Swayles could say.

The other servants gaped.

Awed stares went Morris' way.

"*Good God, man*," gasped Henry. "We could have used you in the Crimean War[68]."

Arthur Holmwood chuckled, "He still shoots as well as he talks."

After a staggered silence, applause mixed politely with the breeze.

"We can shoot in *Texas!!!!*" roared Quincy, engorged with achievement. "I shot out a razorback's[69] eye from fifty steps back once, then put the eye back in and said, 'I'm sorry Mister Hog!' then took a *hunert* steps back an' shot it out again!"

"Good lord," began Ian, "I forget that his accent becomes even more provincial when he's done something extraordinary."

"In his defense, Quincy does do extraordinary things," said Arthur as the applause died.

"Never tell him that," replied Ian.

"Agreed," nodded Arthur. "Loser owes the other a pint."

"Done," said Ian.

Lucy sat there with her mouth open, then threw Mina a quizzical look as if to say, *'How are you going to top that?'*

Mina waved off Lucy's worried expression, stopping instantly when Quincy tried to gain her attention with a triumphant grin. Morris had seen Mina's wave, which only broadened the grin. The Texan tugged on the brim of his cowboy hat at Wilhelmina Murray and cocksure, said, "Your turn, Missy."

Morris coolly pivoted away from Mina like Tom Sawyer way from a freshly painted fence.

"Ready Swayles?" shouted Mina, her nostrils flaring with the fever of competition. Despite her bravado, Mina took a deep breath to calm herself. Missing the next shot in the heat of the moment would be foolish. She strode up to the spot where they had been shooting from, oozing confidence

---

[68] The Crimean War was fought between the Russian Empire and Britain, France, the Ottoman Empire and Sardina between 1853 and 1856.
[69] Razorback: feral pig.

and raised the Henry as Swayles called out, "Ready, Miss Murray!"

As a response, Mina ratcheted the lever on the rifle. The metallic *klatch* that the Winchester made as a round was chambered brought everyone to silence.

Only the breeze fluttered on.

"Go on, Mina!" shouted Lucy.

Ian smiled, thinking Lucy's words of encouragement would break Mina's concentration, but everyone else knew better.

"Pull!" hissed Ms. Murray.

The globe ejected into the bright blue sky, soared, then fluttered sideways as the breeze hit it.

"Skiddin' a little," whispered Quincy to himself, somewhat in support of Mina, despite the contest. Everyone gasped, seeing how Mina had to recalculate her shot.

Mina's blast rang loud.

For a second, the globe threatened to fall to the other side of the gentle slope.

Then it shattered.

Everyone roared with cheer, even the Texan. The audience threw itself instantly in with the underdog. Then Quincy collected himself. "Why is everyone cheering for Mina Murray? I'm the one holdin' the British rifle!"

"Well done, Mina!" shouted Lillian, full of handclaps and pride.

"Indeed," added Henry.

"Yes!" shouted Lucy, full of applause and cheer for her best friend.

"Where's the Texas delegation?" shouted Morris over their applause.

"I believe," heckled Ian as he applauded for Mina, "they are in Texas."

"He's a bit rattled," said Arthur with a nod at Henry, who winked a reply.

"Shut up and shoot, Quincy!" shouted Lucy, smug despite her laughter. She squinted at him in an attempt to throw him off. "Shut up and lose."

Quincy rolled his eyes at Lucy, ejected his spent cartridge and shouted, "I've seen Kangaroo Rats with better stares, Missy. Okey-dokey, Swayles, ready when you are!"

"Yes Sir!" spat Swayles, completely entranced with the joust. "Ready!"

"'Okey-dokey?'" laughed Ian. "What kind of term is that? Is that something that is served with those 'grits' things you love?"

Holmwood chuckled and added, "It's much funnier when he shouts, "'Yee-ha.'"

"It's actually "'Yee-hoo.'" corrected Ian.

"Pull!" sneered Morris. Swayles jerked at the mechanism and the globe launched.

Like Mina's target, the globe soared, then fluttered in the wind.

"I got it," laughed Quincy, lining the shot up.

Morris casually turned back to the others as he squeezed the trigger.

After it fluttered, the globe fell into a distant patch of flowers intact.

Morris turned in disbelief.

The crowd then exploded like it was the end of the world.

Arthur laughed so hard he spat out his pipe. Ian had wine squirt out of his nostrils. Dr. Seward simply fell out of his chair in a titanic belly laugh. Lillian had to hold her stomach so her belly would not burst open, so exuberant was her laughter. Mina simply stood there and shook her head at Quincy before she threw her hands above her head, holding her newly gained rifle in triumph. Lucy and a still-laughing Lillian raced out and embraced her with the deepest admiration and love. Henry rolled in the grass in the middle of a fit of laughter that threatened to make him pass out.

Quincy leaned on one leg, Stetson tipped over his silly face and arms crossed, cradling the Martini-Enfield, somehow not having lost one iota of confidence as everyone around him guffawed at his expense. The Texan then whipped off his hat in the middle of a grand, sincere gesture of courtesy to Mina. "Ya beat me fair and square, Tiger lily."

The others saw this and applauded at Morris' chivalry, even the servants, who somehow had managed to keep their composure through everyone's fits of laughter.

Mina was still shaking her head, incredulous that Quincy had missed. "Morris, can't you hit a glass ball?"

"You should try watching the shot next time, mate," sighed Ian.

"Amen," agreed Arthur, before he plopped his beloved pipe, which he had just picked up off the grass, back into his mouth. He then added a slice of apple, perhaps to mask the taste of soil and grass. "You just cost us a pint."

"Artie," retorted Morris, "Dontcha ever stop eatin'? I swear they're gonna bury you with a mouth full of puddin'!"

The small crowd giggled at Quincy's joke while continuing to celebrate Mina's victory, serenading her with applause. Morris gave her a courtly bow, to go along with another sweeping, polite wave of his Stetson.

Arthur and Ian pointedly stared at an unflinching Quincy as they stood and pulled out their clasped Victorian wallets to hand bills over to the elder Seward, who could not have been happier to receive them.

Henry stood up, walked over and placed his hand on Morris' shoulder with a broad smile on his face as he said, "My thanks for the twenty pounds, my good lad."

Morris snorted at the humor and said, "My pleasure, Uncle Henry."

Lillian then had the last laugh when she intercepted the bills before they reached Henry and put them in her dress pocket, much to the delight of her son, Arthur and everyone else. Lillian then took a bow of triumph as Mina, Lucy, some of the servants and even Quincy clapped in approval. They all took in the afternoon breeze and their friendships, both treasured but the latter far more than the former. The grass around them swayed, as did the flowers, the other rolling hillsides between them and Whitby and the distant sea.

Things had never been better.

"If the target were in the shape of a bison, he would have hit it!" shouted Arthur. Everyone laughed.

Mina and Lucy, arms around each other's shoulders, simply shook their heads at the boys' incessant jousting.

"Buffalo, Artie," laughed Quincy. "If yer gonna insult me and the States, get the animal right."

"Bison is the right term, Texan!" laughed Ian, Henry and Lillian by his side, everyone noticing and admiring the affection between the elder couple. Despite whatever complexities a lifetime of marriage together had brought them, Lillian and Henry Seward still loved each other deeply. As if cheerful at Mina's win, clouds rolled merrily over them as the afternoon extended itself.

"It's the principle of the thing, Sewie," said Morris, shaking his head at Ian. "Ya call it a buffalo in the States."

"If it were in the shape of England, he'd hit it," cracked Holmwood, done with his last apple slice and wiping the edge of his mouth with a napkin.

"Artie, I'd be quiet if I were you," snorted Morris. "You couldn't hit the ground with your own spit."

"Leave him be, cowboy," laughed Ian as he walked to the Texan, slapping Quincy on the back out of love and friendship.

Quincy, stranger to losing, was in no mood for comfort. "That goes for you too, Sewie. You couldn't hit your own cheek if ya tried to slap yourself."

Everyone roared. Ian and Arthur clapped Morris on the back and turned to the ladies.

"Excellent shooting, Mina," beamed Ian, "for a woman."

"Not you as well, Doctor-in-waiting?" laughed Mina.

"Perhaps you want a chance against the best sharpshooter in Whitby?" smirked Lucy, pointing her chin at Mina.

"Steady there, Ian," said Arthur as he nudged his best friend. "You couldn't hit your own cheek, remember?"

"Uhhh, let's head back for some tea, shall we?" said Ian with a nod to the servants, who began to cover the leftover food and pack up the utensils and dishes. "Thanks, all."

Ian waved to everyone to follow him toward the Seward estate, and after everyone gathered their own things, they all began to drift that way. The servants gossiped happily about Quincy's explosive laughter and Mina's marksmanship as they packed the silverware and dishes back up. Swayles placed the target launching mechanism onto a small cart for that purpose, as a few of the other servants packed the table and chairs onto a wagon that had stood on the edge of the scene.

"Ian, would you be so kind as to tend to the patients this afternoon?" said Lillian, slipping an arm around Henry, who had finally regained his wits. "Your father looks a bit peaked by all this frivolity."

Henry scowled as he walked with noticeable exertion. "Nonsense, Lillian—"

"I insist, Dear," said Lillian with a resolute face. Ian was familiar with that look of determination, so he nodded at his parents and said, "Of course, Mother. How is Renfield, Father?"

"Stable, for the moment," said Henry, as his face became a grey cloud from both the effort and the subject of discussion. Dr. Seward's voice came down two decibels. Ian's smile drained away, and he simply gave a sad nod in reply. "But it never lasts."

Arthur and Quincy overheard Henry's observation of Renfield. After a quick glance at each other, they responded, taking out their wallets and shoving bills into his coat pockets. "Your winnings restored, Uncle Henry," said Arthur.

"It's good for a little stop-over in the local tavern next time," laughed Quincy, "If y'all take my meanin'."

Lillian's reaction, steadying her husband as they walked, was a headshake that combined approval and annoyance.

Uncle Henry seems more tired lately worried Mina as she cradled her Winchester, Lucy holding her elbow as they walked.

Ian threw Arthur a wink of gratitude as the cloud over Henry went away. Doctor Seward shouted, "Ah yes!" and elbowed Ian, who chuckled as he too handed over a bill to his father.

"Straight into the Afternoon Picnic Fund," Henry laughed. They all laughed with him, yet somehow Mina's thoughts were echoed in everyone's face. Uncle Henry did look older, the veins on his face were more pronounced, his face a little paler than before, even on this happy occasion. For the first time in a while, the young people contemplated a life without their parents and uncles around. Mina's win gave the late afternoon blue sky even more color, as is if itself trying to liven the youngster's thoughts. As they all headed downhill toward the expansive estate, the youngsters all walked together, lifelong friends that they were. Henry and Lillian lingered, then trailed behind, arm in arm, enjoying the next generation's happiness.

"Are your parents coming for dinner after all, Arthur Dear?" said Lillian.

"They are, Aunt Lillian," said Arthur with a nod. "They are coming with the Harkers."

"If Jonny were here, he'd a beat ya!" said Quincy as he strutted along, holding his rifle like it was a smelly sock.

"Jonathan's the worst shot in the world!" laughed Mina, cradling her gun like it was made of gold, which today it was.

"Most times," interjected Ian, "But you'd be surprised at what your fiancé can accomplish when the bets are down and the money's on the table."

"Agreed," said Arthur as he emptied his pipe and tucked it into his tweed coat pocket.

Mina did not lose a step but turned her head at the Evil Trio, as she sometimes referred to Quincy, Ian and Arthur, and gave them a squinted, suspicious square. "And where may have the money been on the table, Doctor Seward?"

Mina had always had her suspicions about her fiancé's involvement in the Evil Trio's more nefarious adventures but had to this point been unable to prove anything, other than that whenever this subject came up, Arthur and Ian would tense up noticeably, and Quincy somehow became even more relaxed, if that was possible, the classic case of overcompensation.

Before Ian could stammer a response, Quincy waxed, "Ian's referring to the tiddlywinks[70] games we'd play as kids."

"Are you certain you are all not referring to chuck-farthing[71]?" growled Mina.

"I don't know about that," said Lucy, eyes scanning the expansive but deepening blue above, hastily changing the subject. Mina had always suspected that the boys had confided their delinquency to Lucy but not to her and had decided a long time ago to leave that between the five of them, though Mina felt that now that Jonathan was her fiancé, that he should perhaps begin to confess such matters to his future wife. The day was ending in front of them, and Lucy took in the yawning, stretching sky as she said, "Jonny somehow landed you, did he not?"

That brought a sly grin from Mina, and a conspiratorial exchange of glances between the men, and a few filled with gratitude thrown toward Lucy as well, who was only too happy to smile warmly, her mission accomplished.

"That was some fine shootin', Murray," said Quincy, poking her shoulder with his elbow, "although my momma would've given ya a run for yer money."

"Master Quincy," said Swayles, huffing to catch up with them as he pulled the launching contraption along in the small cart. "I must express to you that your father, may the Lord rest his soul, was also a fantastic marksman in our soldiering days, but I don't know if he would have been able to match you."

"When he watches the target," chimed Mina graciously.

"Ya beat me fair and square, Mina," said Quincy with an equally gracious grin.

"Hear, hear," said Henry as he slipped his arm around Lillian's waist in a gesture of love, but also in need of her support, such were his labors in walking. "Well put, Swayles."

"Thank you, Sir," nodded Swayles, having to re-shift his hold on the cart to nod to Henry.

"I can help you with that, Swayles," said Arthur, reaching out to the contraption.

"I'm all right, Master Holmwood," nodded Swayles as he walked. "Thank you, though."

Regardless, Arthur assisted Swayles, taking the cart from the older man, who then nodded to young Holmwood in gratitude.

"Could your mother have shot as well with the Winchester in addition to the Enfield?" teased Mina. Lucy gave an interested look and leaned forward for the answer.

---

[70] Tiddlywinks was an indoor game invented in England in 1889 that revolved around trying to get small round discs into a center pot.

[71] Chuck-farthing is the English term for pitch penny, or penny pitching, a game that involved tossing coins against a wall or into a center area or onto a chair, though the game does go back as far as ancient Greece.

Quincy looked at them sideways and said with a grin, "That woman could shoot a tick off a horse's ass at two hundred paces, excusin' my French, ladies."

They all giggled.

"Oh Quincy," said Lillian from behind, smiling through her exertion to help her husband along. "Despite my inclination to wash out your mouth with soap, it has been such a pleasure having you here with us these past weeks. Won't you consider staying on longer?"

"I'm afraid not, Mother," said Ian, "He has all of that longantler dung to shovel back at his beloved ranch."

"Long*horn*, Sewie. Long. Horn. Stop readin' them picture books," sighed Quincy. "Aunt Lillian, I'm just gonna stay and greet Jonny when he gets back for the wedding, then it's back to the Lone Star State for me."

"As well as harvesting all of that cacti that treated Jonathan so well last time we were there," added Arthur.

"Arthur, do you remember how Jonathan fell off his horse and into all that cactus?" laughed Mina. "I was so frightened. Yet he got right back up and rode back with all of us."

"Tough to ride with cactus needles in your britches," said Quincy with Texan admiration. "That boy's got moxie for a New Yorker."

"Well, aside from cacti, Mr. Morris has other business over in Austin," said Lucy with a sly look on her face. "It was very kind of Consuelo to let us borrow you for a while."

"Well," said Morris with his trademark leer, "As tempting as it is to stay here where cookies are called biscuits, Consuelo is as good a reason as any to head back on home."

Ian cut in with, "Quincy, this is where you usually say something like, 'She's as pretty as—' something. Perhaps cactus."

"Tamales," said Arthur with a smile of remembrance.

"—prettier'n chicken fried steak," finished Holmwood, marching along with them.

Morris laughed, they all did, while Arthur felt he had to defend Morris with, "I, for one, found Texas food enchanting."

Quincy looked at Mina and said, in all seriousness, "Jonny woulda been proud of you today, Mina. Not that he's never not proud of ya, of course."

"Thank you, Quincy," said Mina. "You lose as well as you win."

Quincy gave her a quick, polite bow of his head and a wink followed by, "—and I win a lot."

"Not that he's never not proud of *ya*?" teased Ian as they neared the estate. Lush, manicured greenery adorned pristine brickwork and countless windows. "Can't you speak proper English at all, Morris? There must be a tonic I can give you to cure you of that drawl."

"Ignore the doctor-in-training, Ladies. He's dumber than a box of rocks and a bag full of kittens."

"And an Oxford man, to boot," said Arthur. They neared a large, inviting entrance to the manor. The doors were open and the smell of home, love and tea serenaded their senses.

"I hear tell," roared Quincy suddenly, "that the babies Sewie delivers come out sideways!"

Henry nearly exploded in guffaws. "Quincy! Good God, man! You're trying to *kill* me!" Next to him, Lillian was laughing so hard that a snort escaped her lips, which only deepened everyone's laughter.

They all enjoyed one long, last hearty cascade of giggles as they piled into the manor. Quincy looked at Mina with a serious expression again, and said, "Now, that fiancé of yours took one of my spare Colts out to the Orient with him like I told him to, right? That Webley he's always had couldn't hit an outhouse from the inside. Lord knows what he could run into out there. Lots of wolves I hear."

Lucy turned and without letting Mina see her, threw the Texan the dirtiest look in world history, one that said *You are so stupid! Think of Mina!*

Morris recovered instantly and added, "Either way, he's a sure shot when it counts. Plus, Uncle Peter's with him."

"I'm sure he's run into Uncle Peter and they are just fine," said Mina, still finishing her laugh. "Perhaps they are Mountaineering[72] together.

"Don't worry, Mina," said Lucy. "I'm sure they on they're way home to us as we speak."

The Texan nodded as he waved everyone inside. "Amen to that."

---

[72] The activity of mountain climbing. The 'Golden age of Alpinism' began in earnest in the mid 1800s and culminated in the ascent of the Matterhorn in 1865 by a group led by English Illustrator Edward Whymper.

TWO

A continent away, just before Quincy's second, unshattered globe landed on the emerald velvet overlooking Whitby, a brittle set of wooden wagon wheels ground against a battered dirt road in Eastern Europe, a path traveled thousands of times by millions of people.

A dry, gnarled wrinkle of a road, worn to the bone and bled upon by Roman legionnaire, barbarian marauder, Ottoman infantryman, medieval traveler and peasant of the Renaissance.

A stout, frustrated, yet beaten road.

And yet, the wheels of the wagon moved along, worn knuckles against hard, angry, resentful soil.

Creeeeeeeeek.

Creak.

Creeeeeeeeek.

Aside from the grinding wheels, there was silence.

Somewhere, a raven broke the symphony of creaks by making, not the familiar cawing sound, but the odd and eerie croaking sound that only added to the atmosphere of tension.

Then followed the cawing.

Mothers who had grown up hewing out a simple life at the feet of the Carpathian Mountains threw loving arms around their infants and held them like they might fall off the face of the Earth if they let go.

Old men and women, faces gnarled and backs curved after decades of working angry soil, harvesting bleak crops and eating bitter meals, no strangers to the strange rituals and habits in this land, clutched generations-old rosaries in their withering hands and muttered prayers of safe haven, good fortune and hospice from evil.

Fathers draped their worn, farm-tilling hands over their children, pulling them further into the crumbling wooden walls of the remote, ancient village chapel deep in the mountains of Transylvania.

The roof tiles were either broken clay tiles or worn, exposed wooden beams. The scarlet walls combined ancient brickwork with sections of earthen parapet. An earthen, kneeling angel sculpted out of porphyry[73] before the Old World had met the New wept above the humble wooden front doors. A raven's nest provided the halo for the angel.

Around this tiny cube of faith were miniscule hovels that clustered around the church like fearful chicks under a protective mother hen, with rugged fields of recently planted potato and grain crops that stretched out to the distant edge of the forest, with the Carpathians in the distance like ominous, ever-vigilant sentinels. A cold afternoon had quickly spread out over the village, with a few gloomy clouds stretched out over the homes and the chapel like tattered blankets over a bright, well-made quilt.

---

[73] Porphyry is a reddish groundmass igneous rock. *The Portrait of the Four Tetrarchs*, a sculpture of four Roman emperors that is fixed to a corner of the façade of Saint Mark's Basilica in Venice, Italy, is sculpted from porphyry. The sculpture, which dates back to 300 AD was originally carved and placed in Constantinople, then moved to Venice afterward, probably after the Sack of Constantinople during the Fourth Crusade.

They had seen, heard and told of many mysterious events throughout time in this region, yet this was no fireside fairy tale told to keep the children from wandering in the woods and to keep them continuing to go to mass on Sundays. Paralyzed with fear, the peasants peered out through the weathered front doors that barely hung on hinges from the early part of the last century and through four side windows, each peppered with a little stained-glass mosaic that intermingled roses, candles, a cross and a dove. Through these apertures the small group of very poor and very superstitious villagers watched the angular, worn wagon that slowly wheeled itself though the only road in the village. Once the wagon and its driver had been spotted, all of the villagers had hurriedly crowded inside, some of them still holding their farming tools, a futile attempt at self-defense. A lone, bedraggled priest was all that stood between them and the chapel doors.

Birds had stopped chirping on this fine spring afternoon, almost on cue when the gloom had begun to spread. The grass had paused in its daily reach for warmth and growth. Even the buzzing of the insects of the fields had hushed.

The clouds spread further.

Only the creaks of the wagon wheels, and the distant, macabre croaks of the raven could be heard.

Atop the wagon were coffins, some of them shifting slightly with the sway of the vehicle as it maneuvered the meager avenue that was more path than road. Primus drove the wagon, covered in his shroud of bleak despair, and he nodded at the priest, the bones in the skeleton's neck cracking like knuckles as the ravens that were standing on his skull and shoulder blades adjusted their positions. Without any breath left in their throats, the villagers watched as the shadow passed over the open chapel threshold, with *no horses pulling the wagon*.

"Vechile revine malefice," whispered the old priest. *The old evil returns.*

The priest stood in front of the villagers with arms stretched out sideways, not so much holding the townsfolk back as much as a gesture of protection. He raised his right arm, which held a battered old crucifix, and held it out through the front doors of the church and at the passing wagon. A few old women threw clumps of garlic at the ground in front of the church.

One of the old men held a chalice-shaped silver bowl, then the priest reached out a trembling hand and drew out an aspergillum[74], and he threw water through the doorway and at the wagon as he said, "Propterea accipite armaturam Dei, ut possitis resistere in die malo et omnibus perfectis stare!" *Wherefore take unto you the whole armour of God, that ye may be able to withstand in the evil day, and having done all, to stand![75]*

Primus pivoted his skull and rumbled, "Respondens autem spiritus nequam dixit eis Iesum novi et Paulum scio vos autem qui estis?" *And the evil spirit answered and said, Jesus I know and Paul I know, but who are ye?[76]*:

The wagon bled with hisses as the Holy Water splashed along its battered sides and oblong wheels. Without a backwards glance, Primus drove the shambling wagon on.

Inside the church, held breaths found air.

More sounds, from up the road, following the wagon, moving closer.

Claws raking through soil and mud.

Inside the church, hands and arms held their dear ones ever closer.

Shadows licked the doorstep.

---

[74] A device used in Catholic ritual to anoint a crowd with Holy Water, a small sphere with holes in it that attaches to a long handle.

[75] Ephesians 6:13.

[76] Acts 19:11-12.

A child whimpered, and a mother slid her hand over the boy's face as rows of skeletons marched past the church, in silent, monotonous file.

He pulled it away, more afraid of *not* being able to see.

"Emmisary blestemat," hissed the priest. *Cursed emissary.*

"Lasă-i să treacă și să ne lase să fie, Taică," whispered a trembling old man in the crowd. "Restul lumii poate vă faceți griji despre el acum." *Let them pass and leave us be, Father. The rest of the world can worry about him now.*

The carriage was last, drifting past without horse. Another skeleton, this one tall and thin, drove the coach during the day, as Dracula had ordered, without the shroud that covered Primus. It kept its' craggy head up, watching for any signal from Primus and the carriage before it eerily leered at those inside the chapel, with its gaping orbital sockets, collapsed nasal cavity and overgrown teeth. As the wagon drifted by the chapel doorway, the skeleton, backlit by the grim clouds above him, cast a menacing shadow into the threshold. A few of the children started to cry, and old people had to be kept from falling faint at the ghastly apparition. The carriage windows were open, curtains fluttering, empty. Petra, Venus and Andromeda were all dormant inside their coffins, along with their master, who could, through his gargantuan force of will, control the forward movement of both the wagon and carriage.

More noises, bones grinding and crunching, coming from up the road, and skeletons, raw joints screeching like chalk along a blackboard as the rows of skeletons walked by, looking straight ahead, ignoring the weeping, terrified villagers.

Then, a flurry of motion along the ground along the carriage became a torrent of sinewy, fur-covered revulsion as the wave of disgusting, chirping, mewing, defecating rats swarmed past, with villagers pressing against the altar in the back of the church.

More shadows over the threshold.

The priest took the bowl of Holy Water and splashed it over the church steps, and the rats swarmed *away* from the water, under the carriage and to the other side of the road, where their unholy procession continued.

The sounds of the wicked procession receded.

A few of the ravens flew up and around, back to that lone, dark castle in the mountain range above.

Shadows melted backwards into daylight.

Villagers wept with relief.

Only then, after the last few moments of tension had evaporated, did a lone, brave bird dare to chirp.

THREE

"My engagement is over!" screamed Mina early the next morning as she rode with the fervor of a jockey in the home stretch. Her stallion was bold, powerful, ebony and loved to race nearly as much as his owner.

Lucy raced behind her on a white mare, her hair ribbons flowing in the wind, along a languid bend that was embraced by a grove of beauteous trees. However harsh the winters at Whitby could be, and they could be frigid, today was the day where spring was knighted. The two women had excused themselves from breakfast at the Seward estate to ride out into the day together as they had done many times before, yet careful to explain that they would be heading back to the Murray estate afterward. Mina rode hard along the soft, cool earth, maintaining her lead over a frustrated Lucy, who was clearly more interested in gossip than in who finished first. Both horses pumped air into their lungs as they turned from the bend and into a wide, idyllic country road outside of Whitby. A finer day than the previous one, lush trees in the rococo style that would have made a painting by Fragonard[77] envious whipped by, the wind whistling in their ears, and the inviting stretch of the plush way begged the horses to run as fast and as far as they could.

"You are going to what?" shouted Lucy, air blasting her face and frolicking through her scarlet tresses.

"I'm not getting married!" sang Mina, trying to get her words from horse to horse at full speed. She wore a British equestrian uniform, but with pants. Behind her lagged Lucy, riding sidesaddle and in a furious rush to keep up.

"Will you wait?" shouted Lucy, her baby blue dress fluttering in the air like a dropped napkin and with the beat of her horse's strides. "Must you turn everything into a competition?"

Mina took a glance back and relished the idea that Lucy was not capable of catching her, then pulled back just slightly on the reins enough to slow the avalanche that was her thoroughbred. He resisted, being the competitor that he was, then yielded to Mina's insistence.

"We've won, D'Artagnan[78]," laughed Mina as she patted the stallion on the neck. He neighed a disapproving response, and Mina could only smile in approval as they decelerated into a trot. She loved that horse, loved that he never backed down to anyone but her. Arthur Holmwood Sr. found that out by surprise one summer afternoon a couple of years before, when he tried to mount D'Artagnan and was shrugged off like a bothersome gnat. Everyone avoided D'Artagnan after that, even the Texan.

"You're more mad than usual today!" said Lucy, her frilly white horse matching D'Artagnan trot. Lucy's horse tried to move closer to D'Artagnan, clearly with affection, but D'Artagnan would have none of it, not respecting another horse that could not keep up with him, so he in turn moved

---

[77] Jeane-Honore Fragonard (1732-1806) was a French painter who specialized in scenes of lush foliage with a romantic air.

[78] Charles Ogier de Batz de Castelmore, Comte d'Artagnan (1611-1673) was both a real and fictional character, captain of the Musketeers of the Guard for Luis XIV, as well as an adventurous character based on the real person in Alxander Dumas' novel *The Three Musketeers*.

away. Mina saw this and smiled to herself. Lucy knitted her brow with exasperation and continued with, "Have you ever heard of a simple ride in the country, Wilhelmina Murray?"

"D'Artagnan thinks a horse with ribbons in her hair has no dignity," giggled Mina.

Lucy chortled and said, "Perhaps he's infatuated with my Constance and is desperately trying to hide it."

"I don't want to live a conventional life," replied Mina, turning serious and watching the road in front of her stretch away into the morning mist. "In many respects."

"But Jonny loves you!" It was more of a plea than a statement from Lucy. Shafts of sunlight cutting through the trees tinted their pastoral setting, and they slowed even further, almost as if the horses themselves understood the subject matter.

"And I love him deeply, Lucy," said Mina, focused on the vanishing point beyond the horizon. Her sadness filled the air around them. "But our differences remain the same."

"So, you're just going to call off the wedding? Why would you want to do something as ridiculous at that?" said Lucy. "Jonathan's a good man with a great career ahead of him and kind, warm parents who love you."

D'Artagnan neighed, as if to disagree with Lucy. They moved out of the grove and left the road, riding into a gorgeous meadow draped in lush grass that looked like it was left over from Creation. Butterflies flitted over the greens, and Lucy frowned as she said, "I regret not bringing my collecting nets today."

"You will forever be my best friend Lucy, but what is your point?" said Mina, sharp enough to scan the meadow around them. Lucy noticed this but was still engaged in the conversation as she said, "The point is that you love him, silly. And the poor man is on his way back to marry *you*, you ninny! And those pants look horrible on you."

Mina turned on her mount, threw Lucy a playful yet dirty look as she looked over Lucy's attire. "It's better than flopping about on a horse in that dress, dear."

They had reached the middle of the meadow. Green waves fluttered with the supple breeze. Crickets hummed, birds chirped, and a few brave frogs out for the morning even sang to them from the recess of the tree line. Yet there was still a feeling shared by both of them that was difficult to place, but they both arrived at the same conclusion at the same moment.

They were being watched.

The horses sensed eyes on them as well.

"A highwayman[79]?" gasped Lucy.

Mina shrugged her shoulders confidently, not afraid. "Not for a while in England. Though he'd have to deal with me."

"We should not have ridden without an escort," said Lucy, her horse nearly at a stop. Mina watched D'Artagnan's ears rotate, listening for anything out of the ordinary. After a moment, she could feel D'Artagnan relax as he moved, and so then did she.

Slightly.

"It's all right. I have my escort right here," said Mina as she tapped the Winchester strapped to her the saddle. "Morris kept looking at it so longingly yesterday. He has his Enfield. And yet another bloody Winchester, regardless."

"Same old Mina," Lucy said, chuckling as she relaxed a little at hearing about the Winchester, but the sensation of a secret set of eyes on them would not leave her. D'Artagnan stood relaxed but

---

[79] An antiquated term for horse-mounted thieves who mugged or robbed from travelers. Footpads was also another term for the same type of criminal but without the mounted horse, and lower in social standing than highwaymen. These types of criminals operated in Great Britain until the 1830s, when the roads became more policed. In the American West, they were referred to as road agents.

vigilant. Constance chewed some grass, content and oblivious. Another breeze skimmed them and left but did not take their uneasiness along with it.

Far into the dark groves, a single branch cracked.

Birds stopped serenading.

D'Artagnan cocked his head.

Mina nearly reached for her Winchester.

She scoured the trees for any evidence of someone climbing up and watching them from above but saw nothing. Lucy took her lead from Mina as she felt her best friend's apprehension.

Mina circled D'Artagnan wider into the meadow, and Constance followed suit. "Let's circle the meadow and head back," said Mina, continuing to study the tree line with intensity. She wanted to distract Lucy from their strange sensation, so as she looked around, Mina said, "So, who's in the lead today?"

"Arthur," said Lucy, letting Constance trot alongside a reluctant D'Artagnan. She appreciated Mina's attempt to distract her from the strange tension, and the presence of the Winchester did ease her a bit, so she chimed, "Arthur's in the lead today, and tomorrow, and forever."

"So he's the one?" continued Mina with a genuine smile at Lucy, even as she watched a particularly dark patch of trees. They continued to circle wide and back around the meadow, with the intention of returning to the road. Constance at last caught on that something was amiss and neighed her worry to Lucy, who patted her on the neck as she said, "Yes. I decided yesterday, watching them both during the match. There's just this— kindness about Arthur that is so endearing."

Then out of the bushes, some motion, and the ladies both watched as an enormous raven, magnificent in its ebony, emerged. It held the desiccated wing of a crow in its beak. It dropped the wing to the ground and began to peck at whatever musculature was there to eat.

It looked up at them with enormous obsidian eyes and cawed a warning.

They reached the road again, and whether they wanted to admit it to each other or even to themselves, the riders and horses picked up the walk back home into a brisk trot.

"That was quite strange," said Lucy, taking a deep breath of relief.

"I agree," said Mina, "and I did not know those sorts of birds fed on each other."

Constance's trot had more of a sense of urgency, and D'Artagnan instantly resented this and caught up. As they all went along, the mood left them, and with that, their sense of humor returned.

"Bird cannibalism aside, suppose Arthur's impending title has nothing to do with it," said Mina with a raised eyebrow, firmly in the realm of sarcasm.

Lucy laughed out loud, reaching the forest and pushing whatever was bothering them even further away. "Oh, you're a funny one!"

"It's one of my many talents," beamed Mina as she rode.

Birds fluttered under the foliage of the trees around them, filling them with song, and Lucy sighed, took in the lush grove that they had returned to and said, "I love them both, but Arthur is more set in his life. He'll give my life some *gravitas*, while being silly enough to make me laugh. That's important to me. Should be important to you as well. Ian is a good man. He will be hurt, but he'll grow to accept it."

Mina nodded in agreement. "And Ian is pragmatic enough to not let it affect us all. As for married life, I'm not interested in waiting around for a man to come home to have his shoes taken off and be served his supper."

"Neither am I," said Lucy with a sly glint in her eyes. "The servants can do that."

"So, you *have* thought this out!" shrieked Mina, gently navigating D'Artagnan around and behind Constance so they shielded Lucy and Constance from the meadow side of the road. Lucy was grateful for her friend's gesture, even as a serious wave of expression flooded Mina's face. "What I am interested in is seeing the world with someone who thinks as I do. I want to see the new tower in Paris. Drink tea from a crystal cup in the Holy Land. Take in the pyramids themselves, not just frame a David Roberts lithograph in my library. Teach my students about what I have lived, not what I have read about. Life is not a textbook, Lucy. And Jonathan hates travel and loves ledgers."

"Love matters in this world, Mina," said Lucy, now in a serious mood herself. "It can be argued that there is nothing else, between here, the Holy Land and heaven itself."

They trotted along in silence, Mina deep in thought, Lucy watching her. The trees along the road became less dense, and to their right revealed an endless avenue that led to a proud mansion on a green velvet hill, which D'Artagnan led them onto.

"I must respectfully disagree, my dear friend," said Mina with a long, slow shake of her head. "I have to be as pragmatic about this as you have been with your decision, and with just as clear of an outcome. Whether I love him or not is irrelevant. Jonathan is a brave, kind soul who needs someone else in his life. Someone who can make his life easier. I'm a—"

"—strong personality," finished Lucy with a hearty giggle full of love for her best friend.

"All right, I'll accept that. I'm difficult, in my own way, and that's why I must think for both of us," Mina said as she pointed a gloved finger at Lucy.

They rode up the avenue, perfectly trimmed rows of shrubbery showing them the way toward their homes, all estates that overlooked the port town of Whitby, England below them. Ships of all sizes and descriptions navigated their way into the harbor, where tiny dots that were the working class of Whitby helped load and unload the ships. A stiff sea breeze ran past them, running counter to the Springtime warmth of the road behind them. Mina wrapped her arms around herself to shield her from the frosty gale, then looked at Lucy and said, "I love Jonathan enough to consider all facts and facets of this. I do want him to be happy as well."

"*He* won't be happy without *you*."

The muscles in Mina's jaw tightened with resolve and she said, "Jonathan comes back with Uncle Peter in mid-June, and I'm going to end it."

"So then why did you say yes when he proposed, silly Mina?"

"Silly Lucy," retorted Mina with a bittersweet smile as they trotted along the road, now lined with enormous lawns and manicured landscapes that ended with enormous homes for the wealthy of Whitby.

"So that's it then?" said Lucy, incredulous.

Mina nodded with conviction. "I'll talk to Jonathan when he gets back."

Lucy shook her head with a warm, knowing look. "No, you'll fall in his arms and marry him when he gets back."

"I'm going to let him spend his life loving his ledgers," said Mina with a nod that felt crisp and strong but ended with a chin wrinkled with regret and melancholy.

Lucy took all of this in before reaching across to touch Mina's forearm. "And you will forever have the support of your best friend."

For an instant Mina's wrinkle was there, then was swallowed up by a life-long reticence to show weakness. Yet her eyes betrayed her, because when she turned to Lucy and said, "Thank you, my dear friend," they both brimmed with tears of understanding and friendship. They moved closer to the Murray estate, a two-story grey stone manor that stood proud yet without showing as much ego as did some of the more resplendent estates among the family members. A path of broken old stones that might have dated back to Ancient Rome cleaved a wide and emerald lawn. The Murrays had been teased and cajoled to replace the worn pathway, seen as unsightly, but what the others had seen as unsightly the Murrays had seen as historical and interesting. D'Artagnan whinnied, almost as if he could sense Mina's emotions.

A flash of mischievousness hit Lucy's bright face and she chuckled as she teased, "Do you think Jonny will marry that Fleming girl we went to school with?"

Mina's brows knitted like two clashing swords. She stood a little straighter in the saddle, held the reins a little tighter. "Your sense of humor eludes me."

Horseshoes found the familiar stone path of the Murray estate, and clattered as they moved along. D'Artagnan neighed in anticipation of oats and a brushdown from one of the stable servants, though most of the time Mina insisted upon doting upon D'Artagnan herself. Another dirt path swerved away to the right about halfway up, leading alongside the manor and to the stables in the rear of the estate, and the horses turned onto it.

Lucy's eyebrows were raised high on her forehead, her face full of wit and sarcasm. "Jonny took a liking to her when we were younger. Alice. Alice? Yes, Alice was her name. Dumber than a clump of grass, as Quincy would say. But a pretty if you like that sort of thing. I wager Jonny does."

Pride kicked Mina's head back away from the grey two-story manor that had been her home since her birth, past the oncoming stables and toward the distant sea. "Jonathan fancies intelligent women," was what she said, nearly believing her statement.

Lucy pressed Mina's confidence like a leaf in a book. "Then I presume her blonde locks have nothing to do with the way he looks at Alice Fleming when she flirts with him with her pink dress and blue eyes!" Knowing her emotional dagger had found its intended target, Lucy Westenra giggled at Mina's mask of anger.

"I have not struck another female since grade school," hissed Mina, whirling on Lucy, "but you are tempting fate, Miss Westenra!"

"Don't think I've seen you angrier," mused Lucy, one eyebrow still willing to tease, the other dropped in false concern. "Sounds like love!"

"Jonathan knows a good woman when he sees one!" shouted Mina.

"'The lady,'" quoted Lucy as she wickedly arched her eyebrow ever-higher at Mina, "'doth protest too much, methinks.'"

"Oh, do shut the hell up!" wailed Mina. They both began to shriek with laughter as they neared the mansion.

D'Artagnan tried to trot ahead to the stables, such was his eagerness for his oats, but Mina held back on the reins slightly. In the distance, alone and apart from the other estates above the Whitby port town, stood the forlorn ruins of Carfax Abbey. As if to accentuate the loneliness and isolation of the ruins, a small bank of cloud shadows drifted over the abbey, while everything else around it was blanketed with sunlight and spring.

"I've always enjoyed looking at those amazing abbey ruins," said Mina as she motioned D'Artagnan to the stables.

"Yes, I know," grumbled Lucy, following her in. "And you're all stupid for keeping that horrible-looking stone path up to your home. It's almost like if it's old and strange and moldy, the Murray family will always take interest."

FOUR

That same European morning, a greying hulk of a steamship[80], The *Demeter*, sat on the coast of the Black Sea like a massive beached whale, twin smokestacks pumping smoke amid fore and aft masts, all under the grey-skied dawn. The lone, worn dock was outdated and creaking with age and guilt, more suited for the clipper ships of the past. It sat in the churning sepia waters like a well-kept family secret. The port city of Constanta[81] sat right down the coast for all to use, save this voyage.

Workers had just finished loading tons of coal that would be used as fuel for the voyage and were hoisting the carriage that had carried Jonathan Harker away from the wolves of Borgo Pass up off the dock and down into the ship's open hold, with the coffins taken off the wagon and being hand-carried onto the vessel. The sharp, black coffin sat at the wagon's edge, the crew uneager to touch it. Underneath the clouds, near the eastern horizon of the Black Sea, a cheery sunrise tried to reach out with a warm embrace to counter the frigid morning.

"Load the wagon as well!" said the *Demeter*'s captain, tall, lean and worn by a life forged at sea. He had a scrabbly beard that ran along the line of his jaw, and a dry squint that had developed into a facial tick from trying to find map lines and horizons for decades. Wrinkled, worn clothes covered him. He stood on the deck with his hands clasped behind him, the sun trying to claw its way out from behind clouds filled with rainwater behind him as he watched the crew work.

Some of the crewmen grumbled as they moved the wagon toward the ship. A multinational and multiethnic group of sea-hardened seafarers, some of them continued to mutter fear and disgust, and only after they had taken out washcloths or handkerchiefs would the workers touch the dark sarcophagus. The crewmen struggled to carry it, using six men, all of them making the sign of the cross as they walked the coffin up the ramp and onto the ship.

"This is quite a strange arrangement, Captain Mueller," said the first mate, a small, round and large-eyed man who waddled up to Mueller. His eyes were just a little too far apart on his face, his matted hair was parted in the middle, and he had the nervous twitch of a man with too much money in his pocket, though his were empty. He took a glance at the captain's empty hands and said, "Why are we loading up at this old dock instead of the main port? Where is the manifest for this cargo?"

Mueller coughed a laugh at his first mate's powers of observation and said, "There is no manifest, Remy. I thank you for following my instructions and hiring a minimal crew. Stewards[82] will have to double as stokers[83]. Only one client on this voyage and they paid for the sole right in

---

[80] The 1800s saw the transition from sea vessels with sails to those with steam engines. Steamers, or steamships, a had steam-powered engine or engines that powered the vessel, though the first steamers also had masts. The first transatlantic journey on a steamer had occurred in 1819.

[81] Constanta, also known as Tomis is the oldest populated city in Romania, founded around 600 BC.

[82] Stewards were responsible for the collecting and washing of the bed and table linen on the ship.

[83] A stoker is a worker who constantly feeds coal into a steamship's furnaces, which in turn help power the ship. Some of the larger steamships carried hundreds of tons of coal, as well as fresh water, on each voyage.

advance some time ago. I was contacted anonymously through a correspondence that was sent in the *Demeter*'s name to the Constanta Port. Wrote that there would be no one to meet us today, only the cargo, the money for our compensation tucked into a compartment on the carriage, and no questions. These were the conditions, and they, he or she has paid six times the value for the right to have them."

Remy Chapelle watched the men put the black coffin down as quickly as possible, as if it were filled with scorpions, before he said, "The crew, they are full of gossip and concern since seeing what we are to transport. This is all highly unusual, Captain."

"In our travels," said Captain Mueller, "have we not dragged all manner of strange cargo from corner to corner of this globe?"

"Of course," shrugged Chapelle. "There were those gigantic lizards[84] we transported from Borneo to China—"

"Well then?" said Mueller, shrugging back as he watched the workers stack all of the coffins on top of a net. "We have transported corpses before. Remember the dead natives in Haiti? The murdered diplomat's body to the Canary Islands?"

A winch was lowered, and the net's edges were then attached. Remy watched with intent as the caskets were hoisted as one and lowered into the hold of the *Demeter*.

"The Haitians that loaded the cargo called the bodies *zombis* and said they were still alive. Remember the witchcraft symbols scrawled onto those coffins? And our workers have a problem taking *these* coffins?" said Mueller, throwing Remy a sideways glance. The captain reached into his pants pocket and pulled out a worn but comfortable pipe and a bag of tobacco, which he began to stuff into the pipe. He offered the bag to Remy, who politely shook his head.

"Sir, you know the men. They are a superstitious lot, as are all us men of the sea."

Mueller struck a match along the back of his pants and lit his pipe with a few long puffs. He tossed the match over the edge of the ship and said, "Everyone's share is six times greater this time, no?"

"Yes, Captain," agreed Remy with reluctance laced with anticipation.

Mueller took a long, satisfying drag of his pipe, exhaled a stream of smoke before he prodded Remy gently with the tip. "Well, this client paid six times the regular amount in gold in return for no questions, and he or she will receive six times the privacy. My home is now paid for, Remy, after all these years at sea."

"As is mine, Captain," said Remy, watching the men close the hold. "Theresa and I are grateful, but those coffins smell of old death."

Mueller rolled his eyes at Remy. "As they should! There are *dead* people inside them, my friend! Again, we are being compensated for our silence. Now, get those gangplanks up so we can be on our way."

"Salah said he saw one of the coffins move."

Another sideways glance from Mueller told Remy that the captain was having none of it. "Salah's drunken hallucinations are legendary."

Remy chortled in agreement. "Fair enough."

"How long has it been," said Mueller, taking in another long drag of comfort. "since you've been to England?"

"Lucky seven, Sir."

Mueller clapped Remy on the back and said, "I'll buy you an ale in that godforsaken pub in London, and we'll have a laugh over this ridiculous voyage when it is over."

---

[84] Komodo dragons, a large species of monitor lizard native to a few islands in Southeast Asia, the Island of Komodo being the most prominent.

In the days after the *Demeter* left Constanta, Remy dominated the crew's evening card games as the ship made its way out of the Black Sea, through the cleaving Bosporus and into the expansive Aegean, ever nearer to its fate. The cargo below was cold, damp and housed the corpses in their coffins quite comfortably. Inside their coffins, the skeletons remained in pieces, disassembled bones to untrained eyes. The rats, however, were another matter, their hunger insatiable, and the stronger rats began to cannibalize the weaker vermin, all inside the wooden slats, as their master wished.

Captain Mueller stayed up one night to falsify a cargo manifest should the ship be boarded for any reason, listing the coffins as 'human remains' after lifting the lid of the skeleton-filled coffin and wondering how or why a rib cage would need chest armor from the Roman era. The disassembled skeletons waited for the word from the master's coffin to rise up and stretch their collective arm bones and strangle Mueller, as did the rats await the word to leap out of their shelter to rend the captain's flesh from his bones, but Mueller slammed the coffin lid shut, assuming the others were filled with the piles of bones, much to his temporary respite. He did try one of the other coffins, the large, black, bleak coffin, and it would not open when he pulled on the lid. Mueller assumed it was locked and was too lazy to pursue prying the thing open, but was left with the strange sensation afterward, almost as if there was someone inside pulling at the lid, keeping it shut. The vampires slept, fasting to avoid any kind of disturbance to the crew and the voyage for as long as possible.

They knew that the open sea loomed.

Meanwhile, spring stretched her arms out and began to warm the continent, despite the resistance of the stout and majestic Alps. Mountain ranges melted and wept the fruits of their wintertime aggregate into the plush valleys below. Meadows throughout southern Europe thawed and grew grasses that felt immortal and fertile, too busy romancing with bees and butterflies to dream of the summer heat that would wilt them in the distant months.

Through all of these sunsets and sunrises, Mina Murray taught her class cursive writing, rudimentary arithmetic and the Seven Wonders of the Ancient World. Lucy Westenra concerned herself with her vast butterfly collection and riding Constance around the long roads of Whitby, avoiding the eerie, lush meadow that gave them the crow-eating raven. Quincy Morris taught Ian Seward and Arthur Holmwood how to fish, all of them nearly coming to blows one day over which horse saddle was better, the classic British or hedonistic American, and who was going to marry Lucy Westenra, not knowing that Miss Westenra had already made up her own mind on the subject.

Lastly, upon a particular Sunday after church service, during rounds, Henry and Ian Seward and a few assistants removed the chewed remains of a dozen large spiders out of Montague Rhodes Renfield's gasping, foaming mouth.

FIVE

Somewhere in Southern Europe.

Far away from the *Demeter* and Whitby, England.

Underground, where the soil was cold and embraced the dead.

Where even spring could not embrace with her warmth.

Beneath where lions had fed and gladiators were disemboweled.

They dared not flicker even a single candle, such was their secrecy.

Five undead shadows, cloaked in darkness, emboldened by fury.

Whispering of secrets and plots:

"In nominee Domini nostri Dominus Satanas." *In the name of our God Satan.*

"Bizim efendinin kutsal olmayan isim çağırmak etmeyin! Yeterli değil mi biz karşılamak komplolara Oğlu aleyhine?" *Do not invoke the unholy name of our lord! Is it not sufficient that we meet to conspire against his son?*

"Nous rassemblons sous cette table de boucher chrétien pour discuter à la fois l'attendu et l'imprévu. "*We gather underneath this Christian butcher table to discuss both the expected and the unforeseen.*

"Protege nos, Satanus, servientes tuis mysteriis." *Protect us, Satan, servants of your mysteries.*

"Wir sind hier, das Undenkbare zu betrachten, wie Brutus und seine Verschwörer." *We are here to contemplate the unthinkable, like Brutus and his conspirators.*

"Его безжалостные политикой привел нами здесь, вашего на место сие к этой момент времени." *His ruthless politics have brought us here, to this place, to this point in time.*

"Düşünülemez gerçekleştirilmelidir! Biz başka hiçbir rücu verilmiştir." *The unthinkable must be done! We have been given no other recourse.*

"Les évènements du le dernier voyage de l'héritier ici étaient désastreux. Il défia nos lois, nos coutumes." *The events of the heir's last journey here were disastrous. He defied our laws, our customs.*

"So etwas hat noch nie versucht worden. Kann es getan werden?" *Such a thing has never been attempted. Can it be done?*

"Stulti eloquia! Hinnulus! Nos- tram historiam falces quoniam maturavit cum hasce insidias and conspiracies! Quomodo per nefandas uerendus fides cordibus nostris. Ceruicum messis. Aqua benedicta super cutem. Impaling. Vade retro Satana." *Fools! Fawns! Our history is ripe with these plots and conspiracies! Yes, it can be done. In the manner described by the accursed faiths and feared by our hearts. Decapitation. Holy Water upon the skin. Impaling. Vade retro Satana.*[85]"

"Мы используем обряды Ватикана в этом заговоре? Это безумие!" *We use Vatican rites in our conspiracy? That is madness!*

---

[85] *Vade Retro Satana* is a catholic formula for exorcism from medieval times, incorporated at one point into the Roman Ritual for Exorcism.

"Quis habitabit ex vobis iuvenes accepturas nauigavit justitia eorum apud me, pro me omnibus nobis?" *Who among you young people will take this voyage into justice with me, for me, for us all?*

"Meister, er ist unterschiedlich als der Rest von uns. Herr Satan darf ihn so gemacht haben. Er kann Objekte mit seinen Gedanken bewegen, ganz zu schweigen von seinem verdammten Ratten sagen. Keiner von uns sind in der Lage, dass." *Master, he is different than the rest of us. Lord Satan must have made him so. He can move objects with his thoughts, to say nothing of his accursed rats. None of us are capable of that.*

"Quod sic, adversarius est dignissimus. In rebus huius saeculi sunt dirimenda aut ingénii in curia vel saevitiae, et nunc foderunt in forum novissimis." *Yes, he is a most worthy adversary. In matters of this world, they must be settled in the court of either diplomacy or brutality, and we must now delve into the forum of the latter.*

"Господь Сатана знает, что будем откладывать дажекак мы думаем Это." *Lord Satan knows of what we plot even as we think it.*

"Quis vos postulo intelligere catulos suos quod fruitur eis de rebus convalescit." *What you need to understand, young ones, is that he enjoys and thrives upon these matters.*

"Sie ärgern sich ihm: Meister, wegen der Ereignisse des Schwarzen Pest, und davor, Jerusalem?" *You resent him, Master, because of the events of the Black Plague, and before that, Jerusalem?*

"Ваше негодования ослепляет вас, сестра. Мы должны быть прагматичными." *Your resentment blinds you, sister. We must be pragmatic.*

"O zaman "Konstantinopolis'in düşmek. Sen bunun için ondan nefret ettim." *Constantinople's fall[86], then. You hated him for that.*

"Verum pone moras et historiae nostrae, iuvenili instrumenta. Optimum suggerentes ego agimus solum objectum collective negotia nostra populorum culturae nostrae. Omnes nostri debebant, vel inlicitum legalis, in nostra ripas, et signanter exprimitur inaequali quotus oeconomicas distributione. Esse aiunt omnes facile et contractibus ledgers en eius utilitatem. Nos sistuntur omnia cogitationibus nostris, sensus quod supremum fuit, ad heredem, et risit et dixit, quod eramus nulli autem alii subditis imperium contemplatus ejus regii est servisset quam suae. Nosmetipsi datis et cauteriatam oculos habens optione tecum preented aqua benedicta." *Put aside our history, youthful instruments. I am suggesting that we act only in the best interest of our collective, our businesses, our peoples, our culture. All of our holdings, legal or illegal, are in our banks, and they have pointedly expressed the uneven percentage of financial distribution. They say the ledgers and contracts are all decidedly in his favor. We presented all of our thoughts, our evidence to the heir the last time he was here, and he laughed and told us that we were subjects beheld to his royalty and to no other rule than his own. We insisted and were presented with the option of having our eyes seared with Holy Water.*

"Bu yüzden biz davranmak?" *So, we are to act?*

"Vos talis conversantur de rebus talibus delicata, deficiensque inficetiarum! Loquitur de vobis tuo amplius de quam imperitia derogetur." *You converse of such delicate matters with such dismaying, decaying clumsiness! It speaks more of your inexperience than my opinion of your prowess.*

"'О заговоре! Нозор тебе, чтобы показать твою опасную бровь ночью, когда зло

---

[86] The Fall of Byzantine Constantinople by Ottoman forces, led by 21-year-old Mehmed the Conqueror, occurred in 1453. Mehmed would later become the seventh sultan of the Ottoman Empire. Up to that point, Constantinople had been the capitol of Orthodox Christianity. The capture of the city marked the end of the Roman Empire, which had existed for 1,500 years.

наиболее свободными?"" *'O conspiracy! Sham'st thou to show thy dangerous brow by night, when evils are most free?[87]'*

"Vestra humore non interficies me? Si oportet referre vates Avon, tunc forte versi estis omnes quidem notabiliter iuvenes etiam cherubicus, pro hoc opus subtilis. Ut ad te cum hoc debuisse, obstante hac ingenio et rebus probatisque resplendent. Caedem non politicarum peritus est agrum. Fortasse magis hoc opus debuerit dari procuratorem apud more gerunt in calceati et subtilitatem in artes." *Your humor does not slay me! If you must quote the Bard of Avon[88], then perhaps you are all indeed too young, too cherubic, for this subtle task. I may have been wrong to approach you all with this matter, despite your resplendent and proven talents in this area and these matters. Assassination, not politics, is your field of experience. In hindsight, perhaps this task should have been given to operatives with more wear on their shoes and subtlety in their techniques.*

"Bizim gençlik köstekleyecek değil, sadece bize canlandırır! Neredeyse bütün vergilerden ve arazi alır ve sadece kendisini sanıyor! Biz halkımızın yerli diziler, ne yapılması gerektiği bilmek ve tüm çıkarları doğrultusunda hareket olacaktır görmek." *Our youth does not hinder us, it only invigorates us! He takes nearly all tithes and land and thinks only of himself! We see what ails our people, know what must be done, and will act in the interests of all.*

"Omnia fere mei praecones fere. Recte fortasse deservire potest. loquere nulli. Possimus fœdus homicidii sanguinis vinculo. Estis omnes committere nostris agens meus caprum emissarium, venerabiles in Parisius." *Nearly all, my heralds, nearly all. Very well, perhaps you can be of use. Speak to no one of this. We make a covenant of murder, our blood bond. You are all to engage our agent, my emissary, in venerable Paris.*

"Sind wir nicht zu seiner Festung Annäherung?" *Are we not to approach his fortress?*

"Infantili cherubim! Hassassinic novitiorum institutione! Samaritani! Es sicariorum aut Curiam Jesters? Et triturabitur coniunctis legionibus ex Gallia meus dilectus Bosphoros, sed quæritis occidas draconi qui est in cubili suam? Loqueris ineptias! Nullus exercitus qui ambulat hac tellure penetrabilis quod cor. No— transit in sicut loquimur. Draco fuerit ducta est. Ipse erit in Brittania maturius profecturum." *Infantile cherubs! Hassassinic Novices! Samaritans! Are you assassins or court jesters? He thrashed united legions from Gaul to my beloved Bosphoros, yet you seek to slay the dragon in his own lair? You speak absurdities! No army that walks this earth can pierce that heart. No— he is in transit as we speak. The dragon has been drawn out. He will be in Brittania shortly.*

"Почему я не сообщил? Он не оставил замок так как она." *Why was I not informed? He has not left the castle since she—*

"Non loquamur de illa Non de illius feminae! Eius rebus in furia Balcanicae castellum patens vulnus ferro flammaque supposita. Ineamus evaginabo illius gladii nostra fines!" *Let us not speak of her! Not of that woman! His fury from the events in that Balkan village is an open wound, a sword aflame. Let us unsheath that sword for our own purposes!*

"Comme on l'a fait avec le despote papale?" *As it was done with the Papal despot?*

"No! Hoc non est qui munera libenter accipiunt redibat autocrat ut veneno, no Cardinali ut strangulatus vel Senator esse garroted. Et mortuus est, oportet prope immortalem! Est patris filius! Pugnaturus Gallos agente deinde mandatis litterae. A vehiculo supplebitur pro usu per continentem petierunt. Semel litus Brittania, reliqui sitis vestram refertur pagella." *No! This is no bribery-laden autocrat to be poisoned, no cardinal to be strangled or senator to be garroted. It must be a mortal blow to a near-immortal! He is our father's son! Engage the French agent, then follow his*

---

[87] From *Julius Caesar*, by William Shakespeare (1564-1616)

[88] Shakespeare was born in Avon, England, hence the Bard (poet) of Avon.

instructions to the letter. A carriage will be supplied for your usage through the continent. Once ashore on Brittania, you are left to your collective devices.

"Мы желаем установите право все, что он чем обидел, а все те, которые он была сделанак страдать." *We wish set right all that he has wronged, and all those that he made to suffer."*

"Vade, et noctem et profana patris Satan bibentis animarum inquinatio operiam vos meditationes eius introspicere." *Go, and let the night and our unholy father Satan, drinker of souls, shroud you with his secret purposes.*

"*Ave Satanus.*"

"Obsecro te omnes me adducam super ornatus disco caput. Obsecro vos ne forte vulnera recentia, ut in fertile imaginationes spectare visus esset et sciret quoniam omnium solvit sanctus erat in eo quod machinationes et possem in loco nostro profana sumere sinu Patris." *I beg of you all to bring me, upon an ornate platter, his head. I beseech you that somehow his wounds be fresh, so that in my fertile imaginations he would gaze upon my visage and know that it was my machinations that undid everything holy to him, and that I might be able to take my rightful place at our unholy father's side.*

SIX

Massive, churning waves battered against the groaning, tired hull of the *Demeter*[89], which groaned and shuddered with each blow, rusted iron walls embittered by many journeys to the rigors of a stormy sea feeling that the day when they finally give way might be nearing. She had made good time through the Black Sea, cleaved the mighty Bosphoros, and the Sea of Marmara had been crossed in good time, but the Aegean was another matter. The waves could not be seen through the darkness that enveloped the ocean that night, but they were surely felt, like fists to a battered pugilist's kidneys, and heard as well, deafening wallops full of force and relentlessness. A fierce rain punished ocean and ship alike. Sheets of downpour compounded the weather and furthered the mood as it battered the wet, creaking floorboards of the deck. A single lantern, left behind by a crew too smart to be outside during a thrashing at the hands of nature, flew in the face of all of the darkness, illuminating a center patch of the deck while maintaining its light source as it hung from a lamppost.

Below, the assault of the rain alternated with the booming of the waves outside and echoed throughout the vast, nearly empty hold, which pitched and yawed without mercy. Stray tools and equipment slid along the floorboards, ropes strung along the ceiling swung with the motion, as remnants of broken pallets and boxes clunked and bounced off of the walls and metal support beams.

Among all of this sat the solemn coffins in the gloom, oblivious to the noise or the dizzying movement, as if nailed to the floor, *none of the caskets affected by the swaying of the ship.*

Dracula's coffin was beautiful and new and menacing, while the coffins of the brides were ornate but moldy and brittle, as if they were just dug up and put to use. Venus' coffin was quite ironically decorated with a wooden bas-relief of Cabanel's *Birth of Venus*[90], an exact copy, even down to the fluttering cherubs above the resplendent Venus lying beauteously along the sea rocks and the waves. Andromeda's beautiful, archaic casket had rounded edges, was woven out of wicker, yet was covered with a tightly wrapped canvas along the top that featured a beautiful painted portrait of the *living* version of Andromeda, in the Greco-Roman style that was typically painted upon the mummies of Ancient Rome. Petra's coffin was simple, carved out of a single piece of wood, flat along the top, with a rounded edge around the head yet flat at the base, but with only a simple filigree of papyrus motifs along the outer top, yet featuring an exquisite Egypto-Roman portrait of Petra Ali painted onto a bas-relief impression of her on the coffin lid.

Each of the caskets had ornate handles along their sides in keeping with the styles of the coffins' origins, with the brittle, broken and barely-held-together coffin remnants for the rats and skeletons.

One of the rat coffin lids percolated like it was about to boil over. Enormous tails, claws and

---

[89] In Greek Mythology, the goddess of the harvest.

[90] *The Birth of Venus* was painted in 1863 by French Artist Alexandre Cabanel, and not to be confused with what is arguably the more famous version, which was painted by Italian artist Sandro Botticelli in the 1480s, simply one of the more famous pieces of art from the Italian Renaissance. There exists a second and a third, yet smaller versions of the Cabanel painting, the latter created a decade later.

snouts skittered along the edges of the lid, waiting for the syllable, the word, the hint or even the gesture that would let them erupt out into the night and throughout the hold. Their collective chirping, hisses, squeals and snarls began to build in frustration and anticipation. In the distance, crammed into the recesses of the rusted, inaccessible corners of the hold, the ship's garden-variety ship rats cowered in terror.

"هذه الليلة؟" hissed Petra, hopeful. She lay amid dark soil from the Carpathians that mingled with fertile, dry earth from her beloved Egypt. Mummy wrappings, scarab legs and cobra skins surrounded her beauteous head. *Tonight?*

"Hac nocte," came a dark rumble from the obsidian coffin that challenged the storm to be heard. *Tonight.*

Rats frothed out from their coffin in waves and fearlessly spread out into the dank wetness of the hold, lunging toward the rusted corners of the hold and attacking any rat that was still on this end of the ship. Accustomed to sailors that hunted them with clubs, these common Norway rats were no match for the sheer ferocity of these ravenous, cannibalistic vermin. Squeals from the corners announced the deaths of many tiny mammalians, and the tearing of fur, skin and flesh would precede the breaking of miniscule bones.

The lids of the coffins of Petra, Venus and Andromeda slid open like supple traps. Voluptuous wisps of mist undulated along the floor as they made their way toward the black, ominous coffin that contained their master.

Other older and more worn coffins rattled open to reveal bones, crammed together inside in rows of tibias, fibulas, ribs, clavicles and skulls. Out of the pile rose the darker, stouter skull of Primus, and it floated in the air to about his height, and as the skull of Primus the centurion, Primus the gladiator rose, so did his robust, powerful skeleton, in multiple pieces from multiple parts of the coffin, assembling themselves behind the skull even as the lower jaw set itself into the skull. Leg and arm bones twirled in the air as the spinal column set itself, the humeri settling into the scapulae while the femurs creaked into place between the ischium and the ilium, rib bones twirling into place in, around and along Primus' armor. The bits of hand and foot bone were last before Primus took a single, solemn step out of the coffin and knelt before the black, sharp shadow that was rising out of the larger, bleaker coffin like a cobra.

The shadow blinked twin embers of orange hate.

"Quid variatur voluntas tua?" rumbled the massive skeleton as the other skeletons began to reassemble themselves outside the coffin. *What is thy will?*

Dracula stood straight up, and as his silhouette became more and more bat-like, his voice became an animalistic growl as he snarled, "Et cantavit oportet vivet ad praebere nos apud sanguis et navigatio ut England. Occidere quicumque reliquias." *The crew must survive to provide us with food and navigation to England. Kill whoever remains.*

Above, and overlooking the deck, the odor of oil, fuel, rotting wood and seawater filled the *Demeter's* tiny bridge compartment. From out the window, the surging ocean could be seen pounding against the hull, some of the beheaded waves scattering across the deck, such was the violence of the storm, as if to warn all involved of the awakened malevolence within the hold. First Mate Remy Chapelle was otherwise occupied. He leaned against the side door to the bridge as he poured his large, too-far-apart eyes over a pretty brunette who held the steering wheel as she peered out into the tempest. "I can only see waves out there, Remy! No land! How do you navigate during a storm?"

Remy, no stranger to women or storms at sea, slid his eyes languidly over the girl. "Ermina, I use your beautiful eyes as stars to guide me through the night, my angel. Just hold steady and you will be fine."

"You do not flatter me, Remy," giggled Ermina, her arms tensing, her brows knitting as she struggled to hold the wheel. Ermina, who wore her dark hair pinned up, was a stewardess/laundrywoman and nurse, part of a small staff that Captain Mueller had brought onto the merchant ship for this voyage, men and women who could clean and cook for the *Demeter* and her crew. Individual crews maintained the coal furnace, the masts and the engineering of the ship, while the support staff attended to the crew, cooking the meals from the thousands of pounds of vegetables and meats brought aboard, washing the clothes and cleaning the ship continuously during any voyage.

But Remy Chapelle was not interested in the intricacies of those duties at the moment, focused on how supple Ermina's thigh looked as it caressed her dark uniform dress.

"Let me help you," purred the first mate as he sidled up behind Ermina and slid his arms over her shoulders before he gripped the steering wheel. Ermina's eyes danced; she was young enough to be flattered at having the attention of an older man, yet naïve enough to not consider the ramifications of her possible actions. If Remy or Ermina had been more focused on the ship instead of each other, they might have noticed a small group of ship rats sprinting out of one of the deck cowl vents, pursued by a stream of lethal, possessed rodents. The Norway rats were quickly overcome, writhing as their cannibalistic brethren tore them to pieces.

Ermina did have beautiful almond-shaped eyes, but while perhaps naïve, she was no fool, and she arched a coy eyebrow at Remy and twirled a red scarf around her neck as she said, "I wonder if your wife would mind that you say such things to me?"

"We need not mention it to her." Remy took a big, long sniff of Ermina's dark locks. His hands slid down from the steering wheel to her waist. Ermina let it happen. She was flattered. And interested.

He kissed her neck, and Ermina raised her chin, accepting his affection. She knew Remy was married, but they were at sea, and his wife was Remy's affair, not hers.

"Perhaps you should think of *her* eyes instead of mine," said Ermina with a dry laugh. "I shall think of my daughter Krystyna, perhaps." Ermina didn't mean it, but she liked to keep Remy on his toes.

Remy laughed as he rested his head on Ermina's left shoulder, gazing out into the night and the storm. Through the window, through the rain and through the night, he saw one of the deck hatches move in the wind. The hatch was ajar. In this storm, seawater seeping into the hold could range from a laborious duty to disaster at sea. Remy's eyes popped open as he shouted, "I'm going to kill Salah! He forgot to lock—"

Something stopped Remy from speaking.

Something that was raising the hatch.

It was a shadow.

Enormous.

With glowing, livid eyes.

Stirred out of her arousal. Ermina's eyes widened as she took in the large, dark shape that rose slowly out of the open hold. "Remy, what is that?"

Like the birth of a fallen angel out of a long-forgotten abyss, a gargantuan bat unfurled its massive wings out into the night and began to stride toward them, its scarlet eyes ablaze and its obsidian fur fluttering in the storm.

Mammalian lips unfurled, exposing enormous jagged canines and incisors.

"Holy Mother of God," whispered Remy, realizing everyone on board the *Demeter* was in mortal danger.

SEVEN

While Ermina, Remy and Captain Mueller were dealing with a maelstrom within a storm at sea somewhere between Athens and Crete, elongated shadows stretched over the Valley of the Kings, where some of the most amazing tombs and architecture had been built for pharaohs a thousand years before Christ was born. Everywhere in the valley, revealed to the modern world or as yet undiscovered, lay colossal tombs hewn out of stone for the rulers of Ancient Egypt. Much of this construction happened nearly ten centuries before Cleopatra met Julius Caesar, Marc Anthony and Cleopatra's legendary death at the bite of an asp, between the New Kingdom[91] and the birth of Christianity. In this valley of monuments, pharaohs, queens and mummies wafted many whispers, faint hisses that stretched and clung to the parched hillsides that surrounded one of the cradles of civilization, cotton strands clinging to thorny branches. These sand-laden whispers gossiped fear and the reverence of Ramesses II, the most powerful of the Egyptian pharaohs; known as Ramesses the Great, Ozymandias and The Great Ancestor by his descendants. One of the most prolific builders of the dynastic period, Ramesses capped his legacy with his journey to Nubia with his Queen Nefertari in 1255 BC to inaugurate the spectacular new temple, the great Abu Simbel.

But in this particular, haunted valley, history also whispered of scriptured biblical legend.

History is no different than any other family, and ripe with gossip.

Things to be said about relatives, deeds of good and evil.

Whispers.

Of plagues.

Ten of them.

Of blood in the water.

Of dying fish.

Of frogs.

Of hail and locusts.

Of darkness for three days.

Of death and the firstborn.

Of Moses and the Passover.

And the Exodus.

Of the yawning Red Sea.[92]

Spread out in front of the Valley of the Kings like a colossal asp in search of her next Cleopatra was a titanic brown and blue serpent known as the river Nile, which was not afraid of comparisons with the great monuments that surrounded her. Indeed, the serpentine river had earned a deserved vanity, for she had helped the civilization that grew around her flourish by permitting her curves to be used to carry food, people and even monuments along her sensuous coils. Flowing north, as if in

---

[91] The New Kingdom, 1550-1069 BC.

[92] The life of Moses is presented in the Old Testament Books of Exodus, Leviticus, Numbers and Deuteronomy.

majestic defiance of most of the south-streaming rivers of the world, her only rival for the world's longest river would be the other resplendent serpent from the New World, the Amazon. Yet this asp had two tails, two tributaries, called the Blue and the White Nile, which birth the river from the depths of Africa and the Mountains of the Moon[93]. As the river writhed through the continent and neared the ocean, neared Alexandria, Cairo and the glorious Mediterranean, the serpent's cobra hood spread and became the Nile Delta, to feed her people, slave and pharaoh alike, and for all of history to witness her generosity. She gave to the people her children, the papyrus, the ibis and the crocodile, so they could write, read, contemplate, document, worship and upon occasion, be consumed by her.

And yet, for all of the magnificence of the Eastern bank of the Nile, the Valley of the Queens, the Tombs of the Nobles and even the great boy Pharaoh Tutankhamun, resting in peace in his own, as-yet undiscovered tomb, the eastern bank of the Nile held her own precious marvels. More whispers from the wind, the now-parched but then-fertile sand, from the distant calls of the entombed, mummified Ibis storks, sacrificed and destined as the living embodiment of Thoth, the god of knowledge, whose beak curved like that of the moon.

Egypt, they sighed.

Cleopatra[94], last pharaoh of Egypt, who after exile won her throne back from her brother, then bore children with Julius Caesar and Mark Anthony.

Tutankhamun[95], the boy king who ruled at the age of nine and died nine years later.

Nefertiti[96], queen of the Nile and wife of Akhenaten.

Akhenaten[97], the pharaoh that dared Ancient Egypt to stop worshipping the many gods and deify the sun.

Hatshepsut[98], the woman who ruled Egypt after her husband Thutmose II passed to the afterlife along the river Styx.

Thutmose III[99], warrior pharaoh who would rule with Hatshepsut, his stepmother,

Amenhotep I[100], second pharaoh of the 18th Dynasty, who founded Deir el-Medina, the ancient village that would craft the royal tombs and would end up naming him their patron god.

Khafra[101], Khufu's son and whose name the Great Sphinx was built.

Khufu[102], who would commission the great pyramid of Giza.

Sneferu[103], first king of the Fourth dynasty and builder of the Bent and Red pyramids.

This was Egypt, and this was the necropolis of ancient Thebes.

Amid all of this history and these whispers, the jagged inferno of Egypt in 1899 had decided to ebb into a shimmering, resplendent sunset. Legions of Arab workers, some from Egypt but others

---

[93] Moutains of the Moon, *Montes Lunae* or *Jibbel el Kumri*, is an ancient term used to describe a mythical mountain range that was the reputed source of the Nile, which is now generally accepted as the Rwenzori Mouuntains in Uganda. The actual source waters are primarily from lakes Albert, Kyoga, Victoria and Tana throughout Central Africa. A merchant and explorer named Diogenes reported the location and described the legend, which was accepted by Ptolemy (100-170 AD) and other geographers of the Ancient World. Arabs, Greeks, Africans, and in modern times, Europeans have all explored the region and have come to the same geographic conclusion about the source waters.

[94] Technically she was Cleopatra VII, and she ruled from 51-30 BC.

[95] Tutankhamun's nine years of rule were from 1334-1325 BC.

[96] Nefertiti lived circa 1370-1330 BC.

[97] Ahkenaten reigned from approximately 1353-1336 BC.

[98] Hatshepsut's reign was c. 1478-1458 BC.

[99] Thutmose III was pharaoh from 1479-1425 BC.

[100] Amenhotep I ruled from 1525-1504 BC.

[101] The start of Khafra's rule is unknown, but ended in 2570 BC.

[102] Khufu reigned from 2589-2566 BC.

[103] Sneferu, c. 2613-2589 BC. The Red and Bent pyramids were built in Dahshur, about 25 miles south of Cairo.

from Libya and Sudan, poured over a battered hillside, part of an enormous excavation. From a distance, they looked like ants scouring over a dry patch of someone's back yard, if it wasn't for the fact that they moved over one of the world's most important historical regions.

As the sun was swallowed by the dusk like a rabbit being consumed by a python, the workers furthered the ambiance as they sang:

صالة. القوق[104]انيطعي يذلا تنأ ،يبنلا يلع ةالص .بهذن انوعد ،بهذن انوعد ،يبنلا يلع ةالص"
علی النبی، دعونا نذهب، دعونا نذهب. صالة على النبی أنت الذی یعطینا القوق." *Prayers upon The Prophet/And let's go/ Let's go/ Prayers upon The Prophet/ You, who gives strength/ Prayers upon The Prophet/ Let's go. Let's go/ Prayers upon The Prophet/ You, who gives strength."*

The army of workers' worn shovels and picks gnawed away at a knobby, protruding slope of Egyptian terrain, while other diggers carried the scratched-away earth from a revealed sliver of unearthed ancient architecture that jutted from the hill like a broken femur. Hieroglyphs covered the stonework like brushstrokes. Older laborers, no longer capable of enduring the exposure and pounding of the sun during a work day, brought water in clay jugs to the workers and foremen, grateful that the sun had decided to release its vise grip upon the day. A massive, multi-toned, petroglyph-encrusted cornerstone had been somehow pushed/pulled aside by the army of workers that had covered it with a cobweb of ropes and pulleys in the process. Somehow, the colossal magnificence of Ancient Egypt had been built with many more people, and under even worse working conditions.

Shimmering with heat, the horizon drank the sunset and made the world tangerine. Over the shouting of the men, a few distant jackals yowled with anticipation of the night and the hunt.

Using ropes held stoutly by the laborers, two men, one younger and the other older, were rappelling into the darkness of a hole that was still being picked at by the workers. Torches, both electric and wooden, were being lit all around the opening in the landscape, yet the utter blackness that the two men were descending into persisted.

Pitch dark swallowed them, melting shadow into shadow in the alchemy of the twilight, the evening call to prayer wafting over the desertscape and into the darkness with them:

عراست / هللا لوسر وه دمحم نأب رقأو / هللا الإ هلإ ال هنأب رقأو / .مظعأ وه هللا"
للصالة / تعارع ونحو الرفاهیة / هللا / .مظعأ وه هللا / ال إلإ الا هللا[105]" *God is the greatest/ I acknowledge that there is no god but God/ I acknowledge that Muhammad is the Messenger of God / Hasten to prayer / Hasten towards welfare / God is greatest / There is no god but God*

Inside the darkness of the entombed air, the older, fuller silhouette slid down the rope as if he had spent his life breaking out of prisons and closing out saloons. Enveloped in pitch, he landed like a cat on the cool limestone slab floor like he'd done it a thousand times on a hundred nights, which he of course had. He then looked up to see the second man, a thinner, younger version of himself, still a boy really, unsure, unsteady and a lot more nervous, following him down the rope in staggered, terrified increments. After one particularly abrupt stop, the young man yelped like a puppy. The young man, who somehow wore a tan wool coat, vest and pants in the vicious African summer, landed in an unceremonious heap, scrabbling over on his knees and elbows before bolting upright in a silly, comedic way and dusting himself off, a self-conscious eye on the older man. He wore tan shoes and a bowtie that had no place on an excavation.

---

[104] Muslim prayer.

[105] The Muslim call to prayer is the *Adhan*, or in Turkish the *Ezan*, sung out from a mosque five times a day. The first phrase, 'God is great', is known as the *Takbir*, which is followed by the *Shahada* 'There is no God but God/Muhammad is the messenger of God".

"Sorry," said the younger shape, trying to find the pith helmet that had fallen off in the crash landing. While the young man's clothes befitted a British aristocrat, the older man's garb was lighter and typical of an explorer of the period, though instead of the traditional pith helmet, he wore a *Keffiyeh*[106] upon his head. The older man had a gun belt wrapped around his waist, a Bergmann M 1894[107], worn and jaded with experience, while the younger man wore no weapon.

"Watch for scorpions, lad," replied the elder with a wry, warm chuckle as he strode over to pat the dust off the shoulder of the younger man.

"As if I could see anything in all this," the boyish voice echoing around the chamber.

"Give it a moment, your eyes will adjust."

A fading shaft of light from the hole dug in the ceiling wavered in its illumination, their ropes dangling as if by magic. Echoes from the men above mingled with the bits of dust and dirt that cascaded down upon the two men. Dusk and darkness swirled around the men as they realized that they were surrounded by jaw-dropping antiquity.

Behind them was a mound of rubble and the collapsed entrance to the tomb, a much smaller version of the collection of magnificent crypts that had and would be discovered. They had been lowered just inside, and before them lay what they had not anticipated. Most smaller tombs from ancient Egypt fell into the distinct sections: the entrance chamber, a long corridor and behind that, a burial chamber. Yet instead of walls lined with symbols of death and the afterlife, the entrance chamber danced with beauteous portrayals of swaying papyrus reeds, frothing lotus blossoms, proud chrysanthemums, frolicking ducks, supple fish, elegant waterfowl, graceful ibises, basking crocodiles, bathing hippopotami and relaxing jackals. Browns, ochres and ambers colored everything in the murals except for the water of the River Nile, which was represented by a spectacular expanse of blue, the color that in Ancient Egypt represented the river serpent and her infinite fertility, her sinewy desire to give birth and to create.

"What a celebration of life," gasped the boy, astonished.

"Indeed," nodded the gruff shadow.

The chamber they were in had a concave ceiling blackened with soot from before the time of Christ. The far end featured two ornate Egyptian eyes, the right stylized into the symbol of Ra, the sky god, and slightly above the eyes was the winged sun that represented divinity and royalty. Below the eyes was a rectangular-shaped opening that led to a narrow corridor and more ornate gloom. Visual whispers of papyrus motifs could be glimpsed, amazing imagery from a world long dead.

Into this corridor they went, the younger man following behind, and a few seconds after, the chamber basked in light for the first time in two millennia; it was once again at the mercy of a dying day.

The corridor had a slight incline, down into the bed of rock, the walls lined with tool marks and other evidence of the tomb builders' handiwork. The ceiling was charred black, and it blended carefully into the tops of the beautiful papyrus motifs that sprouted out of the ground, which was also cut from stone, and each side had bits of grey dust, remnants of flower petals, jasmine, daisies and lotuses that had withered and died along with the inhabitant of the tomb.

A small lintel with another winged sun led to a narrower corridor.

Shadows danced with the papyri.

Gloom danced with the impending night.

---

[106] A keffiyeh is a square-shaped garment in Middle Eastern culture worn around the head or shoulders as protection from the elements, and usually made of cotton.

[107] The Bergmanns were a series of early semi-automatic pistols created by German Industrialist Theodore Bergmann between 1893 and 1921. The pistols were capable of firing six to 10 rounds from a magazine.

As the corridor dove deeper into the rock, the temperature lowered, unrepressed by the heat of the African continent.

At the end of the corridor was another doorway, which could be seen to flatten out into a larger chamber.

"This is it," whispered the younger voice.

A satisfied nod from the experienced shadow spoke of his happiness at the find. He patted the younger shadow on the shoulder in a loving, fatherly manner.

The next chamber was rectangular, with massive columns stoutly holding up a ceiling laden with ornate paintings of winged scarabs, human-bodied ibises and crocodile gods. The paintings were created using pigments that bound themselves into the thin layer of plaster that covered the limestone. The chamber reeked of dust, candle wax, ritual and the ancient past. Time had collapsed the far wall, the brickwork bulging outward like interlocked knuckles, though another winged-sun lintel held firm for yet another doorway.

"God," gasped the youth, breathless at the sight of such marvels.

"Not one, many of them," said his counterpart after a dark laugh filled with irony, wisdom and strength. He squinted. "Night is upon us."

The boy gave him a glance filled with esteem before he dug into his own knapsack. "I've got an electric torch here somewhere."

"Never mind," sighed the seasoned explorer as he pulled a long, curved Nepalese kukri knife and some rope out of his weathered, multi-pocketed backpack. He slashed some rope off, then put the rest back inside the pack before he wrapped the remainder around the tip of the blade. He then took a matchstick out of a pants pocket, lit the impromptu torch, pivoted and headed into the depths of the gloom.

"Follow me, lad," he said. "There's probably an antechamber ahead, which then should lead us to the crypt itself. Hopefully it hasn't been looted."

The experienced shadow glided through the half-lit chamber with a purpose, with young Carter in tow, still rummaging through his knapsack for his torch. The rope/kukri torch, meanwhile, flickered in defiance of the silent, mysterious, wondrous bleakness that threatened to shroud it. The older man scanned every crevice of the expansive hallway, searching for signs leading to discovery, but with a special attention to detail, as if there was something he would notice that others could not. Howard Carter fumbled, found his electric torch, activated it and began to nervously wave it around at every nook and cranny. As they passed through the doorway, the next room was even colder than the previous, in stark contrast to the burning, all-encompassing heat that overwhelmed everything outside on a daily basis.

"Stay close to me, Carter, and upon occasion, cast your torch upon the path behind us as well."

"Whatever for?" asked the younger shadow, waving his torch around as if trying to illuminate every crevice in the room.

"Lad, do you remember the conversation we've had about just doing as I ask?" sighed the wizened treasure hunter patiently.

"I'd respectfully appreciate, Sir," said Carter after pointedly clearing his throat to let the other man know he was about to make an important point, "if you could refer to me by my title in front of the workers, especially the foremen. I always refer to you as Professor."

The seasoned explorer gave a long, wry smile. He moved and waved his knife/torch in defiance of the gloom ahead as he replied, "You needn't worry about my title, Master Carter, or yours for that matter. Titles mean very little in the real world. Call me a dew-beater[108] if you'd like. Titles

---
[108] An archaic word for large shoe, an insult meaning an awkward and clumsy person.

only help at teas and socials, events that are important but few and far between. Rather have a true friend behind me in a pub fight than a title, for example. Let's try to keep quiet now, shall we?"

They pushed deeper into the gloom, which undraped itself from a square sarcophagus that sat on an expansive pedestal, in front of an enormous sculpture of a strange, monstrous creature, a bizarre chimera of crocodile, hippopotamus and hyena. Hieroglyphs and symbols carved thousands of years before cascaded off the top of the square, ornate coffin like water off a fountain.

Out of the sullen, magical depths in the chamber came a subtle breeze. The jaded man felt it an instant later and raised his torch to find the general direction it came from and noted it without a word. He faced the sarcophagus, but his eyes continued to scan the room.

"It's Ammit," whispered Carter, pointing at the statue of the beast, "The Soul-Eater. She weighed each person's heart after death to see if it was pure, and if not, she consumed them and kept them from the afterlife. What a find!"

"So much for the usual secret antechamber," said the digger of many tombs with a happy nod, then another acute scan of the chamber. A wave of the flame-lit kukri around the room did little to alleviate the sense of an element of tension in the chamber. Something still troubled him, something that only he could perceive.

Nothing, thought the shadow who had danced in many crypts.

Something just feels wrong.

"This might be that long-sought royal I've been telling you about," spat Carter.

"Patience Master Carter, there are many dead royals in this valley," grumbled the elder as the youth raced past him and up to the sarcophagus. Carter dropped his electric torch and knapsack and began to excitedly push against the heavy stone lid like there was gold to be found.

The lid barely moved.

"For god's sake, p-please help me!" squealed Carter like a child, not quite winning the effort to move the lid. The older man checked the chamber's corners and told himself that it was only the hieroglyphs that were spooking him, yet concern washed over his face.

Standing back in the shadows, the weathered traveler watched as Carter, with one great effort filled with the thrill of discovery, shoved the heavy lid away. Inside was blackness, with an elaborate, inner wooden sarcophagus with a depiction of Ammit the Devourer, the toothy crocodile-faced visage leering at them past the edge of the sarcophagus' stone edge, as if it refused to share any more secrets with the explorers.

Carter reached for the wooden lid of the inner coffin, and a few things happened very quickly:

An obsidian mist exploded out of the inner coffin, which cracked from the violence. The surge was powerful, as if shot from a cannon. A figure, hidden within the surge was human in shape, yet cloaked in a combination of mist and mummy wrappings, and it grabbed Carter with fingertips torn to the bone. The face was skeletal yet covered with green and black patches of desiccated skin. The eyes inside the collapsed orbital sockets were filled with pus and rage, and it snarled like a wild dog as it yanked the Englishman down toward a maw full of jagged incisors.

In the next heartbeat, the older man bolted forward and savagely thrust his kukri torch past the screaming Carter, through the body of the attacking monstrosity and into the open lid of the wooden inner coffin, which cracked from the blow. Obsidian liquid squirted grotesquely out of the wounded being, which shrieked and writhed in agony, nearly matched by Carter's terrified schoolboy wails. Carter recovered his senses and dove onto the creature, helping keep its body pinned to the coffin lid. The thing tore and clawed at the experienced survivor who turned his head to avoid having his face slashed. Struggle as it might, the vampire could not dislodge the old shadow or his deathblow. A grim smile slid over the old face as he took in the struggling undead, whose flailing at last began to lose energy.

"Crux sacra sit mihi lux," hissed the older shadow as he pressed the stake and the knife/torch even deeper into the undead flesh. "Non draco sit mihi dux!" *Cross be my light! Let not the dragon be my guide!*

Vile and wounded, the creature gasped like a dying vulture that had been shot out of the sky.

"Kill it, man! Kill it!" shouted Carter, his body splayed over the body of the thrashing spectre in an effort to keep the thing in its coffin.

"Vade retro Satana!"[109] rumbled the jaded traveler, his weight completely on the blade.

The sarcophagus spectre, covered with an odious, deteriorating garb befitting an entombed mummy, flailed as it tried to rip itself from the carved petroglyph-laden lid, the largest, most evil fly in the world. Its pupil-less opalescent eyes seared a hole through the seasoned discoverer as moldy lips parted to reveal a mouthful of jagged, vampiric canines. A wet, slick hiss slid out of the thing's mouth as the older man shouted, "Don't let it out!"

Howard Carter spasmed in sheer terror, the thing holding onto him like an owl with its talons clamped around a field mouse. The older shadow stomped forward and ripped one of the pieces of wood off of the coffin lid, then with another violent gesture of will, fury and determination, brought the shaft down like a hammer onto the writhing mass of blackness, impaling the disgusting creature through the heart. Somewhere in the middle of the obsidian strands of mist and bone, a canine-laden mouth opened and screamed like a dozen jackals and lions. The roar shook the chamber to its foundation of stone.

"No more newborns for you to consume, coward," growled the world-weary silhouette as he pressed the shaft deeper into the cracking, deteriorating vermin. It gasped fetid air through a meat-encrusted, mold-infected mouth.

Somehow, through its death throes, the fiend leered at him and hissed, "سنلتقي ف.الجحيم قريبا مب فيه الكافية." *We will meet in Hell soon enough.*

Carter rolled off the felled beast in terror, disgust and sheer child-like panic.

With that last thrust of the tomb lid's shard, the animalistic shrieks stopped, and the ghoul released one last dry gasp of undead life before the wretched corpse sagged in its death box. The kukri torch was still aflame, and it flickered and licked the wrappings around the skeletal nightmare's twice-impaled torso until they came alight, and as Carter was at last able to free himself from the spectre's grip and fall backwards to the limestone floor and safety, the blackened apparition in the crypt caught fire. Dust, evil and death squirted out of the thing like pus out of an infected wound, and it spasmed wildly in the coffin like a scorpion in a killing jar.

The older man watched the mummified nightmare burn, his eyes flickering with torchlight and satisfaction.

It reached out for the grizzled shadow with an outstretched, gnarled hand, one last attempt to rip the life out of the other, but then the arm clattered back into the coffin, and the fiend began to die, at last.

The flame that had consumed the body fizzled and died, leaving the charred remains to smolder as it gave up whatever soul was left inside its body, trembling like a raven shuffling its feathers as it passed on. In a matter of seconds, the creature's body melted to ash and began to blow away and mix into the mythical and magical Egyptian twilight. The ordeal left the weary explorer standing but staggering from the effort, yet with a dry, satisfied smile slashed over his face. Carter remained sprawled over the floor, covered in ash and vampiric mummy blood, and with a look of anything but satisfaction.

---

[109] A medieval Catholic prayer for exorcism, the phrase *Vade retro Satana* can be found on the back of a Saint Benedictine Medal.

"Did you know that thing was in there?" sputtered Carter at last, young but certainly no fool.

After a broad shrug, the older man reached out a hand to help Carter to his feet. "An educated guess."

As he stood, Carter looked sideways at the whiskered shadow and grumbled, "So was I to be the bait?"

"Not until you ran past me and opened the sarcophagus in a fever after I asked you to wait." The explorer of a hundred jungles stalked past Carter, slipped his hand around the hilt of the knife/torch and ripped it out of the inner coffin lid in one effort.

Carter was dizzy, covered in ash and in the midst of gathering himself from the shock. "What in God's name was that thing?! How did you know how to kill it?"

His compatriot lowered the kukri's point to the ground and let the burning rope fall to the limestone. It continued to light the chamber, along with Carter's dropped electric torch.

"That, Master Carter," said the old crypt digger as he dusted off the shocked youth, "was a *nosferatu*. A creature of the night. They are very old, known to the rest of the world, yet new to us in England. They feed on blood and sleep in graveyards, as this one did in the sarcophagus. The Mesopotamians called them *lilitu*. The Ancient Greeks referred to them as *lamia*."

Hearing echoes of sandals and boots running down the corridor behind them, they both turned to see the other members of the dig, British, Egyptian and otherwise race into the chamber, torches electric and traditional making the corridor before them incandescent before illuminating the burial chamber.

"Say nothing to the others," said the worn man, smiling at the oncoming members of the dig as though his good will were enough to make them all think everything had gone as planned. Under his breath, he finished with "They would not believe you, regardless."

Shouts of concern cascaded down upon them before a few electric torches wildly scanned the chamber. One beam found them, whistled sharply, then the rest followed suit and converged upon them to form a pool of light around the two men. One completely satisfied at a job well done, the other terrified at what he had *really* just learned about the afterlife. Only Carter's scattered electric torch, pointing to a far corner of the burial chamber, provided any respite from the dark there.

"Are you all right, gentlemen?" snapped a young, thin Englishman with large ears, wavy red hair and an ill-fitting coat and tie.

"As right as a couple of flowers on a spring field, Mister Billows," nodded the older shadow, with a look over to Carter, who was still stunned by the turn of events.

Billows looked askance at the older man before he asked Carter. "What happened here?"

The grizzled elder interjected, "My fault entirely, I'm afraid. My torch accidentally ignited the wrappings on this mummy, and it burnt and evaporated before we could rescue the corpse."

Carter's jaw dropped at the older man's blatant lie, but Billows took this expression as surprise.

Disgust washed over Billows' face, as he gave the experienced man a revulsion-laced scowl. "My word, Sir, this is unconscionable! Your reputation preceded you! I'm afraid I'll have to report this incident to the EAS[110]—"

"Billows, that's enough." said Carter, dusting himself off.

The older man abruptly turned away from the conversation and began to examine the sarcophagus, taking out a small notebook and starting to copy the hieroglyphics.

"But Sir!" argued Billows to Carter, insistent. "This borders on incompetence—"

"Mister Billows," rumbled the explorer as he wrote, "you may report me, do whatever the hell you'd like, just kindly let me do my work."

---

[110] Egyptian Antiquities Service, or EAS, was a department within the Egyptian Ministry of Culture, established in 1859.

"I shall do precisely that, 'Sir'. The EAS will hear—"

"Steady Billows," said Carter with a corrective tone, "you forget you are looking at the chief inspector of the EAS, so kindly help document, then pack the rest of the find, please."

"Certainly, Mister Carter," deferred Billows with a curt nod of his head, which then brought the others around him into activity.

As everyone began to measure, examine and photograph, Carter was still trying to add the just-completed events up in his mind as the older man continued to scour the hieroglyphs on the sarcophagus. The weathered figure saw this and said, "I wonder if this is the long-lost boy pharaoh you've gone on about. The tomb would be much more expansive though."

"You're right, it's not," said Carter as he took the older man's hand and stood up. "Much smaller, but still a good find."

"You'll find him one day, Howard[111]," chuckled the weather-beaten tomb robber, with a crisp nod of respect as he jotted down the outline of a cartouche[112], "of that I have no doubt."

"You are very kind, Professor." Carter's response was sincere and humble.

"Lad," sighed the old shadow. "How many times must I ask you to call me Abraham?"

Carter reverted to the comfort of his rigidity. "You know I prefer formality under professional circumstances."

"Save the formality and the titles and bring me your electric torch, Chief Inspector," said the weathered explorer with a wry, warm smile that brought one out in kind from Carter. "I am having trouble translating[113], my youthful eyes wane."

"Certainly, I only meant—"

The man who had seen it all stopped examining and looked at his younger counterpart with fatherly annoyance. "Howard, if you're going to get anywhere in life, you must learn to not take everything quite so seriously."

He then noticed Billows lingering like a horse with his ears up, instead of aiding the rest of the team in their duties.

"Billows," said the grizzled academic with a glare that could melt iron, "are you a graduate-level archeologist or a professional eavesdropper?"

Billows jolted sheepishly at the man's words. "Sorry, Professor."

The iron glare melted into a laugh. "Or at least learn to be subtle about it!"

The entire crew broke into laughter, including Carter and Billows.

Important for everyone to have a laugh at our own expense once in a while thought the older man. "Now go and measure the corridors like a good lad."

"Of course, Professor," said Billows, now red-eared in embarrassment, but wearing his embarrassment well in front of the crew. "I say, I must apologize for my earlier comments—

"Forget it, Billows. I only take offense when someone pulls a knife on me. Now go on and get those measurements. And watch the corners for sun spiders[114]."

"Certainly, Professor, excuse me."

---

[111] Howard Carter (1874-1939) was a British archeologist who became world famous for discovering the tomb of 1300s-BC pharaoh Tutankhamun, the boy king who ruled at the age of nine, in 1922.

[112] A line that surrounds a series of symbols, usually indicating that the symbols are that of a person's name.

[113] Egyptian Hieroglyphics were disciphered early in the 19th century, aided chiefly by the discovery of the Rosetta Stone by Napoleon's troops during their invasion of Egypt. The stone featured text in both Egyptian and Greek. French scholar Jean-Francois Champollion (1790-1832) compared both language texts, using familiar words like Ptolomy and Cleopatra to finalize the translation, which had eluded translators in medieval Islam, during which time hieroglyhs had been replaced in Egypt by Arabic and Coptic alphabets.

[114] Sun spiders, also known as wind spiders, wind scorpions or camel spiders are very large arachids, neither spider or scorpion, from the Solifugae order of the Arachnida class, which are indigenous to the drier climates of the Middle East, the southwestern United States and Mexico.

"Actually wait," said the older man, bolting to his feet. "Let's not let the moment pass. Carter, a few words."

"Everyone!" shouted the tired shadow, "Gather around! الوح عمتجي! Ngumpulkeun sabudeureun!"

The collective members of the dig surrounded them in that burial chamber which, until just a few minutes ago, had lain mostly dormant for thousands of years. Electric torches brought the chamber to a near-daylight ambiance.

"You all know me," rumbled the crypt defiler as he returned the kukri that had impaled a mummified *nosferatu* just a few moments ago to his knapsack. "Bloody hell, I'm a man of few words. Well done. I thank you, and now turn it over to Mister Carter, who would share a few pleasantries and well-wishes with you all."

Carter's eyes popped over in surprise yet again, yet he was somehow comforted by the large, scarred hand that clapped him on the back by the weathered, seasoned, used-to-danger explorer who stood next to him.

"Congratulations to you all on this magnificent find!" managed Carter, satisfied at the day's discovery and looking nothing like the trembling wreck of a few moments ago. "I thank you all for your help! Our journey here continues, yet as the professor so easily and eloquently just stated, well done! There are more discoveries to be made, but today we have made this one, and I share it with all of you. More pharaohs, queens and amazing mysteries await us. For the moment, let us catalog any artifacts we encounter. Please be sure to place the British Museum of Natural History address on the boxes. Let's have some food sent down here for a proper celebration! Yet before we do any of that I want to acknowledge the true heart and soul of this dig, a man whose ferocity for discovery is only matched by his zest for life. All of you, join me in an appreciative round of applause for my true mentor and the literal pillar of our team, Professor Abraham Van Helsing!"

EIGHT

Remy clenched the *Demeter*'s steering wheel in a terrified stranglehold as he threw panicked glances out from the pilothouse over the grey Mediterranean Sea, which now had calmed to a glass-like tranquility. As if seeking a desert oasis, the first mate sought another ship along the horizon, hoping for a miracle that would allow for their escape, but saw only the dying, gasping sunset along the silhouetted coast of North Africa on his port[115] side. The *Demeter* pushed through the forever pane of glass, a speck of dark grey surrounded by a lighter value of eternity. He could look out over both sides of the ship and see corpses of his dead shipmates floating by, swirls of red turning them slowly as they headed off into the endless grey/blue that claims too many generations of people who dared to tempt the ocean's fate.

Mueller stood next to him, his face a broken brush of fear and tension. They both watched the sun's last rays try to reach through the endless gray slate and claim a few more moments of daylight, only to be rebuffed in their hope that their fear would not turn to terror in the next few seconds. Many bodies lay sprawled across the deck, butchered like farm animals, while a single crewman gave some of the dead crew the opportunity and luxury of leaving the *Demeter* with some sense of peace, even if it meant being thrown overboard and consumed by whatever swam under the deep, cold Mediterranean. Lanky and wearing ill-fitted clothes, the solemn crewmember pulled corpse after corpse, exsanguinated shipmates, friends and enemies alike, to the ship's edge and nudged them one after another into the endless grey, then making a respectful sign of the cross after each one was heaved off.

"Go tell Paulino to grab his crucifix and get back inside before they resurrect for the night!" shrieked Mueller through a mouth that was a slit of anxiety. Paulino, a lanky kid, was in tears as he continued his grim task. Blood saturated most of the deck like a slaughterhouse, which of course it was. Such was Paulino's grief and luck that he did not notice the deck doors swivel slowly open behind him, of their own accord and much to his immediate peril.

"Good God," gasped Remy, his grip on the wheel tightening. "They've risen. Lord, give his soul peace."

Not even the sun wanted to witness the impending bloodshed, so it sank.

Out through the doors, out of the comfort of the darkness came three rats, each as large as full-gown leopards. They saw poor Paulino labor to push the body of a heavy crewmember off the deck into the water below. He was so exhausted he did not see the jagged heads scan the deck and lock in on him, even as night spread its wings beyond the ship, enveloping the sea and the sky beyond. Their eyes glinted with hunger, savoring the moment as they sized the boy up and moved straight for him, crossing the vast deck in seconds. Their clawed feet scratched up the wooden deck as they closed in on the kid.

"Paulino," gasped/whispered/wailed Mueller.

---

[115] Port is left, toward the Bow or front part of the ship's hull. Starboard is the right side of a ship, facing forward.

"We're cowards," gulped Remy as the rats tackled Paulino from behind. His shrieks were infantile and piercing and above all, brief as one of the gigantic rodents clamped its canine teeth around Paulino's throat and ripped it out. The poor boy's body disappeared under the quivering forms of the shapeshifters. Paulino's right hand shot up out of the feast, peppered with blood, gesturing in agony, fingers twitching as they lost life. Then the entire limb toppled back down into the carnage, torn out from its socket as it fell out of sight. As they fed, the brown shapes that had enveloped Paulino then torqued and shifted into the countenances of Venus, Andromeda and Petra. The Egyptian then stood straight, a beauteous, deadly vision. She held Paulino's arm in her hand before she raised it and let the blood drip from the bloody stump of what used to be a shoulder, into her mouth, as if the severed limb was an absurd goblet. She turned to Mueller and Remy, visible to her animal eyes even from a distance, and she beamed a mouthful of canines and blood at them.

Her eyes glowed with supernatural light and feral satisfaction.

Ghostly, feminine laughter brought chills to Remy and the captain.

"So much evil in so much beauty," gasped Remy.

"The horrors never end," gulped Mueller, and his eyes jumped to the hold as he said it. The captain then gulped again as twin, massive wings unfurled, as if mirroring the night in an absurd *pas de deux*.[116] Talons at the end of the wings twitched like Hell's conductor, about to lead a daemonic symphony in a macabre ode to the night.

"We should have killed ourselves when they took the ship," said Remy. "I don't care what the fiend told you, he's going to murder all of us when he sees a sliver of England on the horizon. Those accursed skeletons beat us back every time we try and storm the hold and kill them during the day. As if these beasts need guards."

"Think of your family, Remy," sighed Mueller as he trembled. "We must hope. For them."

With wings larger than the sails of a small boat, the gargantuan black bat raised itself out of the hold, twin sapphire eyes blazing at the captain's window of the ship. The beast then leaped up into the still, cold air of the early evening. It arced for a split second, hundreds of pounds of Hell-spawned mammal in mid-air, before the wings gave twin downward thrusts of immense power, and the thing of the night rose in a crescent arc above the ship. A flash of red, a protrusion of feminine shape and form that dangled from beneath the beast's mouth caught Remy's eye.

He gulped, tears forming in his eyes. "He has Ermina."

"Heaven help us, we've made a deal with Satan himself," was all Captain Mueller could say through a throat choked with terror. The bat swerved around the nose of the ship, outstretched wings forming an absurd triangle as it soared hundreds of feet in the air. But its eyes, thought Remy, its satanic red eyes had locked on them and never blinked as it flew. He could see the jagged white teeth that held Ermina by the throat, dangling like an antelope in the jaws of a leopard as it climbed a tree.

Dracula twisted his body and drifted back down to the ship, settling down right on the nose of the *Demeter*. Remy could sense the ship quiver to have the vampire back aboard. The bat's glare never left them as its majestic wings slowly gathered themselves around Ermina's body. Dracula's massive bat-head began to bob up and down as he drank.

While it looked up at the bridge.

And watched.

Them.

"I convinced her to come," said Remy as he cried. "I told her that she could see the world."

"More than she knew," said Mueller as he gave himself the sign of the cross. "God be with her."

"And with us," signed Remy, trembling as he steered the *Demeter* a little closer to Hell.

---

[116] A French term, a dance duet where two dancers perform ballet together.

NINE

A few days later, while everyone suffered horribly on the *Demeter*, an inconspicuous carriage, followed by an equally ordinary wagon, creaked and groaned along a wet, cold avenue in Paris just before a misty, murky dawn.

The horses that drew the carriage were nervous, but not nearly as much as Philippe Didier, a seasoned carriage driver who had been paid half the agreed-upon amount, in gold, a very handsome reward for what he now gathered was a deal with four devils. Philippe had spent many nights at the fringes of the Moulin Rouge, taxiing customers to and from the infamous red windmill that housed the elaborate dance revue, when he had been approached by a very distinct stranger, a very pale lady in very old clothes. *Is she wearing a nun's habit?* wondered Philippe as the woman approached him. *She's an odd one.* The nun gave him a small cloth bag filled with old gold coins, then instructed him in hushed tones to watch for four strangers who would meet him here one night sometime within the next few weeks. They would use her name, Anne, as a means to identify themselves and engage him for a perfunctory service that would pay handsomely. At one point during their conversation, Anne reached out to touch Philippe's arm, and he almost recoiled, feeling like a wild animal had just clawed at him. The nun noticed Didier's hesitancy, and smiled so sweetly it chilled Phillippe to his bones. But the money was too good, and he agreed.

Thereafter, night after night, Didier moved clients in and out of the Rouge, but with an eye out for the clients. Evening after evening passed, and Philippe had begun to think he would never be contacted. At last tonight, as the last show ended, four very well-to-do strangers approached him out of the crowd and offered much reward for seemingly little work. As they negotiated amid a rambunctious crowd full of revelers pouring out of the cabaret and out into the pre-dawn streets, the strangers gave off an air of tension and mystery, their faces obscured with veils and scarves, but their eyes, their pale, unblinking eyes that seemed more fitting for owls or eagles were what unnerved Philippe. They all seemed to bore holes right through him with their collective glares. The quartet wore clothes that were very finely tailored, something Didier could spot in a potential client right away, for the wealthy made for the best hires, sober or not. And Philippe Didier was not above searching a drunken lady or gentleman for a few spare bills if he had to help them make their way up to their apartment or, in the rare instance, to a *château*[117] outside the city. And their perfume[118] and cologne[119] covered another scent, one that Philippe had a tough time placing amid the many scents and odors of a major metropolitan city and in the presence of these four mysterious customers,

---

[117] *Château*, the French manor or country residence of a noble or lord, usually without fortification. Can also refer to a castle or palace or rural estate throughout Europe. Also associated with wine production.

[118] The history of perfume can be traced to the great cultures of the Ancient World. It was then brought to Europe in the 14th century from the Arab world and into Hungary, where it then spread quickly through France, Italy and the rest of the continent.

[119] Cologne was first developed in Germany in 1709 by Giovanni Maria Farina (1685-1766) an Italian perfume maker. Named *Eau de Cologne* after Cologne, Germany.

but the combination unsettled him. The clients spoke to him in very clipped, very formal French, at a level that Philippe recognized as aristocratic. Yet when they had to discuss other matters in front of Philippe, other languages flowed beautifully out of their mouths, whispers that seemed like commands, such was their intensity and focus. Despite Philippe's reservations, the offer and the gold were simply too good for him to pass up. He could maintain his family for years on one errand. They had agreed upon transportation in his carriage, but his new clients insisted on a second wagon, one for their luggage, which was not part of the original agreement, so after that was re-negotiated Philippe bid them to his carriage, then drove them to his friend Jean's apartment. Jean made his living hauling everything from beer kegs to milk churns, and made his wagon available for service after a brief and heated side-negotiation with Philippe.

Didier was no stranger to the unscrupulous characters of the city's night, having sheparded inebriated mistresses and wounded duelists around the night streets of this most famous city many a time, with no questions asked. Sometime before the dawn started to glide over the city, the drapes inside the carriage gently closed. There would be no need to stop for food or rest, they had stated as he was given the first half of the gold, a discreet dock along the northeastern French coastline was their only objective. *As soon as humanly possible* said one of the strangers, which brought a dry chuckle out of them that raised the hairs on Phlippe Didier's neck. Yet despite the politeness, the assurances, the opulence, the style and the class, he was unnerved, and only the gold in his pocket and lure of the other half kept the nervous Didier from leaping off the carriage and running for his life, even if Jean in the wagon behind him would not be so eager to share.

Yet, after a stop to pick up the luggage, which turned out to be four very large and very opulent trunks, they were on their way.

The horses clanked shoed hooves against the cobblestones. A few meters back, a gaggle of ravens flew down from their customary perches above the streets and followed behind Jean's carriage, run/bouncing the way that type of bird does, just far enough away to satisfy their sense of caution yet curious enough to keep following it.

Creak.

Caw.

Scratch.

Creak.

Caw.

Caw.

Inside the carriage, behind the closed window drapes were four black shrouds that enveloped four cadavers. In an eerie tableau, the cadavers bounced and shook with each movement of the carriage along the cobblestones. The undead sat upright like traditional passengers, not on their backs like cadavers ready for burial. The shrouds covering the vampires were very delicate and very old, almost like doilies[120], woven out of silk and cotton and covered with intricate patterns that flowed out and away from each of the bodies like so many intricate spider webs. Four obsidian ghosts, sitting in a closed carriage that felt at the moment more like a closed casket. Two female vampires sat in the carriage, along with two males. The smallest of them, with only canine teeth visible under full, red lips, turned to the others and hissed, "Custodi me, Dominue Satanus, de manu peccatoris." *Keep me, Lord Satan, in your wicked hands.*

"Et eripe me de caelo mendacium," chanted the others. *And deliver us from the liars in Heaven.*

The smaller vampiress gave the deepest, darkest of sweet, evil smiles and finished with, "Мая сжечь Бог в аду один день." *May God burn in Hell one day.*

---

[120] A doily is an ornament made of cut paper or woven fabric, used for everything from display garnish to food arrangement to head covering.

"Ave Satanas," hushed the others. *Hail Satan.*

The ravens in the distance cawed as they hopped and flapped as they followed.

"Delilik bu," croaked a lithe, gangly male from under his shroud *This is madness.*

The edge of his shroud revealed clawed, emaciated hands under layers of the blackened, withered material that looked more like papyrus than cloth. The hands wringed and intertwined nervously.

"La folie," growled the large male sitting opposite of him. "Nous a conduit ici." *Madness has led us here.*

After a nod of agreement, the smallest turned to the gangly male and said, "Будьте уверены, чтобы убить водителей, когда мы прибываем в склепе." *Be certain to kill the drivers when we arrive at the crypt.*

"Elbette," said the gangly male. *Of course.*

"Und nutzen Sie unser Gold zurück," said the other female, with a smile that mingled with a snarl. *And get our gold back.*

A lone policeman waved the carriage through the Boulevard Saint-Michel, not bothering to look inside the drape-covered windows of the carriage. He was cold and stamped his feet, annoyed at the bulbous scavenger birds that pursued the carriage, eager for any kind of scraps. As the sounds of the horses, carriage and ravens faded, more came up, and the policeman looked up and saw a horse-drawn wagon following, the driver shivering as he nodded to the policeman.

The policeman shook his head in frustration and told himself to get better sleep the next night, because he had thought for a moment that the trunks that the wagon carried were four coffins.

TEN

"The poor continue to remain poor because they are deserving of their fate," said Mr. Collingwood, standing before an open-jawed Mina Murray. "They are unclean, uneducated, and lack the common decency of moral peoples such as ourselves."

Raymond Collingwood was in his sixties, portly, dressed impeccably and lacked for nothing save empathy. Mina was who she always was, and in this case maintaining her composure while seething over Collingwood's narrow-minded statements and within a thread's width from punching him. They stood in a narrow Whitby street that churned with mid-day activity, workers heading to and from the harbor, carrying everything from alum to whale bones to wagons filled with freshly caught herring[121]. Next to Mina and Collingwood, several wagons were being filled with old clothes, canned food and used books. Behind them was a building with a painted sign that read:

CHARITY FOR FAMILIES ORGANIZATION SOCIETY
WHITBY BRANCH

"Mister Collingwood," said Mina past the obvious look of disgust on her face, "we are simply collecting clothes for children that are from families that simply cannot afford to clothe themselves—"

Colllingwood's fat, gloved hand in the air stopped Mina. "It's not just a clothing issue, Miss Murray, it is an issue of moral fiber. I refuse to endorse the lower classes in a journey that has no goal. They are filthy masses that succumb to the lower base instincts and deserve nothing more than what they earn, which is nothing."

Collingwood saw Mina's parents making their way around a milk wagon. He turned, somewhat rudely, away from Mina as he said, "Ah, Murray, ever the optimist."

Andrew Murray was in his sixties, as was Collingwood; also dressed well, but with a kindness in his eyes that went beyond a twinkle, that told everyone around him that they were in the presence of a very well-meaning human being. Judith Murray, still a beauty in her early sixties, had her hand in the crook of his elbow. Andrew had clearly married up, and Judith clearly knew she had given her life to a good, moral man. Andrew slyly cast a beaming grin at Collingwood and said, "Good Morning, kind Sir! Are you contributing to our humble philanthropic venture—"

"Again, Murray? Once more this pathetic cornucopia for the hopeless?" Collingwood was no stranger to being abrupt. He fidgeted in annoyance at being in the presence of the Murrays.

Yet Andrew's beaming grin never wavered. "My daughter has organized this worthy charitable endeavor for the past few years, Judith and I are proud to support her efforts, content to witness her furthering of our personal philosophies."

---

[121] Whitby has a rich history in mining, whaling and fishing.

Mina's smile broadened just a bit wider, reminded as to why she adored her parents so much, her father in particular. There was a strong love between Mina and Judith to be sure, a beauteous one based on an intelligent woman raising an intelligent daughter, but Andrew Murray was such a singularly decent man that his kindness constantly moved Mina.

"And you wonder," sighed Collingwood, "why no one from the club will hunt with you."

Andrew's grin overwhelmed his happy if ambivalent shrug. "If that is the price that I must pay for attempting to make this world an even better place than it is now, so be it. Are you sure you won't contribute? Every bit helps."

As a horse wagon full of firewood moved by, Collingwood checked his watch, which twinkled in the mid-morning light. "This is a dreary ordeal, to be surrounded by swarthy masses unworthy of existence."

Andrew's smile was now peppered in sympathy. "Evil is not what men hold in their billfolds, Collingwood, but what they hold in their hearts, regardless of where they stand in the community."

"Clearly you've never had your wallet nicked in Piccadilly Square," laughed Collingwood. "And spare me the sanctimony."

"They take your money because they have no other recourse," replied Andrew with a gentle sigh of sympathy and politeness. "I'll see you at the club, then."

Judith was no stranger to her husband's confrontations with the coldness that the world's wealthy could offer, and she patted Andrew's arm in quiet, strong support.

Collingwood was finished, and he signified this by snapping his shiny new pocket watch shut so it could stop exploding in pristine highlights. "Not if I see you first. Good day, Murray."

Andrew kept up his silly, resolve-filled grin, mounting a polite challenge to Collingwood's obvious rudeness. It was too much for Collingwood to ignore.

"Murray," snorted Raymond Collingwood as he bounded away, "you play the buffoon far too easily!"

Andrew Murray had to reach out and wrap his right hand around Wilhelmina Murray's left bicep, as she was taking a step in Collingwood's direction with the most serious of intentions.

Andrew patted his daughter's cheek to ease her seething to a simmer, then cast a mischievous eye at his wife and said, "My dear Judith, have I not caught the most impressive fox in England!" He kissed her on the cheek and continued, "And I needed no hounds to do it! Well, save myself of course."

Judith giggled, "Charm has always been the deadliest of your weapons, Andrew Murray!"

Her simmer broken, Mina belly laughed as she enjoyed seeing her parents still so much in love. Andrew could not help tossing a gleeful smile and nod at Raymond Collingwood, who was being annoyed by a kindly fruit vendor just down the street. From afar and during his rejection of the fruit vendor, Collingwood shook his massive head at the Murrays in sheer agitation.

Andrew raised an eyebrow at Judith. "Was it not my chiseled, handsome features that won your heart, my good woman?"

Mina could see that Collingwood was taking no pleasure at observing the Murray family dynamic as he abruptly pivoted away from the fruit vendor before melting into the crowd of pedestrians. She started to pick up a stack of folded clothing that had fallen from the wagon. "Father, I appreciate your defense with Mr. Colling—"

Andrew dove quickly, snapped up the stack and placed it in the wagon as he said, "My dear, amazing daughter, it is Raymond Collingwood and his unsympathetic ilk that need defending, not a kind soul such as yourself. Another matter is whether my impressive daughter has sufficient strength to allow her father the pleasure of speaking up for her once in a great while. In any event, have you given more thought to the subject of your impending wedding?"

"I have Father," said Mina with a deliberate nod, "I've even confided this with Lucy. I love Jonathan, yet I still feel the same way. I'm not fated to be an ordinary housewife. The routine of an ordinary woman simply does not suit me."

"You'll forgive me if I ask you to define what constitutes an 'ordinary woman'," said Andrew, somewhat surprised at his daughter's sudden discomfort.

"Well Father, the male version of an ordinary woman just walked away from us in a huff," sniffed Mina, jutting her nose back in the direction where Raymond Collingwood would have been certainly haunting fruit vendors and aspiring charities.

With a wink and a nod, Andrew nodded, "Point taken."

"Darling," said Judith affectionately to Andrew, "She fool's mated[122] you as a child, and just now used the boorish Collingwood as an analogy against you splendidly."

"Thank you, Mother," said Mina with a viciously appreciative grin.

"Not fair, I get sleepy when I have biscuits with my tea," stammered Andrew, very unconvincingly.

"Quincy refers to biscuits as something called 'cookies'," interjected Judith.

"Quincy needs to only speak when spoken to," snipped Mina, to which Judith readily agreed with a wink of her own.

Judith rubbed her hand on Mina's shoulder and said, "We only want the best for you, Mina, and we will support your decisions until the end of the world," as she gave Andrew, who was none too pleased at his wife taking his daughter's side, a cross look.

"Thank you, *Mother*," chimed in Mina, looking at her father as she nodded to her mother. They turned their collective gazes to Andrew, expecting his conciliation, and Andrew Murray, who had long ago understood his role in this family of strong women, gave it to them.

"You two should form your own football club," smirked Andrew with his palms turned up, that charming smile working its magic. "You make quite the team."

"You'll be all right, Dear," said Judith slyly after she blew him a kiss. "Just do as you're told."

Andrew furrowed his brow, pursed his lips and gave his wife a wry, comedic stare as he said, "I've never considered divorce, but I am presently considering murder."

The crescendo of their collective, roaring laughter made everyone on the street turn and notice them, a father, mother and daughter deepening their bond. When Judith collected herself, she slipped an arm around Mina and said, "To be fair to your father, Mina, I wonder if you are simply suffering from the condition that many an impending bride has faced. Anxiety is no stranger to a bride. Frayed nerves before such a life-altering event is completely understandable."

Andrew arched his eyebrows and nodded in agreement at Judith, then turned his head back to his daughter as if it was a tennis match and it was Mina's turn to volley.

Mina sweetly kissed her mother's check before resuming piling clothes onto the wagon. "It is only that Jonathan is such an extraordinary man that makes me waver. There are many reasons that I love him, and yet there is within me a yearning to see beyond the horizon or map an unexplored region or help people that would have the Collingwoods of the world repossess their meager belongings and place them in a debtor's prison[123], and I simply can't see myself doing that while maintaining a household for a man. And Jonathan Harker is so comfortable with simply going to the same office every day and taking off his shoes when he is done putting all of his columns in

---

[122] Fool's mate, or two-move checkmate, is a checkmate maneuver in two moves that involves two pawns moving forward and exposing the king to the adversary's queen.

[123] Through the Middle Ages and into the 19th century, debtors could be placed in a prison until their debts and court fees were paid off, at times having to perform manual labor as a means to reduce the debt. Forms of debtor's prison exist in the modern day.

cross-references rows, and I don't think that a life like that interests me. I prefer to be mistress of my own fate. Can you understand that?"

Andrew nodded at his daughter, a warm smile pasted onto his face in a way that told Mina that he would always accept her and know her inside out. "We do, dear Wilhelmina. Perhaps your discussions about this with Jonathan needs a different tack. As opposed to his wanting to marry his fiancée and have her do the things that all wives do, should you not tell him that you must live your life the way you believe, and therefore give him the choice to come along with you in life, together, not master and wife? He seems understanding enough that he should at least be given the opportunity to make that choice, if indeed you love him, and he in return loves you. I've seen the way you both look at each other. You both deserve to hear each other out."

Judith patted Andrew on the arm for his good point and nodded warmly to Mina. "If your fiancé wants to be in your life enough, then he will make that choice. Simply ask him when he gets back."

"And if he chooses to not marry me?" said Mina as she stopped loading clothes and stood before her parents, hands on her hips. "What if we have to cancel the wedding, Mother? Uncle Abraham is coming all the way from *Cairo*."

The masses of Whitby, poor, rich, busy and otherwise, drifted around them, on their way to their own appointments, fates and destinies.

Andrew chuckled, "What of it? You speak as if any hint of social scandal affects our decision making, Mina. If that were true, I would be out foxing with other ravenous social climbers and checking my pocket watch in public so that everyone understood I had just bought it! If so, then we will have the continued priviledge of the Rootin' Tootin' Quincy Morris Extravaganza, all the way from the Great State of Texas! Tell me the Lord Godalming would ever abandon you publically. As if Ursula would ever allow him to for that matter! And as if the formidable Abraham Van Helsing has ever given a damn about anyone's opinion. That man has lived five lives in one and would be the first to tell you to do as you will, not live someone else's life. You will always be the most important thing in our lives, and we would cross any ocean or bear any burden for your happiness."

Andrew pivoted to Judith. "Did my response suffice, my wife?"

Judith Murray gave her husband a happy nod of approval and followed it up with, "You, upon occasion, surprise me, Andrew Murray."

Mina breathed a sigh of relief. "Thank you both. And what of the Harkers?"

Arthur's Cheshire Cat grin seemed like it could withstand the Apocalypse itself. "Don't worry about William and Cynthia. They are kind, pragmatic people and will understand. Simply talk to Jonathan when he returns from the Orient, and if he is half the man I think he is, he'll decide to marry an extraordinary woman instead of settling for keeping his ledgers in order. If not, then you'll have your mother's love and your father's jokes to keep you cheery."

Andrew Murray could not resist adding one last joke as he chuckled, "At least until another suitor comes along."

ELEVEN

Captain Mueller trembled in his slogging, drenched boots as he staggered along the deck, toward the bow of the *Demeter*, which continued to churn along the Mediterranean. Mueller could not remember the last time he had slept, and bile kept coming up in his throat as if it wanted to claw its way out of his mouth. The captain could not remember the last time he had changed his clothes, or anything before he had began this horrifying experience. The whole ship swayed in a dark, cloudy, starless night, almost as if the vessel itself was dizzy from all of the tragedy that had taken place inside its bulkheads. Mueller held a small, dingy lantern in front of him in the night and the drizzle, illuminating the shiny, slippery deck that swarmed with the vampire's rat legions. Yet it was not the dreary weather nor the rats that made Mueller quiver this night, another night of horrors in a journey filled with them, rather it was the gigantic black bat that sat on the bow of the ship with its humongous back to him, vast pterodactyl wing arms slung down and spread out like two enormous, dead masts over the nose of the ship, webbed fingers open-palmed and facing the night, the rain and the ocean before it.

Mueller gulped out of fear, loathing and for the loss of his friends and shipmates that his greed and cowardice had cost. But he also gulped simply because, in a short span of time he had gone from moments of horror to continuous unimaginable suffering; had registered the worst trauma that he had ever suffered. Everywhere along the deck were the damnable rat hordes, surging away from Mueller and his lantern, and the captain nearly wretched when he saw thousands of tiny, shiny obsidian pinpoints jumping from rat to rat, as fleas usually do.

He had taken to reciting the Holy Rosary every night, in the solitude of his cabin, more for his own sanity than anything else. Ironically, his encounter with the vampires and their unholy legions had inspired a sense of faith that Mueller thought he never had. Growing up in Germany, his family had gone to Mass devoutly for years, in many instances his father having to find him hiding in a closet or a nook, not wanting, even as a seven-year old, to go to church. Now here he stood, on a cold, dreadful night, scrambling to remember the Rosary litanies in front of a demon from Dante's writings and Doré's etchings.

"Dracula," said Captain Mueller as he held out the lantern. It lit up the drizzle between himself and the bristling *trapezius*, *deltoid* and *teres major* musculature along the back of the Dracula bat. Mueller stood there, waiting for the colossal creature to turn around, wondering which new horror he would experience on this voyage to Hell.

He did not have long to wait.

This was no dragon, chimera or gorgon, some creature of fantasy in front of Mueller. The fur, the skin, the textures of this gargantuan monstrosity were that of a very real yet very daemonic bat. When the Dracula bat turned its massive ebony head, its bone-crunching teeth held a human child, a girl of no more than three or four in its drooling jaws, pearl canines clamped into the girl's neck and chest in a sickening scene. Her blue dress fluttered in the breeze. The complex, lobed nose wrinkled and sniffed the air. The Dracula bat's lips curled back further, into an angry snarl, further revealing the blood-lined mouth of the great bat, which looked at Mueller with hate-filled crimson eyes as its fur-covered throat gulped steadily. Twin ears folded back like those of a predator ready to attack. The creature emanated a powerful, monstrous presence, its breaths coming in deep, strong bursts, and the shapeshifter in its present form seemed like it could leap off the bow of the *Demeter* and rend Captain Mueller to bits of flesh at any moment.

Yet there it sat, on the bow.

Drinking the girl's blood.

Mueller nearly burst into tears. "Ermina's little girl."

Though limp and immobilized, Ermina's daughter was clearly not dead. Krystyna swung out her right arm in a gesture of vague consciousness, which made Mueller nearly wail in outrage. The bat took in Mueller's reaction and snarled at him, then slowly brought the clawed fingertips of its right wing-fingers together around Krystyna's still-moving body. The Dracula bat then closed its lips around Krystyna's neck and with one long inhale, drained the child of the last bit of blood in her tiny body. The Dracula bat then opened its filthy mouth and spat the child out overboard and toward the dark, foaming sea as you or I would discard unwanted gristle or bone in a meal. Krystyna's dress fluttered like a funeral veil before the gloom consumed it.

Mueller heard Ermina's little girl cry out as she hit the water.

Dracula's mammalian foot was padded like a lion, wolf or tiger, and each of the five digits ended on claws four of five inches long, and sharp enough to eviscerate a human being in one blow. The right foot landed with a thud on the wooden planks of the deck, and the rat hordes, fearless of nothing save their master, recoiled in waves of sinuous pestilence. The mammoth bat stepped down from the bow and moved toward Mueller, snatching up a stray rat and swallowing it whole as he loped toward the captain. Mueller trembled as a few rats scrambled over his soggy boots in an effort to elude the vampire, which looked at Mueller like its crimson eyes were trying to boil him alive.

Then the metamorphosis occurred.

Seconds passed as Dracula transformed from bat to human form, fur magically becoming cloth and skin, animal becoming man, or in this case, the undead. Dazzled and terrified at witnessing this spectacular yet sinister shapeshifting, Mueller wondered which countenance of the vampire was more terrifying, the bat, the wolf, the bank of mist or the human, and the way that Dracula glared at him through his animal-like eyes told the captain of the *Demeter* that the human that looked at him so intensely and strangely was the worst of the unholy incarnations. The first thing Mueller wanted to do was to do the sign of the Cross in the presence of something so unholy, yet his second thought was that it would be not in his best interest to do so.

"You will address me as Count or Lord," rumbled Dracula as he licked Krystyna's blood off the fingertips of his right hand, "or I will throw you off this vessel as surely as I threw that child out among the sharks."

"Y-yes, my Lord. My apologies. You wished to know our course as we sailed. We have passed Sicily and are presently crossing the Tyrrhenian Sea, nearing Sardinia—"

"*Sardegna,*" corrected the vampire.

"My Lord?"

The vampire sighed with impatience. "Never mind, Captain Mueller. We pass close to the vacant heart of the Cross, yet I amuse myself with the knowledge that the Holy See hides amid its wealth, hypocrisy and opulence."

"Y-yes, My Lord," nodded Mueller. Never having been in the presence of a royal, he gave Dracula a clumsy, fearful bow that the vampire looked at with a mixture of disrespect and loathing.

"If you will excuse me, I must attend to the ship's duties—"

"Does my presence disgust you, Mueller?" The vampire's eyes blazed in the night like a wild animal's, and for a terrifying second Mueller knew what it was like to be a mouse pinned under the talons of an owl, and to have it consider its prey for a second before devouring it. Mueller trembled with a start, realizing that Dracula was standing there waiting for an answer.

"N-no my Lord," stuttered Mueller, "but there is a leak in one of the boilers that I must see to—"

"Ah!" said Dracula, a slit of a smile opening wider to reveal his canines. He nodded in appreciation at the captain, raised a taloned, dead index figure at Mueller as he said, "Wondrous thing, this vessel of yours. I had not known of the inventions and advancements of the recent years, having relegated myself to my castle. I hear tell of flying balloons and motored trains and other such things. How we sail against the tide simply because of that amazing, interesting machine that moves us through these familiar waters fascinates me."

Mueller stood there for an awkward moment, Dracula reveling in the fear that he caused in the captain. The vampire pointed at the ship behind the captain and said, "There is also the matter of your crew. A few more must be forfeit to sustain us the rest of the voyage. Tell them nothing. We will act as needed."

"*More*? How many more?"

Dracula gave Mueller a quizzical look, as if wondering why his word was even being questioned. "As many as required to complete the journey. Or I could have their throats collectively slit tonight and we could save their blood in vats for the rest of the journey. Have you ever tasted blood pudding, Captain Mueller? A delicacy from all over Europe, even before my birth. Would you like to try some over the next few days? But it will not be the blood of a pig, I can assure you."

"No," was all Mueller could manage in response. He held the lantern out as if it somehow was a charm that could keep the fearsome presence at bay.

Even as Dracula leered in amusement at his fear, Mueller could see the blood stains still covering the vampire's mouth full of canines. "I sense apprehension from you, Captain, and I can assure you that you and some of your crew will return to their families and loved ones. I will not take more than what is needed to sustain my party, and when we land in England, you need be content that we will simply leave the ship and never bother you again."

Dracula followed that up with a grin that was an ice pick through Mueller's soul. Despite his terror, he found the voice to challenge the vampire. "What guarantee do I have that you will keep to what you say?"

Insult poured over Dracula's face, and the vampire snarled like a lion, scattering the nearby rats, who were gnawing on a severed arm that had been lying on the deck. Reacting in sheer fright to the roar, Mueller nearly soiled himself. Dracula calmed himself and rumbled, "Captain, it is rude for a commoner to question the word of a royal. We do not need you. After your crew would be butchered, Primus and his legion could guide the ship to port based on your maps, compasses and astrolabes. Primus sailed this Mediterranean during the height of the Roman Empire. So, I have no need of you, and it is to my generosity you should be appealing, not to my sense of impatience."

"Yes, my Lord." Said Mueller, who wanted to drop the lantern and run. They stood there in the stillness and tension of the moment. The engine could be heard as it labored across the Mediterranean, cutting through the dark waves that tried to keep the *Demeter* from what lay ahead.

After a dismissive nod, the vampire said, "Thank you, Captain. You may go."

Mueller bowed, turned and walked away, Dracula enjoying his fear. He saw a wave of the rats swarm toward Mueller's boots and snarled.

"Nolite tangere eum," growled the vampire. *Do not touch him.*

The rats ebbed away, like an absurd lowering tide. Mueller took deep breaths as he walked, trying to calm himself.

"One last point of discussion, Mueller," rumbled Dracula as he leaned back against the ship's rail.

Mueller froze, too scared to turn around. He held his trembling lantern in his hand, and it bounced from his tremors. "Yes, my Lord?"

After another growl, Dracula said, "Turn and face me, Mueller. Never give a nobleman your back."

"Apologies, my Lord" said Mueller as he pivoted to face the vampire. "What can I do for you?"

Dracula pointed a taloned, bleached finger at the captain and said, "I must ask you not to put to port for the rest of the journey—"

"—but we need to resupply, My Lord!" Mueller had found the voice to speak up.

Dracula's glowing eyes blinked, and he shook his jagged, bone-white face. "Not putting to port will result in no crewmembers being able to abandon ship, hence no one will be alerted to our—predicament."

Somewhere Mueller found some measure of courage in his terrified heart, and with whatever he had left, spat, "This was not our bargain!"

Dracula did not respond or move. He merely blinked again, his incandescent eyes eerily staring at Mueller. For a moment Captain Mueller thought he would be struck dead, and he was at least content that he had raised his voice for once before he was eviscerated, then instantly regretted it when the vampire leaned away from the railing and walked toward him. As the vampire moved, the swarm of rats moved with him, undulating over each other, their fleas jumping from body to body in their insatiable journey for crimson sustenance. Somewhere below deck, screams of pain from one of the crewmembers, undoubtedly set upon by one of the brides, pealed away before they ended abruptly. Dracula had an amused glint in his eyes, as if he had decided to give the captain of the *Demeter* an ounce of respect.

All this, of course, ran more fear through Mueller like fire through kindling as Dracula's face floated just a few feet away, drifting between the lantern and himself.

With a dark smile, the vampire said, "Very well, then I am rewriting the terms, as your temporary admiral. I will leave word with Primus that any motion during the day to put to harbor will be dealt with severely. Is that clear, Captain?"

It was the tranquility with which Dracula spoke that scared Mueller the most, and a fresh wave of shivers came over him as he said, "Yes, my Lord."

"You may leave."

Mueller bowed, backed away, and tried not to run back to the other side of the ship.

TWELVE

Like one long, single brushstroke filled with crimson gouache, the sun set behind a distant fortress of grey English clouds, like hope after an election. The stroke dripped with fate and destiny, held back by the melancholic hope of the absurdly dreary clouds. It was as if the clouds were in a surrealist painting, because the wet tufts that were filled with tears looked like thousands of tiny hands that yearned to hold back that wash of inevitability, as if breaking the hands of a clock would somehow stop time itself.

Wind that had no business being that cold at that time of the year bit into the hillside and grass outside of Whitby, sweeping over the greens like a grand swipe of Samhain's[124] mighty sythe, but the tombstones that had sprung up over the hillside stood tall and defiant, as if they too wanted to help out the grey hands that wanted to hold back that inevitable stroke, as if the markers themselves were not enough monuments to realize themselves. A thin, ragged picket fencing surrounded the cemetery like wagon trains around pioneers and rejoiced in the afternoon's wave of gloom, with white patches of paint peeling away and rotting wood of the fence posts peeking through like bad teeth in a macabre smile.

Oblivious to all this was D'Artagnan, who rode up the hill like the devil himself could have been at the crest and the horse would have run him down under his hooves. Atop him was Mina, covered in a coat that blended in perfectly with the thousands of hand-shaped clouds above and conveniently also matched her mood and expression. Sea salt mixed in with the wind and air like too much creamer in the cup of coffee that was the gale that swept in from the east, as if to push the brushstroke of a sun even further from its aspiration of cheer. A few years ago, Mina had picked D'Artagnan out from a well-renowned stable, as a colt, when he kicked anyone who dared come near him, and as she neared the cemetery Mina remembered her father's concern for her choice of such an untamed and powerful mare for a first horse. But their bond had been sealed early that day when Mina strode past the group of stable handlers that did not want to get kicked, and soothed the muscular black horse into submission with the merest shush from her lips, the tenderness of her hands patting him and the fortitude of her gaze upon him.

Wilhelmina Murray arrived at the front of the cemetery, a rotting, rusted iron mouth of a gateway yawning out to the frothing sea with its decrepit iron maw swung open in a silent scream, defiant of any wicked sirens and prodigious sea dragons that may have been lingering over the horizons. Since she could remember, Mina had sought solace and refuge in this most ironic of places. She knew the latticework of gravestones by heart, and the fact that D'Artagnan was comfortable grazing among the markers also gave her more of a sense of kinship and bond with this silent necropolis. When she was twelve or thirteen, Mina realized that she did not like to come here on a sunny, cheery day. She preferred the dense depths and howling winds of a grey day for her favorite place of comfort.

---

[124] Fall or autumn, the season when things die.

After leading D'Artagnan through the gates and letting go of his lead, Mina let herself drift to the left, up toward the oldest part of the cemetery. There, at her favorite part of her favorite place in the world, did Mina sit down in front of the chipped, worn tombstone with the resident's name worn clear, and that had accumulated more moss and grass atop it than any other tombstone around. Her grandparents and great-grandparents were buried in the newer section of the cemetery, but she just felt more comfortable among the souls that had rested here longer. Wind buffeted her, and she looked with need of comfort toward D'Artagnan, who stood regal in the gale, chewing grass and watching her like nothing in the world could ever bother him. She smiled at her horse and took satisfaction from his strength, loyalty and friendship, even as she sensed movement to her right.

Faster than a cobra could rise and spread its hood, she bolted up straight and gave one quick but powerful Texas-style whistle, courtesy of the tutelage of one Quincy Morris. In an instant D'Artagnan was at her side, and another instant after that she had pulled out the Winchester faster than one could pull our keys out of one's pocket. One pump of the rifle later, Mina had cradled the rifle over D'Artagnan's saddle; the horse standing between his mistress and the rustle of motion that had come over a particularly long clump of grass next to a rotting crypt.

"Come out or I'll blast a hole right through you," she said with her mouth drawn into a simple, straight line.

She scared the wind for a second. Then it remembered it was the wind and collected itself, continuing its frothing around them.

Nothing.

"I mean it!" she snarled.

The grass rustled, and out of it stood a broken rum bottle of an aged man.

"Swayles!" shouted Mina, flush with both relief and anger. She let a glare splash over her face for a moment before the comedy of the scene washed over it, and she laughed, feeling silly for being scared in her morbid sanctuary, as she dropped the Winchester back into its holster along D'Artagnan's saddle. D'Artagnan himself was disgusted with Swayles and showed it by huffing out some air while pawing at the ground with his left front hoof.

"Sorry to scare you, ma'am," said Swayles, standing but shifting his weight like he was on the deck of a ship at sea. His near-empty bottle in one hand and his worn, old hat in another, eyes glazed over with drink, Archibald Swayles was the perfect picture of a tippler. Despite the fact that his nose was a little too large, his hair a little too long on one side of his head and was combed over his bald head, and that he was a little too bow-legged, Archibald extruded a harmless, kind countenance.

A Swayles bender was not news to Mina, as the manservant had a long history in serving the Sewards and had grown up alongside Mina's parents. While the winds kicked up another gale over them, the grass and the deceased boarders of the cemetery, Mina walked over to steady the older man. "Again, Swayles?"

"Sorry Miss Wilhelmina," said Swayles as Mina wrapped an arm around him and tried to tug the bottle out of his hand, with no success. "Thought I'd just sit here and enjoy the cloudy day, and let you be."

"If you fell asleep out here you could freeze to death, Mr. Swayles," said Mina as she walked him back to a leery D'Artagnan, who eyed Swayles the way a dog would eye a tub full of water.

Swayles pivoted awkwardly, swinging Mina with him, and pointed back at the tombstone he had been sitting in front of. "Terence misses me, Miss Mina. At least I miss the bloody idiot. He hasn't told me he misses me yet. He was me mate, ya know. When we was all just little nippers."

Mina staggered, trying to keep her balance, and threw a dirty look at D'Artagnan, who had assessed the situation and had drifted a little further away from them, somehow projecting annoyance while he continued to graze.

"Your father, Mister Murray, Dr. Seward, all of 'em gentlemen," said Swayles, pivoting again back toward the horse. "Wha' a kind man your Pa was— is. They grew up and older with their mates, but I lost all me mates in the wars, both in Crimea an' India. Most of them from this side of Whitby all made it through alright."

"I know Swayles," said Mina, grunting with the effort of holding the man up. "I'm sorry."

Swayles went on as if Mina had said nothing. "Would've given me leg to have Terence make it through, but it didn't work out that way. So, while they sit inside toastin' each other, I just sit here toastin' Terence and talkin' with him and the other ghosts of this place. At least these ghosts got to be buried here and not on the other side of the world."

"That's alright, Swayles," said Mina, with a kind and respectful smile. She had always liked Swayles. "As long as they don't talk back to you."

He tossed the bottle out among the headstones and crypts. "They'll finish it."

After a long, foul and possibly combustible exhale, he said, "Oh they talk back, Miss Mina. And it's the things they say that scare me. Nobody tells the light infantry anything, just line up and charge, so I appreciate what the ghosts tell me. At least they're honest."

"I know the war in Crimea was difficult on you Mr. Swayles. My father told me stories as a child. Too many, perhaps."

As they marched through the tall grass and headstones, Swayles moaned, "It left its mark on the lot of us, Miss Mina, soldier and officer alike. Support the Navy, open up the Black Sea again, they said. We were there at Balaclava for all that Light Brigade[125] business. A bloody mess, it was. Your father handled it better than most. Mister Andrew always made us laugh, he did."

Mina was having trouble holding him up, and Swayles was leaning on her more and more in an effort to stay upright. She nodded, "My father handles most things well, I think."

"As does his daughter," smiled Swayles, in the kind, sincere way that drunks do. "If you don't mind my sayin' so."

"You are too kind, Mr. Swayles," she said, struggling to keep him up as she walked, and looking over at D'Artagnan for help. "And I'm glad most of you made it through."

The horse turned his back on her, and Mina at last gave up and let Swyales slide into a sitting position among the wind, the grass, and the dead.

After a long, resigned sigh, Swayles blinked at Mina with glassy eyes and continued, "Renfield's never healed though. He left his soul behind in all that mess, I think."

Mina stood over him, hands on her hips, gathering her strength to help the older man up again. "The Sewards say that he's taken another turn for the worse, I'm afraid."

Swayles ran his left hand over the broken tombstone next to him and pointed at her with his right. "And he's gonna keep takin' turns, Miss Mina. The war just dragged Monty down like Ahab in the book about the whale[126]. He never made it back with us, at least the good part of him never did. Terence here died but Renfield and Van Helsing took the brunt of it. They was just boys. Officers and all, but just boys."

---

[125] The Charge of the Light Brigade was an advancement of British light cavalry against the Russian army at the Battle of Balaclava in October 1854, resulting in heavy British casualties. The event was immortalized in the poem of the same title by Lord Tennyson, Poet Laureate of Great Britain during the Victorian era.

[126] *Moby Dick; or, The Whale*, written by American novelist Herman Melville, published in 1851.

"War has never been good for anyone, especially for boys," said Mina as she reached down for Swayles' hand, which he gave with a smile. Together they raised him up off the wet ground. Above them and to the west, the sun had hidden, but the scarlet gouache stroke had widened, as if desperately trying to peek from behind the clouds.

Swayles gave Mina a gleaming, lubricated smile. "Terence had a good laugh watchin' you beat Master Quincy at shooting that day, Miss Mina. Good for you."

"Thank you, Swayles," laughed Mina as she slung his left arm over her right shoulder, wrapped her right around his back and began to walk him toward D'Artagnan, who had found a perfectly satisfactory clump of grass to chew on. "Quincy handled it well. He wanted a rematch, but I told him that his further humiliation would have to wait."

"Jackson's boy's a crack shot, that Texan," nodded Swayles in a serious manner. "He's still a Brit by birth if you ask me."

"I don't think he'd feel that way," said Mina with a wry chuckle. They both laughed, Swayles adding a charming snort at the end of his.

Mina could not help glance back to the other side of the estate, towards the knoll where she had beaten the Texan. She could not see it from her view at present, but she knew it was there. Mina had taken care not to show how excited she had been at beating Morris, especially since he was such a good sport about it, but she now regarded that moment as a personal triumph on many levels.

They trudged on.

"Come back here to think again, Miss?" said Swayles, with a grand wave at all the tombstones around them. "You've always loved these piles of stones and bones, even as a lass."

She raised her eyebrows and nodded in agreement. "I have a lot on my mind these days, and it helps me to be here. I don't know why."

D'Artagnan was drifting to the left, away from her, as Mina was reaching out with her left hand at his lead. *Swayles must have been an elephant in a previous life.*

Swayles patted on the sculpture of an angel atop a small crypt with fondness. "It's a good place to think and chase spirits, then have them chase me. I come up here and talk to all my friends long gone, about all of us who are still here and have nothing to regret. Friendship and fellowship, and all that. Me pa told me something I'll never forget, and he told me until he went to his grave."

"I loved your father!" said Mina as she put Swayles' right foot onto D'Artagnan's left stirrup. "What was it your father told you?"

Archibald placed his right hand on the horn of the saddle, pulled himself up onto D'Artagnan, with a none-too delicate push from Mina, and nearly fell right over to the other side, but managed to stay on the saddle and place himself there somehow. "Me pa said, 'Just do your best, Archie. If you done your best, then leave it be. Leave it be and move on. Don't let nothin' chase ya.'"

D'Artagnan had thrown Mina a look that might have been interpreted as impatience with Swayles, and though Mina held steady, she patted her horse on the neck, smiled at the slumped rider in the saddle and said, "I'll take you back."

She took the lead and D'Artagnan began to follow her back to the estate, Swayles holding onto the saddle horn with both hands as he said, "You still need to do your thinkin' Miss Mina. I'll just tend to D'Artagnan, although he still looks at me sideways when I get near him."

"He looks at everyone sideways, Swayles," said Mina, taking in the falling night. Some clouds over the distant coast, but nothing to forecast a storm in the night.

Swayles patted D'Artagnan on the neck, and the horse neighed in disapproval, which the servant did not sense as he said, "Bloody hell, do ya remember the time he kicked young Master Holmwood clear across the stable? I thought he'd killed the lad!"

Mina barked out another laugh, this time an undignified one. "Served him right! Arthur knew that D'Artagnan does not take kindly to teasing."

They walked closer to the Seward Estate, the hospital and the stables. Mina would then ride home after she helped him inside, but she did not feel like her interlude at her favorite place had been spoiled. She smiled, patted Swayles on the leg and said, "You've actually helped me with my thinking for the moment, Swayles, and I'm grateful. Thank you."

THIRTEEN

May 25th, 1899

My beloved Wife and Children,

When you read this letter, I will have been in the Kingdom of Heaven for some many months, and I want to tell you all how much I love you. May God take you all into his arms and care for you in my stead, and my dear children Thomas and Gertrude please mind your mother and grow up to be great people and always use the crucifix for protection to ward off any evil in all of its forms. Be good Christians and always sleep with garlic around your room and your necks. Please do this for your father, for all the old stories are true, my most precious, precious family. To my Dear wife Marie, I am sorry that I cannot hold you in my arms one more time. You have been an honorable wife for all of our marriage and I hope we are reunited someday when I earn my way through purgatory and up to you all.

Your loyal husband and father,
Harald Mueller

Captain Harald Mueller put his pencil down and took a long, slow, deep breath, like it would be his last. Light swayed back and forth in his cabin, the lone lantern above him acting like its only goal in existence was to get off the *Demeter*. Mueller's cabin was simple and plain, like the man himself. The small, worn desk he was sitting at was parallel to the small, lumpy bed he slept in, and a beat-up door was perpendicular to his desk like a broken tooth in a mouth that had taken one too many punches in a bar fight.

Harald could hear the sounds of his crew running for their lives past his cabin door, and the firing of pistols and rifles.

Crack.

Spack.

Crack.

Crack.

Then silence.

Heavy breathing. Exhaustive, desperate, gasping breaths.

Then the sound of claws against floorboards, pads against flooring, then the shouts, screams and curses of the crew. Then the roaring of firearms, which were overwhelmed by the multiple, overlapping snarls of large, enraged wild animals.

A few of the crew could be heard shouting for the captain, their insane screams mixed with the eerie, unthinkable sounds of *skin being ripped off their human bodies*, the tearing of flesh and the roaring of beasts. More inhuman screams followed. The gunshots continued, and a few rounds ripped through Mueller's cabin, but the captain was so distraught he would welcome the stray round that would finish him.

Pencil down, Captain Mueller knew what he had to do next, but loathed it with every ounce of his soul. He reached out past his empty bottle of vodka and a dirty shot glass and cuffed the pistol with his drunken left hand. Mueller took the fingers of each hand, interlocked them in front of his face and clinched them together like he was trying to bend steel. He brought the fists to his head, which bowed to meet them as he said, "Forgive me, Father, but I can bear this no more. Let me one day earn my way out of the inferno and toward my family's arms, but I am a weak man and can go no further."

He picked up the pistol and cradled it in his hand, trying not to hear the shouts, wails and roars that continued in the hall outside. The ship, the light, the cabin and the world seemed to all sway together in misery and destruction around Mueller as he picked up the pistol and held it in his trembling hand. Something slammed hard against the outer wall of his office, and the shouts and roars that had peppered the air a moment ago had dissipated. Mueller's breaths came in rasps, and he heard only one noise over the sounds of the *Demeter*'s groggy motor.

Drinking.

The drinking of human blood.

He heard the opening and closing of multiple throats, and moans of satisfaction and satiation.

"Captain, help us," curdled a whisper from the distant yet very near hallway.

Fingers scratched softly against the outer door, like a last prayer.

This was too much for Mueller, and he cocked the pistol and swung it up toward his trembling head.

Thomas.

Gertrude.

Marie, he thought in rapid fashion.

The door burst open like a hurricane had kicked it in, the force of the blow strong enough to put holes in the walls around Mueller, who could only cringe in astonishment. A mammoth shroud crouched over the doorway, and the Dracula bat reached out a claw-lined hand as Mueller swung the pistol toward his temple, his fate and the ceasing of this madness. The hand clenched the air, Harald's gun flew harmlessly out of his hand and across the dead air in the captain's quarters and into the now semi-human hand of Dracula, who snared it like a crane capturing a fish. His quasi-human face still had mammal fur and bat physiology shifting around underneath the blotchy, pitch-and-pearl skin of the vampire, like vermin feeding and writhing under a blanket. Despite his terror, Mueller marveled at the quickness at which the supernatural creature could metamorphose.

"This will not do, Captain," growled Dracula, his mouth still covered in blood. A bat-like tongue slid out over his now-human mouth and sucked up the blood like a Roman emperor would gold.

Behind him crouched the Venus bat, drinking like a jackal over an elephant carcass but watching them with burning, malevolent eyes. Another crewman lay next to her, clearly the victim of the Dracula bat's assault. His fingers were held out in an eternal, frozen beckon toward the captain's door, the tips of the fingers scratched away upon the just-broken door.

Eyes blazing on Mueller, the vampire roared, "Primus!" out through the hall and the ship.

Venus slowly withdrew backwards, into the ship and the night.

"I've given you the understanding that you will survive this voyage," rumbled Dracula at Mueller, cradling the pistol in his pale, clawed human hands, "even as we pass, the magnificent *Peñon De Gibraltar* [127], the *Calpe*[128] and nearer to the eastern coast of our destination, and yet you try to take the life that I have spared? How utterly ungrateful you are!"

Mueller, trembling as he faced this evil entity, spat, "I am not your fool to think you will not slit my throat as soon as you can see the coast of England over the horizon!"

Primus, the massive skeleton that he was, stepped around the bodies and into the cabin.

"Dominus meus?" he rumbled/whispered at the Transylvanian with a courteous, curt bow. *My Lord?*

Dracula's eyes never left Mueller as he hissed, "Assign a soldier to the captain. Make sure no harm comes to him, or to be completely clear, *make sure he does not harm himself.*"

---

[127] The term Rock of Gibraltar, in Spanish.

[128] The original Latin name of the Rock of Gibraltar

FOURTEEN

Sun.

Warmth.

Flowers.

Grass.

Life.

Cerulean blue skies.

Clouds that would have made a perfect Elysian Fields.

Ocean breezes that shook the soul back to happiness without a second thought.

Trees that swayed with the sheer love on being alive on a day like this. Lying on the plush emerald hillside, enveloped by the supple grasses, the loving flowers, the caresses of the ocean breeze and the divine shade of the tree, was a man, around Abraham Van Helsing's age, and the man could not have been more at peace. Something about the air, the sun, the clouds and the very feeling of being alive stirred happiness in the man, and he lay in the grass drinking in the day. Serenity flowed through his body like fine snow water in a summer brook.

Below him on the sweeping hillside, the man saw a few servants placing tables end to end, pressing down on each corner and placing rocks around each leg until the whole thing felt stable. The man was grateful for the men's attentiveness and made a mental note to compliment the servants later on. The men took down some chairs from a wagon and planted them around the tables, shadows of clouds drifting over them as if to thank them for their efforts.

The servants left the completed table setting and made their way back from the tables to the horse-drawn wagon that had born the tables, nudging each other with kind elbows over rekindled jokes from pub lore, and they joyfully rode off, taking in the scenery as well. Watching them go from his knoll of tall grasses that swayed like palm trees in a tropical breeze, the man laughed at the affable work horse that drew the cart and the servants, an old, sturdy mare that had served them well for years.

Insects buzzed around him, happy to be out on this magnificent day. A few birds flitted above, helping the man measure space between the grasses and the opalescent clouds way above that, if only today, seemed to be gates to heaven itself.

A rustle to the left drew the man's attention.

The servant girl moved with a grace that belied the stack of dishes that she was carrying, the length of her Victorian dress flicking out as her legs pushed her body along, and she barely made it to the table before plopping the heavy stack down. From under the girl's bonnet, red raced out from the curve of her cheeks. He noticed the heavenly garnish of rosebud freckles atop her cheeks.

He watched, appreciative of the woman's efforts, thinking how lucky they all were to have such dedicated people working for them. Societies thrived with hard-working people such as this woman, thought the man. Pyramids in Egypt and walls in China rose with the hard work of the lower classes, he surmised, and how little they have been repaid through history for breaking their backs in their efforts. The woman drew out some napkins that had been carefully rolled around fine silverware and began to place them around the table.

The man smiled in appreciation of her honest efforts.

Maybe he could talk to Old Man Seward and get her a little extra for the holiday season? Surely, she either supported or helped support her family, poor thing. She did her job well, and undoubtedly received a poor wage from the Sewards, who were renowned for both their philanthropy and their thriftiness. Seward would have to be convinced, of course, but merely watching the girl's feverish pace from afar would be enough for the old doctor to know that the extra wages would be well-spent.

He was about to stand and congratulate the girl on all of her fine work and explain his wishes for her well being when he saw her let a knife slide out of one of the napkin sheaths and into the emerald sea of blades.

She picked it up, and the man watched her take a long around look to see if anyone had seen her before she turned and placed the knife safely back into the napkin.

A flash of concern blazed over the man.

How could she do such a thing?

Did she not realize that someone at the table was going to eat with a soiled utensil?

He was shocked at her lack of consideration.

Maybe she'll change her mind in a second and right the wrong, thought the man, but when she went right on preparing the table, his anger festered. His evaluation of her services was perhaps premature. The man could see how he could have been deceived by her appearance, swayed by her charms into an opinion based solely on her allure instead of her merit. She was now placing the dishes, and her casual disregard to her employer's sanitation disgusted him, but he presumed that she lived in squalor with plenty of children and some of them might know who their father was, since this prostitute who was serving dishes with her filthy hands had no business working in such a fine place and with such fine, reputable people as the Sewards. She was stealing wages, lowering the standards for the undeserving cretins from the filthy lower classes that darkened and ruined an otherwise brilliant day like today with their disgusting lack of cleanliness and virtue, especially this broken-down *whore* that served scurvy-infested plates with her filthy hands that had been who-knows-where. He knew of prostitutes who sold flowers on the streets of London, and themselves along with the flora. The lower classes were bloated with whores such as this, trollops who cared not with whom they lay, and birthed multiple bastards from multiple men of similar inbreeding. But oh, how they displayed their wares so easily and cleverly! A daily dance of the seven veils for the unevolved working man, who knew of nothing other than to serve their better-bred superiors. Something had to be done. He had to report her, he concluded, as she flitted around the table again like a tainted butterfly dispensing the plates as easily as she gave herself to any man seeking her meager offerings. Whore! Raging Whore! He had a flush, no, a torrent, no, a flood of anger, fury sweep over him, and the blood in the man's veins began to roar, and his throat swelled in rage but he did not want his prey to hear him. The Sewards would do nothing, *since they themselves were weak and ill suited for any sort of responsibility anyway!* She had her back to the man as he stood tall in the grass, his fingers curled into balls of fury in his palms and he strode down the hill towards her, his blood boiling as he picked up speed and ran down the hill, ready to throttle the stinking prostitute's neck and break it into kindling or slide the very knife she'd placed on the table to gut her like the chicken she was.

He roared as he leaped, and the girl pivoted and wailed. Blood rage pounded through the man, and he was reaching for the girl's throat when someone sprinted in from the left and collided with him, sending them both rolling to the grass. The girl screamed like her throat had been torn, and the man fell to the grass and the ground. The other person flipped up like a cat, between the man and the servant girl.

Above the prone man stood Abraham Van Helsing, breathing hard after a long sprint. He looked down at the man and said, "Hello, Renfield."

FIFTEEN

"When this morning reaches noon, I want all of you to break from whatever duties you'll be performing and swim for the coast," said Mueller. "Swim for your lives, and may God be with you all."

All remaining members of the crew watched as Mueller held the steering wheel like he was trying to keep his soul from falling into purgatory. Dawn had just broken to the starboard side of the *Demeter*, slitting crimson over the horizon that hid the coast of France behind its curvature. Dark, listless water held frigid promise in its open arms.

They were all exhausted, worn from lack of sleep and were jammed around the captain as he steered the ship further northwest, nearer to her fate. They were desperate to hear some kind of hope from their leader. He had none to offer.

"Who did not survive the night?" was all Mueller could muster, looking straight ahead, bleary eyes cracking with tears.

"The last of the cooks," said Remy, also worn from this hell at sea. "The she-devils took them without a struggle."

Remy trembled as he followed that with a hiss. "*She made me watch.*"

"Well, the only struggle remaining is the one within my own soul," whispered Mueller. Convulsing from exhaustion, he reached into his front coat pocket and pulled out a bottle. A cork was affixed to the top of it, pushing slightly down on the letters and rosary that had been stuffed inside. Mueller looked Remy square in the eye as he handed him the bottle and said, "If you survive, give this to Marie. If you do not, then perhaps the letter will make its way to her."

Remy took the bottle and nodded, a world full of friendship and memories flooding between them in a heartbeat.

"Lash the wheel and come with us, Captain," said one of the other men, a Turk. "Do not be a fool!"

"Only a fool would let what occurred on this ship to happen," said Mueller, his mouth a tightened slit. The captain was resolute and knew that if he could at least have a few men get away, it might ease his guilt.

"How could anyone have stopped *this*?" said Remy in a harsh whisper, gesturing with both hands to the dried blood in the corners of the bridge, so much that it looked like the floor had been mopped with it.

"They'll be at their weakest at midday," said Mueller, taking a long deep gulp of air. "They can't catch you all."

Remy and the others began to protest, and Mueller waved them off. "Let me at least try to recover my dignity. I sensed this was blood money and took it anyway. This is all my own fault.

Go, and may God go with you."

SIXTEEN

Below the *Demeter*'s sun-drenched deck, the bowels of the ship squeaked, groaned and shuddered. The engines moaned in the distance as the sea pounded away outside, obscuring the feminine whispers that abounded from inside coffins and hearts alike, dead and undead:

"Lo abbiamo potuto ucciderlo nel sonno. Nessuno ci poteva dare la colpa." *We could kill him in his sleep. No one could blame us.*

"أنت تستأذخ حص قصة، هل؟ واو الزمرق؟ وقد حاولت الجيوش، تذكر؟" *You would take a stake to him, Venus? Armies have tried, remember?*

"Mi ha portato dalla mia famiglia, dal mio Nero, mio vero amore." *He took me from my family, from my Nero, my true love.*

"Την έκλεψε από την οικογένειά της, Πέτρα!" *He stole her from her family, Petra!*

"لقد نجا اعم من لجل كل هذه السنوات، المرأة السلسلة. وأنا أدرك تمام فينوس ومعاناتها. لقد عانينا جميعا في يده." *We have survived together for all of these years, Andromeda. I am fully aware of Venus and her suffering. We have all suffered at his hand.*

"Male parta male dilabuntur." *Ill gotten, ill spent.*

"Πες του ότι όταν ξυπνά, η Αφροδίτη." *Tell him that when he awakens, Venus.*

"Non molto tempo come ha Primus e la sua legione di femori." *Not so long as he has Primus and his legion of femurs.*

Three viper hisses of laughter mingled in the darkness.

"وأ تلكك الفئران الجهنمية," *Or those infernal rats.*

There were no viper hisses of mirth at the mention of the fearsome tide of rodents.

"Dormi bene, sorelle. Noi uccidere l'ultimo di loro quando ci svegliamo. Poi a Inghilterra. Il nostro momento verrà." *Sleep well, sisters. We shall kill the last of them when we wake. Then to England. Our moment will come.*

SEVENTEEN

"You can still tackle with the best of them, mate," laughed Renfield at Abraham Van Helsing as the latter stalked into the room, which gave one the sensation of being in a dungeon rather than the basement of Seward Hospital. Asylums had grown vastly from the nightmarish conditions of the Middle Ages to the Victorian era, and Seward Hospital was one of the institutes with better, more updated facilities, far removed from even a hundred years ago, when it was commonplace for people judged to be 'insane' to be chained to a wall by the neck in a dark, isolated chamber. With some of the more extreme cases though, and Renfield was indeed an extreme case, the extremity meant more severe measures of security and safety, and as Van Helsing moved through the basement, he was overwhelmed by the solemnity, the sense of foreboding, and he quickly realized that those feelings had more to do with the solitary patient sitting inside the suspended cage in the middle of the room more than the decor of the chamber itself. The room was well lit, airy and spacious. A bucket of water and a chamber pot sat in opposite corners of the cage. Only the patient in question darkened the mood.

Next to Van Helsing strode Ian Seward, prim but nervous, a white lab coat over his black suit and pants as he held a clipboard and file, and in their wake followed two large, jaded orderlies and an older but attentive nurse. Van Helsing gave Renfield a large, wry grin that attempted to camouflage sadness as he said, "Not better than you, my friend."

"I think the rugby pitch was invented for you," continued Abraham as they neared the cage. "Tackling you was like trying to move a mountain."

"Is today not Sunday, 'Bram?" slurred Renfield. "Should you not be at service as is your custom? The multitudes of sinners that fill churches disgust me."

"If no sinners were allowed in churches or temples," replied Abraham, "then they would all be empty."

"Righteous as always," sniffed Renfield, who shifted his prodigious weight around in his cell like an elephant would in a broom closet. He glared at Abraham with disgust, but Van Helsing simply stood there and gave a reply of gentleness, compassion and patience, which slowly withered Renfield's cynicism.

"And how are you, young Ian?" rumbled the shadow from within the cage.

"Well, thank you," replied Seward, without glancing up to make eye contact. Ian had always been nervous around the massive Renfield, even when he was a pale, thin boy and Renfield a prodigious, ominous younger man. His medical training had made his anxiety diminish around Renfield now. Somewhat.

"Did you use anything to sedate him, Mrs. Finch?" nodded Ian at the nurse, eager to know and wanting to change the topic.

"Some chloral[129], Dr. Seward," said Mrs. Finch after she checked her charts. "It took nine orderlies" —she glanced at the two orderlies, who nodded in affirmation at Seward, "to put him back in there."

Crouched in the cage like a Kodiak bear, Montague Rhodes Renfield was a brute, six feet seven inches tall. A tan, tattered cotton shirt covered a massive chest and timber-like arms. Suspenders held up sepia wool pants. Large, expressive blue eyes bulged out slightly, framed by full eyebrows, and above that matted black hair that looked like a clump of brittle weeds that had been planted on the vast, neanderthal-like skull. An enormous chest that seemed more suited for an elephant than a human being led to two pillar-like legs and two powerful arms. M.R. Renfield's mouth sprouted a grin that held large yellow teeth and many mortal sins inside of it. Renfield had shoes that looked more like boots covering his feet, and hands that looked like they could either rip a bible in half or rend a bulldog lifeless with a quick twist. His neck and wrists were locked inside a wooden contraption, hence the crouch. Renfield's bulbous eyes locked in on Van Helsing and watched him intensely. His gaze asked for help. The cage seemed too small.

"Is the pillory[130] needed?" asked Van Helsing with a gesture to Renfield's contraption.

Ian nodded in solemn manner. "I was about to have them removed. He twisted free from the handcuffs he had on previous, broke through one of the doors and made his way out onto the grounds. I had given him the run of the basement here until he broke the handcuffs and my trust. That was when you encountered him."

"How are you, old man?" said Renfield, jutting his enormous chin at Van Helsing through the bars. "Sleep well?"

For a moment, Van Helsing studied Renfield. The monster of a man exuded alternating waves of supreme confidence and enormous guilt. Abraham's own pangs of guilt passed through his body, and he noted that Montague Rhodes was, even in his condition, keen enough to sense the guilt and give a contorted smile in return.

"Better these days, old friend," smiled Van Helsing past his guilt. "I think of good things, better times between us all. And I pray."

He meant that, and Renfield knew it. Beside Abraham, Ian, the nurse and the two orderlies watched this conversation with interest.

"My memories are *horrible* things," said Renfield, nearly gagging as he did so, as if he had choked on something. His hair fell over his eyes and forehead, as if to punctuate the massive man's instability. He closed his eyes and clenched his fists in the stocks. Abraham wanted to reach out to his old friend through the bars but knew that it was not a certainty that his arm would not be wrenched out of its socket in return.

"I understand," said Van Helsing with an agreeing, sympathetic nod.

"And yet you and the others recovered, and I have not." Renfield's eyes teared up as he said, "Milady has never stopped kissing me in my dreams. And I refuse to pray."

Renfienld's speech was slurred and mangled. *Perhaps it's the chloral*, thought Ian.

"'*Milady*,'" said Ian as he looked at Abraham with a raised eyebrow and a curious look on his face.

Somehow, in a gentle yet authoritative manner, Abraham pointedly ignored Ian, smiled back at Renfield in acknowledgment as he said, "And in a manner of speaking, I have not recovered either. The war was horrific on all of us."

---

[129] Chloral, or trichloroacetaldehyde, is an organic compound which, combined with water, was once used as a sedative.

[130] A device made of wood or metal that had holes for the neck and wrists, and was used as a form of punishment throughout the world. Also called stocks and whipping posts.

Mrs. Finch, the orderlies and Ian all looked at Abraham for clarity, but he and Renfield were having their own private conversation in front of them all. *A bit rude*, thought Ian, but he trusted Abraham Van Helsing more than any man than perhaps his own father.

"Renfield, can we trust you to remain in your cell, so they can remove the stocks?" asked Ian.

Renfield simply nodded with a feverish grin. Ian motioned to the orderlies and they moved toward the cage in a guarded way, as if a bear or lion were inside.

"We'll undo the lock, Renfield," said one of the orderlies, a red-headed man with a wide moustache, "Just let the stocks drop through the cage to the ground. Don't try nothin' funny, mate."

"All right, Flynn," beamed Montague Renfield, which only unnerved the orderlies more. Flynn reached forward with his ring of keys, and Renfield swung the stocks around so the lock was near the bars.

"Steady, Monty," said Abraham, leaning forward as Flynn's key slid into the lock and turned.

"Always," chimed Renfield as he chewed something in his mouth. The lock opened, and the big man twisted the stock open like it was a child's embrace.

The stocks, as well as the tension in the room fell to the ground.

"Thank you, Renfield," said Ian.

"You're welcome, boy," rumbled Montague, who took a long sip of water from his bucket and wiped his mouth dry with his shirt sleeve before he settled back against the bars on the far side of the cage. "'member watching you youngins when I was younger, when your parents went out to their fine dining together without me, never thinkin' you'd be mindin' me one day. Let you kiddiewinkies ride up and down that stupid American dumbwaiter[131] your pa had put in. It's still here."

Renfield pointed a massive index finger out of the cell and toward the dumbwaiter in the corner.

"We still use it to bring your food down to you," nodded Ian as positively as he could.

Satisfied that Renfield was at ease, at least for the moment, Van Helsing then turned to Seward and said quietly, "In all this haste I have not asked, but how are Henry and your mother? Are they still living here on the estate?"

"They are," said Ian with a nod. "This last bout with our man here made up Father's mind, for which I am glad. Retirement suits him well. And Mother dotes on him so."

"I'm happy for Henry," enthused Renfield, his eyes lighting up in a genuinely warm grin which succeeded only in chilling everyone else in the room.

"I should like to see them," said Van Helsing, even as Ian overlapped him with, "I'll take you to them."

"And Jonny and Peter?" followed Abraham, patting the young doctor on the back.

"Still away on business, due back any day for the wedding," said Ian, giving Van Helsing a warm smile. "Nice to have you back, Uncle Abraham."

Van Helsing returned the smile, and with a nod to Mrs. Finch and the two orderlies, Ian began to lead Abraham to the door.

"Will you come see me again, old man?" called out Renfield, a solemn, soft creak from his cage the only other sound in the vast, dark basement.

"Of course," said Abraham in a half-turn. "We can speak of more pleasant things, Monty."

"Like flowers," said Renfield with a broad, happy grin.

"Even better!" laughed Abraham as Young Seward pointed him to the door.

"I like to pull the petals off them," said Renfield with a huge leer filled with enormous teeth.

---

[131] A dumbwaiter, also called lazy Susan or serving tray, is a small elevator intended to lift objects from floor to floor in a multistory building by use of a rope pulley system, usually involving the kitchen to deliver cooked meals, but also could be used as a freight elevator. Popularized in the 1840s, a patent for a *mechanical* dumbwaiter was given to inventor George W. Cannon in 1887.

Young Seward gave Renfield a sudden, horrified look.

Abraham wondered what had startled Ian, who could only look intently at Renfield's mouth.

Monatgue Rhodes saw this and belly-laughed, his snorts and roars echoing around the basement. Then came a sudden, sharp cough. Dry heaves then followed the cough, and Van Helsing took a few steps forward, more out of concern than the ability to reach in and help. Ian stopped him. Mrs. Finch and the orderlies moved to the cage, but with a wary energy reserved for an encounter with a wild beast.

Renfield had one last dry heave before he caught his breath, but not before he regurgitated a wet, stringy piece of something and spat it out onto the floor in front of the cage.

The hairy, chewn-to-pieces tail of a rat. Horrified, Mrs. Finch gasped, as did Ian. Renfield read Seward's horror, and giggled like a wicked toddler. Van Helsing sighed, gave Renfield a look of admonition, turned and walked away to be let out.

Ian followed, weary.

"Let's talk about flowers next time, Mate!" shouted Renfield. He then started to check the corners of the chamber, and Abraham and Ian simultaneously realized he was scouring each nook for rats.

"Flowers," sighed Van Helsing as calmly as he could, while reaching for the door.

EIGHTEEN

For a brief, fleeting moment, as Remy soared through the air, freedom rushed through him like a strong breeze knifing through an open sail. The wind whistled through, around and past his ears, and the daylight's rays bathed him in a warmth he hadn't felt in days. He arced through the sky, the fear, tension and sadness behind him, and even as he hit the water and was baptized with dark and cold, the first mate felt relief to have finally left the *Demeter* and its horrible fate.

He kicked back up to the surface like the other members of the crew that had jumped off the side of the ship along with him. The silence under the ocean gave way to the froth of the ocean's surface swirling around them, the splashes of the other crewmembers as they began to swim north, toward the distant Mediterranean shore, and the churning of the ship as it pounded by them, on its course and toward its goals.

Remy felt along his neck until he found the string around it, then felt along the string to make sure the small bottle was still tied to the string. He smiled, happy that Mueller's last words would get to Marie and their children. The first mate kicked and swam with the others, not bothering to take a look back at the floating torture chamber that had entombed them until now.

One arm swung over the other as Remy swam farther and farther away from the ship, and the other swimmers had begun to hoot and howl and cry with peals of joy as they pounded against the swell and ebb of the sea. Tears mixed with salt water as Remy thought of his wife, his children, his home, his family and his town. Never again, he vowed, never again would the lure of distant lands lead him astray, he swore, and his smile was cut in half by the water as he sealed his vow with a prayer:

> *Our Father who art in heaven*
> *Hallowed be thy name*
> *Thy kingdom come, thy will be done*
> *On earth as it is in heaven*
> *Give us this day our daily bread*
> *And forgive us our trespasses*
> *As he forgives those who trespass against us*
> *And deliver us from evil*
> *Amen*

Remy sobbed as he swam, eager to put his life of the sea behind him. He would take the farm his parents had always wanted to have him tend, and he would never argue with his wife about going to Mass or praying the Rosary or coming home drunk anymore. And he would stop pursuing other women.

But he had one last thought before he put all of this behind him and began his life anew. Remy swam as he thought of Mueller and all of time they had spent together. They had closed many taverns and explored many ports, and while Mueller had never visited the brothels that Remy had frequented, he realized that he would miss his old friend dearly, and despite Harald's greed at times, he had decided upon an act of nobility Remy had never seen before at sea and he was genuinely proud of his friend.

Remy looked up and saw that land was less than a mile away, and he laughed again at the expense of swallowing some more seawater, and Remy saw the other sailors had seen the nearness of their salvation. But his heart went out to his captain, and Remy had to take one last look back to see the ship as it drifted away. Hopefully Mueller could lead the ship into deeper water and sink it like he had explained to Remy after he had spoken to the remaining crew, and Remy slowed, dog-paddled and turned to look back.

The ship was lit from behind, the sun making its way toward the west and the end of the day a few hours later. When Remy looked up, he saw the dark hulk of the *Demeter* as it drifted by behind them, with a single figure silhouetted against the sun.

Even from this distance, Remy could see the knobby, stocky countenance of Primus, standing perfectly still as he watched them swimming away. The skeleton did not have to move to send a shiver along Remy's spine, but he and the remaining crew had won, and Mueller would scuttle the ship with the dynamite he had on board, and that evil could then spend eternity on the bottom of the ocean floor. As Remy turned to start swimming again, something caught his eye.

The railing of the *Demeter* appeared to be... quivering.

Remy's eyes took a second to adjust, since he was trying to look into the dark area of the *Demeter* that was backlit by the sinking sun, and that was when Remy saw them.

Dozens.

Hundreds.

Thousands.

Of rats.

The vermin poured over the side of the ship like a quivering tide of infested, disease-filled meat, racing by the ever-watchful yet vacant sockets of Primus as they cascaded into the sea like a horrific, surreal waterfall.

Large, small, bloated, sick, pungent, starving, rabid, infected, rancid, the rats hit the water and knifed through the cold and the dark, speeding like fluid, oblong torpedoes toward their intended meals.

Remy's horrible, panicked scream was choked off with seawater. The others heard, looked back and began to swim for their lives, with the understanding that they were moments from being torn to pieces. Remy whirled, swam and began to pray again, clambering over a slower, panicked crewmember who was trying to paddle to the shoreline, now visible in the distance.

The cascade of rats subsided, becoming the frothing of hundreds of thousands of clawed feet and twisted tails as they churned, whirled, swam toward the men, who were screaming beyond reason as they pounded the water furiously in an effort to get to land and run for their lives. Somehow it seemed to them that if they made it to land they could at least have a chance to outrun the disgusting horde that closed upon them.

Remy wailed like a child, in a bright, terrified panic as the first few rats reached him and started to climb up into his pants leg, gnawing and *eating* into the flesh of his legs as he kicked like a sinner trying to soar out of Hell. Other crewmembers began to scream in pain alongside and behind him. His arms flailed as the horde overtook him and the rest of the men, pouring inside of their shirts and jackets, and Remy barely had time to yank the bottle away from his neck and throw it ahead of him and toward the beach as the first few rats, smaller and more nimble, began to gnaw their way into his ears, tear through his cheeks and force their way down his throat.

Bits of gnawed, uneaten flesh cascaded down to the darkness of the ocean floor.

Food for the sea life below.

NINETEEN

The French countryside was a welcome respite from the congestion of Paris, but the travel was still difficult for the four shrouds, as it was for all *nosferatu*. There were always unscrupulous humans around to bribe to assist or guard them during the day, and a few nights had been spent in less than ideal conditions. Cemeteries were and are mirrors of society, some affluent while others varying in degrees of available facilities. The cemeteries that were more opulent had more ideal conditions in which to rest: cool, wet mausoleums and crypts that the shrouds could open easily and gain access in order to rest for the day, while the poorer, working-class cemeteries furnished less crypts, if any, yet had more than a few times some burial plots that had been dug but had not been filled due to a lack of funding. In these instances the four coffins, carved and created with elegance to be perceived as luggage trunks to the unobservant eye, fit in quite nicely. A nice grove of trees or even large crypts could keep the wagon from scrutiny.

Older cemeteries, or older sections of cemeteries, to be specific, were preferable to the undead, since the passing of time had, more often than not, healed the souls and memories of the living and allowed the days to pass with little or no attention from any curious and unwelcome citizens. Other times, citizens that lingered too long at the site of one of their beloved indeed became victims. Weaker souls that came to the cemeteries to pass out and sleep their drunken stupors away also fell prey to the red lust. The occasional pranks of college-age men and women, daring each other to run through the cemetery at night could meet unfortunate consequences as well.

A recent evening had begun with the discovery of an old man at the site of his late wife's grave, yet his grief was so deep that he turned a tearful face to the shrouds and explained that he welcomed them in order to see her again. He whispered the name on the marker as he died.

"We are one at last."

Segments of society that were shunned or put aside for reasons of intolerance also had their places of rest. The shrouds knew this and often sought out Jewish, Moorish and Gypsy gravesites whenever they could, laughing at the humans for their petty categorizations, prejudices and isolations. Like with human society, vampires also created their own feudal system royalty throughout time to mirror that of humanity, and often these undead royals would take residence in or under abandoned castles, deliberately creaking stairs, rattling door handles or slamming windows to scare off any trespassing unwanted visitors, or finally consuming the humans if they persisted. The culture of the undead began to emulate that of the humans, with banks, legal offices, even factories as the Second Industrial Revolution[132] began to intrude upon the world, that were owned by the undead, albeit indirectly in most cases.

---

[132] The Second Industrial Revolution was a phase of rapid industrialization in the latter part of the 19th and into the 20th century, highlighted by advancements in manufacturing, technology, machining and travel, all of which ushered in a wave of unprecedented globalization. Railways, telegraphs, steelworks, machine tools, paper manufacturing, petroleum, maritime technology, chemistry, engines and even the first automobiles all were all part of the innovations of this era.

After a discreet journey across the English Channel, Le Havre to Brighton, in a privately chartered ferry after the carriage had been eschewed and the drivers consumed, the shrouds ran into trouble in Great Britain. One eve, two of the four coffins had been hastily covered with fresh dirt during the day by nervous groundskeepers, somehow worried more about losing their jobs than the consequences of their actions against the undead. That night the other two shrouds had to work feverishly to dig the buried coffins out, even before they could collectively hunt. Once out, the shrouds resisted the temptation to find the groundskeepers' quarters and rip their throats out, discretion being the better part of the need for peaceful travel. Bodies were usually disposed of in smart, experienced ways, in order to deflect the unwanted attention of a police investigation until they were safely out of the area.

Vampires knew better than to trust someone with anything less than the price of gold and understood that the price fetched only the loyalty that could be counted on to wait to inform the local police as soon as they were out of harm's way, so the help that was sought out was often criminal in nature and countenance.

Yet wherever they went, whether country, province or city, the shrouds attracted crows and ravens, and the birds escorted them and their coffins through their area and then left them, flying back to their nests in the trees, and while the shrouds never spoke of it, each one of them wondered whether the birds were paying them respect and tribute, or simply making sure that they left as quickly as they passed by. This day they traveled along the countryside in their coffins, two grizzled local grave-robbers doing them the courtesy of escorting them as far as the price of gold would take them, for the coming night it would be far enough to take them to their appointed, sinister task.

TWENTY

As the wagon of the shrouds rattled along the English country road, two friends stood chest to chest outside of the sprawling Holmwood family manor near Whitby. Above them, clouds decided to bunch up and try to flicker out the candle that was the sun, with intermittent luck, as shadows swam over Holmwood and Seward. Arthur was bigger and burlier than Ian, but the smaller man was emotional and undeterred. He had come out to greet both Ian and Quincy in a huff.

"You're an *alleged* gentleman, Seward," growled Arthur. "You should step aside."

"Gentleman or not, I'm going to ask her to marry me," retorted Ian with a snort. "You've always known how I feel about her."

"Not in my home, Ian, and not if I ask her first!" snarled Arthur, "And you should have acted earlier if you felt this way."

Quincy Morris was busy catching his and Seward's luggage from the driver of the carriage that had brought them to Holmwood Manor. He caught the first piece of luggage with an annoyed look in his eyes. He waved at Ian's driver, who jumped to the front of the carriage, cracked the reins and began to move it and the horses in the direction of the stables. Morris waved thanks to the driver.

Arthur looked at the Texan from the corner of his eyes and said, "What do you think, Quincy?"

Morris shook his head as he caught the second bag and said, "Aw hell, don't haul me into this, boys. The last time y'all asked my opinion with regard to a member of the more delicate persuasion, Jonny took offense to what I said about the Fleming girl and we all got kicked out of that silly bar—"

"—Pub, Quincy," said Ian, unable to help himself, despite the situation. "On this side of the pond, we call it a pub—"

"—What was the name of that thing?" bellowed Morris, eager to change the subject and distract his friends from beating each other senseless. 'The Yodelin' Goat? The Singin' Goose? The Stranglin' Cat?'"

"The '*Lamb*', Morris," said Holmwood, taking the bait. "The pub was called 'The Slaughtered Lamb.'"

This technique usually worked for Quincy; he could count on the national pride of his friends as a subject that would and could distract them from anything he needed them to be distracted from.

"Why can't y'all name your bars like ours in America?" shrugged Morris as he tossed Seward's bag at Ian. "We've got one in Texas called The Mean-Eyed Jackalope!"

Seward caught his bag and spat. "You are clearly the stupidest man in England if you think a pub—"

"—Bar—" interjected Morris with his right index finger in the air. This brought a grin from Arthur, who had balled his hands into fists. He unclenched them.

"—A *pub*," continued Seward with a sarcastic glance at his fellow countryman, "known as the Cross-Eyed Armadillo—"

"—Mean-Eyed Jackalope!" snarled Morris, his mission accomplished. He bounded over to them as he pointed at Ian and said, "Get yer insults right, Sewie! They got whiskey in that place that'll split open your toenails, straighten out yer mustache or clear out your gizzard! My Uncle Billy used to tell me about how in the old days they'd just tie two arguin' men together and give 'em pig stickers[133] to figure it out, but that ain't the point of this conversation, is it?"

Quincy caught his stupidity too late and winced.

"No," said Arthur, his glare returning to Ian, "it is not."

Seward dropped his luggage to the ground and squared on Arthur.

"We should simply resort to fisticuffs to settle this," growled Holmwood, his chin pointed directly at Ian.

"Queensberry Rules[134]—"

"Any term that starts with a term that refers to a king or queen should automatically be disqualified from association with roughhousin'," interjected Morris, attempting to steer the conversation back again to a more neutral topic. "Look, y'all should just both let the lady decide. Just both of ya ask her, and let Lucy make her choice."

"That's what we discussed doing earlier," snarled Holmwood, back to glaring at Ian, who responded by clenching and raising his fists.

"Well," snorted Seward, "that was before she started laughing hysterically at all of Arthur's boorish jokes at the shooting contest."

"She thinks I'm funny!" roared Holmwood, happy to hear his humor had made points with Lucy. Ian fumed as he realized he'd given Arthur's romantic techniques an inadvertent compliment and he surged forward, a fight imminent.

Quincy bolted forward to squeeze between them as he said, "Look, both of y'all should ask her, but it ain't gonna do us any good as a family if one a' ya holds a grudge, and it's you I'm lookin' at, Sewie."

He pushed them apart as he stared at Ian, who was incredulous. "Me? Why are you looking at me, Quincy? I'm not the ruffian here!"

Quincy held out his arms, palms on each of his friends' chests, while he swallowed deeply, about to tell a friend something he did not want to hear. "Cuz I love ya pal and I'm thinkin' she's a little sweeter on Artie than she is on you at the moment, Sewie."

Morris shot each man a glance. Ian had been slightly staggered by this, and Quincy quickly clapped a sympathetic hand on his shoulder. Arthur had cooled into sympathy for a friend who had been given a blow, and Ian's sails had lost their breeze. Before either man could react, Quincy continued. "You've always been sweet on her, cuz she's prettier than a Bible on Sunday, but I seen how she looks at the big, dumb Brit when he makes her laugh."

A dagger in the heart... Quincy could feel Ian's heart sag, and so could Arthur. Quincy thought to give his friend an honorable way out, and said, "But if ya gotta ask her, then ask her, just both a' ya shake hands before and after and let's all stay friends. And family."

Arthur looked over at Ian with sympathy. This was a big moment for Seward, and they both knew it, for he been 'sweet' on Lucy since their childhood, but the present was the present, and fate had played its hand, and was continuing to play its hand, on many levels. After a long moment, Seward reached over and gave Holmwood a friendly slap on the shoulder.

"I wish Jonny was here for this," said Arthur, not happy at his victory if it meant pain for the young doctor. He patted Ian on the shoulder and stepped away from Quincy, an unspoken agreement

---

[133] Antiquated term for a knife.

[134] The *Marquess of Queensberry Rules* are a set of rules created in the 1860s that formed the basic rules of modern boxing.

now agreed upon.

A joke overwhelmed Morris and he spat, "Harker? He'd make y'all hug or somethin' silly like that. He'd take the fun out of a piñata party. You know, I think the fella thinks bloomers[135] are posies in a flower field."

All three men laughed, then stopped as Lucy and Mina burst out of one of the many side doors of the expansive manor. The afternoon shadows had begun to slide over the row of cypress trees that bordered the manor, Seward saw them and thought they looked like gigantic spectral fingers reaching out to envelop them.

"What the hell are you three still doing out here?" shouted Lucy, on the run. Her eyes danced at Arthur, and all three men saw this, and all three men understood that this further sealed whatever agreement they had just made, the silly way that young men think they decide everything and anything, when in fact this was all about a woman deciding what she wanted all on her own.

"Lucy!" shouted an exasperated Mina at her best friend, running fast, gaining. As she ran uphill after her impetuous best friend, Mina noticed how all three reacted to Lucy, took in Ian's attempt at covering his sadness, Arthur's suppressed giddiness at being in Lucy's presence and Quincy's concerned glances at Ian and summarized what had just happened in the blink of an eye. *Men are such simple creatures*, she thought.

"We were just headin' in," said Quincy, who laughed at how commonplace it had become to see Lucy in the more colorful, modern and playful dresses like the pink gown she wore out today, and contrasting it with Mina's reserved, serious, darker colored Victorian wardrobe. *Both of 'em hellcats in their own way.*

He's accepted it, thought Arthur, watching Ian observe Lucy's eyes stay locked on Arthur. *But it will always be something between us.*

It was all for naught, was all that Ian could think. He looked at Lucy as if she were in a fog, drifting away from him. *Perhaps I was not intended for marriage. She was all I wanted. My evening star.*

Morris chuckled as he thought of an analogy for the two women: two wild mares thundering along the southwestern plains of the United States. In a burst of thought Quincy then figured he could make this thought a funny joke when the women were not around, then remembered the near-fight that had just been avoided between his friends, and then he decided to just keep his trap shut and stay out of family arguments altogether.

"Good," said Lucy, as she looked them all over with a sweeping glance and a radiant smile on her face, "because we need help setting up for dinner! The servants can't do it all themselves."

"Arthur, how are you?" she laughed as she looked at Holmwood with fever in her eyes.

"Clearly not as well as you, Lucy," replied Arthur, saddened that he had caught sight of Ian's ability to notice Lucy's glint.

Ian came to a sudden, brutal conclusion as he stiffened up, put his hands in his pockets and said, "I agree, Arthur. She's Venus personified."

"Thank you, Ian," she said with a smile that had a sheen, but not the outright sunrise that she had just tossed at Arthur like a spring bouquet. "We must let you use that train of thought on Miss Fleming at the next social."

It's over, thought all three young men at the same time.

---

[135] Bloomers are loose-fitting underpants and/or pants for women from the Victorian era, down to the knee or the ankle. Also called 'Turkish dress', Bloomers had become a symbol of women's rights in the 1850s, when women began to express the desire to wear pants in public in addition to dresses. Also called American dress or reform dress. Some corsets and petticoats of the period began to literally and painfully shift the internal organs around inside a woman's body.

Quincy and Arthur could both see Ian's pierced heart rolling around on the cobblestone-lined path below them.

"Perhaps we should head inside and help everyone get ready for dinner," said Lucy, slipping her arm into the nook of Arthur's elbow and steering him toward the manor. "I can't *wait* to see Uncle Abraham again!"

"I can't stand a man who brings his mummy to dinner!" spat Arthur, and while everyone cringed and groaned at Holmwood's pun, Lucy pealed with laughter. Ian gave a sad, polite smile of resignation, took his hands out of his pockets and let go of the engagement ring he had been holding in his right front pocket. Quincy saw Ian's stifled pain and clapped Seward on the back. The Texan at that instant felt like he had witnessed the doctor's finest moment.

Arthur very kindly and tenderly slapped Ian on the back as he walked by with Lucy, and Ian returned the slap in a way that all three men understood that they would survive all this as friends.

My god men are so stupid, Mina thought as she noticed the meager attempt at subtlety between the men and decided it must have had to do with their jockeying for position with Lucy, or a bar fight or dirty joke, and let it go as she led everyone toward the manor. As they neared the entrance, Mina shouted to everyone behind her, "And Quincy, for God's sake please clean your boots off this time!"

"Ladies," said Ian with an abrupt stop, "would you both mind if I had one final word with my two alleged gentleman companions?"

"You three" said Mina with a half-turn and a mock scowl, "are more like old gossipy women than young, upstanding gentleman."

Morris retorted with a wink, a grin and a tip of his cowboy hat. "There's a few ladies in Texas who might disagree with ya, Mina."

"Like who?" snickered Lucy, "Consuelo?"

"We've spent time with Consuelo, remember? She is going to throw one of those overwrought American-styled saddles over Quincy and ride him around for all to see after their wedding ceremony," laughed/snorted Mina, which brought even more peals of conspiratorial giggles from Lucy.

"That's for me to know and you not to worry about, ya little hellion in a bustle," snorted the Texan. "You'd meet the devil at midnight and fight him to a standstill. And I prefer the term opulent instead of overwrought to describe saddlery from my side of the pond. Now let us old snake-oil salesmen chat for a second and we'll follow y'all inside in a minute."

Mina noticed the undercurrent of seriousness between the men and looped an elbow around Lucy's free arm.

"Let's leave the ninnies to their games and see if Swayles needs any help," she said as she led Lucy inside. The lights in Holmwood manor had come on as the golden hour neared outside.

Once the door closed, Ian rounded on Holmwood, sighed and said, "Arthur, in all seriousness and honesty I simply wanted to tell you that it's clear to me that you and Lucy have realized all of my fears, and for this tragic yet wonderful reason I must step aside. If your intent is to ask for her hand, then I will stand out of your way freely to wish you luck, dear friend."

Quincy realized he had just witnessed an even finer moment from his friend. A moment of silence, tenderness and sadness later, Arthur simply put his hand out, and Ian Seward took it and shook it with a tender but British stiff-upper-lip resolve. Ian sighed a big sigh and Arthur opened the door for his old friends, and they headed inside.

Quincy patted them both on the back. "Next round's on me, gents."

"You've never bought a round in your life," said Holmwood.

The door closed behind them.

The shadowy, skeletal fingers of the cypress rows stretched ever closer to the estate.

TWENTY-ONE

Captain Harald Mueller woke with a feverish start.

A jolt of pain shot through his skull like lightning through the night, but when he reached up to touch the side of his head, he realized that he could not move. The last thing that Harald remembered was Primus coming at him. The remnants of the crew were all pieces of meat floating around for the seabirds to pick through or being digested inside the voracious rats' innards. Mueller was lashed to the steering wheel, rope an inch-thick wound endlessly around him so he could barely move his head. He faced the window he always looked out of, and he could see the distant but familiar eastern coast of England, with the sunset behind and between the distant, brewing clouds of grey. He could see a map of the coast on the floor, with a red line drawn from the ocean straight toward Whitby.

Between the window and the deep, succulent sunset was Primus, skeleton of the Ancient World, standing at the very nose of the *Demeter*, with his feet slightly out further than his hips and with his bone hands clasped together behind him in a military fashion. Gale-force winds buffeted everything on the ship, but the skeleton stood resolute. Below, the hull groaned, weary from its voyage. The engines banged away in constant complaint.

The ship swayed around him, but the skeleton stood there, barely moving. Watching Mueller. All over the deck of the ship swarmed the accursed rats, content with their meal. They moved freely over Primus, like ants over a statue.

A large, mangy rat stood on Primus' skull and gnawed on a human finger. Primus looked forward to the evening. He had not returned to England since just after the fall of Rome.

He would tonight.

TWENTY-TWO

No one at the party that evening knew it was the night before the end of everything, the way that the season of summer danced with nymph-like joy without a care that autumn and winter would desiccate every flower in every field in a few months.

This night was the last before a group of fine people who had grown to love each other both as a collective family unit and as individual parents and offspring would begin to fall apart, or more accurately, be torn asunder, the very next night. No one knows when a good streak of fortune is going to run its course, and in this case, with a storm looming off the nearby coastline, everyone gathered for what they considered to be yet another fine evening of, above everything else, love.

The Harkers were unaware their son and Uncle Peter had found death on the other side of the world.

Lucy Westenra and Arthur Holmwood knew how they felt about each other and that their love was very strong, but they did not know how deeply that love would be tested in the very near future.

Quincy Morris had finally begun to put the death of his parents behind him, feeling like he needed to travel to the other side of the world to feel the presence of his parents, no matter how much love Consuelo Morera-Lopez and her family back in Texas gave him.

Ian Seward understood and accepted that he had taken on the mantle of Doctor Ian Seward as a result of his father's sudden retirement the previous evening, and that Lucy Westenra was lost to him, yet he did not know how much more heartbreak would happen around him in the near future.

Montague Rhodes Renfield was thrilled anew when he realized how much rats would convulse if he held each end in his hand and began to rip their bellies out with his teeth and begin to consume them while they were alive.

All this was yet to come.

The Harker family hansom[136] was new, with green and black trim. A luxurious contrast to the broken-down carriage that had carried Jonathan Harker to his doom a continent away, this carriage had wide, spotless windows on each side, with two front doors that were elegantly framed at the top by windows, and at the bottom by extravagant leather and lush wood panels to keep the riders warm and in style. Tassels hung proudly from the ceiling, which itself featured embroidered patterns that might have made even the Sistine chapel take notice. Lanterns were mounted just outside the doors, casting a romantic half-light within the compartment. One could open the front doors then step forward onto a landing/splashguard behind the horse, before stepping down on either side. Held up by an early form of suspension, their ride was smooth; indeed they could hear the neighing complaints of the horse outside. Patrick Shearer, the needle-nosed, long-legged coachman who sat behind them atop the carriage shouted, "Come on, Seaweed, we're almost there!" Seaweed was not

---

[136] A hansom cab is type of horse-drawn carriage, smaller than a larger carriage yet stouter than the open-air calash (or barouche) carriage. The hansom was created in 1834 by British architect Joseph Hansom. Meant for two or three people and drawn by a single horse, the driver sat behind the main cab, and could communicate with the riders through a hatch door at the rear of the roof, as well as receive taxi cab fees.

in the best of moods from hauling five people (including the driver) around instead of the ordinary two or three that fit in a hansom, and from being out in the rain, racing down a sand-lined road and toward the sprawling Holmwood estate.

Inside the velvet-and wood grain-lined panels of the hansom were Andrew and Judith Murray, and to their right sat William and Cynthia Harker. Cynthia had to sit on William's lap, quite uncomfortably, in order for all of them to squeeze into the cab. They bounced around in an odd, uncomfortable silence, their last words about how much it had rained that day and Peter and Jonathan's delay in the Orient dangling in the air, laced with an air of tension. The Harkers sat very elegant in their formal wear, while Andrew and Judith Murray projected a more self-assured social confidence. The men wore dark wool coattails and beaver fur top hats, while the women wore evening dresses. Cynthia's evening gown was an astonishing combination of gold and pearl, while Judith's crimson-and-black dress combined with her red-haired beauty to make her blush at Andrew's first glimpse of her that evening.

Before the Harkers had picked up the Murrays on their way to the Holmwoods' for dinner, William and Cynthia had quarreled over the Murrays. As they dressed for the evening, Cynthia Harker had a sliver of temper that could, upon occasion, pierce her insistence for social decorum; she had wanted to discuss with the Murrays what she perceived as Wilhelmina's hesitancy over her marriage to Jonathan. William, a polite, stylish and charming man who was graying most handsomely, managed to avoid many controversies in his life by using his charm as a shield. He thought the subject was none of their business until the Murrays decided to share with them whatever hesitancy Mina had accrued, if any. Cynthia of course was well aware of William's shield of charm and wanted none of it, and in their haste to depart to pick up the Murrays, had forgotten her own hat, a swaying cream-colored compliment to her dress, which hid for the moment under her fur-lined coat.

Cynthia was a blonde, smart, beautiful, even regal woman from Maryland, where she had been an heiress to a Baltimore shipbuilding company. On one of her family's trips to England she had met the dashing, whimsical William after he had returned back from the Crimean War. They had managed to successfully maintain their marriage and relationships on both sides of the Atlantic for nearly two decades since. William was the eager, brave soldier back then, but was more than happy to retire from military life and settle down into running the family business after Cynthia's parents passed away. Now they were both graying naturally and together. They had raised Jonathan on both continents and spending more time in the old colonies naturally had been influential on making Jonathan feel more like an American.

The tension was not just about Mina's hesitancy, or rather Cynthia's curiosity about her future daughter-in-law's concerns about her son, but also about the unspoken competitiveness between the families, or specifically the rivalry that the Harkers had with the Murrays, who were conscious of the efforts of the Harkers to stay what they considered to be a few steps ahead of them, but the Murrays had decided not to care. The Harkers certainly had more money, yet the groundedness of the Murrays had always attracted an admiration as well as resentment from the Harkers, Cynthia in particular. She had the idea that Judith considered her and her family to be *nouveau riche*[137], which of course was not the case with Cynthia herself, as her parents, the Kelly family, had been the ones who had made their family fortune, and perhaps that doubt that lingered was Cynthia's own. Judith's judgement, something never expressed directly but referred to peripherally, remained a point of

---

[137] *Nouveau riche* is a derogatory term, a French word, to describe families who had made their fortune within that generation rather than having inherited it. The term also refers to class, 'breeding' and social climbing in a dismissive manner by the wealthy to differentiate themselves from those of 'new money'.

annoyance between the women. When love began to blossom between Jonathan and Mina at the end of their teenage years, Jonathan began to accompany the Murrays on their charitable pursuits, and the Harkers were also invited, yet it did not sit well with Judith that their invitations had always been coolly declined by Cynthia. This friction led to a hot/cold relationship between the wives, who could bicker with an air of delicacy over *hors d'oeuvres* and drinks so that no one around them could detect their disagreement save their men and their children; so much so that many a time Jonathan and Mina were forced to intervene when the husbands could or would not, or more reasonably, decided to stay out of the affair completely. Yet as in any complex relationship, the love and respect were there, just not without a few issues that nag at any friendship like a pea between mattresses.

William and Andrew's inability to do anything about the friction between the women save to deny that it was present, irrespective of the romance that had grown between Jonathan and Wilhelmina, annoyed both of their wives, who astutely pointed out on many occasions that the husbands seemed to share more secrets with each other than with their families. Both retorted that war experiences did that to men. Yet in the broader sense, Andrew was happy for his friend to have found Cynthia, a woman who he felt meshed well with William Harker, who had come from a family of shipbuilders that had prospered, but not to the extent of those of his intimate circle of friends; the Sewards, the Morris family, the Westenras, the Holmwoods and the Van Helsings. They had also supported each other through tragedies... Quincy orphaned at such a young age, the deaths of Martine Van Helsing and a child during childbirth, which left Abraham widowed, childless and crushed in one fateful stroke. And then of course, there was the strange, horrific case of Montague Rhodes Renfield.

Andrew knew that William had been a little rough about the edges as a young man, despite his abundant good looks, and the late Jackson Morris was fond of stating that William had been blessed with looks at the expense of his wit, yet Andrew took note how Cynthia had knocked William Harker into shape, dressing him even better, pinching him to sit straight, combing his hair in a loving manner with her gloved hand in public, something Judith and Ursula Holmwood had frowned upon at first, back when Cynthia and William were courting, opining that an American woman had no business correcting a British gentleman, but Andrew's response was always that William Harker had been a half-formed gentleman until Cynthia came into his life and polished him into the gem that he was today. And that everyone needed love, especially grumpy English gentlemen.

William and Andrew, who had been through a war together and had been friends since childhood, felt more at ease with the silence that presently floated around them in the carriage, having sat in fields of grass together as children, watching the ships shamble into Whitby Port, or laying as soldiers in the silent aftermath of a battle in the Crimean Peninsula, with the dead and dying all around them.

"Hawkins was always one for an adventure," said Andrew Murray, sitting in the middle of the hansom with a mischievous sideways glance at William that attempted to mask his concern, underscored by his fingers drumming away on the brim of his hat. "They could have been delayed for any number of reasons."

William, simply grunted in agreement, knowing that the wives would see the deeper meaning in Andrew's nervous twitch. *Andrew always does that when he's nervous, and we all know it.*

"But this long without a letter, Andrew?" said Cynthia Harker, her left arm draped over William's right shoulder. William, who thought that perhaps his wife had put on a few pounds since the last time she had sat on his lap, contemplatively traced rain water trails on the front window of the hansom, not realizing he was giving away his own sign of suppressed concern to everyone else.

Rain drizzled down on the carriage and Mr. Shearer was soaked to the bone, despite a heavy coat and hat. Poor Seaweed neighed again in protest. They passed the great oak into which Quincy Morris had shot a gaping hole with a musket round one dawn as a nine-year-old, wearing nothing but cowboy boots and bright red flannels, rear flap open to the world. Arthur Holmwood had roared mightily at the boy, who only sniffed and retorted proudly, "I hit the durn thing at forty paces with my eyes shut, Uncle Arthur!"

The twilight around the carriage faded fast. Clouds wrestled in the distance, to the east and over the ocean, while a pinch of day still remained in the west, past the rain. *Yet another storm off the coast,* thought William.

"We should have heard *something* from Peter or Jonathan by now," said Judith Murray, sitting next to her husband and sharing a look of concern with Cynthia. "It's simply been too long."

The front, windowed doors of the hansom rattled with the rain, and a gust of wind whistled in between the doors and into the cabin.

"Andrew's right, ladies. Travel has a way of making simple things like posting a correspondence a complicated undertaking," said William, looking out along the familiar hedges of the Holmwood estate and remembering his boy playing among them as a child, half-imagining that five-year-old Jonathan would come bursting out of them at any moment to greet him with that all-encompassing expression of love that children could give to their parents. *I love you, Daddy!* Harker turned back to the others and said, "We'll just have to continue to be patient, though I can certainly write to Pattison over at their firm to see if they have received any update"

They all nodded positively at William's idea.

"Let's hope Jonny and Peter get back soon," answered Cynthia as she patted her husband on the knee. "We've got a wedding to plan."

The Murrays were too clever to look at each other in response to Cynthia's statement, which would have pointed out an ever-so subtle misgiving about the marriage to the ever-observant Cynthia, so they were content to find each other's hands and to clasp them together in solidarity, which the Harkers took for love, which was very much there, but also for unity in the face of an impending decision that might upset the balance of the family friendships.

Breaking off an engagement in Victorian England was no simple matter, and many reputations and families had been sullied or ruined by the bitter end of a relationship that had been proposed, accepted, and more importantly, negotiated and agreed upon with the air of a business merger. In this case, everything had been negotiated between the Harkers and Murrays months ago, before, during and after Mina had accepted Jonathan's proposal. There had been a bit of a surprise within the families, as everyone had always thought that Quincy Morris would be the one to propose to Mina, Ian even joking at one point that they could have a two-rifle wedding, but Quincy had fallen deeply for the stunning Consuelo Morera-Lopez in Texas and Jonathan had made the first move for Mina. Despite some of the concern that Mina would turn Jonathan down flat and leave an uncomfortable situation with everyone, she had gleefully said yes, which revealed the depth of their love to everyone. So, the planning for the wedding had begun, with the anticipation that the event would occur upon Jonathan's return from his errand in the Orient.

The Harker carriage made its way through the rain and up along the languid drive and toward the massive, multi-story manor that lay atop the slight hill like a very large, very comfortable Saint Bernard puppy. They could hear Shearer urging the horses along, eager to dry them and himself off in the Holmwood stables, large single-story buildings behind the actual mansion yet expansive enough themselves to quarter many horses, as well as an equestrian staff. The complex, ornate windows in the Holmwood manor were lit up nicely, a warm invitation to hospitality along with the immaculately trimmed hedges that served as visual garnish for the idyllic home for a British lord. William grinned his sideways grin at Andrew and said, "Avoid any mention of the theater in front of Arthur tonight."

"Agreed," agreed Andrew. "Bombastic as our Lord Godalming is under ordinary circumstances, no need to send him to another zenith."

"Especially after he has partaken of his beloved Cognac," echoed William as the hansom stopped. Quigley, the stocky, large-sideburned Holmwood butler ran out of the massive, double-doored front entrance of Holmwood manor with an umbrella.

Shearer, shivering in his seat at the rear of the hansom, took Quigley in and laughed, "Owe you a shilling for the Liverpool/Everton match last week, Quigley. Or a pint if you'd rather."

Before he whipped open the front doors of the hansom, Quigley laughed, "I'm happy to accept the settlement of our wager under either of your conditions."

Quigley snapped open the double front doors, held the umbrella out above the opening and said, "Mister and Missus Harker and Murray, welcome to Holmwood Manor."

"When Arthur is sufficiently lubricated it's impossible to rein him in," finished William, too experienced in marriage to make even the slightest grunt of relief as his wife got up off his legs, which had begun to fall asleep during the trip.

"Ursula manages to rein Our Lord Godalming in every time," said Cynthia with a coy smirk as she stood, silently grateful for her husband's not having made any noise that could have been seen as a reference to her weight, her comment was met with an approving glance from Judith. 'Our Lord Godalming' was Cynthia's nickname for Arthur, a term she could use to simultaneously respect and tease the man, and while the nickname was out of bounds in terms of British forms of address, and it was a bit uncouth for an American such as Cynthia to use the phrase in that context in the eyes of her English friends, they nonetheless enjoyed her ability to do so, and the women in the family always enjoyed the elder Arthur Holmwood being taken down a peg or two once in a while.

Quigley held out his free hand and Cynthia Harker took it after she said, "Thank you, Quigley, most kind of you."

"My pleasure, Mrs. Harker," nodded Quigley, astute enough to lower his head to eliminate the chance of having Cynthia turn and catch him having a glance at her form in motion under the gold and cream gown. He also knew that Shearer, seated right behind him, was watching them step down off the hansom and Quigley did not need one whit of his teasing during their drinking and card playing much later that evening.

"I think we crossed the Black Sea faster than some of you managed to circumvent a few estates!" bellowed a loud, happy, yet bellicose voice as the Harkers and Murrays made their way past a set of doors which had cost the lives of many prodigious trees, and into a foyer with twin swirling staircases and tile-work so polished that one could have used it for a mirror.

At the foot of the left staircase stood a mountain of a man.

Arthur Holmwood, Senior, or The Lord Godalming, was a massive figure with an expansive beard, and a limp that required the use of a pearl-handled cane. All that was matched only by his incredible intellect, wit, vigor and larger-than-life personality. One had the sense when standing next to Lord Godalming that he was Everest now, but Olympus in his youth, a formidable human being. A cigar the size of London perched on the edge of his mouth, held there with the clamped jawlock of a bulldog not afraid to clamp his jaws around anything in life. Steel eyes, filled with intelligence, superiority and ego scanned his guests, for Arthur Holmwood Sr. was a man whose eyes scanned everything. He wore black eveningwear, but with an ebony shirt that furthered his bulbous-but-still-powerful frame. His free hand cradled a cane that looked like it had once belonged to Zeus. Holmwood owned all he surveyed and he acted like it. His father, Jackson Morris was a quiet man when he had been alive, the complete contrast to his son, but one of his more astute observations was to state, "If Arthur does end up in Hell, he would shout at Satan so much that he'd end up in charge anyway."

Next to the now Everest/then Olympus stood his wife, an ethereal sculpture of a woman named Ursula Holmwood, hands clasped together in front of her with regal poise. She was young Arthur's mother and the only human being capable of staring down the Gibraltar of a man next to her. Strawberry brown hair arranged around her willowy neck and head, Ursula was a classical study of feminine dignity, worthy of a Singer Sargent study for her comely allure and mystery-filled gazes; Ursula's looks were completely secondary to her inner resolve. She wore black to compliment Arthur, her evening dress was Victorian, and, despite the long sleeves and high collar, seemed like a step toward the upcoming century. She was the unicorn to Godalming's lion, and as much as he knew that he owned all that he saw, he knew that she owned him. Before she passed, Martine Van Helsing had once noted about Ursula, "From moment to moment my feelings of resentment and admiration vacillate when I am with Ursula, but then again I did state my resentment first, didn't I?"

Next to the Zeus and the Singer Sargent painting stood the Sewards, Henry and Lillian, and one would be hard pressed to find two more opposite, contrasting couples. The direct opposite of the Holmwoods, the Sewards looked like they'd run off-stage if a light was placed upon them, unlike the Holmwoods, who were made for the opera. Henry was diminutive, stout, quiet and older than all of his friends and old soldiers. He had the slight bend at the upper back of a person who had spent a lifetime examining patients. Perhaps it was the experience of seeing Montague Rhodes Renfield recently, but Henry seemed to have aged a decade since the now-infamous Murray/Morris shooting contest the other day. Regardless, Henry's retirement had been sudden, and he seemed not just tired, but spent. Henry had a full beard that never seemed combed, a shock-white head of hair that looked like it refused to be tamed with a comb, both on a head that seemed proportionally too long and large for the body it sat upon. His tuxedo seemed both clean and wrinkled at the same time, with an askew, cream-on-white bowtie nestled firmly under his beard. Yet all this was surpassed by the warm, gentle smile that brought Henry Seward the trust of his patients, his ability to make those ill at ease, or ill period, to feel comfortable.

At Henry's side, Lillian was tall, thin, with gold/silver hair done up in an elegant bun, and much taller than Henry, as if she had straightened out with age as he had shrunk. While Henry was slightly overdressed in a tuxedo, Lillian shimmered in an opalescent Victorian gown. While anyone else in the family tended to worry about things, superfluous or not, Lillian Seward was not one of those people. She managed to stay above most of the political banter and gossip that went on within any group of people that loved each other, and she seemed truly dedicated to taking care of her husband, who was tired beyond his years. They were the same people from the shooting contest a few days ago, and yet Henry stood not as tall, not as straight and not as alert; he seemed tired, worn and spent. It was he who held Lillian's elbow, not the other way around. Henry looked like a polished but worn old shoe. It was Lillian who had passed down her polish to Ian, even as the boy dreamed of following in his father's career. Indeed, if her husband and son were seen as the preeminent alienists of the time, Lillian Seward was certainly the glue that held the family together.

"Must you hold Lillian's arm like an old ninny, Henry?" chided Arthur with a chuckle that attempted to make his coarse comment a teasing one.

"Be quiet Arthur," retorted Lillian in defense of her husband, casting an annoyed glance at Holmwood. Henry Seward laughed off Arthur's comment like he laughed off most of Arthur Holmwood.

Holmwood took a long, confident drag of his cigar, which was the finest that Cuba could produce at that time. He then pointed at Murray as he spewed smoke like a locomotive, "Your mistake, Andrew Murray, was to not set the festivities at your home. Innately, the host's only advantage is that he can retire to his own bed after said party without having to fight his way home through the muck of the night."

"We'll remember that for the wedding," said Judith, furthering the Harkers' contentment with the nuptials with the Murrays, and secretly enjoying the idea that Andrew, knowing Mina's indecisiveness about the wedding, was avoiding her gaze. Judith always did enjoy a good inside joke, and tonight was no different.

"Welcome as always, dear friends," beamed Ursula, and everyone took turns embracing, Cynthia Harker noticing that Arthur Murray wrapped his arm very comfortably around Lillian Seward as she leaned forward to embrace Judith Murray.

"Has Victoria arrived?" asked Judith Murray, in mid embrace, to Ursula's happy, crisp nod.

As their coats were taken by Quigley and the rest of the ever-attentive servants, Arthur Holmwood shouted, "And now, curious people—" more for the effect of hearing his own voice bounce around the grand room than anything else, "—I give you once again our dearest little brother, Abraham Van Helsing."

As if on cue, Abraham sauntered out from the double-doors on the left in a green-brown tweed jacket, vest and pants that would be barely considered fashionable in the social circles that they all dealt with, but Abraham Van Helsing was no normal man and wore the suit well. Clearly Van Helsing was more comfortable on an archeological dig than at a formal dinner, but there was a virility that he carried as he bounded into the room that dispelled any notion of poor fashion. Abraham had shaven yesterday but not today, and that only added a layer of wildness to the man who enjoyed going out and taming the wild, if not the ancient. Van Helsing's coat was for the country, not fine dining and not unlike the Norfolk jacket[138]. His hair was wet and somewhat more combed than it was in Egypt, and his grin had a rapscallion quality to it. Or perhaps it was the Enfield no. 2 Mk1 pistol that he carried strapped under his left arm (which Van Helsing preferred to wear in civilized circles, relegating his Bergmann M 1894 for use during excavations). Most likely it was the grit and toughness that, mixed with his intelligence, made Van Helsing such a formidable man who could wear almost anything and not look silly in it. The others turned, gasped with surprise and showered Van Helsing with applause that was laced with both joy and sarcasm, which they knew Abraham would respond to with a huge silly grin, and he indulged them with not only a grin but with a warm laugh.

Somehow Abraham Van Helsing was treated like the university student coming to visit his parents for the holidays, and he sensed it, found it strange but accepted it, mostly from the wives, because it was based on both love and sympathy, the cosmic, convoluted dynamics that drive all families. With the men, he would always be seen as the boy in their infantry, and it was mostly a generational thing. They had served together in combat, and Renfield was a mere youth through those times, and it did bond them, but they all somehow held their age over him, and Abraham just laughed at their simplicity. Despite his accomplishments, the men still tried to treat him like a child at times, and Abraham had long worn weary having to prove anything to his fellow former soldiers. They in turn had been privately awed by his adventurous lifestyle and professional accomplishments, and in the silly way that men behaved at times, rarely told him of how highly they thought of him. He reeked of travel, adventure, knowledge, and ferocity, yet with a generous helping of tolerance. Abraham Van Helsing had seen it all and lived it all, with the exception of

---

[138] A loose-fitting coat fashionable in the 1860s, primarily used for shooting or hunting.

the family experience, which was the one subject rarely touched upon by his friends, their wives and their children.

"One day," barked Abraham as he hugged Judith Murray, "our dear Arthur will find his true calling, and it will be not in the House of Lords but behind the podium as an auctioneer for Sotheby's."

Even the servants laughed at the retort, along with Lord Godalming, who always saved his biggest guffaws for jokes at his expense, which won him respect from everyone for being able to, above all, laugh at himself. Arthur pointed his Havana-sized cigar at Abraham and shouted, for that was all that Arthur Holmwood ever seemed capable of in terms of speech, his ability to shout to thunderous levels, "I still contest that you are a Dutch National, Abraham, and that your British citizenship should be revoked and your military pension suspended forthwith and with succinct malice and outright prejudice!"

Van Helsing's retort was succinct and elegant as he shot back, "But then who would have shot the Turk that was about to shave that beard right off your neck, oh dear Lord?"

"Why, our dear Montague Rhodes Renfield would have, of course," sang Arthur with open arms and ill timing, his words cutting too deeply and drawing a wince from William Harker. *Did not take Arthur long to step into it.* The collective uncomfortable laughter, which had crescendoed, faded into polite chuckle at the mention of Renfield. Embraces and handshakes continued, but they were now laced with accompanying cringes at Holmwood's inability to rein in his personality at a crucial moment in a social situation.

"Oh, don't turn into sensitive old barn owls in front of me," laughed Arthur, a little too self-consciously. "A quip is just that."

Ursula Holmwood muzzled Arthur with a single, glacial glare before she embraced Abraham warmly. William Harker, patting Abraham on the back, rolled his eyes at Arthur and said, "Never to pasture with this one."

The wives all sympathized with Van Helsing, the lonely widower in their eyes, who enjoyed the warm, motherly embraces that he always received from them. They had all respected that he had not remarried after the death of Martine during childbirth, and time had only explained further how much Abraham had loved his wife. Van Helsing chose to ignore Holmwood's comment about Renfield, saying, "Where are the children? It would make me happy to see the rest of them. Ian looks grand."

"Abraham, they are now children," sighed Ursula, "in name only."

"You have given everyone else a warm welcome, Abraham Van Helsing, but what about me?" said a woman's voice behind Abraham. He pivoted to see a warm, cheery woman in her late fifties, her beauty just past its bloom, standing in front of him in a more traditional Victorian gown.

"It would not be an evening without Mrs. Westenra here to greet me," laughed Abraham with his stupid, sly grin that knew its way around women but was polite enough not to be seen as lecherous. "So happy to see you again, Victoria."

As Victoria stepped to embrace Van Helsing, she said, "If you address me as Mrs. Westenra one more time I shall slap you."

Victoria Westenra was shorter than the other women, a faded brunette who retained her dignity and class even as her dark hair faded. She wore a stunning auburn evening dress that ironically covered yet revealed her figure within the rigid Victorian standards. Victoria embraced Abraham warmly, if just a hair too long and familiar, and far too tightly. Judith, Cynthia, Lillian and Ursula all looked on, understanding that Victoria's infatuation with Abraham went back very far and was unrequited, for the most part. Abraham, with a patient but forced grin, had to pat Victoria on the back to ask her to unclench, which made Judith Murray suppress a giggle. Andrew, William and

Henry were all far too busy taking cigars from Arthur to notice.

"It would not be the first time," chortled Arthur, after a puff of his cigar and a tug of his wit, "that the back of a woman's hand met the face of Abraham Van Helsing."

Abraham said nothing but patted Arthur on his expansive left shoulder and gave Holmwood a sincere grin, one filled with the irony of being happy to see an old friend and wondering why he had come in the first place.

Ursula's pinch at Arthur's right bicep, timed perfectly with Abraham's shoulder clap that said *enough!* and made its point. The warm greetings and conversations of friends who loved and accepted each other through their failings, frailties and insecurities began to mingle together with genuine affection.

Quigley, evening coats over his arms, handed them off to Smythe, yet another Holmwood servant, who whispered that dinner was nearly ready to serve. Quigley nodded to Symthe and moved to close a window that was banging against the sill, pushed around by the growing rain and wind outside.

The coming storm.

TWENTY-THREE

The winds off the English coast yanked at the whitecaps like pulling hair off a scalp, and the night sky and its clouds boiled above the *Demeter*, as if this was a perverse eye of the storm, frothing with violence and intensity. The distant lights of the port of Whitby were swallowed by the pelting sheets of rain, while the shrieking winds begged Mueller to save himself as the ship plowed through twenty-foot-tall crests. The waves seemed to be getting the better of the fight, and the ship seemed to be a tired fighter sagging in a corner during rounds. The lantern beside the steering wheel banged around the ceiling like a fish struggling to breathe air. Mueller's mad, wailing screams of maniacal laughter overlapped the howling winds, the captain knowing that death loomed before him. To his left, a thirty-foot wave grew off the port side, and to his right, near the nose of the ship, swelled a throbbing wave that grew to thirty feet tall off the starboard side. Starboard hit first, then port.

Blow to the gut, then the kidney.

The ship lurched, sheets of steel the size of a small house groaning like they wanted the round to be over about thirty seconds before the bell was set to ring. The metallic shrieks of beams being ripped apart inside the ship like linen was a symphony to Mueller's ears, because he knew they would all drown like the rats they carried. A death at sea would be a relief now. Rivets exploded like rounds out of a Gatling gun[139], shooting out into the crying air or slicing through the raging sea. The entire room shook like Leviathan[140] had taken hold of *the Demeter* and was shaking the life out of it. At the next moment, Primus was next to Mueller, who laughed as the skeleton looked outside and realized the ship was being pushed away from Whitby and up the coast, toward stout cliffs that beckoned like the dark, foreboding canyons of Gustav Doré's etchings.

Somewhere onboard, a boiler exploded. The ship shuddered. The round was over.

"She comes for us! She comes for us, *the sea*!" Mueller raved to Primus, and to everyone in his family that had gone to their maker before him.

---

[139] One of the forerunners of the modern machine gun, first utilized during the Civil War after it was invented by an American named Richard Gatling in 1861.

[140] An ocean monster from the Old Testament and the Tanakh, the Hebrew Bible.

TWENTY-FOUR

"There's the man who taught me how to sharpen my Bowie!" shouted Quincy Morris. The younger generation had collectively risen politely out of their chairs, expecting yet another series of dreary greetings with people from their parents' generation, when the mammoth, ebullient Arthur Holmwood Senior. stepped aside to reveal Abraham as he led the elders into the dining room, the door on the right in the foyer. The dark-wood dining room around them was large enough to play a game of tennis in, with a table fit for royalty, with enough chairs to seat a church gathering. The tablecloth was silk, with sumptuous settings that featured opulent glasses and polished silverware set in the *service à la russe*[141] style. The vast table was framed by an enormous set of French windows that overlooked a spacious back lawn that darkened by the moment. A door at one end led to the kitchen, another, which the elders had just passed through, faced the windows and led to the foyer and the rest of the house. A fire in a large hearth crackled in a far corner. Outside, rain begged to come in and join the good company but was rebuffed by the sturdy architecture.

The children that were no longer children gasped in collective giddiness at the sight of Van Helsing, who rolled his eyes at the attention while laughing at their happiness. The parents laughed as their children raced right by them to get to Van Helsing, offering vague waves of etiquette and courtesy at the Harkers and Murrays.

"Dear Lord!" chuckled Lord Godalming as Arthur II ignored his own flesh and blood in a mad dash to reach Van Helsing, who was being mobbed like a Victorian era celebrity. Mina, Arthur Jr, Ian, Lucy and Quincy overwhelmed Abraham Van Helsing with warm hugs and eyes filled with tearful happiness. As the young people swarmed him, (Mina in particular grabbing Abraham and hugging him so tight that he felt the spine that troubled him so during the excavations pop nicely back into place.) Van Helsing laughed despite himself, at them and at himself, so taken by these people and their love for him. At times he felt so distant from them, especially when they all reminded him of Martine and his Claire, the wife and daughter he loved more than anything else he had ever loved before in the world.

"The man of the world, Uncle Abraham!" shrieked Mina at last, her embrace now tender and sincere. She teared up a bit, and Abraham wiped them like he always had. He beamed and took in her hug and corresponding kiss on the cheek. "And you, my Little Explorer then, now teacher of children, molder of minds and grown woman in her own right."

"You smell of mummies and all the amazing places you always told me about as a girl," giggled Mina breathlessly into his ear while Abraham slapped Quincy Morris' Texas-sized pickpocket fingers from filching one of Lord Godalming's Cuban specials from the comfort of the explorer's right coat pocket. Van Helsing laughed deeply and full of vigor, and he vowed to remember all this naive, provincial

---

[141] The main styles of formal table service in western countries during the Victorian era are *service à la russe*, which in French means, 'in the Russian style', and *service à la française*, or 'in the French style'. In the former, each course is brought out in a pre-set order, while in the latter all the courses of the meal are on the table where the meal is served.

charm the next time he was sleeping in a cold tent on a dig, the next time he thought he was alone in the universe.

Van Helsing was not their uncle by blood, none of the families were actually related, but they had all grown to love each other in an idyllic, perhaps naive way, despite their nagging, gossiping and lingering resentments. Each had their own hereditary tree branches intact and often interacted with them, some had healthier relationships with their blood kin than others, but somehow the Murrays, the Harkers, the Holmwoods, the Sewards, the Westenras, and the Morrises all had bonded into one cohesive, caring unit that lived and loved as a family should, warts and all. Perhaps it was that the men had grown up together from boyhood, then had all served together and seen battle, war and death; or that the wives were all strong beings that ran their families well, or that the children had grown up to be very close friends, but in the end, there was only friendship and love that bonded them. Abraham was their favorite uncle, had been for years, and everyone knew it. They appreciated Arthur, Andrew, William and Henry as well, each for their own fine qualities, but perhaps because Abraham was in between the two generations of parents and children, his archeological pursuits and his warmth and kindness, all combined to bring knighthood to Abraham Van Helsing in their collective, youthful eyes. Any kind of petty jealousy on the part of the elder generation toward Abraham had been washed away when they considered that Van Helsing had no family of his own, so the fawning was seen with kindness and as an emotional replacement for what the explorer had missed in life.

"I've never been told *I* smell of mummies," laughed young Arthur, waiting his turn to greet Abraham.

"You reek of pub and cigar and gin, which is better," retorted Ian, which brought a collective, conspiratorial roar from both of them.

"Arthur smells of lilacs in the fields," cooed Lucy, her chin solidly on Arthur's right shoulder.

"Artie smells like he got sent to Sunday School[142] with his underwear on the outside," sniffed Quincy at Lucy, who stuck out her tongue at the Texan, who then turned to Van Helsing as Mina at last finished giving Abraham one last hug of greeting.

"How are you, son?" said Abraham to Quincy with a warm smile after their hug. Abraham affectionately flipped up the tip of Morris' cowboy hat so he could see more of the young man, and he teared up slightly as he marveled at how much the Texan had grown since he'd seen him last. *Nearly a man now, hell, more of a man than I was at that age.*

His cowboy hat flipped up, Quincy smirked with affection at Van Helsing, since Abraham had been repeating that gesture every time he'd seen the lad since he began his travel to Texas, both before and after his parents' deaths. In a way, Quincy had become a surrogate son to Abraham, since they'd both lost their families. Morris' eyes danced with happiness to see Van Helsing as he blushed, "Mina beat me in shootin' the other day, so I must be losin' my touch in my old age."

Abraham raised both eyebrows in mock surprise and said a little too loudly, "Was this the same Wilhelmina Murray who once took her father's rifle and bounced a round off the church bell as a child?"

"The same!" shouted Mina, standing off to the side as she exchanged funny faces with Lucy. Around them, the parents laughed with the pleasure of seeing their children that were nearly adults so filled with joy. Quincy turned to grin at Mina, and she playfully stuck her tongue out at him again. Lucy, Arthur and Ian all laughed at that; they really were silly children again around Van

---

[142] Sunday School originally began in England in the late 1700s as a place where children working six days a week could get an education and religious instruction. Founded by British philanthropist and Anglican layman Robert Raikes (1736-1811), Sunday Schools predated state-run school systems and became very popular, spreading to America very quickly.

Helsing the explorer, Van Helsing the professor, Van Helsing the favorite uncle.

"They all just melt when he is around," laughed Judith Murray, with a nod of agreement from Cynthia Harker.

"I still do," sighed Victoria Westenra, to a collective giggle from the wives.

"Well then neither should you feel any shame," said Abraham as he slapped a hug onto a beaming Ian, who had forgotten his romantic woes for the moment, as well as the fact that he'd already spent time with his uncle. Van Helsing nodded at Quincy. "Did Annie Oakley cry when you beat her and Buffalo Bill?

Morris did not miss a beat: "Annie didn't, but Ol' Bill did!"

Everyone roared at the quickest wit in Texas.

"Wilhelmina Murray, the shootist," chuckled Van Helsing with a fatherly wink at Mina, who took it in like a sponge takes in water. Lucy decided she'd had enough of waiting behind Ian and Arthur, stepped around them and crushed Abraham with her hug.

"Keeping an eye on everyone for me, like we talked about?" said Abraham as Lucy began to weep with joy, nodding her head in affirmation as she did so.

"That's a good lass," replied Van Helsing, choking back his own tears. "I miss playing at tea with the little girl that you have left far behind."

Lucy was always the most sensitive of them all, and he worried about her above all. Her father's passing had affected Lucy very deeply, far more than it had affected Victoria, who had struggles of her own with Phillip, but Abraham had stepped in gallantly and while Lucy never took to shooting and adventure like Mina had, she relished Abraham teaching her to ride, and quite a few times Abraham Van Helsing, adventurer, could be found in the Westenra living room, helplessly yet patiently playing tea with the delighted Lucy Westenra.

"King Arthur!" exclaimed Abraham to young Arthur, a term he had christened the boy with from infancy, which Lord Godalming had delighted upon, and a nickname young Arthur had carried around proudly throughout his childhood. He once came home from a schoolyard scrap and when asked to explain himself, young Arthur roared, "He made fun of Uncle Abraham calling me King Arthur!" In the blink of an eye, Van Helsing recalled that story, and it moved him once again as he saw this boy, now a young man. With everything else Van Helsing had learned in his world travels, he knew how to love those in his life that loved him. "Is your mischievous streak still intact, or has your adulthood taken it from you already? Or are you still ever rambunctious?"

"Always!" shot back Arthur, the same outward, exuberant personality as his father. Abraham followed that up with a warm slap on the young king's shoulder. "Then all is well and good in Whitby."

Arthur's beaming grin could have split the storm outside in two. His hug was no less constrictive, and Abraham's eyes once more swam with emotion at seeing Arthur so grown up, and he cupped the man/boy's cheeks in his hands, and Arthur beamed back at him. *He'd never let me do that to him*, thought Arthur Senior as he watched them. Even though Abraham had been born and raised in England as the son of a Dutch father and an English mother, he'd been able to evade the stereotypical British reserve, and even Lord Godalming himself had to lean on his cane and clear his throat at the pure emotion. Ursula patted Arthur Senior on his prodigious belly and said, "Now, now, he loves you as well."

"I know," said the Lord Godalming through wet eyes, and everyone around the bombastic man smiled, fonder of the man when humility did not elude him.

Ian was next, and tried to comedically hop into Abraham's arms, which made everyone around them wail with laughter.

"I've already seen you, lad, yet you get another hug whether you'd like one or not!" shouted Abraham to Ian Seward. "Ever the quiet one, yet the brightest mind and quickest wit in Whitby!"

Van Helsing cupped the back of Ian's neck with affection as he continued, "Yet you have the Seward kindness innately with you, young Ian. You're already a hell of a doctor," grinned Abraham, to which Henry Seward, off to the side of the younger generation's greetings, championed by adding, "Hear, hear!"

Ian thanked Van Helsing for his kind worlds with another warm smile. He stepped right up and embraced Van Helsing before abruptly pulling away in mock disgust, then pointed at the holster that hung under Abraham's left arm, obscured by the tweed coat. "What is that you are wearing under your coat, Uncle Abraham? Would that be what is referred to as the cockadoddle holster?"

Perhaps it was the emotion of the moment, but Quincy was quite serious when he darkened at Ian and glowered, "It's called the goddamn Huckleberry[143], Sewie, don't any y'all get started with me."

Ian and young Arthur's eyes met, and they instantly radiated with the idea that they had annoyed the Texan and instantly began to somehow, telepathically plot to spend the evening frolicking through the Texan's temper.

"Ian, I carry this in the city. During expeditions I prefer to carry at the hip. But you know that already, don't you, lad?"

Ian cocked his head at the younger Holmwood and said, "Did I know that, King Arthur?"

Much to Quincy Morris' annoyance, Arthur innocently clasped his hands together in front of him like a devilish schoolboy, arched his eyebrows high and his eyes wide as he replied, "More importantly Ian, can't they name anything in a serious manner in the colonies?"

Quincy retained his patience by closing his eyes and exhaling, and while he held them shut Mina and Lucy both wrapped their arms around him and patted him on the back for his restraint. "Lordy, Lordy help me," he murmured.

Somewhat disappointed that his comment drew no fire from the Texan, Ian continued with, "They could have called it the Dingleberry perhaps. Don't you think?"

Young Arthur knitted his brow in a seemingly serious, completely hilarious expression as he said, "Indeed, Ian. One could wear it in reverse, facing forward, but that might not do when greeting the vicar after Sunday service."

"I've never seen you so patient, Quincy!" gasped Ursula Holmwood.

"It's the British side of him, Mother," needled young Arthur, as he and Ian wrapped their arms around Quincy, and they both began to whistle *Rule Britannia*[144] while they and Mina and Lucy continued to embrace Morris, whose face went from scalding to a slow grin that begat a monumental fit of laughter which was shared by all.

"This is where I last left you all," said Abraham with a chuckle, as they all applauded the gregarious scene; Lucy and Mina both kissing Morris on each cheek to congratulate him on his complete silliness.

None of them lacked for love, and all was right in the world, their world.

"And now, with impeccable timing," shouted Lord Godalming over the din of the applause, "comes Quigley and his ever-stupendous ensemble with our refreshments!"

"I suppose," sighed William Harker with humor and a dash of envy as they watched the younger generation fawn over Van Helsing, "that the Dutchman will forever be the center of these events."

---

[143] Shoulder holsters like the Huckleberry, where the pistol hung under the free arm, were worn throughout the Old West through the 1870s and into the 20th century.

[144] 'Rule Britannia' is a famous British patriotic song, originally a poem by playwright James Thomson, which was then set to music by composer Thomas Arne in 1740.

The servants knew them all so well that they brought the elders their traditional drinks without even being asked what was wanted. The younger generation had lemonade, sheepishly brought to them by the *Quigley-istas*, the affectionate nickname bestowed upon them by the elder Holmwood. Indeed, the Quigley-istas were a little embarrassed to be serving drinks to young adults. Quincy in particular threw a knitted brow and smirk at his drink, only to be shushed by Lucy, much to the amusement of Abraham, who saluted the young men with his fresh glass of malt beer. "We'll make do at the local, what was the term you used last time, Quincy?"

"Watering hole, Uncle Abe," said Quincy after he took a sip of his lemonade, "but Jonny was the one who used it more'n me."

Mina's eyes danced with fire as she hissed conspiratorially, "We have decided to join you upon your next liquor-fueled adventures, have we not, Lucy?"

"Yes," agreed Lucy, "in fact we—"

"Saloon's no place for a lady, ladies," interjected Quincy after another long slug of lemonade.

Mina's brows arched in a surprised, serious manner and she stood straight. "We'll be the judge of that, if you don't mind, Mister Morris."

Morris shrugged his shoulders. "Don't let Jonny find out—"

Mina opened her mouth in shock, as was her custom, even though she had been told by Judith and the other mothers in the family that it was not lady-like, but before she could respond, Ian laughed, "*Pffff*, Quincy, if there's one thing that Jonny Harker always does, is exactly whatever Wilhelmina Murray tells him to do."

"How dare you—," gasped Mina, half-giggling, half-insulted. She looked to Lucy for support, only to find Lucy wrinkling her nose at Arthur with affection and twirling a lock of her red hair, then nodding to her in sad agreement with Ian.

"He always does exactly what you say," said Lucy.

"The truth hurts," agreed Arthur, who then winked back at Lucy, who coyly tucked her chin at her left shoulder with the grace and charm of a young woman in love. Ian noticed this quick exchange in mid-sip of his lemonade, and it hurt him, but a sympathetic slap on the shoulder from the Texan helped dispel the green sliver of envy. Abraham took all this in, as he did everything else, such were his powers of observation, and was fascinated at how the dynamics of the young people around them had begun to play out, seeing them take that next step into adulthood and their lives.

"Bottoms up[145], or Cheers[146], if we'd like to stay out of the saloon talk," said Abraham with a hearty laugh.

Ian, Arthur and Quincy all gave a sarcastic but friendly salute back to Abraham with their lemonades, drawing an even bigger chuckle of irony from the Dutchman.

One of Quigley's greatest qualities, as Ursula Holmwood had oftentimes observed, was his ability to serve refreshments to a party while he and his staff guided them to the hosts' preferred destination, and here they were, all guided by liquid inducement toward the ornate hearth, which sang to them the siren song of cracking firewood and warming flames on a cold night. Lord and Lady Holmwood had taken their customary glasses of champagne, served directly from Quigley, while William Harker nursed his lager next to Cynthia, who was served her usual glass of sherry. A dry martini always worked for Henry, while Lillian had taken a serving of

---

[145] The origin of the term 'bottoms up' is nebulous, yet there are stories of English sailors being tricked into joining the Navy with coins placed at the bottom of their glasses. The men would say "Bottoms up!" so that they could see if any coins were in the glass before they were finished drinking.

[146] There are several origin stories to the use of the term 'Cheers!' during drink. From deliberately clinking hard on a co-toaster's goblet to ensure that any poison in one's glass would spill into theirs, therefore an act aimed at trust, to a toast whose sound would ward off evil spirits. Lastly the Greek term 'Limas!' means literally 'to your health'.

brandy. The Murrays always shared a glass of apple wine. Victoria Westenra had her staple, a glass of emerald absinthe.

Arthur ignored that the younger members of the family, including Abraham had already started to drink, and he raised his own glass and said, "To our Abraham!"

To which everyone happily toasted.

"Well, Lucy tells me you are everywhere between Egypt and China these days, Abraham," said Victoria, settling very lady-like onto a beautiful emerald sofa made of wood and velvet in the shape of flower petals. Everyone else gravitated to the other three sofas and chairs that surrounded the fireplace. Arthur Senior strode around to his customary place where his elbow was cradled nicely by an ornamental corner of the fireplace. The men patiently waited for the women and younger people to be seated, then they sat next to their respective wives.

Abraham, very athletically and against proper social etiquette, took a lone chair into his right hand, leaned it so that three of the four legs were in the air, then spun the chair with a swirl of his arm, turning it backwards. He then settled into the chair, chest leaning onto the chair back, not caring what anyone thought of his breach of politeness, happy that everyone else accepted his eccentricities completely. He rested his right arm on the top of the chair as he continued to work on his malt beer.

"This sofa is new, Ursula, and so beautiful," said Victoria, playfully reaching out and clasping Abraham's left wrist with affection. Everyone noticed, including Lucy, who exchanged knowing glances and subsequent eye rolls with Mina. Victoria let her hand linger for a moment too long before removing it. She was another powerhouse of a feminine personality, and nothing in life had ever dimmed that, not even losing her husband, Philip Westenra, Lucy's father, a decade ago. A good case could have been made among them for her as the dominant female among the women, but that argument would be lost when compared to Ursula Holmwood, a category unto herself, the queen who ruled the king who ran the country. Lillian, Cynthia and Judith were all refined, intelligent women, and they had quietly retained their class and dignity throughout their lives. Victoria's dependency upon the powerful drink that had begun to be called 'the green fairy', had started to assert its toll on her through time, and it had become more and more frequently necessary to have the servants discreetly assist Victoria to her room, earlier and earlier, during their social gatherings.

"The craftsmanship *is* unique," agreed Judith Murray, to an agreeing nod from Cynthia Harker, who ran her supple hands over the plush velvet cover.

"Thank you. It is from Paris," smiled Ursula as she nodded her thanks back to Cynthia. "The gentleman who sold it to me it said it was one of a kind; the artisan is a Spaniard named Gaudi[147], who lives in France."

"So then, Abraham," said Andrew Murray, pushing on in the conversation, as was his style, "was it China or Egypt? You know how much you are missed. Please, update us."

Abraham had always appreciated Andrew Murray and William Harker, both quiet men who led quiet lives in, comparatively, a much less bombastic manner than did their host. After a sip of beer Van Helsing said, "I received your letters, Andrew, and all of you; I appreciate them very much, and must apologize again for not corresponding more consistently. The digs become quite taxing. And vexing, at times."

"The posts we send to you care of the museum do reach you, then? Very good then," nodded William. "We know that you always become more involved as the dig goes on."

"Quite. I do receive them, but you must all know that you are collectively in my thoughts and heart, and while the work to unearth the past for ourselves today continues, understand that only my duties keep me from elaborating upon what my work entails."

---

[147] Antoni Gaudi (1852-1926) was a renowned Spanish architect specializing in modernist design.

"Regale us, little brother," said Arthur, amid a deep exhale of cigar smoke. Holmwood was fond of his cigars, he never offered them to others until after their meal when he hosted, and never apologized for his lack of decorum with his precious smokes.

"As you wish," said Abraham with the boyish smirk that expressed both politeness and bravado simultaneously, and after having that smirk melt into a warm smile at the people most important in his life, he began.

The adults were then able to sit back and listen to Abraham, while watching him hold their adult children in wide-eyed suspense as he recounted his recent experiences. The elders heard the words 'Nepal' and 'yeti' and 'jackal' and 'tomb' hissed by Abraham, augmented by the cracking of the firewood and with descriptions of Tibetan monasteries and Egyptian temples. The elders and servants, those who were not busy preparing dinner, all sat there, spellbound. As Abraham talked, the youngsters all moved their chairs closer, enraptured, while the elders watched them watch the storyteller and his talk of snow leopards and ruins in Southern Asia.

"I could pass on today, knowing that my son would be in good hands with him," said Lord Godalming, pointing his cigar at Van Helsing after taking a long drag.

"Abraham loves our children, but he'd never be around for them," said Judith Murray, who somehow could always cut to the truth of the matter. The other wives nodded in agreement. Rain pelted the windows, and Andrew Murray and William Harker began a side conversation about the weather, and the best way to get back to their homes that night through the storm.

"What about us?" chortled Henry Seward with a sweep of his hand to the other parents. The sweep was a little too wide, he spilled his second martini and his speech was somewhat slurred.

"Too much ether for you during surgery, Henry," chuckled Andrew Murray, pointing gently at the martini after noticing the sweep, the spill and the slur, interrupting his weather conversation with William Harker, who in turn threw a wink of love toward Cynthia, who winked back at her husband.

"And ether is the last thing that Seward would need," followed Holmwood, who, once he began a topic, let it go as easily as a bulldog a bone, "Henry Seward could dress a war wound faster than any of you ladies could wrap a Christmas gift. Remember the time that Stears, God rest his soul, had taken a ball in the stomach and staggered over to us with his intestines hanging out like tripe at the butcher shop—"

"Steady, Arthur," frowned William, gesturing toward the wives. "We talked about leaving the field-of-battle stories back in the field."

"—and Stears' actions as man and soldier," followed Andrew with an annoyed look, "do not warrant nostalgia."

"I, for one," continued Lord Godalming with a wave of his cane and another deep puff of cigar, "have gone on the record that I do not regret a moment of my endeavors with the light infantry, and neither should any of you."

Arthur's words hung among them like a hung corpse at the crossroads. The men all gave Holmwood a look which meant *stop talking*.

"I for one," announced Ursula, mimicking Arthur Senior, "would like to know what said endeavors in the field of battle were—" to everyone's collective yet uncomfortable chuckle. "Might I have some more *champagne* served to you in an effort to let you loosen your conversational purse strings?"

Arthur merely arched a friendly eyebrow, sighed conspiratorially and covered his glass in mock fear when Ursula gestured for one of the servants, ever on the ready, to refresh Arthur's drink.

Abraham had just uttered the word 'vetala[148]' to the younger generation, who sat collectively entranced with his storytelling.

"Good luck, Ursula," said Judith Murray after a sip of her apple wine. "At the mere mention of the war, our husbands' mouths always shut faster than clams with the tide." She shot Andrew a sideways look. Andrew, no novice to the marriage game, pointedly and comedically locked his eyes out past the windows to the rumbling storm.

"What a lovely evening!" he announced, to the guffaws of the older men and the annoyed silence from the women.

Judith playfully slapped Andrew's leg and said, "In all the years we've been married, I've never been able to pry a single mention of his time in Crimea."

Cynthia Harker had already given William a look that made him want to melt into the fabric of his couch, "Regardless, talking about it might let them sleep easier. At least my William."

"I agree," said Victoria, floating the iceberg of tension out among them again. "They should share. The children are entertained at the moment. Would any of you care to at least give us a single memory of your collective lives during that extraordinary experience?"

The women then just sat there, waiting through solemn, weighted moments for any of the men to venture forth with anything that might resemble an attempt to communicate about anything, good, bad or indifferent, that they had lived through during their soldiering days, but Andrew's comedic stare out the window had made its point among the men and had taken effect. The marble column that was Arthur Holmwood just stood there near the hearth, yet at the periphery of the conversation between Abraham and the children, a silly grin splitting his beard but nothing but cigar smoke chimneying its way out of his mouth. He took a long, languid puff and winked at his beloved to say *you'll get nothing from me, Ursula.*

"Of course," groused Ursula bitterly after the wink, encapsulating the wives' collective feelings. "Typical."

The men chuckled uncomfortably.

The women did not.

"I think," began Andrew in a rather dramatic fashion, giving the impression he was going to put forth a topic about the war, and the wives instantly leaned forward, even Ursula Holmwood, so eager was she to hear any of the men in the family broach a topic that up until now had been considered taboo. But instead, and after his long, dramatic pause, Andrew Murray arched a comedic eyebrow and pointed at the grand French doors and exclaimed, "the door handles here are different than the handles in Henry's dining room? Do you agree, William?"

The husbands began to collectively beam in conspiratorial satisfaction, while the wives instantly sat back, simmering in frustration. Andrew Murray received a deserved pinch from Judith, even as William Harker raised both eyebrows in a facial expression worthy of a theater actor, and nodded his head vehemently as he said, "My good chap! You are quite right! Henry, had you noticed these new door handles on Arthur's beloved French doors? Finally, we can put aside the rumor that the Holmwood and Seward dining rooms are blasphemous mirrors of one another!"

"My dining room floors are wood, Arthur's here are stone," laughed Henry, glad to be off the previous subject. "And my rafters are exposed, while there is a ceiling in this room."

That was all that Henry would say in order to change the subject, and they all sat there, the women taking advantage of the quiet tension that happens when the conversation lags, or in this case, when one group is trying to pry secrets from another. The wives hoped that the silence would cajole any of the husbands to at last speak.

---

[148] *Vetala* is the Indian word for vampire, from Hindu mythology.

But the men just sat there, closed crypts all.

Nothing.

Silence.

"A pox on you all," sniffed an irritated Cynthia Harker at the men, which drew agreeing nods from all the wives.

Meanwhile, the servants were almost finished adding to the table a centerpiece of beautiful candles that danced a flickering romance in the room, warming hearth, heart and home, a lovely counterpoint to the tempest outside.

"But enough about *vetalas* and whatnot, how are all of you? No Jonny yet?" said Abraham, pivoting and looked around the gathering. "At least that is what Ian tells me."

"He's away on business, along with Uncle Peter," said Mina with a finger's pinch of worry. "We're expecting him at any moment."

"I should hope he would be here for his own wedding," chuckled Van Helsing at Mina, to reassure her. He succeeded. Then he shot a sly grin at Quincy, Arthur and Ian. "He's not at the Slaughtered Lamb, is he boys? Sipping lemonade like the rest of you?"

Quincy greeted Van Helsing's wit with a hearty American guffaw.

Fathers smiled.

Mothers did not.

"Goodness no," said Lucy as she beamed at Abraham, happy he was back, "he's with Uncle Peter in the Orient."

"Peter's a good traveler, they'll be fine," said Abraham with a grin that was meant to further ease Mina's concerns, which it did, but the thought of Peter in the Orient slid a frigid sickle of memory through Van Helsing's mind. *It's just me*, he thought, looking at the elder men. *Being around them. It brings the memories out of me.*

Of what we did.

A dark cloud of worry rippled over Van Helsing, only to be suppressed after the briefest of exposures. Abraham didn't look at Mina, who would read his glance like a homily on Sunday.

"Dinner is served," announced Quigley. "Quite a row out there."

TWENTY-FIVE

Below the *Demeter* grew the mother of all waves, forming out of the black, frothing waters like nature itself wanted to rip the freighter to pieces, to keep it from its mission. Inside the bridge, Mueller felt that power surging under his vessel. Knowing the sea as he did for all of these years, he understood when an undercurrent was set to tear a ship apart or shoot it halfway around the world on a whim of the seas, and his laugh crescendoed into triumphant hysterics. Next to him, Primus held on to a railing, his decrepit bones clattering against his ancient armor. He had seen countless ships sink with everyone or no one to tell the tale. A wry, dark chuckle floated out of the skeleton as he waited for either situation to occur, knowing he would survive regardless. It was as if Poseidon himself had decided to rid his seas of the vile countenance that the *Demeter* carried, and the ocean wanted to cast aside this daemonic cargo.

The wind and the rain pummeled the ship as it began to rise, pushed heavenward by the biblical, apocalyptic wave. A scattering of seabirds skimmed over the deck, on their way in to the sea cliffs, their collective shelter against the pounding storm. The ship groaned in agony from its beams to its hull. The scene was like a Doré etching, with distant lightning and cloud and light and dark combining in the background to silhouette the black, monstrous wave as it picked up the relatively tiny *Demeter*, darkened save for the single lit lamp on the ship's bridge, open like a hypnotized eye. Moans from the beams, from port to starboard, filled the freighter as it was slowly spun by the wave, until it was no longer perpendicular to the coast, but parallel to it. Inside the eye, Mueller stopped screaming and watched the rocky shoreline pivot away from the nose of the ship.

Then, a few things happened simultaneously. The horrid infantry of vermin poured by the thousands over the edge of the *Demeter* and into the frothing sea, and the ship itself was hurtled away from the storm, away from the sea, away from everything save its destination and the fate of its inhabitants. The *Demeter* gave one, long, final groan, from stem to stern, which terrified everything and everyone in the ship as it was shot toward the craggy shore.

All save one, in a black, bleak coffin below deck.

TWENTY-SIX

"Little brother Abraham, please continue your tales of deed and danger!" thundered Lord Godalming after they had all been seated and he had taken in a large spoonful of warm turtle soup. "Did you sail down that God-damned canal[149] in the Holy Land?" Arthur Senior turned to one of the servants and said, "Bloody Hell, Smythe! This soup is your finest moment!"

"Why, thank you, My Lord," was all Smythe could answer as he took the empty serving bowl away from the table and toward the kitchen door. Smythe, like Quigley and the other members of the serving staff were accustomed to Arthur's thundering compliments and admonitions. Arthur Holmwood Senior thundered on because that was his way, his monumental banter the impetus to the many warm, rollicking conversations that were had when the friends and families were together. Young Arthur, who had chosen to sit across from Lucy at mid-table rather than at his accustomed seat across from his mother and next to his father at the head of the table, had long since grown accustomed to his father's bellowings, yet no one reveled more in skewering Lord Godalming than Lord Godalming himself. He was like a massive puppy that craved attention in any form, whether compliment or criticism. Once Jonathan Harker had famously said at a Christmas gathering, "If I ever die before Uncle Arthur, he'll just shout at me during the burial and make me jump out of the casket out of sheer fright!"

"I did sail upon the canal, Arthur," replied Abraham, enjoying his soup. "Though I have never become quite accustomed to the humidity throughout the region. Yet one has a job to do, and we found some fine relics. I am happy that I was able to receive an invitation to this wedding, though I don't know how you found me."

"I telephoned your office at the British Museum[150] to inquire as to where to send you an invitation in great haste," followed Cynthia Harker, who sat next to Ursula, who in turn sat next to Arthur, who sprawled out languidly at the end of the table.

"Yes," said Abraham, "and I knew I was dealing with the capable Cynthia Harker when I received both the invitation and a telegram."

Andrew Murray, no stranger to dry humor, sighed, "What's all this about a wedding?"

Judith laughed and playfully slapped at Andrew's shoulder, secretly grateful that her husband was trying to steer the conversation away from the actual wedding. Mina saw this subtle loyalty from her father and appreciated it, nearly as much as she did the soup, which was as Lord Godalming rambled, delicious.

"Uncle Andrew," began Quincy after he had inhaled the soup like it was vapor, "You're my favorite uncle 'cuz I can't get in trouble for what I say as long as you're around!"

"Goddammit Quincy you are right!"

"Uncle Andrew!" scolded Lucy from the younger end of the table, trying to keep pace with the

---

[149] Arthur is referring to the Suez Canal, a waterway created in Egypt in 1869, connecting the Mediterranean and Red seas. There were canals in the region before, including the remains of a canal discovered by Napoleon Bonaparte in 1799.
[150] London's Museum of Natural History was referred to as the British Museum for many years after it opened in 1881.

speed of the conversation.

"—I do not consider weddings to be frivolous," said Abraham as he pointed a soft, kind nod at Mina, who nodded back in happiness.

Martine Van Helsing, thought the women at the table.

The Lord Godalming pounded on, like a train with no brakes, somehow *louder* than before. "I merely wanted to be updated as to the wanderings, cataloging and general goings-on of the current *wunderkind* of archeological society, our indomitable Abraham Van Helsing!" he turned to Mina and shouted, "—and of course Mina knows her uncle Arthur is a melancholy blowhard—"

"—on that we can all readily agree!" said a sly Andrew Murray as he finished his soup, which drew a quick cackle from Ursula, who loved her husband but might have enjoyed these verbal jousts even more than he did.

"I second the motion," nodded William Harker, followed by a cascade of laughter from the rest of the table.

Arthur feigned injury and sent a wounded squint toward the younger generation, which was the wrong thing to do. "I am injured by this youthful mutiny—"

"—Uncle Arthur," said Ian, placing his spoon in his empty soup bowl, "It is impossible to hurt you."

"My son, one must first have feelings to have them hurt," sang Henry Seward, surgical in his timing.

Judith Murray and Cynthia Harker exploded in simultaneous, parallel giggles, which were absorbed by Arthur Senior's and Junior's explosive rolls of laughter.

When the laughter quieted, Quincy spoke up, "Well, I wanna hear more of what Uncle Abraham has been up to."

"On that we agree," interjected Arthur Senior, trying to rein in the conversation. "I've always been an outspoken advocate of archeological—"

A collective sarcastic yet loving groan came from the table, anticipating more of Arthur's endless pontificating.

"—and zoological expeditions throughout the world!"

"I love you, Father," shouted young Arthur with a laugh, "but do kindly shut up!"

An explosion of applause erupted from the table, even the servants laughed as they brought in more dinner rolls and butter to compliment the soup.

"Clearly nothing has changed since I last left you all," laughed Van Helsing, reacting nonchalantly as he buttered a dinner roll while avoiding the gaze of Victoria Westenra, who had been trying to rub her calf against his shin for the past few minutes. She took in Abraham with a mixture of attraction and frustration at trying to get his attention above and below the table. Whatever love Abraham had, it belonged to the souls of Martine and Claire, his stillborn daughter. Abraham might have been a widower to the world, but in his mind and heart he was still a married man, a family man.

William Harker, master of parrying conversations in new directions, leapt into the fray with, "The zephyrs and gales of Lord Arthur aside, I do hope your work has been fruitful for you, Abraham—" to a round of words of agreement and encouragement from the others. 'Lord Arthur' had always been William Harker's teasing response to Abraham's anointing of young Arthur as King Arthur, all four men enjoyed the teasing in a good-natured way, and the terms had spread to the rest of the family, with either of the Holmwoods being referred to by their nicknames at any given moment.

"Aunt Victoria is constantly alerting us to articles about your expeditions in The *Times* of course," said Mina, down and across the table from Abraham. Mina, along with everyone else, had long-since sensed Victoria's fancying of Van Helsing, and delighted in teasing her uncle about it. He found Mina's teasing with regard to Victoria to be not a laughing matter, yet permitted her to continue, doting uncle that he was.

"I prefer the *Whitby Gazette*," said Henry Seward as he was served some roast pork with potatoes. "No need for news of further congestion in London or more foreigners coming across our borders."

"Of course you would, Dear," snipped Lillian Seward after a sideways glance at her husband.

Victoria knew that Mina's teasing of Abraham had its roots in herself, as did most of the table around them, but the respect was so high for Abraham that it was left right there for everyone to notice, but never to be acted upon.

"That's very kind of you," said Van Helsing, at last looking to and nodding at Victoria in appreciation while continuing his meal. Victoria bobbed her pointed chin right back at Abraham, satisfied that she had finally earned his attention.

He continued, "And thanks to you all for your kind words and interest. As a matter of fact, before Egypt, I was in the Cuzco region of Peru seeking a long-lost Incan city[151]. Our search was fruitless. Perhaps this was all rooted in Conquistador legend in the end, yet afterward I ended up being set upon by a school of these ferocious man-eating fish[152] in one of the tributaries of the Amazon. They are tiny, but have teeth like sharks, and when they travel in large groups, will chew anything down to the bones in seconds. My boat had been cleaved in two by a falling tree and I was desperately trying to make it to shore.

"Good God, man," gasped Holmwood. "What did you do?"

Abraham had a gleam in his eye as he sipped from his refreshed malt beer and said, "I ended up throwing petrol onto the surface of the water, then igniting it to keep them from me as I rowed my way to the edge of the river."

---

[151] Abraham is referring to the ruins of Machu Picchu, an abandoned Incan city in the Andes Mountains. Built in the 15th century, the site was ultimately found by American Hiram Bingham in 1911.

[152] Piranha are freshwater fish that inhabit the rivers of South America.

TWENTY-SEVEN

The starboard side of the *Demeter* slammed against the jagged, worn, ancient cliffside that was the eastern coast of England in a collision that should have been felt on the other side of the world. Seawater frothed up along the hull and surged over the deck, which threatened to crumble to pieces at any moment. The ship moaned a long, singular, colossal death wail, and a half-dozen holes were torn, punctured or split open along the hull. Seabirds that had nestled along the sea cliffs for the night scattered over the ship to try and find a place that did not now reek of engine oil or ancient evil. As the minutes passed, wave after wave pounded the *Demeter*, and if rain could erode continents and mountain ranges, then a single ship was no match. It began to come apart under the pounding, relentless waves. In the midst of all this, the rain had halted.

Night had opened its singular eye over everything.

Four huge bats flew out of the bridge, between the beat of the waves. Three of them carried a flailing, untethered Captain Harald Mueller with their clawed feet as they soared through the fog that had rolled in like Judgement Day after the four horsemen. Flapping vigorously to gain altitude, they soared toward a jagged, flat-on-the-top protrusion overlooking the sea. While this was happening, hundreds of skeletons and thousands of rats had poured out of the ship's corpse and were climbing along the cliff's walls, with a small crew of skeletons carrying the coffins up the rocks like tiny ants carrying huge leaves and twigs up along a vast, Amazonian tree.

Primus ascended the rocks, his fingerbone tips scratching against the exposed strata like fingernails on a chalkboard, but he did not follow the other skeletons or the rat horde up to the cliff tops and firmer land. The skeleton had looped a sack around his armored shoulder and was making his way by hand up to the outcropping above him, where the four bats were about to land.

Mueller was thrown onto the jutting ledge by the bats, where he landed, wet, cold and terrified beyond all sane thought. The vampires then clung gracefully to the sides of the ledge and climbed up to the top as they began to transform back into the feminine forms of Petra, Andromeda and Venus. The ledge sat about halfway between the frothing storm waters and the top of the seacliffs and the surrounding English countryside just north of Whitby. The biggest, darkest bat then found footing against the seacliff wall and Mueller shivered as fur became skin and cloth, animal took human form. Dracula of Transylvania stood before him, tearing Harald apart with his gaze like an eagle tearing a dove.

Primus reached them and immediately took some rope out of the sack and began to lash Mueller to the rocks. The captain resisted, but a brutal, skeletal elbow to the gut silenced him, and the ancient Roman tied Harald's wrists and ankles to the weathered sea rocks. The rain somehow paused, and the wind noticed this and hesitated.

Then, the moment arrived.

Clouds parted.

The moon glinted its smile.

As did Dracula, without a ripple of mercy inside him.

Primus had begun to light small, strange, obscene candles that he had taken out of the sack, placing them at the base of each foot, each hand and above the area where Captain Mueller's head rested.

The horror of this purpose dawned over Harald Mueller's face.

He was about to become a human sacrifice.

Dracula reached into the multitude of rats slithering up the rocks away from the ruins of the *Demeter* below. He ripped one of the rats from the torrent of writhing vermin and in one motion ripped the rat's head off completely. Blood spouted from the animal's headless body, and Dracula let the blood of the rat drip all over the body of Captain Mueller.

"Patri Satanus," growled Dracula with a tender smile over his face as he crouched over Mueller, "suscipe benedictionem hanc inferiis homines immolabant—" *Father Satan, accept this human sacrifice—*

"You swore the oath of a noblemen!" screamed Mueller, out of his mind with grief and pain but thinking of his family, all at home right now, his children being tucked away by his loving wife. "My wife! My children! You gave your royal word—"

"Surely you know, Captain," said Dracula as his fiendish grin widened, "history tells us that all royals are born liars?"

Petra, Andromeda and Venus, anticipating the feast, had crouched down to all fours, still in human form, and each was creeping forward along the rocks, Petra to Harald's neck, while the other two neared his wrists. Their eyes glowed, ravenous she-leopards in the moonlight.

"You are not invulnerable!" screamed Mueller. "There's too much good in the world for you to survive! Someone will kill you—"

"I *am* dead," whispered Dracula as his clawed right hand shot out and knifed through Harald's chest cavity while Venus, Andromeda and Petra savagely tore into Mueller's neck and wrists, feeding like lionesses on the Serengeti. Primus stood impassively while Mueller struggled, gurgled and cried louder than the waves crashing around them. With Petra's head buried in his neck, Mueller wailed, cried, and called out his wife and children's names as Dracula ripped out his heart, raised it above his head like a beating, crimson wineskin and poured Mueller's blood down into his throat.

The sky darkened again, as if Hell itself was on the way.

A zephyr swept up.

All the candles were blown out at once.

Dracula of Transylvania had arrived in England.

TWENTY-EIGHT

Ting, ting, ting, sang Lord Godalming's glass as his fork rapped against it. Arthur stood in the majestic, melodramatic way he always did, and everyone's attention gravitated to him. "I'd like to make a small announcement—"

"Yes, My Lord," laughed Abraham, "Your pants are undone, we know that, now would you kindly sit down?"

Everyone roared, even the servants that were bringing in the cake, coffee and preserved fruit. Arthur's laugh bellowed at Van Helsing's quip, even louder than did everyone else. He then dutifully stood at attention and gave Abraham a deep, chivalrous bow, to the thundering applause at everyone in the room.

Lord Godalming started to speak, then held his breath as he slyly and comedically checked the front of his pants with his cane to see if any of his buttons had indeed become undone as he threw Abraham a humorous dirty look. Lillian nearly snorted up her serving of coffee, so deep was her laughter, and the applause, which had abated, now soared, renewed. Arthur Senior stood there, one eyebrow majestically in the air to signify his complicity with the humor until the applause passed. He cleared his throat, then said, "Now that we have experienced the sundry juvenilia of our evening's entertainment, we have an informal announcement to make, and to do this, I give the floor over to my dear wife."

He turned to Ursula and said, "Beloved?"

Ursula stood, her eyebrows arched in comedic complicity with Arthur, then playfully slapped his shoulder before turning to the others and saying, "We'd like to explain to our loved ones something that has been decided upon, though we are not quite ready to announce this publicly—"

With this, Lucy, Victoria and Arthur stood up and began walking toward Ursula at the head of the table. Mina sat there, curiosity flowing through her, only to be overwhelmed by a dawning realization that their movements had been rehearsed.

"—but to you, our family, we'd like to announce the engagement of our son Arthur to Lucy Westenra."

Everyone was stunned, then stood with a round of applause that dwarfed the round just given to the Van Helsing/Holmwood comedic duo.

Lucy pulled a ribbon from her hair and gave it to Arthur, along with a sweet, simple kiss, which the future Lord Godalming took in with a beaming, satisfied smile.

Arthur took a beautiful, elegant engagement ring that sparkled with the love between them and slipped it onto Lucy Westenra's ring finger.

TWENTY-NINE

Dracula savored a long, gulping drink from the wineskin that was Mueller's heart, blood overflowing his canine-lined mouth, down his jaws and neck, a truly horrible sight. He blinked as he drank, incandescent eyes turning off and on as he did so, like a vulture. Petra, Andromeda and Venus voraciously sucked, ripped and swallowed blood, meat and bone from the dying man, turning his neck anatomy into frayed skin and flesh in seconds. And as he sputtered to his death, Harald locked eyes with Dracula, who bored a hole through Mueller's head with his glare as he hissed, "Go to your 'maker' knowing that I will find your wife and children to eat them *alive.*"

Satiated, the vampiresses stopped drinking and ripping the musculature off the carcass and looked up, their lower jaws covered in crimson, their eyes glowing in the night like horrific, eerie owls' eyes, their beautiful, haunting clothes fluttering in the zephyrs. The winds had whipped up around the vampires on the jagged cliff, with the *Demeter* moaning while being pounded to bits by the relentless surf below them, and skeletons and rats swarming over the cliffs above the crumbling metal hulk.

The moon had hidden behind a glowering bank of clouds, ashamed.

Without a word, Dracula threw Mueller's ragged, empty heart out into the night, the froth, and the depths. He then cleaned the blood from his fingers with his lips and tongue as Petra picked up Mueller's still-convulsing corpse by the neck and threw it down among the clashing waves and rocks.

Dracula sighed and said, "Concubines, be certain that—"

Then his eyes went wide open with sudden shock.

The vampire staggered, silent.

Waves churned, the ship moaned and the gusts howled.

Watching Mueller's corpse being consumed by the waves, the vampiresses realized the silence and turned back around when Dracula did not finish his thought.

From above, with a vicious trajectory, an arrow had shot out of the night and had thrust itself into the base of Dracula's neck. Shocked and surprised, the vampire staggered, then roared like a wounded lion as a second arrow followed the first and plowed between his shoulder and neck. Blood spewed and hissed from the wounds and over Dracula's black clothes. The vampire staggered again but stood tall and looked up in the direction of this sudden, brutal attack.

Soaring down through the gloom like four birds of prey diving toward their next meal, were four black shrouds, the four *nosferatu* from the carriage traveling from Paris, bolting down through the night and toward their intended target: Dracula of Transylvania.

The four shadows dropped like stones.

The air changed from that of blasphemies ceremony to that of a pitched battle from one moment to the next.

Within the flutters of the mid-air shrouds, a bow was drawn.

From the flowing, mingling folds, a third arrow hissed viciously down at Dracula, their intended target of assassination.

The son of Satan, no stranger to attempts on his 'life', stepped aside in a blur and caught the arrow in mid-flight with his right fist. Dracula smiled wryly even as he stumbled, respecting the boldness of the attack despite the two arrows still buried deeply into his upper torso. The smile melted as shock bled all over his face while blood billowed out over his dark-as-pitch clothes.

Venus, Petra and Andromeda, mouths covered with blood and bits of flesh, bolted straight up in alarm, then shot into the air to intercept the shrouds. Petra's leap took her from human form to bat in an instant as she ascended, swiping at the most massive shroud with the clawed fingertips of her left wing. But the shroud was as deft and quick as he was powerful and fearsome. He avoided her blow, swirling around the Petra bat and plummeting down toward the wounded Transylvanian.

The smallest of the shrouds screamed, "Держите меня в, Господи Сатане, от руках этих грешников!" *Keep me, Lord Satan, from the hands of these sinners!* as she pulled another arrow from the quiver strapped to her body and nocked it into her bow. But before she could let the arrow loose, Andromeda, still in human form, knifed up through the air and tackled the shroud in mid-fall.

"Bizim despotun bize kurtulun!" *Rid us of our oppressor!* Shouted the gangly male shroud, as it turned into a disgusting albino bat and clawed at Venus, who had become her formidable bat form as she soared to attack him. The two forms collided in mid air and engaged in a vicious dogfight, both clawing and tearing at each other with their canines and clawed feet while their wings flapped ferociously in the air, each trying to gain the upper hand while attempting to rip one another's throats out.

The Petra bat, having missed the huge male shroud, twisted around and tore into the fourth shroud, a lithe female, who shouted, "Zerquetschen ihn! Kreuzige ihn!" *Crush him! Crucify him!* as she turned into a thin, tall bat with a pale gray tinge to her fur. The Petra bat caught the lithe shroud bat by the back of the neck as she fell past her, and the two bats plummeted down toward the carnage-stained ledge below.

As the massive shroud hurtled down at Dracula of Transylvania at great speed, the cowl on the shroud flew back to reveal a fearsome young male vampire. His eyes were tiny, his face and canines huge, and he roared like a bear. His clawed arms reached out, anticipating a high-speed collision with the wounded vampire. He anticipated the Transylvanian taking another step aside, as he had when avoiding the arrow, and grinned as he braced for impact.

Dracula simply looked up, the dawning realization that he had nowhere to go all over his face, like the blood that was spreading all over his clothes.

Then came the collision.

And the unexpected.

Dracula was gone.

His body had exploded, violently, with the impact.

Into many small, dark, shiny pieces.

Small pieces.

Small bats.

Bats.

Tiny obsidian bats...

...which shot out in every direction, an explosion of fur, bone and flesh.

Vampiric flesh.

Like perverse sparks from the impact of an anvil, the tiny bats spewed and twisted out in every direction, surprising and stunning the young vampiric behemoth, who fell down past where Dracula had been a moment ago and crashed on the ground in a stunned, wounded heap, shocked at not having crushed his target beneath him.

The arrows that had pierced Dracula clattered as they fell against the cold sea rock.

"No!" roared the huge vampire shroud, swiping at the obsidian sparks with his huge arms. "Il devait être le nôtre!" *He was to be ours!*

As violently and as quickly as the huge, shrouded vampire had landed, the black sparks around him fluttered back toward each other, like dirt to an invisible magnet, coalescing around the crouching behemoth vampire's neck to re-form Dracula's body, head, arms and hands. A bat's head formed into the right hand of Dracula, planting itself on the chin of the vampire, while the left hand formed around the back of the shroud's neck. With a lone, ferocious twist, Dracula wrenched the head around with a sharp, dry crack. The huge, young vampire's face echoed stunned shock, looking back at Dracula *even though his body was facing the other direction.* It was a stunning turn of events.

Feigning sadness, Dracula nodded, "Vale in patri armis, iuventutis Halim." *Fare thee well in my father's arms, young Halim.*

Halim's mouth was wide open, in a silent, mammoth scream of agony and failure.

Dracula reached out for one of the fallen arrows. It obeyed and flew of its own accord into the Transylvanian's hand. Dracula savagely sank the arrow through the big vampire's jugular, the tip bursting out from the other side of the neck. Blood followed. The vampiric assassin stared in silence at Dracula as he died, and the son of Satan only said, "'Et omnes hii in supplicium aeternum.'" *Then they all go away to eternal punishment.*[153]

Halim the assassin could only gaze up at Dracula and the night with complete shock, both looming over him as he began to disintegrate, skin and flesh to ash and dust. Such was Halim's agony at failure that even as he died, he began to cry. The tears in the big vampire bled into his ashen cheeks as he fell backwards, rather forward, and when he hit the ground, he crumbled apart as softy as cool embers after a forest fire. A few sparks and scattered plumes of smoke were all that remained. Ribs, femurs and a skull, all made out of a hardened ash, poured out onto the rock and began to be whisked away by the breeze and whim of the sea.

Watching it all, morbidly delighted, his face a focused mask of triumph, was the son of Satan.

"Contra id quod possit legisse, est Italici erat iniuriam," chuckled Dracula to the memory of Halim as he turned away. "Non est nonus circulus, vel alio modo ut paradiso. Non est nisi Inferno." *Contrary to what you may have read, the Italian[154] was wrong. There is no Ninth Circle, or any way out to Paradise. There is only Hell.*

Landing in front of him, against the sea cliffs, were Andromeda, Venus and Petra. Each of them held a struggling, captured shroud, forcing them into a kneeling position in front of the shadow from the Carpathians. The shrouds hung their heads in abject failure, for they had had the moment and the opportunity, and in seconds it was gone as surely as Halim's ashes were scattering across the frothing seas and the disassembling *Demeter* below.

Venus blinked at Dracula, deeply impressed, and in total fear.

"Non ho mai visto alcuno di noi trasformare in quel modo," she whispered, referring to his metamorphosis into small bats. *I have never seen any of us transform in that manner.*

It was a whisper filled with awe.

"I am the son of Satan," hissed Dracula. "I do as I will."

---

[153] Dracula is using Matthew 25:46 to mock Halim. "Then they will go away to eternal punishment, but the righteous to eternal life."

[154] Dante Alighieri 1265-1321, one of the most famous poets in history, an Italian whose most famous work, *The Divine Comedy*, describes Heaven and Hell in great detail.

THIRTY

Abraham Van Helsing's problem was that he was always thinking. Even as he watched young Arthur Holmwood stand, Abraham had already recounted the windows of the room they were in, and as he counted them he made a mental note to re-check the Whitby cemetery graves, as was his habit every time he returned from abroad. He glanced at all of the door handles and locks for the expansive French windows that opened up into the darkness and rain outside, making yet another mental note to check them again after the servants had turned in. He had an itch to place garlic and/or crucifixes at the doors, but resisted the urge to do so, given the row it would cause with the Lord Godalming. The staffs of each of the families had learned a long time ago that these sorts of eccentricities were Abraham's habit, and Arthur Holmwood Senior had quietly instructed his own servants that very evening to 'let the adventurer do as he pleased' with his sometimes-strange manners and customs. Years ago, Abraham had concluded that the time for raising a family had passed him by and that he would live out his life alone, yet he was at peace with this because he simply could never see himself with anyone else but his wife, and though he never met Claire, he always felt that his daughter was irreplaceable.

As he stirred milk into his freshly served coffee and watched the dynamic of the room sway from the elder Holmwoods to King Arthur and Lucy Westenra, Van Helsing reminded himself to borrow that antiquated book of Eastern European folklore from the young writer Blackwood[155] he'd met in London a while back, and to also try and meet with that Gérôme [156] fellow who had been painting all of those wonderful scenes set in Jerusalem. Abraham's professorship at the University of London[157], where he had earned his doctorate and had taught Archeology and History for years now, along with his association with the recently founded British Museum[158] had opened many social doors to Van Helsing. Henry Seward and the Lord Godalming had both attempted to sway Van Helsing into attending their own universities, Oxford and Cambridge, respectively, but in the end, Abraham had chosen to go in his own direction. As a result of his relationships with both the university and the museum, Abraham's thirst for knowledge seldom went unquenched.

Van Helsing was always in an uncomfortable middle position in the 'family,' too young for the elders yet too old for the younger generation, so as a consequence he never felt like he fit into either group of dear friends completely, though he did always feel loved. Occasions like this were even more cumbersome for him, firstly because he was more accustomed to the company of mummies and ruins than attendees of social teas, but also because the two age groups broke so decisively into the two factions, leaving him stiffly sitting alone and becoming the object of pity or gossip for all involved. His solitude was always noticed and was often followed by the customary scout sent at

---

[155] Algernon Blackwood (1869-1951) was an English writer of supernatural short stories, in particular "the Willows" and "The Wendigo."
[156] Jean-Léon Gérôme (1824-1904) was a French artist whose depictions of the Holy Land and Greek mythology became incredibly influential.
[157] The University of London was founded in 1836.
[158] The British museum of Natural History was founded in 1881 and was often simply referred to as The British Museum.

the behest of the others to either see how he has been feeling, why he is sitting all alone, or worst, to pry into a subject of disagreement between the two parties. *No*, he thought, what was even worse was when they would, in the hope of 'making him feel better,' bring up subjects in his past that were uncomfortable for him, much less to discuss with someone else. Of course, there were occasions where he ended up sitting, by sheer conspiratorial coincidence, next to a lovely woman he barely knew at one of the larger social events, when the god-awful mainstream of Whitby society was involved, and he would politely converse with the lady in question and sidestep Arthur's subsequent blusterous, blundering but well-intentioned queries as to why he had not pursued said widow, old maid, spinster or social harlot.

Then there was the time that the male elders had crossed the line with him. They all had formed a manly cabal and arranged for a 'lady of the evening' to call on him one night at his London flat, 'courtesy of the fellow members of your regiment.' This had led to quite a row with his comrades in arms and in life, nearly to blows with Arthur, and though their falling out was brief, they never quite understood why Van Helsing had chosen to leave his 'gift' unopened. Harker and Murray had to stop him from separating Arthur from his jaw when Holmwood questioned his manhood, yet the steady stream of flirtatious widows and heiresses had quieted any questions about the charm he had upon the opposite sex. He was a desired man, but he desired only to be alone. He privately and quietly felt that his wife and his daughter, such as they were, would be all that he would ever need, and that the wives of his friends and their daughters were all the female company that he would require. One brief word to the wives during a subsequent gathering was enough to have the subject of an evening gift never to come up again.

Abraham's mother was the English daughter of a wealthy railroad and shipbuilding magnate, while his father was the son of a middle-class Dutch family of educators, and since his mother's family had all the money, he grew up in England, with his father teaching primary education. Abraham grew up seeing his father chafe at the trappings of wealth and they grew very close, and while his mother's side of the family never spoke an ill word about his father, Abraham, because he noticed everything even back then, began to prefer tinkering with mineral samples or plant specimens that his father and he would collect in their 'scientific expeditions' through the English countryside of Abraham Van Helsing's youth. As he became a young man, Van Helsing yearned to know what could be found on the other side of the hill, the country and the world, and encountered all of that all too well with his friends during their military service. After the passing of Martine and Claire, the teacher that was Abraham took to tutoring the children of his friends, in many different ways. Abraham and Quincy, even in the Texan's youth, always bonded over the subject of firearms, while Arthur and Ian always were keen to talk about advances in the sciences. Lucy had turned out to be quite the competitive spirit, and she and Abraham had many fierce duels over the chessboard, to the point where Lucy would not speak to Abraham for a day or two if her loss was particularly bitter. And Andrew Murray appreciated Abraham lending his books of travel to his young Mina. It was a tender moment in all their lives when Abraham's father retired and Mina took on his old class. Mina's qualifications were beyond question, even to those few who objected to the idea of a female instructor. As time had gone by, Abraham's stature at the museum and the university had grown to the point where he could start to form his own expeditions instead of following other explorers around like David Livingstone[159] and Heinrich Schliemann[160]. Even during the war in Crimea, he

---

[159] David Livingstone (1813-1873) was a Scottish explorer and missionary. He explored Africa extensively and was one of the more significant figures in Victorian era culture.
[160] Heinrich Schliemann (1822-1890) was a German businessman and a significant figure in archeology because he basically used a copy of Homer's *Iliad* to find the actual site of Troy.

was one of the waifs of the regiment, and treated so back then by Harker, Murray, Holmwood and Seward. Even Archibald Swayles, the working-class man who would end up working for Henry Seward, and Renfield, who was only a year older than Abraham, treated young Van Helsing like he was closer to wearing a cloth diaper than to carrying a weapon.

Abraham watched Arthur Holmwood Junior, still at the head of the table with the others, turn to Ian Seward and say, "The only way this wedding is going to come off as planned is if the best man at this table agrees to be my Best Man."

Young Arthur pointed to a stunned Ian Seward and beckoned him forward.

The room went quiet as a church wrapped in the arms of dawn. Ursula Holmwood nearly burst into tears, but the silly, titanic Arthur Senior beat her to it. Arthur Junior clamped his hand on his father's broad shoulder, steadying the Victorian mammoth, who began to weep openly. King Arthur slipped his arm around his mother's waist and patted her on the back. Ursula was much more reliable under these circumstances than her husband, who lacked the steadfast British composure but made up for it by being a force of nature.

"My boy," blubbered Lord Godalming, wiping his eyes, "My young man."

Ian Seward, deeply touched, nodded in acceptance, stood up straight and walked around to the head of the table. With more nobility than anyone had ever given him credit for, Ian Seward happily shook young King Arthur's hand, and said, "It would be my pleasure to be the *second*-best man at this wedding."

"Goddammit Ian," said Quincy through streaming tears, "you've gone ahead and made this Texan cry."

Ian held in his emotions as he raised his drink, his lemonade, and as he did he saw Abraham tease him by raising his now-empty glass of beer. Ian laughed at Van Helsing's fun and gathered himself. He had lost the woman he had dreamt of since childhood, everyone in the room knew it, and yet he wanted happiness for all of them.

"If I may do so in your house, My Lord," Ian said to Arthur Senior, who reveled in being called Lord, "I propose a toast to the bride and groom, the future Mr. and Mrs. Arthur Holmwood!"

Lillian and Henry Seward led the round of applause and cheers. The room was a hearth of good will and love. Even Mina, who knew not her future and fate because of the decision she'd secretly come to, could only applaud in genuine good cheer for her friends. Judith Murray shot her a reassuring glance as she applauded, and Mina could feel her father's eyes on her as well. *We're with you, regardless*, Judith's eyes said, even as other faces at the table looked her way. Lucy's eyes found Mina's, and they were full of apology. *I'm sorry*, they said to her.

"We shall have a double wedding!" bellowed the Lord Godalming with raised arms, to a collective groan from the others.

"You're just trying to have poor Murray pay for the whole thing!" shouted Abraham, to more peals of laughter, complete with a snort from Victoria Westenra, who was quite enjoying her absinthe.

When the cheers managed to wither, Mina tossed a sly look at Morris and said, "Quincy, save your crocodile tears for the bachelor party—"

"—at the Slaughtered Lamb!" Morris roared back. The men in the room heard that and bellowed like a herd of ridiculous, semi-inebriated elephants, led by Arthur Sr. and Abraham, whose hearty, dry and sincere cheer soared around the room with zest and gusto.

Watching young Arthur and Lucy assist an inebriated Victoria back to her seat, under the ever-vigilant gaze of Ursula Holmwood, Van Helsing was genuinely happy for them all, yet it was in perspective. His travels had taken him to places where the poverty of what would be called Victorian

England's more undernourished regions made a stark contrast to the comparative luxury of the scene before him now. But watching this scene play out in front of him made Abraham relish seeing the children of yesterday become the husbands and wives of the near and distant future. He laughed, yet the irony of wealthy people making pomp and circumstance in the face of what most of the world had to offer was both a tribute and a curse of his broadened frame of reference.

The last part of Van Helsing's laugh was lined with cynicism and reserved for himself, his self-disgust at ranking and comparing human suffering, whether a family in India which has to cook their meal in a flooded house has endured more suffering than any starving orphan picking pockets or resorting to prostitution in Piccadilly Circus.

"What have I done?" giggled Mina in response to the Texan's bellow. She sat across and to the right of Abraham, and he snapped back to the present, her laugh having changed little from childhood, when he had taught all of them to shoot, indeed making up contests for the children of who could hit the farthest target accurately, whether it be an old shoe or milk bottle. Young Quincy had won nearly all of them, yet Mina was the one who had come closest to besting the Texan, so her recent triumph was no surprise to him. Ian was the worst shot, though he had a sporting time of it. Jonathan Harker had been a steady if unspectacular marksman. Even Lucy and Arthur had found their targets consistently, despite some laughing and joke-playing that left Abraham warning them to take a pistol in their hands seriously. And how these two were getting married.

"Not to worry, Mina," said Lucy, on her way back to her seat. "Their bachelor party will only be topped by our hen party[161]!"

It was then the turn of all the women at the table and in the room shriek with glee, over the fascinated, stupefied silence from the men. Victoria Westenra slid back into her seat and gave Abraham another angry-yet-interested grin. Abraham had known Victoria well enough to know when she was teetering on the edge of sobriety, so it was no surprise to him when she slurred, "Tell me, Abraham, did you perchance imbibe of any of the native women in your recent travails?"

She searched for her goblet of absinthe along the table, found it already in her hand, and took a long, wet sip.

Abraham gave her a kind but annoyed look before he took a long sip of his coffee and said curtly, "None. You know that."

The room went quiet, for a beat, everyone hearing Van Helsing's stiff rebuke of Victoria. He winked at Lucy to let her know he was fine. Everyone noticed the wink and went back to the merriment of the evening.

"Victoria," said Abraham with a gracious smile," let me pour you some fresh coffee."

---

[161] Hen party is a Victorian Era American term for a bachelorette party.

THIRTY-ONE

Three Crucifixes.

Inverted, but crucifixes nonetheless.

Three shrouds, crucified.

"Vos non possunt transmutare!" shouted Dracula, his open hand extended out over them, his spell cast. *You cannot transform!*

Splayed out on the rocks, the three remaining assassins had been forcibly restrained and stretched out on top of the trio of intersecting wooden beams that had been resurrected from the ruins of the *Demeter*. The ornate black hoods had fallen from each shroud to reveal three young vampires: a gangly male with a long face, named Sarnai, a leonine female with a rapacious mouth full of canines, known as Imma and a shorter, voluptuous female with large, piercing owl eyes, named Alina. Dozens of Primus' skeletons held them all down while their wrists, torsos and ankles were being lashed to the beams with rope, blasphemous versions of the three crucifixes that were placed at Golgotha[162]. Their hands had been raised over their heads and tied onto the main post, the crossbar at their knees, with their feet where the head would sit on a standard crucifix, where INRI[163] would have been found on a Catholic cross. A bulbous, fertile moon illuminated the night, casting a cyan ray of light down onto the craggy, jagged ledge.

Clouds churned above, filled with evil thoughts.

Petra, Venus and Andromeda had each clamped their feminine, deadly hands around the throats of their prisoners, while squirming to keep the shrouds atop their respective crucifixes. Dracula, his face still bloodstained from Mueller's blood, had moved to a rocky perch above the cliffside protrusion. His taloned hand stayed outstretched, his spell upon the three shrouds intact. The trio of undead writhed in agony, hands lashed over their heads on the upside-down crosses, at both Dracula's spell and their predicament. Waves of rats sat, crawled or slithered on every available and conceivable ledge, edge and protrusion, watching with a million red-hateful eyes, a hideous sight.

"Schonen Alina und Sarnai!" shouted the lithe Imma at Dracula. Her eyes shimmering with tears and terror. "Sie haben zueinander gefunden haben! Halim und ich waren die wahre Verschworenen!" *Spare Alina and Sarnai! They have found each other! Halim and I were the true conspirators!*

A grotesque tide of rats, pulsing with fleas and ticks, surged violently out of the rock wall, rapacious in their intent of shredding the vampiress for daring to speak to their master, their tiny

---

[162] Golgotha, or Calvary, was the place outside of Jerusalem where Christ was crucified, according to biblical scripture. Supposed to resemble the top of a skeletal cranium, Golgotha is loosely translated to mean 'The place of the skull.'

[163] INRI, the inscription traditionally depicted atop a Catholic cross, written in Latin, the language of the Roman Empire, means *Iesus Nazarenus Rex Ivdaeorvm*, Jesus of Nazareth, the King of the Jews. Biblical scripture John 19:19 reads: *And Pilate wrote a title, and put it on the cross. And the writing was, Jesus of Nazareth The King of The Jews.*

crimson eyes savage with hunger. A disinterested wave from Dracula sent them coiling back to the nooks and cracks of the cliffside, waiting to quench their bloodlust.

"Imma, σας όλη πέθαναν τη στιγμή που συνωμότησαν εναντίον του πλοιάρχου," snipped Andromeda. *Imma, you all died the moment you conspired against the master.*

The brides stood in unison, satisfied that the three shrouds were secured, as were the skeletons. A blue, fungus-infested skeleton finished tugging at all the bindings and nodded to Primus, who in turn lowered his head and said to Dracula, "Thy will is done."

Dracula relaxed his outstretched hand and the prisoners, leaving them gasping with ragged, dry heaves. Their eyes showed only hate for their captors.

"Egli è il nostro marito, non nostro maestro," said an indignant Venus, her chin high, leading them all away from the three crosses and behind Dracula. *He is our husband, not our master.*

"Tu ne id quidemst, Italian meretrix et concubinam," snarled Dracula at Venus with a sudden, vicious sneer. His eyes danced with malice. *You are not even that, Italian whore and concubine.*

The three *nosferatu*, creatures of the night, then reacted like any mortal women would have. Venus, Petra and Andromeda gasped in astonishment at Dracula's insult and bowed their heads, embarrassed. Petra reached out and placed her hand over Venus' shoulder out of instinctual sympathy. Venus nearly swatted Petra's hand away, but knew her anger was with Dracula, not one of her sisters, and restrained herself, retaining her dignity with silence and her raised chin, though she glared a hole right through the back of the Transylvanian's head. He sensed Venus' eyes on his and relished her seething resentment.

"Дурак алгебры А женщине!" shrieked Alina at Venus, who ignored her, still flustered and trying to retain her composure in the face of public humiliation. "Он даже не звать тебя его жене! Ты своим *шлюха*! По крайней мере, мы боремся за наших близких! Это варварское деспот десятину нам все сухие, дает нам ничего и берет вас как девочку с вашей собственной семье-*aiiiiii*—" she shrieked in triumph and vindication. *Fool of a woman! He does not even call you his wife! You are his whore! At least we fight for our loved ones! This barbaric despot tithes us all dry, gives us nothing and takes you as a girl from your own family— aiiiiii—*

Alina held in her pain as Dracula clenched his hand again. He felt their agony and devoured it with heartless joy.

"Morsus poena," growled the Transylvanian, his right hand extending and tightening even further. *Sting, penance.*

The three shrouded vampires wailed, rolling their heads side-to-side as pain built throughout their bodies, still frozen by Dracula's spell. The Transylvanian relaxed his hand, keeping them under his spell that restricted their transformation, but releasing the pain incantation. The three shrouds sagged and vented cries of relief.

"Helfen Sie uns, Venus!" wailed the lithe, leonine Imma, her face porous with pain and fear. *Help us, Venus!*

Imma's plea embarrassed Venus, and the bride was shamed into looking to the east, to the night-filled ocean's horizon, helpless and shocked at how deeply she was moved by Dracula's torture of the shrouds. Petra and Andromeda also understood the situation and stood rigidly, never moving to help the shrouds though every fiber in their bodies beseeched them to do so.

Dracula gave them a slow, gleeful nod over his shoulder before he growled, "Excellentior vestrum, Graecam et Aegyptiacam maleficas excellens! Fidelitatem tuam et nihil aliud ad mecum! Tu sororibus venatum, sed ego sum dominum tuum! Si vos umquam sustinere Italian meretrix supra mecum, I fore epulabuntur vestris poplites manuum super altare Catholicus!" *Excellent of you, Greek and Egyptian witches, excellent! Your loyalty is to me and no other! You are sisters of the hunt, but I am your master! If you ever support the Italian whore over me, I would feast of your wrists upon a Catholic altar!*

Dracula turned back to the shrouds.

"Nail their palms to the wood," he said casually to Primus, whose neck bones cracked with ancient dust as he nodded. The macabre soldiers then brought out metal shards from the shipwreck and began to spread the fingers of the shrouds out from their clenched fists, holding rocks in their bony hands as makeshift hammers. The three victims maintained their silence through this, though the grim expressions on their faces revealed their collective pain. "Their feet as well."

All three shrouds had their feet pinned to the wooden beams at the crossbars and lashed at their ankles. Imma spat upon one of the smaller, more decayed skeletons, but the morbid servant tied the knot around her ankles very tight, oblivious.

"Per manibus ejus, non in manibus," instructed Primus. *Through the wrists, not the palms.*

Dracula shifted his weight, eager to get a better view of the torture, but then winced with sudden pain and surprise. The Transylvanian instinctively reached for his source of pain, his neck, the arrow wounds still not completely healed. He snarled in annoyance at the three shrouds, and they in turn defied them with their stares of resolve.

"Insidiator sagittae intincti essent in aqua benedicta," railed Dracula, still clutching at his shoulder. *The conspirators' arrows were dipped in Holy Water.*

"Sic Christus aquam nocebit vobis," sneered the gangly Sarnai as the blue, fungus-covered skeleton raised a rock over the improvised nail, held by another skeleton just above his outstretched palms. "Nos nihil nostrum revelare insidiarum, tyranne!" *So, the water of the Christ does injure you! We will reveal nothing of our plot, tyrant!*

"Et quod peto nihil, Sarnai puer insidiatorem, jam scio enim qui misit vos, adeo aegram est 'coniurationem' tuam," sneered Dracula. "Ego Venari quoniam requirens sanguine utrumque Parisiorum Romae, juvenes stultus, Postquam fuero negotium meum deducite in terra ista." *And I ask nothing, Sarnai the boy conspirator, for I already know who sent you, so feeble is your 'plot.' I will hunt for blood in both Paris and Rome, young fool, after I conclude my business in this land.*

The first rock slammed into the nail, and Sarnai wrenched with pain through his palms and wrists. He tried to get up but was held down by both the dozen skeletons around him and Dracula's incantation. The other skeletons began to pound rocks against the nails that had been set above his bare feet. The nails ripped through undead flesh and into the decaying wood of the *Demeter.* Alina and Imma also agonized as nails penetrated their palms and feet, their blood spilling out over the cross and the rocky ledge. A few bold rats ran out from between the rocks they were hiding between and lapped up the spilled ichor. Alina struggled mightily and managed to rip her right hand free before another skeleton yanked it back in place next to her left hand, which was in the process of being staked, and another nail shard was driven through the base of the wrist. Bones broke in the wrists, and Alina shrieked in unbelievable pain. Her blood squirted grotesquely over the cliff rocks, and more rats surged forward in sickening waves to lick it up. Alina, Sarnai and Imma began to weep, alternately screaming and wailing in searing agony, their sounds washed away with the thunderous noise of the rising tide, which had continued to tear the *Demeter* below to pieces.

As the shrouds sobbed and shouted, a small sweet smile formed on the mouth of Dracula, his glowing eyes dancing with morbid glee. "Flectere clavum semel carnes penetretur." *Bend the nail once the flesh has been pierced.*

"Вы трус, не король!" screamed the leonine Alina between shrieks and tears of pain, her rapacious canines flashing in the night. *You are coward, not king!*

Imma, the oval-eyed voluptuous vampire, raised her head as the skeletons pounded her ankles and wrists with blow after blow. In a moment of frenzy and defiance, she spat viciously onto Dracula's coat.

His reply was to lean forward and leer with joy.

Dracula extended his hand out over the three shrouds once again.

"Dolor," he said. *Pain.*

He clenched his fingers once more.

Again, the trio arched their backs in utter, torturous agony.

As her palms and ankles spattered gore all over the ledge, Alina flashed a feverish glare of contempt at Venus, Petra and Anrdromeda, who collectively stared back at the lithe vampire with dark sympathy in their eyes but they dared not move. "И вы трое! Вы нет королев! Истинные члены королевской семьи не смотреть невинные люди умереть! Брось вызов его! Вы не шлюхи он говорит, что вы!" *And you three! You are no queens! True royals do not watch innocents die! Defy him! You are not the whores he says you are!*

Frozen, but with holes burning in their hearts, the brides began to feel an alien sense of empathy pulling at them, and their chests began to heave with guilt, their predatory eyes brimmed with tears.

But not one moved, knowing the price to pay for any action but silence.

"ты трусы!" shrieked Alina at the brides. *You are cowards!*

Klick!

Klack!

Click!

The skeletons continued to hammer, while the shrouds sobbed, wailed and screamed. Dracula savored the moment, his eyes dancing with supernatural light and evil joy as a small bone cracked in Imma's wrist. She shrieked in complete agony that brought a soft, delighted chuckle from the Transylvanian.

When the victims were at last secured to the crucifixes, Primus nodded to his master, who raised his left hand and growled, "Accipe sacrificium tuo nomine Patris mei." *Accept this sacrifice in your name, my father.*

Dracula made an inverted sign of the cross gesture over the three victims with the left hand as he kept his right hand up and clenched, his spell of transformation and torture still intact.

Dracula threw a grim nod of affirmation to Primus, who in turn nodded his knobby, vacant skull at the skeletons.

"Sie Jagd die Sie wie das Mischlings Sie sind gibt!" shouted Imma, still whimpering from her broken wrist as the skeletons began to push the crosses toward the edge. *They will hunt you like the mongrel you are!*

"Est naturae meae, ut hostes impugnant et coniuratorum primum," chuckled Dracula, his right hand still outstretched above the three. *It is my nature to attack enemies and conspirators first.*

"Senin için ben ver gerçek aşkı, Alina!" screamed Sarnai as he started to slide off the rocks, the boiling seas and submerging *Demeter* beneath them. *To you I give my true love, Alina!*

Alina, wailing like a wounded cat as she bawled, "И моя душа твоя, добрый и скромный Sarnai!" *And my soul is yours, kind and humble Sarnai!*

At Sarnai and Alina's proclamations, Venus gasped in astonishment. The magnificent, beautiful predator then raised her fingertips and ran them lightly to her breast, so touched was she, so racked with guilt. It was all she could do not to act out, to run over and save them simply for their gestures of love in the face of oblivion. Or to shout to the lovers her admiration for their eternal devotion. And to Imma for her strength in the face of extermination. That these two *nosferatu* dared to profess such love for each other in front of the son of Satan was an astonishing, overwhelming event for Venus to experience.

"Halim sevdi sen, Imma!" shouted Sarnai, nearly over the edge. *Halim loved you, Imma!*

"Und ich liebte ihn!" wailed Imma, "Ich träumte davon, Gebären seine kind—" *And I loved him! I dreamt of bearing his child—*

"Scortum!" roared Dracula with a mighty yet angry laugh, his right hand still holding them with his incantation. "Ego solus pater potest, apud utri equa canis exprimamus aut meretrixI opportunos esse. Reliqui inficiat efficio sic debetis, symbolica regium agrestiumque distinctionem." *Harlot! I alone can sire, with whichever mare, bitch or whore I deem worthy. The rest of you must infect to do so, symbolic of the difference between royalty and peasantry.*

Venus had to fight to compose herself, so that Dracula would not see her chest heaving, her eyes brimming with tears, and she dared not look at either Petra or Andromeda for fear that their eyes meeting would send them all to tears, and to their collective doom.

"Et vos tres mulieres sordidis voluptatibus derelinquet hoc campestris existentiae siccis, sterilis, absque liberis vulvam!" snapped Dracula, his eyes burning with pointed loathing toward his three brides. *And you three filthy women of pleasure will leave this plane of existence with dry, barren, childless wombs!*

Venus, Petra and Andromeda, humiliated once more, could only keep their glowing eyes fixed on the crucifixes, their victims and the skeletons that were pushing them over the ledge and away from Dracula. In the gloom of the night, the foam of the tides, the thin sheets of rain that garnished the cliff wall, the three women stood in silent union, their incandescent eyes blinking back tears of silence, empathy and sadness. This was not the first time they had been made to feel unworthy or suffered humiliation at the words of their master. Satisfied that his words had wounded the vampiresses sufficiently, Dracula turned back to the shrouds, who were still convulsing with pain.

"Iamque coniuratis infernus te manet!" hissed Dracula. *And now, Conspirators, Hell awaits you!* With a forward thrust of his right hand, all three shrouds and crosses were jerked out of the hands of the skeletons and off the rocks, arcing down toward the seawater and the battered metal hulk of the ship.

Alina and Sarnai both screamed simultaneously to each other as they fell.

"я люблю—"

"Severim—"

I love—

Venus, her chest heaving from the torrent of feelings inside her, nearly burst out in tears. Next to her, Andromeda and Petra stood in tortured silence as the crosses all plummeted from view, puncturing the waves and knifing underwater. Then, somehow, supernaturally, from under the water, three unholy fires began to burn.

The tide churned.

And swelled.

And ebbed.

Wind swirled around the brides, and at last they glided silently, solemnly, around Dracula of Transylvania, and toward the edge. The three undead women watched the underwater fires rise from the frothing depths of seawater and toward the surface, surreality come to life.

Petra's face pulsed revulsion.

Venus did not bother to hide hers. "The water, especially from the ocean, corrodes us."

Andromeda, the youngest of them, simply wept, her ember eyes riveted on the underwater fire.

Primus and the skeletal legion all stood in eerie silence, winds whistling through their hollow skulls.

Then the three shrouds, each of them burning from unholy fire, burst back up through the surface on their wooden crosses, all boiling in liquid agony, the water peeling their flesh away like staked pigs on a split. All three wailed in limitless pain, boiling and scalding with the water that was acidic to the undead.

Alina, Imma and Sarnai's screams threatened to tear their lungs to shreds as they burned alive; skin crinkling off them like paper, their eyes melting and bursting like grapes in a woodfire, flames blossoming out of their gaping mouths, their muscles fraying like kindle, their bones cracking and shattering like wood inside an old stove.

"Cinis cineris cinis cinerem," sighed a delighted Dracula, who had not moved to the edge of the precipice, satisfied in taking delight in the screams of the shrouds, a warm grin smeared across his face as if he had just skipped a pebble across a pond. The grin was followed by a satiated, satisfied sigh from a beast whose only pleasure was derived from the suffering of others.

"'For dust thou art[164],'" said Primus with a crisp, creaking nod.

"'—and unto dust thou shall return,'" finished Venus, whose predatory instincts were being overwhelmed with the expressions of real, eternal love that she had just witnessed. She was not just quoting, she was stating a sense of perspective that surged through her.

A sense of emptiness.

A void.

A longing.

Dracula felt no such longing. Vapor swirled around the vampire, water whisps that were still digesting the *Demeter* and the shrouds yet were not enough to harm the Transylvanian. Dracula grunted and rotated his wounded neck and shoulder area in an attempt to relieve the throbbing pain from the still-healing arrow wounds, which were not quite right yet, despite the collective vampiric ability to heal from most wounds, even mortal blows, nearly instantly.

"Ad nostram prædictas fatales," he grunted. *To our fates.*

In the following, breathtaking moment, he was not an undead man anymore but a bat, a horrid and gargantuan bat again, as Dracula of Transylvania turned into his bat form and spread his magnificent, expansive wings and leaped up into the air. The zephyrs caught his wings, and the beast soared upward to the top of the cliff, toward the English countryside beyond.

The skeletons followed, abandoning the *Demeter* to its death, then clambering up the cliffside, raising the wagons from the ship, hand to skeletal hand. Surging among all of the moving bones were wave after wave of the voracious rodent pestilence. Some rats dragged pieces of the crew in their mouths, scratching and clawing for every scrap of flesh available.

The brides, however, did not follow, and lingered.

Clouds boiled above, tide frothed below.

They stood transfixed at the precipice, the abyss, with their incandescent, carnivorous eyes fixated upon the funeral pyres burning away amid tide, wave and surge. Six cat eyes blinked back tears that mixed raw empathy, the combustible bloodlust of a rival's conquest, and the festering hatred of their master.

Their husband.

His *whores*, they fumed.

---

[164] Genesis 3:19: "In the sweat of they face shalt thou eat bread, till thou return unto the ground; for out of it was thou taken: for dust thou art, and unto dust shalt thou return." The exact phrase "Ashes to ashes, dust to dust, is not found in the bible and is based on the English Funeral Service in the Book of Common Prayer, originally published in 1549, a product of the English reformation following England's break with the Vatican.

More than zephyrs swirled.

Embers within all three, particularly Venus, had been reignited by the wind of dishonor. Of disrespect.

Venus blinked back tears of not just vanity, but the memories with which the tears came.

Of long ago.

A memory.

An experience.

A love.

A tragedy, the reminiscences of a love now gone amidst time. That hurt danced in Venus' heart. Something had changed.

A *nosferatu* had a soul. A carnivorous thing of the night thought of when she was not a beautiful beast, but when she was simply a beauty.

She was not the only one.

Her Egyptian and Greek sisters felt it as well, for if he did this to his own kind, would he not hesitate to crucify them as well?

The crucifixion of the shrouds, three of their kind, had staggered them, made the women feel what they each had not felt in an eternity. Bitterness, anger, sadness, resentment, all swam through the women.

Andromeda and Petra were less conflicted, still young enough to have their carnivorous urges remain their strongest instinct, they were nonetheless sad and livid while watching the lovers in agony, and it was Andromeda, the youngest who finally spoke what they had all been thinking.

"1 τον μισούν," she hissed. *I hate him.*

Without another word, Andromeda and Petra transformed and flew away, to their master.

To their fate.

The Andromeda bat screeched for Venus to follow as they soared up along the sea cliffs and onto land.

Venus ignored the screech, instead continuing to watch two burning corpses reach out for each other one last time before the water burned them like hate could consume a soul. For a moment, she yearned to be one of them. To have burned like they did, to have loved like they had. To have died for their love. For a moment, she yearned to help them. Her face was a mask of scalding hate and boiling envy.

At last even the crucifixes began to burn, upside-down crosses of fire, three macabre markers of blasphemy, unholiness, and somehow, spoken true love.

She wept, the depth and bitterness of her tears surprising even her.

Then she composed herself.

Venus shook her head in frustration, angry at herself for being touched so, watching the three crosses, burnt to charred blackness, sink under the churning waters, which continued to digest and vomit the remnants of the *Demeter*, and wondered why their acts and gestures of *love,* she thought, for she could not say the word out loud, had touched her so profoundly.

Then she remembered why.

She let herself enjoy the memory, in her solitude.

An echo, a dark echo through time.

When she was not a carnivore.

When she was a mortal woman.

Filled with the overwhelming joy of love.

That fire, that love had consumed her, but in a beauteous, profound way.

Such a fire was a delight to be consumed by.

I have forgotten.

Amare.

Nero.

Love.

And the stars in the sky.

And the flutter of her heart.

Amare.

She gave pause.

And grieved for that love.

She nearly sobbed.

But she contained it.

She was a queen, a wife, not a concubine.

Then came anger.

Then came her new lust.

Blood.

Her comparatively new love.

Her addiction.

Her hunger.

Her curse.

Her fate.

The never-ending, unsatiated desire to feed, to drink of others, to drain from the living so that she may remain undead, that too pulsed through Venus, and then she remembered that she was not just a woman, she was also a thing of the night.

But she had indeed remembered that she was a woman.

After one last, long look, she too melted into bat form and flew up along the rocky wall to join the others in flight and bloodlust.

Yet forever changed.

Or simply renewed.

Reminded.

THIRTY-TWO

Wilhelmina Murray sat alone in another of her favorite places in the world, another garden of graveyard markers, moldy tombstones and decomposing corpses. In this case it was the Holmwood family cemetery, complete with old tombs that held Arthur's ancestors as well as a freshly laid elaborate tomb for Lord Godalming and his wife. The moon was nearly gone behind her, to the west, while Whitby sat below her, and beyond her port, the open sea. The storm earlier in the evening had passed and the skies seemed to yawn like they had just woken for the first time. Lost in thought, Mina idly pulled on blades of grass while she tucked a loose strand of her raven hair behind her ear, smiling as she recalled telling Lucy when they were both children that she did not want to allow the piercing of her ears, explaining that she liked her ears just fine and preferred not to wear rings in them. Both Lucy and Judith begged Mina to pierce her ears, and in the end, she acquiesced, but in the years since she had rarely worn earrings.

The night had been both triumphant and frustrating. The announcement of Lucy and Arthur's engagement had been brilliant, but Victoria's descent into alcoholic clumsiness through the night had been depressing, especially after the announcement. Everyone had grown accustomed to Aunt Victoria's incessant inquiries into Uncle Abraham's romantic life, and his answers had never been rude in response, yet tonight's episode had brought down a cascade of humorous needling from the other 'adult' men, especially Lord Godalming, which Abraham had parried effortlessly and with good cheer. Indeed, it was difficult to tease a man who told of hiding under the decomposing corpse of a mummy to avoid a group of murderous tomb robbers, and the younger generation relished the ease and confidence with which Abraham Van Helsing carried himself. He and Aunt Ursula seemed to be the only people capable of putting the gigantic persona of Arthur Holmwood in its proper place, and 'Original Artie', as the Texan Morris had dubbed him, knew this, yet he refused to stop his incessant baiting of Uncle Abraham at every turn. Mina had expressed her annoyance to her uncle before, and Abraham only chuckled and said that if he could handle the stuffed shirts down at the British Archeological Association or armed mercenaries in the Congo, then he could certainly handle the Lord Godalming.

Mina then remembered she was alone and unescorted at night and D'Artagnan was at rest in the Holmwood stables, so she searched her purse for the Remington-Elliot Pepperbox Derringer pistol[165] that Uncle Abraham had given to her as a present for her fifteenth birthday, over the objections of Andrew and Judith. She found the revolver and comfort at the same time. Four rounds sat in four chambers, and the trigger would pop out with the pull of the hammer. Mina relaxed and kept her hand in her purse with the satisfaction that she would either not need it or would relish using it. An envious Quincy Morris (whose own weapons collection bordered on zoological) had

---

[165] Pepperbox revolver: A very small repeating pistol, easily concealed, used predominantly for self-defense, particularly by the wealthy during the Victorian era. The original single-shot version was invented in 1852 by American Henry Deringer. The Philadelphia Derringer was the pistol used by John Wilkes Boothe to assassinate President Abraham Lincoln.

offered her a tidy sum for it at first, before purchasing a Sharps Derringer[166] for himself in Philadelphia and trying to trade with Mina, then attempting to convince Mina that his was the superior weapon. She laughed out loud at the memory of Jonathan's rebuke of the Texan.

"If Mina's is the inferior weapon," said Jonathan at the time, *"Then why did you offer her your piece in trade to begin with?"*

"'Cuz guns are like posies[167] in Texas," snipped Quincy. *"Ya can't have too many of 'em."*

Jonathan's words and his eye roll at the Texan's quip brought Harker back to the forefront of Mina's mind, and she allowed her eyes to swell with tears, out here with no one around,—no one alive anyway—to see her cry. Mina's lips quivered with emotion. At times like this she missed Jonathan Harker, the fool who dashed off to the Orient and the only person who seemed to understand her completely. It was not the surprise announcement of Lucy and Arthur's engagement that had sent her out here, she told herself. Perhaps most other women might feel intruded upon by the timing, but their engagement seemed to only put pressure on Mina to cancel her own wedding, something she was still very conflicted about, she realized. Holding her left hand out, Mina looked at the sparkles her engagement ring, a curvy gold band with diamonds surrounding a large sapphire, made as it searched for any moonlight it could refract. She wondered if making Jonathan and everyone else happy by becoming a wife and nothing else was indeed the wise thing to do. It would certainly be the easiest thing to do.

Then she realized why she was really upset.

I saw my future tonight in Uncle Abraham. He is growing older, and he remains alone. Do I really want to see the world on my own? He has journied to all four corners of the world, and to what end? How many empty train cars has he sat in? Slept in? How many will I sit in alone if I walk away from Jonathan?

Mina sniffled, trying to pull her tears back into her eyes. There, at the Holmwood dining table she had just left, was her future, embodied in the man she grew up admiring so much, the man whose father had given Mina her teaching job, the man who had taught her how to shoot, how to use a knife, how to be self-reliant, much to the early discomfort of her parents, who never imagined that their princess would someday prefer to touch the ground of all the continents rather than settle for a domestic family lifestyle.

When she was growing up, she had heard the gossip about Uncle Abraham, the loss of his own wife and daughter to childbirth after he came back from the Orient and the war, and how he aggressively then staked out his career. Professor. Doctor. Anthropologist. Author. Marksman. Archeologist. Researcher. Scientist. Occultist. Grave robber. Lecturer.

Having discovered that what everyone thought about her meant nothing compared to what she thought of herself, Mina found herself at her own crossroads, wondering if she indeed was brave enough to be an Abraham Van Helsing, to see everything that he had seen, live what he had lived, cheated death so many times and yet come home to an empty home full of research and knowledge and nothing else.

Mina was aware Lucy Westenra was there before Lucy sat down on the tombstone next to her.

"I think I was born in the wrong time," sighed Mina, looking out into the boil off the coast.

Below Mina and Lucy, the dead held their own silent debate and agreed. And disagreed.

Lucy watched the night clouds swirl over the sea and sighed, "Mother has the tact of a buffalo at times, and no more so obvious than tonight. All this came about just before dinner. I had no idea they were about to announce it, Mina, and I apologize, completely."

---

[166] Sharps Derringer: Another type of small, four-chambered, repeating pistol.
[167] Posies: flower bouquet.

"I understand," said Mina, reaching out and patting Lucy on the shoulder.

"No, you should not," sniffed Lucy, annoyed. "It was completely rude and inconsiderate of the present circumstances of your engagement."

"Lucy, as far as anyone knows, I am to be married within days. I am not an old maid-to-be."

"What kind of talk is this? You are no more an old maid than my future father-in-law is a meager spinster. I do not know too many old maids who could split an apple off my hat at ten paces, Mina."

They laughed, their bond renewed.

They did not know what to say to each other after that, but both of them were so comfortable with one other they could sit in endless silence. Mina then remembered the game they had always played as children, and she began to hum, then sang softly:

"Quanno fa notte e 'o sole se ne scenne,
me vene quasi 'na malincunia;
sotta 'a fenesta toia restarria
quanno fa notte e 'o sole se ne scenne."

When night comes and the sun has gone down,
I almost start feeling melancholy;
I'd stay below your window
When night comes and the sun has gone down.

Lucy thought, clapped and shouted, "That's 'O Sole Mio'[168]!"

"Dammit, you're good!" spat Mina past a wicked grin.

"Do you remember the first time they brought Uncle Monty to the Seward Hospital?" said Lucy, reaching out and holding Mina's hand. "Or shall we call it what it *really* is: Seward Asylum? They thought we'd never find out but you and I snuck a peek through the dumbwaiter and caught Uncle Henry and Uncle Abraham shackling Uncle Monty to the wall?"

"You were too curious to be scared," said Mina with a laugh, along with a shudder. She poked at the dead grass beneath her with her boot.

Lucy swung her and Mina's hands back and forth as she said, "And they heard me yelp when Uncle Monty spat up a human finger and we ran away and they rounded us children all up and asked us who had disobeyed them? Asked who had said that he was there? Who took the blame, Mina? For you."

Mina rarely said someone else was right, so she simply said, "There's no doubting Jonathan's qualities, Lucy. The issue is me, and what I want out of life and how fair I am being to him."

They sat there as the waves of grass stirred among the tombstones, sisters from different parents.

Then Mina jerked her head back in a mixture of annoyance and anger. "How was that even bloody normal?! Watching our uncle spit up a human finger!"

"Was it a human finger, Mina?" said Lucy, tugging on Mina's hand. "I always thought it was just one of the animals he'd just started to catch and eat."

"I'd have bet my life it was human," said Mina with a vigorous headshake. "I don't care what the lot of you thought."

Mina then reached out with her other hand and affectionalty tapped the top of both of their clasped hands. "Go inside and rejoin the frivolities. I'll return in a moment."

Lucy just looked at Mina in the night, all the way into her soul. "You don't have to, you know."

---

[168] "O Sole Mio," by Eduardo di Capua and Giovanni Capurro, is a popular song of the time, published in 1898.

"I don't have to what?"

"You don't have to *not* marry Jonathan. He'd support whatever you want to do. He loves you. Truly. I've seen it. He'd let you go anywhere and do anything you'd like and allow you to drag him anywhere in the world with you."

"That's the whole point, Lucy. He should not be dragged anywhere."

"You should have married Quincy, then," teased Lucy.

Mina scoffed and said, "So I could spend the rest of my life dragging him out of saloons or arranging for his bail in my golden years? No thank you. I do love Morris as a brother, but he is the eternal child. Consuelo will soon discover this, if she has not done so already."

"I have seen Consuelo's fire when Quincy lapses," said Lucy with an arched eyebrow. "And I have seen Morris roll over to her like a puppy under those circumstances."

"Ah, yes, that's right," said Mina with a warm smile. "The not-so-secret secret drinking binge with the lads when we all arrived in Texas. Good Lord, it was hot there!"

"I don't think she objected to the bingeing as much as the, well, indiscreet entertainment that accompanied said drinking."

Mina crinkled her nose, yet she was able to retain the charm in her smile as she said, "Didn't Ian squeak like a mouse when she pulled a knife on Quincy and told him if he ever did that again she'd gut him like a pig?"

They both laughed.

"Did she actually say that?" asked Lucy. "She was speaking in Spanish, if you remember."

"I caught the gist of it," nodded Mina with a wide, appreciative grin. "And Consuelo herself gave me her own translation later, after Morris waited on her hand and foot for the entire day. And her knife was sufficient evidence, I think."

"Difficult to do that when one is hung-over," laughed Lucy.

They let the wind and grass converse for a few moments. The grass had heard what was on the wind and wished dearly that it could tell the women what was nearly upon them.

"Uncle Arthur has been making fun of your father and Uncle Henry again. Though Uncle Andrew has quite the rapier wit. You know how much you enjoy their banter." It was Lucy's way of asking Mina to come back inside with her.

"I'll be in soon," said Mina, and this time it was with a hint of dismissal; Lucy knew when her friend needed a little more time alone, regardless of how much she could make Miss Wilhelmina Murray laugh.

"You know I love you— we all love you," finished Lucy, shaking the hand she was holding before releasing it.

She stood, turned and walked past Mina, pinching her nose in another sign of love.

"I know," said Mina, and she was alone.

With the dead.

ARRIVAL

The tide rises, the tide falls,
The twilight darkens, the curlew[169] calls;
Along the sea-sands damp and brown
The traveler hastens toward the town,
And the tide rises, the tide falls.

—Henry Wadsworth Longfellow

It was as if the night understood that this was a special passing from dusk to dawn, the event of an invading force arriving in England was, unto itself, a reason for the remaining hours before that sunrise to linger. Indeed, as the night wore on, a few more important events happened before and after Mina and Lucy briefly left the party. The *Demeter*'s encounter with the cliff wall had not gone unheard or unnoticed. A few local policemen on their routine night patrol in Whitby proper heard the collision and relayed word to the fire brigade, which eventually responded, arriving with horse-drawn steam engines that could pump hundreds of gallons per minute. A few local officials, some policemen and the fire brigade arrived at the edge of the cliff to shine lamplight down into the empty, collapsing hulk that was being pounded to pieces by the surging tide. A few brave souls cast ropes and rappelled down past Mueller's ledge (licked clean by the rats) and to the ship, only to find it empty, the *Demeter* having given up her ghost upon her death.

Among the inner streets of Whitby, lost amid the distant sounds of the shipwreck and subsequent rescue efforts, were the few concerned citizens who were wakened by the commotion but did not participate in the rescue efforts. Those citizens, still in their sleepwear, took notice of a series of strange, eerie presences moving at a languid pace past the bookshops and apothecaries. Those brave enough to push aside a curtain or shutter took in the bleak, weary wagons that were being drawn slowly through the cobbled old streets, each with a very gaunt-appearing figure seated at the front seat yet being drawn by *no horses*. Coffins rattled away in the back of the wagons, which were followed by dozens of emaciated, bony figures that scraped their bare feet along the stone streets, and waves of rats that frothed and undulated among the walking corpses. Somewhere along the way, a skeletal hand covered in a Roman gauntlet slipped an envelope of an antiquated style through the mail slot of one of the main solicitors in Whitby, whose sign read Sears, Hawkins and Harker. The envelope contained the completed deed for Carfax Abbey that transferred ownership to a very old, very anonymous company with holdings throughout Europe and what used to be referred to as the Ancient World. Above the port town, blending immaculately with the night, flew four enormous bats, high enough not to be seen yet able to simultaneously take in the futility that was the ship's rescue efforts and the progress of the wagons. The macabre procession made its way out of Whitby

---

[169] A curlew is a long, thin-beaked wading bird of the sandpiper family.

and toward a crumbling, decayed edifice on a hilltop that loomed over the township with no one taking deeper notice. A few of the townspeople decided the parade sight was a result of their liquoring, others saw it as an omen that only they could see, something evil that loomed in their near future.

Oblivious to the events at the shore, the dinner party at the Holmwood estate rambled on. Van Helsing, after much prodding by the Murrays and Harkers and after another glass of malt beer, described his most recent expeditions in Egypt, while deliberately omitting the specific supernatural circumstances of the tomb-opening along the Nile. Mina was enthralled, reminding herself that she needed to see the pyramids of Giza before she became a 'withered old biddy', as she described herself to a giggling Lucy.

In turn, at Abraham's insistence, they all updated him as to their own recent life events, and he turned a raised set of eyebrows at the Texan after the results of the recent shooting competition were relayed. Ian and Arthur II cheerfully volunteered to fetch said Winchester trophy, which annoyed Quincy to no end. Lord Godalming himself led a toast to the new shooting champion of the family, to which Ian, Arthur Junior and Quincy drank heartily, lemonade and all. The Texan, no stranger to mischief, discreetly produced a flask that he shared with Ian and Arthur, but not with Mina and Lucy, who signaled their displeasure at being excluded with a series of not-so discreet finger gestures, which made Abraham Van Helsing laugh so hard he thought his sides were about to split open. William Harker and Andrew Murray, perhaps buoyed by their partaking of alcohol, stood up and sang "Three Fishers went Sailing," "The Old Arm Chair" and "I come from the Beautiful Rhine[170]" together, much to the delirious, snorting laughter of their wives, and even Henry Seward joined in to a not-quite-on-key version of "Oh Mother![171]," which sent everyone into near hysterics. Victoria Westenra's screaming, laughter induced even more laughter from everyone but Lucy, who could only watch with a grim smile while her mother had to be held back physically by Ursula Holmwood and Judith Harker as she attempted to join the men in more vocal merriment. Arthur had to step in when Ian, Mina and Quincy began to whisper a teasing version of the latter song at Lucy, who gave them such a withering glare before being reduced to laughter by Ian's ridiculous, clownish facial expressions.

At a moment that was less than boisterous, amid the rollicking conversation and laughter, Abraham asked Ian if he could observe Renfield again the next morning, to which Ian replied with only a grim nod. Everyone enjoyed themselves so much and so late into the night that Ursula had the servants prepare rooms for all, and the entire party decided to call it a night only to reconnoiter, as Lord Godalming put it, for a late breakfast the next morning.

Lucy and Mina shared a room and gossiped into the night, about both of their weddings, Lucy asking if a double-wedding was a complete impossibility, while Mina's heart continued to surge back and forth between her love of Jonathan and her own dreams of whatever lingered beyond the horizons. William and Cynthia Harker simmered as they readied for bed, annoyed with what they perceived to be poor timing with the announcement of Lucy and Arthur's engagement. As he kissed his wife goodnight, William told her he'd bring up the matter privately with Arthur Senior in the morning. In their own room, Andrew and Judith Murray whispered quietly about the announcement, Mina's reaction of discreetly leaving the party for a bit as a result of said clumsiness, and their own doubts and fears about how the engagement with Jonathan would turn out. Ursula Holmwood scolded Arthur Senior in their bedroom for wrapping his arm a little too much around the waist of Lillian Seward during the merriment and requested that her husband sleep in the adjoining room, to

---

[170] Popular Victorian-era songs.
[171] Another popular song of the times.

which Arthur silently obliged. Henry and Lillian prayed quietly and fell asleep instantly, the elder Seward not wanting to hear the answer to the question of why his wife allowed the Lord Godalming's arm to linger. Ian, Quincy and Arthur Junior enjoyed some Cognac, dirty jokes and Wild Woodbine cigarettes on one of the terraces (much to the silent appreciation and laughter of Arthur Senior who was eavesdropping from his banishment to the sofa) before retreating to their own rooms, with Morris not bothering to do anything other than to flop face-down, fully clothed onto the bed, asleep before his head hit the linen. Exhausted, the servants went to sleep instantly and soundly.

Abraham Van Helsing, of course, could not sleep. He waited until there was silence in the manor before leaving his room, carefully avoiding Victoria Westenra's door before proceeding to check the locks of all the windows and doors in the cavernous home.

As everyone in the Holmwood estate slumbered, in the distance, beyond the town and overlooking all of the estates in the area, sat the crumbling, decayed Carfax Abbey in dead silence, hiding from the world, hiding the secret that was about to be revealed. Broken brown bricks covered sad memories and forgotten love. Dry grasses bustled with the writhings of rodent waves as the solemn, macabre procession of wagons arrived at the knob that overlooked Whitby. Among the collapsed orbital sockets that were castle towers landed the four bats, gigantic wings closing as they melted into the shadows. The skeletons tirelessly dragged the coffins from the wagons, through the dilapidated doors and into the depths of the ruins.

Gliding through the rooms with a ghostly elegance, the brides transformed from bat form to wisps of mist and melted down through their coffin lids to their night's rest, their hunger satiated by Captain Mueller. An unfortunate squatter, a fisherman who'd had no money for an inn and snuck into the ruins of the abbey woke to see the Transylvanian moving by him, also having had his fill from the wineskin that was Mueller's still-pumping heart. The vampire took in the doomed fisherman, waved a clawed hand and the poor soul's mouth was full of biting, tearing, flesh-eating rats before he could even scream for his life. Moving toward a collapsed window along the second story cloisters that gave the vampire a broad view of the area, Dracula permitted himself a long, satisfying look over the distant sea, the town and the window-lit manors before allowing a single, wry grin of supreme satisfaction to spread across his face. The vampire nodded with near-glee. Peter Hawkins' map was not only among his possessions but engraved in his mind. The storm clouds had begun to clear. Primus strode out of the shadows to tell Dracula that the abbey was secure. He could see the lights of the rescue efforts and laughed at their futility. A church bell in Whitby tolled four times. Instinctively, Dracula scoured the city for the cemeteries, both public and private, as well as the location of the estates significant to his journey the locations of which he had memorized from Hawkins' maps. In moments he had found them all.

Another smile.

A leer.

Beyond everything, even the sea, the last moments of the night began to fade into morning. A satisfied Dracula stepped backward, into the darkness of the abbey he now owned and resided in, with the assistance of the now deceased Peter Hawkins and Jonathan Harker.

He knew that the next few evenings would be, at the very least, eventful.

The next morning, the following article appeared in the *Whitby Gazette*:

Mysterious Shipwreck
off Whiteny Coast

EMPTY VESSEL WASHES ASHORE
CAPTAIN'S MUTILATED CORPSE FOUND ASEA

Last night the *Demeter*, a merchant ship out of the Orient, was found wrecked off the coast of Whitby. Said ship, en route from points east, was discovered at midnight with no crewmembers to be found, or any cargo to speak of. Ship's log has been discovered to be missing. Ghastly details, including the mutilated torso identified as that of Captain Harald Mueller was found not on the ship but in the sea. Inquiries will be made as to how such a large ship was able to make the journey through the Mediterranean without her crew. Suspicions that this tragic event was the result of piracy or other foul play have to be put off until more details are accumulated.

ONE

Upon the last peaceful dawn that followed, everyone woke up very slowly in Holmwood Manor, the effects of the delirious events of the previous evening ringing inside their heads like church bells. Servants stirred first, albeit slowly since they had peripherally partaken of the previous evening's liquid festivities. Arthur Senior had always disliked a party in which only the celebrants celebrated. So, the staff of Holmwood Manor rose and the kitchen staff prepared a sumptuous breakfast of warm cakes, fruit juices of various kinds, hot coffee and/or tea, eggs both scrambled and fried, smoked bacon, fried tomatoes and mushrooms, sausages, fresh rolls drenched in butter and marmalade as well as cakes of various sizes and flavors.

Everyone in bed, even slumbering Quincy still in his clothes from the day before and in the depths of a drunken slumber, sniffed out the sprawling scale of the morning feast that was being prepared and stirred to order. Everyone cascaded down from their rooms, with Arthur Senior complaining to Ursula about not being allowed to sleep in his own bed, a complaint to which Mrs. Holmwood coolly decided not to respond before a social breakfast. She would have plenty of time to masticate Arthur for his 'Arthurness' later on.

A spacious patio, adjoined to the massive home and in front of a back lawn that could have held a Rugby pitch, hosted the breakfast. Egg-white clouds slid between the lawn and the high-hanging sun. The setting was less formal than the night before so the friends could eat in their own social circles, which in this case meant the younger generation, the men and the women all sitting apart. Tiny, soft meadow pipits[172] flitted around them, anticipating crumbs and being rewarded with unexpected treats. A supple breeze from the distant sea romanced the shrubbery. The smell of freshly mowed[173] grass tangled with the aroma of strong, black coffee, which the three hung-over youths took to right away, much to the distant amusement and reminiscing of the older generation. Arthur chided William Harker about having spilled the brewing coffee early one quiet morning during their tour of duty, and he was instantly scolded in return by Abraham, who teased his former regiment leader about the volume with which he snored during one particularly frigid night. Andrew Murray and Henry Seward spent the meal discussing the expansion of Whitby from the small whaling town that it had been to the ever-growing port that it was blossoming into. Meanwhile, Ursula Holmwood impressed Lillian Seward with her recent discovery of green tea from the Far East. As the tea discussion went on, Cynthia Harker, Judith Murray and Victoria Westenra all wondered why Uncle Peter and Jonny had been so long in returning, especially given the impending wedding, now plural. It was easy for Judith Murray to keep Mina's ongoing doubts about her own wedding to herself.

Once breakfast was consumed, the Lord Godalming broke out cigars to the quiet content of the other men, while the wives joined their separate conversations about tea and weddings into another about how to gather everyone's extraneous wardrobes into offerings for the poor. All this while the

---

[172] Small birds.
[173] The lawn mower had been invented by Englishman Edwin Budding, who was granted a patent in 1830.

younger members began a half-hearted game of croquet, more to distance themselves from the adults than anything else.

"So, was he in London?" whispered Ian as Quincy Morris, still a little rumpled from last night, lined up a shot with his mallet. Mina, Lucy and Arthur looked on, feigning boredom.

"You took my turn again, Morris," said Arthur Junior, a little too loudly, so the elders would think they knew the youngster's subject matter.

Arthur nodded affirmatively at Quincy, a dark look over his face.

"Sorry, Mina," shouted Quincy, so over-the-top that everyone around him cringed. Morris saw their reaction and came down a decibels he finished with, "you have a go twice next time."

"He was in London for *all* of them?" whispered Lucy.

Another nod from Arthur.

"You went alone?" came Mina's hushed interjection.

"No, I went with Morris," whispered Arthur. He then shouted melodramatically, "Uh, my turn!"

"Good heavens, could any of you be more obvious?" hissed Lucy. "Try and keep your raised tone somewhere below soprano-conspiratorial."

"Did you speak with Lestrade?" asked Ian as Arthur marched around him to take his turn. "Was my letter of any use?"

Arthur promptly struck his ball through the arch. "Good shot!" said Lucy in a controlled, slightly louder-than-normal tone. She then proceeded to stick her chin out proudly at the men, happy at her ability to feign a conversation.

Quincy rolled his eyes at her and sarcastically said, "You could work for Pinkerton[174], Red."

Arthur, under his breath, said, "No, he would not see me. Father must have spoken with him, or at least instructed Lestrade not to speak to me."

Mina shouldered Arthur out of the way and said, "My turn!" then whispered, "And Abberdine?"

Arthur shook his head. "Retired. Or at least, not actively working for Scotland Yard anymore. I was told that he had a security job in Monte Carlo or some such."

After a long, quiet moment, Arthur leaned against his mallet as he followed his last statement up with, "There's more."

"More what?" said Mina as she lined up her shot.

"More than the five cases that we know about," said Arthur gravely.

Their collective jaws dropped.

"Good Lord," gasped the Texan, leaning against Ian, still not on solid footing with his hangover.

Mina deliberately missed her shot.

"You missed!" shouted Lucy, far too sing-songy and loudly. She whispered, "Could it be someone else—"

Morris simply shook his head.

"Are you certain?" said Mina.

"Yes," said Arthur, "It was *him*. It's all hush-hush, but there were more, at least five. Uncle Abraham took the lead, but they all assisted in finally capturing him. It was an incredibly violent arrest, but it happened." Arthur looked up at Ian and added, "Uncle Henry was able to arrange for quarantine up here. Quincy and I will head back to London again with Jonny for more information after he returns."

As he watched the Croquet players, Lord Godalming was exhaling smoke from his cigar as he said, "Gentlemen, this is a Flor De Sanchez y Haya cigar. Made by Cubans in Florida. The best in

---

[174] The Pinkerton Detective Agency, founded by American Allan Pinkerton in 1850, is a private security and detective agency which is still in business to this day.

the world." He was also thinking *those children are growing up far too quickly. They're digging into our secrets. I thought this would all lay until our passing.*

"They're far too loud between their whispers," giggled Arthur Senior, admiring his cigar.

"They're so young," said Henry Seward, with a nod toward the kids, and a loud cough afterwards. The oldest of the elders, he was never much of a smoker, though he usually partook of a cigar with his old infantry mates.

William Harker nodded at Arthur. "Perhaps they are inquiring as to the London happenstances again."

"Let them," replied Holmwood with confidence. "I've communicated my feelings on the matter to everyone involved in London, especially Lestrade. And we need not worry anymore about Abberdine and his inability to keep his mouth shut."

"I simply don't understand their need to know," said Henry after a long cloud of cigar smoke billowed out of his mouth. "They should look ahead in their lives, not backward."

"Were you not that age once, Henry?" interjected Abraham, relishing his Sanchez y Haya. He arched an eye toward Seward. "Did you not at one point in your life need to know everything?"

"I would not have needed to know *this*," hissed Henry Seward, with a curt, angry wave at the young ones. Arthur nodded, as did William. Abraham frowned. It was always like this, all of them against him, all of their secrecy against his honesty, all of his lack of understanding against their protection of their children's innocence. *They think I know nothing because my child lies buried*, thought Abraham, *and yet I know their children better than they ever could, save perhaps Andrew.*

"Eventually they are going to put the pieces together," ventured Van Helsing, knowing the path the conversation would take before he even opened his mouth, but hoping once in their adult lives these obstinate fools would see reason. "Everything that we lived *and did* will come out."

"If it has not already," said Andrew Murray, to everyone's genuine surprise. *There*, thought Abraham, *Murray's stepping out on his own. I see Mina in him right now.*

They all laughed for a moment as they watched Ian futilely try to knock his call through the nearest hoop, only to have young Arthur finally push him aside and finish the job for him.

"If they had," continued Andrew Murray, who thought he knew his child better than his friends knew theirs, "they would have asked us by now. Mina certainly would have asked me."

Arthur Senior chortled as he watched Quincy shoot his ball right over Mina's in a trick shot to take the lead. In a grand gesture, Arthur Junior waved for Lucy to take her shot, like a true gentleman. He saw love in his son's eyes and said, "I want my boy to marry without the shadow of all that, like Damocles' sword. For Mina and Jonny as well."

"You should just tell them," said Abraham before a puff, perhaps a little too sharply.

Arthur felt the blade and retorted, "Spoken like a childless man, Abraham."

Van Helsing's eyes tightened, as did his fingers around his cigar.

"Arthur!" hissed Andrew Murray. The croquet players and wives pretended not to notice. "That is enough!"

"Hear, hear," agreed William Harker.

Abraham's face flared, and for a moment Andrew Murray thought that Van Helsing was going to launch himself at their host, but then Abraham's face softened into sad resolve. "I should expect nothing less than that from you, Arthur. These conversations always lead to those sorts of comments. I now remember why it has been some time since I've returned here. You and I play silly schoolyard bully games, and I tire of them."

Arthur sighed, embarrassed. He ran his thumb over the top of his pearl-handled cane, shook his massive head in shame and patted Abraham's arm with his hand. "My apologies, Abraham. That

201 ARRIVAL • ONE

was uncalled for. I was rash. I still speak as a child at times. Last night I was castigated out of my own bed for my mouth running over. I have remained the child, and you remain the better of us both."

Abraham softened as well, patting Arthur's hand in love and appreciation as he said, "It seems like our destiny is to squabble until we are in front of Saint Peter's gates, my friend." Van Helsing then turned to Henry Seward and said. "I would like to see Monty."

"Of course," sang Henry, glad to change the subject. He hated the competitive bickering that always seemed to envelop Abraham and Arthur.

Henry Seward then turned to William Harker and said, "Please allow me the honor of hosting our dinner tonight, William?" Harker, having grown weary of both his cigar and the theme of the conversation, was watching Lucy put her ball through the wicket with the assistance of Arthur Junior. William looked forward to seeing his own son return home, not knowing he would not live to see the next dawn.

Henry pressed on. "If you don't mind, that is, William. That way Abraham can see Monty and—"

"Done," said William. "If for no other reason than to just move this conversation away from the previous topic."

"I don't know whether to be offended that our husbands think we do not know about the circumstances regarding Monty in London, or to simply to let them think they are all marvelous conspirators," sneered Ursula Holmwood, sitting not a stone's throw away from the men. Lady Godalming was smart enough to sit with her back to the husbands and astute enough to know where her husband sat with relation to Lillian Seward's line of sight. In the distance lingered the croquet game. The wives' table had been swept clean of breakfast, but the hot tea remained, along with some biscuits that sat untouched, such was the expansiveness of the first meal of the day.

"I don't think they could be more obvious," said Cynthia Harker. She laughed as she watched the youngsters frolic, then saddened as she caught William watching them and knew he was thinking of Jonathan.

"At least our children remain children," laughed Victoria Westenra.

"I don't know about that, Victoria," said Lillian, taking a sip of her tea while distinctly avoiding Arthur Senior's eyes as she looked at Ursula. Mrs. Holmwood seemed a tad more observant lately. "Young Arthur traveled to London with Quincy a few weeks back, you know."

"Yes," said Ursula, sensing the tension with which Lillian fought to look *at* her, and not past her. Ursula laughed with a mixture of amusement and bitterness as she replied, "I presume it was for the usual inquiries. If nothing else, my husband prides himself on keeping his secrets and his family quite separate."

Ursula Holmwood really did relish using sarcasm as a weapon.

"It's a terrible secret," interjected Judith Murray. She, like the other women at the table, was aware of the tension between Ursula and Lillian, and she had made her assessment of the situation based on her quiet observation of the two, and had decided long ago not to inquire, but to let the dynamic between the two very powerful personalities play out without her involvement. Family, of course, was another matter in her mind, and it made it easy for her to brush incidents like this aside when she had her daughter's complex feelings about marriage on her mind. They had always been close, Andrew, Mina and herself, and this allowed Judith to deal with whatever the world had to offer, both good and bad, with a steadier hand.

"It's not his keeping the secret from his son that I resent, Judith, it's keeping it from *me*." Ursula fought to not snarl as she spoke.

"I suppose we should simply tell the children ourselves," responded Judith. "If the men have not told them by now."

"You forget that they have not revealed all of this to *us*, Judith," interjected Cynthia Harker as she straightened the folds of her dress. Judith mused that it was the time in their conversations for Cynthia to align with Ursula again. "They are like tombs," finished Cynthia, pointing her chin at the men, and the women collectively fumed over that thought.

"If Arthur had not conferred the duties of attending to the post[175] to you a long time ago," laughed Lillian to Ursula, "we would know nothing of any this."

Ursula, the boldest and most emotional of all of the wives, took a long sip of her tea to try and conceal her annoyance at Lillian's laughter. *She wasn't laughing at you*, The Lady Godalming reminded herself before she added, "Then we are co-conspirators, ladies."

There was a moment of silence between the women, when the laughter of the croquet players and the guffaws of the husbands could be heard. It was Lillian who broke the silence. "If everyone in London is to be believed, the crimes were those of a monster."

Behind Ursula, Arthur Senior roared at his son shooting his ball past Ian's for the lead. She turned her head sideways, gave him a sliver glare of anger and said in a matter-of-fact way, "There are times I wish he had died in the war."

Two tiny pipits fluttered on the table, tugging after a piece of bacon. They all watched and giggled at the birds, even Ursula. The pair tore the piece in half and flew away, contented.

"Don't you think it's a burden for the men?" said Cynthia, ever the diplomat. "Whatever happened between them all in the war, it must have been incredibly significant for them to care for Monty like this—"

"Cynthia", "said Victoria, "He *mutilated* them—"

"Victoria! Please!" said Judith. She nearly shouted.

"We should simply tell the children," said Ursula.

"After the weddings," said Judith, ever pragmatic.

"I agree," said Cynthia.

"Before they leave for their honeymoons?" said Victoria with a snicker that all the women took to be in poor taste.

"Goodness, Victoria," chuckled Cynthia. "Does a perpetual furnace burn within you?"

Annoyed with Victoria, who she thought of as a silly poppy, Ursula picked up the porcelain tea kettle nearest her and cleared her throat as she said, "No, when they all return. We'll sit them all down and tell them."

"It's not like they don't strongly suspect anyway," said Cynthia, in support of Ursula once again, noted Judith. *I hope she'll be easier to deal with after we're both grandmothers to our children's children.*

Lillian looked nervous as she said, "Then they'll tell our husbands—"

"—who have never taken the time to tell us anything anyway," hissed Ursula as she raised her freshly poured cup of tea to her lips.

The tea and irony were both perfectly steeped.

The children who were not children—nor would they ever be again after that upcoming night—played on.

---

[175] Mail.

TWO

During the rest of that day:

In the distance.

In the ruins of the crumbling, invaded Carfax Abbey.

In the tender embrace of darkness amid daylight.

In the four coffins:

"Nocte nostrum, Domine Satanus, tuis mysteriis servientes," rumbled Dracula, restless within his wooden womb, eager for the impending evening. Outside, rats swarmed all over the dark, dank room, protecting the vampires while they reposed.

In their own coffins, three female voices hissed a morbid, delicious chorus:

"Προστατέψτε μας απόψε, Λόρδος ο Σατανάς, υπηρέτες των μυστηρίων σου."

"حمايتنا الليلة اي رب الشيطان، عبيد أسرار الخاص بك."

"Proteggici stasera, Signore Satana, servitori dei tuoi misteri."

Protect us tonight, Lord Satan, servants of your mysteries.

"Benedicam benedicentibus tibi pater in nomine meo magno, Satan," whispered Dracula, eyes closed, almost in a meditative state. *I bless you all in the name of my great father.*

"Gratias agimus tibi propter benedictionem," whispered Andromeda and Petra, thinking of crucifixions and disrespect.

"*We thank you for your blessing,*" sighed Venus, thinking of blood and love.

"*Ave Satanus,*" sighed Dracula, his prayer bringing him to the point of sleep.

"*Ave Satanus,*" sighed the brides, eager to rest.

"Satanas vobiscum," said the Transylvanian.

"*Satan be with you, as well,*" whispered the three.

And they slept.

THREE

I understand why no one speaks to Renfield anymore, thought Abraham Van Helsing as he stomped through the tall grass and toward the small cemetery at Seward Manor. The day had been eventful in an odd way for Abraham. After the breakfast, where it had been decided that they would gather again that night at the Seward estate for dinner, Van Helsing had made his way to his guest room, one of the many in the Holmwood estate. Somewhere in the middle of packing, he began to consider returning to London, regardless of Holmwood's apology over their cigars. He knew Arthur too well, had been at too many of these gatherings to know that their tacit peace, however long, would not last. And Abraham was getting older and much less patient with the sort of games that Holmwood enjoyed playing. What was it about Lord Godalming that made him seek out these jousts, to say nothing of himself, thought Abraham, who plopped his Enfield no. 2 MK1 into his bag instead of carrying it on his person, especially if he was going to spend any time with Montague Rhodes Renfield that day.

The wives and younger generation had taken up a fierce game of badminton, Ursula and Mina becoming quite competitive at one point, while the men were inside examining the Impossible Bottle[176] that Arthur had just completed. After making his way past everyone, promising to see them later that afternoon after he had visited Renfield, Abraham rode to the Seward estate and hospital. After an informal lunch in the kitchen courtesy of the staff, which also peppered him with questions about his travels, he paid his visit to Renfield.

A reasonable conversation with Montague Rhodes Renfield had proven impossible, the huge man raving about how sane he was even as he explained his curiosity as to how delicious cat flesh might taste when eaten off the bone.

Abraham remained steeled as Montague Rhodes tried to extract a reaction from him.

"Tell me of your travels, Abraham. I've never seen the world like you have."

"You have, Monty," nodded Abraham past a dry smile. "You've seen some of England."

"Yes, you're right," said Renfield. "I did see the north. Stonehenge. And London. London, of course. Colder than bloody hell. That's where I spent the best time, gutting those whores that deserved to be slit open like pigs, sharing their wares with whoever had a spare shilling to tempt them with, or a pint to buy them with. They'd kiss me in a coffin for a shilling. I'm glad I cut them, their stupid look of surprise when my hand found their throat or my knife found their bellies. I'm glad I cut them. They would eat children while they kissed me. I surely am glad I cut them. Their bellies slit like stinking cheese. I love cheese. Their tripe warmed my hands in the night. Cut them like they were virgins. They probably bled like virgins. You know how cold London can get, Abraham. Made the world a better place, I did. A better place. Vermin. *Vermin*. They turn into vermin as well. Bite us. Like fleas. You know. You've seen. We've all seen. That way they can't continue

---

[176] An Impossible Bottle is another term for a Ship in a Bottle, the pastime of placing a miniature replica of a sea ship within a glass bottle.

to be vermin and infect the rest of the world. That way the world would be clean. There would be no blood in the gutters. If I could have killed them with a cross I would have, but it would have been blasphemous. I'm glad I cut them, glad I bled them, and I'm glad I went to London, mate."

Abraham said nothing.

"I'm glad you were the one who caught me, mate."

"I'm not," said Abraham, staring straight into the massive man's enormous, fragile eyes. "Wish there had been no need in the first place, my friend."

"Butterfly kisses in the dark. All in the past."

He'd left the basement cell after Renfield's rant as quickly and politely as possible, not letting on that Montague's rants had repulsed him. Abraham had taken a few moments to collect himself outside of the metal door to the basement floor, Mrs. Finch patting him on the arm for support.

"You have to leave what he says in there with him," she said.

"Indeed," smiled Abraham, reassuring Mrs. Finch that he was fine, but Renfield had been the last straw in a long day. Van Helsing then headed back through the hospital and into the room that had already been prepared for him at Seward Manor, where he scooped up the night bag. He'd intended to head to the stables, retrieve his horse and then head back to London, perhaps staying at an inn along the way if darkness fell. As he was deciding whether or not to leave a note with the stable hands for Henry, he saw Mina in the distance, in the cemetery, and he headed out to say goodbye. The afternoon breezes swayed the trees, shrubs and grasses on the sprawling grounds. The nearest place of residence could not be seen.

Looking like a black orchid in a sea of emerald and grey tombstones Mina's consistently bleak choice of wardrobe style stood out as she plucked flowers from among the graves on the soft hillside. Mina Murray was plucking flowers, but her furrowed brow told Abraham, even at that distance, that she was absorbed in thought. Swayles also sat nearby her on a tombstone, smoking the same brittle pipe he had smoked the last twenty years. He waved warmly at Abraham as he said, "How you be, Master Abraham?!"

Van Helsing was happy to see Swayles, and as he drew closer, he waved as he said, "Archie, I should think it no good to remind you that childhood friends do not refer to each other with such formality, in my mind at least, and that I should always be 'Bram to you."

"Yes, Sir," chortled Swayles, his ignoring of Abraham's requests for informality were standard operating procedure between them, and they both laughed at the humor and at each other. "How is Monty?"

From her nest among the swaying grasses, Mina looked up, her concentration moving from flowers and whatever else she was thinking about, before seeing that Abraham had his night bag. "You're leaving?"

"Bloody hell, Mina!" laughed Van Helsing, "Do you never tire of spending your free time with corpses?"

Ever the sharp one, Mina cocked her head, raised an eyebrow and planted her hands firmly and dirtily on her hips as she retorted, "I could say the same thing about you with all your mummies, Uncle Abraham!" She would not have her question go unanswered. "Do you tire of our company?"

He neared Mina, and she could not help but break character in order to greet him with a warm embrace and a kiss on the cheek. She was still concerned over her observation of the night bag and did not hide it.

"I realized I was not going to miss your wedding, Mina," said Van Helsing with a wry smile and a glance at his bag. "Because there would be no wedding after all. Arthur and Lucy will wed when the time is right. I'm happy for them and would gladly return for that event."

Mina was not an easy person to surprise, so Abraham had to suppress a smile as her mouth dropped open. "How did you know?"

"How could I not?" shrugged Abraham as he poked her chin with one of the knuckles of his right hand. "A bride celebrates her day, and your face has told me all that I needed to know."

Mina looked away from Abraham's piercing, inquisitive gaze, searching for the ocean in the distance rather than at the father figure in front of her. He had always had that look, those hawk-like eyes crammed with the attentiveness and alertness behind them that seemed to notice *everything*. She let a few flowers rise in the soft breeze and be blown away from them. "It's not Jonny, it's me."

"No need to explain," he cut her off in a crisp, kind way, and Mina's eyes returned to him, free from whatever mixture of shame or guilt that had forced her to look away. Van Helsing reached out with his right hand, and she clasped it warmly with her left. He gave her that slanted grin of comfort that he had always given her as he said, "Perhaps it's just not the right time, dear one. It may be the right time for Lucy and King Arthur."

Mina's eyes glazed with tears, as Abraham was one of the few people in the world to whom she could reveal herself like this. Abraham put down his bag and patted the top of her hand with his left palm, his grin going from warm to a pang of loneliness. "You know, I think of you all as my sons and daughters, the children I never had."

"We know, Uncle Abraham."

Abraham patted her hand again in a warm, fatherly manner and let go. He watched Swayles continue to smoke as he resumed weeding the tombstones. "I grow weary of whatever seems to always invade me when I come here, Mina. There is much love here, but there is also much in the past that haunts us soldiers, some of which you already know about, and some of which you are all undoubtedly discovering for yourselves."

He knew, from knowing Mina has he had her entire life, and without looking at her, that she was giving him her patented Wilhelmina Murray once-over, which is long on contemplation and short on words. Finally, when she had tumbled enough thoughts around in her brilliant but stubborn mind, Mina said, "Do you think it wrong for us to discover said secrets?"

Van Helsing laughed as he watched Swayles shoo a few crows away from one of the crypts. He looked back at Mina with a flat, trusting expression and said, "On the contrary. Part of the reason I'm leaving is that I'm weary of suppressing all of those ghost stories and how they have haunted us for all these years. They have certainly overwhelmed poor Renfield. In my mind, you're all old enough to know, but I'm not your parents. It's not my place to tell you."

The crows fluttered out of Swayles reach and settled on another crypt lid. Mina smiled grimly. "I should try to see poor Monty."

"Candidly, it's best to avoid him if you are not in the best of spirits," rumbled Abraham in the tone Mina always took as fact, not opinion. "These matters, among others, have somewhat muddied the waters between your Uncle Arthur and myself, speaking boldly. It's best that I go before matters become worse between us."

"Father seems to want to tell mother and I, but always hesitates—"

"He's also loyal to his regiment," said Abraham with a respectful nod, "which I understand to a point, but in time this shall all come out and we will all be the healthier for it. Some of the old ways are stupid and foolish, and others are for the better. Soldiers' ways are always among the last to change. When one is trained to do one thing, we do it, but we are not trained to deal with the consequences. Perhaps I am the impatient one. In any event, I'll head back to London and they'll send for me when Lucy weds King Arthur and I'll be back then. In the meantime, I've a few sarcophagi to catalogue—"

"Let me come help you." It was a plea and a wish rolled into a whisper.

Van Helsing nodded his head at her as held up a finger while he picked up his night bag with his free hand. "Stay here, wait for Jonny and tell him whatever it is you need to tell him, for better, worse or later. Then, if you wish, you may join me. But you must follow directions this time, Wilhelmina Murray! No unwrapping of the mummies without the consent of the lead archeologist!"

"That was all Carter's fault! He's such a ninny!"

"That ninny will be England's leading archeologist one day! Mark my words."

"I shall believe it when I see it," Mina said with a laugh, which was followed by a serious but loving look that pierced right into his soul.

"You're a good man, Uncle Abraham. You deserve a family who loves you."

Van Helsing gave her a look that was filled with irony, pity, peace, sadness and love. After a short, bitter shrug, he said, "I mourn Martine and our Claire to this day. Perhaps it is respectful, perhaps unhealthy, I do not know. I have known other men in my situation who have moved on, remarried, raised other children. Such is not for me. There are days on which I reflect that I should have taken a different direction in my life a long time ago, but in all honesty I am more at peace this way. Sometimes the paths in front of you in life are not the happiest, perhaps even melancholy, but I've learned to choose the path which makes the days simple and peaceful. Another wife and child would not have made me happier or replaced them both. It was just never the right time. Like you and Jonny. It's just not the right time. It may never be, but for God's sake do not be motivated by other people or forces around you. Make your own decisions."

"What is the meaning of you packing your things, Van Helsing?" rumbled a familiar voice from behind and below them on the hill. Van Helsing groaned to himself as he pivoted to take in the Lord Godalming and Henry Seward side-stepping their way among the grass and rocks toward them, Arthur depending on his cane to get him along, and Henry struggling with the exertion at his age. Mina sadly noticed both of these things. Arthur's large, wide coat blew open with the breeze, and Henry had to hold onto his hat to keep it on his grey head.

Abraham looked at Arthur Senior and said with his eyes *I am weary of our constant jousting.* Mina watched Van Helsing say without emotion, "It's best I leave. I'll be in London at the museum. Call for me when the weddings are given a date. I would not miss them for the end of the world."

He's not telling them that I'm planning to put Jonny off, thought Mina with even more respect for Van Helsing.

Arthur took all this in, a wide oak of a man who was not used to being challenged, in the midst of being told something he did not want to hear from one of the few men in his life who could challenge him. After a moment of brittleness, the big man softened. "Abraham, please forgive this old, drunken buffoon. I thought we had settled this at breakfast. You are my good friend, my brother through spilled blood if not actual blood, and are loved by all here—"

"—Yes, Abraham, please stay," interjected Henry Seward. "It would not be the entire family together if you were not with us."

The words moved Abraham, if only a little. He stood there and said nothing, which to them all meant that he was considering.

"I'll have a pheasant prepared for dinner," teased the elder Seward, attempting to ply a smile from Abraham, "Your favorite."

For a few seconds, they all watched Swayles shoo crows and clean markers. Mina knew that Abraham could be a hard man at times, and he confirmed it by saying, "I already sent word to my staff that I was returning."

Arthur Senior, who could be an oaf so easily upon so many occasions, could also be refreshingly gentle at times, and he proved it again as he stepped forward, closer to Abraham, and patted him softly on the shoulder. "Then send a note that states your change of mind and heart, dear friend."

Still sitting down behind him, Mina reached out and clasped Abraham's hand again. Suddenly Wilhelmina Murray needed Van Helsing there, needed his wisdom, perspective and honesty. There were no follies, politics or shenanigans with Abraham Van Helsing, and Mina realized that she needed that in her life right now. They all did. "Please, Uncle Abraham."

She waggled Abraham's arm with her hand, in a kind, nostalgic manner that reminded them both of their lost youth.

The crows all cawed a laugh at Abraham Van Helsing's expense.

"Very well," said Abraham with a sudden, tension-releasing laugh. "You're all bloody ridiculous."

The Lord Godalming tenderly slapped Van Helsing on the back, took his night bag from him with the intent of carrying it back for him. Arthur spied a moleskin ledger protruding from one of the pockets. Abraham saw that Arthur had noticed this and said simply, "It's Peter's."

Another emotional shift in their conversation, all three men understood that, and more importantly, Mina noticed this, as she had many of these tiny-but-significant gestures and incidents as she was growing up. She had been trained all too well by her Uncle Abraham.

"Did you speak with Monty?" said Henry Seward, so desperate to change the subject that he referred to a usually uncomfortable topic.

Abraham nodded his head with a soft sadness, and they all knew what he meant by that as well.

"We'd best be heading back," continued Henry. "Have to let the kitchen know that there's an addition to the dinner guests."

"Swayles!" shouted Arthur, waving at him to join them. "Dusk is coming!"

Swayles nodded and said, "I shall follow you sirs in but a moment!"

As they headed in toward the sprawling Seward estate and hospital, Swayles lingered, not knowing why, cleaning the tombstones, smoking his pipe, shooing crows and above all, watching the distant sea.

Behind him, the day died a little more.

FOUR

The last light of the day flickered over the western horizon.

Whitby was doused with night.

Crumbling, dilapidated chambers in the decomposing ruins of the cavernous Carfax Abbey melted into darkness like oil paint mixing upon a canvas. A moment after the last light dissipated within the abbey's ruins a maelstrom from within blew open the great, black lid, scattering the pile of bones that lay upon the coffin, the skeleton zealots that shielded their master during the day hours. The abbey reverberated with sound and fright, and a great, malevolent dark shadow rose out of the obsidian sarcophagus, half form and half fog. Mist poured out and followed the shadow, cloying to the shadow, whose eyes glinted like a predator caught in a lantern, focused with the rage of suppressed anticipation. The form then pointed to the coffin lid and closed it with a single gesture of his right hand before bounding to the nearest craggy, worn, open window like a lion rushing through the Colosseum gates, anticipating Christian morsels within. As he walked, the form hardened into the human form of Dracula, though no less a predator than his leonine counterparts.

From within every hollow and crevasse surged the rat legions, frothing in waves of pestilence and ravenous famine. Some of the skeletons had begun to morbidly re-form themselves after being scattered like ashes around the room, the bones dragging across the cold, dark room toward each other, connecting themselves back together in an awkward spell of evil and wickedness. Primus was one of the first, his armor-laden bones forming the prodigious shape of the skeletal centurion. He pivoted to Dracula's direction and bowed with Old World respect and honor before his master even as his gauntlet-covered left arm crawled up his body like a spider before it settled into the arm socket.

The brides' coffins swung open, and the three beautiful, deadly corpses rose up like cobras as they then slid out of their death boxes, silently gliding along the stone floor, following Dracula's shadowy form as it began to metamorphosize yet again. They felt as they did the night before, but the hunger beckoned them. The vampire reached out with arms that were growing into the wings of a blasphemous pteranodon as he neared the yawning, cobweb-laden window.

Somewhere in mid-transformation, Dracula's dark voice roared, "Primus! Collige omnia ostendi vobis maps super sequi! Stemus in loco ignis videtis et colligere us!" *Gather everything and follow the directions on the maps I have shown you! Stop where you see fire and collect us!*

The word 'us' in Dracula's last sentence was never finished, because the last word was not completely enunciated, it was roared from the feral beast that uttered it. The Dracula bat had reached the window and he clasped it with his jagged talons. The monstrous bat leaped out of the window, majestically unfurling its great, wicked wings, which caught the wind and opened like the sails of a galleon seeking the New World. Behind the black, bleak bat followed the three women, who in their haste to keep up with their master leaped out of the window still in human form, metamorphosing into the triple set of brown bats in mid-air before gravity could catch them completely.

Below them lay the abbey grounds, and all of the roads that wound in, out and around Whitby. As the young night air slid over the Dracula bat's face, in the vampire's mind he superimposed the map that poor, stupid Peter Hawkins had shown him when the Englishman came to Transylvania thinking he'd be selling Carfax Abbey to a wealthy foreigner who was interested in renovation. It was as if the entire area had turned into an enormous table-top model, complete with blinking nights from the town and the ships at port.

Here's the road that I take out of Whitby, said Uncle Peter in Dracula's memory, *and as you pass Carfax Abbey you'll head out for a stretch past the moors, then follow that one road out and you'll see all of the Whitby estates lined up, and we're all among them. We shall be neighbors after you move in!*

Dracula saw a strange caravan moving in from the northwest, toward Whitby. He did not know what this strange new vehicle was, since the vampire had never encountered a train before. Dracula brought his wings together as he dove, falling like a brick, wind whistling through his large, wide bat ears, which he pivoted backwards along his great, shaggy skull. He spread his great wings, catching the air and stunting his fall, and he swept up along dirt, shrub and fog along the moors and soared above and past the passing train, and he purred with the joy of a hunter at seeing the passengers in the train, all bloated with blood that he could pour into his mouth like bottles of wine. This was nothing but a moving vineyard. The train bells went off as the bats all banked above and around the brake van.[177]

They all rose again with the night air, flying fast. Fields and fences swept below them, as did barns and sheds and groves of trees. The tabletop model zipped by at incredible speed then, and the brides chattered and chirped like bats do behind Dracula.

He had other matters to concern himself with.

A familiar road lay perpendicular to their path.

He banked to the right, the bride bats followed.

Dracula growled with delight as he recognized property lines along each side of the road, manicured lawns, shrubs and gardens that clung to the large mansions that funded them. A lone carriage headed underneath them and toward Whitby, away from his wrath. Dracula hissed with glee when he heard the horses that drew the carriage neigh in fright when they saw what soared above them. If he were human, Dracula's pulse would have raced when he recognized the sprawling Harker Estate. *This will be unlike any other siege, any other battle, any other conquest, because my wrath has been earned*, thought the Transylvanian. The manor was dark, windows black and empty. No carriages or wagons, no signs of visible activity. Hunters that knew their job well, the bats soared over and past the Harker home, eager for light and evidence of activity.

"Quincy Morris, you are so disgusting!" squealed Lucy, in a laughing fit of hysterical proportions. She sat next to young Arthur, just across the table from the Texan, who had stuck two pieces of carrots up his nose, his cheeks full of pudding and was crossing his eyes in the most immature yet hilarious combination of tomfoolery that his audience had, apparently, ever witnessed. They all sat in the expansive dining room in Seward Manor, which was, despite what Henry Seward had contested the previous evening, an eerily similar design to the Holmwood dining room, complete with beautiful wooden floors and a languid elegant table with a prodigious feast set upon it.

Both generations roared with laughter at Quincy's frivolity, even Abraham, who was a little drunk but nevertheless was out-roared by the bombastic Arthur Senior. The ladies also giggled like

---

[177] The brake van is the British term for caboose, which in America is a railroad car at the end of a freight train, which provides shelter for the crew.

lunatics, Judith Murray so hard that she spat out her last sip of wine. The meal, which indeed had featured pheasant, which unlike the night before was served *à la française*[178], placed in front of Lillian Seward before it was carved and served. A dessert pyramid[179] was the star of the meal, brought with a round of applause from servant and audience alike.

"Uncle Abraham!" shouted Ian, who, along with Quincy formed the bachelor faction of the family. "Will you indulge us in your card trickery? I surely miss that about you when you are away."

Van Helsing beamed at Ian fondly for remembering. "Magic, Young Seward. It's not card trickery, it is magic."

"There's no such thing as magic!" giggled Lucy, slapping Ian's shoulder, her good, golden mood overflowing as much as the wine had over dinner. All the older men caught each other's glances before grinning in a wry, bitter way, since they knew that what Lucy had just stated was not true. All the elder women noted the exchange with resentment in their hearts for being excluded, as well as a familiar chill in their spines for the implication. The younger generation was too busy regaling each other to notice.

Outside the expansive French doors behind them, decorated delicately with cranes, tulips and rosettes, with a second story of opulent class windows hanging above, the night and the wind danced together to a nocturne that only they could hear and fall in love to, a contrast to the previous night's storm.

Nearby, Archie Swayles again sat among the dead, an empty bottle of rum in his hands and a stomach full of it. His face felt warm and his eyes were glazed over, such was his intoxication. The night around him was new, but cold and hard. Tombstones were his friends and the distant, collective laughter from inside the manor filled him with both happiness and loneliness. He envied, hated, loved and admired everyone inside.

His eyes were so glazed that they could not focus properly on the four ghost-like figures that had swept down from the night above. Three brown forms and one black, it was as if John Singer Sargent himself had painted a scene just for him, with bold, beautiful out-of-focus paint strokes. The forms all blinked with crimson, glowing eyes.

And brushstrokes that were canines, rendered in bold hues, four off-white mouths and white, slavering teeth.

And those eyes, the crimson eyes, all eyeing poor Swayles.

The Sargent painting shifted in focus, and the oily strokes began to form and frame beautiful, eerie, classic human faces framed by dark, stark, elegant clothes. The faces were unfinished, still forming, still being painted, underpaintings all. The process of underpainting appeared live before Swayles in these four undead portraits. The malevolent, black, jagged form before Swayles shifted somehow, brush strokes twisting and flowing as they did, and became a man.

A shadow man.

Menace.

All black, with a ghostly white face and eyes of an owl or a leopard. A man who looked like he could crush a kingdom, which in fact he had, many times. The ghost/owl/leopard painting man glared a hole right through Swayles. Like he was made out of chocolate. Or flesh and blood.

The other three brown forms had been re-painted as well, and there were now three beautiful women that looked old and new at the same time, with the same stare that a carnivore has as it closes in on something it is about to consume. Their collective faces had been borne out of angry,

---

[178] *À la française* is the formal dining habit of serving various dishes of a meal at the same time, hence 'in the French Style'. Serving food at the table from a platter to a dish is called 'English service' or *service à l'anglaise*.

[179] A dessert pyramid is a fanciful arrangement of small cakes and sliced fruit, topped with sugar, in the familiar triangular form.

obsessive brushstrokes, where a woman's gaze was a bold challenge, not a demure exploration. The angriest, a classical Italian face of exquisite beauty and ferocious countenance, snarled at him like a panther.

The shadow man smiled like he knew there would be no tomorrow.

This did not surprise Archie Swayles.

Gales, zephyrs and gusts all pirouetted in the night around them.

All trying to warn him.

"I knew you'd be arriving," chuckled Archie. "From that moment back in that horrible village, I knew some of you would come for us."

"We have never had the fortune to meet until this moment," said the Singer-Sargent painting's main figure, in a clipped English reserved for learned aristocrats. He seemed almost amused at Swayles' last statement. The man had clasped his hands behind him, looking like he could command an army.

"That's right," said Swayles, starting to laugh and cry, such was his fear. "But I reckon you know all about what we did, back when we did it, and though we wuz just boys at war, I figure we deserve everything you done bring with you. All of us. But she deserved to die as well. That I will tell you."

The man in the painting grinned again, and despite being intoxicated, Swayles knew that the man's grin meant death.

"I almost want to let you live," beamed Dracula after a few profound nods and taking in the swirling clouds above him. The women did not, they only stared at Pat, and they were not blinking.

Only glaring.

"I want you to know I'd have done it again," gasped Swayles, no longer drunk, the last bit of defiance left in him. Adrenaline pumped through Archie, he burst into tears. He wet his pants in terror.

The Singer-Sargent Painting Man gestured to the three women, and as Swayles gagged with horror they leapt at him. He was shoved to the ground and he felt his intestines being ripped out of his stomach by luscious lips. Clawed feminine fingers pulled his rib cage apart with a deafening crunch. Feminine forms writhed over him as they consumed him. One of them twisted his head and buried a mouth full of canines into his neck, pulling out his jugular and his neck muscles with one bite. Swayles heard a macabre feminine giggle as the women began to feast on him *while he was still alive*.

Blood and tears filled his eyes, and in the moment before Swayles' organs were pulled out of his torso, he relived a lifetime full of friendship, abandonment, war, loneliness and an empty bed beside him.

Dracula eyed the Seward estate, with its manicured lawns, elegant architecture and multiple carriages sitting in wait.

And beautiful French windows.

"'Bram," slurred Victoria at Van Helsing, "come by tomorrow and for tea with Lucy and me."

Everyone then knew which moment this was in the chronology of family festivities. This was the Victoria-makes-a-fool-out of-her-drunken-self moment of the evening's entertainment. Mina's laughter from watching Ian try and examine Quincy's ear with a pheasant bone was curtailed. She put her glass of wine down and looked into it. Mina didn't need to look to her immediate right; she knew that Lucy would have already noticed her mother's condition and must have been flushed red by now. Instantly Mina's eyes shot to the other end of the table, where her parents were already trying to steer the focus away from Victoria's antics, with the thought of outright ignoring her second on the list. The Murrays' conversational inertia was further enhanced by both the Holmwoods and the Sewards, while Ursula shared a knowing, conspiratorial glance with Lillian Seward and Judith Murray. *This is why we seat her with the children.* The Harkers remained in their own universe, quietly sipping their wine and reacting to the bluster that was Arthur Senior.

"I think not, Victoria," flared Abraham. His gesture indicated Victoria's inebriated condition. "I thought you were past all this."

Mina suppressed a small, tight smile. She had always admired Van Helsing's bluntness, especially in social situations that others treated more with an aim toward preserving their reputation than of furthering the truth. He was like her parents, but with a sharper edge. Victoria took in Abraham's words with a simmering stare, knowing he was right but hating him for speaking his mind and embarrassing her like this.

After a moment of rebuking Victoria with his stare, Van Helsing softened. *I've made my point.* He followed with an effort to change the subject, "Lucy reminds me more of her father every time I see her. Phillip would have been proud."

They both turned to Lucy, who looked like she could commit matricide at that moment. Victoria took a swig of wine and hissed, "You remember my husband better than I do, Abraham."

"He saved my life," shrugged Van Helsing. "Many times over. I was just a boy at war. I had no business there. Phillip was a man. A true man. A good man."

Victoria Westenra planted her chin on the palm of her right hand in a sarcastic gesture to Abraham, who simply nodded at her politely and turned away to the rest of the guests. Victoria sighed and wistfully kept her eyes on Abraham, who began to trade strange faces with the Texan, all the time knowing that Phillip's wife was watching him. As did everyone else at the table, and whatever else they all thought about Abraham Van Helsing, they respected him for choosing not to be ordinary.

Normal conversation started to resume again along the dinner table. Mina had to tease her dearest friend. She leaned over and whispered, "You are clearly your mother's daughter, Lucy."

"In the respect that I am a drunken tart like the mother who bore me?" smirked/hissed/giggled Lucy, who even in her present mood could enjoy a joke at her own expense. Lucy glared a hole right through her mother as she said it. Her mother may have heard her comment, but Lucy Westenra was not in the mood to care as she bandied with Mina.

"No," said Mina, "in the respect that you do not back down to anyone, not even to Professor and Doctor Abraham Van Helsing. Or is it doctor and professor?"

"She's always fancied Uncle Abraham," nodded Lucy after another sip of wine. "Ever since I can remember. She says Father was a kind man, but far too often enjoyed a silent life in our tomb of a house—

"—and I presume that Uncle Abraham represents the antithesis of that—"

"—I wonder," said Lucy, "if they've ever—"

"Good Lord," said Mina after a sharp gasp.

She was looking past Lucy, who turned to see her mother rising up and out of her seat, holding her glass of wine up higher than she might have intended if she were sober. Abraham noted this and covered his face with his hand, more out of embarrassment for Victoria than anything else.

Victoria Westenra was struggling to stand and make an announcement.

Lucy reached for Victoria's sleeve, to pull her back down to her chair. Victoria pulled away and threw her daughter a dirty look as she semi-shouted, "I suppose this is something that is accustomed to be done by the man of the house, the host, but I'll break tradition in this instance and salute my daughter and Young Arthur on their impending wedding."

Mina reached out and held Lucy's hand, who was just livid. She shook with rage as she whispered, "God, Mother you're quite drunk."

"Don't you worry about my drunkenness Missy," winked an always-sunny Quincy Morris from across the table in an attempt to lighten the mood. *Good Lord, Quincy's an idiot*, thought both Ian and young Arthur at the same moment.

Lucy brightened for a second before she heard her mother go on with, "I'd also like to take the moment to salute Miss Wilhelmina Murray on her impending marriage to her betrothed," and here Victoria swayed as she swung her glass of wine toward Mina, who could only flush with crimson embarrassment, even as Victoria giggled, "as soon as Jonny can arrive from whatever passionate romp he is having in the Orient—"

Lucy's jaw hit the ground.

Everyone's eyes turned toward Mina, who died a thousand deaths in a second.

Lucy bolted to her feet and reached out for Victoria's glass. Victoria swung it away and said, "Let me finish my toast, Lucy!"

"That's enough Mother!"

Victoria raised her glass again, staggering as she did so while trying to keep it away from Lucy, who was clawing her way up her mother's arm to retrieve it.

Victoria cleared her throat and shouted, "To the lovely schoolteacher and her handsome husband-to-be!"

In one motion, attempting to save face for everyone, Abraham stood, whipped his arm out and took the glass from Victoria. He raised it and said loudly but politely, "To Victoria's intentions for Mina, regardless."

They all toasted to that.

"Hear, hear," said Lord Godalming, toasting Van Helsing's actions as much as the toast as well. He winked an apologetic, grateful wink to Abraham, which Van Helsing returned in kind.

"Well deserved," said Henry Seward, followed by an eye roll from Lillian.

Lucy was trying to get Victoria back into her seat, but Mrs. Westenra was intent on getting her glass back from Abraham, who tossed back the rest of the wine in one shot and sat down, with a look at Victoria that read *sit down and shut up*.

"Sit down, Dear," said Judith Murray to Victoria, softly.

Ursula Holmwood nodded curtly and succinctly said, "Indeed."

"Please," whispered Cynthia Harker.

Mina was beet red, sitting stiffly, like she was alone in the universe. Andrew saw how his daughter was feeling. He stood and said, "We'd best be on our way for the evening."

"I agree," said Judith, who started to walk over to Mina.

"Not so soon, Andrew," said Arthur. "Victoria meant no harm. Tempest in a tea cup, old man."

Lucy at last was able to force her mother back down into her chair as she hissed, "Mother, you have embarrassed Mina—"

"She's alright, silly," giggled Victoria. "At least she'll able to break hearts again now that she's available. Perhaps it's that Fleming girl Jonny once fancied?"

Aw crap, thought Quincy. *Shouldn'ta said that, Aunt Victoria.*

She's just the crow that would not shut up, thought Judith as she moved to comfort her daughter. Mina just sat there, staring straight ahead, humiliated and overwhelmed. All of her feelings of confusion with her marriage, Jonathan and life itself began to boil inside of her, and she began to cry, hating herself for showing weakness like this and hating herself for not being who everyone thought she should be. She brought a trembling hand to her lips, to cover their quiver. Ironically, she hated Jonathan Harker at that moment, because when he was here she could always talk to him and he could wipe her soul clean of whatever ailed her at the moment. Where was he when she needed him the most?

Then a streak of pride, anger, independence and frustration exploded inside of Mina, and she bolted to her feet, in tears. Out of the corner of her eye, she saw Van Helsing, looking at her with an expression that said *don't do it.*

Don't do it.

Mina became calm, cleared her throat and said, "Everyone, I'd like to announce that my marriage to Jonathan—"

Wilhelmina Murray's words were cut off by a thunderous explosion of glass that shattered the moment and the grand window behind them.

A two thousand-pound carriage was hurtled into the dining room with brutal, violent force, as if it was shot out of a cannon.

The carriage raked across the room, collided with the dining table, pinning it to the inner wall, killing some of the diners instantly.

The Golden Age was over.

FIVE

Utter bedlam.

Screams of terror erupted.

Glass covered everything.

Pandemonium lanced with abject horror.

The carriage lay on its front end, wheels facing out toward the window. The driver's box had shredded the dining table, throwing the meal and everyone aside with tremendous force and violence. The gas burner lights in the room had blown out, as had most of the candles that were on the table but now littered the wooden floor. Candle wax dribbled over broken table and carriage seat.

In the half-light were moans, shouts and wails.

Silence between screams and within flickering-candle darkness.

The frame of the great French window collapsed.

Cynthia Harker was viciously pinned to the table by the top of the carriage. Her back, neck and skull had been horribly crushed by the weight.

The carriage's front had pressed against William Harker's chest until his heart exploded, then it continued to crush him into the chair and to the wood floor.

"Cynthia! Cynthia!" shrieked Ursula Holmwood after seeing the crushed bodies. Only William's broken, bloody legs were visible from under the carriage. It was as if they were grain seeds pulverized under a great stone mill.

Judith Murray valiantly held Lillian Seward, who was tearing at her hair while screaming at the top of her lungs.

Lucy and Victoria, cast aside by the momentum of the carriage, began to scream hysterically, while Young Arthur and Ian Seward, themselves shocked beyond words, held the women back from aiding the Harkers, whom they knew were lost. The carriage groaned as it started to lean to its right.

"Move!" shouted Van Helsing, somehow calm in a sea of panic. He glanced back at Quincy and roared, "Keep them back! It's about to tip over!"

The carriage moaned again, and the rear began to slowly rake a downward arc along the wall. No one saw poor Henry Seward laying on the spot where it would land, semi-conscious among the rubble.

"Help Henry!" bellowed Arthur Holmwood Sr., sprawled out on the other side of the cresting carriage. Like a shot, Quincy Morris dove in, and while the carriage hastened its path to the ground, dragged a barely-conscious Dr. Henry Seward away from the shadow of the dying carriage, which thundered and cracked when it slammed down onto the table and the splintered floor. The entire floor buckled with the weight and the agony that everyone was feeling.

Victoria vomited and passed out, with Lucy and Mina in tears as they held her limp form.

"Oh my Lord, help us!" screamed Judith Murray, collapsing into the arms of Andrew, even as she herself restrained Lillian Seward, who wailed an insane, trembling, tearful smile at Quincy, grateful to the Texan that Henry was still alive.

Having fallen to its left side, the carriage completely revealed the crushed bodies of William and Cynthia Harker.

"William!" shouted Henry Seward, still in the arms of Quincy Morris, who had tears streaming down his face. Henry reached out to the body of his old friend, the bloody pulp of a form barely recognizable, when the heart that had borne Dr. Henry Seward so well for so many years suddenly turned on him. He began to tremble and could not stop. Henry felt the pain and began to scream, then could not stop screaming, as it seemed that Vesuvius itself was erupting out of his chest. Seward arched his back, then fell over, and in an instant Ian was upon him, screaming "Father!" over and over again as convulsions overran Doctor Henry Seward. Lillian Seward, who had freed herself from Judith Murray, raced in to see her husband whisper, "Forgive me, Darlings," and he was dead before Ian could act, tears pouring out his eyes as he held his son while the room and the world around him darkened forever.

Fire had caught where the candles had fallen from the tables.

A servant ran in from the kitchen to astutely turn the main gas light switch to the dining room off, but then turned and ran when Dracula turned his glowing, crimson eyes upon her and snarled like a jackal.

The carriage began to flicker with fire as well. Shouts and wails set the tone of chaos and terror in the room. Quincy slid his hands away from Henry's body, and let his friend mourn his father.

"Uncle Henry," sobbed Morris, reaching over and planting his palm on Uncle Henry's forehead, a last gesture of love.

"Good Lord, Good lord, Good Lord," was all that Arthur Holmwood, the Lord Godalming could repeat over and over. He had fallen to his knees, and held a sobbing, distraught Ursula Holmwood.

Abraham saw that Henry and William's bodies were close enough together so that he could hold both of their hands, which he did. Van Helsing scanned the shattered French doors, eyes moving back and forth like a hunter, even as tears ran out of them, as he prayed, "'In company with Christ, who died and now lives, may they rejoice in Your kingdom, where all our tears are wiped away. Unite us together again in one family, to sing your praise forever and ever. Amen[180].'"

A cold, bitter thought ran through Abraham Van Helsing.

They know.

Someone knows.

And they are here for us.

After all this time.

The room had gone silent, save for wails from Lucy.

Van Helsing continued, "Oh God, admit him to Paradise and protect him from the torment of the grave and the torment of Hell-fire; make his grave spacious and fill it with light[181]."

Abraham thought he saw movement outside, past the broken windows. He ignored the hollow feeling of dread that crept over him as his prayer continued. "For certain is death for the born, and certain is birth for the dead; therefore over the inevitable thou shouldst not grieve[182]."

Mina also thought to look away from the inert carriage and outside, past the enormous, destroyed window.

She was the first to see the vast, bleak, iridescent shadow drift through the broken frame like a plague through Biblical Egypt.

---

[180] Roman Catholic prayer for the dead.
[181] Roman Catholic prayer for the dead.
[182] Chapter two from the Bhagavad Gita, or simply Gita, part of the Hindu epic Mahabharata.

Then the shadow advanced.

Death swept into the room.

The Singer-Sargent painting in motion, a great rendered shadow of Old Testament pestilence was among them.

All the men still alive that had gone to war and come back and left that memory behind, all of them knew at that moment that their deed had come back.

Their ghosts had come back.

Someone knows.

Three other shadows followed, drifting in through the broken-glass frames, and the whole scene became surreal, dreamlike and menacing as Van Helsing, resolutely, eyeing the shadows all the while, continued to pray, "The Everlasting is their heritage, and they shall rest peacefully upon their lying place, and let us say: Amen[183]."

"Amen," replied everyone, and as they did, Abraham Van Helsing let go of William Harker's and Henry Seward's dead hands and stood, eyes locked on the lead shadow, the plume of maleficence that stood on the other side of the destroyed table.

A tremor ran down Quincy's body as he watched the shadow move toward them.

He realized that it was a tremor of fury. That fury snapped the Texan back into reality enough to snake his Colts up out of their holsters and at the shadow.

In tears, he squeezed the triggers.

All of the rounds exploded out of the barrel of Quincy's Colts.

One, one, two, two, three, three, four, four and a double-five[184].

Small tufts of material and dust harmlessly appeared and disappeared on Dracula's coat and shirt. Holes cut into the walls that held the broken, massive window frame behind the shadow.

A dark chuckle wafted from the malevolent silhouette, which stepped forward into a flicker of light from the burning room.

Van Helsing's blood ran cold, as did Lord Godalming's, as did Andrew Murray's.

Four corpses glided into view, three deadly women and one monster of a man.

Dracula's eyes danced with evil glee.

Venus, eyes glowing like all of the vampires, held something behind her, bleak, elegant dress. Teasing them with what it could be and with her electric, ferocious leer.

Andromeda snarled like a wild dog, and Lucy nearly fainted.

The shadow hissed, "I am Dracula of Transylvania. I am a king, a nobleman, and your natural superior."

Venus revealed what she held, casually throwing the dismembered head and torso of Archibald Swayles out in front of them. It landed in a wet pile of blood on the remnants of the table and the dinner.

Lillian Seward screamed bloody murder.

Blood over ceramic.

Torn intestines over tablecloth.

Candle wax bleeding over exposed brains.

"Omylordhelpus," gasped Ursula Holmwood, her composure gone, quivering in fear.

"I am *nosferatu, strigoi, vampyr*," said Dracula proudly, his taloned right hand splayed out against his chest. "A being of legend, myth and reality. I existed when this world had rules only for peasants, whores and slaves. I am master of all that I have owned and seen. I have survived more wars than you have had all your years of existence. My titles of Count, Cardinal and Royal

---

[183] Van Helsing is reciting from El Maleh Rachamim, the Jewish funeral prayer.
[184] Quincy's Colt is a six-shooter, and many gun owners at that time only loaded their revolvers with five rounds to avoid accidental misfires.

Heir were granted to me by three beings: Vlad Tepes of Wallachia, His 'Holiness' the fool Pope Alexander VI, and my Most Hateful Father. You have no defense, no recourse against myself or my concubines, for Satan is my blessed father and I am his only revered son."

"Quincy," whispered Abraham, "Do you have your Bowie knife with you?"

After a single nod and a tap at a sheath wrapped around his thigh, Quincy whispered back, "Oh, yeah."

Despite the situation, Abraham nearly laughed out loud in gratitude. He whispered, "I have a bottle of water in my pocket—"

"We've done nothing to you!" shouted Ursula Holmwood at the vampires as she rose to her feet. With a sweep of his massive arm, Arthur Senior stood, stepped forward and swung his wife behind him, away from them.

We deserve this, thought Andrew Murray as he shielded Judith from the undead.

But not the women.

Or our children.

Dracula looked at Ursula like she was a dove in his hawk's eyes.

The Transylvanian growled like a leopard as he turned to the Holmwoods.

"Touch her and I'll kill you!" bellowed Arthur Senior.

After another angry chuckle, Dracula whispered, "I stand here before you because years ago, on the other side of this continent, amid my beloved Carpathians, the old men in this room murdered *my wife*!"

Dracula's eyes danced with fiery hate.

"And for this sacrilege, this blasphemy, *this insult*," roared Dracula, "I am here to exact revenge upon you and all that dare to love you. My only regret is that there are no grandchildren here to slaughter. I have already taken the lives of both Peter Hawkins and Jonathan Harker, and *none of you* will see the upcoming dawn!"

Dracula then composed himself before he reached into his inner coat pocket and pulled out the small, framed photograph of Mina that he had taken from Jonathan Harker. He glanced around the room until he found Mina, who looked shocked when the vampire recognized her. Dracula held out the photo by his fingertips for everyone to see before he savagely crushed it and casually tossed the remnants to a shocked Mina. Wilhelmina Murray, teacher, lover and dreamer, caught the fragments, took in her own visage, shouted out of raw agony and burst into horrified tears as the loss of Jonathan Harker hit her like a freight train.

The vampire drank in Mina's wailing pain. "You were to wed. I take great satisfaction in your suffering, whore."

Savoring the moment, the vampire again looked over the room, locking his owl eyes with everyone, one at a time, sizing them up until he settled upon Arthur Holmwood, the Lord Godalming. The look in Arthur's eyes told Dracula everything he needed to know. "Yesssssss. You look to be their leader, the one who would have commanded the execution of my wife. You remember your eradication of my woman very well, do you not?"

As the invader snarled at Uncle Arthur, the shock and horror in Mina knew no bounds. *I have already taken the lives of both Peter Hawkins and Jonathan Harker,* the monster before her had gloated. She staggered, lurched to the side and vomited.

He's dead, she thought, *my Jonathan is dead and they took him!*

A single, raging scream erupted from Mina, and she drew her Remington-Elliot Pepperbox Derringer and angrily emptied all four rounds at Dracula, the bullets passing through him like a welcome summer night's breeze.

"Woman," laughed Dracula, "Did you not see that your weapons will do us no harm? Now, you will discuss your disrespect with my Venus."

The look that Venus gave Mina was enough to make Lucy want to wither with terror into young Arthur's arms, but she stood strong, resolute and unafraid.

"Per manus autem mea non omnis moriar!" snarled Venus. *By my hand you will all die!*

Mina calmly took rounds out of her purse and began to reload while she kept her eyes on Venus. The vampiress snarled like a wild dog, canines fully exposed and eyes bloated with bloodlust.

An awakened Victoria lay at Mina's feet, sobbing, with her head in her hands and trying to retain her sanity. Lucy and Arthur gently helped her mother to her feet, propping Victoria up so she would not collapse.

Through all this, Abraham Van Helsing had remained calm, taking everything in, where everyone was, how many adversaries, which windows were broken, how many doors to the house were still closed... all of it. When he was done taking everything into account, he stood, took a step forward, swung his arms out wide and bellowed, "Everyone! Move behind me! Now!!"

Then, without the slightest hesitation, Abraham whipped out his Enfield, pointed it at Dracula's chest and squeezed the trigger.

Once.

Twice

Three.

Four.

Five times.

And each time, each round punched the vampire in the chest, moving through him, their trajectories altered, yet each one a solid blow to his body.

Gut punches from a pugilist.

Each 'punch' staggered the vampire back a step.

The Transylvanian gave Van Helsing an astonished look.

"These bullets are silver, blessed with Holy Water," smiled Abraham through the gun smoke, with a nod to Quincy, so the Texan could understand. "The regular rounds would wound your women, but they affect you enough for my purposes."

Staggered into a crouch as a result of Van Helsing's blasts, Dracula reared back and spread his arms and as he did so, the vampire became the moving John Singer Sargent painting again, texture, skin and fur shapeshifting all over his black silhouette. His arms became the massive black wings of a bat as Victoria, Lillian and Ian began to wail in fear and astonishment. It was a terrifying, yet beautiful moment, and when the moment had past, he was once again the Dracula bat, enormous, primeval, and completely intimidating.

As the vampire was transforming, Abraham had reloaded his pistol and spun the cylinder into place, ready to go. Quincy Morris started to reload his Colts as well. The round, crimson eyes blinked with ferocity at Van Helsing. Abraham was unbowed, coldly raising his Enfield again.

One round punched the vampire's head before it sang up and lodged itself somewhere in the ceiling.

Two.

Then three.

But the colossal bat did not charge Abraham. Instead, it took the remaining blows from the pistol, raising its left arm to protect its face. Powerful musculature was at work while the creature moved, like a grizzly or a lion, and the others were astonished. The monstrosity pivoted and leaped not at Abraham but at a terrified Lord Godalming, who had no recourse but to further shove himself in front of Ursula as the bull-sized Dracula bat expanded its enormous wingspan fully during its leap, a frightful sight. Ursula shrieked in terror and Arthur picked up his cane from the floor. The Lord Godalming was an imposing man, and he was not unprepared for a situation such as this. He wrenched the top of the handle from his cane off and from inside the cane came a hidden sword. Arthur swung it at the beast, but the Dracula bat was faster, it had already begun to swing viciously with its right arm/wing. Arthur tried to raise his left, holding his swordless cane to try and parry the blow, but the force was so ferocious, so violent and so savage that it broke both the cane and Arthur's left arm.

Then the blow collided with Arthur Senior's head

And tore it completely from the neck.

The violence of the blow was shocking and horrific.

One moment Arthur Holmwood, the Lord Godalming, was fighting for his life and protecting the woman he loved from attack, and the next, his head was ripped cleanly from his body and slammed down against the polished floorboards, a burst of blood shooting out of the torso volcanically as his body collapsed backwards onto poor Ursula Holmwood, who screamed maniacally as one and a half gallons of blood that had been inside her husband's body exploded over her face.

Blood continued to squirt horrifically from Arthur's severed head as it skidded along the floorboards, into a corner of the dining room, leaving a trail of ragged crimson in its wake.

Arthur Holmwood's life left as quickly as his blood did.

Everyone screamed in absolute horror and disbelief.

As his friend's blood splattered all over him, Abraham aimed his Enfield and emptied the last three rounds at the Dracula bat, who in one fluid movement lunged over the falling, decapitated body of Lord Godalming and bit savagely into the neck of Ursula Holmwood, his foaming canines sinking into her delicate neck. The monstrosity soared over her body, his wing claws skidding along the varnished floor, before yanking her backwards, away from the still quivering, headless body of her husband. Ursula had not even been given the opportunity to scream at Arthur's decapitation. Then the Dracula bat crouched, powerful muscles contracting and bulging underneath the fur, before exploding upward in a tremendous leap, catapulting himself and Ursula high in the air, up into the rafters of the dining room, like a leopard jumping up into the safety of a tree, holding a baby antelope in his possession.

Sickle-like claws raking at the exposed beams, the gigantic bat clung to the rafters, upside-down, wings splayed out like twin spiderwebs. Ursula's body hung limply from the enormous canines that held her.

Everyone looked up as a spasm of twitches from Ursula made Judith Murray wretch in overwhelming disgust and horror. Lady Godalming dangled from the Dracula bat's mouth like a fresh kill in a tiger's maw. Then she gave a long, single moan *because she was still alive*. Hearing the moan, the Dracula bat gave his shaggy head a violent shake and broke Ursula's neck like a twig, the crack reverberating around the large room like thunder from a nearby lightning strike.

"You Goddamned coward!" shouted Abraham in defiance as he reloaded his revolver as quickly as you or I could strike a matchstick.

The Dracula bat gave a long, dark, satisfied hiss in response before he looked down and over to the brides.

They in turn were watching his every movement with their candle-light, owl eyes.

He then gave a single, silent nod at his women before twisting his head and spitting Ursula Holmwood's corpse to the ground.

Arthur Holmwood II, not yet aware he was now the Lord Godalming, gave out a long, mournful scream as his mother's lifeless body's bones broke as it collided with the floor.

Petra, Andromeda and Venus needed no further invitation.

Three undead women became three oil paintings.

Three horrific, beautiful portraitures.

Macabre, extraordinary works of surreal, shimmering death.

Skin, fur, cloth and texture moved and flowed.

Three heads that were sculptured pieces of undead art melted like candlewax, then hardened like clay, and when it had hardened, they were not human heads. Hands had become wings, dresses had supernaturally melted into skin and metamorphosed into fur, and like three cobras twisting out of a basket, the brides rose in liquid motion.

The bride bats bellowed eerie, inhuman shrieks as they attacked everyone in the room.

Everything then happened very quickly, simultaneously.

The Petra bat was upon Quincy Morris in a heartbeat, her canines and eyes flashing in the firelight, her wings spreading out gracefully out to envelop him in a death embrace. But the Texan had ripped the Bowie knife from its sheath and he whipped it around viciously to slash at the monstrous bat.

In the same moment, Abraham swung his Enfield, now fully reloaded, at the Petra bat's head as she embraced Quincy, but she pivoted and kicked out savagely with her right leg, planting it brutally against Abraham's rib cage and knocking him toward the back wall of the dining room. The blow was tremendous, and Van Helsing slammed against the wall, stunned. Quincy's knife slash passed harmlessly through Petra's rib cage, as if it was made of wax, leaving a wound that healed instantly. Petra was more annoyed than injured by the knife parry and she raked the air with the clawed fingers of her left wing, a powerful blow meant to rip the Texan's face clean off. She missed, and Morris countered by punching the Petra bat in the face with a right-hand cross while still holding the knife. The Petra bat swayed back away from the blow, snarled ferociously at Morris, and charged again.

"The others need not suffer," said Andrew Murray, holding his hands up in a gesture of surrender as he backed away from the Dracula bat. As the monstrous beast landed back down on the floor, making the boards groan, it began gliding across the floor towards Andrew like an oversized cat toward a mouse. The look on the Dracula bat's face was that of pure malice and ravenous hunger. Its ears lowered and pivoted to the back, ready for the kill.

Andrew, having decided to maneuver the creature away from the others before yelling for his loved ones to run, as the monster had at him, reiterated, "They need not pay our price!"

Andrew glanced over at Judith, who along with Ian was helping a shell-shocked Lillian Seward to her feet.

Mina and Arthur were shielding Lucy and Victoria Westenra from the Venus bat, who had lowered her head and was moving at them, savoring the moment of attack.

Murray thought, *that was my last glance at my wife and child, may God bless them and give them another day.* He nodded at Dracula and almost pleaded. "The deed was ours. Let us pay."

Bones shifted, fur supernaturally melting back into the texture of cloth, and the human form of Dracula gave a death grimace. "As you spared my wife?" snarled the vampire, his now-human face curled up into an animalistic snarl. "As you spared my own wife?!"

Another servant burst into the dining room with a meat cleaver raised, only to have Dracula emasculate him with one horrific blow to the body. The pieces of the corpse flew onto Andrew, splattering him with gore.

The Andromeda bat bounded on all fours toward Lillian, Judith and Ian, its winged hands and mammalian feet leaving claw marks along the wooden floor as it moved, hundreds of pounds of undead flesh on the run. In a panic, Ian Seward grabbed the end of the broken dining room table while pushing a terrified Lillian behind him. The Andromeda bat opened its foaming maw and hissed like a cobra as it leaped. Ian took the table end and flipped it over, then held it up with all his might as Andromeda rammed into it with the force of a runaway bull.

The Venus bat leaped and plowed into Arthur Holmwood like a locomotive into a woodshed. He felt the right side of his body slam against the wood flooring, the air expelling from his lungs. His head banged against the wood, blunting his hearing, so Lucy and Victoria's screams became muffled. Arthur put up his hands just in time to feel the weight of the bat press against him. The beast's huge, jagged teeth flashed in Arthur's face, his bent arm holding her off. It was only the adrenaline surging through him that kept the beast off him. Eyeball to eyeball with the she-bat, Arthur felt the heat and stink of the animal's disgusting breath, and in that moment, he saw her fury, her hate, the malice in her expression. He noticed a shadow pass over them, and when he looked up, the new Lord Godalming braced himself. He watched as Mina hoisted a dining chair over her head and with a vociferous, primal roar, brought it down like thunder on the head and neck of the Venus bat.

What little light left in the room began to flicker amid the darkness of the deepening night, casting an eerie, dramatic pallor throughout the dining room. Then a few hisses and pops from the burning carriage signaled the expansion of the flames toward and around the combatants. Firelight began to illuminate the Holmwood dining room in a strange, candlelit aura.

The Petra bat burst toward Quincy Morris at incredible speed, grabbed the Texan by the neck and picked him up bodily off the floor in her clawed, auburn bat wing. Quincy swung his knife wildly around at Petra's face, but the she-bat evaded the blows, whirled, and in one serpentine motion threw Quincy aside as she ferociously kicked at the hulking carriage with such force that it careened right at the staggered Van Helsing. The wooden floor hissed as the flaming carriage shot along, slicing inch-thick grooves along the slats as it slammed into Abraham, pinning him to the inner wall and knocking him out instantly. More flames started licking the far wall as Van Helsing sagged into unconsciousness.

One of the dining table legs was aflame, and Andrew Murray wrenched it from the table, then whirled it at Dracula, who walked calmly toward the blinking flames, eyes glowing in the unfolding darkness of both the room and the circumstances. Andrew charged at Dracula and swung the piece with all his might, but the vampire easily side-stepped the blow, tore the table leg from Andrew's hands with his left hand, then slammed his right into Murray's chest. The blow was brutal, took all of the air out of Andrew Murray's lungs and sent him hurtling across the floor, banging his head against the far wall.

Andromeda's charge was so powerful that she knocked Ian back from the shield that was the fractured dining room table, Lillian Seward and Judith Murray along with him. Judith's head collided with a broken piece of table, knocking her out instantly. The Andromeda bat swatted the wooden debris away with her right wing, then with a grand sweep of her left wing, she swatted a stunned Ian Seward so hard he plowed against the door of the carriage, which disintegrated under the impact as he fell inside, as unconscious as Van Helsing, who lay nearly next to him, pinned to the wall by the carriage.

"Leave us alone!" shrieked Lillian in absolute terror as the Andromeda bat turned its attention back to her, jagged opalescent canines flashing inside the curled, blackened lips and gums. The enormous mammal's ears pivoted backwards as well, as it prepared to charge Lillian. Ian's mother sensed it and screamed out of fright and fury. She picked up a metal poker in her trembling hands, wailing, "Just go away! We didn't do anything to any of you!"

The Andromeda bat crouched, ready to pounce, eyes blazing with savagery.

Mina snarled in fury as she brought the chair down on top of the Venus bat's skull. The staggered she-bat emitted something that combined a screech and a wail of pain as she crumpled forward and onto the prone Arthur. Holmwood then reacted in an animalistic fervor, scrambling out from underneath the bat, then grabbed the broken chair pieces, and joining Mina, started to repeatedly pound the Venus bat over the head and back.

"I'll send you back to Hell for what you did to my Jonathan!" Mina roared, through rage and tears.

Mina whirled at Lucy, gestured at Victoria and yelled, "Get her out of here!"

That one wrinkle of hesitation on Mina's part was all the opening that Venus needed. In one whirling, powerful motion, the Venus bat's right wing whipped around incredibly fast and swatted the chair pieces away from them. Then the bat bolted upright and gave Mina Murray a vicious head-butt as her left wing swirled around and knocked Arthur's feet out from under him. Arthur fell backwards. Mina also landed hard onto to the creaking flooring, but she shot right back up to her feet, bleeding from her nose. Wilhelmina Murray was livid as she picked up a chair leg and charged the Venus bat, who had pounced back onto Arthur and was trying to tear the flesh off of his face.

"Arthur!" shrieked Lucy while trying to scramble a lucid Victoria Westenra away to safety.

"Let go of me and help them!" screamed Victoria.

Abraham was still pinned between the roof of the carriage and the interior wall of the dining room. Mayhem surrounded him, smoke from the various fires began to choke the room, as did the evening mist that poured in from the great broken French windows. Van Helsing was inert and unconscious, his head hanging limp and his arm dangling freely, fingers tickling the floor boards. He was completely unaware of the charging Petra bat, who swung her curled-up wings out in front of her like a gorilla as she bounded at him, her great canines and jagged molars yawning open in anticipation of tearing Abraham's arm out of its socket.

Charging in and sliding along the ground between the oncoming Petra bat and the unconscious Van Helsing was Quincy Morris, knifing along the wood floor, with his freshly re-loaded Colts ready to go. Ten rounds, all of them, shot through the Petra bat's face, passing harmlessly through her body but forcing the huge bat to squint and put her wings up, her vision obscured by the trajectory and subtle wake of the bullets. Quincy finished his slide, ending up under Van Helsing's dangling arm. The Texan watched the Petra bat continue her blind charge, such was her hunger and fury, right into the path of the Venus bat, who in one violent movement had yanked both Victoria and Lucy away from Mina and Arthur.

The Petra and Venus bats collided like runaway bulls in the streets of Pamplona.

As she rolled over the stunned Venus bat, Petra roared and unfurled her huge fangs at Quincy, who bellowed, "And I got more of that for ya, Missy!"

I just need Mina and Judith to escape thought Andrew Murray as he lay in the far corner of the dining room, head split open from the impact with the wall behind him, blood rivulets obscuring his vision. Andrew watched Dracula bound toward him, right hand open like he was going to rip Murray's heart out. *I just need to distract him enough so they can get away.*

Reaching around the floor around him, Andrew found another piece of the shredded dining table and picked it up. The varnish on one end was on fire, but it would be enough, Andrew decided. As Andrew Murray staggered to his feet, he dared a look past Dracula to the mayhem that were the other battles in the room, and found his wife, trying to get a barely-standing Lillian Seward out of the room. Mina was with Arthur, evading slashes from the clawed wings of the Venus bat.

Then a million memories of Mina and Judith flooded Andrew's mind and heart:

Holding a newborn baby girl.

Thanking his wife for giving him the greatest gift of all.

Tickling an infant daughter.

Hugging her after her first step.

Laughing with them over breakfast.

Her first day at school.

Their outings in the country.

His proposal to Judith.

The torrent of shimmering, beautiful memories brought tears to Andrew's eyes.

He'd always known it would all end one day, everything does, but when confronted with that end, at least in this plane of existence... well, that is another matter.

"Mina, Judith," blinked Andrew through tears of blood.

Baby to girl to young woman.

Betrothed to beloved wife.

About to die.

Not tonight.

Me yes, but not them, Lord.

Let them live more days, many, many more.

May they never forget me.

Dracula noticed the momentary distraction in Andrew's eyes, and the vampire's left arm snaked out with blinding speed to snatch the flaming table piece out of Murray's hands as his right arm brutally grabbed Andrew Murray by the coat. With a wry, satisfied grin, Dracula tossed the table piece into some drapes, which bloomed with more flickering crimson. He yanked a poker-faced Murray toward his pale, dead, predator-like face and said, "Your melancholy weakness disgusts me."

A defiant Andrew stared into Dracula's piercing eyes and said calmly, "I'm glad we killed her. Your wife was a vile thing."

Dracula replied simply, "After I murder you, I'm going to devour yours."

Around them, the grand room was being engulfed in fire and violence.

Venus was staggered by the collision with the Petra bat, and she stumbled backwards, a momentary opening which Mina and Arthur seized. Driven into a frenzy by the mayhem, they both leaped onto the Venus bat, along with Lucy and Victoria, both of whom had picked up serving knives from the floor. Arthur fell upon the enormous bat and thrust his left hand under her chin, pushing the great foaming fangs away from them and leaving the neck exposed.

"Now!" shouted Arthur. "Kill her now!"

Like otherwise docile herbivores driven to bloodlust in the face of an attack by a meat-eater, Mina, Lucy and Victoria fell onto the Venus bat's chest and began to stab her repeatedly along her neck, chest and stomach.

"Die! Die! Die!" shrieked Victoria Westenra as she repeatedly stabbed the thing through the neck.

Mina snarled and ejected spittle as she punctured the rib cage over and over.

The knives sank in, raked, then rose out of the thrashing body of the Venus bat having left barely a mark, which then faded away.

To no effect.

Harmlessly.

Not silver, remembered Mina.

Arthur had the Venus bat's head pinned to the floor, his body splayed over hers to keep the she-bat pinned to the ground, but with a vigorous wrench, Venus twisted her face free, then one of the crimson eyes locked with Arthur's from between his fingers.

You had your chance was what the livid eye screamed to Arthur.

With a powerful swing of a right wing that was capable of lifting a three-hundred-pound bat off the ground and into the air, the Venus bat swatted all four of them off of her, sending Arthur, Mina, Lucy and Victoria flying into the smoky air of the Seward dining room.

"Don't you dare! Don't touch me! Leave us alone! Leave us all alone!" shrieked and begged Lillian at the top of her lungs, swinging the poker around awkwardly like someone who did not know how to swing a baseball bat. Ian lay next to her, inside the carriage and beside the inert Van Helsing. The Andromeda bat crouched before Lillian, her vast wings splayed out along the creaky flooring.

Watching Lillian swing the poker.

Back and forth.

The bat hissed as she waited, timing the swing of the poker, back and forth.

Waited.

Waited.

And leaped.

The Andromeda bat's pounce startled Lillian. The beast grabbed the poker in mid-swing, then ripped it out of Lillian's hands before backhanding her with a savage blow across the face with clawed hands. Lillian crumpled to the floor, her face ripped open by the blow and pouring blood. Andromeda loomed above Lillian, swinging the poker around in her winged hands, staring at Lillian Seward with animalistic fury. In moments, Andromeda transformed back into her humanoid form, whirled the poker around as she raised it and ferociously rammed it down through Lillian's torso and through the floorboards, breaking wood beams and vertebrae simultaneously. Lillian Seward wailed with agony. The wooden floor underneath her groaned, as much from the loss of the lady of the house than the blow itself. Andromeda leaned on the poker, ramming it down through Lillian's body and the wooden floor, until she came face to face with the dying woman, the vampiress with a salacious grin on her face while the poker slid ever downward.

Blood began to pool and slide down onto the end of the poker.

On the other side of the carriage, Petra's bull rush at Quincy was much faster than the Texan had calculated. She was on him in a lightning bolt of motion and enveloped him with her wings. The Petra bat's left wing swung wide, and she landed a tremendous blow to Quincy's right side. He flew backwards, slamming against the wall next to the inert Abraham and Ian, but the Texan managed to keep his wits about him. Petra leaped with the intent to kill, but Quincy somehow managed to slip his Bowie knife out and began to rip at the vampire's face with the blade, the only thing that was keeping the bat's teeth from tearing his face to pieces. As he slashed, Quincy hoped against hope that the blade had been forged of silver, but while the edge seemed to slash across the bat's face, the cuts along the face, nose and mouth began to heal nearly instantly. Only a pounding heart and survival instinct helped him keep the bat off him. What Quincy had not calculated were the two clawed hands that had stopped trying to rip him to pieces but had gripped his neck and began to strangle him.

A satisfied glare from the Petra bat soaked him in futility. *I've got you*, her eyes gleamed.

The Texan tried to say *Go to hell* but nothing came out of his mouth.

Tighter, thought Petra.

Quincy began to black out.

Even tighter, blazed the Petra bat's eyes and claws.

A bone popped in Quincy's neck.

Like a goddamned noose, thought Quincy, as he began to quiver from the pressure of the strangulation.

At that moment, a now-conscious Judith Murray ran up to them and slammed a serving tray against the base of the Petra bat's neck. "Let him go!"

More annoyed than hurt, Petra kept her gaze and her right hand around Quincy's neck as her left wing savagely swung out at Judith Murray.

But the she-bat was staggering.

The air was knocked out of Judith, and she almost fell over, but such was her fervor, her fire to combat these fiendish creatures to whatever limit lay ahead, that she remained on her feet.

And felt warmth.

Heat.

Overwhelming.

Judith dropped the tray.

More warmth.

Heat.

Around her stomach.

And moisture.

Wet.

Then searing, jagged pain.

When Judith looked down she saw that the bat had torn a massive hole in her abdomen.

Before Judith Murray could scream, the Petra bat violently yanked her blood-soaked intestines from inside her. As blackness swept Quincy Morris into unconsciousness, the last thing he took in was a disemboweled Judith Murray.

Mina thought Judith. *Andrew.*

Judith had just reached for her stomach when Petra's next blow came, brutal and swift, with the same bloody wing and with such force and violence that it ripped her throat out completely. Judith Murray dropped her shard of wood.

Another punch from the Petra bat came, and Judith's body flew across the room.

And fell to the floor like a broken puppet, her clothes afire with blood.

At Andrew's feet.

Andrew looked down at the shredded body of his beloved.

Waves of shock ran over him.

He looked back to find Mina.

But found Dracula's ghostly, horrific countenance instead.

"Delicious," said Dracula with the sweetest yet most evil leer ever.

Mina and Judith, I'll see you both in Heaven was the last thing that Andrew Murray ever thought in his life.

Dracula ferociously grabbed both sides of Andrew's head and savagely crushed his skull in an instant, like an eggshell.

The crunch was loud and brutal, reverberating above the sounds of the rest of the massacre.

The vampire let go of Andrew Murray's bloody pulp of a skull and caught his body by the collar, holding it out in front of him in disgust, like an exterminator would hold a dead rat.

Dracula then disgustingly licked his bloody right hand clean like a tiger after a kill.

With the exception of the unconscious Abraham and Ian, everyone still alive saw Andrew Murray's death and were mortified.

Mina, who was scrambling to her feet after the Venus bat's blow, took all this in.

Her scream of outrage knew no bounds as she realized that her mother lay dead at her father's feet. Wilhelmina's face trembled with rage, terror and unrestrained anguish.

"My father!" she wailed. "My *daddy*! M-my mommy! M-my parents!"

Her last, long, lingering scream brought the world to a halt. It shook the entire building, and when it was over, Mina's shoulders slumped, and she wept into her palms.

Through tear-rimmed eyes, Mina said, "God damn you."

A whisper from under the palms.

God damn you.

Without blinking, Dracula snarled, "He already has."

Dracula whirled and threw Andrew's headless body aside like it was garbage next to the disemboweled Judith, who in her last, gasping breaths, sought Andrew's twitching hand, and as they lay dying, their hands found each other, their fingers interlaced, and their blood mixed together as they died at the same moment.

Judith, for both of them, thought of their daughter.

The Venus bat took in Wilhelmina Murray's anguish and seized the moment, lunging forward and clamping her massive jaws around Victoria Westenra's neck. Her jagged canines sank through a stunned Victoria's throat, her voice and breath cut off instantly, and before Mina, Lucy or Arthur could act, the Venus bat planted her 'hands' firmly on Victoria's head and throat before savagely ripping her throat out.

Victoria Westenra's final scream was silent.

Lucy was stunned, she emitted one ear-splitting scream of terror. Victoria was dead before she even realized her throat had been torn out. So savage was the bite that her head hung limp, exposed to the neck vertebrae.

"Oh, my dear mother. My mother, my *mother*! MY MOTHER!" bawled Lucy, her eyes shut from the horror of her mother's near-decapitation. Arthur ran to hold her, his eyes flooding with both shock, sadness and rage.

The fires roared around them.

Andromeda, still in her human form, lunged onto Arthur, tearing him away from Lucy and pinning him to the floor, ready to rip his head from his body. Venus threw the dead Victoria onto a screaming Mina, who was still overcome by the death of Judith, Mina was caught off guard by Victoria's body, an absurd, morbid tackle, and she fell to the floor, covered by the weight of her dead aunt. Blood poured over both dead body and grieving niece.

Mina, pinned by the weight of Victoria's still-quivering corpse, reached a trembling hand out to her dead parents, half a room away but on the other end of existence now.

"Mother. Father," she muttered, half-unconscious from all the shock, numb to the idea of her parents' deaths.

Mina sagged into a place between consciousness and unconsciousness.

Whatever fight or battle this had been, it had reached a sudden, jarring violent end.

This was not a fight.

It was a massacre.

The golden days were over.

Arthur and Ursula Holmwood, Cynthia and William Harker, Judith and Andrew Murray, Lillian and Henry Seward were all dead.

Ian Seward, Quincy Morris and Abraham Van Helsing all lay unconscious.

And everyone who was not dead was about to be.

Dracula stalked over from where he had just murdered Andrew Murray; he stood straight, proud and satisfied. He saw the end had come, having known nothing but war, pestilence and destruction for his entire existence.

"Nunc autem occidere me in mortem animam viventem," whispered Dracula with glee, more like a snarl than a whisper, yet full of satisfaction and wickedness. *For now they kill me with a living death[185].*

"Young Ones," announced the vampire with a dark chuckle, "it is fitting that you all now die by my hand, as did my wife perish at *their* hands." He pointed a taloned index finger at the bodies of the elder generation.

The Petra bat glided over to the unconscious Texan with murderous intent. The enormous, repulsive mammalian face slid up close to the immobile Morris, her saliva dripping all over his face in salacious glee. Her complex, membraned nose sniffed him as if he were a flower, her inches-long canines softly sliding along his cheeks and brow. She blinked, taking in the handsome visage of the unconscious young man, and her head cocked in deep thought. The Petra bat then purred like the largest kitten ever created, a deep, satisfied purr of interest and hunger. Her long mammalian tongue snaked out of her tooth-filled mouth and slid all over Quincy's face.

Mina, stirred back to awareness, sobbing as she tried to push Victoria's corpse off her.

The Venus bat, seeing that Lucy was vulnerable as she wailed over the body of her mother, bounded over with the intention of ripping her head off with one clean blow when a voice like a bolt of lightning from Mount Olympus, halted all of the motion in the room.

"Stop!" screamed the new Lord Godalming. He was pinned to the ground like a hog by the human form of Andromeda, her long flowing hair sliding over Arthur's body, backlit by the fires that had begun to devour the dining room. Other than the crackling of the burning wood, the room was silent.

Except for Arthur's sobs.

"Don't kill her," he wept.

The Venus bat was startled at Arthur's shout, but then yanked Lucy to her canine-lined maw, ready to tear the poor young woman's face off in one bite.

With a simple hand gesture, Dracula stayed Venus' fury.

The Transylvanian stared blankly at Holmwood, disgusted but curious. "Have you no dignity, young fool? She is worthless. Dogs have more value."

"Please. I beg you," wept Arthur, as if asking for his heart to be kept whole.

Fires all along the room crackled and blazed, casting long shadows behind Dracula as he took in everything around him like a child takes in a candy store. Mina somehow made her way to her feet after pushing Victoria's body off of her. She was on the edge of exhaustion, all of her friends at the mercy of the merciless, herself beaten, dirty, defeated, and surrounded by dead family members everywhere. Dizziness overcame her, and Wilhelmina Murray dropped back down to the floor, to her knees, her eyes boring hate through the Transylvanian, who merely laughed at her folly.

The vampire nodded at Mina and said, "We ate Jonathan Harker as ravenously as you consumed your dinner tonight."

"You never had him, but we did," chuckled Andromeda, and the brides all laughed at a humiliated Mina.

Dracula beamed with wicked glee.

---

[185] *Richard III*, act one, scene two, by William Shakespeare.

Mina burst into angry, hate-filled tears, and her eyes never left Dracula, who turned back to the pinned Arthur Holmwood. He saw the concern he had for Lucy, and it filled the vampire with loathing.

"Do you truly love this creature?" Dracula asked Arthur, nodding at Lucy, his arms behind him now, a regal vulture.

"Yes! Yes," bawled Arthur, still in the iron grip of the human version of Andromeda. The new Lord Godalming stretched his hand out to Lucy, and she, in the claws of the Venus bat, bawled as she reached back. "She is to be my bride. We announced our engagement just last night."

"You love this pig of a woman? What would you give for this English whore?"

"I'll give you all that I have," moaned Arthur. "Everything! I'll give you my very life! Let my death give her and my dearest friends life. You've taken whatever measure of revenge you say you needed to take against our fathers, our parents. Just let her and the others go!"

Dracula stood there, relishing the moment, the roaring flames his throne.

Consideration never crossed his face, only more disgust.

"Did you not love your wife, Sir?" whimpered Arthur into the floor, exhausted and beaten.

A knowing, contemplative expression swam over the vampire's face. Dracula smiled, his decision made.

"No."

Dracula exchanged a glance with the Venus bat, an understanding, a silent command passed between lion and lioness before he nodded to her.

And while the vampiress gave Dracula a look of doubt, she nonetheless nodded in solemn affirmation.

An order had been given, and Venus was to do as instructed.

Dracula then raised his left index finger without turning around, as if to say *now*, and the Venus bat promptly plunged her teeth savagely into Lucy's throat.

"Ar-aggghhhh!" shrieked Lucy Westenra as the jagged canines did their work.

"Lucyyyyyy!" screamed Arthur.

The door to the kitchen slowly pried open. Quigley, Shearer and a few servants, expressions of fear wrapped around their faces, tried to peer out into the smoke and dust and mayhem of what used to be the Seward dining room. A man and two women, clearly more comfortable in a kitchen than anywhere else in the estate, held cleavers and knives.

"God in Heaven," squeaked Quigley when he took in the massacre.

Andromeda and Petra turned and snarled like ravenous pack animals at the servants.

"Run!" screamed young Arthur at the top of his lungs before Petra clamped her left palm on his head and pressed down.

Arthur screamed with pain and the kitchen door shut with finality on the servants.

The new Lord Godalming took in the Venus bat's supping of Lucy and tried to squirm toward her.

Andromeda held him down, her owl eyes relishing Venus' feast.

Lucy Westenra quivered like a dying zebra, but Venus kept her powerful wings around Lucy like an absurd parasol as she continued to drink.

Arthur, helpless, bawled and seethed at the same time.

As did Mina.

She also tried to move to Lucy and Venus, rage leading her.

"Stop or I will behead you and violate your corpse!" roared Dracula at Mina, and it was his voice that now shook the building.

They all watched.

Petra stood up from the inert form of Quincy as she transformed back into her flowing, Egyptian female form, a large, bloody leer stretched over her fruit-like lips. She moved like a panther toward her master as macabre sucking sounds filled the paralyzing silence of the wrecked room.

Holmwood, never to be young again, lowered his head, unable to watch anymore.

With a single sweep of her hand, Andromeda grabbed Arthur by the nape of the neck with her left hand. Then with her right, she yanked his hair and forced his head upward, pivoting it toward Venus and Lucy.

Toward the Venus bat's feast.

Lucy's eyes fluttered, half-open, half-closed.

Half alive, on her way to death.

Venus drank slowly, lovingly, very softly, devouring Arthur's anguish as much as she was drinking the life out of Lucy Westenra. They could hear her swallow Lucy's blood, gulp by gulp.

"Do not kill the commoner," sang Dracula casually at the Venus bat, gleefully taking in Arthur's suffering.

A somewhat surprised Venus withdrew her bite, leaving bloody marks on Lucy's throat but still held onto her with her endless, elongated wings. Lucy convulsed like a lamb in the process of being slaughtered, her face coming back to a semblance of consciousness. As she bawled and bled, Lucy could only look at Arthur for help and began to sob. Lucy Westenra then turned to look at Dracula, confused by his overwhelming evil. Her blood swam down along her dress and onto the floor slats.

"You love your woman," said Dracula, gesturing at both Lucy and Arthur. "I will spare her life. I am not an unfair royal."

Arthur began to weep and grin through his pain at this happiest of news, despite the vice grip of Andromeda forcing him to watch.

"Give her new life," said Dracula, and after a long pause, "My life."

Venus, Petra and Andromeda collectively gasped, and even though Venus was still in her bat form, her gasp was the same as the others, a reaction of shock and unanimous objection.

Dracula darkened at their hesitation. It was a whisper laced with violence. "Existimatio non putatum est." *Your opinion was not considered.*

The Venus bat gave Dracula a dubious look as she turned and dug her teeth into Lucy's neck again. Lucy wailed in pain once again. Arthur, still in Andromeda's clutches, began to sob, softly. "What is she doing?"

"What more can you take from us?" sobbed Mina, still on her knees, hands out in a gesture of helplessness.

"Your very lives, child," gushed the son of Satan. "Your very lives."

Venus drank silently, even though her eyes darted back and forth from Lucy to Dracula, frustration mixed with confusion, if not outright defiance.

The fires in the room grew, took larger, stronger forms.

More wood began to crack because of the flames, which licked everywhere now.

Holmwood watched his fiancée being fed upon, violated like a deer in the wild by a thing of the night. Arthur tried to yank his head away but Andromeda savagely pressed it harder into the wood.

Holmwood closed his eyes.

"Why look away, human?" taunted Dracula. "Your woman lives!"

"You're killing her!" shouted Holmwood, beside himself. "Does your word mean nothing?!"

"You coward!" shrieked Mina. "You and your women are cowards! You've murdered her!"

Dracula gleefully cackled, "She lives! For me!"

Arthur's eyes shot open at Dracula's shout, his tears bleeding into the wood. He simply could not look away if those were to be the last moments of Lucy's life, for Arthur Holmwood believed that Dracula was taunting him again, and despite appearances, was murdering Lucy regardless.

Venus withdrew her bite, and the she-bat let the pale, lifeless form of Lucy Westenra collapse to the ground, next to her mother's corpse.

Inert.

Dead.

Arthur's eyes desperately sought to see Lucy's chest heave, as did Mina.

It did not.

Nor did Lucy blink.

She lay there amid the blood and the fire.

Eyes wide awake in her death.

Red hair furled around her head like textured flame.

Dracula laughed, and when a livid Arthur glared at him with all the hate in the world, the vampire pointed him right back at Lucy's corpse.

With one violent motion, Venus slit her own left wrist and held it over Lucy's lifeless mouth. Blood dripped onto and into Lucy's open lips, and seeped in.

Arthur watched.

Drip.

Drip.

Drip.

Then.

Somehow, the lips twitched.

And parted.

She drank.

Lucy's body then went into brief if violent convulsions, her arms and legs quivering like those of a mangled soldier on an operating table.

Then the tremblings stopped.

Lucy Westenra lay inert for a few more seconds, *then began to breathe again.*

"I have been true to my word, Englishman," said Dracula. "She will live."

Lucy Westenra blinked her eyes open.

Then closed them.

Then open.

And again.

She lived.

She breathed again.

Alive.

Still.

Arthur and Mina cried out of sheer relief, so glad their friend was alive that they did not notice the strange anticipation of the vampiresses.

No one else in the room cared or noticed, but simmering resentment swam through Petra, Andromeda and the Venus bat.

Lucy quivered again.

Then went still once more.

Eyes open.

"For me," rumbled Dracula. "She lives for me."

Lucy's left arm moved.

Her fingers trembled.

Strangely.

Then the beautiful cat-like eyes of Lucy Westenra closed once again.

She slept.

A strange, ominous feeling crept into both Arthur and Mina, and they looked to Dracula for answers.

He had anticipated this moment, having done this very cruel thing over and over throughout the centuries.

"Your woman will now be mine," gleamed Dracula. "Such as in the days of the feudal lords, I exercise my will and desire over my servants and any woman I may take as my mate. She will firstly know a nobleman before any peasant."

Mina's face contorted in rage, and she pulled her Pepperbox Derringer out of her pocket, lined it up with Dracula's forehead and fired, all in one motion, more out of frustration than anything else, for the chambers were all empty.

Click, click, click.

The vampire shrugged his shoulders at Mina and laughed.

As did the brides, even the slathering Venus bat.

Exhausted and beaten, Wilhelmina Murray collapsed down to the floor, her elbows the only thing keeping her up.

"Your betrothed will be given the privilege to share in my rest this dawn," teased Dracula with a leer that was full of malice, lust and cruelty. "And for as many dawns as I require."

Petra, Andromeda and the Venus bat, three women from three ancient cultures of the Old World exchanged glances that combined hate, envy and petty jealousy, but they remained silent.

Arthur took in the implications of Dracula's statement and tried to bolt up to charge at Dracula, but the power of Andromeda's grip held firm yet again.

After several violent but futile attempts to wrestle out of the Greek vampiress' grasp, Arthur gave up. He plopped his forehead down onto the floor, crying from the death of his parents, the murder of his uncles and aunts, and the loss of Lucy to as evil an entity as the world had ever seen.

Happiness overwhelmed Dracula, giddy at the turn of events. He sang, mockingly, "An eye for an eye, a tooth for a tooth[186]."

Only the sounds of crackling fires around the dining room, and of the wind kicking up outside and whistling its way through the broken, enormous French doors wrapped their arms around them all.

Dracula sensed that this all had ended and sighed, more out of boredom than anything else.

"My interest wanes, thus the raping and pillaging must commence," said Dracula, starting to turn, waving his hand. "Slit all of their throats, burn their bodies, and set the manor ablaze. Bring my new woman—"

Dracula's thought was interrupted.

He turned to watch as a tattered, dark form bolted in from the night, through the remnants of the shattered window and slid into a crouch in front of Dracula.

The figure was *filthy*, with dark, torn and rumpled clothes that had never been washed, a face so dirty that it was covered in soot, grime and frustration, yet with eyes that boiled with hate.

Crouched down but full of violent energy, like it wanted to explode up at Dracula but thought

---

[186] Biblical scripture, Mathew 5:38.

it better to protect the others, the figure resolutely held an object out in front of him, at Dracula and the brides, poised between the Transylvanian and Mina.

Who was this stupid miscreant?

Some loyal servant?

Or brazen kitchenhand?

Some ignorant groundsman with jangling keys somehow protecting his employers?

Annoyed, the vampire took a murderous step toward this new interloper, then abruptly stopped, genuinely shocked.

The figure held out in a lone, grimy hand.

In the hand, an ordinary, wood-carved crucifix began to glow bright in the night.

Illuminating and revealing.

A worn, exhausted, battered young traveler.

Known as Jonathan Harker.

SIX

Dracula stared down at Jonathan with a look of stunned, wide-eyed shock. The vampire threw his arms out in a gesture of surprise and astonishment. The expression and gesture lasted a few, long seconds, then melted away to one of humor and if possible, appreciation and respect. "C'est impossible! I must congratulate you, Master Harker!"

Jonathan stayed in a crouch in front of the great vampire, trembling and crying as he held the incandescent cross out in front of him. The crucifix glowed from within, like Venetian blown glass, and while it was completely harmless to Jonathan, the cross clearly agitated the *nosferatu* around him. Jonathan Harker was exhausted, shorn to his last wit and at the edge of sanity. His clothes looked like a dog had dragged them around for days.

"Jonathan!!!!!!!!" he heard Mina shrill behind him. Her voice, knowing that at least she was alive, gave him great joy and strength.

Mina began to sob with both joy and loss.

Harker never let his eyes leave Dracula, and he smiled coldly at the vampire.

"Stay back, sewer rat!" screamed Harker, still holding the crucifix out like a torch in front of wolves. He whirled his free hand around behind him, to show the others that he was referring to them. "All of you! Don't come near us!"

Dracula stood calm amid the fire and destruction like someone who had done nothing but cause such events since the beginning of his existence. The crucifix's intensity increased when Jonathan took a half-step toward Dracula.

A flicker of concern danced across Dracula's face, but the Transylvanian was no stranger to confrontation, and his warm smile of death returned in the next moment.

"You have accomplished two goals that are nearly impossible to attain, Master Harker," started Dracula, pointing at Jonathan during the word 'two' for emphasis.

Dracula gave Jonathan a few nods of respect as he said, "You have both surprised *and* impressed me. None of any of the empires on this world were able to accomplish this. Not the venerable noblemen of my youth, Sir Richard nor Salahadin. Not the Medicis, the Borgias or even the simpleton who came to call himself the Doge of Venice. Fools, all. Nor could the procession of Papal pseudo-royals and frauds that have alternately attempted to either usurp or enlist me. Ferdinand and Isabella would prove to be ever so predictable and typical. The Draculs, renaming themselves and not knowing I would so delightfully betray their entire Order of the Dragon, proved to be filled with ignorant zealotry and nothing more. An accumulation of royals of this misbegotten continent revealed themselves to be mere nothings. But you! Jonathan Harker, lowly commoner, solicitor from Whitby, England, son of an inbred soldier who murders defenseless women, you have managed to take me aback! I salute you!"

"Filth," seethed Jonathan. "You're utter filth."

"You have somehow managed to survive the fall from my castle, and you have gone to, pardon the phrase, Biblical lengths to pursue my party on our humble excursion, all the way back to your banal, incestuous hovel and to this precious tableau. I must say that I am astonished to see you alive, for I thought I had rightly killed you, and I am impressed at your fervor of pursuit—"

Dracula stopped speaking.

He reached for his right temple as if a white-hot poker had lanced through his skull.

Two spots suddenly grew on the vampire's face.

Two spots that began to smolder.

A few droplets of water, thrown from somewhere on his left, made Jonathan Harker blink and clear his eyes.

Then a tiny glass bottle sailed past Jonathan like it was pitched during a cricket match.

It swirled as it shot through the air and shattered against Dracula's forehead.

Glass and Holy Water splashed over the surprised vampire, who covered his face as he howled, "Ralhhhhhhhhhhh!!"

Jonathan shot a glance to his left and saw Abraham Van Helsing with his right arm slung forward in a baseball pitcher's follow-through. And a bedeviled smile across his face as Abraham reached for Ian, who was stirring to consciousness inside the burning carriage.

Dracula's wolf howl became the enraged snarl of a tiger. When the vampire whipped his hands off his face, a smoky scar remained above and below the right eye as he glared maniacally at Van Helsing as the latter grabbed Ian by the collar.

"In nomine patris et filii et spiritus sancti, amen," said Van Helsing as he made the sign of the cross at Dracula. *In the name of the Father, and the Son, and the Holy Spirit, Amen.*

"Succendent in Infernum!" shrieked a livid Dracula, his face still scalding. *Burn in Hell!*

In a few breathless seconds, Dracula metamorphosed back into his bat form, exposing jagged canines as he snarled ferociously at Abraham, who laughed in the vampire's face as he tucked his hands under Ian's armpits with the intent to pull him out.

"Watch it, Uncle Abraham!" shouted Mina as the vampire bat girded itself to pounce. And the vampire did leap, frighteningly quick for such a large animal.

But not at Van Helsing.

Dracula was far too smart for that.

And far too savage.

The Dracula bat sailed past Abraham and landed in front of the carriage. The monstrous bat wrapped his winged 'fingers' around the base of the carriage.

The carriage that still held Ian Seward.

Two thousand pounds of wood, metal and Ian Seward were thrust up into the air by the Dracula bat, a feat that astonished everyone still alive in the room, even the undead brides.

Yet through this Herculean effort, Dracula's eyes blazed with hate at Van Helsing.

Barely coming to consciousness, Ian was thrown around inside like a bean in a jar that was being shaken.

Dracula held the carriage high over his head, wings splayed out magnificently under the carriage, so high that the front end scraped the second-story ceiling. Burns from the Holy Water still smoking, his eyes projected nothing but fury.

Van Helsing bellowed, "Ian!!"

Jonathan took this all in and realized that Dracula's every intention was to slam the flaming vehicle onto Van Helsing and crush him like a roach.

The exhausted wooden floor groaned like a dying whale.

"Dive!" screamed Jonathan, and Abraham did so.

Dracula slammed the carriage down like it was Thor's Mjolnir[187], just missing Van Helsing and Seward. The room exploded with the violence of the impact, and what remained of the dining table and the dinner itself was blasted to pieces. The burning, wooden floor, holding up like Atlas before this, splintered and shattered into a billion pieces.

Stunned and taken completely by surprise, the brides screamed and shrieked in unison.

The entire floor moaned one last time and gave in.

Everyone fell.

Amid fire, wood and Holy Water.

Baptized with the flaming carriage.

Down became indistinguishable from up.

Mina and Jonathan fell.

As did Abraham, Arthur and Quincy. As did the bodies of Arthur Senior and Ursula Holmwood, William and Cynthia Harker, Andrew and Judith Murray, Henry and Lillian Seward, Victoria Westenra and the shredded torso of Swayles.

And Ian Seward, the bean in the jar, felt the world erupt with the violence of the carriage smashing against the wood, felt the loss of gravity.

For all of them, there was falling, then flame then dark.

Then nothing.

---

[187] Mjolnir is the hammer of Norse legend, belonging to Thor, the god of thunder.

SEVEN

Claws embedded like hooks into blocks of ice, the gigantic bats clung to the inner wall of the ruins of what used to be the Seward dining room, which was blackening with flame. When the floor had given away, all four vampires had leaped for the walls, and in the case of Andromeda and Petra, they leaped in human form but landed against the walls in their bat forms.

Below them raged a fire that was starting to consume the basement and ground floor. With pops and crackles, flames from the burning mound of debris had begun to lick at the walls and started to burn through the piles of broken wood floorings.

Lucy Westenra hung unconscious and motionless in the air, her right hand above her, with the left 'hand' of the Venus bat clutching Lucy's wrist and keeping Arthur's fiancée from falling three stories into the enormous bonfire that was the Seward basement.

Right about this time the Venus bat wondered what she was doing holding on to Lucy in the first place and raised her arm in a motion that indicated she was about to let go.

A curt and vicious snarl from the Dracula bat made her hold on.

They watched the fires burn. The Petra and Andromeda bats chirped between them, softly enough so that Dracula could not hear, with the sounds of the wood burning starting to rise.

He should have killed her like the rest of the humans.

Yes, I agree. We should kill her at the first opportunity.

Before she manifests.

Agreed.

The Venus bat lifted Lucy Westenra back up before her and looked over the young lady who was somewhere between life and death. Dracula's most ferocious woman took in Lucy's perfect crimson hair, immaculate makeup and stunning dress and her mammalian bat nose crinkled in disgust. Venus had a mind to rip the woman's head off in one blow.

As she held the limp figure of Lucy Westenra before her, wanting to bite the skin from her face and spit the chewed remnants back onto the skinless skull, the Venus bat began to wonder.

Why would the master force me to drink from the human woman?

His revenge had already been taken.

Surely, he knew we would resent this!

Is he punishing us?

The entire floor below was now a raging inferno, with sections of flooring mixing more and more with the crumbling walls and basement.

Groans, cracks and snaps from the burning wood filled the air along with the smoke, dust and floating embers.

The Dracula bat looked intently for signs of life for nearly a minute before he melted into mist form and poured down the wall toward the broken French doors. He congealed around one of the ornate door lintels, ebbed along the frame down to what used to be the ground floor before bleeding out into the night.

Once outside, the mist slithered and cloyed just above the open area where the carriages were stationed before he became the Dracula bat again. Massive wings snapped open reflexively, and the huge bat let out a long, hard screech/roar/bellow of satisfaction as he glided across the expansive Seward lawn.

Behind him came the brides, still in their bat forms, crawling out through the French doors, Venus having to conspicuously avoid letting Lucy Westenra's skull be fractured as she made her way past broken glass and metal framework. The Petra and Andromeda bats bounded across the sand-covered drive and the remaining carriages, while the Venus bat soared upward, Lucy dangling from her clawed, padded feet.

Wails, screams, shouts and cries cascaded out of Seward manor and hospital as nurses and attendants rushed to help patients out of the burning buildings. The hospital was a wing attached to the two-story manor house, and the fire that had started in the main building had begun to spread to the hospital. Chaos ruled as patients in various states of care and incarceration were whisked out of the doors and out onto the spacious lawns of the estate for their own safety.

Dracula landed gracefully on one of the distant lawns, away from the manor, pivoted while he transformed back to human form so he could observe the outer wall of the dining room give way and cave inward, crumbling into the flame and smoke with a great crash. Fire and destruction were nothing new to the vampire, yet he watched this ruin with particular satisfaction as the Petra and Andromeda bats bounded toward him, with the Venus bat dangling Lucy until they had nearly reached him, whereupon she flew ahead and dropped the body at Dracula's feet while she banked back around to land.

As her world burnt or lay dead around her, Lucy Westenra was semi-conscious and her lungs expelled air when she landed on the soft, manicured grass. Her eyes rolled over underneath her eyelids and she began heaving ragged breaths while the still-drying blood from Venus' attack bathed her face, neck and chest in crimson. The bite mark on her neck was vicious but had already begun to heal itself.

With one quick motion, the Transylvanian sliced open his right palm with a talon from his left hand. As Lucy lay at his feet, Dracula made a fist with his cut hand and let his blood drip into Lucy Westenra's open mouth.

"Ego dabo vobis in vitam aeternam, hoc illis a me profanum benediction," hissed Dracula. *I give of myself to you, to give you eternal life. This is my unholy benediction.*

Lucy, though she still lay barely awake, began to eerily lick up the blood in her mouth and on her lips. She began to moan, quiver and writhe in an odd, surreal manner, as if under some sort of diabolical, hypnotic possession. She vomited some blood mixed with bile, then gave one long tremor before her body went limp, unconscious once again.

"Est factum," said Dracula. *It is done.*

Petra and Andromeda transformed from bat to human form as they approached Dracula, and Venus landed next to them and metamorphosed from bat to woman. As if they did not exist, the vampire stared past the brides, enraptured with the burning of the main residence and hospital.

Venus looked down at Lucy, smiled at Dracula and began, "Dovremmo mangiato lei—" *We should have eaten her—*

After an abrupt turn of his body, Dracula stepped forward and gave each of them a cold and brutal slap across the face that left them crumpled on the grass, Venus the recipient of a particularly vicious backhand.

They all sprawled on the lawn, their collective glares hating him in silence.

Dracula roared, "Concubines! Din Cipru! Tu întrebarea directivele mele în faţă a prada noastră? التمست ارائكم أدبا!Siete popolani, prostitute, seduttori e ladri! Τους ρόλους σας αποτελούν να υπηρετήσει τον πραγματικό βασιλιάδες!" *Concubines! Cyprians!*[188] *You question my directives in front of our prey? Your opinions were never solicited! You are commoners, streetwalkers, seducers and thieves! Your roles are to serve true royalty!*

With a savage growl, Dracula snapped his right hand around Venus' throat and lifted her off the ground as if she were a paper kite. His eyes blazed hate and fury while he held her aloft. His grip was of iron and would have killed a human in a few heartbeats. Venus gagged, dangled and choked, spewing nameless, silent hatred right back at Dracula's, eyes of fire reciprocated the hate right back at her.

A metamorphical quiver writhed over Venus' body as she readied to transform.

Dracula had anticipated this.

"Vos non possunt transmutare!" shouted Dracula, his incantation cast upon Venus. *You cannot transform!*

"Prostituta Romana!" hissed Dracula. "Non ho chiesto il vostro parere nei confronti delle quali ho scelto di concedere il dono di quasi l'eternità!" *Roman prostitute! I did not ask for your opinion regarding on whom I choose to bestow the gift of near-eternity!*

He let her dangle from his vice grip, then hissed slowly, "Noi siamo non morti ma in qualche modo posso soffocarla come se fossi viva. Come se tu avessi un cardiaca."

A few vertebrae made popping sounds in Venus' neck.

"Ciò che," he continued, "è stato dato può sempre essere portato via. Sapere che." *We are undead, yet somehow, I can choke you as if you were alive. As if you had a heart. What was given can always be taken away. Know that.*

"Do not kill her, Good Sir," rumbled a form in the shadows, in the shrubbery that surrounded the estate. The vampires all whirled at the sound, hunters unaccustomed to being observed.

Out of the darkness stepped the huge form of Montague Rhodes Renfield.

He had his palms out to explain visually that he presented no threat.

Renfield cleared his throat and said, "And you shouldn't kill me for two very important reasons, my Lord."

"Explain before I have these streetwalkers pull your intestines out like garters," said Dracula.

Renfield continued as if nothing out of the ordinary was occurring, as if he were not conversing with four *nosferatu*. "Before I explain, I should express that I myself have cut a few intestines out from the human torso, and as it so happens the 'ladies' in question were themselves questionable women, M'Lord. And not so much garters as much as pig tripe, they was. I call you Master because I aim to dedicate myself to you, in your service, for as long as is required. You see, I know you, Master and Count. I know you through your most charming wife, M' Lord."

"Charming is not a word I would use to describe my late wife, commoner." But Dracula's voice had softened. He was intrigued, not offended. His glowing eyes blinking in the night, Dracula stood there and watched Renfield like a wolf might watch a mouse. "How did you know her?"

"I knew your lovely lady during the regretful episode that resulted in her passin', Master. I knew her and she knew me. She whispered to me of you, M' Lord," and before Dracula could react, Renfield hurriedly added, "in the most respectable of circumstances, my Master."

Montague added flatly, "Your wife was my first love."

Renfield then turned to the brides and said with a nod that combined respect and sarcasm, "But I don't remember her ever mentioning any of you ladies, though."

---

[188] Cyprian is an antiquated term for prostitute.

If the three female monsters had been cats, their backs would have arched and their fur would have risen, such was their hostility at Renfield's words. But before the vampiresses could react, Dracula waved them off with an ironic chuckle and a subtle sweep of his hand. Somehow the mountain that was Rhodes Montague Renfield had calmed the storm that was Dracula of Transylvania. The subject and mood of Venus' discipline had passed.

"You were present at her murder?" rumbled Dracula. The vampire's stare was penetrating, truth-seeking.

Cracks and pops continued to emanate from the fire upon Seward manor, which had reached the roof, which it began to consume.

"Yeah, but if you don't mind me sayin' so," said Renfield, "the fire's gonna draw some interest pretty soon and it won't be doin' us any good to stand here talkin' when I could be drivin' you and yours back to safety, wherever that is. I'm good with me hands, great with a knife and I don't ask too many questions, if you take my meanin', Master."

They all reacted to the squeaking sounds of metal-on-metal behind them. They turned to see Primus driving up with the wagon, right on time. The wagon was filled with coffins and the ever-eerie skeletons, all on the look-out for any possible attackers. Behind the wagon, the ground rippled with the legions of rats. The huge skeleton bowed his head only to his master, which brought a sarcastic grin from the vampire and further infuriated the brides.

"Bloody hell," was all that Renfield could manage at the sight of the skeletons, and a shiver of revulsion at the rodents. And hunger.

"I am here to serve you, my Master," said Primus after he stood up. He gestured to the skeletons in the wagon. "We are all here to serve you. What do you need of us?"

Dracula simply turned back to Renfield and said, "Primus has been in my servitude—"

"—not too convenient," interrupted Montague with a nod at the skeleton, "for takin' the ol' wagon through the crowded streets of Whitby or Whitechapel during the mornin' rush, with all due respect to your man here."

Primus gave Renfield a nod in return, to explain that no offense was taken.

The brides waited for the vampire to attack the enormous, stupid brute for daring to interrupt him, but that moment never arrived.

Dracula then nodded in agreement, as did Primus.

The vampire stood there for a moment, boring through Renfield, sizing him up. Then he began to nod.

"I offer you thirty pieces of silver for your soul[189]. You will then pledge your life to me, and to my unholy Father Satan, when you die. Do you accept?"

"I've never felt more alive, Master. Yeah."

Dracula strode to his coffin, raised the obsidian lid and pulled out a small cloth bag from the lining, and handed it to Renfield as he said, "With this covenant, you shall belong to my Father. Like Judas Iscariot so many years ago."

Renfield took the bag, nodded in affirmation, and pocketed the coins.

"Very well," Dracula then said. "We all leave. Now."

"Our destination?" said Venus, looking sideways angrily at this hulk of a human who had rudely insinuated his way into their group.

"My plans, furthered," was the vampire's mysterious reply.

He pointed at Lucy, lying unconscious on the lawn.

"Bring her with us."

"Of course," slavered Renfield.

---

[189] In the Gospel of Matthew 26:15, Judas Iscariot betrays Jesus for thirty pieces of silver.

EIGHT

Jonathan Harker's consciousness swam to clarity.

He realized that there were stars above him, and that they were in motion. The movement of the stars meant that he was outside, that he was alive and that he had somehow survived the collapse of the dining room. He then felt his left arm in pain, and he realized that it was raised over his head, and that he was being dragged across the ground by his legs. Despite the lawn's immaculate appearance, Jonathan Harker's head bumped along the turf like it was littered with bricks.

Harker looked up, not at the stars but over his head.

The world was upside down from his perspective. Familiar silhouettes standing on the lawn, and the distant sky dropping to infinity. The silhouettes were all watching the flaming destruction of Seward Manor and hospital with gestures that reflected total and abject horror. Whoever had been dragging Harker let go of his legs, which fell onto the dark, wet, upside-down grass. Still somewhat dazed, Harker looked down, that is, up, and saw the sharp countenance of Abraham Van Helsing walk into view. Abraham stopped and watched the fire.

Motion came from the silhouettes.

One of the shapes ran to him.

Covered in black.

A half-second later, Mina landed on top of him, crying with pain, joy, sorrow, mourning and relief. She was livid and deliriously happy at the same time, wrapping her arms around his face and head and squeezing so hard that he could not breathe, and in that moment, despite everything that had happened to him, Jonathan Harker was the happiest man in the world, even if he was being suffocated by his fiancée.

"You're alive, you idiot! You're alive! You're alive!" was all Mina kept screaming. He could feel the hands of the other silhouettes grab him roughly around the shoulders and arms.

He heard a Texas drawl say, "Yer gonna smother him before he even tells us how he got here, Mina!"

Jonathan was yanked to his feet, and he staggered, his eyes blurry from having just been awakened, and by the smothering Mina had just given him. He saw some bleary figures in front of him, smiling at him, backlit by the enormous blaze behind them. The blurry figures he recognized as Mina, Quincy, Ian and Arthur were all speaking over each other.

"Goddamn, it's good to see ya!" mixed with "We're glad you're back, mate" to "This is the worst night of our lives."

Jonathan slurred, "How did we get out—"

"—'member that old dumbwaiter that we rode up and down to the basement as kids?" drawled Quincy, but Jonathan was too woozy to hear the rest of it.

All of the voices melded together as Jonathan focused on the writhing sea of red, orange and yellow behind his dearest friends. They all saw what he was looking at and they slowly turned around to watch the inferno. They were in a thicket outside one of the lawns, and Jonathan realized that the nurses must have let the patients out of the burning building, because he could see figures chasing each other between them and the blaze. Jonathan thought of all the memories inside of that building, the Christmases, New Years and Easters they had spent growing up there. Quigley and Shearer sprinted past, too engrossed in chasing patients to notice them.

Abraham had his back to Jonathan, in front of all of them watching the fire, because a second later he came to the same realization as Jonathan just had and shouted, "The patients have been freed by the nurses! They're running around—"

"—Renfield—" Ian gasped.

"We'll have to check the grounds," grunted Abraham.

"I saw him lopin' away a few seconds ago," said Quincy. "Couldn't miss him, he's so big."

Without turning, Abraham said, "Then, as you all full well know, Monty is a murderer, and he has been freed tonight. I hope he has not encountered our attackers."

They all stood there, in silence, knowing all they knew, as their world burned.

"Where," said Jonathan, "are my mother and father?"

He saw Mina cover her mouth and begin to sob. She stepped toward Harker and enveloped him in another hug, openly crying in his arms. Confused, Jonathan looked at Ian and Arthur, who cried silent tears; Quincy avoided his gaze while checking his Colt.

"Where..." repeated Jonathan, even though his bones and his gut had already begun to explain the answer to him, "...are my parents?"

At that, Abraham turned and faced him, his face suffused with rage and sadness. He looked at Jonathan fiercely and said, "Be strong at this news, my boy. They are in God's hands now."

Arthur sobbed, "He killed— they killed all of our parents, Jonny. *All of them.* Just now. Tonight."

"They're all gone," said Ian through his tears.

All of them wept and mourned for a few minutes, some silently, some not, while another section of Seward Manor and Hospital crumbled inward in a flaming storm. Hot wind swept past them all, their futures all in doubt. Jonathan wrapped his face with his hands even as he held Mina.

Orange light danced over Abraham's face as he watched the inferno. He nodded, "You'll all have to be brave and accept adulthood as of now. Out of the nursery. Fiends abound in the night."

"I never saw them again," was all that Jonathan could say as he cried, and Mina held him even tighter. "He made us all orphans."

"'When the wicked came against me to eat up my flesh, my enemies and foes, they stumbled and fell,'" quoted Abraham. "Psalm 27:1."

Van Helsing then cleared his throat and said, "I have to track them all down and kill them. Even Lucy."

"What?" shouted Jonathan, who had not witnessed the vampiric assault upon Lucy.

"Dracula," began Ian to Jonathan, "took her as one of his own."

Arthur whirled to Van Helsing, his face warped with insult. "She's to be my wife!"

Abraham clapped his hard, calloused palm on Arthur's shoulder. "Steady lad. You know I love you, and this is hard for you to hear, but she's no longer your fiancée and she's no longer *alive*. Not after tonight, Arthur. Lucy is a *nosferatu*, a supernatural creature of the night, as were those other four things. Their type of creature feasts on humans, or in rare instances, turn humans into their kind. It is difficult for me as a man of science to attempt to categorize the supernatural, but that is what they are. Tomorrow after sunset she would drain you of your blood as sure as we stand here in front of this burning edifice. I'll kill her quickly, my boy. I am sorry. I loved Lucy like she was my own daughter, you all know that. I can never look at a butterfly without thinking of her collections."

They were all incredulous at Van Helsing's statement.

Mina pointed and shouted, "You'll do no such thing, Uncle Abraham!"

"We do not have time to debate this!" hissed Van Helsing. He gestured out to the night. "They are headed in one of three directions as I see it: a cemetery to shelter themselves for the coming day, the road to London by way of an acolyte that will take them, disguised as actual corpses, or lastly to the docks of Whitby where they have already arranged passage to the continent. We bleed time and opportunity."

"The ruins!" shouted Jonathan. "I—we leased him the old Carfax Abbey and grounds."

"A ruse," interjected Abraham, "to get Peter and yourself to divulge all that he wanted to know about this area. Or a temporary shelter for his arrival. Dracula is an old being, older than you can imagine, and not foolish enough to stay there this night, knowing you would know to search for him there."

They all quieted again, understanding Abraham's point, so Van Helsing finished with, "Yet, it is my intent to intercept them before the next dusk. I will write to you as I can after the deed is done."

He patted them each on the nape of the neck in a gesture of goodbye as he said, "This does not need to involve any of you. Mourn your parents, they were good people. Better than most of their social class anyway. The rich are usually the scum of the Earth, taking all and leave nothing for anyone. But not your parents. They were my friends, and I shall avenge them."

He began to walk out from the thicket and toward the burning building. Mina shook her head in anger at him and said, "And if they murder you instead?"

Abraham stopped and turned. He looked at them flatly and said, "It would be a fate I deserved, given that I have eradicated as many of those vermin as I have, without paying a price yet."

"So you have encountered these creatures before?" said Ian, incredulous.

Abraham gave the youngsters all a wry nod as he stepped toward them. "What *you* encountered tonight are unholy things, and I use holy methods from my travels to rid this earth of them. They are things of the night, Satan's seed, but they are not invulnerable. All of the beings from ghost stories and fables you read about, they exist like species in the animal world. Some are good, others are evil. This Dracula, and his women, are examples of such things. He might be the most powerful of his type that I have ever encountered, but no matter, he must sleep after the dawn, and I will end him in his sleep."

Arthur, emboldened by Van Helsing's brave talk said, "I pledge the entirety of my estate if it means ridding the world of this filth and avenging our parents' deaths."

"As do I," said Ian.

Mina nodded in agreement.

"What they said," followed the Texan. "Get them sonsofbitches."

Abraham shook his head, walked up to Holmwood and slapped him on the shoulder with tenderness and respect. "Stay here, help put out these fires, arrange your parents' funerals. Your patients need tending to."

"No!" shouted Jonathan. "These creatures are overwhelming! How would you deal with them by yourself?"

Abraham looked behind him at the burning building, knowing that he needed to leave, then turned around and said quickly, "I'll leave word at my office with a letter addressed to you all as to my destination."

At their still-questioning looks, Abraham impatiently hissed, "We cannot debate this any further! Time escapes us like sand out of an hourglass! I must take my leave—"

Arthur begged, "They murdered our parents! They took Lucy! That fiend took *my fiancée*!"

Jonathan stepped out of Mina's arms, stood in front of the others and locked eyes with Abraham as he whispered, "He put Uncle Peter on an upside-down cross and threw a lance through his heart. I witnessed it."

The manor burned fiercely behind them.

Beams cracked in the roaring fire while they all took Jonathan's words in.

Mina gave a long, deep sob, as did Arthur.

Ian ran his fingers through his hair in agony, while Quincy looked at the burning manor to hide his tears.

Their collective anger burned bright.

"Sweet Jesus," said Quincy, for all of them.

"We're comin' with ya, Uncle Abraham," said Quincy, stepping forward. "You're all we've got left."

Ian, Mina and Arthur also drew near, and Abraham was surrounded. The fire frothed behind him, the night ran away above him. Van Helsing stood there and thought about these now-grown children whom he had known since infancy, and now, without the daughter he had sired but had not seen through birth, Abraham Van Helsing was surrounded by his new children, his surrogate family, and he sighed with resignation. He watched the manor continue to collapse in on itself.

"This journey," said Van Helsing flatly, "could lead us around the world and back, if not to Hell first—"

They all grew ear-to-ear grins, despite the ash, dirt and disaster that had enveloped them. Ian raised a finger in a curious gesture, as if he had just remembered something. Young Seward then turned and disappeared into the shrubbery. Jonathan took in Mina's inquisitive glance regarding Ian with a shrug.

"Debating this only allows their escape," said Ian. He was right, and while Abraham knew it, he was still concerned with their well-being.

"There is more to all this," sighed Abraham, "than all of you may know."

"Then we'll have some interesting conversations along the way," said Mina with a crisp, firm nod.

Abraham decided to attempt to dissuade them one last time, and as he looked over the raging blaze that was Seward Manor an hour ago, he sighed, "I would prefer that you all not suffer as we all did, your fathers and I. Would it not be best that I deal with all of this myself and leave you all to bury your parents and begin your lives?"

"The odds would be against you, Uncle," said Arthur. "There's four of them and one of you."

Ian slid back out of the shrubbery, holding a small, dirty bag in his hands, and said nothing, a conspiratorial expression all over his face.

"If we are truly adults in your eyes," said Jonathan, "then it is our choice as to how best live our lives."

Mina nodded in agreement.

"Very well, then," said Abraham with a final nod of agreement, "I have warned you."

There are those smiles again, thought Abraham as he watched them rejoice and congratulate each other even though they had lost everything an hour ago. *Truly, youth is not wasted on the young.*

Abraham nodded at them as he turned and walked out of the brush, gesturing for them to follow him as he said, "There is much to discuss on this journey. We have daemons to track. Gather your things. Quincy, take our horses out of the stalls. We leave at once with what we carry. They would head for the continent, I surmise."

At that point Ian ran up and handed Abraham the small bag. "Father always hid some gold on the grounds in case of dire circumstances—"

"Ha! Of course he did," said Abraham, who kept walking as he smiled wryly and patted Ian on the shoulder. "What a rascal he was! That sounds very much like your father and my friend."

Abraham stopped, looked at them all and said, "I loved them all like my brothers. We surely argued like brothers to prove our love."

That brightened the lad, and Ian continued to walk and talk, "I'm going to give this gold to you so that you may begin your pursuit well-funded. I will handle arrangements here and join you all as soon as I am able."

"Good," said Abraham. He led them to the doorway of the manor, which had been ravaged by the now-ebbing blaze. Van Helsing pointed his right thumb over his shoulder and at Wilhelmina Murray. "Give the gold to Mina. She would be the most difficult to rob."

Mina could not help shoot a satisfied leer at Morris, who in turn could not help but take the bait.

"I dunno about that, Uncle Abraham," quipped Quincy instantly. "Got my Colts on my hip and my Winchesters in my luggage, ready to hum a diddy or three."

The heat around the doorway had subsided by the time Abraham neared it, and Van Helsing wasted no time in putting his boot through the door, which yawned wide open, with darkness and soot inside. "As well-armed as you are, lad, you would be the first anyone would think holds anything of value."

Arthur chuckled as Ian handed the small bag to Mina, who then slipped it into her purse, sitting next to her Remington-Elliot Pepperbox Derringer. Abraham walked just past the doorway and leaned down to pick up his baggage, which was smoldering, but still intact.

"At least the Fates be with us," said Abraham as he cradled his luggage. It was still hot inside the crumbled foyer, but it had helped that the whole roof had collapsed and let most of the heat out. As he held his bag out to open it, Van Helsing sensed Arthur's renewed anguish, but decided to ignore it and let the others handle each other's well-being. Someone patted Arthur's shoulder in sympathy, perhaps it was Ian, but Abraham had other things in mind.

After he opened the clasps, Abraham Van Helsing held out his bag for them to see the contents.

Inside were medallions, charms and medals of various sizes: mezuzahs and Stars of David from the Jewish faith, Hindu Aums and Sri Chakra Yantras, Wheels of Life from Tibetan Buddhism, Zen circles, crescent moons for the Islamic faith as well as assorted and varied Crucifixes and Crosses for Christianity. Also in the bag were small bottles that contained Holy Water, silver knives of various sizes and a few broken pieces of wood with sharp edges. And his ever-present *kukri* knife.

"An omen," smiled Abraham. "I first thought that only Christian symbols would keep them at bay or harm them, but as I traveled along the world I realized that all good and purity repels all evil. We are surrounded by the brightness of life, not the other way around."

Quincy simply nodded and quipped, "And here I just thought you were really religious, Uncle Abe."

They all laughed, and they all needed it.

Abraham then said to Mina and Jonathan, "Quickly. To the stables, bring us horses, and then, to our task."

Van Helsing looked at Ian and added, "Make sure you find Renfield first."

"I'm sure," said Arthur, "that Monty's on the grounds somewhere."

"I surely hope so," said Van Helsing to Ian. "Join us after all has been arranged. Pay off the servants well for their silence, we must leave before any authorities arrive. Good luck, my lad. I love you."

"Where to?" shouted Jonathan, over his shoulder as he and Mina raced to the stables.

"We shall check the Whitby docks," said Abraham. "Then the roads to London, then to the continent."

On the other end of the estate, the Dracula bat bounded across the cemetery, the distant remnants of the Seward estate behind him. Self-satisfaction further bloated an ego accustomed to hundreds of years spent crushing foe after foe under his heels. Tombstones littered the clumpy grass, while blood and gore from the attack on Swayles still wet the monuments to death. The bat chortled and deliberated between the three possible paths they could take to Paris, and further mayhem.

Dew grew on the grass, as did the sliver of orange in the distant eastern horizon, over the ocean.

He looked ahead, and saw Renfield, having readied and loaded the coffins onto the wagon, awaiting his command like a large, feral dog. The brides, rats and skeletons were all packed inside, ready for travel. Renfield would make a good servant, decided Dracula, if Primus, the rats or the concubines did not tear him to pieces along the way. In either event, it would be amusing to see how the situation played out. Dracula thought to inquire as to Renfield's personal history, but then concluded that he simply did not care. The large Englishman would be useful until he was not, and at that point he would be disposed of.

A hint of movement caught the Dracula bat's eyes, and he turned his massive, shaggy head to the left.

There, floating among the tombstones and grave markers, lingered a spectre.

A ghost.

Swayles.

They took each other in for a few seconds, ghost and vampire, as the bat never broke stride and made his way toward his coffin and rest.

Archibald Swayles nodded his translucent head at the massive bat and quoted, "'Cowards die many times before their deaths; the valiant never taste of death but once.[190]'"

In a matter of moments, Dracula was in human form again, and he chuckled as he glided away from the ghost and the cemetery and to his waiting coffin, which M.R. Renfield held open for him.

"G'bye, Archie," nodded Renfield, finding it not at all strange that he was conversing with a spectre.

"Go to Hell," replied the Swayles ghost.

"He is on his way," smiled Dracula.

"Coward," reiterated Swayles.

"If only a bar of gold could be bestowed upon me for every wretched ghost who attempted insult after they had caught my wrath."

"Me mum taught me that quote as a nipper[191]," chuckled the Swayles ghost. "Loved to quote the Bard, she did. A good woman."

"Your dog of a mother had a womb that was a play yard for mongrels far and wide," hissed Dracula, sounding angrier than he cared to admit as he neared the wagon. Renfield laughed the laugh of a simple person as he held the coffin open for his new master.

In his own way, Montague Rhodes Renfield had never been happier in his life. He now had a purpose, and from his perspective, a respectful position of employ. He accepted the presence of these supernatural beings with no surprise whatsoever.

He'd had experience in these matters.

---

[190] From Shakespeare's *Julius Caesar*.
[191] Colloquial British term for small boy.

Dracula looked at Renfield and said, "There are bags of gold hidden in the lining of my coffin. The arrangements had been made before your servitude. Pay the captain in my name and he will take us to the agreed-upon destination. If you fail or steal I will feed you to the women. You are not to touch the virgin."

Dracula gestured to Lucy.

"Understood, my M'Lord," rumbled the mountain of a man. "Ten shillings, or the equal, per week for my services, Master?"

Dracula nodded in agreement, then took one last look around at Swayles, the burning manor in the distance, and England.

Swayles laughed as he drifted away, "Remember me and the Bard's words when your time comes, lad."

In their coffins, the rats and skeletons convulsed, and for a moment both coffins rattled like teakettles. The brides were already asleep, laying in their native soil at the bottom their coffins. Something about the way Swayles responded bothered Dracula as he slid like a serpent into his coffin next to Lucy, who lay there, eyes closed, as if in a trance.

He stared at her, fallen innocence personified, and he relished the idea of how much this new concubine would continue to hurt and create tension with the other brides. Dracula could feel the hate for her pulsing from the other coffins. He gave the new vixen a week before they tore her apart, then another few days of their punishment at his hands.

Dracula smiled, sweetly, relishing both Lucy and the future conflicts that would arise from his whim.

As Montague Rhodes Renfield closed the coffin lid, Lucy whispered one hushed word laced with love, agony and regret.

"Arthur."

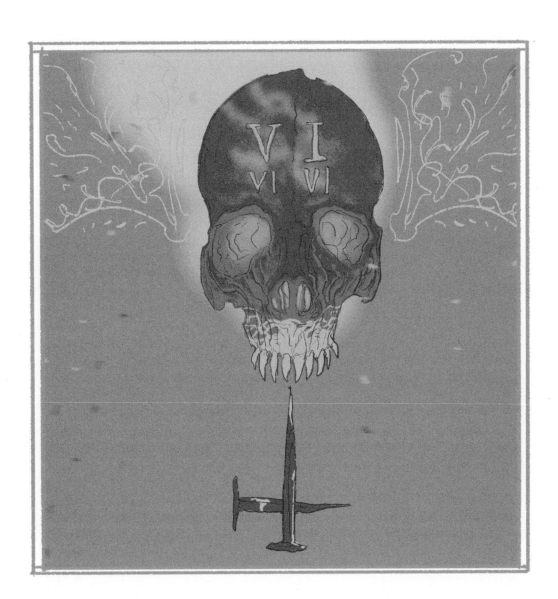

THE CONTINENT

Crossing the Bar

Sunset and evening star,
And one clear call for me!
And may there be no moaning of the bar,
When I put out to sea,

But such a tide as moving seems asleep,
Too full for sound and foam,
When that which drew from out the boundless deep
Turns again home.

Twilight and evening bell,
And after that the dark!
And may there be no sadness of farewell,
When I embark;

For tho' from out our bourne of Time and Place
The flood may bear me far,
I hope to see my Pilot face to face
When I have crost the bar.

— Tennyson

Dawn mixed with an angry fog, while seabirds fluttered as cloud banks billowed and the ocean frothed around them. The deck of the fishing boat, a speck in the wide swath of ocean blue, pitched and yawed like capsizing was an inevitability, not an option. To their port side, a seed of tangerine horizon had bloomed into a crimson morning. Arthur, who had been very quiet since they had left Seward Manor, had vomited overboard twice already, and Morris had mercilessly teased him until Quincy too left his last meal in the ocean between Great Britain and the European continent. Mina simply sat there, holding Jonathan, the man she had all but decided a few days ago she was no longer going to marry; but presently she could not see a future without him. Their destinies seemed forever intertwined now, for when Dracula boasted to them of Jonathan's death, Mina's heart had withered at that very moment. She was still very much her own woman, but when Jonathan burst into the Seward's dining room, he had reminded her like a lightning bolt how deeply she loved him. They had both become orphans together, both wept and mourned together. The others mostly ignored them out of respect for their relationship, and began to deal with their own emotions in their own ways. Arthur found his own corner of the boat and held the ribbon that Lucy had given him only two nights before, when it seemed like they had eternity in front of them. Abraham found his own corner and smoked in silence as he rustled through his bag or contemplated the ocean before him. Quincy settled in at the front of the boat, wrapped his arms around two Western-style rifles and scabbards that he'd rescued from the Seward estate, leaned on his knapsack, then lowered the brim on his Stetson to slumber away for a while, or at least to deal with the pain on his own. They were all in shock and mourning while moving forward with the ancient act of vengeance. Mina held Harker on that boat like he was her soul, and he let her, and she felt the comfort of his undying need for her that made their love fit together like a wanting hand within a willing glove. They held each other, mixing the satisfaction of their bond while continuing to mourn for their parents. Mina thought of Lucy, but pushed those feelings aside for now, if only to find comfort in the friends that were still alive and use that to try to heal from the massacre that had occurred the recently deceased night.

Abraham had engaged a fishing boat that was preparing to set out for the day's catch to, instead, take them from Whitby to the coast of France. Some money and questions spread along the docks had netted them the information that a merchant vessel had left for the Port of Calais, quickly and quietly, but an hour before. The quietness and the quickness of the launch had attracted a few inquisitive minds along the port of Whitby, and pounds, furnished by Arthur and Quincy, had loosened a few previously clamped mouths.

Arthur had hastily scribbled a note for Ian and had engaged a young, sleepy-eyed dockhand to take it to Ian Seward, care of Seward Hospital. The fire had attracted attention, and the unusual event was already the talk of Whitby port when the group arrived there. But, from the gossip that they had heard around the port, Ian had somehow succeeded in casting the story as simply a fire in the hospital that had gotten out of hand, a prevarication for which they were all grateful. A few uncouth questions regarding their leaving so soon after such an unfortunate event as the burning of a friend's home went coolly unanswered and were sorted under the category of improper manners. Quincy's tendency to flare his nostrils, which occurred when the Texan felt insulted, was kept under control. He did not take kindly to the implication that they had left their friend in a tough spot, but they had, and Quincy's pride had to be muffled for the greater good. Further discussions and innuendoes regarding the shipwreck of the Demeter *two nights before only heightened the group's cautious air, as well as giving them a vague understanding of how the vampires had arrived in England in the first place.*

Arthur had managed to arrange for the local banker to make available some of his funds at an ungodly and untimely hour, for which said banker was discreetly and generously compensated, while Quincy had boisterously pounded on the doors of the local gunsmith ("Only an American gets away with that sort of rudeness," opined Arthur) and had emerged with plenty of rounds for his weapons, which Abraham had instantly blessed with Holy Water. "It will not kill them, but with the Holy Water it will be a blow as if a horse had kicked them."

Now they huddled on the starboard side of the boat, the sails above gliding them toward France, toward the continent and toward Dracula. The ocean had smoothed out, and they were cutting through the water nicely. On the port side stood Van Helsing, alone, smoking his pipe quietly as the coast of England faded away. A few gulls wafted above them, waiting perhaps for the catch of the day that would never come this day.

Abraham turned, took a puff of his pipe as he measured Jonathan with his eyes and said, "How'd you get out of his castle alive, lad?"

Jonathan's response, which was to shake his head at Abraham, surprised the others, because they had never known Jonathan to ever say no to anything that Abraham had ever requested. As far as they all could remember, Abraham Van Helsing was gold in the eyes of Jonathan Harker, a fact that both bonded him further with Mina and did not go unobserved by everyone, especially by William Harker. But then, this was not the Jonathan of Whitby so much as the Jonathan who had survived Transylvania.

"Not now, Uncle Abraham," said Jonathan. "I'll explain later. Right now I'd really like to hear why we are out on a fishing boat, pursuing supernatural beings that murdered our parents."

As Jonathan finished his last sentence, one of the deckhands came above with some coffee and bread and passed it out to all of them. Abraham tapped his pipe along the outer edge of the boat and smiled at them as he took his food with a grateful nod of his head to the deckhand. They all realized they were famished and ate quickly and quietly.

When they were all done, Abraham turned and pulled a book from his knapsack, then walked over to them. He handed the book to Mina and said, "Read this to them. Start at the marked page. Then all will be clear." He then returned to his side of the boat, refilled his pipe and re-entered his solitude.

Mina dutifully took the book in her hands, turned in over and looked at its cover. Jonathan, Arthur and Quincy each looked at her quizzically as she opened the book, found the page marker and began to read aloud:

November 5th, 1895
A Confessional:
From the Journals
of
Peter Hawkins

I murdered a woman.

Her blood is on my hands, eternally.

I killed her.

Or, at least I helped kill a woman.

And I am glad for it... to further damn me.

Forgive me, Lord, for my mortal sin.

I do not think I can go to my maker without first writing about the worst experience of my life, and how at the end of it, we took a life, however wretched and vile a life it might have been. And even though I witnessed death and experienced killing on the field of battle in the name of God, Queen and country, nothing prepared me for the actions that I am about to confess to in these pages. The experience has eaten away at me like acid through the years, and now, seeing how it has affected all of us participants to lesser or greater degrees, most of all young Master Renfield, who has failed in his battle with his inner daemons and is incarcerated in Henry's asylum.

Cowards are we!

Van Helsing was right. His secrecy was only bought by his own loyalty to the friends that he now resents for doing this to his best friend, Montague Rhodes Renfield, but the fact is that we all performed a service when we rid the world of the most evil being I have, or will ever encounter. But by doing so we lost the lives of a few men, and all this, fostered upon young Abraham and Rhodes, mere children under God, no matter what the Queen's militia may state, were the events that forged Abraham and broke poor Monty into shards. However much Seward may try, even an alienist has limitations.

If she was Hell itself, I would rather suffer eternal torture rather than to meet her Lucifer.

In the summer of 1856, a fraction of our regiment, about thirty of us, at least the thirty of us that were left after the campaign against the

Russians, marched into a tiny village embedded so deep in the foreboding mountainous ranges of the Oriental region known as the Balkans that I doubt I or any other expedition could ever find it again. Near the Black Sea, our decimated regiment was preparing to embark on our journey homeward, our participation in what is now known as the Crimean War over, when we were dispatched by Her Majesty's High Command to investigate reports of barbarous acts by the Turks upon remote villages in the region, even after they had lost the war, and as good, young, foolish (I may write that now, I have lived long enough) soldiers, we obeyed without delay.

Under the command of Maj. Arthur Holmwood, whom I had known in friendship since childhood, a man who would receive one of the first Victoria Cross medals and become the Lord Godalming for his efforts during the afore-mentioned campaign, we departed and found that while none of the reported barbarous acts were false, each village pointed us not in the direction of the Turks but further and further into the depths of first Wallachia then Transylvania. Reports of gruesome deaths circulated by word of mouth by the villagers, who seemed to be filled with silly superstition and folklore. Or so we thought. However, from all accounts the perpetrator of all these events appeared to be an individual.

As we moved inward, the forests grew labyrinthine, dense and full of silence and mystery. The near-perpendicular mountains around us seemed to creep closer and closer to the edge of the gnarled roads we marched through, with Harker and Murray busy either telling jokes or complaining the entire time about the extra duty. The shadows of the Balkans kept us cold while we made a wide sweep through the provinces, if they could even be called that, in this strange part of the world. Each village seemed to take a step further back in time in both appearance and culture. At our surprise to see remnants of medieval life in one village, we were then astonished to see meager places that could not be called anything less than remnants of the Dark Ages. The forests seemed to absorb everything, including daylight. Evidence of the belief in the supernatural permeated our every encounter, from roses in the mouths of the about-to-be-buried to the unearthing of the previously-deceased in order to decapitate the corpse.

We began to see wooden crucifixes of all sizes and origins at crossroads, indeed we witnessed a few scraggly villagers burying a young man standing up, adorning the departed with roses and garlic before placing the cadaver feet first into the grave. I remember Renfield, such a large boy for a fifteen-year-old, expressing disgust at the desecration of the dead. How ironic, given the reasons for Renfield's future incarceration at the Seward Asylum.

Folklore from the villagers no doubt contributed to our state of mind. Stories of skeletons hitchhiking at crossroads, entire cemeteries that shifted slightly overnight, cats with no eyes scratching at the back door and lamias hiding under pulpits fed our imagination, but it was not until Holmwood ordered us to halt late one twilight so we could watch an opalescent spectral being float across the road in front of us did we all realize we were in a place of great mystery and supernatural presence.

The ghost waved at us as it melted into the tree line.

The following experiences are true and happened in the order I've written them here:

We found ourselves at another crossroads one morning. There was a crucifix that had been mounted on a stone pedestal in the middle of the dividing roads. Its eyes were bleeding.

Not one bird had been heard in the forests for days.

Our blood ran cold one afternoon when we watched a single tombstone bounce around a graveyard that dated back to the Dark Ages.

In the middle of one of the nights, Private Williams, the man on watch, shot a round out of his musket. The sound woke us all, and we watched the intended target, a human figure in the distance, as it transformed into a wolf and loped away.

Phillip Westenra saw the wolf another night and shot at it. The wolf ran away, laughing like a woman. Had we known who this might have been, we might have considered turning back. But we did not.

The soldier in all of us refused to express our fears, and yet we counted the days until we would complete our duty, return to sea, and to England. A quiet terror began to grip us all.

It was under these conditions that we found ourselves when we discovered the tiniest of villages hidden at the feet of colliding mountain ranges and swallowed by an oppressive forest that fought the hovels for space. A few farm fields supplied what was barely needed for sustenance.

We made our way in.

In the dark, oppressive trees had bags of cloth hanging from branches near the tops.

Van Helsing pointed to one of the bags.

A child's dead arm hung from inside of it. Flies of all sizes and descriptions swarmed over it.

We all presented our swords and Enfields and made our way into the middle of the collection of huts and worn, old buildings. Some of the roofings looked to be older than we could ascertain. The stone roadwork looked like it could have been built by the Romans. Surrounded by sad crop fields, a lonely, crumbling church sat at the edge of the small town like a guardian to keep the adjacent cemetery from somehow rising up and engulfing the entire hollow.

As we drew near the center of the village, peasants emerged from their tiny, humble abodes to humbly bid us welcome. Given the strife we had just endured in Crimea, any warm welcome from citizenry in the region would have been a delight. The town leader, an older and particularly rotund fellow, informed us that he was the elder of the village in a very rustic version of broken English, which some of us could make out. He was harried, and through tearful eyes explained enough so that we knew that it was his child that was suspended from the tree and that a horrible Strigoi had been hunting and killing their children for weeks on end.

We perceived the suspect as a wild beast native to the mountains.

How right we were.

Arthur conveyed the particulars to us (He had taken a first in Oriental Languages, of course) but we knew enough from the gestures of the man and the weeping of the other townsfolk around him that we had found our place and assigned duty. Arthur asked us to make camp. The burgomaster, or whatever the town elder was, told us that this Strigoi was only active at night, and we should make preparations to confront this vile thing after sunset, which we did. The townspeople seemed renewed in their vigor, happy that they were being protected, and everyone prepared for the night. We formed a camp in the middle of the ancient town square, with our muskets and bayonets pointing out in a radius and the villagers squatting amidst us. The horses had been put into a small barn toward the edge of town.

We thought ourselves prepared.

We were wrong.

Mere moments after the day fell behind the mountains, a bat came fluttering toward us, over the village rooftops, mixing in with the stars in the sky.

It was huge, the creature, the size of a man.

Or a woman.

We all gasped.

The wingspan was gigantic.

The townspeople recoiled with terror, some of the children crying out like they had been struck with a rod. With its foot claws, the enormous bat held the limp body of a child. One of the mothers began to shriek in unholy peals and screams.

She had recognized her son.

We were splattered with droplets of wetness.

But it was not rain.

It was the ichor of life.

Baptized with blood, we were.

The bat threw the body to the ground in front of our circle, and the corpse crashed in a wet splatter in front of us. Renfield exclaimed in fear. The bat then landed like a dandelion in spring, about ten paces away from us and, well, I might be judged as worthy of an alienist as Monty, but the bat, by some wicked act of devilry worthy of Mephistopheles, transformed into a woman before our very eyes.

From one moment to next, she went from bat to woman.

This I swear to Christ, Our Lord.

Yet she was no woman, beautiful though she was, there was no beauty in her, she was a creature from Hell itself. Her countenance and presence was one of pure and complete malevolence. No mercy lingered in that heart, for surely there was no soul to occupy that hellish husk either. Her tresses were as long and curled as the Gorgon Medusa in my beloved Ian's book of mythology, and her skin was devoid of all color, but her feline-shaped eyes glowed with the ferocity of Vulcan's fires. She wore an ornate black dress that seemed out of antiquity. The daemoness' ruby lips smiled as she asked us why we had ventured this far out to protect her livestock. Her smile revealed teeth that belonged in the mouth of a leopard or other foul thing. Her mouth and blouse were covered with the child's blood, and the blood of a hundred other victims before. She roared like a lion and the peasants around us joined the mother in screaming for their lives.

Arthur's response was to instantly stand and fire his musket at her. His shot was true and the ball found its mark, through the eye of the cursed hellion!

She staggered, and we all cheered Arthur's aim.

The villagers roared in triumph.

But she did not fall.

Our cheers died.

Then, the only way to explain what happened next is to simply write that the wound on the daemon healed in a few blinks of her hellish eyes. She spat the round out of her mouth and smiled wickedly at us.

"What kind of daemon are you?" gasped Holmwood.

The hellion then spoke.

"I am nosferatu, vrykolakas, strigoi and vampyr," she uttered with the Queen's own English, but with a thick Oriental accent, her taloned right hand splayed proudly out atop her blood-encrusted breast in a gesture of pride and royal arrogance. "A noblewoman of legend, myth and reality. I am mistress and own of all what you see. Both Ferdinand and Isabella from the House of Trastámara, and His Holiness Pope Alexander VI issued a proclamation to announce my nobility. You have no defense against me, for I am a superior being in every way and Satan is my unholy father through marriage to my beloved!"

Poor Williams, he was always impetuous, even for a private. Outraged against this satanic filth, he impetuously stood and discharged his Enfield at the she-daemon. The ball hit her squarely in the chest yet passed right through her. Williams then raise his bayonet charged the woman with the intent to impale the beast, but she easily parried the blow with her arm. Then she tore the poor man apart so violently, like a dog tears apart the carcass of a dinner pheasant, to the renewed screams of the villagers and to our collective horror.

After throwing Williams' rifle and bleeding left arm back at us, she cackled like Poe's infernal Raven and hissed, "If you take leave tomorrow and do not take my prey with you, I will allow you to depart. If you chose to stay and defend my prey, then none of you will leave this village alive."

"Ave Satanas."

She then bewitched herself back into a bat again and fluttered away like Lucifer's herald.

Toward the black silhouette of the church.

Renfield in particular began to quiver in fear. The villagers began to wail, moan and cry, and we had a dire choice to make. In the end, despite some fearful resistance from the younger members of our regiment like Renfield, Westenra and Van Helsing, boys still, Holmwood decided to have us stay, a decision that he would wrestle with for the years that followed.

Then, the village priest, a young Hungarian man named Tibor, then came forward and explained to us that this woman, this strigoi, was a vampyre, and though she was powerful, these creatures were not indestructible. She had arrived one hellish night, murdered the town watchmen and desecrated the town church with his corpse, skinning the poor man and reciting Satanic incantations while she spread the body parts throughout the dilapidated place of worship, thus claiming it for herself and Lucifer. The next eve she fought off the determined priest and the villagers to claim the church permanently.

Father Tibor had managed to continue services in one of the local homes. He opened a worn, old illuminated manuscript and read the rules to us in Latin. As I took dictation he said:

A vampyre may only walk by night.

Daylight can burn or kill them.

Their food is blood or flesh, either from a mortal soul or an animal.

They can take the form of creatures of the night: bats, rats, wolves, owls, ravens, cats and serpents.

The bite of a vampyre can infect a mortal soul and turn them into said creature if they survive into the next evening and drink the blood of a vampyre.

They can take the form of mist.

All holy relics can burn or kill them.

They cast no reflection.

Silver can wound or kill them.

Their strong minds can hold influence over the weak-minded.

They bathe in blood and avoid bodies of water.

Fresh water will burn and peel their skin.

Sea water will set them afire.

Garlic placed in the mouth will prevent a corpse from rising again.

A vampyre will blaspheme the holy language of Latin.

Faithful prayer from a believer keeps them away.

They prefer to sleep in a coffin lined with the soil of their native land.

To sleep without the native soil will weaken the creature significantly.

The touch of a crucifix can scald them.

A stake of wood through the heart kills and reduces them to ash.

The vampyre can command wicked things like wolves, owls, rats, ravens and bats.

Holy water is like fire to them.

Weapons cannot harm them unless they are blessed.

A blessing of their coffin will purify it and kill them if they cannot find similar shelter by dawn.

An exorcism can kill a vampyre.

The Holy Word of God, read from the Bible will keep them at bay.

Holy scripture from any book of faith will have the same effect.

Vampyres cannot sire children through natural means, they can only create other vampires with their bite.

They are the origin of the Black Plague.

An iron stake through the heart of a human corpse will keep it from rising.

An exorcism before the first dawn will restore a mortal soul bitten by a vampyre.

A vampyre ages very, very slowly, then withers to ash when final death comes.

Roses in a coffin will serve as iron bars in a prison and keep a vampyre from rising.

The Holy Communion is poison to a vampyre.

As the dawn neared, we had decided to fulfill our duties as soldiers. I suggested we track the creature to the church and dispose of it before she woke for the night, but the villagers explained that since we were in the creature's native soil that she could sleep in a different place every night and therefore was nearly untrackable.

Hearing all this from the priest, Arthur formulated a plan. We would hide the horses in one of the nearby barns, as if we had ridden away, obeying the command of this lamia woman. Holmwood then instructed the town elders to gather everyone in the center of the village that night, and he would dress in their native garb and hide among them. When the vampyre approached, Arthur would step forward and shoot her with a wooden arrow which he had hewn, one which lacked a metal arrowhead. Holmwood felt that at close range he could kill her with a shaven arrow fired out of a crossbow that one of the villagers had supplied.

If he somehow failed to kill the feminine monster, Arthur asked the priest to soak our .577 ball rounds in holy water so we could fire at her and the blessed rounds would finish off the beast. I remember young Abraham listening intently to this discussion.

We then reposed at one of the homes, offered by one of the grateful villagers. After a warm but humble meal cooked by the women of the village, we all slept, with Van Helsing taking turns at the watch with Renfield.

Rested, we woke early afternoon. Arthur asked William Harker to test the antiquated weapon, to assure him that it would not fail that night. Arthur had decided to heed Hawkins' earlier opinion and double the trap—they would seize the moment now and attack the vampiress while she slept in the desecrated holy place, and if she somehow survived our onslaught, we would then regroup for the previous plan.

The priest indeed blessed our .577 rounds, bayonets and pikes with holy water, and he accompanied us toward the church, which upon closer inspection was more of a chapel. Adjacent, in the cemetery, a lone, large crucifix lay cast aside, amid the gravestones. The chapel doors had been torn apart and ripped off their hinges, with pieces of human fingers stuck along the doorframe and dried blood smeared across the top of the doorframe in Latin, which read:

Ave Satanas

Arthur whispered to everyone to ready their weapons as we passed through the vestibule[192] and into the chapel. A huge hole in the roof cast a long, dramatic ray of sunlight down into the nave[193]. Every pew had been rended to kindling by this brutal creature. The altar had been broken into pieces, with human bones and blood scattered across the table top. Along the walls, the Stations of the Cross had been defecated upon. The statues of Mary and Joseph had been decapitated and bled upon, but the most horrific sight was the crucifix, which had been torn down and turned upside-down, with the head of the victim, a young child, placed upside-down over the face of Christ our lord.

This infuriated Murray, the most devout of all of us, and he ran ahead, ripped one of the broken pews out of the pile and whirled it around in an attempt to find and dispose of this heathen presence that had desecrated this holy place.

It was then that Westenra spied the dark, angular silhouette suspended upside-down from the rafters, behind us, near the back of the chapel. Her scarlet eyes lit up with childlike glee at seeing our torment. Arthur also spied the huge bat and pointed for us to open fire, and we did. The she-bat shrieked horribly in pain as the .577s ripped into her. She launched herself across the room, but in doing so was exposed to the rays of sunlight from the broken roof, and the hellion was scalded instantly, the heathen creature's back sizzling like cooking meat. She could not fly out through the vestibule and into the afternoon sun, nor could she flap out through the roof, so she soared around the chapel and us. Those of us that had not already opened fire already proceeded to do so. Most of us could manage to load and fire three rounds in a minute, with the gifted Jackson Morris averaging nearly five in the same time span. We showered the chapel walls with ball rounds in an effort to eradicate this beast from Hell. She alternately flew and clambered along the wall of the chapel, tearing holes in the walls and ripping at the

---

[192] A vestibule is a small room with inner and outer doors that separate the exterior of a building from an interconnecting main room inside.
[193] In Judeo-Christian church architecture, the nave is the main room of worship in a church, often in a long diagonal shape, with another rectangle, called the transept, intersecting the nave and forming, when viewed from above, a cross.

delicate stained glass windows. Her animalistic roars filled the air. She destroyed the desecrated Stations of the Cross in the process, leaving gashing claw marks on the columns, like the prehistoric Pterodactylus I've since read about in scientific literature.

The bat saw an opportunity and dove. She took Hughes-White, one of the lads with a pike instead of a rifle, into her rancid claws and flung him viciously against the aforementioned statue of Mary, crushing his body and reducing hers to rubble. The vampyre went for Van Helsing as well, but Westenra shoved him out of harm's way. Murray dove forward with his wooden stake and pinned her to a column, and a few other pikesmen skewered her as well, and she wailed with agony, and we thought we had her, but to our astonishment she turned into a sliver of mist before our eyes and 'bled' out of the hold of our weapons. She then transformed yet again, this time into a gigantic rat and stumbled, for she was slightly wounded from our thrusts, toward a fissure near the base of a small, ornate pulpit. She clawed her way through the wood and stone base in seconds as we continued our volleys and she disappeared under the floor. The priest led us down a dark circular staircase in a mad chase, thinking we were about to end this monster's 'life' at that very moment, but when we arrived in the basement we were in for a surprise, for a large, jagged fissure had been clawed over time in the far basement wall. Inside the fissure was a black, dank hole with broken, ancient caskets and coffins scattered about a crypt that seemed to have been built sometime in the Dark Ages.

In the fissure's bleak pitch, we could hear the scrapings of an animal slithering through tunnels, coffins and chambers. From somewhere in those depths we heard her hiss, "Ecce ego interficiam omnes."

"I will kill you all," translated the Priest.

"In nomine Satan."

We all shuddered.

Never one to panic, Arthur ordered a makeshift explosive to be made, and while a few of us began that task, Holmwood had Tibor bless the basement, to much distant hissing from the now-unholy depths of the catacombs. He also blessed the rest of the chapel and replenished the holy water. We laid the gunpowder-filled extra canteen onto the crypt floor right beside the mouth of the fissure and lit the fuse at the base of the stairs before we ascended to the ground floor and ran out of the chapel. A few seconds later an explosion ripped through the base of the chapel and collapsed the nearest part of the cemetery.

"Father," said Arthur to Father Tibor, "bless the interior of the church. At least she will not be able to get back inside. And the weapons as well, anoint them all."

"And tonight?"

"Tonight we behead her and scatter her ashes," snarled Holmwood.

We did not have to wait long. As the last sliver of sun let the night begin, she burst from somewhere in the recesses of the cemetery and came for us, but we were at the ready. She was in her bat form when we saw her from our position in the middle of the village, and Arthur instantly gave the command to open fire. We did, and Jackson Morris in particular was able to fire two rounds at the beast; her twin eyes of red fury locked upon us all.

I have seen battle in my years of service to Her Majesty, and I have seen the inhumanity and brutality of the field of battle, but I have never experienced the intensity of a conflict more than I did that night. She landed among us like the burst of a cannon, and with her great wings this unnamed vampyre threw us around like we were children. Instantly we were in a combat that would have only one outcome: either she was going to kill us all or we would end her existence on this world.

It was as if we were fighting a lioness on the dark continent, or the dreaded tiger from my days of serving in India, for this creature had both great fangs and powerful claws at her disposal, and while we used our rifles, bayonets' and pikes on her, her savagery more than matched the overwhelming odds in our favor.

With one swing of her left wing, the she-bat cut Turner's torso in half.

Foaming, massive jaws open, she bit into Mitchell's head and ripped it right off of his neck, his scream continuing as she flung it aside.

We swung at her with swords, fired at her with the Enfields, and she bellowed with fury as she yanked Walker's entrails right out through his uniform.

She continually transformed, from bat to wolf to something in between both forms and back again as she bit, clawed and roared her way through us, and we became as she, we became animals to match her ferocity, God help me for admitting this. We lost our human souls in this battle with this, this hellish witch of Satan, and we were never the same after. My hands tremble as I recollect the fury in that chapel!

Pray for me, reader!

Pray for our souls.

Then, a few of the pikes, led by Harker and Seward, were able to pin the beast to the wall of one of the village homes, while the citizens screamed in bloody terror inside, and Murray flew in with a broken pike and impaled the satanic creature through the chest.

She roared deeply, like a skewered bear, our damage deep and telling. The vampyre staggered, under the strength of the men that held her there, before turning to mist. I simply have never seen the like since. But the daemoness was wounded, and when she was free of the pikes and became her human form once more, she staggered, deathly injured.

Holmwood then shot her with his crossbow and she somehow caught the wooden arrow in mid-flight, and we were further shocked when the holy water-covered arrow burst into flame in her hand! The vampyre screamed in agony as her entire devilish arm went alight with fire! Arthur bellowed for us to rush in and finish her! Then the she-creature did something unexpected. Her arm still burning, she transformed into a bat again, dove for the youngest among us, the boy Renfield, and flew away, carrying her prey in her clawed feet.

Monty boy screamed like a small child, the wounded she-bat's barely-aflame wing scraping across the top of the chapel as she flew over it and toward the darkness of the cemetery.

"I will kill him if you pursue us!" shrieked a ghostly female voice from among the tombstones.

"Better Renfield die right now than at her mercy!" rebutted Arthur to us.

In the depths of the night, we chased them.

The priest screamed that she would bite Renfield and that we had only until the upcoming dawn to find and exorcise him. I feverishly asked the boy Van Helsing to bring spades and picks. Once past the chapel, we were all brought tools with which to dig, and so we began.

Though exhausted from the battle, we nevertheless excavated

through the rest of the night, uncovering tombstone, crypt and grave marker alike. Villagers stood along the sides of the cemetery for a time, holding torches and lanterns with which to illuminate our macabre duty, before some of the men began to help. Superstitious whispers of daemons and ghosts were squelched by the priest, who began a rosary with some of the village elders. We spent the hours breaking crypt seals, ripping apart caskets and destroying caskets, slowly revealing a network of freshly-dug tunnels in the process. The tunnel walls were lined with claw marks, explaining what we already knew about the identity of the culprit.

As the night ebbed, we had torn the cemetery completely apart. Villager, officer and soldier alike were near the end of their energy and wit. We had scattered bones of revered ancestor and criminal alike. At last we reached the final coffin. We were all filled with dread at the prospect of opening the coffin. The priest uttered something in his native tongue and left. Abruptly, Van Helsing also staggered off, Arthur nodding and explaining that this all might be too much for a boy and for a man of the cloth. Our group then gathered 'round this last symbol of mortality, as did all the villagers, to see if a young boy was still alive inside. At that point Harker, Seward and Murray all pried open the crumbling coffin lid.

Inside were the two of them, and above everything else I've written here, nothing else still fills me with more dread and horror than the sight that was revealed to us all.

The boy Renfield lay sideways, trembling and quivering and crying in absolute insanity as he stared into the wide-open eyes of the vampiress, who lay next to him in the coffin, her unblinking wide-open eyes staring blankly and horribly into Renfield's own.

His own eyes.

Her clawed, human fingers held Montague Rhodes Renfield's boyish face to hers like a lover, their lips locked in a horrific, morbid kiss. Monty had lost all sense of reason and sanity, shaking uncontrollably like a freezing dog, his mouth in a long, single, silent scream.

She then turned to us and hissed like the infernal serpent of Eden, when the priest shoved in between us and poured the entire contents of the chapel aspersorium, the holy water, into the coffin.

The coffin burst into white, holy fire.

As did the vampiress.

Yet, to prove without a doubt the Lord's prowess, the boy did not.

He lay quivering next to her, but only the she-devil burnt with God's touch.

She scrambled to claw her way out of the coffin, to stay alive, even as she burnt away, in agony, and that was when Van Helsing burst past us and savagely planted the cemetery's crucifix right through the daemon's body.

Harker pulled the wailing Renfield out of the coffin and away from his captor. Monty screamed and shrieked away, his soul scarred for life. It was at that moment when we lost Montague Rhodes Renfield.

Van Helsing leaned on the symbol of Christ and kept it right there, in the breast of our unholy foe. The crucifix began to glow inwardly with holy light, and in that horrible moment, we understood that we were in the presence of the Lord Our God. She clawed at Abraham as she withered, aflame with holiness, and Van Helsing's face danced with fury as he pushed down even harder on the crucifix, refusing to let her get out of the coffin, the symbol of the Crucifixion not letting this beast from Hell back out among the living. Abraham then unexpectedly began to bawl like a boy as he held the crucifix in place as the woman at last died a horrible death, a horrible thing herself, as we all watched like spectators in Rome's ancient games.

Van Helsing was never a boy again.

We had won.

We had murdered her.

And lost ourselves in the process.

No one cheered.

We all wept from the effort, save Arthur, who sometimes I think feels nothing.

The village was spared. Yet we all know, as we collectively watched the fiend burn away, that we would all never see the world the same way again. Renfield was unbitten, and therefore unaffected in that sense, but he was never the same again.

A few days later, after much rest and appreciation from the village, we left the Balkans for the Black Sea. We made our way back to Her

Majesty's Army and returned home to England and Whitby, and we were never the same. Rarely did we discuss our collective experiences in Crimea, and even less did we discuss the events in the little village. As the years went on and we carried on with our lives with marriage, children and life in general, we all seemed to somewhat heal from our encounter with the woman, and 'the woman' is the term I will use to refer to her since we were never told her given name.

Of all of us, Monty suffered the most and he was the one that unfortunately bore the deepest emotional scars of our experience. Renfield began to show more and more signs of distress and mental agitation as the years went on, until he was institutionalized by Henry Seward, by then a doctor and practicing alienist, in the mid 1880s. Under Seward's care, Renfield revealed an obsession with the food chain of life, stuffing insects, frogs, sparrows and rats into his mouth. Then came his escape in the spring of 1888 and his subsequent recapture in 1891, with the realization that our Montague Rhodes Renfield was free during the events that came to be known as the Whitechapel Murders.

Should we have let justice take their course with Monty? Certainly we debated this among us, with Van Helsing being the lone voice for giving his childhood friend over to Scotland Yard, despite how much it pained him to consider such action. When I remember being at sea on the journey home from this experience, it now reminds me of one of Tennyson's poems, the one about sea and death. Cannot recollect the title of the piece now. To this day, I struggle with the perspective on this experience. Should we have simply left the villagers as is, in the grip of that ferocious beast? We have all stated negatively to that question on the rare occasion that the topic has come up, but I do not think there is one among us who wishes that experience had never happened.

In the end, I helped save a village, but lost part of my soul.

May all of you who read this in future generations come to forgive us for the misfortunes that befell us as a family as a result. The rest of this journal will chronicle the rest of my comparatively mundane career in serving Her Majesty as a soldier, and my career as a solicitor.

Yours in God,
Peter Hawkins

Mina closed the book like she had just been given the secrets of the universe and they all looked at Abraham with a blend of acceptance, resentment and understanding. Van Helsing had been in the midst of finishing a letter, his fountain pen[194] swirling over the paper as he finished with a flourish. Abraham Van Helsing gave them all a sad, sly conspiratorial grin, as if they were all part of something greater now and looked them all over as he puffed on his pipe. Van Helsing considered them for a moment with another mixture of emotions, those of happiness and parental concern.

He said, "Now you know everything," before turning to look out to sea.

The coast of France was in the distance, with the wind.

---

[194] The development of the fountain pen traces back to the Arab world in the 10th century and began to be popular in 17th century Europe, while the ball point Pen was invented in 1888 by American John J. Loud.

PARIS, THE CITY OF LIGHT
EARLY SUMMER 1899

Secrets travel fast in Paris.
—*Napoleon Bonaparte*

In Paris, our lives are one masked ball.
—*Gaston Leroux*

London is a riddle.
Paris is an explanation.
—*Ernest Hemmingway*

When good Americans die, they go to Paris.
—*Oscar Wilde*

Paris, France in 1899 pulsed and resonated with events:

Paris, and Western Europe, for that matter, swam in the glow of *La Belle Époque*, or 'beautiful era', a time of peace and prosperity that abounded with cultural and scientific advancements, all this despite the abject poverty in Paris that did not allow many to similarly enjoy these times. This golden, gilded age would run from the early 1870s and into the twentieth century, not knowing that two world wars awaited the entire continent.

The Treaty of Paris of 1898 had just come into effect that April, in which the United States paid Spain $20 million dollars to gain possession of the Philippines. This, along with Spain giving up control of Cuba, Puerto Rico, Guam, and parts of the Spanish West Indies effectively ended the Spanish-American War. This signaled both the end of the Spanish Empire and the beginning of America as a global power.

A year later the 1900 Summer Olympics (known later as the Games of the II Olympiad) would be held in Paris, without opening or closing ceremonies. The games were part of the 1900 World's Fair, also known later as the Exposition Universelle of 1900.

The Eiffel Tower itself had only been completed ten years earlier, erected in 1889 for the Paris World's fair. Named for Alexandre Gustave Eiffel, an engineer whose company designed and built the structure, the tower would remain the tallest man-made structure for another forty-one years, until the Chrysler Building in New York City was finished in 1930.

A hundred years before, in 1789 to be specific, a civil protest regarding the dismissal of a reform official erupted into what is now known as the French Revolution, which transformed France from a monarchy to a republic and culminated in the beheadings of both King Louis XVI and eventually his queen, Marie Antoinette. In the aftermath of the Revolution, which ended after thousands of executions by guillotine, considered a merciful form of capital punishment at the time, the different factions of the revolution took turns seizing power until Napoleon Bonaparte, a young general at the time, seized power and named himself first counsel.

Auguste and Louis Lumière, known as the Lumière Brothers, began using the first motion picture camera, the Cinematograph, to make moving pictures. The camera, invented by Léon Bouly in 1892, gave birth to the art and business of film.

In 1899, Alfred Dreyfus was pardoned for his involvement, or lack thereof, in the Dreyfus Affair, a political scandal that began in 1894 as was not completely resolved until 1906. Captain Alfred Dreyfus, a French Military officer was unjustly accused of passing secret information to Germany and sentenced to Devil's Island, an infamous prison colony in French Guiana. He served five years before he was recalled to begin a series of trials, sentencing, and pardons, all while his family sought to clear his name. All of this happened as evidence came to light that another officer was the guilty party, and in the end, Dreyfus was pardoned and reinstated, but not before France was divided under the shadow of anti-Semitism. Alfred Dreyfus would serve in the First World War before dying in 1935.

The infamous cabaret Moulin Rouge, a can-can dance revue had been performing nightly for a decade and would continue to do so for another thirty years.

1899 was the year that Claude Monet, founder of the French Impressionist style of painting, would begin to paint water lilies in his home in Giverny.

ONE

Wilhelmina Murray woke up in a bed in Paris. It was warm, and from the sound of the city outside, it was middle of the day. She took a long, deep breath, and tears came with the abrupt thought that her parents were indeed both dead. A lifetime of memories with them were behind her now, and her throat swelled with anguish at the thought of them never seeing her wed, never holding her children, and of never again being able to tell them that she loved them.

Mina was not wearing any clothes, her innocence lost. She laid an arm over her eyes and cried a little, silently, lest she disturb the person in bed with her. Right then and there, Wilhelmina Murray decided to contain her feelings of mourning until all of this was over, and if she survived, then at that point she would give her parents a proper remembrance and burial.

Next to her, Jonathan lay silently, and she realized that he had been watching her sleep, and now wake. They smiled at each other in silence, a warm sense of comfort flowing between the two young lovers.

It had seemed an eternity, not a day and a half since the attack on Seward Manor. After the journey across the English Channel, they had landed in Calais, the French port town that had been the natural landing place for all travel to and from England for centuries. Sitting snugly before the Strait of Dover, the narrowest point of water between the two countries, Calais had been founded by the Romans, who had named the settlement *Caletum*. Inquiries similar to those in Whitby, this time around resulted in the knowledge that a certain vessel had just come in from England. It took a significant 'inducement' to that ship's captain to garner the explanation that, while he had asked no questions regarding the passengers and some ornate 'boxes' that were part of the arrangement, he certainly seemed content that the massive man named Renfield with whom he had conducted business had been on his way with the boxes, after having engaged another wagon.

A wave of sorrow had passed over Abraham's face at the mention of Renfield, confirming his worst fears of Monty's involvement in this affair. Van Helsing theorized that the captain had been rewarded with enough gold to pay off his boats or any other debts in life, further explaining to them that vampires often used gold as a method of international currency that was untraceable and easy to carry in the lining of a coffin.

Another curious fact of discovery was that a coffin, filled to the brim with human bones, had, avoiding customary procedure, been sent ahead to a location in the distant Orient, written in Romanian; an address which Abraham surreptitiously noted and subsequently translated for confirmation from Jonathan. The name of the specific train station and the intended destination thereafter was bought for another tidy sum of money, which Arthur continued to supply with the understanding that the objective was to track down their quarry as quickly as possible. His efforts got a strong pat on the shoulder from Jonathan, who seemed to be pulling out of his exhaustion from his furious cross-continental journey. Before they left for the train yard, Quincy telegraphed[195] word to Ian, also leaving a note for him at the ticket window. Abraham wired Paris for hotel rooms.

After a breakneck journey to the railyard by hired carriage, the group discovered that the mid-day train to Paris had left with a load of 'boxes'. Enough awkward silences from the porters and ticket-takers began to explain to the group that Abraham's theory of golden payoffs was indeed more than a hypothesis. The only worry at the moment for the train station employees was concern for a young porter who had been working at the station for months and had suddenly vanished before the end of his shift.

Given the circuitous route of the train through France, the group decided to dine upon some less-than-satisfactory croissants, which Quincy wolfed down so quickly that invariable humorous comparisons of the Texan to an open furnace were made.

They then took the last train to Paris.

Before everyone knew it, Arthur and Morris had retired to their rooms, as had Abraham, which left an exhausted Mina and Jonathan to discreetly take her room together, both flopping fully clothed onto the bed, too exhausted to do anything but sleep.

Or so they thought.

Afterward, they fell asleep near dawn, not married but bonded for life.

Outside, the activity of daytime in Paris was not enough to wake any of them.

Now, they looked at each other, in bed, in love, wrapped in tragedy and destiny, and it seemed to them, impossible to live without each other.

"How did you survive the fall?" asked Mina, a brave smile back on her face.

"I thought of you," was Jonathan's reply.

Mina rolled her eyes and laughed at Jonathan's remark, but she accepted it.

Then, two confident brisk knocks at the door.

They knew by the brisk, quick tempo of the knocks, who it was.

"Yes?!" shouted/screeched Mina at last, over a few panicked expressions thrown back and forth between herself and Jonathan, who was scrambling to get dressed. An unmarried couple sleeping together in a hotel room was something that was still frowned upon, even this late in the 19th century's modern age, even in the modern city of Paris, France.

"It's Van Helsing." Abraham's voice. "Meet us downstairs in the lobby for dinner, please."

"Did we miss lunch, Uncle Abraham?" answered Mina, shaking her head and rolling her eyes at her own stupid question, gathering her wits while searching for her clothes and her dignity. Jonathan stopped his own search and simply laid back to watch her with a mischievous smirk on his face.

"My dear, we missed the entire day!" laughed Abraham, and after a long pause while Mina anticipated that her uncle would ask if there was a man in her room, they both heard Van Helsing simply say, "See you both downstairs," before they heard him saunter back down the hallway.

"This," said Abraham Van Helsing about an hour later, "is not going to be pleasant conversation for supper, or whatever this meal is, and I apologize beforehand."

Forty minutes before, they had met in the lobby of the Hotel Paris Ritz, a sprawling, luxurious hotel that had opened the previous year. The eyes of Van Helsing, Morris and Holmwood were firmly upon Mina and Jonathan when they arrived in the lobby. They were all too polite to speak of Jonathan and Mina's obvious rendezvous. In fact, Arthur nobly distracted everyone by insisting that they make their way to a restaurant a few blocks away for dinner. Between them was always respect, one of the pillars of their friendship.

---

[195] Telegraphs were introduced in 1849. By 1950, cables had been laid in the ocean between England and France, and the first transatlantic cable was installed in 1857. Contact was made between England and the United States on August 16, 1858.

Arthur playfully nudged Jonathan with a smile on his face, and Mina took the moment to tickle Holmwood, cognizant that he, among them, had lost not just his parents but had had his fiancée taken from him. Indeed, even as Mina tickled Arthur and he laughed even harder, she knew that Lucy remained on all of their minds. She saw Abraham give them all a warm grin, happy at their youthful pranks, but she knew what Van Helsing's thoughts were about Miss Westenra's fate.

The thought sent an icicle through her.

Jonathan was surprised when they left the hotel as the afternoon ebbed; the streets teemed with the bustling populace of the city. They hailed a carriage and weaved through and around the storm of traffic. Abraham lugged his bag, and Quincy carried a knapsack and long leather rifle scabbards, complete with Western-styled tassels.

As the horses pulled them along the tall, narrow, crowded streets, they all instinctively took in the long shadows and knew that the evening and everything that came with the night lay only a few hours ahead. After they found the cafe, and were seated, they ordered in perfect French, (although Quincy's Texas accent, attempting French, was a linguistic marvel).

After the waiter slid some perfectly delectable fried chicken in front of them, Van Helsing said, "As I stated before, I apologize in advance for the gruesome topic of our meal. And as I stated before, I have had previous experience with these creatures. The second vampire I murdered, after Dracula's wife in the Balkans, and I say murder because it is, plainly speaking, murder, was a member of Her Majesty's Constabulary. He had been infected by another *nosferatu* some time before and had been preying on flower girls, inebriated bar patrons and other lost souls."

Mina, Jonathan and Arthur could only gape at Abraham's directness, though it only stopped Arthur for a moment or two before the aroma of the chicken called to him.

"I was a mere child compared to all of you now, and yet I was able to come upon the disgusting thing during the witching hour. He was feasting upon an old woman as they both sprawled on a London sidewalk. I threw Holy Water that I had procured from the local parish onto him. I'm afraid he dissolved over the poor woman like baking powder in a stream. After that, it became an obsession, really. Holmwood's father, your grandfather," he said, nodding at Arthur, "Wrote me a letter of introduction to Sir Richard Owen[196], who has only recently passed on, and I volunteered for a time in the department of archeology in the British Museum before later being bequeathed a position in the position in the department while I completed my studies at the University of London.

"I began work at the museum while I continued my nocturnal activities. I learned where to look for them, and as I traveled abroad as a member of the museum, pursuing cultural enrichment for Her Majesty, I began eradicating every vampire I encountered. It took time in the beginning, but I found them. A Swiss grave keeper. He slept under in one of the empty crypts he tended. A French lawyer, not far from this very restaurant. I beheaded a university librarian in Florence who had been eating children in his spare time. I learned to diligently pursue every folktale, every myth, every parable, every ghost story, every superstition, as if they were clues in a mystery fable from Doyle in *The Strand*[197], and when folklore combined with disappearances and murder, invariably I would find a vampire. Or something else.

"Other times, I found an actual apparition. Or a banshee. Upon a rare occasion, a shapeshifter or lycanthrope. There are villages in Old Spain and in the New World where the inhabitants transform into leopards or jaguars. In Africa people turn into leopards, hyenas or lions. An Indian

---

[196] Sir Richard Owen (1804-1892) was an English biologist most famous for the term 'Dinosauria' (terrible reptile).
[197] *The Strand* was a monthly magazine that originally published, among other pieces of fiction, the Sherlock Holmes stories by Sir Arthur Conan Doyle. The first issue was published in 1891, the final in 1950.

princess who could shapeshift into a tiger nearly ripped me to pieces. I learned the rules to deal with these beings, how to eradicate them if need be. Some of the shapeshifters were not evil, simply making their way through their existences, and those I left alone. Any being supporting Satan, his minions or that hunted humans became the object of my hunt. The supernatural is a very real thing, sits on human society's fringes, and nourishes itself on the wealthy, the poor, the ignorant and the wise alike. I learned of the evil that was behind it. My academic career grew. I married. My wife and daughter died during childbirth as you all know, so I was left alone. I buried my family and then buried myself in teaching, exploring and my macabre pursuits. I became an instructor, then a professor. Your fathers all knew of all this but decided to stop asking me about my... mission. In the name of the museum I sought out farther corners of the world in search of these *nosferatu*, whose appetite for humans knows no bounds. In India they are called *vetâla*. Armenians refer to them as *dakhanavar*, and in China they are the *jiangshi*. I became learned in the different ways to kill them, accrued said methods as a horticulturalist might gather planting techniques. I made friends and acquaintances along the way, good and bad people who knew of vampires because of personal experience and who had also pledged to stop them. Old Saiful in India. Malaquias Rivera in Central America, Father Tibor Kovacs, yes, from the story, with his dragon-statued monastery in Budapest. The late Henry Jekyll in London. The venerable Yasuke Shimura in Japan. You would be surprised at how many forces I could muster to aid us, if need be, and with very few questions asked, especially among the holy people of every religion in this world. Good is good, regardless of faith. Don't forget that. We all want a better place, a better existence. This all leads me in a roundabout way to the events of the immediate future. You've seen the wanton destruction these things are capable of. Have any of you had a change of heart?"

They all looked at each other, searching their youthful faces for any trace of doubt. They could not find any. Abraham began, "It would not be held against you if—"

"We're all in this," said Jonathan flatly.

"And honestly," said Arthur, "we'd appreciate that our resolve not be questioned from this moment forward. He killed our parents. He took *my wife*."

There was such fervor from Arthur that Abraham reached out and patted his arm. "I would never question your resolve, King Arthur, and all of you for that matter, yet it is quite another thing to climb into a dark crypt at the witching hour[198] with nothing but a candle and a sharpened piece of wood in your hands."

"I'm here to kill 'em all," whispered Quincy, and they all looked at the Texan, because when he did whisper, it meant the most serious of his oaths. He gave them back a stare that could sear metal. "An eye for an eye.[199]"

"I disagree with that philosophy, despite my observation that I am living that verse," said Abraham as he took a bite of chicken. "We should consider the possibility of digging our own graves as we begin this endeavor. If I perish during this campaign, set me upon a pyre and set me alight. I need no burial."

This took them all back a bit, and their youthful eyes danced again between each other again, exchanges of glances and covenants, before Jonathan said, "For us also."

"Very well," said Abraham with one long, sad nod of his head. "A burial for us all."

"Not without me," said Ian Seward as he walked in from the street and out of nowhere to plop down into the empty chair at their table. They all took a moment to recover from their shock before

---

[198] The witching hour is usually between three and four at night, when supernatural beings are most active and powerful. Today the witching hour usually refers to midnight.
[199] A biblical quote, from Mathew 5:38. "Ye have heard it hath been said, An eye for an eye, and a tooth for a tooth."

collectively roaring with joy. Warm handshakes abounded, as well as a loving hug from Mina. "The *concierge* gave me three ideas as to where you might be dining. This was my first choice."

"Brilliant, mate!" beamed Arthur, before emotion swamped him. Teary eyed, he clasped Ian's arm and said, "How's my best man?"

Mina nearly burst into tears, as did Abraham. Jonathan gulped deeply to hold his in. A fierce quiver crept over Quincy's lips.

Ian blinked back tears of his own as he slapped Arthur's shoulder and said, "Well, now that I'm with you. And I'm *famished*!"

They cobbled together some chicken pieces for Ian to eat, and Seward dove in, not realizing how hungry he truly was.

"Somehow, I've put everything in order at home," said Ian as he ate, his voice growing lower and lower with emotion. "With all of our homes. Spent a few hours with the local authorities, explained all of that as a fire, somehow hiding all of the bodies before they arrived. I received your note from the lad, then made it to Whitby Port and hired the next available boat. Got your note at the Calais train station as to your destination here."

Ian took another eager bite of chicken, then he trembled and said, "It was difficult to pull the bodies out of the collapsed basement."

"Ian," gulped Mina in sympathy.

"That," sighed Arthur, "was our collective responsibility."

"We all shoulda helped ya, Sewie."

Ian shook his head at Quincy, then took a moment to force back some tears before he continued. "Our parents are all out of the country, you see. At least that's how I had them explain to anyone who would inquire. Spoke to all of the servants, retained all of them and paid them a year's advance to care for our respective estates without any questions until our return. The blaze at my home was explained to the authorities as simply a house fire. I explained to the servants in your respective homes that we'd be away, as well as paying their wages for the year in advance. They'll talk with our nurses and such, so the truth will be gossiped about. Nothing we can do about that but hope that our loyalty to them all these years and the wages paid so far in advance will also retain their consideration. Managed to discreetly place our parents at rest in the Holmwood Family crypt, temporarily."

"We'll give 'em all a proper burial when we kill these sons of bitches," snarled Quincy through a mouthful of fried chicken.

"Amen," said Ian. "What have I missed since I saw you all last?"

"We prepare to hunt that which hunted us," said Abraham Van Helsing with a grim, knowing nod.

TWO

In another section of Paris.

Dark and wet.

Lucy Westenra opened her eyes for the first time in two days.

Once she did, Lucy knew what it was like to be reborn.

Yet this time she was not born as an infant but as an adult.

This time as a thing of the night.

Nosferatu.

She blinked, and her eyes gained clarity.

A series of wooden planks stood but a few mere inches from her eyes, but now Lucy's vision was different, more focused, as if she could see through a microscope[200], examine the texture of each plank, each knot in the wood, and every fibrous texture was revealed to her as she could never have seen before. She was able to notice the nails that held the planks together in near-infinite detail, each tinge of rust, each notch on the nail and she knew how many blows it had taken to thrust the tip of each nail through the wood, whose grooves looked like gaping labyrinths to her now. But the amazing part was that she could see all of this in complete darkness. Lucy realized she had somehow been moved to another coffin, not the dark, svelte coffin that she had shared with the Transylvanian.

She was underground, Lucy knew, but she could sense a room, a chamber, outside of the coffin, with wet ground. She reeled at her newfound abilities. But more important to Lucy of Dracula at the moment was the heretofore unknown, succulent aroma that overwhelmed her. She lay in the darkness of the coffin, but the smell that wafted through the planks and to her delicate nostrils was enough to make her salivate instantly and begin to heave her chest in breathless anticipation. This sugary, lovely smell was irresistible! Yummier than baking bread, more delicious than candy! She had experienced all manner of delicacy and dessert in her day, from the banket of the Netherlands, panzarotti from Italy, the legendary croissants of France, and Uncle Abraham had even brought her a lotus seed bun once, from China of all places, but Lucy had never smelled something as amazing and delicious as this!

Surely this was a feast beyond measure!

Her mouth watered, anticipating.

Thirst unquenched.

She salivated.

Someone walked around the outside of her coffin, around her head, and lifted the coffin up at that end. Lucy felt her head and torso rising along with it. After a few forceful tugs at her coffin lid by someone of tremendous strength, the lid creaked slowly open.

Once again, that delicious aroma wafted through Lucy's nostrils, even stronger now, like the

---

[200] The invention of the microscope goes back to the Netherlands in the late 1500s, as well, and Galileo Galilei's compound microscope was named by Giovanni Faber in 1625.

scent of a home-cooked meal. At the periphery of her vision, even in the gloom, she could see piles and piles of skulls and bones, femurs, tibias, ribs and fibulas. All lining the strange, odd-shaped room in rows, like an absurd library, but one filled with bones instead of books.

The Catacombs of Paris can be best described as a labyrinthine ossuary, with chambers that spread for miles along seemingly endless tunnels, both modern and ancient, that extend under the city. This underground cemetery houses the bones of millions of Parisians that have died over the centuries, and as the city grew and the above ground graveyards had to be moved to make way for new buildings, the disinterred were moved to the underground cemetery. Endless stacks of bones stretch along endless tunnels, sleeping in endless darkness.

The air in the chamber was one of diffused, eternal dusk, with the generations of dust that were not covering the skulls filling the air.

With darkness.

And yet not complete darkness.

A dust-drenched pool of light.

Upon wet, dank soil.

Inside the pool, was a pentagram of perverse, oddly-shaped candles, and inside that, a moldy mound of wet bones. Centuries-old, piled upon each other.

Atop the putrid mound: a young man, tied and helpless.

In black clothes.

Wearing a white, *clerical* collar.

The priest stared at her, wide-eyed and full of terror.

He shrieked, "Protégez-moi, Seigneur Dieu, de ces créatures maléfiques!" *Protect me, lord god, from these evil creatures!*

Dracula's voice rumbled in the ink of darkness. "Il faut avoir la foi pour être protégé, prêtre." *One must have Faith to be protected, priest.*

Lucy stared back at the young man, famished and flush with bloodlust, for Lucy Westenra had the explosive realization that the delicious scent was *that of the priest.*

She could take in the scent of his blood *through his skin*.

Bloodlust exhilarated her.

Lucy's senses had become incredibly acute, like an uncontrollable tide. Saliva poured into her mouth like creeks into a river, and the thought of sinking her mouth into the priest's supple, ready neck was so overwhelming she tensed to leap at him, even though every fiber in her rational mind told her that this was the wrong thing to do.

She did not care.

Lucy Westenra of Dracula only salivated.

The allure was irresistible.

She knew she was not starving, but her craving for the blood rushed through her like fire. Yet she sensed something else, a feeling of foreboding around her, then she felt the presence of complete malevolence, it tugged at her soul, pulled at her and poured into her like ink into a cup of water, or blood into Holy Water. The sense of lust was overwhelming to Lucy, still naïve in many ways that did not include two nights in a coffin with a being of unspeakable evil, and she choked on the corruption for a moment, overwhelming and quenching her fever, her fervor to devour. She teared up in fear, and yet the corruption and the bloodlust then began to combine.

From the darkness around the room, Dracula's dark voice snarled, with the menace of an animal behind it, "Ne attingas antequam iuberet." *Do not move before I command it.*

"Yes, my husband," said Lucy, tremors of fear and anticipation searing through her.

A trinity of insulted feminine snarls and hisses filled the chamber, then ebbed.

Somewhere in the gloom, unseen, the brides seethed.

"Yes, my *Master*," corrected Dracula. The tone stated that the correction would only happen once. "You are never to be my wife, regardless of what I have taken from you."

"Yes, my Master," was Lucy's reply. She choked back tears, for innocence and paradise lost.

"Ego invocant nomen Domini profana patris mei," rumbled Dracula's voice. *I Invoke the Name of my Unholy Father.*

"In nomine Domini nostri profana patris," choired the voices of Petra, Venus and Andromeda, unseen as well. *In the name of our Unholy Father.*

Candlelight danced morbidly.

Darkness flowed like wicked ink all around them.

"S'il vous plaît, chère demoiselle, détachez-moi!" shrieked the priest, horrified at the daemonic incantation, while he struggled with the ropes that bound his wrists and ankles. *Please, dear young lady, untie me!*

Lucy looked past the priest and sensed a surge of motion amid the distant piles of bones before she realized that thousands of rats scurried in and out of, through and around the labyrinthine bone stacks that lined the chamber. Dracula's possessed vermin were chasing the normal sewer rats throughout the stacks of bones, *killing and eating them as they caught them.* The tiny screams and wails of rats being devoured, some while they were still alive, lent an even more macabre air to the chamber. Death echoes dancing around them.

Lucy's thoughts swam to her foggy memory, to her past, to Arthur, Mina, Ian, Quincy, her mother. There was a feeling of empathy that began to seep into her heart, but the wave of corruption came crashing in like the tide and washed them away. *You belong to me now.*

"—et profanum filius," continued Dracula, and Lucy could hear him nearly laugh at his own irony. *—and his unholy son.*

"—et profanum filius," chanted the vampiresses.

"—*and his unholy mother*," rumbled the voice of corruption.

"—et sceleratis matrem," finished the three

Dracula snarled like a feral dog and continued, "Puer nox texisset per Satan vero sumus de crucifixione Christi secundum mentientibus. Itaque asseris vota Indoctrination Impia quam opera renunciabit Deo servire promisimus Impia Diabolus et Satanas in Ecclesia." *Child of Darkness, through Satan's truth we have been shielded from the lies of the Christ after his crucifixion. And so, let you state the vows of Unholy Indoctrination, which you will renounce God and his works and promise to serve Satan in the Unholy Satanic Church.*

"And so I ask you, Lucy Westenra, do you renounce the Christ, Moses, Buddha, Mohammed or any other prophet of morality?"

Breathless with blood hunger and corruption, Lucy gasped, "I do."

"Qui es-tu?" sobbed the priest, desperate to untie his ankle bindings. *Who are you?*

Dracula barked, "Je suis tout ce que vous êtes, mais représente le contraire de tout ce que vous semblez être." *I am everything that you are yet represent the opposite of all that you appear to be.*

"And do you reject all of the works of God in this world and the next?"

"I do."

Blood trickled, in sympathy, out of the eye sockets of the rows of skulls.

"And all of Heaven's empty promises?"

"I do."

The priest undid the ropes around his ankles, blood pounding through his body as he anticipated sprinting away into the next chamber.

"Do you renounce all acts of good will, so as to live as an enemy of the Christ?

"Yes."

"Do you renounce the lie that is good, so that no apostle or prophet may have mastery over you?"

"I do."

The priest bolted upright, his wrists still bound, and as he did so a dark wave of vermin surrounded him and the altar of bones. The rats ripped at the front of the priest's shoes, and he had to scramble back atop the altar to avoid having his feet gnawed off his legs, screaming in shock at the ravenous wave of pestilence. Obeying silent commands, the rats retreated, and Dracula's voice hissed, "Do you renounce God, who twists the truth for his own gain?"

"I do."

"Do you believe in Satan, the Unholy Father Almighty, Creator of truth and darkness?"

"I do."

The priest's jugular pulsed with blood and fear and Lucy saw it surge with microscopic precision.

"Do you believe in Dracula, Satan's only son, your Lord, who was born of the Demoness Lilith and his Unholy Father?"

Lucy's breaths came in heaves. Her mouth watered as she said, "I do."

"Do you wish for the dimming of the Star of Bethlehem?" rumbled Dracula.

"Yes."

"Tu blasphèmes, ma fille!" shouted the priest. *You blaspheme, girl!*

"That the Seventh Seal be torn asunder? For the seven-headed, seven-crowned dragon to crush Michael and his accursed angels? For the destruction of the Great Lamb, and the corruption of all that is good in this and any world?"

"Yes, I do," whispered Lucy, her mouth overflowing with saliva. Her appetite was ravenous, and her skull pounded like a storm against a flimsy dock. She would have sold Victoria's soul at that moment to feast.

To say nothing of her own.

"Then you are now a child of Satan, and you may partake upon this sacrifice," chuckled Dracula. "Daughter of my father."

No longer able to control herself, Lucy leapt out of her coffin and at the priest, and as she did so, she began to change, and it was not Lucy the human being that landed on the screaming, terrified priest, but rather it was Lucy the giant grey bat who began to tear apart her first victim, gulping blood and chunks of meat from atop the altar of bones, even as the priest screamed for his life. She growled like a starved leopardess, parched for food and ravenous at her conquest.

From out of the darkness that was the perimeter of the chamber walked Primus, the skeletons, the rats, the brides and Dracula, son of Satan. And Montague Rhodes Renfield, eyes shining brightly at the sight of butchery. Venus, Petra and Andromeda watched the birth of this new bride, this new competitor, his new *vampyre*, with a mixture of envy, nostalgia and loathing. They watched her feed and drink. The claws of Lucy's wings and legs tore at the priest, and her huge canines ripped through flesh, bit through bone, and she drank blood like it was water in an oasis. After she had eaten her fill, the Lucy bat raised her grey, blood-soaked face, her ears pinning back, eyes blazing as she gave one long, ferocious hiss.

She then bowed her shaggy, mammalian head at her master, who nodded contentedly at the show of respect. "You are mine to command, until I banish or kill you, my new bride. This is your oath to me."

The Lucy bat stepped away from the torn-asunder torso of the priest, whose arms were still quivering since *the victim had not died yet*, and as she did so her body metamorphosized from bat to human, Gothic painting to watercolor, in seconds, but her mouth, hands, and dress were all soaked with blood when she stood, then kneeled before Dracula and the brides as she said, "I am yours to command, my Master."

"These are my brides, concubine, you answer to them in my absence."

Lucy bowed her head to them, her formal Victorian etiquette guiding her as she said, "I am yours to serve, my ladies."

"And serve us you shall," said Venus in cold fury. Petra and Andromeda's canines glinted smiles of satisfaction as they sensed Lucy's anger. She did not break expression, but they all read that she took insult. There was a moment of electric tension between the women, which Dracula ambivalently ignored, which then faded.

Dracula noted the hunger with which the brides were looking at the corpse of the priest and said, "This sacrifice was not for you. Let the rats have it."

At his word the rats poured out from all of the bony recesses of the stacks around them and began to envelop the carcass of the priest with a revolting fervor that made the body actually twitch and spasm as the daemonic rodents began to gnaw, cut and tear away, at times clawing away at each other so as to get a better morsel from the unexpected feast.

"I found him on *Rue Saint Denis*, searching for prostitutes, just as you said, Master," giggled Renfield, a chuckle that would have sent chills down the spine of any reasonable human being.

"So you have stated and has been since the time of the Romans, Mister Renfield," replied Dracula.

"Will you be needin' anything else, Master?" said Renfield, his head bowed in respect even though he was taller than Dracula.

"That will be all for this evening, Mister Renfield," said Dracula as he turned and tossed a few gold coins to the ground in front of the massive man. "Make what use you may want of your time. Primus and the skeletons will guard the coffins."

"And what of our evening, Master?" said Petra.

"Tonight is my blood sport," hissed the master, "and you are to be my hounds."

THREE

"They are here somewhere," said Abraham Van Helsing. He smiled as he took in the Parisian night. "We look for anything or anyone out of the ordinary and pursue it. Most times we will end up with routine human situations, the theft of a money purse or public drunkenness, but once in a great while, strangeness will take us to the macabre."

Abraham, Mina, Jonathan, Ian and Quincy were all standing just outside the restaurant, their meal behind them. The crowds had begun to swell with the night. It was a warm Saturday evening and people of all walks of life were making the best of the late spring and early summer and were flocking along the streets. They could smell fresh bread from some nearby bakery, as well as perfume, alcohol and sweat from passers-by. Abraham continued, "*Nosferatu* in larger cities are highly organized and will prey upon the weaker members of human society that are more easily missed: the drunkards, prostitutes, elderly couples as well as orphans. Outcasts. Upon occasion a member of the French police will go missing, then will turn out to be a corrupt member of law enforcement, perhaps without family. Or it may turn out that he was an older man without marriage or children, then one can assume that their hunters had done their research thoroughly. They own banks, have old money, and constitute their own economy."

"How long have there been vampires in Paris?" asked Jonathan. They all had their eyes on the crowds as they poured by, watching with a new, different sense of purpose.

"How long has there been a Paris, Master Harker?" replied Abraham without hesitation. At their wide-eyed reaction, Van Helsing chuckled wryly and continued, "farthest back I have been able to track them is to the time just after the Emperor Constantine, but that is another matter. Tonight we are here to hunt down Dracula before he moves on to another city, if he is even still here. We have a window of opportunity if he thinks us dead."

"Why is he even here in France?" said Quincy.

"That's a good question, young man, and I hope we find out shortly."

"Either way, I got my sweet *mamacitas* by my side," hummed Quincy with a malicious twinkle in his eyes, as if he was going to a dance with two girls instead of one. He patted the Colts he had slung on his hips and the rifle scabbards.

"I thought Consuelo was your *mamacita*?" teased Jonathan. The others chuckled, and it was a welcome relief from everything. Abraham saw Jonathan's tactic and appreciated it.

"I kiss these *mamis* g'nite after I kiss Consuelo g'nite, if you know what I'm sayin'," leered Morris, to the collective groans and eye rolls of everyone else. "Call ya'll a liar if ya tell her, though. I'm not afraid of my woman!"

There was a slight squeak in Morris' voice as he annunciated the word 'afraid'.

"Uh-huh," replied Abraham with laugh-filled sarcasm, and it spoke for everyone.

"I gotta picture of my li'l Darlin' here somewhere," said Morris, fumbling among his many pockets.

"You photograph your guns?" teased Mina with and arched eyebrow, which brought smiles to everyone.

"No, Tiger Lily," growled Quincy as his pocket search intensified. "A picture of my woman."

"Ian and I brought our Webleys," said Arthur. He didn't say, *the weapons our fathers gave us.* "And I know Mina always carries her Derringer."

At that those words, Mina slipped her hand into her purse and fingered her pearl-handled pistol and her extra rounds of ammunition. "I'd rather have Quincy's Winchester, or rather, the Winchester I won from Quincy."

At this, Jonathan Harker turned to Mina in genuine surprise and mouthed the words *I won from Quincy* at her, only to receive a proud, arched eyebrow from his fiancée and confirming nods from Arthur and Ian.

"The Tiger Lily[201] beat me fair and square," shrugged the Texan, ever the gentleman, and he gave up his search for Consuelo's photograph and shrugged sheepishly. Abraham gave one of his patented pats on the shoulder to Mina, who reveled in it, poking her chin proudly at the Texan to continue.

"Hell, I guess this is as good a time as ever to tell y'all I brought both *your* Winchester and the Enfield, ya British bell-ringer," smirked Quincy and they all had their second laugh since the tragedy. Morris raised the two scabbards, patted them like children and handed one of them to Mina. He kept the more garish, Western-styled version for himself. "Pulled 'em out of the carriages after the fire."

"Have we no ammunition?" murmured Ian.

"I got us covered, Sewie," said Quincy, patting his knapsack. It rattled, metal-on-metal.

"Pistols and rifles won't do against these creatures," interjected Jonathan as the crowd of passers-by swelled around them. "They are supernatural, as Uncle Abraham explained, like ghosts. We saw what happened during their attack. Ordinary weapons are useless against them."

"Unless they are blessed by Holy Water or other such residue of light, kindness and spirituality," said Van Helsing flatly. "The smaller caliber seems to go right through them, but they react to the bigger weapons all right. The male *nosferatu* we encountered is formidable, perhaps the most powerful I've ever seen. The rounds barely affected him. Bullets won't kill them, but will act as a blow of sorts, it can stun them, and you can rush in and finish the job with a sliver of wood or a blessed knife through their heart."

"Good thing I brought my li'l Bowie then," beamed Quincy, tapping his left thigh, where his enormous, sheathed knife was strapped.

"Good Lord," gasped Ian. "Once you've disposed of our adversaries you can then cut the Texas panhandle off from the rest of the Americas, Quincy."

"If I get another chance," hissed Quincy nicely, "I'll dot Dracula's eyes. Get it, dot his 'I's'? 'Eyes?'"

As Morris' pun languished, Jonathan added, "Thank goodness you didn't lose that horrible sense of humor while I was away."

"All right," said Van Helsing after the laughter died. *They are so young and pivot from tragedy so quickly* he thought. "Let us see what the evening brings us."

As they began to move through the crowded streets, he said, "If we find one of them and we get separated, meet back at the hotel, and make doubly sure that *nothing follows you back.*"

Night had fallen.

---

[201] Morris is referring to *Lilium catesbaei*, a flowering plant known throughout the American southwest, referred to also as tiger lily, leopard lily, or southern-red lily. The story of Peter Pan, with its Native American princess character also named Tiger Lily, was not created until 1904.

FOUR

Coagulating up through sewer pipes, surging through crevasses and finally out upon broken cobblestone, the serpentine mist that was Dracula of Transylvania slithered its way up onto a cold, damp Paris street. Once it reached the cobblestones, the more solid front end of the mist reared up like a cobra's hood, looking around for any observers, seeing without eyes with a venomous countenance. White as bone and liquid as an eel, the mist found a direction and purpose before sliding around and along the darkened *rue* until it stopped at the broken sidewalk of a smaller, more private and even darker side street. The mist then began to convulse, to form into the jagged, feral, royal countenance of Dracula's human form. As he bled back into human anatomy, as his eye sockets went from being filled with milky white to the pupils of a night bird, the vampire looked around with an expression of nonchalance, taking in the scenery around him.

Then, of all things, a surprise.

Dracula's eyes widened.

Lights began to blink around the son of Satan.

Blinked to life around the undead.

The night had been newly birthed, and the streetlights around him, the so-called Yablochkov candle[202] or arc light, danced electric all round him.

The *nosferatu* was astounded.

In his near-millennia of undead existence, Dracula had seen birth, life, death, baptism, marriage, divorce, murder, betrayal, innocence, decadence, seduction, triumph, failure, corruption, family, friendship, infidelity, insanity, virtue, faith (which he particularly abhorred), blasphemy (which he particularly appreciated), joy, pestilence, miracles, curses, absolution, regret, sorrow, loneliness, selfishness, famine, gluttony, and most distastefully, love.

Dracula had existed, such as he was, through the Middle Ages, the Renaissance and into the early Modern Age. He had delighted in the conflict that split the Eastern and Roman Catholic Church in 1054. He had been but a child when Jerusalem fell, and watched the Christians and Muslims spill blood throughout the Holy Land in the Crusades. He had been a witness to the birth of the Order of the Dragon, which had taken their name in his honor before he so ferociously betrayed and crushed them. Dracula had been at the Massacre of the Latins, had met popes and anti-popes. He knew Joan of Arc; whose fierce zealotry matched his boiling hatred. The vampire had battled the Hongwu emperor in China and had been taught how to use a samurai's blade in Japan, out-maneuvered the Bank of Medici and its owners, observed the discovery of the New World even as Jews and Muslims were expelled from Spain in 1492. He appreciated the artistic explosion of Da Vinci and Michelangelo during the High Renaissance, relished the Spanish Inquisitions, delighted in the Black Plague, reveled in the destruction of the Spanish Armada in the English Channel in 1588, personally

---

[202] An early form of the electric street light, invented in 1876 by Pavel Yablochov and installed for the Paris Exhibition of 1878. Also referred to as the electric candle.

knew Cervantes, Dante, Shakespeare, Rembrandt and Mozart. Dracula enjoyed the British Civil War, was present at the beheadings of Louis XVI, Marie Antionette and Robespierre as well as for most of the American Revolutionary War.

In his unearthly life, Dracula had observed many people and events.

And yet there were still things in this world that managed to surprise him.

Some of the older streets still had gas lighting, but 1899 Paris was transitioning to lighting by electricity. Rare was something that could cause the formidable vampire to be taken aback, but he gazed in awe at the incandescent posts of light. His widened eyes followed the lights down the street until he came upon another jaw-dropping sight.

In complete shock, he took a step back.

"Uimitor!" exclaimed Dracula, astonished. *Amazing!*

Sifting out of the cracks in the cobblestone, the brides formed out of mist behind him, but Dracula's attention was absorbed with a structure in the distance.

"Timpul de miracole este asupra noastră din nou," he said. *The time of miracles is upon us once again.*

"Non ho mai visto una cosa del genere," gasped Venus, agog. *I have never seen such a thing.*

"Οὔτε ἐχω," whispered Andromeda. *Nor have I.*

"الجيزة ربما," finished Petra. *Giza, perhaps.*

Stretching above them was a mammoth achievement of ingenuity, steel and engineering, a metal pinnacle which had been built a decade before. Dominating the skyline, the monolith stood proudly in its dark splendor, as of yet without lights, while ironically surrounded by the City of Light. The structure seemed to reach up and touch heaven, magnificent in its dark silhouette against the incandescence of the streets below.

The Eiffel tower.

For the first time in centuries, Dracula was awed.

"Opinari," said Dracula after catching his breath, "primum ego in hanc urbem, in medio platearum occidendus sum apertas venas cloacas currebant sicut septem post annos post Parisiensis inluminati ut versus platearumque et turres ferro." *To think that the first time I was in this city, the sewers ran like open veins in the middle of the streets, yet seven hundred years later, Paris has illuminated posts that line the streets and towers of iron.*

"Je voyais la tour quand il a été en cours de construction," chimed in Lucy, happily taking in the scene behind them all. *I saw the tower when it was being built.*

"The only rule that you have, Lucy of Dracula," said the Transylvanian without taking his eyes off of the tower's silhouette, "is that if you speak ever again without being first addressed, I will have the three women around you tear you to pieces."

Lucy was taken aback at Dracula statement, and with genuine surprise looked around her and found the brides leering at her like birds of prey, eyes glowing in the new night and with an eagerness to tear her to shreds. Lucy knew enough to simply stand and say absolutely nothing.

"Well done," snarled Dracula at her after a beat. "You will keep your tongue in your mouth for at least tonight. Now, we hunt." The vampire took a step, and before he took another, Dracula was in mid-transformation, and Lucy watched the other brides begin to transform into bats. At that moment, Lucy also wanted that gift. Lucy Westenra looked at her hand and thought about how it could become like that of a bat wing, and in an instant, her arm began to melt like a candle. It lengthened, grew dark grey fur and expansive, membranous wings in between her fingertips. Her dress melted onto her body as fur grew out of her skin, and her face pushed forward, her mouth and teeth expanding. Her ears grew out, and she began to hear not only the screeches of the great bats in front of her, but she also began to *hear conversations within the buildings around her.*

Lucy watched the brides follow Dracula's lead and launch themselves into the air. She then realized she was a bat now and leaped up into the air, as high as the second story flats around her. She stayed in the air with a savage flap of her wings. Her wings began to churn, and a rush of air greeted Lucy, as did the sudden change in the perspective in the buildings around her.

Lucy of Dracula, formerly Lucy Westenra was airborne.

Acceleration and drunken exhilaration bolted through Lucy, and in seconds she had shot above the buildings on the Paris street and was following the brides as they themselves pursued the massive black bat over the city of romance. Rooftops were square blurs. She had never been higher in her life, and the speed made Lucy's head swim, and she was thrilled at being a bird, then she remembered she was a bat, and that she had taken vows, dark vows, to receive this dark gift.

Below her, buildings and streets swept by, her wings beating faster and faster to catch up with the others, but the view of the streets from this height, and the idea of flight thrilled her, and in that moment any fragment of humanity that Lucy Westenra still had left in her flew away with the breeze that was carrying her through the night air. She was a hunter now, and the gift of hunting was the greatest gift she had ever received, and Lucy knew where she was supposed to be, fated to be, meant to be. They banked hard to the left, flew straight along *Avenue Mont Parnasse*, then banked right, high above the crowded *Avenue Sulfren*. There they maintained their trajectory until they soared to the right, flew through the *Champ de Mars* and toward the colossal structure that was the Eiffel tower, looming in darkness before them.

Lucy heard the bride bats screech out in astonishment as they all soared through the gargantuan lower level of the tower, with the ground far below. The massive space loomed above and around them, beams that could crush carriages and clipper ships created a labyrinthian web of shadows that cloaked them. Beams groaned above them and Lucy could understand the brides' chatter.

Andromeda screeched like a bat, and Lucy somehow understood and heard, "Δεν έχω δει ποτέ κάτι σαν αυτό που!" *I have never seen anything like this!*

Petra hissed, "القبر في الهند، ربما؟" *The sepulchre in India[203], perhaps?*

"Si," chirped Venus, "il santo sepolcro che scottato i nostri piedi quando si è cercato di entrare." *Yes, the holy tomb that seared our feet when we tried to enter.*

Lucy almost shouted for them to slow down, remembered the edict just placed upon her by Dracula, and in an evening filled with extraordinary events, another occurred. As the other brides screeched, Lucy could *hear* the surroundings better, like an echo, even as the noises from the others rang around under the massive edifice. Somehow, even the structures around her became visible in her head, *even though she was not looking directly at them.* She pivoted her ears and the structure became even clearer in her mind!

What wonderous gifts these be, bestowed upon her!

They all flew out from under the Eiffel and Dracula made an abrupt and hard right, leading them right along the shimmering Sienne, in all of the glory that a major river of the world could hold on a young summer's eve. Lucy could see tiny people walking along the banks, some of them holding hands or holding each other, and even though her bloodlust had ebbed for the night now, she panged slightly at the thought of Arthur, the promise they had made and their lost love. But Arthur could never have given her wings, and Lucy now soared above the world.

---

[203] Petra refers to the mausoleum known as Taj Mahal in Agra, India. It was built in 1648 to house the tomb of Emperor Shah Jahan's preferred wife, Mumtaz Mahal.

She was too intoxicated with the thrill of flight to think to think of the others. They were dim memories that swam in the back of her mind, kind thoughts that reverberated in the distance, and Lucy of Dracula was soaring about the streets of Paris, and her only thought at the moment was to relish the incredible things that she had done only in the last few moments since her awakening. What miracles would the future hold for her?

Far below, the river twisted to the right, and so did they, the Dracula bat's fearsome shape twisting easily in the wind. Again, she could hear the screeches of the she-bats, perhaps in the wind that they left their conversation in, and Lucy realized that Dracula might not be able to hear them if he was up-wind of them.

The Dracula bat then began a sudden, steep descent, swerving to the left side of the river, and they all followed, the four brides, as they descended, all of them watching Dracula as he banked around a tall arch, then toward a complex of multi-storied buildings, which held out its wings to their left and right like two welcoming arms. With a beat of his wings, the vampire flew above a beautiful, intricate façade, and into a dark, expansive courtyard, where he landed, the three other brides following suit. The ground rushed up at Lucy, but she spread her wings in imitation of the others, and it slowed her descent, and she landed lightly.

She was joyous! *I've never known such marvels and thrills! This is incredible!*

The courtyard was three stories tall and overflowed with classical architecture. Venus transformed into her human form, her eyes glowing as she shot Lucy a foul look, as much to show her hate as to make certain she had not gotten lost. Petra and Andromeda had melted back into human form as well, also moving in Dracula's general direction.

As soon as Dracula had landed, the huge black form began to shift, twist, pulse, coagulate and became an opalescent mist again, cloying to the ground as it serpentined its way across the pavement toward one of the court's many doors. Even while he was still in bat form, Dracula did not look around, did not take in any of the architectural splendor, nor did he look around in a cautionary manner. He seemed filled with nothing but intent.

Night and the busy Paris restaurants had peeled away any possible witnesses, so the mist slid in through the shut front doors and into the museum.

Lucy had followed the other bats to the same set of doors, and they had turned to mist to melt through them. At her mind's whim, she thought of being mist, and in the next moment she too began to melt into cream-colored vapor. *Another miracle!* Lucy's vision and consciousness somehow stayed clear and she simply pushed herself, however impossibly, through the slots between the doors and into the cavernous pitch of the darkened Louvre.

FIVE

Three thousand years ago, twin prodigious obelisks stood magnificently in front of the Luxor temple, site of the ancient city of Thebes in upper Egypt. The river Nile flowed then in front of Thebes, as it does now in front of Luxor. At the western bank of the south-to-north flowing river lay the grand necropolises of the Valley of the Kings and Valley of the Queens, filled with death, culture and lost wisdom. One of the Luxor obelisks weighed more than 250 tons and stood over seventy-five feet when it was installed in Paris' *Place de la Concorde* in 1836, a gift to the French by Muhammed Ali, Viceroy of Egypt. Its twin stands guard over Luxor temple to this day. Covered with hieroglyphics that describe the reigns of both Ramses II and III, the obelisk was placed in the very center of *Place de la Concorde*, which, before the French Revolution was called *Place Louis XV*. During the revolution, the square was renamed *Place de la Revolution*. King Louis XV would never know the irony that his own grandson, Louis XVI, would eventually be guillotined at that very spot along with his wife, Marie Antionette and thousands of others. It was not until the 1830s with, after the Reign of Terror, the fall of Napoleon and the return of Louis XVIII would the name *Place de la Concorde* be reinstated.

Two monumental fountains, the *Fontaine des Fleuves* and the *Fontaine des Mers*, respectively, were placed to the north and south of the obelisk. Every corner of the octagonal space featured a statue that represented French cities: Bordeaux, Brest, Rouen, Nantes, Marseille, Lyon, Strasbourg and Lille. The entire plaza had the Sienne to its south, the Tuileries Garden to the east and the *Champs-Elysées* to the west. The Tuileries Garden is a public garden between *Place de la Concorde*—and the *Louvre* museum.

Wilhelmina Murray, Abraham Van Helsing, Jonathan Harker, Ian Seward and Quincy Morris, now stood at the base of the Obelisk of Luxor, not knowing how close they were to their quarry. Mina play-boxed with Arthur (quite well, actually, landing a solid left hook nearly instantly to Holmwood's right cheek), Abraham pulled out his pipe and began to stuff it with tobacco, Quincy shooed away a dog that looked like it wanted to urinate on his scabbard. Ian impulsively kept cutting a fresh deck of cards that he'd bought along the way, and Jonathan just stuck his hands in his pants pockets and looked out over the streaming crowds, matching Van Helsing's vigilance. People and carriages poured all around them in the early evening, which was lit by the nearly sixty thousand street lights in Paris at the time.

People, rich and poor, married and single, old and young, thin and rotund, merchant and worker all moved around them, on their way to dine, pray, listen to a concert, gamble their pay away, buy clothes for their children, dance with their girlfriend, drink themselves into a stupor, read an old book again, buy a gift for their spouse, get their infection checked, clean their apartment, smoke some cigars with old friends, beat their dog, hug their dying mother, employ a prostitute, propose marriage and everything else that happens in any city anywhere in the world. Night had unfurled itself, yet the Sienne glowed with her own supple illuminations that reflected the last ribbons of fleeting light in the sky. As it was blanketed with velvet, Paris illuminated itself with her own glittering jewels, like a Jean Béraud painting, dark-garbed Victorian silhouettes moved wherever fate and the night would take them.

Abraham Van Helsing seemed to be able to scrutinize each one of the passers-by as he said, "We're going to stand here and watch, all of us, in front of this obelisk."

"Shouldn't we split up?" started Jonathan, eyes darting over the sea of top hats and bonnets.

"That's the worst thing we could do," said Abraham. "If we divide and search, then encountered one or all of them, we would be ill-prepared, at their mercy and with no manner with which to alert each other. We stand here, watch, and conserve our energy. This is the heart of the city; we simply need to observe the masses as they move by us. Watch for the oddities, then differentiate between what is simply odd and what then becomes macabre. That's where they are always found. A prostitute luring a wealthy man to a beating and robbery at the hands of a group of ruffians is considered an everyday occurrence in such a large city, but always observe closer. Does she have the pale skin of a corpse? Do her eyes glint like those of a wolf? In Paris it would be odd for her to speak Latin to the ruffians, for example. Would everyday ruffians know Latin, the language of royals and the Ancient World? A nun walks past you, is she alone? At night? Does she carry pagan relics? Why? Details. Details! Look for the morbid after the oddities are observed, and we will find, if not our *nosferatu*, then at least their kin and potentially, a means to get closer to our quarry."

"How do we know they haven't moved on?" asked Jonathan.

"If they have," nodded Abraham, "then we have lost them, but I do believe they are still in Paris, if only for the night. Secondly, in the event we do not encounter them tonight, their leader, their master, is too significant in their culture to not be traceable. We would simply find one of their kind and interrogate her or him. Either way, we will find them."

"You've heard of this Dracula then, Uncle Abraham?" asked Mina as she stopped her fisticuffs and focused on the passing crowd, adhering to her uncle's edict of looking for the strange, for the out of the ordinary.

"Rumors and fearful gossip mostly," said Abraham. "He is their king, simply put."

"So we'll just have to kill him that much quicker," said Arthur, rubbing his right cheek, surprised at the agility of Mina's left hook.

The others did as Van Helsing said, their eyes drifting to the passing citizens, and they continued to watch the crowd.

Minutes passed, as did the night.

A few tough-looking youths made their way to Mina and Quincy, who was starting to eye a baked goods stand not far away. In the midst of all the Victorian fashion, the youths were dressed out of the norm. Despite appearing to be from disadvantaged upbringings, they all had shined shoes, large pants, striped but rumpled shirts, caps on their heads, opened jackets and distinctive tattoos around their dangerous eyes, which collectively fixed on Mina's purse.

The largest of the bunch pulled a significant knife from his coat and pointed the end of it at Mina's purse. Quincy casually flipped his coat aside to reveal his Bowie Knife and Colts. He then slid his knife out of its sheath, winked at them and used the tip of it to push his Stetson back on his head, all the while with an enormous smile draped over his face.

"When your momma gives you a real knife, then come back and talk to me. This here's a Texas knife."

"I don't think that chap speaks English, Morris," said Mina, also watching them with intent.

"Oh, he understands me just fine," laughed the Texan, patting with his left hand his rifle scabbards, which he held with his right. The youths looked to Mina, who pinned her own scabbard between arm and ribcage as slid her Derringer coyly out and back into her purse, a sly glint flashing in her eyes. Arthur and Ian, in the middle of breaking out a set of playing cards, casually took their Webleys out with their free hands and nodded respectfully at the youths, who backed away into the crowds of the night.

"You should have twirled your Webley with your index finger, American style, like Morris does in his silly pistol exhibitions," said Ian to Arthur, who was about to cut the playing cards.

"Shootin' shows," sighed Quincy helplessly under his breath.

"And put a bloody round in my thigh?" laughed Arthur, which brought laughter to them all. Five cards in each hand, Ian and Arthur began to play, one eye on their hand and the other on the passers-by.

"Are you playing cards or watching for the unexpected, gentlemen?" drifted Van Helsing's voice from over Ian's shoulder, to which Seward replied, "Both!"

Mina shot them a discouraging glance, which she shared with Quincy, who had taught them all five card stud[204] back in Texas, much to the consternation of the women in the family and the keen interest of their fathers. Quincy, no stranger to the hunt, shrugged his shoulders at Mina and continued to watch the pedestrians.

"Uncle Arthur loved it that you taught us to play, Quincy," said Ian abruptly to them all, and they all had to spend the next half-minute trying to swallow lumps in their throats. Jonathan turned and gave Mina a glance filled with love and kindness, also wanting to know she was well, and she returned it in kind.

Abraham just continued his watch.

As did Jonathan.

People drifted by.

A troupe of young children skipped by, their parents following, beaming and holding hands.

As did a rotund older gentleman, somehow reading a newspaper while walking.

Three middle-aged women, clearly sisters, strode by, giggling and trading love, gossip and friendship.

Two lovers, arm-in-arm, gazing into each other's souls, no one else in the city or universe around them, moved by. He dared a public kiss, and she rewarded him with one in return.

An exhausted worker, pushing a wheelbarrow full of coal bricks, huffed and puffed by. As did a bulbous-nosed priest, in a hurry.

A young boy somehow walking four dogs, all on leashes, all barking and yipping at each other passed by. Abraham and Jonathan and Mina and Quincy watched them all.

"Anybody interested in sharin' a fruit pie with me?" said Quincy, himself eyeing the food stand. "God damn, that smells like Christmas dinner!"

Arthur looked up from his hand, incredulous. "We *just* supped, mate!"

"Aw, that was just the first course, mate!"

Ian shook his head at Morris. "Are Texans even allowed to use the word 'mate'?"

"Only when they got a Bowie to back 'em up," sniffed Quincy as he made up his mind and bounded over to the food stand. The woman running the stand looked at Morris' cowboy hat and boots for a comedic beat as the cowboy sized up the available merchandise.

"So, we are hunting Lucy as well as the others," said Jonathan to the shadow that was Abraham Van Helsing, smoking his pipe as a wagon filled with groceries ambled by. It was as much of a statement as much as it was a question.

"Yes. Mind the crowd."

"And when we find her?" asked Jonathan, watching the ember of light go on and off as Abraham smoked.

---

[204] Poker apparently originated in ancient Persia, played with twenty cards of five designs and named as-nas. The modern form was played in New Orleans and subsequently, on the Mississippi river and through the Civil War, during which the deck went from 20 cards to 52, when the draw, the wild card and the straight were added as the game evolved to its current form.

Arthur and Ian turned slowly in Abraham's direction at this question, as did Mina.

"I will kill her," nodded Van Helsing, matter-of-factly. "You all are to concern yourselves with his wives, as much as you are able. See that they do not interfere. I will also kill the lead *nosferatu*."

Arthur gulped. "Is there no path to recovery and redemption for Lucy?"

"No, there is not, and she is your fiancée no longer, Arthur. I am very sorry, my boy," said Abraham as he wrapped his arm around Arthur in a loving, fatherly way. "You've always been drawn to her, even as a child, I know. But she and whatever is inside her belongs to Dracula now. In every way, if you take my meaning. Forgive my boorish, forward talk. She has been infected, and her survival of that infection means that she is now *nosferatu*. She would kill you tonight, any of you, upon sight. I have seen it happen. In other parts of the world, corpses are buried, then *disinterred* when others become ill after a death. Have you ever seen a corpse dug up and beheaded? I have. You would be best served to see her as you would a lion or panther."

"Do you remember when you taught her how to dance, Uncle Abraham?" said Ian, eyes filling with tears. *He was always the emotional one*, thought Abraham.

"Yes, I do, child. I remember tea with little Lucy and will mourn her, as we all should. Yet when you meet her next, she will only try to eat you. Remember that."

They all stood there, around the obelisk, unsure of what to say, somewhat stunned at Van Helsing's bluntness.

"What if she approaches me, or any of us?" asked Arthur, going back to reading his hand of cards, but his heart still filled with thoughts of Lucy.

"Defend yourselves, or she will murder you," was all that Abraham could say. They could all sense Arthur's frustration toward Van Helsing, who also sensed it but knew he could do nothing to ease the boy's pain.

As if on cue, Quincy Morris bounced back to them with his mouth filled with an enormous chunk of pie and a silly, sly grin over his face. And a cup of coffee in his free hand. They all shook their heads at the Texan, none more grateful than Jonathan, who saw that Arthur needed a laugh to get him to stop thinking about Lucy.

Mina threw up her hands in happy exasperation and semi-shouted, "But we *just* ate, Morris!"

Quincy Morris somehow swallowed the massive chunk of pie and beamed, "I didn't get any dessert after dinner, Missy, y'all rushed me so much."

Van Helsing had resumed combing the crowds with his glacial stare, but he smiled as he said, "Doesn't your well have a bottom, lad?"

Jonathan pointed at an odd-looking man pulling a wagon of scrap furniture, but Abraham shook his head.

"Thank you, darlin'," said Quincy with a wave at the lady street vendor for the completed sale. She waved back, having been charmed, Quincy-style. Morris took another whale-sized bite of his pie and followed that with a splashing slug of his steaming cup of coffee. He tossed Van Helsing a jagged smile and said, "Uncle Abraham, let's just say that if you throw a pie into my well, it's gonna take a minute before you hear it splash."

"You were not always so Texan, Young Quincy," said Van Helsing, watching the crowds ebb and flow, his eyes steady as they moved from person to person. "In your younger years, before Jackson settled you all in Texas, there was a British accent within you."

"I would pay a significant sum to hear that," said Ian with a smile at Arthur, meant to relieve Holmwood's frustration, and the quip did result in a brief grin from Arthur, before he went back to his hand and his forlorn thoughts.

"Not possible, Uncle Abraham. Once a Texan, always a Texan."

"Good Lord," was all that Mina said, with a crisp laugh.

"Shut up and eat your pie, Morris," laughed Jonathan, who then said, "So, this is our strategy, Abraham? Stand here for the rest of the evening and hope to catch a glimpse of someone who can turn into a bat?"

"If you know what to look for, usually the wait isn't long. You see, young Harker, they are out hunting as well and do not suspect that they themselves might be hunted. The trick is to observe them observing others, if that makes sense. A falcon watching an owl as they both watch for doves. Their intent is different. Not to snatch a purse or a necklace, or a wallet. Not to sell something, scrupulous or not. Lions watch for the sick, the very young and the elderly. Wolves make chase, separating and isolating the weakest, even through the snow. Tigers offer the element of surprise in their technique, attacking when they have moved so near to the intended prey that there is little chance of escape."

"Coyotes watchin' for quail," mumbled Quincy as he finished his pie in a large, nearly inhuman gulp.

"The gullet of a crocodile," was all that Ian could manage, marveling at the Texan's appetite.

"And which of the techniques do the vampires employ?" asked Mina, watching the crowds with Van Helsing, and their conversation lured them all into watching the masses walk, run, stumble and skip by.

"All of them," said Abraham, eyes locked, "as well as the element of the lure. An enticement. The approach can involve the prospect of commerce, food, shelter, sex or money. The attack comes after the subject is lured to the appropriate venue of privacy."

Arthur shook his head, and with a little too much frustration, said, "That's no different than any other nefarious solicitor anywhere."

"Point taken, Arthur," said Abraham, ever patient and understanding, "save the final element: Every *nosferatu* will avoid any symbol of purity and goodness as if it would sear them to the touch, which as you now know will. We observe for the moment, then make a descent to the ossuaries under the city after dawn. Usually guards watching the ossuary are paid off to leave the bone graves be at certain times of the night, no questions asked."

They all looked at him with surprise.

Mina started with, "The vampires pay off the guards to look the other—"

"—let us table this discussion," said Abraham with a sharp, sudden gleam in his eyes. Everyone saw this and whirled to scan the crowd as he continued with a wry smile of satisfaction, "We waited we observed, and in this instance, we find not what we seek, but *that which will lead us to our prey*."

He nodded, to the left, to the distant edges of the drifting crowds, and as he did, Abraham Van Helsing picked up his bag, which clunked with wood and metal, among other things.

They all knew.

This is it.

He was right

We begin the chase.

Well, there's a platter full of biscuits and gravy.

The street lights lit the crowds, obelisk, fountains, statues and plaza in pools that varied from amber to white.

A multitude of people flowed in different directions through the jammed Parisian square.

But above them all, knifing through the masses was an unmistakable hulking profile.

That of Montague Rhodes Renfield

SIX

Sometime in the 12th century, before it became a museum, the Louvre was a fortress.

As time went on, the kings of France modified and altered the original square design of the fortress into a palace, throughout the Middle Ages and Renaissance, which was when Francis I acquired the first important pieces of the collection, including da Vinci's *Mona Lisa*. Gradually during the 18th century the Royal Collection became a public museum, and when Louis XVI was himself imprisoned during the French Revolution, then the collected works became property of the country. The museum itself opened to the public in 1793, for a few days per week. Two wings, to the north and south, that attached to an elaborate west face, were built as the palace transitioned, some aspects of the construction beginning during the reign of one king and ending during that of another. By the 1800s, the palace had survived Catherine de' Medici's chateau and Napoleon's Arch while continuing to assemble one of the world's great art collections.

Silence and darkness enveloped the vampires as they prowled through the cavernous Louvre interior. In front of Lucy, the other brides had already transformed from mist to bat forms and were following the human form of Dracula down the large, endless galleries, silent and filled with malice. Paintings from masters from all over Europe stared at the intruders with blank, ghostly stares over their painted faces, rendered malevolent by the night. The vampires moved without sound but with unspoken purpose. The Lucy bat could see clearly and knew that if she were still human she'd be lost in the dark. She felt giddy at yet another miracle. She chirped very softly, and it was as if a ping went off in her head, as she somehow *heard* the room around her, behind her, where her eyes could not possibly see. The Petra bat pivoted her head and threw a silent snarl at Lucy for opening her mouth, and for her presence in general.

To explain that Dracula strode through the dark, shadowy museum galleries like both a king and a jungle cat would be simplistic, but that is exactly what the son of Satan did, moving with a leonine confidence that was distinct, mesmerizing and menacing all at the same time, a cadaver walking among some of the greatest works of art known to man.

It was like watching a raven stalk over a freshly dug grave.

The Transylvanian then arrived at a particular painting and paused to contemplate it.

After a moment, the bride bats arrived behind him, and Dracula said, in an awed whisper, "Steti coram accepta hac pictura haec mulier. Fui porticus in bis ante et in singulis totus efficior melancholiae anxius risus. Modus quo spectat ad me cum me tanquam supremis Italiae depinxit quam potuisse datis libris Florentiae, admonet vel solis occasum quod nunquam vidit nisi per of picta. Illudit per me quidem post tot annos post mortem. Et tamen, motus fuero omni tempore video La Gianconda[205] sciens mundi corrodit multo magis at omne intervallum inter nostros arcerent." *I*

---

[205] The painting that Dracula is contemplating is Leonardo daVinci's *Mona Lisa*, which was painted by the artist in Florence, Italy between 1503 and 1506. The piece was painted on wood and the model was Lisa del Giocondo, wife of a wealthy Italian silk merchant. The Mona Lisa is arguably the most famous piece of art in Western civilization.

have stood here before, taking in this painting, this woman. I have been in this gallery twice before, and each time I become absorbed in her melancholy, poignant smile. The manner with which she gazes back at me, as if the Italian was thinking of me when he painted her, which he might have been, given my history in Florence, and reminds me that I have never seen a sunset or sunrise except through that of a painted picture. He mocks me through her, even after all these years after his death. And yet, I am moved every time I see La Gianconda, knowing the world rots all the more at every interval between our meetings.

Without another word, the vampire continued to prowl through the gallery, the dark and the night, in the way only a cat can move through a room at the witching hour without disturbing or touching any furniture. The bats followed in his wake, a macabre parade through hallways lined with some of mankind's greatest works of art. Then the vampire paused abruptly, spied something in front of him, then smiled a deadly grin as he hissed, "'Amen, amen dico vobis, quia unus ex vobis tradet me.'"[206] *'Truly, truly, I say to you, one of you will betray me.'*

In the distance, in the middle of a pool of moonlight. lay a figure on the wooden floor.

A museum guard.

Splayed out in death.

Dark forms moved over the body.

Sucking sounds in the blackness.

Secret.

The guard convulsed, grotesquely.

The paintings surrounding the feeding all watched, offended or enthralled, but collectively helpless.

Death of the Virgin by Carravagio took the scene in, silently.

Others enjoyed the mayhem.

Red ichor spread over parquet flooring.

Above the corpse loomed two shrouded, black human figures.

Nosferatu.

One was old and masculine, the other middle-aged and feminine.

Spying them, Dracula of Transylvania instantly snarled.

They bolted up at Dracula's dog growl, their eyes glowing like those of feral dogs, open wide in shock and surprise. The two vampires both wore very old, very outdated clothes from the Renaissance. He had a long, grey beard and a floppy grey cap. She wore a frayed, formal gown, her brown hair up to frame her face, which was that of a faded beauty.

Both of their open mouths were scarlet with blood.

"M-mon Roi!" shouted the old vampire. His shout was nearly a scream. Surprise, shock and fear bolted through him. *M-my King!*

He managed to continue, "Je suis indigne d'une visite de la royauté—" *I am unworthy of a visit from royalty—*

"Epargnez-moi votre langue d'argent, Nostradamus[207], prophète de tous les contrats à terme, mais votre propre," snarled the Transylvanian, advancing. *Spare me your silver tongue, Nostradamus, seer of all futures but your own!*

The vampires sensed that Dracula was set to attack them and began to panic. They looked to

---

[206] Dracula is using a biblical quote in a blasphemic way. John 13:21- *After saying these things, Jesus was troubled in his spirit, and testified, "Truly, truly, I say to you, one of you will betray me."*
[207] Michel de Nostradame, or Nostradamus (1503-1566) was a French prophesier, seer and apothecary whose prophecies became known worldwide. His written works remain in print to this day.

each other, their blood-soaked faces terrified at the turn of events.

The body of the museum guard twitched once as his life ran out onto the flooring.

"Certes," hissed Dracula, "vous ne prévoyait pas mon survivre à un assassinat. Ou mon vous déchirer dans ce musée très pour votre rôle dans l'affaire!" *Certainly you did not foresee my surviving an assassination. Or my tearing you to pieces in this very museum for your part in the matter!*

Nearly in hysterics, the female vampire shrieked, "Pardonne-nous, Maître! Nous ne savions pas qu'il vous était qu'ils avaient l'intention de tuer!" *Forgive us, Master! We knew not it was you they intended to kill!*

"Ferme la bouche, Anne[208]"! wailed Nostradamus, who turned to Dracula with his arms out and his palms up as he pleaded, "Elle ne sait pas ce qu'elle parle, mon roi!" *Shut your mouth, Anne! She knows not of what she speaks, my King!*

The Venus bat hissed, "Mensonges!" which Lucy understood, in her bat form. *Lies!*

Dracula pointed to them and hissed, "Votre complot a rattrapé avec vous, blasphémateur! Et pulvis et citra proximam Luna sub scabillo pedum." *Your plotting has caught up with you, blasphemer! You will both be dust at my feet before the next moon rises.*

Like blurs, the mated vampires bolted toward the nearest doorway, transforming as they moved, he into a billowy grey bat and she into a huge albino rat. The she-bats scrambled along the floor, sprinting behind Dracula, who had begun his own transformation, on the move, into the massive black bat. Lucy trailed them and saw the grey Nostradamus bat blast into the door at full-speed, splintering the frame and the door into shards as they found the night air of Paris.

As he transformed, Lucy saw the Dracula bat turn to them and roar, "Interficerent eam, aut i voluntas trucidabunt te!" *Kill her or I will cut you to pieces!*

Dracula reached the outer frame of the door and began to unfurl his sail-like wings in pursuit of the grey bat, which had whooshed a few times along the grounds before taking off into the night sky.

Claws clattering along the ground, the albino rat scampered out into the open area between the wings of the Louvre, pursued by the brides, who somehow transformed from bats into rats while on the run, Lucy trailing behind. The brides were driven more out of fear of failure than the possibility of the female escaping, knowing the consequences of failure. Sprinting under the *Arc de Triomphe du Carrousel*, the monument Napoleon had erected at the beginning of the century, Venus closed in on the albino rat, only to lose her as the rat knifed to the left and toward the Sienne.

The grey bat chose a sharp upward angle as it soared away from the museum, but when he dared peek back over his shoulder, the Nostradamus bat realized that the Dracula bat was nearly upon him. A savage torque to the right was the only thing that saved Nostradamus, the Dracula bat screeching ferociously at its failure. Nostradamus had underestimated the speed of his pursuer, twisting then to the left and shooting down to the crowded streets of Paris. Dracula was a wicked heartbeat behind him, the wind whistling around them as if in warning to Nostradamus. Banking left and right from street to street, skimming above the crowds, twisting and turning from second to second. Nostradamus was able to keep the larger, faster but less agile Dracula at bay, but the black bat thrust out with jagged, taloned fingers and clamped a winged paw around the Nostradamus bat's lower right foot, and they both tumbled and slammed down into the packed street and into some tables and chairs set outside of a crowded café.

Screams from the shocked patrons ensued. Nostradamus was able to wrench his leg free and bolt back up into the night air. As the panicked patrons spread away from the massive black thing that snarled at them with crimson eyes and canines that looked like broken pieces of iron, Dracula

---

[208] Anne Ponsarde Gemelle was Nostradamus' second wife. They were married from 1547 to Nostradamus' passing.

grabbed a piece of broken wood from one of the demolished chairs, spread his expansive wings and raised himself up into the indigo Paris night, leaving a crowd of stunned patrons behind, some of them performing the sign of the cross on themselves and muttering words and phrases like, "*vampir*," "*goule*," and "*deterreur de cadavers*!"

Dracula's wings thrust down again, and it was enough to propel him above the city, the lights below becoming jewels on velvet as he banked in search of the grey bat, which he quickly located. The monstrous bat then dove slightly to gain speed and momentum before knifing upward continuing its pursuit. The Nostradamus bat saw the incoming shadow silhouetted against the City of Light and, in a panic, swept up, which took the pursuit higher, higher and higher still.

All the way up to the top of the Eiffel Tower.

SEVEN

The albino rat sprinted along the railing of the *Pont du Carrousel*, an arch bridge that had been built at a time when suspension bridges were the standard. Right behind her, shrieking and snarling with bloodlust were the bride bats, eager to shred Anne Ponsarde, wife of Nostradamus, to ribbons. Clearing the bridge, she jumped off the railing, ran for a sewer cover, tore it from its position and dove for the deep, dank depths.

Anne could hear the rapid-breath inhales and exhales of the four bride rats on her heels.

As it gathered more speed, momentum and frenzy, the chase through the sewers was even more frantic than the pursuit above ground, four rats chasing the albino rat at a breakneck, rollercoaster speed through the fetid, dank, dark pitch of the sewers. They ran over enormous pipes filled with flowing, pressurized water. The screeches and movements of the chase broke the silence of the Parisian subterranean world. Through the tunnels they raced, along the rounded ceilings and vaulted chambers, their claws holding them upside down as they all raced along the tunnels, which ranged from tiny to wide enough to pull a boat through. Lucy the dark grey rat lagged behind them, all of their glowing eyes like moving pinholes in the dark subterranean tunnels.

Venus, Petra and Andromeda were all brown rats, with Petra the darkest and Andromeda the lightest. Venus, who had the largest incisors and claws, dove for the albino rat and missed. Anne squealed in fear, twisted away and shot down into a narrower tunnel, walls lined with slime, fungus, corrosion and waste, simultaneously matting her fur with the dust and grime. Terror filled the Anne rat's heart, pursued by four hellions that were afraid of the consequences of failure as well as anticipating the kill. Venus howled at her missed opportunity while the Andromeda rat clambered over her in a bloodlust frenzy to kill her assigned prey.

Nostradamus' wife surged ahead, terrified of the prospect of never seeing her beloved husband again. As Petra surged by Lucy in pursuit, Andromeda closed in on the darting albino rat, trying to gauge the moment to lunge and end the chase.

Far above the rat chase, two enormous bats neared the top of the Eiffel Tower.

The night and the stars above Paris glittered and pulsed, determined to match Van Gogh's *Starry Night over the Rhone.*[209]

Terrific gales from different directions buffeted the tower, swaying it back and forth, rather eerily given the enormous amount of metalwork involved. As the Nostradamus bat landed, exhausted and clinging to the structure as he metamorphosized into human form. He did not need to look back, Nostradamus felt the mass of the great black bat as attained the top of the tower, which was a semi-domed shape above the hundreds of tons of steel below it[210].

---

[209] Vincent Van Gogh (1853-1890), was a Dutch painter and one of the most important artists of the 1800s. *Starry Night over the Rhone* was painted a few months before Van Gogh committed himself to an asylum. In that asylum, Van Gogh then painted *Starry Night*, his masterpiece and most famous painting. The greatest irony is that *Starry Night over the Rhone* was painted at night, while *Starry Night* was painted by day.
[210] The Eiffel Tower weighs 73 million kilograms or 10,100 tons.

"Votre femme m'a trompé!" screamed the old vampire over the winds, clinging to the top rail. *"Your wife deceived me!"*

The huge black bat clung to the rail in silence, like the first pterodactyl in the primordial Mesozoic, eyes blazing crimson hate at the old man. His free right foot claw held the broken piece of chair from the café.

"Elle nous a promis la vie eternelle quand elle me fait donc, pas la servitude eternelle a vous!" railed Nostradamus, *She promised me eternal life when she made me thus, not eternal servitude to you!*

"Je vous ai soutenu dans vos relations avec l'alliance des butées!" *I supported you in your dealings with the banking covenant!*

"Ils voulaient vous tuer pour ne pas partager les taxations et nos avoirs dans toute l'Europe, et même alors, je l'ai dit, 'Non, nous ne pouvons pas tuer notre roi!'" shouted Nostradamus, his body trembling with the creeping chill of night and the fear in his heart. *They wanted to kill you for not sharing the taxations and our holdings throughout Europe, and even then, I said, 'No, we cannot murder our king!'*

The great black bat crouched as he swayed with the tower, still without a word, before it began to slowly change to human form. Dracula's eyes never left their quarry. Nostradamus looked down and Paris swam below him, seemingly right below his feet.

Nostradamus quivered with cold and fear as he said, "Tout a changé lorsque vous avez pris les châteaux et les terres que nous avons utilisés pour voyager à travers le continent. Il a changé lorsque vous avez pris la femme Médicis que votre concubine contre son gré, et la honte le nom Médicis dans le processus. Ils ont tous réalisé, les banquiers, les barons, ducs et l'ensemble de notre peuple, que tout ce que vous vouliez était tout pour vous-même." *It all changed when you took the castles and lands we used to travel through the continent. It changed when you took the Medici woman as your concubine against her wishes, and shaming the Medici name in the process. They all realized, the bankers, the barons, the dukes and the entirety of our people, that all you wanted was everything for yourself.*

"Vous ne nous permettez de changer, de grandir avec notre proie!" *You never allow us to change, to grow with our prey!*

"Nous allons mourir a moins que nous negocions—" began the old vampire. *We will all die out unless we can negotiate—*

The shard of wood shot from Dracula's hand as if from a cannon, where it had been moved when he had taken human form, and across the top of the tower structure in a heartbeat. The shard punched deep into Nostradamus' chest like a cutting knife through a fresh tomato. The old vampire's mouth opened wide in agony, and his hands dug at the piece of wood as he teetered off his perch.

"Sed quid huc vos me occidere," hissed Dracula as he watched Nostradamus twitch in agony. *I am not here to do anything but kill you all.*

Nostradamus staggered, at the precipice.

He thought of Anne, what would become of her, and how he had failed them both.

Nostradamus' body began to crumble to ash in its death throes.

Yet as he died, as his ashes began to scatter even though he was still able to think and reason, Nostradamus looked at Dracula and whispered, "Vous n'etes pas pour longtemps." *You are not long for this world.*

The wind began to take Nostradamus' ashes and scatter them over the City of Light as what was left of his body fell.

The piece of wood sounded occasionally as it clanked and bounced toward the ground. Dracula watched the ashes scatter as he became a bat again, then he flew back out over the starry night. Nostradamus never finished his descent, but his ashes did, soaring all over the air of Paris.

The City of Light.

As ashes sprinkled and spread over the Sienne, the albino rat burst out of a large sewer pipe and into a much larger underground room in the gargantuan and ancient Parisian sewer system. Twisting as she leapt through the air, the albino rat had her left hind leg caught in mid-air by the Andromeda rat, who screeched in triumph, finally catching her prey. As they tumbled in mid-air, the albino rat became mist, thrashing about in an effort to escape, yet to her surprise the grip on her mist form held firm. Anne twisted backwards to see how this was possible and saw that the Greek vampiress/rat had also become a tendril of mist, was clinging to her gaseous state, and that the other she-rats were right behind them and transforming as well.

A moment in mid-air became the length of a day in complexity and action.

They transformed into four ribbons of mist, twirling over and around each other in beautiful synchronicity with the most horrible of intentions. Four ribbons writhed through the fetid air together, Anne and Andromeda and Venus and Petra, intertwining watercolors spreading over the parchment of the chamber's air. The room they tumbled through was oblong, dark, vaulted with stone and brickwork, clearly the foundation of a building above. Yet, as in the other chambers, along all of the walls were more piles of human bones. Bluish light drained into the room from another craggy, forlorn sewer tunnel above. Various rickety wooden posts along the damp walls somehow held up the foundation.

Flutter.

Swirl.

Movement.

Even though they were still in mid-leap, held afloat by their state's resistance to gravity, Lucy was the only one that had not become mist. She instantly recognized that they were nowhere near the same chambers from earlier in the night. The Lucy rat landed on all four footpads, skidding along wet sand and soil, and looked back to watch the four bride ribbons of mist coagulate back into human form again.

When they did reform, the violence was blindingly quick and brutal.

Anne Ponsarde became flesh and blood human form once again, as did Venus and Andromeda. Fur became skin, sewn threads lifted out from in between the fur and became cloth. They rolled forward along the dark chamber floor, three *nosferatu*. Venus acted first, viciously grabbing Nostradamus' wife by the throat, pushing her backward and slamming her into a stack of tibias and fibulas. Mud and mildew spurted out from the atrophied pieces of anatomy, bones crumbling and crumpling. Anne wailed in pain while her arms where pinned to either side of the pile by Andromeda and Petra.

"Ciao, traditora Anne!" roared Venus, hair like Medusa's tresses cascading over her face, which was lit up with a hellion's fury. *Hello, traitor Anne!*

She rammed her hand against Anne's throat, let her gag for a moment, then decreased her pressure.

Slightly.

"'*Et tu, Brute?*[211]' Li mandato di ucciderci tutti!" shouted Venus. *You sent them to kill us all!*"

"Non! Nous avons reçu l'ordre!" spat the French vampiress through her closed throat. *No! We were ordered—*

---

[211] This phrase appears in William Shakespeare's play *Julius Caesar*, in a scene where Caesar is assassinated by his friend Brutus and other conspirators in the Roman Senate. Spoken in Latin, *Et tu, Brute?* expresses a betrayal by a friend.

"Da dove, la mia cagna di un amica?" *From where, my bitch of a friend?*

Silence. Anne struggled violently against Petra and Andromeda, who kept her pinned against the pile.

"Eri il mio buona amica," whispered Venus with a sudden hurt that surfaced out of her depths. *You were my good friend.*

"Che ne è stato l'amicizia tra noi." *What happened to the friendship between us?*

Venus' eyes rimmed tears. Her chest heaved, her grip lessened.

Anne felt the hurt from Venus and turned her head, averting her eyes.

"Era Roma?" Venus' hiss was filled with the weight of suspicion. And fear. *Was it Rome?*

Silence. Anne's eyes tried to resist but circled back to Venus and whispered.

Yes.

The weight of this new information swept over Venus, and Petra instinctively reached out to hold Venus' free hand with her own, while Andromeda simply whispered, "Να είσαι δυνατός." *Be strong.*

Complex emotions swept over Venus. Fear, envy, distrust, disgust, longing, and at last, the remembrance of love past, the longing of love's missed opportunity and the sadness of love lost. Then, in a circuitous way, the return of the feelings of betrayal at the hands of a friend.

A long, angry grin grew over Venus' lips. "Il nostro Maestro vi ringrazia." *Our master thanks you.*

"Il a tous vous tuer! Il ne sera jamais vous marier et vous donner l'honneur et le titre! Vous êtes des putains à lui!" roared Anne, spitting at Venus. *He'll kill you all! He will never marry you and give you honor and title! You are whores to him!*

Rage flooded Venus' beautiful, cruel face. She picked up a tibia, broke a third of it off, whirled it in her hand like a throwing knife, then ferociously plunged it deep into Anne's chest. Anne screamed, and Venus' eyes were crimson slits of fury and evil joy.

Petra and Andromeda continued to hold Anne down as she spasmed. Venus was their leader, their elder, their confidant; they followed her devoutly in Dracula's absence, but doubt crept into their minds as they took in Anne's thoughts. They had trusted each other over tens of thousands of nights in those coffins, at the behest and control and violence of their master, but did they indeed believe in each other, or was one of them a possible conspirator? Andromeda looked over to Petra, who glanced back over to Lucy, who was watching in shock and bloodlust at the tableau before her. They all turned to Venus, who was thoroughly enjoying the torture of Anne Ponsarde, wife of Nostradamus, vampiress, former friend to Venus of Dracula of Transylvania, and co-conspirator.

No, thought the Egyptian and the Greek, seeing Venus' strength and resolve, *We are always sisters. She would never betray us, and we could never betray her.*

"Deux judas et mon mari sait que je ne suis pas le seul traire dans cette salle!" groaned Anne, blood and ash pooling inside of her mouth. *Judas and my husband both know that I am not the only betrayer in this room.*

Venus pushed down on the tibia even harder, her anger driving the bone deeper.

I understand, said Anne's expression. *I betrayed you, and us.*

Anne winced as her body, her clothes, became cinder. Her eyes began to bleed. She slipped her hand over Venus', over the tibia that was killing her, and her eyes whispered *forgive me* before they said no more. Venus blinked tears that said *I do,* as the entire body was consumed.

Blood and body became soft ash, and the chamber filled with blackened petals of resentment and betrayal.

Then Anne Ponsarde was gone.

With hate and regret spread over her, Venus picked up Anne's skull as it too became black and ashen.

"Addio, vecchio amico e rivale. Salutate nostro padre diabolica in mia vece," whispered the Italian vampiress. *Goodbye, old friend and rival. Greet our unholy father in my stead.*

"سوف يسيد يكون الصبر اذا وصلنا إلى التوابيت بعد ان يدعي فعل," said Petra to Venus, looking to the adjoining chamber tunnels more anxiously than she would have cared to admit. *The master will be impatient if we arrive at our coffins after he does.*

"Ποιος ήταν ο Γάλλος γυναίκα αναφέρεται με το σχόλιό της για προδότης?" said Andromeda, who slid her sandals over the pile of ashes that was Anne Ponsarde as she looked at Venus with the same concern for Dracula's arrival that Petra just expressed. *Who was the French woman referring to with her comment about a betrayer?*

The Greek vampiress then jerked her sharp chin at Lucy as she hissed mockingly, "Perhaps the child?"

"Je ne suis plus un enfant que vous êtes une vierge," hissed Lucy, rather boldly, but she was tired of being spoken to so rudely. *I am no more a child than you are a virgin.*

Her French was rusty, and for a split-second, memories of lessons and trips to France from her childhood flashed through Lucy's mind, and the ripple of memory that was Arthur Holmwood seared her heart again with fleeting melancholy. It was a brief moment, for as she finished her words Venus' strong feminine fingers had savagely clamped around her hair, and she was yanked to the right. Lucy shrieked in pain and had to bend to her right if she wanted to keep her hair on her scalp, which she did. Venus' leonine eyes loomed right in front of hers, blazing with hate, jealousy and intimidation. The Italian had moved like a blur across the space between them. Lucy's confidence emptied out of her like water out of a broken vase.

"Putain! Votre bouche ne reste jamais fermé! Votre famille est de nouveau à la richesse? Combien de langues pouvez-vous parler? Combien de terres avez-vous vu? Vous êtes, mais un enfant!" snarled Venus, nose-to-nose with her. *Whore! Your mouth never stays closed! Is your family new to wealth? How many languages can you speak? How many lands have you seen? You are but a child!*

"Rappelez-vous les paroles du maître. Nous pouvons vous tuer à notre caprice," sneered Venus with a wicked nod as her free hand clamped around Lucy's neck. *Remember the master's words. We can kill you at our whim.*

Lucy tried to use her fingers to try and pry the Italian's grip loose, but this only furrowed Venus' brow, and she, without any effort, raised Lucy off the ground.

"وقال هنا حجاة اللستماع أفضل لسبب أخذ حياتها،" whispered Petra. *He would need to hear a better reason for taking her life.*

The Egyptian, along with Andromeda had appeared on either side of them. Glances were exchanged quickly between them all and read with the intricacy and intimacy that women possess and eludes most men. Andromeda and Petra were trying to calm Venus down, keeping her from murdering Lucy right then and there. Lucy read this as support for her predicament, which the Egyptian vampire noticed and bristled at, even as Petra and Andromeda began to press down on Venus' arms to slowly lower Lucy back to the ground.

Petra threw Lucy a sharp glance and hissed, "Vous allez apprendre votre place parmi nous, déflorée chienne d'un serviteur. Vous n'êtes pas de notre classe. Nous sommes tous descendus de redevance ou l'aristocratie. Nous devons recourir à vous adresser la parole en français, la seule langue aristocratique que vous connaissez." *You will learn your place among us, deflowered bitch of a servant. You are not of our class. We are all descended from royalty or aristocracy. We must resort to addressing you in French, the only aristocratic language you know.*

"Ou nous allons l'arracher de votre visage, enfant," interjected Andromeda, also glaring at her. *Or we will tear it from your face, child.*

Lucy somehow managed a nod while averting her eyes from the three brides, and the powerful grip was released. Lucy fell like a wet laundry sack, coughing and hacking as the others walked away.

"Suivez-nous à la chambre de cercueil et le maître," said Venus, pointing backward at Lucy. *Follow us to the coffin chamber and the master.*

As Venus, Andromeda and Petra glided toward an ancient, darker-than-dark sewer tunnel, the Italian finished with, "Et comprenons que nous adressons à vous que nous le aborder un roturier." *And understand we address you as we would address a commoner.*

Lucy Westenra took a few moments to compose herself, thinking *We shall see who is the servant and who is the royal.*

As she stood and began to take a step to follow the brides, a long, wooden blade slid in from behind Lucy and across her pale throat.

"Good evening," chuckled Abraham Van Helsing.

EIGHT

The brides whirled about to face Abraham and Lucy, the anger of seeing Abraham alive mixing with the shock of how easily he had captured their newest member.

All six of their incandescent eyes blazed with surprise.

Lucy tried to wrench herself free as Van Helsing pressed his crucifix with a sharpened base so deeply against her right jugular vein as to nearly puncture the skin. That stopped her. Abraham held Lucy's scarlet hair in his left fist like she was a wild mare, and they locked eyes for half a breath.

In that instant, Abraham's heart broke. The child he had known for all of her life, the little girl he had taught how to dance, had become that which he had dedicated his life to eradicating. Her pale blue eyes, which had looked at him with such love during their tea playtime were now the cold-blooded raptor eyes of a *nosferatu*.

She snarled at him ferociously, like a jackal.

And sent chills up along Abraham's arm and neck.

But Van Helsing had lived a thousand lives in his own, single lifetime, and could put his feelings of anguish aside.

"Know this," rumbled Abraham into Lucy's ear, "whatever you are now, you are no longer my niece. I would gut you from stem to stern."

"My dear Uncle Abraham," gasped Lucy, sarcastically, overwhelmed by the intoxicating scent of Abraham Van Helsing's flesh and blood, her eyes aflame with hate and her mouth full of incisors that could rip his throat out in an instant.

"Transform into mist, whore," snarled Venus at Lucy.

"Can she do it before I puncture her throat?" snarled Abraham right back, the jagged crucifix wedged deeply against Lucy's neck.

Footsteps in the near-darkness of the chamber.

"Our husband was rude when he did not introduce us when we first met. I am Venus, and my sisters are Andromeda and Petra."

"I don't give a shit who you are," snarled Abraham.

Venus began to reply, then cocked her head like a hawk at movement behind Van Helsing.

She heard something.

Shoefalls, in the night.

In the gloom, shadows gained from behind Abraham.

Jonathan, Quincy and Mina then drifted into view from behind Van Helsing, out of the darkness. Jonathan held his Webley and another sharpened crucifix, while Mina cradled her Winchester, her own crucifix tied to the outer part of her left hand. Quincy was ready for bear, with his own Winchester out, and his coat flipped behind the Colt on his right hip. As they moved around Abraham and Lucy before settling in between the brides and Lucy, Mina and Quincy exchanged glances of alarm upon seeing Lucy in her vampiric condition.

Not Jonathan.

His eyes were locked on the brides.

"Remember me?" said Jonathan with a caustic nod at the brides.

"Yes, child," said Venus, too dignified to be ever caught off guard. She sensed the connection between Jonathan and Mina, "We enjoyed your kisses and sighs and love-making."

All eyes danced to Mina, whose grip on her Winchester tightened.

The brides all giggled like vicious schoolgirls at Mina's attempt to hide her frown.

No one else did.

Mina saw Lucy, the Lucy of her childhood, in the clutches of Abraham and took in her blinking, glowing, supernatural eyes.

Mina choked tears.

"Lucy," she gulped. Lucy twisted in Abraham's grip, locked eyes with Mina and snarled like a livid panther.

"She is our Lucy no longer," said Jonathan, as Van Helsing nodded, not taking his eyes off the brides for a second.

"I had the pleasure," continued Venus, "of impaling your dear uncle Peter's hands onto the cross on which he died."

"Tonight you'll be the ones impaled," hissed Mina.

"Amen," said Quincy, to her left, holding his Winchester like it was his firstborn child. "Like Rattlers on fenceposts."

"Why not just slit her throat" said Venus to Abraham. "We do not need her."

"Because he wants your attention diverted," spouted a voice behind the brides, from the darkest dark.

The brides whirled again, surrounded.

Their eerie, glowing eyes blinked in surprise again.

Ian Seward held a Webley and a lantern, filling the room with a strong light. Arthur was beside Ian, holding his own Webley. King Arthur locked eyes with Lucy, as did their friends, and they all felt for young Lord Godalming. Lucy had been taken from his arms, killed and had been reborn. Lucy's beauteous face cast long, macabre shadows because of the strong light from Ian's lantern, her terrifying visage more animal than human as she hissed at him, perhaps more strongly than at the others because she recognized Arthur. Staggered at Lucy's ferocity, Holmwood stumbled as the earth under his left foot gave way and collapsed down through a small crevasse in the dirt floor. He pulled his foot out and regained his balance. An even darker chamber loomed below.

"Mind the ground around you," said Holmwood, his eyes never wavering from Lucy's. "It feels unstable."

He moved closer and took in Lucy, her hair in the left fist of Abraham, and his sharpened cross ready to punch through into her neck, and the young man was overwhelmed. Arthur's eyes danced with lantern-lit tears.

"Darling Lucy, what has become of you?" whispered Arthur. He tried to find his fiancée in Lucy's fierce eyes, but they only burned with the eagerness to rip his neck to pieces. Holmwood's eyes brimmed with tears. "Do you not remember our love? Our betrothal?"

Ian reached out with his lantern hand to nudge Arthur in a gesture of support.

"All that was ours has died," hissed Lucy, her cold heart convulsing with confusion at seeing Holmwood, and her confusion caused hate to flare from her and she added, "You will not see the next dawn!"

"Sounds like they've been married for twenty years," chuckled Morris.

No one thought that was funny at all.

Tension bloated the chamber.

"Wound them with your weapons, then kill with the crucifix through the heart!" shouted Abraham, escalating the tension.

"'Cowards die many times before their deaths,[212]'" whispered Andromeda, her hate blazing through her glowing eyes. The brides were beautiful, haunting and deadly as they moved into a semi-circle. Venus looked Van Helsing square in the eye and said, "Behead her. She means nothing to me."

"They are quite fast," warned Abraham. He tightened his grip on Lucy, preparing to punch a hole into her throat. Jonathan and Mina exchanged a look that said *he's going to kill Lucy right in front of us!*

"I'm faster," beamed Quincy, cocking his Winchester.

Then it all happened.

Andromeda's' charge was a blur, incredibly fast, but it was halted by an invisible punch, and for an instant she was suspended in the air, a round from Quincy's Winchester having pounded against her chest like a hammer to an anvil.

"Told ya," nodded the Texan as he re-cocked his Winchester.

Andromeda fell right by Morris and at the feet of Abraham Van Helsing, who did not hesitate. He leaped forward, Lucy in tow and thrust his crucifix out.

He pounded it deep into the fallen Andromeda's chest.

A mortal blow.

"Sterven, hellspawn!" he shouted. *Die, hellspawn!*

The vampiress convulsed like a punctured scorpion, arms and legs flailing in the air, her eyes and mouth wide open. She struggled to pull the crucifix out, but Jonathan and Mina both followed Van Helsing's blow with a shot from each of their weapons, which bored into Andromeda's heart.

Lucy used that moment to wrench herself free from Abraham's grip and leap upward onto the ceiling of the chamber, turning into a bat during the leap. She watched upside-down as Andromeda began to spasm eerily and shriek at the top of her lungs, mortally wounded. Andromeda then let out one lone, unholy howl.

As the mournful cry echoed around them, blood began to pour out of Andromeda's eyes, and as she wept blood, a small wicked flame erupted from the dying vampiress' mouth, licking her lips and canines.

After Abraham pulled out his crucifix knife, blood spurted out of the wound in the chest, and then Andromeda's entire body began to crackle into ash.

As she bled tears, Andromeda turned to Venus.

She could not speak.

Life, undead life seeped out of Andromeda Philaras.

With one last whisp of breath, she whispered, through her dying flame, to sister de' Medici.

"Αδελφή?" begged Andromeda. *Sister?*

"Mia sorella!" shrieked Venus, eyes wide with horror and shock. *My sister!*

Andromeda agonized, crinkled and withered.

She reached out to her sisters

Venus and Petra's expressions frothed with both sorrow and rage.

---

[212] *Julius Caesar* by William Shakespeare. Act II, scene 2. *Cowards die many times before their deaths. The valiant never taste of death but once.*

Petra was so livid that her eyes flooded with tears, and when she screamed, it became a roar, and for that moment, her face took the countenance of a bat before it melted back to human form.

She burst out, "حبي، اي أنردموادي! أختى!" *My love, my Andromeda! My sister!*

"Θα σ᾽ ᾽αγαπώ για πάντα και οι δύο," cried Andromeda to Venus and Petra as her face withered, her eyes stilled. *I will love you both forever.*

The flame died out in Andromeda's mouth, and she melted into a pile of ashes and was no more.

No one moved as they took in the vampiress' death, curling up like a speared serpent on the damp, dark sewer soil.

Venus and Petra wept openly.

"Hell yeah," nodded Quincy, quite satisfied.

Abraham walked over and pulled out his crucifix, pointing both it and his Bergman at the other *nosferatu*. "Your turn."

The Egyptian and the Italian stared death at Quincy with their wet, glowing eyes, and snarled like wolves.

Morris simply winked at them and said, "Got some more right here for ya."

Lucy halted her crawl along the ceiling and dropped down to the ground next to Venus and Petra. Sensing Lucy's reinforcement, the she-bats charged forward with the intent of rending the Texan to shreds, but Jonathan, Quincy and Mina held out their crucifixes. The three *nosferatu* had to cover their faces with their hands and arms and retreat, hissing like vipers as they did so. Ian's lantern brought long, strange shadows to the chamber, an eerie ambience of the supernatural to the dank chamber. The brides' retreat brought Lucy back closer to Arthur, who was a torrent of conflicting emotions.

"What has he done to you, Lucy?" cried Holmwood, more to himself than anyone else.

He took a step forward.

Not a step with the intent to injure maim or murder, but a soft step, a gentle one.

Lovingly.

And King Arthur lowered his Webley and crucifix.

The vampiresses sensed movement, Lucy turning to him, blinking at the Lord Godalming with incandescent eyes.

Arthur was adrift, not in the moment, his thoughts on what had been Lucy instead of the Lucy that was before him, calculating a leap at him with every step Arthur took.

Arthur choked back tears as he pulled some fabric from his pants pocket. "Here is the ribbon of love you gave me the other night."

Arthur's words alerted Jonathan and Mina, who saw that Arthur had lowered his weapons. Mina shouted, "Arthur! Step back!"

Lucy of Dracula lowered her head at Arthur like a lioness about to pounce, her eyes glowing ravenously in the gloom.

"Uncle!" spat Jonathan.

Abraham, ever calm, deadpanned, "Ian, keep Arthur from Lucy."

Ian had to put the lantern down and grab a hold of Arthur to keep him from walking right to his fiancée. "Arthur! She'll kill you, mate!"

"No, she won't," said Holmwood, who smiled at Lucy and said softly, "You still wear your engagement ring."

Petra and Venus, despite their predicament, smiled with glee at Arthur's pain.

"She wore it while the master ravaged her," laughed Venus, meaning to sink a dagger into Holmwood's heart, but she furrowed her brow when she realized her words did not affect Arthur, who lifted his arm to wrench free from Ian's grip.

Ian held on, Webley at the ready.

"Come to me, darling," leered Lucy, like a leopard.

"She'll kill you!" shouted Jonathan.

 "No, she won't," said Arthur again, tears running down his face as he shook his head. "Please, don't hurt her."

Ian pulled back on Arthur's right shoulder as he took a few more steps in his near-somnambulistic journey toward having his throat torn open.

Seward used that moment to let go of Arthur and pull out a crucifix, just as Lucy was tensing to leap forward with the intention of decapitating Arthur, and Ian thrust out his crucifix.

It stopped Lucy in her tracks.

She snarled at Ian before whirling to projectile-vomit a pound of bile and blood onto her fiancé's face and chest, like a spitting cobra.

Arthur stood drenched and in shock as Lucy snarled like a wolf at him. "Murderers! I could never love you, you whimpering eunuch!"

"Step back from her, Arthur!" shouted Abraham, who was using his free hand to instruct the others to spread out to form a semi-circle around the brides.

"Stay strong, Arthur," said Ian, nudging a distraught Arthur back while holding his own crucifix and Webley at the vampiresses.

"We move in as one and kill them all!" roared Abraham, and he saw fear in Venus' and Petra's eyes, and that brought a sharp grin to his face. "Contain them with the crucifixes! Shoot at the chest to stun them! I'll impale them before we *cut off their heads!*"

Venus hissed and tried to rush at Van Helsing, but he waved his crucifix blade to keep her back. "No, animal! Tonight you die!"

Petra did the same and found Mina's crucifix blocking her way. She backed away and snarled like an enraged tiger in a trap.

They closed the circle around the brides.

"Pour the Holy Water at their feet!" roared Abraham, growing in confidence. "Force them back against the wall!"

Jonathan and Ian splashed Holy Water at the feet of the brides, and they backed up toward the far wall of the dark chamber. Ian's lantern light cast a hellish pallor, and when Seward scooped it up, it swayed in his hand, the light swaying over the chamber and its inhabitants, casting waves of light and dark.

Venus's face began to melt into the features of a bat, but Abraham raised his crucifix and shouted, "Vos non possunt transmutare!" *You cannot transform!*

She roared in unexpected pain, and stayed in her human form; both of them were cornered. The brides wore surprised expressions on their faces, all looking at Abraham Van Helsing, who nodded at them with a smirk. "Yes, I know the spells of your kind!" to the others he ordered, "Shoot to stun, then step back so I can impale them! Shoot them upon my mark!"

Livid fear, then outright panic flowed through the eyes of the brides.

"Andromeda died like the vermin she was," chuckled Jonathan, holding his crucifix. He had to re-adjust his footing as the ground below him began to crumble like dry cheese.

"Arthur's right," he said to everyone, "watch the floor."

Petra's outline shimmered as she began to transform into mist, but Abraham shot out his crucifix and repeated, "Vos non possunt transmutare!" *You cannot transform!*

Petra's form solidified and she screamed in agony, pinned to the wall, trembling with outright fear. She reached out and found Venus' hand, and they held onto each other fiercely, trembling.

Mina, Ian, Jonathan, and Abraham converged.

Kli-katch!

Mina chambered a round in her Winchester even as she held her crucifix in her left hand, under the weapon.

"Help me, beloved!" cried a panicked Lucy as she reached out to Arthur, who trembled with feelings of sorrow, anger, loyalty and love.

Lucy's fooling him, trying to lure him closer so she can cut him to shreds, thought Ian, even as he sensed echoes of sincerity in Lucy's voice.

"Mina, shoot the Italian," growled Abraham with fervor, "Ian, you have the Egyptian. Jonathan, shoot Lucy."

Abraham sensed hesitancy in his pupils and reached for his holstered Bergman when Arthur barked "No!" from behind Ian.

Abraham tried to shove his way around Ian, but Seward managed to hold his friend back by shoving back with a raised right arm while maintaining his crucifix upon the brides.

Arthur was beside himself and bawled, "Lucy, tell them you still love me! We can help you! They'll kill you!"

Lucy's face stayed as hard as sculpted marble, but the softening of her eyes betrayed her. She swallowed hard as her eyes suddenly melted, waves of memories overwhelming her. She never opened her mouth.

Her eyes did all the talking.

Yes.

I love you.

I am so sorry, beloved.

Venus saw the effect that Arthur was having upon Lucy, and vice-versa, the intangible chemistry between people who truly love each other. She took this in and snarled at young Holmwood, out of both rage and jealousy, as she spewed violent animalistic sounds. Petra pulled Venus back from the closing circle of hunters, into an embrace.

Lucy, staggering and trying to hold her own swirling feelings in check, reached over and tried to help Petra but Venus savagely swatted her hand away in a fit of rage. "You are no sister to me, whore! Do not touch me!"

As she crept closer, Mina cocked her Winchester and held it strong and cold, right at Venus' head. "You get the first round, bitch. Right in the head."

Venus turned to Mina and raised her head in proud defiance. *Shoot me if you dare.*

"This," said Ian as he took another step toward them, raising his Webley," is for killing our parents."

Another step closer.

Abraham knew that with one more step, he'd be in range for a blow to Venus' sternum.

He thought to shoot first, then stab during the reaction to the blow.

Then, a scuttle.

A sound.

At their feet.

More.

Then a filthy, enormous, crimson-eyed rat crawled over Jonathan's shoe.

Harker flicked it off with a kick as another slithered in over his other shoe.

Then another.

Two more, clambering up Quincy's leg, and he kicked/shook them off in disgust.

Three fell onto Mina's rifle, and she flung them off in horror.

Then ten, flowing from a protruding piece of timber and over Ian's head, shoulders, arms and rifle, and he flailed his arms around, yelling out in fear while nearly dropping his Webley.

A few leaped into the air at them, and Mina shot them in mid-air.

One.

Two.

Three.

"Quincy!" she yelled, and the Texan joined her, helping to disintegrate the leaping unholy vermin.

Four.

Five.

Six.

Seven.

Eight.

One right after the other.

A hundred advanced from behind Van Helsing, scratching and clawing the ground as they squirmed through every conceivable hole, nook and cranny in the dilapidated walls.

Mina emptied her rifle and was about to reload when, in a moment of absolute horror she took five hundred *more* squirming into the chamber from the darkness, becoming a living, moving, writhing wall of pestilence that undulated along the wall behind the brides.

"Sweet Jesus in Sunday School," said Quincy, as he finished chambering a round in his Winchester before he realized the futility and lowered his weapon.

They all, human and undead, looked at each other, knowing what was coming.

Undead smiles.

Living frowns.

Petra let go of Venus, who pointed at Abraham with glee and said, "The master has arrived."

Abraham remained collected as he pivoted around, holding his crucifix stake out, and the brides' faces began to split wide with grins.

"Viviamo un'altra notte, la mia sorella!" disse an excited Venus to Petra. *We live another night, my sister!*

More vermin poured in, the floor alive with motion, every nook and cranny alive with beady eyes, swollen fur and swishing rat tails.

Abraham took out a small decanter and shouted, "Quincy, Mina, Jonny, around me! Quickly!"

When they gathered around him, Van Helsing took the metal decanter and poured the clear liquid in a circle around them, shouting, "Ian, do the same! These are not ordinary rats. Use the Holy Water! Quickly!"

Seward did as he was told, pouring from his own decanter, and the rats scattered outside the perimeter of the circle.

"I will tear you to ribbons for Andromeda!" seethed Venus at Abraham, as rats flooded the chamber, crawling in from above, below and all around them. As the group tightened into a circle around the Holy Water circle, Venus and Petra moved away from the wall, both smiling, both anticipating. The entire room was writhing, frothing with vermin by the thousands. Dozens of them tried to cram their way through a hole in one of the walls, and the moldy section of the dilapidated chamber wall broke off and slid through the dirt floor, landing with an unseen crash in the unknown emptiness below.

Then, a shadow followed them, black as night save for twin, piercing red embers.

Dracula glided into the room like an obsidian dragon.

Underlit from Ian's lantern, Dracula was hellish. He took in the scene, pausing without emotion at the pile of ashes that was Andromeda, before sliding his wicked eyes over to Van Helsing, the only human that wasn't holding a crucifix at him.

The Transylvanian said, "Femina iam Graeca patre meo." *The Greek woman is with my father now.*

"*Ave Satanas,*" chanted Venus and Petra together.

"*Ave Satanas,*" whispered Lucy, and at that moment, Mina knew she had lost her best friend.

Dracula pointed at them and nodded with respect as he said, "You are all stout of heart, surviving our first encounter, your trial by fire, as it were. Yet you all might have had a chance to tell of that experience if you had retreated after you had killed my Greek concubine. It is, however to my great satisfaction that your pursuit allows me the opportunity to witness your passage into the next realm."

"Godamm," Quincy laughed morbidly. "You're uglier than the ass cheeks on a broken-down donkey!"

No stranger to insults, the vampire curled a faint smile, chuckled darkly and replied, "I have never met your mother."

He then stared like a stone at Van Helsing. "You were not conscious at our formal introduction. I am Dracula. I am *nosferatu, strigoi, vampyr*. My titles are that of count, cardinal and royal heir. You have no defense against me or my women, for Satan is my blessed *pater* and I am his only revered son. Who might you be, intrepid guest?"

Abraham did not bat an eye as he replied, "I am Abraham Van Helsing, and all you need know about me is that as a boy I had the joy of planting a crucifix right through your wife's cold black heart. Remember forever that your wife died *by my hand*. As I will do to you this very night."

Quincy and Jonathan looked at each other as if to say *good God*.

Dracula looked right through Van Helsing with the wide-eyed gaze of a bird of prey for a few long, dry seconds before he broke into a canine-filled grin that was even more terrifying than the glacial stare.

"You have courage, Abraham Van Helsing. Real courage. It will serve you well when you and these children meet my father in but a few short moments. He does not quite have my patience."

Abraham's stare was glacial. "Dead rats in a gutter have more worth than either of you."

As quickly as his smile vanished, Dracula's tiger-like roar filled the chamber, scattering rats in its wake. He lunged toward Abraham Van Helsing like a hurricane at a coastline.

Abraham stood resolute like a lighthouse and threw a wicked left cross at Dracula.

It shot forward and met Dracula's charge head-on, square on the face.

To everyone's absolute astonishment, the punch connected with terrific force.

The accompanying sound was like hammer meeting anvil.

The blow knocked the Transylvanian backward, arms flailing; the vampire had to put his arms out to avoid falling to the ground.

Dracula took a moment to clear his eyes, but then had to cover them, had to bring his hands up to cover his eyes, in fact.

A strange new presence had entered the room.

It was bothering Dracula, in fact bothering all of the *nosferatu* in the chamber.

What was bothering them was a supernatural glow.

It came from the sharpened wooden crucifix that glowed white-hot but harmlessly in Abraham Van Helsing's hand.

NINE

Everyone stood in awe, not at the blow struck by Van Helsing, which had nearly felled the vampire, but at the incandescent crucifix in Abraham's left hand.

"Did that hurt?" mocked Abraham with a quirky, ridiculing leer.

"Holy shit!" roared Quincy.

"Master!" shrieked Petra, and she moved forward to help Dracula, but was angrily waved off by the vampire. Venus and Lucy snarled like jackals at Abraham.

"These simple crucifixes burn only for you and yours, blood-drinker," chuckled Van Helsing, eyes jumping from the brides to Dracula and back. "No other. It has always been a simple matter to rid this earth of you vermin."

"The collected armies of the European continent have tried and failed," laughed Dracula, having gained his composure. "And you will address me as a nobleman, serf."

"Should a dog be called anything but a dog?" chuckled Van Helsing," the only thing you are deserving of is a quick death."

Dracula did not bat an eye as waved to the rats and gestured to the group. "Eat them."

From every corner came waves of flea-infested bodies with crimson eyes.

"Hold your crosses out!" screamed Abraham. "These are unholy vermin! The Holy Water protects us!"

Mina, Ian, Arthur, Quincy and Jonathan all whipped out their crucifixes, lowering them closer to the ground.

All of the crosses began to glow, in concert, beacons that illuminated the chamber in warm light. Shadows ran, as did rats.

As each rat met the line of Holy Water in the soil, they were scalded into writhing pain or consumed instantly into puffs of satanic smoke.

The brides saw an opening and attacked.

Wide-eyed night owl with talons open, Lucy led the way, bloodlust re-fueled by the attack on her master, followed by Venus and Petra.

Arthur stood with his arms and weapons down as Lucy bore down on him.

Mina saw this, wrenched Arthur's Webley from his hand and shot Lucy point-plank in the chest, stopping Lucy of Dracula in her tracks. She turned and howled at Mina with animalistic fury, the light from Mina's crucifix giving the young vampire a ghastly countenance. Tears streamed down Mina's face as she pulled the trigger again to knock Lucy back a few steps.

Petra and Venus swerved around the retreating Lucy, intent on ripping Mina's arms off, only to have the white-hot crosses held by Ian and Jonathan repel them.

"The crucifixes scald *them*, but do not burn us," gasped an amazed Mina, her face underlit by the beautiful cyan light emanating from the crosses. The others saw this as well, and kept their holy weapons held high.

"Incredible," whispered an astonished Jonathan, his cross searing one of the larger, bolder rats. It mewled, staggered, and withdrew over the swarming tide of rodents.

"It is the presence of holiness," rumbled Abraham. "We have all goodness behind us."

"I don't believe it," gasped Ian, his own crucifix holding off a disgusting wave of unholy rats.

"Lordy, I believe it," nodded Quincy, who was waving his own crucifix at the rat waves, with multitudes of them retreating with every swing of the Texan's arm.

Van Helsing threw a confident grin at Dracula, who said nothing, stood in the shadows, a huge shadow himself, the only lights coming from him and the brides were their red, vicious eyes. He watched Abraham and his cohorts fend off the rats and brides with growing confidence. They felt fortified, renewed, emboldened.

Like a living wave, the rats frothed at them from all sides, falling, biting, squirming over each other like a fur and lice- tsunami that could not land on the beach, being held back by the circle and the crosses. Some rats fell from above, or clawed from below, and they were all incinerated by white-hot holy fire. The circle held firm, their crosses out in front of them, but the rats did not cross the circles of Holy Water that surrounded them all.

Arthur took in Lucy's rage over the blinding dust. He reached out to her with his free hand, and she spat upon it, her saliva scalding Holmwood's cross.

Dracula stood in the midst of the turbulence, watching Van Helsing like an eagle would watch a lamb. The vampire was watching for the first opening, the first opportunity to attack. Van Helsing threw Holy Water out on either side of the distance between himself and the vampires.

"I rebuke you in the name of all that is good in this world and the next!" shouted Abraham.

The rats squealed in pain and scattered. As they did, a section of the floor below sagged significantly.

"Uncle Abraham!" shouted Ian over the din of the rats and the animalistic snarls of the brides, who were turning into huge bats again, their wings sliding over their eyes like shields against the crucifixes. Van Helsing waved to Seward to show that he was alright. Arthur recovered enough to repeat Abraham's act with the Holy Water, and the rats in their path to the brides parted as well, some of them mewling in pain at any contact with the blessed liquid. The humans moved forward, waves of rats frothing on either side of them, eager to eat the humans down to their bones.

Abraham Van Helsing had literally turned the tide.

"Mina, Quincy, weapons!" shouted Abraham over the din as Mina scrambled to reload hers. They raised the Winchesters, both at Dracula. They anticipated some action from him, but the vampire did not react, staying where he stood, straight and proud.

"You have us, Abraham Van Helsing," said the Transylvanian, "you must attack."

"Move in and impale their hearts with your sharpened crosses!" shouted Jonathan, feverish with anticipation.

The humans pressed in on either side of the vampires, the rats not daring to trespass over the paths of Holy Water. The brides began to shriek and chirp in fear as the crucifixes closed in on them. They looked to their master, who stood tall in the middle of the commotion, the crosses seemingly unaffecting him.

"We've got 'em!" shouted Quincy in his exuberant drawl. "Feed 'em to the hogs!"

Closer still, Van Helsing leered at Dracula, who stood strangely passive, staring straight back at Abraham, who raised his sharpened wooden crucifix from his bag in anticipation.

"En el nombre del pardre, del hijo, y del el espiritu santo!" shouted Van Helsing as he readied his thrust. *In the name of the Father, the Son and the Holy Ghost!*

"Now," said Dracula with a plain wink and grin.

It was then that Mina, who was almost close enough to shoot the vampires point-blank, felt a massive hand clamp around her throat.

"Hello Tiger Lily," whispered Montague Rhodes Renfield into her ear.

TEN

Renfield smiled tenderly as he picked Mina up off the ground. His enormous right hand wrapped around her neck, Montague wrenched the Winchester out of her hand with the other. Mina whirled Arthur's Webley around but the brute brought his Winchester-laden hand back around and knocked the pistol out of her hand with a backhand slap. Mina gurgled at the chokehold but had enough fortitude to find the Pepperbox Derringer inside her purse, torque her body and thrust the Remington-Elliot under the chin of the huge man, glaring at him with eyes overflowing with defiance.

She pulled back on the hammer and coughed, "Squeeze and I'll splatter your brains all over the ceiling."

Jonathan saw this and shouted, "Renfield!" and lowered his Webley and crucifix stake, just enough. With a singular, dynamic thrust, Dracula shot out his left arm seized Jonathan Harker by the nape like a small dog and savagely pulled him close, the arm of his coat catching fire in the process. Jonathan nearly blacked out, such was the vampire's strength, but he kept focus, his eyes on Mina.

Abraham moved forward to thrust, and as he aimed his blow at Dracula's neck before the vampire could take hold of Jonathan completely, a powerful force yanked him sideways. Abraham Van Helsing was forced to his knees even as he thrust upwards with his crucifix, which was aimed at whichever unseen person or vampire held him, but the blade and blow strangely slipped between what felt like an empty rib cage. The strength of his hidden foe was incredible, something Van Helsing had never experienced before, and he was helpless in the possession of whoever was now holding him.

"I have you, Sir," growled Primus in Abraham's ear.

"Good God," was all that Ian could say as he took in the animate, armored brute of a skeleton before him.

Quincy pivoted to meet the Petra bat, who had sprung out at him, wings spread wide, and he fluidly pulled one of his Colts out of his right holster and shot once, twice, three times, blowing her backwards with each blow, the Texan was quick as liquid gold, as if he was born to do it, which of course he was.

Quincy then turned and pointed the business end of his Winchester at Renfield, chambered a round and drawled, "Put 'er down or I'll put a hole in ya bigger than yer mamma when she birthed ya. Yer no kin of mine."

Renfield lowered Mina to the ground but did not let go of her neck.

She could breathe, but Montague still held her.

"Let go of me, Renfield!" commanded Mina.

"Not 'till the master gives the go-ahead," beamed Rhodes.

"How about a bullet in yer brain, 'Uncle'," challenged Morris.

"Then I would go to my glory with the master's father,' replied Renfield.

His grip on Mina tightened.

As did Mina's on her Derringer.

Dracula, with Jonathan still in his clutches, drew a sly grin at Renfield's dedication. Harker remembered he had his Webley, and he whipped it around, pressed it against Dracula's belly, pulling the trigger over and over, emptying his rounds into the vampire, through whom the shots rattled like they were blows from a small child. The trajectory of the bullets was altered, but the Transylvanian stood stout, and his grip held firm.

"I am not my concubines, boy," growled the vampire. "I have girded myself. It will take more than water sprinkles or your projectiles."

The chamber, filled with nothing but night a few moments before, was quite cramped now.

The Venus and Lucy bats then charged Ian and Arthur, but were repelled back with crucifixes; the battle line held.

"Try me and find out!" roared Ian, and he shot Venus twice, pushing her back from him, the bullets embedding themselves in the moldy, crumbling wall behind her. The huge mammal snarled in rage as she raked the ceiling with her claws as de' Medici transformed back into her human, livid form.

"Lucy, I beg you, think this through!" shouted Arthur to the Lucy bat, even as he held his crucifix out at her. "I love you! We are your family!"

Lucy had also finished her transformation back into his young former fiancée and screamed, "I will kill you first! I could never love you!"

A section of wall behind her that crawled with swarming rats, cracked and sagged.

"Uncle Abraham!" shouted Mina, still holding her Derringer at Renfield's chin. "This entire chamber is unstable!"

"Your pawns have fallen, Van Helsing," said Dracula, sensing the tide in the room changing. "You are in checkmate."

Abraham could barely raise his head to look at Dracula, on his knees with Primus' weight pushing down on him. "Gahhhhhhhhhh!" screamed Van Helsing, struggling futilely against the skeleton's grip.

"You will not leave this room alive," beamed Dracula, who tightened his hold on Jonathan, about to rip Harker's head clean off. "And I will laugh at your memory from the Eternal City."

"Nostra danza è finita," said Venus thickly, slowly, with long pauses between words as she seared Jonathan to pieces with her glare, enjoying Mina's silent, jealous eyes. *Our dance is over.*

Renfield licked his lips as he tried to draw Mina in for a kiss. She pulled back the hammer on the Derringer, but Montague whispered, "To die, to sleep.[213]"

At that moment, Van Helsing thought they were all finished. He thought of everyone, his wife, unborn daughter, his friends and their children who were about to die tonight, led to their deaths by his incompetent leadership.

Dracula hissed, "I have you all!"

And he was right.

This thought snapped through Arthur like lightning.

He knew that while he loved Lucy deeply, that he could not let anything happen to the others. He knew that he could not let the murderer of his parents go unpunished, and in a moment of reckoning, realized his purpose in that moment.

Even if it meant Lucy's life.

And his.

---

[213] From Shakespeare's *Hamlet*. "To die, to sleep– To sleep, perchance to dream– ay there is the rub, For in this sleep what dreams may come..."

"NO, filth, you do not!" roared King Arthur.

And Arthur Holmwood Junior, Arthur Holmwood II, King Arthur and the Lord Godalming realized that his life on the earth was about to end. He thought of his mother and father, both at rest, and he had one long heartbeat of a moment where he regretted not being able to avenge their deaths, but then a sense of tranquility came over him, and Arthur accepted that perhaps the next plateau would be with his parents in heaven.

Along with his fiancée.

So long as his dear friends could live on.

In one motion, Arthur Holmwood strode forward, ripped Lucy into his arms and in an astonishing moment, poured his bottle of Holy Water all over her. Lucy screamed in uncontrolled pain as her face, body and dress burst into white-hot flame, scattering the rats throughout the chamber.

"Nooooooo!!!" wailed Mina as she futilely fought against Renfield's iron grip.

Abraham simply shut his eyes before tears of mourning began to fill them.

The Holy Water did its work, and Lucy Westenra became a beacon of light in this somber, dank chamber. A corner portion of the floor crumpled into the dark nothingness below. Lucy screamed in agonizing pain, even as she wrapped her arms tenderly around her fiancé.

"Arrrrrthhuuurrrr!!!!" she shrieked like an angel on Judgement Day.

She resisted his bearhug, which he knew would happen, but then her love for him flowed out from inside once more, and she embraced him as if they would never see each other again. He returned her embrace, and they found peace.

"I'm right here my love," he said through tears. "At your side, as always."

A flower field of fire raged over Lucy of Dracula.

Beautiful flame petals covered her, an unseen wind swirled around her, cleansing her.

Lucy was one of flame, one with fire.

Yet the flames did not burn Arthur.

But the fire lit up the chamber.

The brides retreated.

The holy light made even Dracula of Transylvania squint, and take a step back.

Waves of rats were burnt, and they recoiled back to the multitude of recesses amid the bone piles.

The flare and hisses of the holy fire shocked Jonathan Harker, still in Dracula's clutches.

Mina fought off tears just as much as she resisted Renfield, and if she could have screamed, she would have.

Abraham, for one of the few moments in his life, was taken completely by surprise.

Arthur bawled openly as he held her tightly, and whispered, "Go to Him, Lucy, rest in peace, my one, true love! I would have married no other. Let not the troubles of this world hurt you again. Seek my parents, find your mother! We will love again in heaven, if I am worthy."

"Arthur my love!" screamed Lucy, "It burns! It kills me!"

"No Artie!" shrilled Quincy, his rifle still locked onto one M.R. Renfield.

"Pull away from her, Arthur!" screamed Ian, desperate to help his friend but keeping Venus and the Petra bat at bay.

Arthur slowly shook his head at Quincy and gave Ian one long, happy smile, "You're still my best man, mate."

"عذراء-" gasped Petra, reverting in an instant to her human form, moving to help Lucy. *The virgin—*

"—has earned no loyalty from us," replied Venus, stopping her. "Only from him. Only from his love."

Yet Venus was staggered.

Overcome with Arthur's sacrifice.

With his love.

For his beloved.

Venus was envious.

Of the love between these two.

The love.

L'amore.

"Solo dal la sua unica amore," Venus nearly sobbed. *Only from her one love.*

Dracula watched Lucy scream in pain without a hint of emotion.

Astonished at Holmwood's bold move, Renfield's iron grip on Mina relaxed.

Just a little.

Quincy, his Winchester still trained upon the behemoth, took a few steps back, away, but more to be able to take in the burning of the former Lucy Westenra. Morris began to weep, even as his trigger finger ached to blow a hole right through the back of Montague Rhodes Renfield.

Mina watched as well, her chest heaving in silent, mourning sobs while still in Renfield's grip, her Derringer still under his chin.

They all watched her become a holy, undead spirit.

Abraham wept as he at last took in Lucy aflame in Arthur's arms, had his soul explode with memories of them as infants, as children, as young adults, and the emotion that welled in his heart brought him to heaving tears, seeing the little girl that he had played tea with now burn to death, and his King Arthur, but he blinked tears away knowing that at least she had not had the fate that had befallen the other undead in the room. Then the pressure came from Primus above him, pushing down on his shoulders to keep Abraham's entire arm locked, then Van Helsing remembered that his wooden blade was also a crucifix.

Abraham re-gripped the crucifix from the top to down around the corpus and thrust it up into Primus' face. The Roman gladiator of old took in the Christian symbol and was startled. The pressure released, and Abraham Van Helsing stood and turned to see the brutish skeleton backing away.

Abraham's crucifix stake was alight with inner radiance.

Jonathan saw what Abraham had done, whipped his crucifix stake around and right into the face of Dracula. The light within the crucifix brightened and the vampire released him immediately. Jonathan gagged and staggered while he made his way over to Abraham, who was standing beside Quincy and Ian, who were in the middle of catching their breaths as well. They were all watching Arthur and Lucy. Between them were Renfield, who still held Mina, surrounded by Primus and the vampires.

Lucy, comforted by being in Arthur's arms, wailed as her face and hair were overrun with flames.

Her eyes opened and were twin incandescent beacons.

Holmwood shouted to his friends, "Leave this place! Now!"

"Not without Mina!" shouted Jonathan, and when he tried to attack Renfield, the huge man clenched her throat even tighter. *Don't do it, man.*

Mina bravely held up her end of the détente by pushing the barrel of her Derringer up into Renfield's chin.

Whatever was inside the massive man, Renfield was not quite ready to meet his master after all, and his eyes remained locked with Mina's.

Dracula pointed at Arthur and roared, "Consume him!"

Thousands of the vermin swarmed in from every corner of the chamber and bore down upon Arthur.

Lucy, so aflame that her skull could be seen through her face, took Arthur's face into her glowing hands and said, "Je meurs avec vous, mon amour." *I die with you, my love.*

Arthur Holmwood's soul was seared with his love for Lucy Westenra.

The white-hot flames burnt through Lucy and kept the rats at bay. They gnashed their teeth, swirled and circled Arthur, looking for their moment to tear him to shreds.

Primus took a step back from Van Helsing's sharpened crucifix.

Abraham pushed the others toward the chamber entrance.

"Arthur!" shouted Ian as he was pushed. "Escape the other way! Let her go!"

"Save yourselves!" screamed Arthur, pivoting to avoid the closing circle of rats and vampires while maintaining his embrace with his beloved. "Run!"

"Dearest," whispered Lucy, herself once again, as the fire purified her, "Your love saves me in this world and the next. If I am in your arms, I could never die."

Arthur blinked back tears and replied, "I'd rather spend eternity with you than to see you like this, my wife eternal."

Her flame began to die.

Lucy Westenra began to wither.

And die.

She became ashen.

The rats at last surged at Arthur.

Holmwood raised a hand away from the ashen corpse of his fiancée and braced himself, about to have his flesh ripped from his bones.

But Abraham pointed his Bergman.

"Goodbye, my good, good, boy. My King Arthur."

And fired, once, into Arthur's chest.

The bullet punched into the young Lord Godalming.

Jonathan screamed, "Abraham, you COWARD!" as they all surged forward to help Arthur, Abraham doing his best to hold them back.

Arthur staggered, hit, but was steadied by the dying Lucy.

Ashen Lucy, dead Lucy took one last deep breath and held her man as her eyes closed, "I have you, my love."

"Aucun autre," whispered Arthur as he died. *No other.*

Her flame ebbed, as did Lucy herself, and as their souls became one in immortality, the rats overwhelmed them, bursting past Lucy's ashes and pouring into the dying Arthur's mouth. Thousands of satanic vermin began to gnaw, tear and feast upon Arthur's flesh, even as the animate, undead ember that was Lucy Westenra Holmwood crumbled down upon the body of her beloved.

"Si amavano," gushed Venus in admiration, despite herself, deeply moved. *They loved each other.*

"أنا أحلم عن هذا النوع من النار,," sighed Petra, barely able to contain her tears. *I have dreamt of this kind of fire.*

Abraham whirled and fired, point-blank, at Dracula, shouting, "Shoot Dracula! Now!"

Jonathan and Quincy began to pound Dracula with rifle rounds, Morris' Holy-Water-blessed rifle rounds doing the most damage, pushing a defiant Dracula backwards. Renfield roared with outrage, but when he turned to scream, he had given Mina the opportunity and she took it. Mina turned, fired her Derringer into Renfield's twisting shoulder, then planted her crucifix blade deep into his thigh. He released her, doubling over in pain. Now free, Mina coughed heavily from Renfield's grip as she scooped up Arthur's Webley and fired at Dracula. She emptied the Webley then picked up the Winchester that Renfield had dropped and began to fire that.

They were overwhelming Dracula with firepower, blessed firepower and the vampire was weakening. Dracula doubled over, holding his left hand out to block the rounds, which passed right through him, but *with their velocity slowed*. The blows were having effect.

Venus surged forward and was punched back by a round from Mina right into her chest. She gasped in pain, the round squirting out though her body, before retreating back away from Dracula and toward Petra. They watched as their master was pummeled by rifle and pistol rounds.

Dracula sagged, in deep pain from the assault.

Ian held off Venus, Petra and Primus with his crucifix, and Dracula was pelted into a wet, damp corner of the chamber. Van Helsing crept closer with his right arm raised and holding his crucifix stake, ready to plant it into Dracula as the barrage continued.

"Keep it up!" shouted Abraham over the sounds of gunfire.

Round after round beat against Dracula's head and torso, and only a vampire with the strength of the Transylvanian could have survived such an assault.

Dracula was pinned deep into the corner when at last Abraham Van Helsing saw his opening.

He lowered his arm, raised his right, holding the sharpened cross, and charged the Transylvanian.

A battered, exhausted Dracula took in Abraham's charge, turned and threw a tremendous punch with his right fist through the moldy, bricked-up corner wall behind him.

Bricks and piping exploded out of the hole, followed by tons of water, erupting into the chamber, and overwhelming everyone in an instant.

ELEVEN

Black.
Nothing.
No light.
Then a light.
Lights.
From above.
The street above.
From gas and electric streetlights.
And the ebbing day.

Out from a corroded sewer cover came wisps of mist in various shades of grey. The bank of mist slid and coagulated along the wet, cobblestone-lined Paris street with unseen eyes with clear vision, looking around for any possible eyewitnesses. The tentacle of vapor then sculpted itself into a coughing, heaving Venus de' Medici. Stray tendrils became fingers clawing along the ground, writhing in agony. Her skin smoldered, patches of skin all over her body hissing from the heat of the contact with the water. She tried to stand but staggered, then fell onto the cobblestones, her ribs expanding and contracting as she fought the searing effects of the water. Venus was still wet from the flooding, and her skin burnt and dried and peeled and died and flew away like sunburnt human skin, the effects of exposure to the water. Venus' clothes, whose fabric remained magical as long as she wore them, began to dry out, and as she lay, she gathered herself and looked around the empty street out of concern not for her master, but rather her sister.

The darkened street brooded around her.

Venus breathed and heaved unsteadily as another column of mist rose out of the sewer cover, slower than Venus' was, and with convulsions and twitching and painful knots in its vaporous form, until the column became the burnt, exhausted form of Petra Ali, laying out on the ground in such pain that she clenched her teeth and growled until it started to pass.

Both women took a few moments in the darkness to recover. Their hands found each other and intertwined. Petra's eyes found Venus' and they smiled at each other, even through the boiling water that was still covering them with agony. Venus had the worst of it, Petra saw.

"أختي الجميلة!" whispered Petra as she stroked Venus' forehead with her free hand. *Sister! My beautiful sister!*

Venus struggled to speak, but Petra shushed her with pursed lips and looks of concern. "بقية، وشفاء نفسك. وسوف يسهر على كل." *Rest, heal yourself. I will watch over you.*

Venus moaned in pain and her eyes filled with tears as she whispered/cried, "Andromeda! lei è andata, la nostra bella principessa greca. è colpa mia." *She is gone, our beautiful Greek princess. The fault is mine.*

Venus lay on the street, Petra holding her hand, they both cried to and with each other. Petra clasped her other hand over Venus' and said, "ديان أن أي أنا خذي عناية من بعض الـبعض. انت تسلـتـحدك، الشـقيقة." *We must take care of each other. You are not alone, sister.*

Venus nodded through her tears as she said, "Aiutami a miei piedi. Egli mi ucciderebbe se mi ha visto in uno stato di indebolimento." *Help me to my feet. He would kill me if he saw me in a weakened state.*

"إن كان على قيد الحياة," said Petra, as she threw an arm around Venus and pulled them both up. *If he survived.*

Both of them having recovered, they watched one last tentacle of black mist etch its way out from the rim of the sewer cover and begin to slither toward them.

Standing straight, now completely recovered, Venus took in the black mist and sighed, "Sopravvive sempre." *He always survives.*

As the mist drifted in their direction, it also convulsed in pain, twitching and dragging as it moved along. The form was somehow a combination of mist and flesh, which smoked from the various burns that eminated from the main body as it grew eight or nine hands of different size and zoological species, and those hands, whether they were clawed like animal or ended in fingers like humans, dug its nails into the street as it pulled the weight of its mass along. Along the melting anatomy somehow grew a strange vertabrae, and along the back formed agonizing faces; bat-like, humanesque, wolf-like and physiology from a rat, all into a disgusting stew of animal and human anatomy.

A mouth grew at the front of the body, and the mouth grew misshapen teeth that combined molar and canine, fang and human tooth, It roared in pain, echoing along the lonely street, daring any citizen of the City of Light to leave their home and investigate. The mouth heaved and vomited, nearly upon the women, then it lay on the ground in a state of pain and exhaustion, until finally it began to form back into the anatomy of a human, the smoke still seeping from along the body, until at last Dracula of Transylvania was reformed.

He stood, finally.

Dracula looked tired, in pain, and his skin peeled and fell from his face, as he looked at them with an expression of absolute exhaustion.

A dark, deep laugh rang out behind them.

Hefting up the heavy sewer cover was Renfield, giggling maniacally as the still-surging water sloshed around just below him. He has completely drenched and he swept back his greasy black shock of hair as he squeezed out of the sewer opening, so large a man that he was almost too large to get out.

"They've gotta be drowned, Master," said the massive man to Dracula. "I could go down and search for them, put a knife into their corpses and cut 'em up a bit if that would help, especially that Mina. Rearrange her loins and play with her body a smidge."

Dracula nodded in deep satisfaction even as he waved off Montague's request. Then Dracula looked back over and saw Petra and Venus both staring at him, and he was struck by the way the two women took him in, full of intensity after having transformed into their bat form once more, their large raptor eyes glowing in the dark, and for a moment Dracula did not understand the emotion and intonation that was behind the way they were looking at him.

After a blink, their emotions became clear to him.

Dracula had grown accustomed to the hate that was cast upon him for ravaging most of the cultures of the world, but the raw emotion that the two remaining brides were giving him surprised Dracula of Transylvania, for what the vampiresses were projecting at him was nothing short of absolute contempt.

Dracula could not have cared less, and the brides knew it. He turned to Renfield, who was helping the soggy-boned Primus out of the sewer, and barked, "Both of you, retrieve the coffins, bring them to the *Arc De Triomphe* and wait for us there. We must gather ouselves before journeying to Rome."

As he spoke, the rat legion followed Primus and crawled out through the open hole in waves, having endured the flood in the manner with which rats usually survive anything, which is to simply endure. The supernatural vermin crawled over their master in waves, over his clothes, arms, legs and face. The clawed feet clambering over his body bothered Dracula not in the least. The vampire only gave a broad, canine-laced grin as he said, "They are not to be found, say the rats."

"Essi avere sopravvissuti. Dovremmo eliminare ogni possibilità—" said Venus, who did not hide her scorn. *They may have survived. We should eliminate any possibility—*

"Non sit tempus," snarled the Transylvanian. *There is no time.*

"Nescierunt destinatum. Vom lua concediu de noastră," said Dracula, his patience ebbing after he saw the brides' questioning expressions. *They know not our destination. We will take our leave.*

"Yes, my Master," replied Primus, a sentence echoed a moment later from the lumbering behemoth Renfield.

Dracula then turned back to the twin furies, still gazing at him without the customary fear that he had beaten and instilled in them for years now, and growled, "Follow me, *concubines.*"

Venus and Petra were both livid and looked like they were about to attack Dracula.

He ignored them and began walk along the street, though the vampire limped a bit and had to swivel his shoulders, in pain from the assault in the sewer. As he did, cloth and skin became fur, and once again a magnificent dragon of a bat, Dracula unfurled his gargantuan wings, swept them downward to give him the impetus to soar upwards, toward the dust clouds, the gathering French citizens and the night.

A moment later, enough to give their collective pause weight but not enough to infuriate their master, the Venus and Petra bats followed suit.

The bats soared away, elegant slivers of evil seen only by a few citizens that had run out of their homes to find out what the cause of the sounds from the street were.

Underneath another Paris street and not too far away, surging water and human forms poured out of a large sewer pipeway. Tons of water gushed down into an open channel in a larger tunnel. Arms, legs and torsos splashed head over heels down into the channel, which was without any source of light and therefore darker than midnight. The first was Abraham Van Helsing, and he surfaced in fetid, dank sewer water, coughing violently as he used his fingertips and forearms to cling to an embankment as the rest of the water that had exploded out of the pipe spilled itself out of the ossuary chamber. The tunnel itself was cylindrical with a curved ceiling, about two meters tall, and with cement embankments on either side and countless years of grime covering every inch of it. Van Helsing spat, coughed and as he pulled himself up and out of the water, gagged, spat and shouted, "Who is still alive?"

Echoes, then silence.

Silence.

"Come on then," said Abraham, still coughing. "Anyone?"

More silence.

More darkness.

He worried.

Losing Lucy and Arthur like he just had was horrible enough but having the rest of them drown on his account terrified Abraham to his bones, and Van Helsing was about to yell out into the darkness around him when he heard some splashes and coughs and wretching nearby.

"I am, Uncle Abraham. Filthy but alive. You alright?"

"Yes, Ian. Nothing more than a bruised scalp and a twisted ankle, I should think."

"I'm fine, thanks for askin'," stated the most recognizable drawl in Western Europe.

"Where are you, Quincy?"

"Behind ya, Uncle Abraham. Down a ways, Only thing hurt's my pride, them gettin' away an' all. Mina? Jonny?"

"Jonathan?" cried Mina's voice, upstream from them. "Jonathan!"

"I'm here, Mina. I'm fine. Nearer to you than the others, I think. I'll swim my way over to you."

"Don't," echoed Mina's voice. "Get out of this filth as soon as possible!"

"Aw this ain't filthy," coughed Morris' voice. "There was that one time that we fed the hogs all them chicken parts—"

"Shut *UP* Quincy!" shrieked Mina's voice, intermingled with her efforts to climb out of the channel. "That is the vilest story I've ever heard and I never want it to be repeated again!"

"That story places third on my Vile Ranch Story list," muttered the drawl in the dark, amid his own efforts to clamber out.

"I thank our Lord for your collective survival," sighed Van Helsing, out of the water now.

"Arthur. Lucy," sobbed Ian's voice in the pitch.

"They're gone," said Quincy.

Mina sobbed. Once. Loudly.

As did Jonathan.

Ian wept, openly.

"We can mourn them now," said Abraham, sitting with his elbows draped over his knees and his head down.

As Van Helsing tried to stand, a dark shape charged at him through the gloom and the muck.

It was the silhouette of a livid Jonathan Harker.

Abraham took in the youth's furious body language in an instant and understood it.

Van Helsing stood up straight and planted his feet just wider than his hips.

Abraham swung his hands out and *behind* him and away from Jonathan, clasping his left wrist with his right hand.

Van Helsing made sure his toungue was not in between his teeth and awaited the first blow.

And sighed, expelling his pain and guilt and taking in patience.

He would need it.

The first punch was a roundhouse right, and it found Abraham's left cheek cleanly. Van Helsing took the blow and his first thought was to find contentment in the idea that Jonny had one fine right hand.

"Coward!" roared Jonathan, his accusation echoing through the sewer. "Murderer! He would have lived!"

The left came as an uppercut and found Abraham's neck, just underneath his jawline. Abaham had seen the blow coming but did nothing to block or deflect it. Part of it was patience, the other part guilt.

"You murdered Arthur!" shouted Jonathan as he swung his fists around in twin motions of fury and pain. "What kind of man are you?"

"NO Jonathan! No!" shouted Mina, nearly in Abraham's ear, after she had chased Jonathan down the waterway and stepped in between them, bodily blocking Harker's follow-up right jab.

"Easy Jonny—" hissed Quincy, who had come around from the left, along the water's edge.

"You shot him in cold blood!" raged Jonathan, throwing wild punches, all of them landing on

Abraham's face, neck and head. "He loved you, and you put a bullet in his heart!"

"And in doing so spared him a worse fate," said Abraham as an overhand left found his right temple. His hands remained clasped behind him, his stance innert.

"No mate, this isn't the way!" shouted Ian as he looped his right hand around Jonathan's neck and his left under his armpit. Each of Seward's hands clamped together and he tried to pull Jonathan off Abraham, which was not easy.

"Could ya take a step back, Uncle Abraham?" coughed Quincy as he struggled to push Jonathan off while catching one of Harker's flying eblows along the way.

But Van Helsing did no such thing.

In the dark, in the gloom, in the sewer, he locked eyes with Jonathan as the others finally held his arms in theirs.

Harker's glare found Abraham's. "He might have survived."

Van Helsing held his own stare. "No he would not, nor would the rest of you. He gave his life for us."

Mina's right palm found Jonathan's cheek, and he felt her love and it calmed him somewhat, but he still fumed, "So you would shoot any of us if this happened once more?"

"In a heartbeat," said Abraham flatly, which turned everyone's gaze to him. "Rather than have you become *nosferatu*."

Van Helsing continued, knowing they were hanging on every word. "This is no game, Lad, need I remind all of you once more."

That did it, and they all calmed even more, but Abraham continued, "I would rather any of you kill me instead of suffering or becoming one of their kind, is that clear?"

His arms still locked around Jonathan, Ian Seward gulped.

Nodding grimly, Abraham locked eyes with each of them individually as he said, "If you cannot accept these terms, then perhaps it is best that I resume this present course on my own."

The youths all stood silent, watching him somehow in all that blackness.

They all blinked, considering, and said nothing.

A moment's hesitation was all Van Helsing needed.

"Be well," said Abraham as he turned to walk away.

"NO!" shouted Mina. "We will join you, Uncle."

"Do you accept the stakes and terms?" reiterated Van Helsing before looking each of them in the eye. "This is no churchbell that you shoot at, my Wilhelmina."

"Yes," said Mina Murray with an added nod.

"Yes," said Jonathan.

"Of course," sighed Ian, at last releasing Jonathan.

"Hell yes," winked the Texan.

"Very well then," sighed Van Helsing as he turned and began to make his way down the tunnel. Without looking back, he beckoned them with a 'Come on' gesture.

They trudged along the sewer tunnel behind Van Helsing, who after all that had just happened to have the idea to search his coat pockets for his pipe. Abraham found his pipe, then realized that all of his matches were soaked.

Mina stopped, looked around and said, "We've lost our things."

"I got mine," said Quincy with a silly smirk as he double-checked his Colts.

The Texan's expression changed when Mina wondered, "Where's your rifle?"

They all started to look around for their possessions, both inside the water and out, their eyes further adjusting to the pitch.

Van Helsing felt a hand find his shoulder.

It was Jonathan, a once livid balloon now deflated. And sorrowful. "I'm sorry Uncle Abraham. I was caught up in the moment."

"I know Lad," said Abraham, reaching out and giving Harker a few fatherly pats on the cheek. "This is ghoulish business. I was once as young and headstrong as yourselves. I understand."

"Thanks."

Abraham's right hand went from a pat to a pointed index finger, and he put it squarely against Jonathan's chest as he said, "If I'm ever compromised on this venture, you're to put a round in me. Without hesitation. Is that clear?"

"It is," said Harker, even with the chill that ran through his bones for saying it.

"And anyone else in our party, for that matter, growled Van Helsing in matter-of-fact manner that was somehow fatherly and not intimidating. "Even your beloved."

Abraham threw a look of determination at Mina until she too nodded in affirmation.

"I hope we are clear."

"Crystal," said Ian, trying to slap his coat against the cement to somehow dry it off. "You certainly have a way of coming to the point, Uncle."

"Comes from years of getting my arse handed to me out on the field," muttered Abraham, resigning himself to having to wait to purchase tobacco and matches above ground.

"We got our fancy-pants asses handed to us by the blood drinkers," groused the Texan.

"We took and we gave," shrugged Van Helsing as he searched below his left ribcage for his worn-but-faithful Huckleberry holster and with relief found his Bergmann. "Though it came with a price."

"Artie," sighed Quincy.

"Lucy," gulped Mina.

"And Lucy," reiterated Ian with a quiver of his lips.

"Yes," said Abraham, clasping a gnarled hand onto the young doctor's shoulder. "I know you loved her lad. I'm sorry. She's in a better place. I of all people can understand how you feel."

Ian felt his uncle's pain, and he returned Abraham's pat, feeling a deeper sense of empathy between them.

"We will mourn them all in time when we have finished this. Though I do not regret them, I will carry the weight of my actions with King Arthur with me."

They all looked at Abraham, whose own voice quivered when he said the word *King*.

"Let's retrieve our belongings," sighed Abraham, "and begin the hunt anew."

They all started to scour the tunnel and waterway for their possessions, each of them with tears seeping out of their eyes.

The tunnel echoed with the soft sorrow of people weeping for their loved ones.

TWELVE

Like an absurd combination of hell-spawned winged prehistoric monstrosity and broken kite, the gigantic Dracula bat descended unsteadily toward the massive Arc De Triomphe[214], his sore limbs struggling to maintain control, wings fluttering unsteadily through the night air. The Dracula bat was silhouetted by the lights from countless carriages making their way around the expansive archway, even at this time of night. Dropping through the sky, his wings swayed ungainly, like an airplane struggling to level before landing. Still feeling the effects of the assault of his attackers, Dracula's left wing folded up in pain, and the vampire landed hard, staggered, and crumpled to the top of the arch in an undignified crash landing. After a moment of lying still like an injured athlete on the football pitch, the Dracula bat collected itself and raised its shaggy mammalian head, fangs bared in case he was attacked. With labored breathing, the creature then rose to its feet as it transformed back into Dracula's human form. He looked even more worn and haggard than he had when he left the sewer. Vanity took over in a ridiculous moment, and the monster who almost conquered Europe at one point in his existence glanced around like a school child, hoping that no one had seen him tumble.

Behind Dracula landed the Petra and Venus bats, gracefully and lighter than demonic angels on snow. They had seen Dracula's crash landing and looked at each other with as much glee as two massive vampire bats could muster. If they were both schoolgirls, Venus and Petra would have laughed out loud.

The sounds and lights of the city below them blinked, honked and buzzed.

As she transformed, Venus stepped forward, becoming a biped, simmering bat eyes becoming livid human eyes, and those cat-shaped eyes were boring a hole right through Dracula's back; she was still livid at her sister's death.

Venus strode right to him as she shouted, "Andromeda è morto per te! Non ti lutto lei? Lei ti servito fedelmente— *"Andromeda died for you! Do you not mourn her? She served you loyally—"*

Dracula whirled and gave Venus such a vicious punch to the face with his right fist that if not for the parapet wall around the top of the monument, she might have fallen to the ground below. De' Medici recovered, glaring at Dracula as she helped herself up. Blood ran down out of Venus' mouth, her own. She wiped it away, her glare refusing to wither in the face of Dracula's fury. Spent though he was, the Transylvanian was still an imposing presence.

But the women were too livid to care.

Petra, still in the form of a bat, instantly rushed at Dracula in Venus' defense, such was her rage. The Egyptian let out a single, unrestrained roar as she opened her wings and claws at the vampire as she flew across the rooftop. Worn as he was from the encounter in the sewers, the vampire nonetheless grinned serenely at her audacity, side-stepped her attack as his left hand snaked in like a blur to wrap itself like a vice around her throat.

---

[214] The *Arc de Triomphe de l'Ètoile* (Triumphal Arch of the Star) is an internationally reknowned monument in Paris. It honors soldiers that fought and died for France in the French Revolution and Napoleonic Wars. Construction, in the Neoclassical style, began in 1806 and was completed in 1836.

"Ausus es!" roared the vampire as he raised the Petra bat bodily off the rooftop. *You dare?* Their challenge had stirred his inner fire. Her wings flailed in vain, clawing at Dracula's clamp of a hand, which seemed more interested in pulling her throat out instead of strangling her. Petra flailed even more, her wings becoming human arms in the process.

He turned to see Venus, who was sprinting toward him as she yelled, "Dimittam eam!" *Release her!*

"Ataca pe mine! Aceasta este ocazia dvs!" shouted the Transylvanian, boring a hole through Venus with his incandescent eyes while he choked the supernatural life out of Petra, whose flailings were lessening as Dracula's pressure was growing. *Attack me! This is your opportunity!*

Venus pounded to a stop, her dress swirling around her, but Venus' hate for Dracula could have engulfed all of France. She snarled at this beast of a man in front of her. Venus' eyes darted up in sympathy to her sister and confidant, then back down to Dracula in silent supplication.

Dracula smiled. "Rogo tunc. Vitae enim suae. Rogo mihi, *Cipriota*!" *Beg then. For her life. Beg me, Cyprian!*

Eyes blazing with hate, Venus hissed, "Supplico, il mio Maestro." *I beg, my Master.*

Dracula spoke fire right back at Venus and snarled, "Numquid non est terminum contemnant? Super pectus tuum genua!" *Is there no end to your disrespect? On thy knees!*

"Supplico della sua vita, il mio Maestro!" said Venus, dropping to one knee and lowering her head. *I beg for her life, my Master!*

He whirled and threw Petra across the rooftop and on top of Venus, the two colliding with vicious force. They both rolled to an intertwined stop before they cast eternal hatred at their master. Dracula glanced over them with disgust before he hissed, "Avrei avuto più rispetto per te se tu fossi morto cercando di uccidermi." *I would have had more respect for you if you had died trying to kill me.*

"And I would have more respect for you if you had not retreated from the human, Van Helsing," said Venus in plain English as she stood, helping Petra to her feet as well.

As her eyes glowed macabrely, Petra giggled at him in the manner which a woman humiliates a man.

It worked.

Dracula's eyes grew large with rage.

"عجارت," repeated Petra, mocking. *Retreated.*

A river of fury poured over Dracula's face; he was embarrassed and exhausted.

Dracula snarled, stomped over and spat at their faces before he roared, "Whores! The both of you! Not queens, countesses or duchesses, but whores! You are to do my bidding as the servant wenches you are, in silence and at every beck and call!"

Appalled, the women were nearly moved to tears as they cleaned the spittle off their faces.

They were all silent, fuming at each other.

The women absolutely *seethed* at Dracula.

For a long, weighted moment, they threw hate at each other.

Many tides, many nights, many mistakes and many histories had led to this moment.

Venus began to shout, "Andromeda non meritare—" *Andromeda did not deserve—*

Dracula waved her off. "Eu decid ce voi toti merita, prostituată, și că ea greacă-porc merita nimic, dar praful de sub cadavru ea! Siete entrambi i miei servi, non i miei spose! Ego solum unam uxorem habuerunt, et quicquid est in anima præ aeternumque adytis effert animae patris mei pabula odio." *I decide what all of you deserve, prostitute, and that Greek she-pig deserved nothing but the dust under her corpse! You are both my servants, not my brides! I have had only one wife and whatever was in her soul is the nourishment for my father's undying hate.*

"Allora perché Lei chiede a noi di vendicarla?" spat a livid Venus as she clenched her fists and stood straight. *Then why do you ask us to avenge her?*

Dracula gave them a long, incredulous look, then a single, wicked laugh before he grinned at them like an open wound and said, "Vindicabo illam? Eam? Uxor mea? Profecto utrumque intellectum petrarum. Hoc semel, eo stupidiores equos arare ambo, mihi exponam tibi. Huc tu *mihi* ulcisci auxilium. Non *eam*. Eu am fost cel care a fost insultat când acei soldaţi idioţi cumva ea terminat." *Avenge her? Her? My wife? Truly you both have the intellect of rocks. This once, because you are both more stupid than plow horses, I shall explain myself to you. You are here to help avenge* me. *Not her. It was I who was insulted when those idiot soldiers somehow finished her.*

Venus snarled, her contempt growing. "Allora non avete fare questo per il suo amore?" *Then you do not do this for her love?*

"Dragoste?" chuckled Dracula. "Venus de'Medici, de Medici căzuţi, cu siguranţă ştii cu cine te culci într-un sicriu? Nu există nici o dragoste în mine. Nu există decât răutate în sufletul meu, şi am poftească numai pentru mai multă putere." *Love? Venus de' Medici, of the fallen Medicis, surely you know with whom you lie in a coffin? There is no love in me. There is only malice in my soul, and I only lust for more power.*

The two brides stood there, in shocked silence.

Broken hearts broke even further.

Dracula continued, "Oricine ar putea jigneşti vreodată de mine, sau de a lua de la mine un obiect pe care am deţin, cum ar fi noblem woman care a fost soţia mea, va fi zdrobit sub pentru picioarele mele, cum ar fi paraziţii care le sunt." *Anyone who could ever disrespect me, or take from me an object that I possess, such as the noblewoman that was my wife, will be crushed beneath my feet like the vermin that they are.*

Venus cried as she shouted, "Allora perché mi rubare da la mia famiglia! O Petra da lei vita e di amore in Egitto? Perché non ci date avere bambini? Perché se tu non hai ci amano? *Then why steal me from my family! Or Petra from her life and love in Egypt? Why do you not let us bear children? Why if you did not love us?*

"Pentru că a fost plăcerea mea să facă acest lucru," sniffed Dracula, uncaring. "Şi nu veţi mai avea copii, cu atât mai puţin de la mine, fost încă dacă aibă vreodată fruct de pe un bărbat umane atunci te voi ucide, că copilul, amantul tău şi întreaga sa familială. Nu va exista niciodată iubi în mine, şi nu va exista niciodată un copilul în oricare dintre aţi." *Because it was my pleasure to do so. And you will never bear children, least of all from me, yet if you ever bear fruit from a human man, then I will kill you, that child, your lover and his entire family. There will never be love in me, and there will never be a child in either of you.*

Dracula leered as he pointed to them, and to his feet. "Es utraque iam sit canibus." *You are both my dogs.*

He spread his arms wide and grandiose, mocking them as he laughed, "Vel potius Ego sum canis es canicula." *Or rather, I am your dog, and you are my bitches.*

Dracula casually stepped to the edge of the parapet, looked down, then back at them, his eyes aglow with the hate that he had given them. "Renfield habet eduxit coffins quasi pius retardare. Sit nobis relinque Romam. Ibi indignatio mea germinabunt." *Renfield has fetched the coffins like a dutiful retard. Let us take our leave to Rome. There, my wrath will flourish.*

Petra was in tears, "كناخ دق تمت امور يف يف عيمجلا نأ ضرتفت نأ كنكمي فـيك كنأ؟" *How do you presume that everyone in Rome has betrayed you?*

"Concubine mele murdare," sighed Dracula, pretending to be weary of the conversation when he relished crushing the brides' spirits once more. "Nu-mi pasă sau nevoie de a investiga. Tot ce trebuie să faceți în Roma este reafirmă că am pronunțe absolut. Eu am fost neglijent pe parcursul acestei materia țin de asasinarea soției mele, dar acum că materia a fost soluționat, asa ca acum diplomații, avocații și toți ceilalți vor muri, astfel să pot prospere." *My dirty concubines, I do not care or need to investigate. All I need to do in Rome is reaffirm that I rule absolute. I have been negligent during this matter pertaining to my wife's murder, but now that matter has been settled, so now the diplomats, lawyers and everyone else will die so that I may thrive.*

Venus gathered herself, shook away the tears that threatened to run down her face, and said, "Richiedo che il mio Maestro mi licenziamento. E 'chiaro che io non soddisfano." *I request that my Master dismiss me. It is clear that I do not satisfy.*

Petra nodded in agreement. "نتمنى ان في جرفـي اهنع من استعباد، لأن خادمة هو كل انأو رأيت ان يكون. باسم عفـل" *As do I. We wish to be released from servitude, since a servant is all I am seen to be.*

"Optime," said a solemn Dracula with a returning nod. "Tu mihi servitute liberum. Scribam ad legisperitos in utraque et ripae Cairo Florentia. Dotem mercedes suas propere cessabit huiusce aetatis." *Very well. You are both free from my servitude. I shall write to the lawyers and banks in both Cairo and Florence. The dowry payments to your respective families will cease as of this moment.*

The two women's eyes went wide with shock. Venus shouted, "Questi termini devono essere negoziati! Lo sai le nostre famiglie dipendono dal reddito—" *Those terms must be negotiated! You know our families depend upon the income—*

Taking in a huge breath, Dracula of Transylvania laughed out loud in the faces of the women before him and shouted, "Fortium domus Medici! Ali est dynastia! Utrumque reducitur ad mendicans in platearum occidendus sum Sciebas quod ego pacisci." *The mighty House of Medici! The Ali Dynasty! Both reduced to begging in the streets! Surely you know that I do not negotiate.*

Both Venus and Petra stood there, hating him, knowing they had no choice.

He stepped closer to them and hissed with satisfaction, "Id quod vobis meretur propter quae dimitterem temperare viro qui similis mei finis." *This is what you deserve for letting a man like me control your fate.*

"Vos nobis abduxerunt!" shrieked Venus. "Scripsit familiis nostris arbitretur quod vos occideres nos, tunc tractaverunt nostris dotes magnam quaerunt! Habuerimus non electio!" *You kidnapped us, wrote our families that you would kill us, then negotiated our dowries! We had no choice!*

"Veniet," said Dracula. "Ego non quaeritur iterum." *Come. I will not ask again.*

With that, Dracula turned, became the grand bat he was, and flew down, wings once again steady, toward the waiting Renfield, who already had Lucy's old coffin open for him. Inside the coffin lay a disheveled woman who had seen too many nights on the wrong streets of Paris.

She had been eviscerated.

Renfield gave Dracula a conspiratorial leer. "Feast for your journey, Master. Found her on Rue Saint-Denis, Sir. I was chuffed to do it."

"So long as your activities do not reveal any of mine, you may do as you will, Renfield."

"Thank you, Master."

"The moment you are revealed, I will rip you to pieces."

"Understood, Master."

Before they transformed to fly down, Venus and Petra exchanged a look that combined resignation, anger and conspiracy.

"Era debole dopo la battaglia con Van Helsing," noted Venus before she began to change. *He was weak after the battle with Van Helsing.*

"بنعم، ويمكن ان طير بصعوبة," agreed Petra. *Yes, and could barely fly.*

A new understanding flashed between the two women.

Perhaps not new.

A new realization perhaps.

A page had been turned.

Or had been turned for a long time, and only now completely accepted.

A wound that would never be healed.

Cold hearts that had fluttered with love, now even colder.

Bats again, they then flew down to him.

The Paris night lights blinked, somehow thankful that the vampires would be leaving.

Meanwhile, as he pried open a sewer cover, Abraham Van Helsing rumbled, "Finish your tears and leave them here. We are going to find a bathhouse to clean ourselves up, then make our way to Rome so we can plant a wooden stake through Dracula's cold, dead heart."

FROM THE JOURNAL OF MONTAGUE RHODES RENFIELD

In the span of a few days, weeks or months since I have been 'reborn' at the hands of my Master, my life has taken on new meaning, the likes of which I never knew in all the years before, especially in my time of incarceration at the hands of the people I thought I knew as my family. And I am not referring to me mum or dad, but the men I thought were my brothers and fellow soldiers. Yet now I am a servant of the Master, who is taking me 'round the world with him, for reasons of kindness I know not.

Our journey from Paris to Rome was not an easy one, especially since the Master demanded that we avoid the traditional route to the southern coast of France, then by sea to Venice. Before we left Paris I had the unpleasant duty to procure a large box for old Primus, a jolly though morbid fellow, and I sent him and his lads ahead through Post back to the Master's castle. Instead of the sea, we made way by land, using the railways when we could, but also using the roads, both rural and main. The Master seems tired these days, taking a stretch to recuperate after the injuries given to him by Van Helsing and co., my former family. My Master told me that a journal was useless and might even lead to our capture, but my life is not meant to be long regardless, and I will soon be in the presence of the Unholy father himself, whom has blessed me far more than the lying God who only had me suffer through a miserable life, and I can serve my Master's father eternally as I serve his son.

After the row we had with my former brother Abraham in the French sewers, I am glad they are all dead, even the luscious children that he had fooled into service, but I will miss Abraham Van Helsing the most, he who was me mate through me troubled childhood. But even Bram betrayed me, conspiring with the others to incarcerate me after my temporary cleaning of the filthy Whitechapel streets. The travel has been difficult for me, since I am the one who must care for the coffins and find suitable meals for the Master and his two concubines.

It was when we were on a lonely road leaving France that I managed to overwhelm a tollbooth guard for the three to feast upon, though I had the sad duty of burying the dismembered corpse afterward, which was unfortunately partially consumed, such was their appetites after a few evenings without a meal. I pride myself in being able to approach stray children, or children leaving their jobs at factories near dusk, which Venus de' Medici in particular seems to delight in feasting upon. Petra Ali prefers young men and women, particularly young lovers which she happens upon during moments of their indescretion. She tells me that at times the couples resist in a forceful way, which the concubine handles with equal force. She broke the neck of one of the young men who nearly escaped her. She drank from him in bat form, atop a barn as we waited. The rats stay in their coffin until they are so starved that they begin to consume each other, and at that point the Master releases them, and they are a formidable sight to see, moving in waves toward any horse, dog, cat or infant. They also eat from forest animals, deer, even wolves. They prefer to gnaw down to the bones. The Master himself usually prefers to do his own hunting, bursting out of his coffin with force and disappearing over the horizon, usually along one of the toll roads that he prefers taking these days. I myself am only able to eat sporadically, at times the Master gives me gold with which to purchase eggs or vegetables from a farmer, which I then cook at my leisure, my campfire careful not to bother either the Master or his women. Their kind are averse to fire, and water, and relics of holiness, which confuses me as to the order of things if I ponder enough. If the Master's father is all-powerful, why then do they cower in presence of the reliquaries of the enemy? I am but a mere servant and not capable of understanding such matters. I myself am far from perfect, evidenced by my weakness during these times of inconspicuous travel. Medici and Ali, they remain distrustful of me, and one night when they were all away I found a woman making her way past the cemetery we were sleeping in, and I managed to slip away and judge her to be the whore she was and I did what every good man would do and rid the world of such a harlot. Well, the two concubines found me as I was having my way with her and they admonished me as I washed off the blood in the river as if I were a mere child to be scolded by his nursemaids! I thought to slash them to pieces in their sleep and feed them to pigs in the next farm! The brides keep to themselves these days, more and more managing for themselves, hunting for their own food alone, not disrespecting the Master outwardly, but they seem distant from him now. I at first would find the Master slipping into either of their coffins after they had feasted and before daybreak, but this happens less and less these days. These weeks.

My loneliness is a bit much at times, and I think of taking my own life, but then I am cheered by the Master's good will as he tells me that my time with his father will be at hand when I pass from this world and move from serving the son to serving the father. I only hope that my servitude to the father has been as pleasureable as that of my work for his son. Days seem the same, and I feel the weight of my solitude. I would have loved to have started a family at one point, but I could never trust a woman more than I trusted me Mum.

I had a problem at another tollbooth as we passed into Italy, the guard having the misfortune of insisting, upon inspecting the contents of my wares, only to have the Egyptian sit up abruptly and smile at him sweetly when he opened her coffin. How cunning are these seductresses, the way they use their feminine wiles to maneuver us good, brave Christian men to our doom.

We near Rome, I am weary, and what good fortune we have earned we will put to good use there.

I am told this city is an amazing sight to behold.

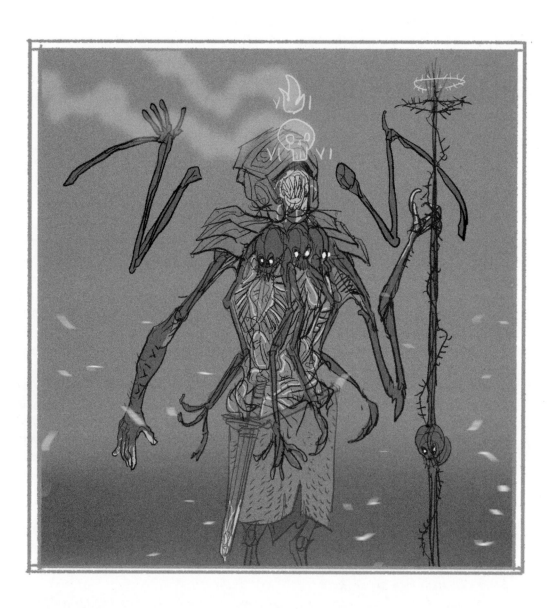

ROME, THE ETERNAL CITY
LATE SUMMER 1899

Veni, vidi, vici.
—*Julius Caesar*

Rome will exist as long as the Colosseum does;
when the Colosseum falls, so will Rome;
when Rome falls, so will the world.
—*The venerable Bede*

From the dome of St. Peter's one can see every notable object in Rome…
He can see a panorama that is varied, extensive, beautiful to the eye,
and more illustrious in history than any other in Europe.
—*Mark Twain*

Rome — the city of visible history,
where the past of a whole hemisphere seems moving in funeral procession
with strange ancestral images and trophies gathered from afar.
—*George Eliot*

Everyone soon or late comes 'round by Rome.
—*Robert Browning*

Rome, Italy in 1899 had a history that was full of life, love and death:

The city that had birthed the Roman Empire, which once stretched across most of the Ancient World, had become the capitol of Italy again only thirty-nine years before when, on July 1, 1871, the capital of Italy was moved there from Florence.

From 1871, the Pope was a self-imposed prisoner of the Vatican as part of the so-called 'Roman Question', the status of the papal office and the Holy See in general during the transition. Italy had reunited twenty years before, and the papal office had attempted to maintain the Vatican's independence throughout. This led to decades of tension between the Italian government and the papal office. All would be settled in February of 1929 when the Holy See and the Kingdom of Italy signed the Lateran Treaty, thereby creating Vatican City. The treaty was signed by Cardinal Secretary of State Pietro Gasparri on behalf of Pope Pius XI, and Axis leader Benito Mussolini, representing the Italian Government. (Mussolini, born in the southern Italian town of Predappio, was a sixteen-year-old boarding school student in 1899.)

Vatican City would become the smallest country in the world.

Fifteen years later in 1914, Cardinal Basillo Pompili, Vicar General of Rome, representing the Pope, publicly denounced the dance known as the tango. "The tango, which has already been condemned by illustrious bishops, and is prohibited even in Protestant countries, must be absolutely prohibited in the seat of the Roman Pontiff, the centre of the Catholic religion."

The Seven Hills of Rome, the area upon which Rome had been originally built, are located east of the Tiber River, forming the geographical heart of the Eternal City. They are The Aventine (*Aventinus*), Caelian (*Cælius*), Capitoline (*Capitolinus*), Esquiline (*Esquilinus*), Palatine (*Palatinus*), Quirinal (*Quirinalis*) and Viminal (*Viminalis*). North of the Tiber and not considered part of the traditional Seven are are the Vatican (*Collis Vatinus*), Pincian (*Mons Pincius*), and the Janiculum (*Ianiculum*).

Ground was broken on the Sistine Chapel in 1473, and was finished in 1481, twenty years before the 'discovery' of the New World.

Saint Peter's Basilica, built upon the site where the apostle Peter was martyred, was refurbished and expanded, with ground breaking in 1506 and completion in 1606.

The longest recorded conflict in human history was between the Romans and Persians, which lasted over seven hundred years, starting in 92 BC.

Guiseppe Fortunino Verdi, composer of operas such as *Requeim*, *Otello* and *Aida*, would only have two more years to live in 1899.

King Umberto I had even less time and would be assassinated in 1900.

Rome is also known as 'Caput Mundi,' coming from Latin and meaning 'capitol of the world'.

Concrete was not a Roman invention but was used on many structures such as the Pantheon, the Colosseum and the Roman Forum, which are still standing today, thanks to the development of Roman cement and concrete. The Romans first began building with concrete over 2,100 years ago and used it throughout the Mediterranean basin in everything from aqueducts and buildings to bridges and monuments.

It is thought that over 500,000 people lost their lives and over a million wild animals were killed throughout the duration of the battles at the Colosseum. The last gladiatorial fights took place in 435 AD.

Julius Caesar introduced the modern 12-month calendar, known as the Julian calendar, in 46 BC. Up to that point Lunar or Arabic calendars had been used.

The abbreviation SPQR can be found on many Roman statues, buildings, and military standards. It stands for "*senatus populusque romanus,*" meaning "The senate and people of Rome."

Rome's population of more than a million was not matched by any other European city until London finally overtook it in the nineteenth century.

Rome's first university, La Sapienza, established in 1303 A.D., is one of the oldest in recorded history and the second largest in the world.

For the Romans, a "circus" was a chariot racetrack, not the tented entertainment venue of today.

There are over two thousand fountains in Rome, over fifty major and hundreds of smaller versions. Perhaps the most famous is the Trevi, which was built in 1762 after Pope Urban VIII found the previous version unsatisfactory.

Most of the over 900 churches in Rome are Roman Catholic.

ONE

A few nights after Renfield's last journal entry, Venus de' Medici and Petra Ali sat comfortably in a private balcony inside Rome's grand *Teatro Costanzi²¹⁵*, watching the finale of *Aida²¹⁶* with Dracula of Transylvania.

The *nosferatu* enjoyed the opera, any opera, and had been eager to take this particular performance in since this specific opera was relatively new. Written by Verdi thirty years before, *Aida* was set in Ancient Egypt and had first played in Cairo in 1871. The opera house itself was relatively new, having opened in 1880. It held three tiers of boxes, just over two thousand seats, all under a lavishly frescoed dome and a gargantuan chandelier.

When they had arrived in Rome three nights before, Renfield and the vampires had all seen the notices posted throughout the streets. Venus and Petra became quite excited at the prospect, as did their master, despite Dracula's failed attempt to suppress his enthusiasm, as was his custom to hide any expression of happiness or contentment. Before that dawn, Renfield had extravagantly bribed the concierge of the Grand Hotel in Rome, which had opened but a few years before. The enormous Englishman then discreetly moved the coffins up one by one to three expansive, adjoining suites. Renfield was then given gold to convert into *Lira*, which he dutifully did the next day through the network of clandestine money exchangers that exist in every city, large or small, in every time throughout history. He then procured the balcony seats for *Aida* by heavily bribing the box office worker at the *teatro*. For two days they rested, leaving only in the night to feed, discreetly slipping into open windows throughout the city, having drunk enough blood to keep the victim alive but not enough to kill or transform them. Discretion was imperative for their arrival in the Eternal City, and for many reasons.

Throughout the centuries, Dracula of Transylvania had acquired an interest in the arts, the only thing for which he could respect humans, and he had frequented concert halls, exhibitions of paintings, publications of works of literature. He was the only person presently 'alive' who could claim to have witnessed performances by, or had met personally, Beethoven, Mozart, Brahms, Bach, Wagner, Mahler, Chopin, Schubert, Handel and Haydn, among others. Dracula knew this and smiled with arrogant satisfaction as he sat at the front of the box, his predatory bird eyes not needing opera glasses as he appreciated the daylight tableau of the spectacular fresco that depicted blue skies, pearl white clouds and pastoral hills. The arts were a way for the vampire to see what he could not, in reality. Artistic depictions of daylight fascinated him endlessly, whether they be by literature, opera or painting. Petra and Venus customarily preferred to be seated behind him, and they thoroughly enjoyed the anticipation of the performance and the cacophony of conversations that flowed up and around them at every

---

²¹⁵ The Teatro Costanzi would not be known as Teatro dell'Opera di Roma until 1946. From 1926 to 1946, it was known as Teatro Reale dell'Opera.
²¹⁶ *Aida* is an Opera in four acts, with the *Libretto* (Italian for little book; text for an opera) written by Antonio Ghislanzoni, and the music by Guiseppe Verdi.

opera house they had ever been to. The two women also relished commenting on the performance as it took place, which annoyed the Transylvanian greatly. This would be the first opera that they would take in without the presence of Andromeda, and the thought of her made deep love ripple through them.

As he had become accustomed to doing, Dracula had his servant, in this case and point in time, Renfield, overpay for the seats in exchange for a 'no questions and no attendants' type of service. There would be no one to attend or interrupt them, or risk being feasted upon if the temptation arose. The vampires preferred discretion in these situations; they did not need the death of a theater attendant to spoil or complicate their enjoyment of the evening.

Indeed, most times the vampires preferred to dine before the opening curtain, but in most cases ended up, like the humans around them, supping after the show. In large cities such as Rome, the vampiresses would, on nights like this, find an orphanage with an open window with which to placate their bloodlust for the evening. Dracula preferred the anonymous prostitute, old couple or lonely widow, whose death would not be investigated vigorously. A discreet bite along the back of the neck could cause the death to be mistaken for a heart attack by the tired or incompetent doctor.

The vampires had arrived just before the performance, riding with Renfield, who drove them in a very handsome carriage, also purchased in gold the morning after their arrival in Rome. They left after sunset and had ridden through the wet, candle-and-gas-lit streets of the Eternal City, Renfield careful to avoid crossing the Tiber and coming anywhere near the Vatican. The moon was huge and luminous, and the city was just coming to life around them. Streets, taverns and restaurants overflowing with people, lights everywhere, with people laughing, yelling, enjoying the night. Once they arrived and disembarked, Dracula whispered some discreet instructions to the massive servant, who sauntered out into the night and to his own ominous affairs. Venus' query as to where Renfield was headed went unanswered, and in the night shadows near the opera, the vampires transformed into bats, flew from the street and landed on the building's rooftop. They then melted into mist to gain entrance to the theater.

The *nosferatu* made their way down the lush hallway and to their private box, then sat in silence as the well-heeled crowd of Rome's elites poured into the opera house, polite crowd noise beginning to reverberate in the air. Dracula in particular enjoyed the orchestra's awakenings, the strings and wind instruments' first expressions of the evening as the musicians warmed up. Though the tension from Paris and before was still palpable between them all, as Venus took in the opulent frescoes above them, she said, "Sia possibile che altri della nostra specie siano qui, e ci potessero essere riconosciuti." *It is possible that others of our kind are here, and we could be recognized.*

Despite their collective enmity, Dracula was in a coy, mysterious and strangely jovial mood as the lights dimmed. "Hac sero foret aliter quam vanitati." *Tonight would be too late for anything other than futility.*

Then the curtains parted.

During the first three acts, Venus and Petra were overwhelmed by the extravagant sets, lush costumes, sumptuous music and powerful vocal performances. As the story crescendoed in the final, fourth act, symphonic harmony swelled from the orchestra pit, revealing that Aida, the Ethiopian Princess, had hidden herself in the underground burial chamber that her love, Captain of the Guard Ramades, had been sealed in. The vampiresses that could devour an infant in seconds now both wept silent tears of enjoyment and irony as they realized that Aida had sacrificed her life to be with the man she loved.

And the soprano playing Aida sang:

Presago il core della tua condanna,
In questa tomba che per te s'apriva
Io penetrai furtiva…
E qui lontana da ogni umano sguardo
Nelle tue braccia desiai morire.

My heart foreboded this, thy dreadful sentence,
And to this tomb that shuts on thee its portal
I crept unseen by mortal.
Here from all where none can behold us,
Clasped in thy arms I resolved to perish.

"La principessa etiope deciso di essere sepolto vivo in modo da essere con lui," sighed Venus. "Lei sarebbe preferito morire con il suo amante." *The Ethiopian princess chose to be buried alive so as to be with him. She would rather die with her lover.*

Amid the heights of the cavernous Egyptian crypt set, an Egyptian Princess named Amneris whose love for Ramades went unrequited, wailed in silence onstage, broken-hearted.

"Amneris, la principessa egiziana, anche lei lo amava!" gushed Petra. "ومثل هذا وسيم المصري! طيب المذاق!" *Amneris, the Egyptian princess, she also loved him! And such a handsome Egyptian! Delicious!*

And the tenor playing Ramades sang to Aida:

Morir! sì pura e bella!
Morir per me d'amore…
Degli anni tuoi nel fiore
Fuggir la vita!
T'avea il cielo per l'amor creata,
Ed io t'uccido per averti amata!
No, non morrai!
Troppo io t'amai!…
Troppo sei bella!

To perish! so pure and lovely!
To die, thine own self dooming,
In all thy beauty blooming,
Fade thus forever!
Thou whom the heav'n only for love created
But to destroy thee was my love then fated!
Ah no! those eyes
So dear I prize
For death are too lovely!

"Il suo sangue deve essere come il modo francese vino utilizzato a piacere!" whispered Venus, and they both giggled like evil, smitten schoolgirls. *His blood must be like how French wine used to taste!*

Aida sang her reply:

Vedi?… di morte l'angelo
Radiante a noi si appressa…
Ne adduce a eterni gaudii
Sovra i suoi vanni d'ôr.
Su noi già il ciel dischiudesi…
Ivi ogni affanno cessa…
Ivi comincia l'estasi
D'un immortale amor.

See'st thou where death in angel guise
With heavenly radiance beaming,
Would waft us to eternal joys
On golden wings above!
See heaven's gates are open wide
Where tears are never streaming,
Where only bliss and joy reside
And never fading love!

Dracula said nothing, sitting straight and regal in his seat and remaining focused on the technical and artistic aspects of the performance; the first chairs in the orchestra, the opulence of the costumes and the quality of the singing in the darkened theatre. Onstage, the entombed lovers overheard dancers and singers representing the temple priestesses.

Aida wept:

Triste canto!…
That sad chanting!

Ramades held her and sang:

Il tripudio
Dei Sacerdoti…

'Tis the sacred dance
Of the Priesthood!

Aida held Ramades and sang:

Il nostro inno di morte…
It is our death chant resounding!

As Venus watched the actors exude agony and tenderness toward each other as the orchestra's music danced with their voices, she marveled, "Il modo in cui tengono a vicenda, cantare una all'altra, anche come morte arriva per loro." *The way that they hold each other, sing to each other, even as death comes for them.*

Rebukes in the form of a few sharp shushes came from older, well-dressed women in the boxes on either side of them, unaware of they were quieting two bloodthirsty romantics.

Ramades stood and tried in vain to move the enormous stone that sealed them in the crypt:

Nè le mie forti braccia
Smuovere ti potranno, o fatal pietra!

Cannot my lustful, strong arms
Move from its place this fatal stone?

"الحب يلتهم حتى الموت!" sighed a moved Petra, placing her hand over her breast, overwhelmed, as her eyes glistened. *Love devours even death!*

Soprano Aida held her arms out for her lover, wailing like a songbird:

Invan!… tutto è finito
Sulla terra per noi…

'Tis vain! All is over
Hope on Earth have we none!

Venus blinked back a few tears herself as she sighed/hissed, "Their love becomes eternal."

Ramades realized their fate, and moved to his beloved's embrace:

È vero! è vero!…
I fear it! I fear it!

In the dark, the two vampiresses' hands found each other and fingers that ripped human hearts apart intertwined in shared enthrallment. Venus' eyes danced with longing. Regret and fire. "Che avrebbero preferito morire l'uno tra le braccia piuttosto che vivere separati." *They would rather die in each other's arms rather than live apart.*

Aida and Ramades collapsed, holding each other in the darkening crypt as they both sang:

O terra, addio; addio valle di pianti…
Sogno di gaudio che in dolor svanì…
A noi si schiude il cielo e l'alme erranti
Volano al raggio dell'eterno dì.

Farewell, O Earth! farewell thou vale of sorrow!
Brief dream of joy condemned to end in woe!
See, brightly opens the sky, an endless morrow
There all unshadowed eternal shall glow!

"ما أتمنى أن يمنحني مثل هذا الحب،" hushed Petra, opera lights dancing over her damp eyes. *What I would give for such a love.*

"Qualsiasi cosa," whispered Venus, shaking her head with affirmation and emotion, "Vorrei dare e fare di tutto." *Anything. I would give and do everything.*

Then, in a stunning black robe of mourning, Amneris, unloved Egyptian Princess reappeared. Touched deeply, Venus and Petra openly wept as the mezzo-soprano playing Amneris sang mournfully:

Pace, t'imploro — salma adorata…
Isi placata — ti schiuda il ciel!

Peace everlasting, lov'd one, mayst thou know
Isis, relenting, greet thee on high!

The stage was enveloped in sudden, final darkness.

An overwhelmed Venus de' Medici covered her mouth with a trembling hand so as to not sob out loud.

The orchestra fell silent, the curtain closed, and the entire *teatro* stood en masse to thunder its approval. Waves of clapping hands poured over the audience like waves at high tide. Shouts of "*Bravissimo!*" and "*Bravi!*" frothed over the applause as the cast came out from behind the curtain to take their bows.

"Brava!" shouted Petra at the soprano as she came on stage stood and applauded, her eyes filled with fire.

"Bravo!" screamed Venus at the tenor, her mouth rippling emotion and her palms thundering together.

Dracula turned and gave them a bewildered glance. They had taken in many such works, and while the brides had always enjoyed them, never had they reacted this strongly before. The Transylvanian then stood and clapped three or four times, slowly, before he clasped his hands behind his back as he stood in solemn contemplation of the outpouring of emotion below him, an enormous silhouette in front of the motion and color of the audience.

Teatro Constanzi shook to its foundation with the roar of the crowd.

Roses and flowers were flung out from the crowd and onto the stage.

Then, without any notice and at the flick of his hand, Dracula pointed at each of the curtains that surrounded their balcony box and slid them shut of their own accord, even as the encore continued.

Venus and Petra stopped clapping and shouted, "Che cosa hai fatto? Stiamo godendo il momento!" and "اظهظحللا هذه عتمتت نحنو ؟تلعف اذام" their anger flaring. *What have you done? We are enjoying the moment!*

"Opus meum fatisque," said Dracula, walking by them and toward the rear of the box, his body already shape-shifting. *My work beckons.*

"È il vostro unico piacere della vita a negare noi la nostra?" snapped Venus. *Is your only pleasure in life to deny us ours?*

Petra cringed and waited for Dracula's rage.

It never came.

He moved by them, his mind elsewhere, as if he had not heard the outburst. The brides had seen that expression and mood drift over Dracula's face many times. His thoughts were focused on another task, yet another adversary. The look of distraction melted away into one of focus. Before he began to shift into bat form, Dracula said, "Nocte est Baccha. Nos adesse festinant tempora." *Tonight is the Bacchanal. We make haste.*

The two vampiresses were stunned and looked to each other, suddenly understanding their reason for being in Rome, the pace of their journey from Paris, and Dracula's plan all in one moment.

As much as the women wanted to enjoy the last moments of the applause and curtain calls, they understood the greater purpose and knew not to question Dracula when such a purpose was revealed. As the shower of applause throbbed at the casts' individual curtain calls, Petra and Venus metamorphosized into giant bats and began to climb the walls of the balcony suite on the way out of the *teatro*. When they reached the top of the box, they all turned to mist and melted through the cracks in the ceiling, drifting through the roof structure of the opera house and materializing on the roof top.

A soft breeze buffeted them, there on the dark rooftop, the sound and vibration from the celebration going on below rippling across the top of the building. Below them were the lights and sounds of Rome on a late summer's eve, bustling with shouts from citizens and the clatter of horseshoes and carriages. Venus and Petra watched the vampire observe the activity below him, a resplendent shadow among shadows, with glowing, vicious eyes that frothed with conspiracy and vengeance.

"Essent congregata ad omnes ad hanc horam," said Dracula with a soft smile. *They would all be gathered at this hour.*

"Che cosa dobbiamo fare, Maestro?" said Venus, who knew better than to distract the Transylvanian when he was this focused. *What are we to do, Master?*

"Mantenete dei celebranti dal lasciare finché non avrò ucciso ogni singolo uno di loro," he said, melting into bat form again, great vampiric wings growing out of his shadowy visage, silhouetted against the Rome city lights, and with a great sweep he was off and up into the night sky. *Keep the celebrants from leaving until I have killed every single one of them.*

The women followed suit, becoming bats again before they spread their wings and flew up and toward the low clouds hanging bulbously just above the city. Somewhat healed from the injuries suffered in the Paris sewers, the son of Satan flew with great purpose. Below them, the city swam by, an impressionist painting of its own as they rose, the sounds of the city dimmed before melting away. In front of them, the Dracula bat soared above the nearest, pillow-like formation and used it for cover, banking to the left, Venus and Petra following dutifully. The great bat gave one short satisfied growl, and the bride bats looked at each other, knowing the the vampire usually expressed such a growl in satisfied anticipation of great bloodshed. Dracula's vast wings buffeted in a sudden warm gale, but then he folded his wings and dropped like a rock through the other end of the cloud. Venus and Petra knew where they were going, and they squinted their eyes as they closed their wings and cut through the cloud as well, and when they came through it, they saw what no one had ever seen up to that point in human history.

Below the female bats and the distant, fluttering wings of the Dracula bat was the view, from the skies, of the Roman Colosseum.

It was alight with torches.

TWO

Dracula did not knife down toward the innards of the Colosseum, but rather veered, twisting his vast wings to bank around the ancient structure, approaching the world-famous building from the northwest and flying around the spectacular outer wall. The vampire torqued his body, still sore from the Van Helsing attack, and turned his thoughts to the spectacular ruins he circled and flew even lower as he reached the east side of the monolithic edifice. Having 'lived' through centuries of war and conquest, Dracula had become a scholar of the art of the battle. He'd read many of the medieval chronicles that involved battles that he had taken part in, and it was with much irony and relish that the vampire could, hundreds of years later, re-read accounts of warfare from both sides of the clashes that he had participated in. This experience both in the battlefield and in subsequent historical research gave him a particular field of expertise in approaching any possible battle or skirmish.

The Colosseum had been built before the end of the first century, within forty years after the life of Christ. The structure could, in its prime, seat upwards of fifty thousand citizens to watch gladiators battle each other, slaves fed to ravenous animals and even naval battles, since the amphitheater was capable of being filled with water for those such occasions. Underneath the arena was a labyrinth of chambers and catacombs, filled with prisons and platforms that could lift combatants up onto the field of battle, or lower their corpses after they had perished or been fed upon.

Now the amphitheater had been abandoned for many centuries since the fall of Ancient Rome, more of a relic than anything else.

Dracula spiraled downward toward rooftops of the neighborhood surrounding the amphitheater in a wide arc and at a dizzying speed, landing deftly along a darkened wall in a darkened street, within sight of one of the wonders of the world[217]. The Venus and Petra bats touched earth behind him as the undead son of all that is evil became man once more. The bride bats became women and stood regally against a brick wall while he watched the ruins.

Nothing moved on the street, no pedestrians, no dogs or cats.

Such was their fortune.

They watched, three pairs of glowing raptor eyes in the shadows.

Petra started, "Abbiamo il vantaggio di aggressori—" *We have the advantage of attack—*

A quick, angry glance from Dracula silenced her.

They waited, in the dark, anticipating.

Lights within the Colosseum flickered eerily.

As they waited, the brides noticed that Dracula's body was relaxed, and not waiting to pounce. He was simply waiting.

In front of them, a lone cat did slide out of the pool of darkness that was one of the rooftop shadows

---

[217] The Colosseum is *not* considered one of the Seven Wonders of the Ancient World. That honor goes to the Great Pyramid of Giza, The Hanging Gardens of Babylon, Colossus of Rhodes, Lighthouse of Alexandria, Temple of Artemis, Statue of Zeus at Olympia, Mausoleum at Halicarnassus. It is considered one of the Seven Wonders of the Modern World, along with The Great Wall of China, Petra, Christ the Redeemer, Machu Picchu, Chichen Itza and the Taj Mahal.

cast down upon the old street stones, and Petra had to resist the impulse to chase it down and eat it.

They watched, eyes aglow.

As did Dracula, a shadow of a man himself, the son of Satan.

A dog barked, blocks away.

A noise.

In the distance.

Sounds of carriage and hooves clattered through the streets.

"Ȋn sfârșit," said Dracula. *At last.*

At that moment, Renfield, driving the wagon they had all taken from Paris to Rome, slowly clattered into view.

The vampires drifted out to the middle of the street, their graceful strides making them appear as if they were gliding across the wet cobblestones.

Dracula reached the wagon and started, "Servant, did you—"

Montague Rhodes Renfield's face, sleeves and coat were soaked in blood. "Just as you said, Master. Right on time."

Renfield's leer was ear to ear, and the only thing on his face not crimson with splatterings of blood. Dracula's eyes danced over the wagon, searching for a corpse, but it was empty, save for one coffin. He glared at the massive man, who grinned back shyly like he had just been caught with candy before dinner.

"One of these nights, when your meanderings cost me, it will be the death of you," said Dracula, point blank. "I remain clear?"

"Master, just a bit of fun—"

"I do not care. Expose us and I would feed you to them," said Dracula pointing behind him toward the brides, whose eyes glinted with anticipation at Renfield. "And they would feed from you while you still kick and scream."

Venus and Petra simply smiled at Renfield like he was a freshly-cured ham.

"If you were a man, we would castrate you," laughed Petra, and Venus joined in her giggle, teasing. "But you are not."

"Dirty tarts," began Renfield, nostrils flaring at the insult, but a single raised hand from Dracula was sufficient to silence them.

"Enough," he nodded at Montague. "I see you accomplished your given task."

Renfield nodded enthusiastically, his Neanderthal head bobbing up and down comedically like a massive puppy. His savage leer was enough to inspire shivers.

Dracula pointed to the shadows behind him.

"Sit. And. Wait." His point was clear. "Be ready to leave at any moment."

Dracula had to add, "And do *nothing* more."

"Of course, Master," said a crestfallen Renfield, who relished being part of any impending bloodshed, and he began to solemnly steer the horses and wagon around the vampires and toward the distant night.

The crowd in the amphitheater roared again. It echoed around the darkened street.

"Dunno how the locals and the bobbies don't hear the ruckus," fussed Renfield as he drifted away, a petulant child with his toy taken from him.

"The authorities have been paid for their silence, and the locals prefer to not be eaten," replied Venus.

A large lick of flame from inside the ruins caught their eyes.

"Pater meus adest," said Dracula to the brides, his eyes flickering with heightened interest. *My father is here.*

THREE

As Renfield guided the wagon toward a darkened end of the street that stared right at the Colosseum, Dracula pointed to the coffin lid, and it rose slightly. Inside were a thousand incandescent red eyes, shrouded by blackness. They squealed, hissed and shrieked with starvation. The lid percolated like an overheated tea kettle, all but whistling.

"Ecredere, et multiplicabo," said Dracula with a dark chuckle. *"Go forth and multiply[218]."*

A fountain of black rats poured, slithered and twitched over the edge of the coffin, off the wagon (which startled the horses momentarily) and onto the old cobblestone street.

They streamed toward the ruins, fleas horribly flicking off their bodies.

They moved wide around the brides but clambered over Dracula's clothes, the Transylvanian twisting his head as a few rodents jumped off his shoulders and back onto the irregular, worn cobblestones below.

Dracula of Transylvania watched the torrent of vermin swarm away from them before he turned to Venus and Petra and said, "Singulis vestrum lato patefecit limite ruinas in sinistrum et dextrum eius, et eradamus vigiliis. Tacete paulisper in situ tuo occisione facendum. Quondam vos consummati tu et me vobiscum coniungam simul ingredi voluerimus Flaviae amphitheatro." *Each of you take a wide path, to the left and right of the ruins, and eradicate any sentries. Be silent in your killing technique. Once you are finished, I will join you and we will enter the Flavian Amphitheater[219] together.*

Venus nodded once, crisply.

Despite her resentment of her master, she enjoyed the adrenaline rush of killing. Petra gave a charming, deadly, canine-filled grin.

With a casual wave of dismissal, Dracula sneered, "Adesse festinant tempora!" *Make haste!*

At his wave, each of the brides began to transform, their red eyes blinking from human to bat shape as they melted and rearranged themselves, and the two brown bats raised their wings and soared off into their appointed directions, just above the street, using the buildings for cover. Nearly synchronized in their movements, they flew in great, wide arcs, rising just above the rooftops, their eyes locked onto the ruins for any hint of movement. Half of the top façade of the Colosseum had been lost, to decay, theft of the stones themselves and the occasional earthquake, so the ruins formed an oddly shaped silhouette against the lights of late summer's Rome.

Venus and Petra soared among and through the crumbling ruins of Palatine Hill[220], which overlooked the Colosseum. The two bats raced to the base of the amphitheater, then split apart,

---

[218] Dracula is mocking the biblical scripture from Genesis 9:7, "Be fruitful and multiply."
[219] Another name for the Colosseum.
[220] Palatine Hill, or *Palatino* in Italian, is part of the Seven Hills of Rome and one of the oldest archeological sites in the city. In the Rome creation myth, Remus and Romulus, two twin brothers were found there by the she-wolf Lupa. Palatine Hill stands near both the *Forum Romanum*, a plaza surrounded by government buildings that was used for public speaking and gladiatorial matches, as well as *Circus Maximus*, the ancient Roman Chariot racing stadium.

Venus flying to the right and Petra the left. Each then sharpened their respective trajectories and swept very low and very fast around the gigantic structure. They could hear the roar of a crowd inside, and flame light tickled the broken tunnels and arches. They flew even lower, within ten feet of the ground, at high speed, their large eyes able to take in everything around them despite their trajectory. Columns and levels were blurs, melting with sheer velocity.

The two huge bats shot past the Colosseum, Venus from the north and Petra from the south, both in silence. Any chirps of communication would be picked up by any other *nosferatu* in the area, and despite Dracula's stealth, the amphitheater was most certainly being guarded. The two female bats banked toward Palatine Hill, with Venus having the longer journey, and they met again atop the Arch of Titus[221], where they landed on the grounds lighter than normal-sized cats. Venus glanced to her left to snarl at the Basilica di Santa Francesca Romana[222] before they looked straight down at the Colosseum in the distance.

They crouched in silence, listening to the crowd.

"Ave Satanas," came a collective moan from inside.

Scarlet eyes blinked, scouring around them for movement.

"Nos protegat, satanam," rumbled the crowd. *Protect us, Satan.*

The hunters watched. Otherwise the grounds, the sky, the city seemed inert.

Then, in the distance, two other huge bats flew in and landed on top of a huge archway near the Colosseum that was nearly parallel to their position. Their silhouettes melted into human form, both female, both younger. The Venus and Petra bats crouched in the dark, watching the two women.

In the inky dark, Petra chirped, "امبر اوناك قد أني ان يطي ريامب." *They might have seen us fly by.*

To which Venus responded, "Avrebbero già allertato gli altri." *They would have already alerted the others.*

Both of them watched the other *nosferatu* women, one in a Kimono, and the other, a blonde-haired woman in clothing from the mid 1700s Spain. Both of their dresses were black, despite opulent lacing and details on each dress. Their hair was elaborate, refined and perfect. Both beautiful, the women turned and their mouths were red with fresh blood. They were in the middle of a conversation yet keeping watch.

That was when the Petra bat noticed two bodies, two men, two human victims laying on the ground below the arch, inert. She gestured with her left wing to the Venus bat, who nodded while she watched the Japanese and Spanish vampires giggle like old friends.

Venus leapt into the air, Petra following. They both drifted in the air for half a football pitch, their eyes never leaving the two *nosferatu* they were hunting.

The Venus and Petra Bats landed ever so gently on Via Sacra. [223]

The cold wide stones that lined the road were nearly as cold as the two predators that coolly crept along them.

Bloodlust began to surge through Petra and Venus.

One of the nosferatu on the arch giggled, "しかし、私はそれらの両方を愛します! *But I love them both!*

Venus and Petra crept along the ground and toward the giant stone arch, like huge cats that had spied mice.

The Spanish vampiress turned to her Japanese counterpart and said, "Así entonces nunca te

---

[221] The Arch of Titus, or *Arco de Tito*, is a triumphal arch built in 82 AD by the Emperor Domitian to honor the life and victories of his brother, the recently deceased Titus.
[222] Basilica di Santa Francesca Romana is also known as Santa Maria Nova, and was constructed in the 10th century.
[223] *Via Sacra*, or Sacred Road, was the main street of Ancient Rome. It begins at Capitoline Hill and ends at the Colosseum. In the fifth century BC, the road was covered by a superstructure, but paved over with colonnades, a row of columns that support a roof, added during the time of Nero (37-68AD).

casarás?" *So, then you will never marry?*

"私は誇り高い女性です," she said, brushing her kimono with her pale, delicate hand. "スレーブではない." *I am a woman, not a possession.*

"Podria tratar," said the European noblewoman, "de pagar lo suficiente a su padre para casarse con usted contra de sus deseos." *He may try to pay your father enough to marry you against your wishes.*

"その後、私は、私たちの結婚式の夜に彼の頭蓋骨を通して私のヘアピンの1を置きます." Then *I would put one of my hairpins through his skull on our wedding night.*

They both giggled as Venus and Petra glided closer, the shadows a blanket over them.

Venus's eyes glinted with anticipation.

The Spaniard licked her lips and said, "Entonces podría casarse con el chico Irlandés que se te antoja tanto!" *Then you could marry the Irish boy you seem to fancy so much!*

"私は決して結婚しません," said the Japanese woman, her kimono fluttering in a sudden, momentary breeze. "彼は短すぎる." *I will never marry. And he is too short.*

The two sentries continued to laugh, talk and occasionally glance around as the Venus bat melted into mist form, which then coagulated and began to move forward on its own. Petra followed suit, and twin tendrils of mist drifted along the ground.

Nearing the Arch of Titus.

More chanting from the amphitheater. The sentries heard the chant and broke off their conversation and looked around, their eyes twin embers, blinking in the night.

The two banks of mist paused.

"El irlandés trató de darle una bebé humano para alimentarse la última vez que lo vimos," whispered the flame-haired vampire as she took one last look around, everywhere but at her feet. *The Irishman tried to give you a human infant to feed upon the last time we saw him.*

Venus and Petra pooled around the hems of their dresses.

"はい、" replied her companion. "キスと引き換えに. 私は彼にそれを与えました—" *Yes, in exchange for a kiss. I gave it to him—*

In a burst of transformation, the pools of mist became human, bolted up and clamped their hands around the sentries' mouths and the back of their heads. With synchronized savage twists, Venus and Petra both whispered, "Cinis cinerrm," and the two female vampires turned to ash in their hands. *Ashes to ashes.*

"Cenere alla cenere,'" quoted Venus, her victim's eyes turning to ash as she looked upon her murderer.

"من تراب إلى تراب," gushed Petra as she wiped her hands clean of hers. *Dust to dust.*

In the distance, still among the street's shadows, Dracula released a thin smile. His vision was so acute that he could see from the street he was hiding in, past the Colosseum and all the way to the massive parallel arch where the Japanese and Spanish *nosferatu* had just been murdered. He could have seen the event from twice the distance. Dracula transformed into the ebony, massive bat once again, and with a glare of warning to Renfield to do as he was instructed, soared out past the monument, flying low, to the reach the brides.

The ashes of the Japanese and Spanish vampiresses cascaded down along the top of this particular arch, which was erected by the Roman Senate in 312 AD. Passing through the arch in ancient times was *Via Triumphalis*, the road by which emperors entered the city in triumph. The archway itself featured one main, large arch, with two smaller arches on each side, and was covered with columns and sculptures depicting Roman life, war and conquest. Nearly seventy feet tall, eighty-five feet wide and twenty-four feet deep, the arch was decorated with artwork taken from other monuments and repurposed for this piece of architecture, as well as work done originally and specifically for this massive tribute. The central archway alone was thirty-eight feet tall, while the two other arches were twenty-four feet tall each. Four columns with Corinthian capitals held up the top portion, or attic, of the archway. Amidst an elaborate inscription, one word stood out among the others, the person whom the entire arch was dedicated:

CONSTANTINO

FOUR

"Protege nos, Domine Satanus, Tuis mysteriis servientes," hissed the shrouded figure with gnarled, outstretched arms. *Protect us, Lord Satan, servants of your mysteries.*

Logs and scraps of wooden beams used to frame houses, ceilings and rooftops in 1899 Rome made up this sacrificial pyre, nearly a thousand years later, and the pile of dead, burning trees cracked and snapped with the heat as the fire roared through it, rained ashes down along the sections of broken floor of the Colosseum.

The history of the *Colosseo* parallels the history of human civilization. There were six elevations of the amphitheater, starting at the bottom with the *hypogeum* which means 'underground' in the word's original Greek. These levels also separated the classes in Roman society. Above was the arena floor, where blood was spilled in the name of sport for centuries. The first seating level above the floor was the *podium*, a level for the political elite of Ancient Rome, the senators and ruling class, or *patrici*, who wore white togas bordered with purple, the most expensive color to create. The toga was a thick wool wrap measuring five or sex meters in length. Above the podium was the *maenianum primum*, which seated the *equites*, or equestrians, the secondary layer of the aristocratic class wearing purple-striped tunics. The level above the *maenianum primum* but below in social order was the *maenianum secundum inum,* the largest section in the arena. Reserved for plebians, or commoners, the wealthier of the Roman common citizenry were seated there, as well as soldiers. Above that, similar in social standing, but with less money, were the *pullati*, who sat in the *maenianum secundum summum*, where those who could not afford expensive togas but wore tunics instead, the poor citizens like freed slaves and the poor of Rome. At the very top of the Colosseum was the *maenianum secundum in legneis*, where women of all classes, as well as slaves and non-citizens, could sit. Above everything was a large canvas awning along the rim that could retract during windy days but be opened to supply shade from the heat.

In 1744 Pope Benedict XIV proclaimed the Colosseum holy ground to prevent any more of the brickwork to be taken from the amphitheater, and also placed Stations of the Cross within the Colosseum, consecrating the structure in commemoration of the Christian victims of the gladiator games.

Tonight, the edges of the levels were lined with black shrouds masquerading as celebratory bunting. Strange candles were everywhere, made of black wax but filled with strange objects like animal skulls, human eyeballs and broken crucifixes. The candles underlit the entire Colosseum.

It was a haunted atmosphere on a haunted night.

On nights such as these, the population of Rome would hear the blasphemous revelry from within the Flavian Amphitheater, but few would investigate, and those that did would never see the light of the next dawn.

During nights like these, the Colosseum belonged to Satan's legions.

This night, the scavenged woodwork was now a pyre, spanning the caved-in openings of the arena floor, the revealed *hypogeum*, hissing as it burned. Long since had the actual floor of the Colosseum collapsed, revealing the hypogeum's labyrinthine network of tunnels and chambers underneath, exposed to the weather and the world. How the actual amphitheater had been able to fill the arena for naval battles was a marvel of planning and engineering in the Ancient World. Now, nearly two thousand years later, huge, deformed black candles smoldered atop five different protruding wall remnants that radiated from the bonfire. Sparks blew and danced out from the bonfire's frenzy, tiny yellow runes in the black, bleak night in a stiff, strange sudden breeze.

In front of the bonfire, tied to a beam with ropes made of thorny branches and ropes, lay a woman, an unfortunate victim of vampiric Rome who was screaming in silence. Her screams could not be heard because of the tied rags that were covering her mouth. In front of her, standing on the crumbling top of one of the arena floor's many support walls was a lone figure draped in an ornate, crinkled, black shroud. Twin pinprick eyes glowed supernaturally under the hood, which was a disgusting quilt of human skin, animal fur, raven feathers, all stitched together over the finest obsidian silk.

Gnarled, bony fingers covered with mottled grey/green skin twitched in a macabre manner as they reached up and pulled the hood back, revealing Flavius Valerius Aurelius Constantinus Augustus.

The despot of old stood very still, like a lizard fearful of discovery, twitching occasionally like a cadaver eager to walk like Lazarus. His desiccated, flaking hands twitched and rubbed against each other in anticipation like mating lizards or dying, plucked birds. No longer the dying tyrant, Constantine was now a living, vampiric skeleton, his head a bald skull covered with familiar symbols that had been seared onto his scalp and face:

VI

VI   VI

Deep, blackened eye sockets were filled with the glowing crimson eyes of a bird of prey. Thin, blackened reptilian lips could not hide outrageous canines and incisors that looked like they could have bitten an angel's head clean off. Constantine's throat was a mass of wrinkled thin lines between his bulbous skull and emaciated body. Veins spread over his face like infinitely delicate cobwebs, blood somehow pulsing below the seared symbols of Satan. A once-mighty beard was now scraggly and spread like desiccated vines from his chin. Gone was the tyrant, the conqueror, the Roman emperor who had helped forge Christianity.

In the distance behind Constantine was an obscene throne built of bone, blood and gold. Fashioned after the curule chair, an x-shaped and collapsible seat in which senators and dignitaries in Ancinet Rome seated themselves, this throne was a complex thing, ornate, with an embroidered cushion, and unlike most chairs of this type, had a back rest, carved out of wood, like a Dante or Savonarola chair. This back rest depicted in its carving the devouring of suffering angels by a ravenous yet pious three-headed dragon. Golden rays of Hell radiated out of the dragon's eyes. The throne sat in the Colosseum's Imperial Box of old, in the middle of the northside's podium. On either side of the throne were oblong black, glowing, evil candles made of wax and the skeletons of children. Ornate weapons racks filled with satanic versions of daggers, spears, shields, pikes and maces stood behind the candles. On the right-hand side of the throne was a thorn-encrusted pedestal. On the pedestal was an upside-down Christian Bible with a cruel, metal spike punched through it.

Behind the weapons rack were three gaunt figures, all draped in endless, opalescent shrouds. The shrouds on these deacons were all encompassing, save the upside-down crimson crosses emblazoned down their torsos. Upon closer inspection, the upside-down crosses were made up of embroidered, tiny demons from the Dark Ages. The shrouds themselves were covered with barely distinguishable patterns as well, as much filigree as a rococo sculpture or pattern, but the ornamentations were lacings that combined skulls and crucifixes with the Christ in an upside-down pose. The only openings in the shrouds were to show the mouths, which were swollen purple lips that hung half-open in an effort to hold back mouthfuls of jagged, vicious canines that dripped unclean blood. The figure in the middle was a particularly gaunt and horrific being. It held a round, black pillow embroidered with elegant scenes of Satanic worship with taloned, infected hands that were meant for ripping the innards out of sacrificial victims and other *nosferatu* alike.

On the pillow was the most jagged, disgusting knife ever created. The ornate handle was made out of a human baby's mummified arm, the hand grasping a black pearl, while the shoulder socket intertwined with a wooden handle that depicted the vomiting of Satan upon the cross. The blade itself was black, jagged and twisted beyond human design and recognition, and it was made of different, horrific substances; melted iron with decapitated angels engraved onto the surface, as well as obsidian thorns that protruded out from each side of the insane, blasphemous blade. The knife edge was laced with blood, Holy Water, demonic urine and human excrement.

Behind all of this fluttered twin, long, black, silk banners that had languid, long, red upside-down crucifixes woven into the fabric. The night sang to the banners, and flattered, they serenaded the night back.

Bacchanal Vampirica, in the Colosseum.

The so-long-ago emperor's clawed right hand extended up, out and over the crowd of perverse spectators as he shouted, "Ego vos benedictio in Nomine Magni Dei Nostri Satanus." *I bless you all in the name of our great god, Satan!*

An insane roar bellowed forth from the crowd of vampires: small, large, tall short, thin, old, young, child, adult, aged, African, Asian, Indian, European, healthy, diseased. They all crammed among the ruins of the ancient grandstands, tens of thousands of glowing eyes in the darkness. Among them sat the resplendent, horrific Unholy Mother.

"Ave Satanus!" screamed Constantine.

"Ave Satanus!" shrieked the things of the night.

The Colosseum shook with the roar of collective malevolence.

"Silentium!" bellowed Constantine, and silence slit the throat of the crowd. After a moment engorged with insane stillness, the emperor then raised his arms and shouted in an eerie, sing-songy way, "Placeat tibi, Domine Satanus, obsequium servitutis meae, et praesta ut sacrificuum quod occulis Tuae majestatis obtuli, tibi sit acceptable, mihique et omnibus pro quibus illud obtuli." *May the homage of my service be pleasing unto you, Lord Satan, and grant that the sacrifice I have offered in the sight of Your majesty may be acceptable to you and win forgiveness for me and for all those for whom I have offered it.*

The middle deacon stepped forward and proffered the obscene sacrificial knife, and the old tyrant took it into his broken-knuckled, gnarled hand. As the crowd bellowed again amidst the haunting, candle-lit Colosseum, Constantine glided forward from his perch along the podium and toward the victim, with an eerie, staggering gait, as if he were walking backwards instead of moving forward. Constantine quivered with age and oddity as he pointed the knife at the woman. The victim saw this and she burst into deep, sobbing tears. She was in terror as the vampiric old conqueror neared her, his arm raising the black, unholy blade over his bulbous, misshapen head.

"Nos hic in commutationem pro anima, a facie tua, Domine Satanus," hissed Constantine from the depths of his bleak garment, his scarlet eyes glowing with bloodlust. *We exchange this soul for your presence, Lord Satan!*

Black night then rushed, poured into the amphitheater. The night poured into the fire, which fizzled down to a few embers. The macabre crowd whispered in fear and anticipation. For a moment there was nothing.

No sounds save the victim whimpering.

Then the bonfire then exploded back to life in a wave of sound and fury. The flames boiled into a vast inferno that threatened to turn the ancient edifice to cinders. Two twin hooks rose from the rippling heat, followed by two gargantuan wings that slowly spread out like manifestations of all that ails the world. Sulfurous stench streamed out from the wings, and some of the vampires were overcome with nausea. Others fell to their knees or became completely prostrate in silent, malevolent prayer. Trembling like a newborn calf, the sacrificial victim continued to scream, simply and completely overwhelmed.

The massive, jagged head with three sets of horns that changed shape from goat to antelope to bull to kudu and back to goat raised itself out of the inferno. Twin sets of eyes blinked as the head turned slowly, looking over its zealots. Ragged breath raced in and out of multiple nostrils, infernal smoke stacks. A mouth filled with countless obscenities and glowing, dripping lava-like blood snarled at the vampiric crowd and they all shrank from his visage.

Silence overwhelmed everyone.

"Ego solacium omnis mali, I sum filius perditonis, donum esset vanitas," purred the voice of a thousand lions. *I am the comfort of all evil, the son of perdition, the gift of vanity.*

The crowd trembled. Some burst into tears and backed away. Others threw their arms out in adoration. The beast rose from within the fire, and the daemon of all demons floated before them all, engorged with their worship.

Constantine shrieked, "Pater Satanae qui tibi offerunt hoc sacrificium—" *Father Satan, we offer you this sacrifice—*

Satan pivoted and shot melted fire out of his maw, fire that became a tongue of magma that engulfed the poor woman. The flaming appendage wrapped around the body and pulled it and the victim back into the prodigious, disgusting mouth, which slammed shut with bile and hiss. His lips dripping with magma and blood, Satan turned to the vampires, roared like a hundred beasts and shouted, "Ego consolator peccatorum, innocentium seductor, magister fraude, intentator Christus! Sum et scelesti patris!" *I am the comforter of sins, the seducer of the innocent, the teacher of treachery, tempter of the Christ! I am your unholy father!*

Once again, his taloned hand produced a whip from a belt of skulls over stretched-out human skin, and the hundred-tails whip lashed out over the prostrated crowd. A few vampires were instantly decapitated, disemboweled or cut in half by the lashings before they disintegrated to ash. The vampires that survived the lashings screamed with agonized ecstasy.

"Ego Samnu!" roared Satan as he continued to whip them. *I am Samnu!*

"Ave Satanus!" shouted Constantine.

"Cultus nullum aliud!" bellowed the monster. *Worship no other!*

"Ave Satanus!" shouted the crowd, in a bleeding frenzy.

"Ego Marduk Babylonis, primum angelum perspiciunt lapsum, Moloch, Hades Graeciae, tentator Christi, qui accusaverant Danielem ad unum et insipientes inconpositos sine Mephistopheles!" *I am Marduk of Babylon, Moloch, Hades of Greece, Tempter of the Christ, the Accused One and your merciful Mephistopheles!*

Sobs and wails were suppressed.

Satan's bellowing laughter shook the ruins around him. He whirled to Constantine, leaned toward him and snarled, "Mihi vos vocant in ordine ad finem, Peccator de Peccatorum! Loquere, Constantinus olim Byzantium, Primo Vampire, et dlator Christianitati!" *You beckon me for a purpose, Sinner of Sinners! Speak, Constantine of old Byzantium, First Vampire and Denouncer of Christianity!*

Constantine nearly gagged, his throat empty of bile but full of fear. He took in the hideous, massive form in front of him and gathered the vigor and belief to say, "Magister, volumus ut dem vobis congregabo adulationibus attollitur—" *Master, we gather to give you adulation—*

"Subdola canis ego sum primus, mendax est," reminded the massive shadow. *Sly dog, I am the First Liar.*

"Sic Dominus meus," whispered the vampiric emperor. *Yes, my Master.*

After a long growl full of thought, Satan said, "Quantum ad actionibus filium meum Explica, Hypocrita." *Explain your actions with regard to my son, Hypocrite.*

As Constantine struggled with an answer, Satan added with a rumble, "Mentiri mecum et ipse lotus meo malitia sua." *Lie to me and bathe in my malice.*

The shrouded, old tyrant trembled in fear, but ever the diplomat, ever the emperor, ever the politician, Constantine composed himself before he lowered his head in respect and said, "Morte sua necessaria esset. Vos semper firmae voluntatis egredietur praedicamus. Quidam erat novam eget vocem. Ille tecum vivit et si non propter hoc planum existential." *His death was a necessity. You always preach that the strong will out. There was a need for a new voice. He lives on with you, even if it is not on this plane of existence.*

"Fili mi tuus non sit mecum in inferno foeda et caduca imperatorem," said Satan. *My son is not with me in Hell, foul and fallen emperor.* The First Liar then pivoted his shaggy head past everyone and stared directly at Dracula who was hidden in one of the western entrance tunnels of the Colosseum.

"Fruor caedibus, etiam quando deficient," added the father of Hell. *I relish assassinations, even when they fail.*

Whatever amount of blood was left in Constantine drained out of his skull-like face.

In the shadows, Dracula grinned like a proud son.

"Et filius meus cum omnibus vobis huc per noctem," beamed Satan. *And my son is here tonight with you all.*

Satan melted into a black plume of smoke and flame and disappeared.

A hush fell over the crowd.

Dracula stepped forward out of the shadows of the ruined western entrance, flanked by Petra and Venus, who surveyed the crowd with keen interest, as if searching for familiar faces.

Everyone gasped, none more so than Constantine.

The old tyrant was visibly staggered and took a few unbalanced steps before he nearly fell back into his obscene black, gnarled throne of gold, thorns and bones.

He fumbled for words, the old politician searched to find his serpent's tongue.

"Maiestatis!" he coughed at last. "Quae causa inducat suam Celsitudinem humilitatis nostrae configuratum epulis praesumebat?" *Majesty! What brings his Highness to our humble festivities?*

A small, goblin-like vampire ran in from his place next to the deacons and announced to the audience, "Aggeniculor eius tenebris majestatis et filius Satan, Dracula Transylvaniae!" *Kneel before his Dark Majesty and Son of Satan, Count Dracula of Transylvania!*

Around them, the entirety of the vampires in the Colosseum faced in their direction and knelt. All save the vampire on the throne, the vampiric goblin continued, "Ac conjugibus suis, reginae Venus de' Medici and Petra Ali!" *And his wives, the queens Venus de' Medici and Petra Ali!*

Petra and Venus bowed with smooth, aristocratic grace to Dracula, who returned their bow with royal formality. The brides then turned to bats and flew toward the center podium in the southern side. Out of the crowd came forth two plush curule chairs, brought forward by two minor, knobbed demons covered with pestilence and vomit, yet the two brides remained standing, out of courtesy, and looked to their master, their husband, their fiend. They would not sit until after Dracula was seated. They knew better.

The Transylvanian remained where he stood, near the west entrance.

The same small, strange vampire began to recite, "Volumus puros dempta stella Bethlehem." *We wish for the dimming of the Star of Bethlehem.*

As he continued, the entire audience of satanic worshippers chanted, "Volumus lacerandos sigillum septimum. Et volumus habet capita septem et cornua decem et septem diademata draconem opprimere Michaelis Angeli damnati. Speramus magnum exitium Agno pugnabunt, et in iudiciis corrumpendis exercitati, omnia bona et alterum—" *We desire that the Seventh Seal to be torn asunder. And we wish for the seven-headed dragon with ten horns and seven crowns to crush Michael and his accursed angels. We hope for the destruction of the Great Lamb, and the corruption of all that is good in this and any other—*

The goblin vampire stopped reading because Dracula had transformed into a bat, bounded over from his perch during the reading and cleaved the *nosferatu*'s head off with a single, powerful blow from his clawed wing. The knobbed head arced gracefully through the air, spraying blood in a wide arc before it plopped to the ground and rolled over to Venus, who picked up the head and began to sip from the flowing blood like it was pouring out of a wineskin.

After a beat, Petra joined her.

They feverishly lapped up the blood like ravenous birds.

The crowd stopped reciting and gulped in both thirst and shock.

The Dracula bat crouched magnificently upon of one of the crumbling remnants of the hypogeum and the colosseum floor as he melted back into the refined, cultured human form of the Transylvanian. He then nodded in amused satisfaction, understanding that he had set the tone for the evening's proceedings.

"Maiestatis," said Constantine, who sat up straight and nervous in his throne, "quod humiles consolationem potest offerimus tibi hoc tempore celebrationis?" *Majesty, what humble comfort can we offer you at this time of celebration?*

Everyone was silent, watching Dracula, who loomed without a word, ignoring the polite, diplomatic greeting with Constantine. One of the pearlescent deacon vampires slid out of the imperial box with a goblet in his hands. He rippled over the broken, open sections of the arena's floor and offered the goblet to Dracula, who snatched it from the deacon's clawed hands.

The Transylvanian glared contempt at the entire court.

"Non est cur non hie bacchantis," announced Dracula to the crowd. "Sum profecto et hic super inquisitione." *The bacchanal is not why I am here. I am here upon an inquiry.*

The Transylvanian pivoted to Constantine and hissed, "Primum, relinquere throno meo et procidámus ante Filium satanae tuum regi, insidiantem canis!" *Firstly, vacate my throne and kneel before the Son of Satan and your king, plotting dog!*

Stunned silence from everyone.

Constantine's face was a bubbling concoction of revelation and terror.

"Insidiator!" shouted Dracula, and the entire arena quaked. *Conspirator!*

Dracula took a long, bloody sip from his goblet and snarled through blood-stained teeth, "Cito flexis genibus coram me et ego dabo vobis morte nobilis." *Kneel quickly before me, and I will give you the death of a nobleman.* The Transylvanian threw the goblet at the deacons, splattering blood over their pure-white shrouds and hoods. The farthest deacon caught the goblet and snarled contemptuously at the Transylvanian, who terrified the deacon and the crowd by snarling a retort so ferocious that it sounded like it came not from a lone wolf, but an entire pack.

Dracula turned back to a horrified Constantine, who was clearly too old to be a match for the Transylvanian.

"Genua!" howled Dracula. *Kneel!*

"Egli farà nessuna tale cosa!" roared a deep, dark voice from the eastern entrance. *He will do no such thing!*

Everyone turned to the voice, save Dracula.

A massive male vampire sauntered out from the shadow-filled eastern entrance of the Colosseum. The young *nosferatu* was enormous, taller than Dracula and dressed completely in black. His clothes were a fascinating combination of Italy in the Victorian era and Northern Africa of the past, complete with a keffiyeh wrapped around the powerful neck and shoulder muscles. A clawed hand reached up and pulled the keffiyeh down off the face, revealing a head that was shaved and a short beard that lined the long, sharp jawline. Handsome features on ghostly-grey skin cradled piercing eyes of an owl that boiled confidence. A sharp but short nose hung over an angry slit of a mouth, which opened up into a ferocious snarl filled with jagged canines when the mysterious interloper took in Dracula. The stranger actually spat in Dracula's direction before becoming a sprawling, massive black bat and flying over the ruined, open floor with one sweep of its sail-like wings. He landed a few meters away from Dracula, on another one of the crumbling arena floor supports. Fur begat skin, wings begat arms, and the young male's musculature rippled as he moved, his clothes defining his handsome, intimidating countenance.

The young male turned, his sharp chin pointed right at Venus as he said, "Il mio amore." *My love.*

Venus de' Medici was staggered.

Petra, mouth agape, had to reach over and steady her Italian sister.

"*Il mio amore,*" gasped Venus, as if she had spoken those words for the first time in her life.

Venus nearly took a step off the south podium and toward the stranger, such was the effect the newcomer had upon her, and Petra had to tighten her grip on her arm. There was raw, tender emotion radiating from Venus toward him, and the young vampire reciprocated the feeling, tenderness seeping from his eyes to her like blood from a wound. The crowd sensed the flurry of emotion and rumbled with seething compassion.

"Prenda ad un passo e io ti tagliuzzare a pezzi!" snarled Dracula at Venus without turning. *Take one step and I will shred you to pieces!*

His command echoed over the crowd and the ruins. Venus froze, then regained her composure before she slid her eyes away from the enormous, handsome stranger. Petra stared only at the Imperial box, but she slid her arm around Venus' back in sympathy and support.

The Transylvanian pivoted to face the monstrous vampire, and as he did, Dracula chuckled, "Aniantem parvulus." *The lovesick child.*

"Questa è la tua ultima notte come re," said Nero, who was clearly larger and more powerful than the Transylvanian. He oozed confidence. *This is your last night as king.*

The crowd rippled with further mutterings and whispers in support of Nero.

In a gesture of complete sarcasm that combined ferocity and humor, Dracula gave Nero a frown and a fearful, wide-eyed look, "Quid ita?" *How so?*

"Hij is onze koning!" shouted a voice from the darkened crowd. *He is our king!*

"他是我的暴君," shouted another. *He is our tyrant!*

A few, brave smatterings of applause snaked through the audience.

Thousands of glowing eyes watched them.

Raptor eyes aplenty blinked with morbid tension and curiosity.

One even dared to shout, "Zabij go dla nas, Nero!" *Kill him for us, Nero!*

Venus and Petra dared not raise their mouths into the slimmest of grins.

Dracula threw up his arms in a sarcastic gesture of accepting adoration from the crowd. He pivoted around at the shadowy, macabre audience as he laughed, "Dar eu sunt deja mort, prietenii mei, romanii mei, neamul meu!!" *But I am already dead, my friends, my Romans, my countrymen!*[224]

Constantine, still languid on his throne, was cunning enough to not move a muscle, not make a sound, not to do anything other than have the politics bleed out.

"Io non sono più un ragazzo," snarled Nero, "avere il mio promessa sposa presa da un tiranno!" I *am no longer a boy to have my betrothed taken by a tryant!*

Dracula gave Nero a nod and smile laced with menace. "Si haberes punctum facietis mihi puero potuisses simpliciter ad castello meo." *If you had a point to make to me, child, you could have simply come to my castle.*

"Vos furata est de familia," shouted Nero, gesturing in youthful frustration with both arms, "Nostra imminente nuptias pollueritis eam mundo. Nunc quia hominis requiro nostrum honorem!" *You stole her from her family and our impending wedding, dishonoring her in front of the world. Now as a man I seek our honor!*

"A duel!" shouted Constantine to the crowd, seizing the opportunity, "Nero Passi wishes a duel!"

Everyone roared their approval, and Constantine completely hid his delight.

Dracula gave a sly nod laced with an expression of respect toward Constantine. He spoke low enough so the crowd could not hear him, "Bene lusit, veteres politicus. Si perpetrata caede pergere defecit, velim hic reagunt et itineris, qua vos et zelantem puerum me opperiebatur." *Well played, old politician. If the assassination failed, I would react and journey here, where you and the jealous child awaited me.*

Constantine nodded once at Dracula, with the oblique expression of a politician and king that had knived through politics for nearly two millennia. He hissed, "έχετε επιβάλλεται η δεκάτη, οι τράπεζες μας για τη σχεδόν ερείπιο, αλλοιωμένα γυναίκες μας και δολοφόνησαν δικούς σας ανθρώπους στην ιδιοτροπία σας. Η συλλογική μας φως θα ήταν σβήσει αν έχουμε συνεχιστεί υπό τον τίτλο «μοναρχία» σας. Αυτό είναι για την επιβίωσή μας." *You have tithed our banks to near-ruin, corrupted our women and murdered your own people at your whim. Our collective light would be extinguished if we continue under your 'monarchy'. This is for our survival.*

"Quello dici che, antiche, autocrate gonfio!" roared an impatient Nero at Dracula. *What say you, old, bloated autocrat!*

The ruins of the *maenianum secundum summum* shook with his thunder. "Arrestare chiedere l'elemosina per la tua vita a la nostra vera, proprio capo e affronta il tuo destino! Affronta il tuo meglio!" *Stop begging for your life to our true, just leader and face your fate! Face your better!*

---

[224] A play on a famous quote from Shakespeare's Julius Caesar. "Friends, Romans, countrymen, lend me your ears; I come to bury Caesar, not to praise him." Dracula is back-handedly accusing the audience of plotting against him.

Dracula turned to Nero and said flatly, "Cum matre fossuris illis in situ tuo domesticum patris sui mei, dixi ad eam hanc esses in lapillo soleam." *I told your mother when I mated with her that you would be a pebble in my shoe.*

The audience gasped at the insult.

Nero roared in a fury as if the world had split open.

Dracula beamed with satisfaction.

"Credam in cunis fuerunt ululatus momento," sniffed Dracula. *I believe you were wailing in your cradle during that moment.*

"Alla morte!" bellowed Nero, raising a fist to the crowd. *To the death!*

The crowd would have it, and roared approval.

The ruins shook with the thunder.

"Perbene," said Dracula, matter-of-factly. *Very well.*

Dracula was standing upon one of the hypogeum's support sections, about a third of the way toward the northern podium, where Constantine was seated. Nero was behind him and to the right. Dracula reached his empty hand out to the weapons rack near the throne. Obeying a silent commend, a very long pike soared out of its place on an elaborate wooden rack and shot across the space. The pike's grip smacked against Dracula's open palm.

The audience quieted.

Nero's grin shrank a bit.

As did the crowd.

The Transylvanian took the pike, whirled it over his head with startling speed as he stalked in a wide circle toward Nero, taking care to move gracefully, like a panther, from foundation wall to foundation wall. Dracula turned and glared at Nero and said, "Hoc meum non sit primum duellum, puer." *This is not my first duel[225], boy.*

"Et non estis nobilem," added Dracula. *And you are no nobleman.*

After a courtly bow toward Constantine but not Dracula, Nero turned to bat form and soared over to take another pike from the rack with his mouth. He turned to mist and slowly drifted back to a spot opposite Dracula, atop one of the hypogeum walls. It was a strange, eerie scene as the mist carried the weapon out to the center of the arena. As he transformed back to human form, Nero's hands materialized around the pike. Eyes fiercely fixated upon Dracula, Nero took the pike and whipped it around his head, no stranger to the weapon, and held its point out toward the Transylvanian.

"Qui ductor est vester Secundo?" asked Dracula, now in the formal manner of a duel. "Solus sto." *Who is your Second? I need none.*

Nero leered at the Transylvanian and laughed as he shouted, "La mia Seconda è Venus de' Medici!"

Another torrent of gasps from the undead crowd.

Dracula remained unphased, his back to Nero, Venus and Petra.

Venus stood rigid, frozen by Nero's words. He turned to find her gaze, but her eyes avoided his, understanding the protocol in these matters. It would be traitorous for Venus to even glance at Nero. She then raised her chin and spoke to the crowd, "Io sono Secondo a mio marito, Dracula di Transilvania." *I am Second to my husband, Dracula of Transylvania.*

---

[225] A duel is an Old World formal combat between two people, primarily nobility, with equal weapons with a set of rules. Swords, then pistols were used throughout history. A duel between women was called a petticoat duel. Complex rules of behavior were enforced, along with the role of 'seconds', advocates for each person who negotiated terms with the involved parties. Perhaps the most infamous duel is the Burr-Hamilton duel, in which American Vice President Aaron Burr killed Alexander Hamilton, former Secretary of the Treasury, in New Jersey on July 11, 1804.

Applause of support for the dignity of Venus de' Medici. Petra also held her head high and avoided Nero, but the crowd drank in the tension and attraction between Nero and Venus.

A loud scoff from Nero as he glared at Dracula. "Meus dilectus dat vos quando reverebuntur dignus es nihil! Tractabatis eam vapulabit petra sicut meretricibus! Et salvos eos faciam de ponendo verbum hoc per pilum mortuum tuum corde!" *My beloved gives you respect when you deserve none! You treat her and Petra like whores, not wives! But I will free them from their word by putting this pike through your dead heart!*

Enjoying Nero's rant, Dracula said coolly, "Illam plene percipere eam loco apud nobilitas. Vos ex sanguine numulariis sicariorum. Aurum in ripa numquam aequiparat quale regia sanguine." *She understands her place among nobility. You are from the blood of bankers and assassins. Gold in a bank never equates the quality of a royal bloodline.*

Constatine stood and raised his bony arms, shouting, "Sorelle! Fratelli! Una piega inaspettata presso la nostra baldoria! Un *affaire d'honneur* tra Maestà, Dracula di Transilvania, e la nostra Nero Pazzi di Firenze!" *Sisters! Brothers! An unexpected turn at our revelry! An affaire d'honneur between our Majesty, Dracula of Transylvania, and our own Nero Pazzi of Florence!*

The daemonic crowd danced and roared with delight.

"Uruchom za nim przez Nero!" cried an old vampire. *Run him through, Nero!*

A tall demon spat, "Gure aitak semea errespetatu behar dugula!" *We must respect the son of our father!*

"امش ىارب ام مبارزه، Pazzi!" *You fight for us, Pazzi!*"

Pike in one hand, Dracula gestured to the brides. Venus and Petra became mist and poured over the broken basement supports until they reached the Transylvanian. They then took human form as Dracula watched them with his raptor eyes. Dracula was trying to find disloyalty in the eyes of both Petra and Venus, but he could find none. Both women were true royals and diplomats, with strong yet proud faces held high, both projecting their dignity back to one who may never have known what it means for others around him to have dignity. He took his coin bag from the folds of his clothes and handed it to Venus. She took it from her husband without a word, and with a neutral expression upon her face. Petra was next to her, watching Dracula in silence.

Dracula eyed them both and decided to test them again as the crowd roared in anticipation of the duel. "Forte liberavit te de verbum tuum nocte Concubines?" *Perhaps you are to be free of your word tonight, Concubines?*

Venus looked at Dracula like she wanted to spit upon him. "Lo non sono concubina." *I am no concubine.*

"امش داتسا ام تسا و ام رد تمس دوخ ىا رد داتسی،" said Petra, equally neutral, placing her hand over Venus' in a calming gesture. *You are our master and we stand at your side.*

"Essi non sanno la vostra forza. C'è una ragione tu sei il nostro re," said Venus. "Non hanno visto da quello che che abbiamo vissuto." *They know not your strength. There is a reason you are our king. They have not seen from you what we have lived.*

Behind Dracula, Nero stood with his arms raised with the fervor of the anticipated duel.

"Nu Recent Cautare," Dracula nodded. *Not recently.*

He pointed at the button of his cloak, which unfastened itself, then the cloak slid into the crook of his left elbow before it floated into Petra's hands. She took it and held it, her face still expressionless in the face of the roar of the crowd around them.

"Tu nu favorizează dragostea ta logodită, Medici?" asked Dracula with an ironic twist of his head to Venus. *You do not favor your betrothed, Medici?*

The Transylvanian was teasing Venus in a cruel, sly manner. His knives of words twisted into her soul, yet she refused to reveal her pain, and the vampire nodded his proud, sharp head in respect toward her. His eyes shot up, trying to catch a sympathetic glance from Petra, which would have meant her instant death, even in front of this crowd, but the Egyptian stood tall in the solemn pose of a noble in a position of duty, but not consent.

Dracula spun the pike in his hand as he looked back at Venus.

"Tu sei sempre mio marito," said Venus, ever so flatly. *You are ever my husband.*

About to walk away, Dracula raised his eyebrows and said, "Chiar dacă ceea ce a declarat este adevărat prostul? Că te-am rapiti, tu violeze şi niciodată măritat cu tine?" *Even though what the fool says is true? That I kidnapped you, violated you and never married you?*

Petra became livid, her eyes exploding with hate, and she nearly struck out at Dracula, but Venus swung her arm around Petra's own waist to stop her. The public gesture became one of love as both women smiled at Dracula, their arms settled around each other's waists. They both watched him laugh at them, united, hate blazing in their eyes even as they smiled ever so politely back at him.

Unable to bait them, Dracula gave the brides the thinnest and sweetest of smiles as he said, "Loialitate seara asta, în ciuda resentimente dvs. clar, este ceea ce tu ambele salvează de la dezmembrarea care vă aşa merită." *Your loyalty tonight, despite your clear resentment, is what saves you both from the dismembering that you so deserve.*

He bowed to them.

The brides bowed back, then became bats and flew to the Imperial box, metamorphosizing back into human form just behind Constantine's barbed throne and next to the deacon vampires, who gave them a uniform, courteous bow, to which the brides replied with a polite but curt nod of their heads.

Constantine turned and gave the women one crisp nod of acknowledgement.

Venus and Petra returned the nod, their faces remaining like stone, expressionless.

"Μπορούμε όλοι να κερδίσουμε απόψε. Και οι δυο σας, πάνω απ 'όλα," said Constantine with a warm, macabre grin at the brides. *We may all win tonight. Both of you most of all.*

The women ignored the last comment, and Constantine turned his politics-filled head back to the duel.

Dracula bounded across the broken arena floor and toward Nero and the duel, the vampiric version of a regal, evil lion.

The roar of the crowd engulfed them, and the undead began to chant Nero's name. "Ne-ro! Ne-ro! Ne-ro!"

"دق ورين كب تفـعل المسـتحيـل،" hissed Petra, a raven's caw in the crowd. *May your Nero do the impossible.*

"Concordato. Per Andromeda anche," hissed Venus. It was nearly a snarl. *Agreed. For Andromeda as well.*

They watched the crowd, twin coiled serpents, unblinking.

Then, Flavius Valerius Aurelius Constantinus Augustus stood out of his throne and waved for silence.

"Queste armi siano ritualmente immersi nel Sacro acqua del Cristo!" announced the bleak shroud. "Έτσι, οποιαδήποτε πληγή με τα όπλα απαγορεύει επίσης μετατροπή σε οποιαδήποτε μορφή, διάρκεια της μονομαχίας." *These weapons are ceremonially bathed in the Holy Water of the Christ! Thus, any wound with the weapons also prohibits transformation in any form during the duel.*

At this the crowd howled in an orgy of evil revelry, the likes of which had not been seen in that arena since the last days of Ancient Rome.

"Sit nobis a Satana legare victoris!" sang Constantine with raised arms. *May Satan bequeath us a victor!*

The crowd concurred with a deafening roar and continued to chant Nero's name.

With Constantine, the deacons, the brides and the audience taking in their every move, Dracula and Nero faced each other, pikes in hand. Each stood upon one of the craggy dungeon walls that rose from the darkness of the hypogeum. Venus and Petra stood on Dracula's side. Nero tried to catch Venus' eyes, but she would not allow their eyes to meet. Petra, concerned for her fellow wife, reached out to steady Venus with a supporting arm from behind, but Venus gently and respectfully took Petra's hand, patted it with affection before she pushed it away. From inside his shroud, Constantine produced a crinkled, black, ornate handkerchief that hung from his hand like a dead tarantula. He held it out before him with gnarled, taloned fingers. *This has worked out perfectly.*

"Hoc tetigerit terram usque ad mortem." *Once this touches the ground, to the death.*

"Combatto per la mia Firenze!" roared Nero, twirling his pike with confidence. "E per il mio amore, Venere de' Medici!" *I fight for my Florence! And for my love, Venus de' Medici!*

"Et dimicare pro me," leered Dracula, spreading his feet out and his pike in front of him. *I fight for me.*

Constantine the Great released the handkerchief, and it fluttered to the ground of the podium.

"*Ad tuam mortem,*" laughed Dracula at Nero. *To your death.*

"Bahhhhhhhhhhhr!" bellowed Nero with the full of his soul, and he leaped off his perch and at Dracula. Nero swung down his pike with vicious power, but the Transylvanian stood stout with the weapon facing out from his left hand and easily twisted his pike to block the trajectory of Nero's. The wooden staffs collided and slid against each other with a tremendous clatter. Nero landed upon the same support wall that Draula stood on, and both men used prodigious strength to force the pikes against each other, the spearhead tips rising high in the night air. The crowd roared with a loud bellow of adrenaline and hate. The power behind Nero's pike thrust was tremendous, and at the moment their staffs clashed, Dracula knew he faced a formidable, powerful, if inexperienced opponent.

Nevertheless, Dracula parried the blow while holding his ground, then viciously head-butted Nero away from him, then using the wooden back end of the pike to slam viciously against Nero's massive skull. But Nero was fast, and he swung his spearhead down savagely, only to have Dracula step toward him and turn into mist. Miraculously, Nero's pike pushed Dracula's mist form out to the embankment wall nearest him.

The Transylvanian's arm stayed solid as it held the staff, while avoiding the spearhead dipped in Holy Water. Dracula solidified into human form and whipped his Pike around, trying to surprise Nero with the speed of his counterattack, but the young vampire also melted into mist. Only Petra could hear Venus gasp in fear as Dracula's staff swirling through the Florentine vampire's body with no effect.

As did the crowd, collectively and decidedly in favor of Nero.

Then Nero grasped the back end of his staff and thrust it savagely down upon Dracula's hand, and the Transylvanian groaned as he dropped his pike. The wooden staff clanked as it fell between the crumbling arena floor walls, toward deeper darkness.

The crowd leaned forward in anticipation.

With a wide, arcing blur, Nero swung his spearhead around, roaring as he did, anticipating the kill, but Dracula leaped back toward the wall that Nero stood on, and as he did, he reached out his hand.

The pike froze in mid-fall, then magically yanked back up to Dracula's hand as he landed on top of the wall, and the son of Satan became mist in a blink, swerved over and under the blow, while his outstretched arm and pike defied physics and reason; a surrealists' vision, a bank of fog with an outstretched arm. Nero's blow shot through the mist, Dracula's body then materialized, swung his pike up and shot the spear tip straight at Nero's head, and only a lightning-quick-jerk of his head saved the Florentine.

Filling the jewel-encrusted goblet to the brim from a black leather wineskin[226], the second deacon passed the opulent cup to Constantine, who hid a satisfied grin when he raised it to his lips. *Perhaps today the son of Satan falls.* Constantine the Great sipped, sighed with satisfaction and nodded to the goblin *nosferatu* with appreciation.

"Sanguinis et vinum, ut solet, permixta est vera maiestas," croaked the deacon through a mouth full of pig-like teeth. *Blood and wine, blended as usual for our true majesty.*

Dracula bounded backward like a majestic leopard, his pike swirling in an expansive arc. He landed atop another broken floor support, feet set to meet the onrushing Nero, in mid-leap himself, his own pike behind his head. Dracula's arc finished and his spearhead collided with the stout pike of Nero's own weapon as it came down at him, the steel pike tips glinting against each other and the firelight.

Dracula leaped sideways onto another wall support and thrust out his own pike, aiming to rip the musculature out of Nero's right leg, but the enormous vampire was quick enough to drop the spearless end of the pike down to block the blow.

Roars from the crowd swirled through the decrepit grandstands.

"Bokun o korusu!" shouted a ghostly vampire in the podium. *Kill the tyrant!*

"Stuur hem naar zijn vader, Nero!" bellowed a bulbous vanpire from the maenianum primum. *Send him to his father, Nero!*

"Afjaro dulmi ah!" screamed a robed, long-haired vampire. *End his oppression!*

The pikes clashed again and again, youth against age, ferocity against experience, insurgent against royal. The crowd's roars melded with Nero roaring and bellowing his hate in youthful fervor, while Dracula remained focused and calm, the memories and moments of many such duels behind him. They parried each other, between Constantine and the crowd, dancing like dueling flames over the floorless arena, standing upon the remnants of walls that once held up a Colosseum's floor.

Dracula whipped his pike around and sliced Nero's back, and it sizzled at the touch from the Holy Water-laced metal. Nero wailed at the wound but parried, twisted and thrust out his pike, nearly catching Dracula gloating over his blow. They then stood back, pikes held out in front, then the pikes rammed together again, Nero using his superior strength to press against Dracula's pike, rotating it backward as Nero stepped forward. His arms trembling, Dracula stepped backward, his pike rotating clockwise in his hands, against his will.

The arena itself sensed this and snarled for blood; sand from the Ancient World had fallen to the hypogeum floor, thirsty and anticipating one more bloodbath.

Constantine passed the goblet back to the deacons, who took turns sipping the alcoholic red living ichor.

The third and last deacon offered the goblet to Venus. "ہمیں اس کی موت پر پئے" *Let us drink to his death.*

---

[226] A wineskin, zahato or bota bag, is a portable liquid container from the Old World, made out of leather, stitched together, inflated and filled with pitch to enable it to carry fluids like wine and water.

"Si parla prematuramente. Egli è il nostro re per una ragione," snapped Venus, her regal head held high. *You speak prematurely. He is our king for a reason.*

"La tua bocca non parla per il tuo cuore," snarled the last deacon, leering disgustingly with broken, bloody dog teeth and craggy, wind-chapped lips. *Your mouth does not speak for your heart.*

Venus ignored the deacon and continued to watch the duel, her heart on her sleeve. Memories of her youth swam through her soul, of the first glances of curiosity, the first kiss of attraction and the consummation of love with her beloved, and the searing pain of love lost. Yet now, love fights for her against he who could never love her, and the waves of emotion frothed throughout Venus' mind, heart and soul, yet the proud queen that she was, de' Medici never flinched, remained stoic, and Petra was the only other person in the area that knew what she was going through.

"لاقو انه يمكن نكفت لعفت لذلك," whispered Petra. No one else could hear her. *He can do it.*

"Abbiamo potuto essere esente di lui finalmente?" whispered Venus back. *Could we be free of him at last?*

"συγκράτησης σας είναι αξιοθαύμαστη, δεδομένου ότι ήταν η επιστολή σας που με ειδοποίησε για το ταξίδι του στην Αγγλία για να αρχίσει με," whispered Constantine to Venus as he watched the combatants. *Your restraint is admirable given that it was your letter that alerted me to his voyage to England to begin with.*

Venus did not bat an eye as she said, "La prima fedeltà di una donna è per se stessa." *A woman's first allegiance is to herself.*

The firelight flickered on the polished wood of the pikes.

The combatants danced over the broken sections of arena floor as they parried and slammed the pikes together again and again. Nero was the stronger, but Dracula the sager, and nearly as fast.

And both danced in the eyes of Constantine the Great, awaiting the outcome like a vulture for carrion.

Macabre all, the undead crowd lived and died with each blow and parry.

Then came the unexpected.

In a powerful move, Dracula tried to wrench Nero's pike from his hands, but with a ferocious parry and thrust, Nero shot his newfound pike forward and punched it savagely into the upper left of Dracula's chest. The pike's spear tip shot clear through Dracula's body, impaling him. The thud that the pike made as it punctured Dracula's body brought an enormous gasp from the crowd. Dracula roared like an impaled bull in pain as the Holy Water sizzled over the wound. Nero roared triumphantly with the crowd, in a frenzy reserved for the fall of a gladiator from the Ancient World. Constantine shot to his feet and bellowed in triumph, and Venus clasped her hand around Petra's wrist as a surge of elation swept through her.

In an instant she saw her life changed, her love fulfilled and tears of hope swept into her eyes.

Dracula's eyes blazed with defiance as blood vomited out of the wound.

Nero swung Dracula's body out over the dark, cavernous hypogeum below.

"Qual dici che Tiranno!" screamed Nero. *What say you, tyrant!*

He had just become Saint George and had slain the dragon, wresting the kingdom of vampirism away from the Transylvanian. Nero's massive hands gripped the pike like twin vices, and he began to lift the deposed royal off of the craggy, ruined ground they had fought on as he shouted along with the crowd in a siege of clamor and celebration. The wound around Dracula's torso smoked with holy fire.

Dracula, king of the vampires, hung like a corpse at a crossroads.

Gasps like a fish on land emanated from the shocked Transylvanian.

His blood sizzled as it ran along the blessed wood of the pike. It bled down into the labyrinth below.

Nero raised his head up and shouted at the heavens like a triumphant lion.

The crowd bellowed with him.

Petra began to reach for Venus, to hold her share in release and comfort, but Venus stood straight, held Petra's arm down and hissed, "Non fino a quando non è completamente morto!" *Not until he is completely dead!*

Dracula coughed, his mouth scarlet.

He began to close his eyes.

The hopes of a culture soared.

Constantine gripped the throne's armrest tightly, in an attempt to wring victory out of it.

The deacons squealed in glee like perverse owls feasting on a baby rabbit.

Petra burst into tears of joy.

"Controllare voi stessi!" said Venus, remaining stout and holding the Egyptian next to her. *Control yourself!*

The Transylvanian gripped the pike in a gesture of futility.

His body trembled with effort.

His palms sang smoke.

The crowd laughed at their fallen king's feeble attempt.

"умереть старая шлюха," screamed an old, worn vampiress. *Die, old whore!*

"Não, Senhor! Não morra! Viver para nós!" wailed an adolescent, well-heeled nosferatu. *No, Master! Do not die! Live for us!*

"Keur Venus, pikeun urang sadayana!!" roared a young vampiress. "Sadaya raja jahat maot dina jalan kawas anj aranjeunna keur aya!" *For Venus, for us all! All tyrants die on the street like the dogs they are!*

On the horizon, the upcoming dawn peeked over the crumbling lip of the Colosseum, then decided to wait.

"É fatta?" gasped Venus. *Is it done?*

Somewhere in the distance, a raven cawed.

The caw was only audible for a mere moment, because the collective bellow of the audience overwhelmed it.

As did Constantine, who shouted, "Όλα χαλάζι νέος βασιλιάς μας—" *All hail our new King—*

Dracula pulled the pike toward him, thrusting himself forward.

And down.

Toward Nero.

His left arm gestured, and a wooden sword on the rack responded, leaping to the Transylvanian's hand. Dracula swung, and on one blow, cleaved the head of the stunned Nero off of his neck. The pike was still in Nero's hands, and it trembled with the spasms of the decapitated body.

"لا," whispered Petra. *No.*

"Για άλλη μία φορά," sighed Constantine. *Yet again.*

"Addio amore mio," cried Venus. She somehow suppressed the urge to burst into tears. *Goodbye, my love.*

Hush, said the crowd.

Another caw, this one for Nero.

A lifetime of memories flooded into Venus' heart, her time with Nero from childhood, the faded promise of love, and now his death at the hands of her master. Nero's head slapped the ruins when it landed with a bloody splat, then tumbled down among the ruins of the hypogeum.

"Mai. Mai questo sarà finito," moaned Venus. She nearly burst into tears. *Never. Never will this be over.*

Ash-filled smoke, Nero's smoke, began to billow out from the bottom of the Colosseum.

The first deacon slid a hand onto Venus' shoulder in sympathy.

Petra's hand found de' Medici's.

They clasped in sorrow, companionship and love.

Dracula swung the sword back around, and he flung it violently blade-first right through the heart of Constantine, slamming him backward and pinning him to his throne. Constantine gasped like a lizard at the end of a stick.

After his feet hit the broken wall that Nero had been standing on, Dracula brought his right hand down savagely onto the pike, shattering it right in front of his bleeding torso. He pulled out and threw both pieces aside. Blood in his mouth, Dracula turned to the crowd as he screamed at the top of his undead lungs, "Ego Dracula fili diaboli regis gustas lamia et vos indignatio mea!" *I am Dracula, Son of Satan, King of the Vampires and you will all taste my wrath!*

He raised his bloodied, burnt and taloned hands into the air.

To give out an invisible but deadly cue.

Then:

Hundreds.

Thousands.

Millions.

Of frothing, ravenous vermin.

Rats exploded out of every possible crevice and overwhelmed every vampire in the arena. The amphitheater filled with screams of torture and death, waves of rats from below ravenously overwhelming all of the vampires they could reach.

"Maledicentibus vobis, soricesque! Tu nos sanguinem siccum furari interficiat nos et vos nos miseros omnes," shrieked the deacons at Dracula in an unholy chorus, their high-pitched, unearthly voices overlapping each other, their mouths spitting blood and spite. *Curse you, vermin! You bleed us dry, you steal us poor and you kill us all!*

Dracula leaped, and in midair began to transform, blood spraying from his wound, and the bat landed like an earthquake tremor on the podium. The Dracula bat wrenched the wineskin from the main deacon and ripped the top of the container off with his enormous canines. The monstrous bat drank deeply and darkly but did not swallow, for he then snatched one of the obscene candles from the podium and proceeded to spit out the entire contents of his mouth at the deacons, sending it through the candle's flame.

Instantly the trio of satanic deacons were engulfed in fire.

They squealed like pigs who were being butchered as the blood-and-wine-fueled fire scorched them. Arms flailing like the wings of beheaded game birds, the deacons staggered to the edge of the podium as they frantically tried to put out the flames. The first deacon fell into one of the collapsed hypogum passageways under the arena floor, and the Dracula bat swung out a wing so viciously that it ripped his head and shoulders clean off. Below them, the two remaining deacons squealed in pain less and less as they burned away. In a moment the son of Satan was in human form again, but Dracula sagged, gasping for breath from his efforts and injuriy, then pointed to Venus and Petra and whispered, "Vestra fides pepercit tibi oculus meus." *Your loyalty has spared you.*

Though he was wounded, the Transylvanian turned and watched with satisfaction as the rat hordes consumed the other vampires, some of them trying to fly away in bat form only to be dragged back down by the sheer number of rodents weighing their bodies down, gnawing and ripping at skin, muscle and bones.

"Pestis tu es cum tuis omnibus converseris!" gasped a weary voice behind them. *You are a plague to your people!*

Reveling in the masses writhing in agony in the arena stands, Dracula said, "Nequaquam veteres proletarianae tantum iter Romam satis locupletes celebrando secreta spes morte remittam." *No, old proletarian, only to those wealthy enough to journey to Rome with secret hope of celebrating my demise.*

Dracula and the brides turned to see Constantine gasping like a fish, still alive despite being impaled to the throne. Blood pulsed out of the old tyrant's mouth in eerie spurts. The Holy Water that laced the weapon began to eat away at Constantine's body, flame and smoke turning undead flesh into ash. The old conqueror coughed blood and ash as he rasped, "Είστε μια μάστιγα για εμάς." *You are a plague to us.*

"Tantum ad eos qui resistunt mihi," said Dracula. *Only to those who oppose me.*

Constantine took agonizing, gasping breaths as he said, "Μετά από όλα μάχες μας, αυτό είναι το πώς τελειώνει." *After all of our battles, this is how it ends.*

Dracula stood and watched, relishing Constatine's agony. The first vampire turned his burning eyes toward Venus and Petra and gurgled, "Αφήστε τον. Είστε βασίλισσες και αξίζει κάτι καλύτερο." *Leave him. You are queens and deserve better.*

The fire began to blossom out from his wound and all over his body. Constantine quivered like a dying bird and when his eyes blinked, they cried flame. "Εγώ επόμενη θα σας υποδεχτεί δίπλα του πατέρα σας." *I will next greet you at your father's side.*

"Εκείνος ποτέ δεν θα σας δείχνουν την αγάπη," hissed Constantine. *He will never show you love.*

"Είστε πιστοί σε έναν πατέρα που ποτέ δεν θα σας αγαπήσει," agonized Constantine at Dracula. *You are loyal to a father who will never love you.*

Dracula stepped forward, leaned down and looked at Constantine with the unblinking eyes of a bird of prey. "Εγώ είμαι πιστές μόνο στον εαυτό μου." *I am loyal only to myself.*

Flaius Valerius Aurelius Constantinus Augustus, Titan of history and first vampire, whithered and crumbled into cinder upon his throne of gold and bone.

Dracula stood straight, yanked the sword out from the throne and the body with his right hand, wincing in pain from the effort, then he thrust it back through Constantine's withering skull, melting it to dust.

"'Είμαστε στην βασίλισσες,'" quoted Venus in a whisper as she took in the ember-filled, decapitated body of Nero. *We are queens.*

Among the ruins of the old arena were piles of ashen corpses everywhere, and waves of rats retreating back into their secret, dark recesses. She and Petra both turned back to watch their master with hard, unblinking eyes. Never had they hated anyone more than Dracula of Transylvania.

"Călătorie sprâncenată, dușman vechi," said Dracula as he watched Rome's soft evening breeze take Constantine's ashes. "Mai tatăl meu sărbătoare pe sufletul pentru eternitate." *Good riddance, old enemy. May my father feast upon your soul for eternity.*

Dracula pointed to a tattooed, knobby-headed vampire who was was cowering in the stands behind the throne. "Instruere reliquias seniorum eligere candidatorum ad repone Constantine sicut vicarious profana. Eligam successoris hic ver." *Instruct the remaining elders to select three candidates to replace Constantine as Unholy Vicar. I will select the successor here in the spring.*

"Et erit sicut iubet magister," replied the vampire after he stood to salute with a deep bow. *It will be as you command, my Master.*

Though exhausted, the Transylvanian turned back to the brides and said past ragged breaths, "Nox mihi."

The night is mine.

FIVE

Renfield sat in the wagon, smoking patiently, the night ticking away around him.

He thought of dirty jokes, roast mutton and slitting women's entrails.

Montague Rhodes had been puffing on a makeshift cigarette when abruptly the crowd noises pouring from the Colosseum had died abruptly a few minutes ago, and the huge brute had nothing to do but continue to drag and puff in silence. A few doors along the dark street east of the Colosseum had cracked open during the commotion, but the sight of the enormous man leering at them in a macabre fashion had been enough for them to be slammed shut instantly.

Renfield took another drag and exhaled slowly, enjoying the expulsion of the smoke from his lungs. He had picked up the habit as a boy, during the Crimean War, mimicking Turkish soldiers by rolling his tobacco in pieces of newspaper. He had also been thinking about how this time had been the happiest in his life. He'd even started to write again, something he had barely done since the war. Montague shuddered as the memory of the woman and the crypt raced through him like a cold draft, but the Master had explained it all away, her touch of understanding and sympathy. No one had ever cared for Montague Rhodes Renfield in this manner before, not his drunken soldier of a father and certainly not his whore of a churchgoing mother. His beatings at her hands were so commonplace that they had done nothing but embolden him at school, where M.R. Renfield became a first-rate schoolyard bully.

But here, with him in Rome, despite the tension-inducing presence of the brides, who always looked at Montague like they wanted to consume him like owls that would rend a mouse to pieces, Renfield felt that at long last he had found his station in life.

He flicked ashes at the horses. One of them felt the burn and shifted its right leg, irritated.

A rat scurried by the horse, who then stepped sideways to avoid it.

And another.

Yet another, a trio of searing red eyes.

Renfield looked up and saw the tide of rats slithering toward him along the dark street, infinitely smaller than the horde that had just consumed an entire amphitheater of nosferatu, followed by three huge bats in the sky, a bride on either side of the Dracula bat. Renfield grinned, knowing his master had once again defeated anything or anyone in his path. The bat opened its massive wings as it neared the street, then the Transylvanian touched ground.

And crumpled.

The Son of Satan lay like a sack of dirty laundry upon the darkened streets of Rome.

His wings trembled like those of a dried, dying crow.

His right shoulder bled out over the street, and his right wing trembled.

The Dracula bat gasped for breath into the cobblestones like a beached shark.

Renfield bolted upright in the wagon, filled with concern.

The brides landed and transformed instantly, shocked expressions over their faces at seeing the

Transylvanian lying so weakly upon the street.

The Dracula bat sagged, tired and bleeding from its wound.

"Master!" shouted Renfield as he bolted out of the wagon to help Dracula. He ran around the horses, who neighed out of terror at the bat's presence, to help his master up off the ground. But before the brides could warn Montague, the Dracula bat pivoted and opened its great jaws.

Taken by surprise, Renfield was too shocked to react as the Dracula bat savagely clamped its great foaming maw around his servant's left shoulder.

In one heartbeat, the enormous Englishman was yanked off his feet.

The Dracula bat snarled furiously as he shook his servant as violently as a dog would shake a rabbit.

The brides' incandescent eyes blinked nonchalantly in the darkness.

They were no strangers to this kind of outburst.

Victims, in fact.

Many times over.

Montague bellowed in pain, the sound reverberating along the dark and lonely street. The monstrous bat shook Renfield side-to-side in his jaws before flinging him bodily down the street.

Rhodes Montague Renfield tumbled head-over-heels, like a bag of rubbish, onto the battered old cobblestone street in front of the horses. He gagged, the wind knocked out of his body.

Still slumped over, the Dracula bat was like an open parachute over the wet, cobbled Rome street, but gasping from exhaustion and bleeding from the wound inflicted by Nero.

Petra and Venus simply watched, knowing all too well the price for showing any love or compassion to the Son of Satan. They then looked to the bruised, inert form that was Montague Rhodes Renfield.

For a moment the women thought him dead, still as he was, but after a few seconds the enormous man stirred, found his breath, then moaned. Dracula's canines had done their work, and Renfield struggled to sit up, like a beaten, bleeding dog. His coat and shirt were ripped apart, and crimson and skin intermingled in a ghastly way. For the first time since they'd known the Englishman, Venus and Petra sympathized with him. Renfield's wounded eyes searched Dracula for answers, but the Dracula bat held no mercy in his crimson pupils, hissing fiercely at his servant.

Petra took this all in and was disgusted.

She was disgusted by the way that Dracula had treated Renfield, she was horrified at how the Transylvanian had treated Venus but more than anything, Petra Ali was more disgusted at herself for tolerating this kind of treatment from anyone.

She spoke with a cold, even tone but boldly.

"Domine, tu dominaris absolutum. Verum hoc est enim pinnaculum. Tibi gratulor. Placet, concede nobis tuae libertatem servitio nostra iaspidem et quaeremus." *Master, you rule absolute. Truly this is a pinnacle for you. I congratulate you. Please, grant us freedom from your servitude, that we may seek our own pinnacles.*

For a moment, Venus stood petrified, shocked that Petra would even consider such a request much less utter it. She sensed Petra's anger, her resolve and the end of her sister's patience.

De' Medici then braced herself, ready to leap in front of Petra to protect her, even with the prospect of being torn to shreds by her master, anticipating that the great bat would leap at her instead.

The leap never came.

Instead, the Dracula bat gasped air raggedly as he stood from a semi-crouch in the darkness and began to form into human shape, but not completely, and Dracula stood there, half humanoid/half monstrous bat, staring at the Egyptian with one human and one oblong bat eye. Both eyes blinked but oddly, with the larger eye opening slower, eerily and with pus sliding out of its tear duct. The Dracula thing favored his injured left shoulder, which was healing, not bleeding, from the wound suffered in the Colosseum, but much more slowly.

Not as quickly and not as cleanly.

"Vide ad eum," gurgled the wounded vampire oddity, his eyes hallway closed as he pointed to Renfield. *See to him.*

The Transylvanian stayed half-transformed, just for a moment, in order to catch his breath, before he melted, de-evolved back to his bat form, his more primal form, his birth form. The vampire turned from them as the brides moved to aid the still stunned and shocked Renfield. Then the great bat flapped his wings, favoring the injured left wing, gaining altitude with the first sweep of his wings, and then with the next downstroke Dracula had the night, and flew toward the Rome moon.

He soared away, favoring the wounded wing.

Yet the great dragon easily rose above the city with which he shared so much history and contempt.

The brides relaxed and looked back at Renfield, and with a mixture of empathy, loathing and following orders, they moved to him.

Renfield coughed, wretched and vomited horribly, through both his mouth and nostrils, which restored Venus' usual level of revulsion toward the Englishman.

"Are you well, human dog?" asked Venus as she reached down to pick Montague up, which she did easily, bodily lifting the man up with one hand by his collar despite his tremendous size and height advantage. Venus exchanged a tiny look of pity with Petra, who looked toward the vanishing silhouette of the Dracula bat to remind Venus that they had more important things to concern themselves with.

"Yes, just follow the Master," gasped/gagged Renfield, straightening his clothes and pointing to the shrinking silhouette of the vampire. "He is the important one."

"Allow him to fly ahead," sighed Petra as she watched Dracula soar away, "I would rather keep my distance from him at the moment."

Venus merely nodded in silent, hate-filled agreement.

The women exchanged a glance between them that was a further understanding, which neither of them needed to explain to each other, especially in front of Renfield.

He is weaker now.

In the distance, the city swung below Dracula, appearing to kneel below him in awe after the vampire's spectacular triumph in the great amphitheater of old.

Rome would move at my whim tonight, thought the Son of Satan with an inner satisfaction. The Eternal City yawned beneath him, like the subjugated metropolis that Dracula had always known it to be. Below lay his food, his victims or his pawns; all at his beckon. His wound was healing but still bit at him, and Dracula grunted and endured the pain. Despite his injury, which the vampire knew would be slow to heal because of the accursed Holy Water, Dracula was content for a being that existed for nothing other than his own personal satisfaction.

In two bold strokes, Dracula had avenged the murder of his wife by the Englishmen and wiped out the naive insult of a conspiracy propagated by his cadaver-like rival Constantine. Now the Transylvanian nobleman could retreat to his castle and rest and plan and accept the usual shallow correspondences of support by the other vampiric politicos throughout Europe and the rest of the world, as if they themselves did not at the least know of the plot and had decided not to intervene.

He banked down toward the hotel below, seeing the balcony of his suite as it neared him, and the ground seemed to rise up to make his landing as smooth as possible. He drifted down through clouds that were lit from the city's incandescence. Dracula closed his eyes, did the gigantic bat, and felt the moisture from the cloud surround, embrace, then release him. He took in the smells and sounds the city: food cooking, people laughing, horseshoes clattering against the streets, bread baking.

As the gigantic bat drifted to the balcony window and his usual rest, his thoughts ran deep.

The first order of business is to decapitate the Egyptian whore upon arrival to the castle, thought Dracula as he spiraled downward. *After she has served her purpose on the return voyage. Or have the rats peel the flesh off her bones. Then crucify the Italian wench to an upside-down cross for the vultures to feed upon. Petra for her insolent request for release, and de' Medici for her blatant favoritism of her failed lover Nero during the duel. Then wipe out the townspeople for clearly aiding Young Harker. Or merely execute the village children to ensure future cooperation. Then kidnap new concubines.*

The Transylvanian was angry to see that Renfield had left the suite's windows open, the breeze pouring in to the room through the parted, curtained French doors and into the solemn, dark room. The curtains whispered with the night breeze. Inside would be their expansive suite filled with dark wood furniture and flooring.

I'll beat Renfield senseless for this latest stupidity thought Dracula as he stepped through the door, still in bat form. The vampire was so angry at the huge Englishman that he hissed in frustration, and that hiss made the Dracula bat not hear the sound of a pistol, positioned right at the very edge of the inside window pane, being cocked.

A heartbeat later, the Pepperbox Derringer went off in the right hand of Wilhelmina Murray.

SIX

Shot in the left ear, the Dracula bat fell to his right.

Crimson splattered all over Mina's black Victorian dress.

Dracula's left wing swung out and up, six-inch claws nearly ripping the right side of Wilhelmina's face clean off.

Before the huge bat had a chance to land on the hotel suite's wooden floor, Quincy Morris and Ian Seward, who were positioned just to the left of Mina Murray, ran out from behind her. They slid to a crouch in front of the staggered bat and began to pound the Dracula bat with blasts from Morris' Winchester and Ian's Webley.

"We've been waitin' for ya!" shouted Morris as he blasted away.

The power and momentum of the shots actually lifted the Transylvanian back upright. The impact of the Holy Water-dipped rounds, despite the fact that they went through the bat and punched into the ceiling of the suite, kept Dracula staggered and off-balance but on his feet. While the wounds did heal, they healed at a slower rate, and the wound from being impaled at the Colosseum burst open, with blood bubbling and oozing out in disgusting spurts. The winged apparition staggered and fell with a dark, hollow, thud.

"Stop!" shouted Abraham Van Helsing from the right side of the window frame.

Quincy and Ian held their fire and stepped back.

"Now," whispered Van Helsing, and out from the shadows from behind Abraham charged the furious, livid, enraged underlit form of Jonathan Harker.

He held the wooden, broken handle of a shovel in his hands.

This ends now, thought Abraham Van Helsing as he pivoted on the tableau and shut the French windows, carefully wrapping a rosary and garlic around the handles. He held a lantern in one hand, creating the only light source in the gloomy room where presently a murder was being committed.

Or attempted.

The great Dracula bat had fallen, its huge wings waving like sails in a strong crosswind.

Harker let out a roar from the depths of Hell as he screamed, "For our parents, you fiend!"

Jonathan slammed his weapon down at the Vampire's heart, but the Dracula bat coughed and twisted enough to that the shovel handle punched right into the wound from the pike, which spurted grotesquely.

The vampire had avoided a death blow but bellowed like a dying bear.

Harker jerked the shovel handle out of the wound and and tried to put all of his weight onto the shaft and ram it down through Dracula's heart. But the bat rolled away from the blow and swatted Jonathan away with a vicious swipe of his enormous right wing. Mina charged in and picked up the shovel handle to finish the job, but she was also thrashed away with a sweep from the left wing. Jonathan was thrown against a large sofa while Mina slammed into a bureau drawer.

Shock and fury rippled through the Dracula bat, but when the vampire stood as he pulled the shovel handle out of his wound, Quincy Morris bolted in from the left and slammed his Bowie knife right into the base of Dracula's neck like he was trying to split the world in half. An infernal yowl of pain erupted from the Dracula bat, which staggered backwards, the knife embedded up to the hilt in his neck. Red ichor belched from the wound, over the bat and the floor.

"Now, Sewie!" shouted Quincy as he sprinted away, "Hit 'im with them holy rounds!"

From the shadows sprinted Ian, who pounded the Dracula bat with more Webley rounds, emptying the revolver into the vampire, who flopped backwards onto the floor, bloody, beaten, and weakened. The Transylvanian coughed, and blood mixed with saliva sputtered out.

Abraham Van Helsing stepped forward while pulling an old book out of the recesses of his coat, the lantern in the other hand. As he did the sign of the cross over his face, Van Helsing said, "In nomine parties, et filii, et spiritus sancti." *In the name of the Father, of the Son, and of the Holy Spirit.*

The Dracula bat, though he lay like a bloodied rag in a dank alley, reacted to the words of prayer with fire. His brow furrowed, eyes dancing with fury, relit with the mere mention of the sacred.

The Son of Satan, bolted up and swung his massive left wing at Abraham, knocking the lantern out of his hand. It clattered to the wood floor.

Then Dracula vomited.

Into Van Helsing's face.

Bats.

He vomited bats.

Black, hairy, tiny and disgusting.

Writhing, squirming and flying.

Out of the vampire's fetid mouth.

All over the room.

The squirming bats all screeched horribly as they poured out of Dracula's mouth, and only then did Mina see that the outside form of the vampire was dissipating with the exit of the bats, in a surreal manner turning himself inside-out as the bats left his mouth. As the body dissipated, the head itself, turned into small bats themselves that hurtled out from the mouth and pelted Abraham with wet, matted fur and slimy, leathery skin.

The Bowie knife fell out of the neck wound and clattered harmlessly against the wooden floor.

The lantern fell on its side, ghostly shadows erupting from the change in lighting and crawling up along walls, shadows of bats multiplying the winged visions by double.

Jonathan dove on top of Mina, who had crumpled at the bottom of the bureau as the bats swarmed over them, clawing and snapping their tiny, canine-lined jaws at them.

"Godammit, he barfed himself into bats!" spat Morris as the tiny mammals swarmed him., filling the room with vermin. "Shoot 'em, Sewie!"

Ian Seward, an empty Webley in his hand and hundreds of bats frothing toward him, dove behind another drawer, a hundred bats on his heels.

Through the hailstorm of bats, Abraham stood and pulled his crucifix stake out from his coat, and when he thrust it out among the swarming, screeching bats, the holy object became incandescent, a beacon of purity in the gloom.

He shouted, "Crux sacra sit mihi lux! Non draco sit mihi dux! Vade retro satana! Numquam suade mihi vana! Sunt mala quae libas! Ipse venena bibas!" *Let the Holy Cross be my light! Let not the dragon be my guide! Step back Satan! Never tempt me with vain things! What you offer me is evil! You drink the poison yourself!*

Instantly the bats, who were circling around Abraham like hundreds of dark stars around a sun, scattered from the cross and back along the walls of the suite. The collective shrieking of the bats was overwhelming. Mina and the men all began to cover their ears with their hands, in the midst of a maelstrom.

"And when he had called unto him his twelve disciples, he gave them power against unclean spirits, to cast them out, and to heal all manner of sickness and all manner of disease![227]" railed Van Helsing, oblivious to the lightning storm of bats, waving the crucifix out around him, searing bats that flew into its trajectory. The seared bats left plumes of smoke as they flitted away, scorched by holiness. The bats, who had scattered to the corners of the room, now swept toward the center and floor of the chamber, working in union, as one single mind. They began to gather into one large, dark shape, all black but still textured from the tiny, crawling vermin.

Twin glowing eyes formed and bloomed where a jagged, predatory head was molding itself out of the flying vermin like a blasphemous Renaissance sculpture.

"Everyone!" shouted Abraham, and Mina, Jonathan, Ian and Quincy all looked up from their places in the room, swatting away flying mammals. "Out of the room! Lock the doors as we planned. Now!"

"He's too strong!" shouted Jonathan, his voice and face etched with concern.

"Stick to the plan, Jonny!" shouted Abraham, the dark shadow still massing in front of the beacon-like crucifix, twin eyes blazing right at Van Helsing. Most of the bats were shooting at and into the re-birthing form of Dracula.

Abraham girded himself, staring right back at the vampire roaring, "Get them all out and *lock him in with me!*"

Seward stood up and ran toward the French doors that separated Dracula's suite from the one to the left. He wrapped a crucifix around the handle before he closed it behind him. A glance by Van Helsing to the right revealed Jonathan closing the opposite door behind him. A crucifix and garlic dangled from that handle as well.

Abraham Van Helsing and Dracula of Transylvania were alone in the room.

The rustling of the bats over the body of the vampire made for an eerie wave of sound in an otherwise silent room.

Dracula, which had nearly re-formed, cast his jagged chin back toward the front door of the suite. It too had a crucifix around the handle, and garlic as well.

With the lantern illuminating the large room in an underlit, surreal fashion, more of the chamber became visible. The room was big, more of a salon. Three of the four walls had French doors linking that room to the other suites and were lined with cramped bookshelves. The wall behind Dracula had a regular doorframe leading to the hotel's hallway. Framing the door was an enormous, elaborate mirror, and Van Helsing could see himself, alone in the room without the vampire's reflection, in the mirror. The furniture consisted of two couches, two bureaus and chairs, which had been pushed to the corners of the room. In the middle of the room sat Dracula's huge, black coffin. Clearly the room had served as some kind of library for the hotel, or a venue for social gatherings.

When the Dracula bat realized the plan was a confrontation between himself and Abraham, he glared a hole right through Van Helsing's skull as he snarled wickedly. With his experience in dealing with the undead, Abraham would not be intimidated, and the vampire sensed this. As the Transylvanian leaned forward to pounce, Van Helsing noticed that the wound from Quincy's knife attack had not fully healed. He stared right back at Dracula before he slowly read, "'Now the names of the twelve apostles are these; the first, Simon, who is called Peter, and Andrew his brother; James the son of Zebedee, and John his brother—!'"[228]

---

[227] Biblical verse Matthew 10:1, King James version.

As he spoke, Abraham quickly slipped the crucifix into his coat pocket, sensing what was coming.

And he was right.

With a savage roar, the massive bat launched itself at Abraham, its leathery wings spread out nearly as wide as the room, but in one motion, Van Helsing drew out a small circular glass container and threw Holy Water at the vampire before crouching and rolling underneath the outstretched right wing. The bat shrieked in sharp pain as it swept by, smoke hissing out of its upper torso and neck.

Abraham bolted up, putting the bottle away and yanking out his crucifix knife again as the Dracula bat pivoted sharply to face him, incandescent eyes boiling hatred and rage. Behind him were Mina and Jonathan, both visible from behind the locked French doors, their faces pasted onto the glass doors in absolute terror and concern.

"That's the bravest man I've ever seen," gulped Mina.

"Amen," agreed Jonathan, both of them riveted on the combat.

"'Philip, and Bartholomew; Thomas, and Matthew the publican; James the son of Alphaeus, and Lebbaeus, whose surname was Thaddaeus![229]'" continued Abraham Van Helsing.

He took the initiative and did the impossible.

Van Helsing then charged at the demonic bat.

Taken completely by surprise, the Dracula bat took in the onrushing glowing cross and *retreated*, folded-up wings clawing and clambering over the sofa, up onto the wall and past the mirror, which eerily only reflected the charging Van Helsing.

"Simon the Canaanite, and Judas Iscariot, who also betrayed him![230]" bellowed Abraham as the bat's torso skidded back along the mirror, such was the vampire's eagerness to evade the cross. The mirror astonishingly reflected only blood trails and the pursuing Van Helsing. Abraham slipped the book away as he jumped onto the sofa, holding the cross up in his left hand, his right hand threw more Holy Water at the vampire, the drops sizzling wherever they landed on the huge mammalian. The son of Satan hissed in pain and anger at Van Helsing as its clawed fingertips latched into the bookcases that lined the right wall, and the bat clung to the shelves as it tried to crawl away from Van Helsing, who jumped off of the sofa, his glowing crucifix knife now held high as he shouted, "'These twelve Jesus sent forth, and commanded them, saying, Go not into the way of the Gentiles, and into any city of the Samaritans enter ye not![231]'"

As it climbed and clawed its way along the bookcase, the vampire dislodged the contents of the shelves. Abraham continued to pursue it, white-hot crucifix blade safely held in his firm grip.

Heart of Darkness and the Congo Diary by Joseph Conrad fell onto and off of Van Helsing.

"But go rather to the lost sheep of the house of Israel—[232]"

As did *The Time Machine* by H.G. Wells, followed *The Invisible Man*, *The War of the Worlds* and *The Island of Doctor Moreau*, which punched Abraham in the nose.

"'—and as ye go, preach, saying, the Kingdom of Heaven is at hand![233]'"

Abraham swung and blocked Kipling's *The Jungle Book*, before it could hit him.

"'Heal the sick, cleanse the lepers, raise the dead, cast out devils: freely ye have received, freely give![234]'"

---

[228] Matthew 10:2, King James version.
[229] Matthew 10:3, King James version.
[230] Matthew 10:4, King James version.
[231] Matthew 10:5, King James version.
[232] Matthew 10:6, King James version.
[233] Matthew 10:7, King James version.
[234] Matthew 10:8, King James version.

Dracula, still crawling along the wall, reached the right French door and reached for it, but the clawed mammalian's wings sizzled when it tried to rip open the handle with the rosary and garlic hanging from it. Abraham continued his pursuit, crucifix all the while in front of him as the bat rained more and more books down off the shelves onto him with its massive wings. Abraham could see through the French doors into the next room, taking in the concerned looks of both Quincy and Seward, but had to ignore his instinct for their concern and focus on the task at hand.

"Bloody Hell," gasped Ian, who could not believe his eyes.

"Ya got 'im on the run!" ya-hooed Quincy. "Get 'im Uncle Abraham!"

Wilde's *Picture of Dorian Gray* did not dissuade Van Helsing and fell aside.

"'—and the seventy returned again with joy, saying, Lord, even the devils are subject unto us through thy name—[235]'"

Cyrano de Bergerac by Edmond Rostand.

The Interpretation of Dreams by Sigmund Freud.

"'—and these signs shall follow them that believe; In my name shall they cast out devils; they shall speak with new tongues—[236]'"

The Great God Pan by Machen plunked Abraham on the forehead, but he was unbowed.

"'—and there was in their synagogue a man with an unclean spirit; and he cried out—[237]'"

In rapid succession cascaded *Dickenson: Poems*, *The Anti-Christ* by Fredrich Nietzsche and *The Red Badge of Courage* by Stephen Crane.

"'—saying, Let us alone; what have we to do with thee, thou Jesus of Nazareth? art thou come to destroy us? I know thee who thou art, the Holy One of God—[238]'"

The Watcher and other Weird Stories by Joseph Sheridan Le Fanu fell.

Quo Vadis by Henry Sienkiewicz was cast aside in a fury by Van Helsing, who shouted, "'And Jesus rebuked him, saying, Hold thy peace, and come out of him![239]'"

The Dracula bat whipped his shaggy head around, bellowed and vomited crimson gore all over Abraham Van Helsing, who shut his eyes, did the sign of the cross over himself and threw more Holy Water onto the great bat, which then fell off its perch along the front wall and onto the floor, splaying out, wounded, bloodied and exhausted.

Ripe for the picking thought Van Helsing as he charged, pulling out a large wooden stake from his bag.

The moment to impale had arrived.

---

[235] Luke 10:17, King James version.
[236] Mark 16:17, King James version.
[237] Mark 1:23, King James version.
[238] Mark 1:24, King James version.
[239] Mark 1:25, King James version.

SEVEN

As soon as the Venus and Petra bats landed on the wide, moonlit balcony of Dracula's suite, they heard the unheard-of, which was a booming scream of pain from their master. They crossed the balcony in a heartbeat, their wings along the ground, where they saw through the French doors Van Helsing leaping at the Dracula bat with a sharpened wooden stake. Venus instantly lashed out with her left wing to smash open the doors, only to have her claws hiss and burn from the touch of the glass and wooden frame. She tried to punch through with her right wing closed into a fist, but while the glass within the frame crumpled, it did not fall out. They both saw the rosary and garlic lashed around the inner door handle and knew their entry was being prevented. Petra growled and put her shoulder into the door, which produced a burst of supernatural flames over her. The Petra bat's thrust should have been enough to break open any other door, but they held as the ethereal flames dissipated.

The supernaturally-protected door held and kept them outside.

Inside, the weakened Dracula bat lifted its right leg and desperately kicked out at Van Helsing as he charged with his wooden stake. Abraham somehow twisted so his left ribs did not take in the full impact of the blow, but it was still vicious enough to shoot him across the room and slam him into the near-empty bookshelves. A clean blow would have been enough to kill any human.

As he regained his feet, Abraham winced as he felt the sting in his ribs. A glance out through the broken glass doors explained that the brides had arrived, so he shouted, "Visitors abound!"

To Abraham's right, the doors to the hall outside of the suite began to pound with knocks. "Il personale dell'hotel, si prega di aprire la porta!" accompanied the knocks. *Hotel staff, please open the door!*

Behind him, on the other side of the see-through doors, Jonathan shouted, "Understood! We're ready!"

"We're ready Uncle Abraham!" shouted Quincy from behind the far door. "Gut 'im like a razorback!"

"What the hell is a razorback?" he heard Ian add.

Outside, the Venus bat bolted to the left, clambering over the railing, along the wall of the hotel and toward the next balcony over, while the Petra bat spread her wings, lifted off the balcony and soared to the right, knifing in through the open French windows. Petra knifed right into the gunsights of Mina Murray, who sat in the darkness of the adjoining suite with her Winchester at the ready, next to Jonathan Harker, who had his Webley pointed out at Rome's rooftops.

They both unloaded into the silhouette of the she-bat.

As the gunshots went off on the other balcony, the Venus bat crouched near the edge of her French doors, which were slightly ajar as well. She very carefully started to peer around the doorframe, her nose protruding onto the window, sniffing for scent when she heard a rifle chamber a round.

"Come on in, li'l lady," she heard a voice chime with a twang, "the water's just fine."

After taking a step back, the bat stood upright from its crouch as it metamorphosized back into the nubile, feminine form of Venus.

Amid all the noise around her, from the other suites and the hallway inside, Venus de' Medici stepped in through the window and the fluttering curtains. Crouched in the dark, behind a desk and settee, Morris and Seward took in the voluptuous silhouetted form with the glowing pupils before them. Her hair and dress swayed with the incoming breeze.

In the library, Dracula flipped over from his back onto his bat-winged clawed hands, his shaggy mammalian head dropping with exhaustion and spent energy. He gave out a long, slow hiss at Abraham Van Helsing, who stood roiling with energy, his crucifix back out in front of him, "'And when he was come out of the ship, immediately there met him out of the tombs a man with an unclean spirit—[240]'"

The bat viciously slammed a chair aside, leaped up and snapped its white jagged teeth at Abraham, who jerked the cross out at the bat like a right jab, and the bat reared back in fear and instinctual respect.

"'For he said unto him, Come out of the man, thou unclean spirit! [241]'"

The Dracula bat dropped back down to all fours, and started to bare its canines, its back raised, its head low to the ground, and it began to growl, and that growl deepened.

And the bat began to change.

"'—and he asked him, what is thy name? [242]'"

As the Dracula bat circled Van Helsing, it began to metamorphosize again, and as the body boiled with demonic change, the satanic visage of Dracula of Transylvania roared in a deep, unearthly voice, "'Legio nomen mihi est, est quia multi sumus!'"*My name is Legion, for we are many!*

Wings became forelegs, clawed feet became padded feet, a tail grew out, fine fur became denser and a snout full of canine teeth had grown in what was now a massive, black wolf. It snarled savagely at Abraham, great foaming jaws gnashing in primal rage as it stepped bodily over Dracula's coffin, such was the size of the beast. It was a quadruped, with enormous shoulders and forearms. Its eyes were small but focused and full of liquid hate. Sharp, triangular ears topped the massive head, but right now they had dropped and pointed backward in anger. The snout resembled a wolf's in every way except it was shorter, but the teeth inside the mouth were all so pronounced it was difficult to imagine how they could fit inside the lips of the monster. Bigger than a man, the Dracula wolf was larger than a Bengal tiger.

Yet Abraham Van Helsing was unbowed.

The knocking from the doors in the hallway had given way to pounding, with shouts in Italian now mixed in. The roars and gunshots from inside quieted them momentarily, then the pounding resumed, accompanied by distant whistles associated with the *Polizia di Stato*.

Inside the suite to the right, round after round from Mina's Winchester blew the Petra bat backwards, the enormous beast flailing its expansive wings and knocking over furniture, framed paintings and even wallpaper, which the bat clawed off the walls with her razor-sharp talons. The she-bat recovered during a moment's respite from the bombardment. She saw that Mina was reloading and charged, but Jonathan stood and ran toward Petra, his Webley aflame. The Petra bat rose up, lifted just off the ground, and when Jonathan's Webley clicked empty, the bat brought her head down

---

[240] Mark 1:25, King James version.
[241] Mark 1:25, King James version.
[242] Mark 1:25, King James version.

savagely at Jonathan, with the intent of biting his head clean off. From behind Jonathan came Mina, and she thrust her rifle barrel just past Jonathan's head and shouted, "Leave him alone, bitch!"

She fired, as Harker covered his ears. The round blew back the Petra bat's head and battered the monster bodily against the far wall.

In the third suite, Ian Seward bolted up from behind the settee, and from out of his coat pocket came a sharpened crucifix. Ian held it out in front of the dark, feminine form with the blazing pupils and sensual countenance that glided toward him across the wooden floor of the suite.

As Venus neared, the crucifix began to glow.

Still crouched behind the desk, Quincy Morris saw the glow and his jaw dropped. "My Mama was a Baptist, so I dunno if she'd have liked me thinkin' that this Catholic stuff was workin' fine, but it is, Sewie! It is!"

The undead woman in front of Ian Seward was the perverse embodiment of the masterworks by Botticelli and Cabanel. Venus de' Medici would never be described as demure. She let Ian notice that her eyes drifted over him in appraisal, and her eyes hardened in disapproval. "My mother was a wealthy patron of the arts in Florence when your grandmothers were birthed in brothels."

"My grandmother knows who her father was," smirked Ian, showing more bravery than he really felt.

Venus ignored the insult, her smile lovelier than cream in tea.

"You are both young men, not boys," she said with a grin that was born in a convent. Venus' dress, translucent and backlit by the moon, fluttered in the night breeze along with her raven tresses. She glided closer to Ian, and her eyes began to beckon.

De' Medici reached out, away from him, and ran her hand over the French door to Dracula's suite like it was an old lover.

Her fingers flickered with profane flame.

Ian's smile wavered at her stunning majesty, entranced.

The mouse in front of the cobra.

He backed up, touching the French door as well, with no divine fire.

Venus had her answer.

A wolf's snarl and a subsequent crash sounded from the adjoining suite.

Closer, she snaked.

"Sewie," whispered Morris as he cocked the Winchester, "Kindly get outta my line o' sight, ya lovesick puppy. I wanna shoot this two-dollar bar dancer."

The Dracula wolf snarled again as it crept around Abraham Van Helsing, who stood strong, holding it at bay with his crucifix. The incandescent light from the crucifix dominated the fallen lantern that blanketed the suite with somber shadows.

An unbowed Abraham shouted, "Crux sacra sit mihi lux!" *Let the Holy Cross be my light!*

The Dracula wolf snapped enormous, jagged jaws, its ruby eyes fixed directly on Abraham, who continued, "Non draco sit mihi dux!" *Let not the dragon be my guide!*

Many things then happened very quickly:

Anticipating that the Dracula Wolf was about to try and leap over the crucifix and attack him, Abraham slipped his book into his coat pocket as the wolf dove to its left to avoid the cross.

Van Helsing pulled out a fistful of medallions: a Jewish mezuzah, a copper Ganesh- medallion from the Hindu faith, Islamic prayer beads, a Tibetan Buddha all-seeing eye, a Saint Benedict's medal, and threw a wide, strong and vicious left hook.

Medals and a fist connected brutally and cleanly with the Dracula wolf's right cheek.

The wolf flew sideways and crashed into the door to the hallway.

The flame that erupted from the rosary and garlic-covered handle on the front door was the only thing that kept the wolf from smashing through and plowing into whoever was pounding at the door to the hotel hallway.

Screams could be heard from the hallway in reaction to the wolf's impact, as well as shouting in Italian and more police whistles.

The wolf squirmed in anguish as it pulsed like a metamorphosing cocoon. It yowled in pain, canid features melting and bubbling grotesquely as it shakily rose. Hindquarters quivered and forelegs skated along the floor.

But this was no ordinary being, and the Dracula thing found its resolve, fueled by a wounded pride.

A transformative instant later, in a breathtaking metamorphosis that even impressed one Professor Abraham Van Helsing, Dracula was the form of a bat again, and it snarled in embarrassed anger as it began to climb up the door, toward the ceiling.

"Coward!" roared Van Helsing. "Face this humble instrument of all that is good in this world!"

Now upside down along the ceiling, the Dracula bat hissed spittle at Van Helsing, and began to crawl along the top of the room, its claws sinking into the painted and frescoed ceiling, a literal demon clambering over an idyllic painted scenery of trees, flowers and fields as Van Helsing held the cross in his right hand, the medallions in his left as he shouted, "Vade retro satana!" *Step back Satan!*

Dracula heard this and sent out an unholy shriek of rage and launched himself right at Van Helsing, wings spread out, with talons spread at the end of each webbed finger.

A horrific vision that wound terrify even the most hardened soldier.

Yet this was no mere man.

Abraham Van Helsing swung his right fist, holding the crucifix, and ferociously punched the Dracula bat in the sternum with a terrific blow.

The room filled with a bright light from the crucifix and the medals, and the bat flew head over heels, colliding with the bookcase, causing *Pride and Prejudice, Jane Eyre, The Picture of Dorian Grey, Great Expectations, Little Women, Sense and Sensibility, The Adventures of Huckleberry Fin, The Count of Monte Cristo, Crime and Punishment, Les Miserables, A Tale of Two Cities, War and Peace, Oliver Twist, The Scarlet Letter, The Adventures of Tom Sawyer, Mansfield Park, The Three Musketeers, David Copperfield, Bleak House, Around the World in Eighty Days, The Adventures of Sherlock Holmes, Uncle Tom's Cabin, Alice's Adventures in Wonderland & Through the Looking Glass, The Importance of Being Earnest, Treasure Island, The Portrait of a Lady, The Idiot* and *The Last of the Mohicans* to cascade down on the bat.

Venus was taken aback when she heard the books collapse upon Dracula, and his resulting yowl of pain.

Her instinct kicked in, despite the nature of her relationship with her husband or master or whatever he was to her at the moment.

The protective portion of Venus de' Medici took over.

Her hands shot out in one lightning-quick move, grabbed a startled Ian by the lapels, and before Quincy could react she pivoted and hurled him bodily through the French doors and into the other suite.

Glass, wood framing, garlic and rosary beads blew through the air like autumn leaves in a gale.

Ian Seward plowed and crashed. into the library.

He soared past the charging Van Helsing and collided with the black coffin in the middle of the room.

"For all of your countless victims, for all the children you have devoured!" roared Abraham as he yanked the wooden stake out of his bag and raised it over his head. Dracula yelped pathetically as he scrambled along the bottom of the book case, not trying to hide his fear of being impaled. More books rained upon the shapeshifting form, which was twitching intermittently between wolf, then bat, then rat, then mist, then wolf again, panic written all over Dracula's bubbling, changing face like bursting boils from a victim of the medieval plague.

Dracula, conqueror and terror of the Old World, crawled away from Van Helsing like a feral dog with a broken leg.

"For all of the cities you have razed!" screamed Abraham, bringing down his stake in a savage blow, missing the Dracula form as it twisted away, eyes drowning in fear.

"For all the women you have dishonored!" spat Van Helsing, this blow swatted away in panic by a malformed wolf's leg.

"And for all the churches you have desecrated!"

This blow tore a piece of Dracula's belly skin off as the vampire desperately tried to flail away from his attacker.

They locked eyes, and the predator had become the prey, the hunted was now after the hunter. Dracula was beaten.

"Kill him!" screamed Ian as he lay where he had been thrown into the library.

The splayed-out vampire was a monstrosity, resembling a bubbling mass of animal body parts as it dragged itself away from Abraham.

Dracula's pride was gone, his confidence was gone, and his existence on Earth was about to be taken from him.

The Son of Satan pathetically raised a half-formed bat wing in a meek attempt at self defense.

Abraham Van Helsing raised his wooden stake up for a final, fatal blow.

Just as the dark, nubile form of Venus de' Medici slammed into him.

The blow was tremendous.

Abraham shot through the air.

Van Helsing was sent flying across the library, the wind knocked out of him.

He slammed viciously against the mirrored wall, sending a million spider web cracks and reflections out before he collapsed down onto the sofa, rendered unconscious.

Venus landed deftly, then turned and shouted to Petra in the other suite, "Gettate uno degli esseri umani attraverso la porta! Si romperà l'incantesimo!" *Throw one of the humans through the door! It will break the spell!*

The sound of a charging she-bat emanated from the adjoining suite, and a moment later, the opposite French door exploded.

Mina flew into the library, hurtled by the snarling Petra bat.

Wilhelmina Murray skidded along the wooden floor and to the coffin where Seward was just gathering his senses.

Frothing rage, the Petra bat bounded into the library, followed by Jonathan, who gathered Mina's semi-conscious body and pulled it toward the front of the room. Morris also bolted into the room and past Ian, his Winchester ablaze. He shot at the still-reeling, yet re-forming Dracula but hit the brown blur that was the Petra bat, who had run over to shield the Transylvanian with outstretched wings. Quincy's aim was true and wicked, yet Petra held her ground and deflected the rifle shots to the wings, head and body. She wailed with pain at the gunshots. The Holy Water in the rounds left hissing burns where they had landed, but the she-bat's protection remained intact. Her clawed wingtips scratched handholds along the wooden floorboards.

Quincy pelted the Petra bat with gunfire, but she would not budge.

Beneath her lay Dracula, nearly formed back into his human shape.

Mina sat up and shook off broken glass from having been thrown into the room, then her jaw dropped.

"She's got him!" she shrieked in a semi-panic, so loudly that they all turned to the sound of her voice and saw an unconscious Abraham Van Helsing in the iron grip of Venus.

Everyone stopped.

De' Medici leered wickedly at them as she held him aloft, effortlessly holding the large man over her head.

She abruptly dropped her arm, and a now-standing Ian gasped as Van Helsing's head banged sharply against the floor.

Abraham lay on the ground like a broken puppet, held by the neck by the vampiress.

She glided over to Dracula and the Petra bat, dragging Abraham along. In her clutches, Van Helsing at last stirred and gurgled, unable to breathe with the vampiress' human-form hand around his throat.

As Venus regarded everyone else in the room, she eased her grip.

Somewhat.

Abraham, still groggy, coughed and gagged from the pressure.

At least he's still alive, thought Mina. But the thought of her uncle being murdered flooded back memories of the massacre at Seward manor, and she attempted to lunge for Abraham, but she was pulled back by Jonathan. They both stood in front of the doors to the hotel hallway, which were being pounded on heavily from the outside, accompanied by continued shouting in Italian.

"Portare la chiave!" shouted an officious-sounding woman's voice from the hallway door. *Bring the key!*

"Chiama la polizia qui!" shrieked a falsetto male voice. *Call the Police up here!*

"Find Tibor," moaned a half-conscious Van Helsing.

"Rompere la porta!" *Break open the door!* ordered a baritone-voiced male.

At that moment, a gust swept in from the night, from the opposing suites, and blew the lantern out. The room was plunged into the stillness of night, except for the glowing embers that were the eyes of the vampires.

After a long moment, with only the sounds coming from the hallway outside, Dracula collected himself, seething as he stood.

The Transylvanian was exhausted, wounded, beaten badly but with his well of resolve replenished. Dracula's eyes dancing with fury as he hissed, "Your opportunity is lost, your leader is ours and—," he paused as he took a menacing step forward, "Your faith is an empty vessel."

An air of dread and death filled the hotel's library.

The brides also glided forward, lionesses ready to leap.

Quincy tried to chamber a round of his Winchester but there was none.

Jonathan found his Webley.

Ian and Mina found their weapons.

They all pulled their triggers.

Repeatedly.

At nothing.

Into emptiness.

The only sounds were the hollow clicks of empty gun chambers.

As the pounding of the door rang louder, a sense of panic grew over the young ones.

"Delicious," said Venus, holding a still-dazed Van Helsing up off the ground with one arm as she moved to them.

She meant them.

Her food.

Then, a light.

In the darkened room, there was light.

Not from the vampires.

Nor from the guns.

But from the cross in Jonathan's right hand, the one that was thrust out before the undead.

Light.

Full of brightness.

Light, full of faith.

Light that brought hope with it.

And further enlightenment.

And encouragement.

And a smile to the face of one Jonathan Harker.

A crisp nod of resolve from Mina Murray.

A few tears of appreciation from Ian Seward.

And a stupid leer from one smirking Quincy Morris.

The light burned enough, breathtakingly enough, to make the *nosferatu* take a collective step *backward*.

"I've seen Hell, so now I know there is a Heaven," snarled Jonathan at Dracula, the crucifix lit from within like a candle in a lantern, a beacon in the gloom. *"Vade retro Satana, numquam suade mihi vana!" Step back Satan! Never tempt me with vain things!*

"Let him go!" shouted Mina as she gestured at the immobile Van Helsing.

"We take our leave," said Dracula, who eyed the hallway door and the constant pounding behind it. "But not before I cut off the head of the serpent."

With that, he turned, ripped a still-shaken Abraham from the arms of Venus and hurtled him through the French doors and out onto the balcony. Van Helsing tumbled helplessly and did not move after his body landed.

"Ya damn filthy pig!" roared Quincy, his eyes full of tears.

Ian held the livid Texan back. "We're out of rounds, mate!"

"Uncle Abraham!" shouted Mina.

"God damn you!" screamed Jonathan, full of venom.

"He already has," leered Dracula.

As the Transylvanian backed away, he began to melt and grow into his bat form. He and the Petra bat turned and ran, followed by the transforming Venus. They knifed through the open French doors and out to the Eternal City's night.

"Uncle Abraham!" they all shouted together and bolted for the door, but Van Helsing was a wet load of laundry on the balcony floor. As the two bride bats began to flap their vast wings to gain air, the Dracula bat leaped onto the still form of Abraham Van Helsing. Then the bat thrust its winged knuckles onto the ground, then pushed off and leaped off the balcony and out of view with the body of Abraham in its wicked lower claws.

As they ran out of the suite, Jonathan, Mina, Quincy and Ian heard the doors breaking open behind them. They watched out, over the darkened city of Rome, where the gigantic Dracula bat was rising up between the two flying bride bats, still carrying the dangling, limp form of Abraham Van Helsing.

Flying away.

Away.

With their adventurer.

Their leader.

Their uncle.

Their light.

Gone.

Mina burst into tears, as did Jonathan.

Quincy, the stout Texan, bled silent tears, as did Ian as they watched the Dracula bat ascend, ascend and ascend more until he let go of Van Helsing, whose inert form then tumbled through the sky.

The bats flew on.

Mina screamed silently as Abraham fell through the night.

The crowd from the hotel hallway reached them. A woman behind Jonathan screamed, and he found and held the whimpering Mina's hand as the silhouetted body of Abraham Van Helsing fell down and into the distant skyline of Rome.

Gone.

FROM THE JOURNAL OF MONTAGUE RHODES RENFIELD

In the hours left before dawn here in Rome, there were a few events that have puzzled me, and it was in those few moments of eve's end that I first began to question my master's reasoning. Said events began at the bloody Colosseum, which saw the master come out in a strange state of mood, temperament and injury. I then was instructed to meet the master and his loathsome, stinking concubines at the hotel at which we had been residing, and I returned to a scene of complete chaos. Crowds was thick as thieves along the exterior of the hotel, and I knew not what my next step was to be, when I was summoned to a darkened corner of the opposing street, and at the mouth of an even darker alley was Venus, the disgusting harlot of the master. She slid onto the wagon next to me and directed me to a cemetery outside Rome, where Petra and my master waited among the shadowy crypts and tombstones.

To my great surprise, the master appeared even worse than he did when he had flown to the Colosseum. He was in the shape of a bat and his injuries had been furthered, yet I had to suppress the urge to aid him, knowing the master's reticence for assistance, which I had experienced earlier that evening when my offer of help was met with my nearly being torn apart.

The Venus concubine started to elaborate to me on the evening's events and was silenced by a savage growl from the master, who them transformed into his human form and, despite his clear state of exhaustion, relayed to me that I would be readying us all to return to his homeland, a prospect that excited my greatly. He gave to me another small bag of gold and asked me to inquire discreetly and procure for us three coffins from the nearest cooper[243], as their old coffins had been left at the hotel amid the circumstances that remained a mystery to me. I was curious, but I learned a long time ago not ask any bloody questions that are not any of my bloody business. I was to bring them coffins back to the graveyard for the trip home, and that he would wait with the harlots and rats in a nearby crypt. In the meantime I placed the remaining coffin, that of the delicious, juicy rats, in one of the larger, cooler crypts, and without hesitation the master slid into the coffin to rest, while the rats went forth to eat what they could find, always at the master's beck and call. The insufferable brides retreated to a dark corner of what was clearly a sniffy crypt used by an Italian family with a bit of coin. The tarts seemed even more resentful of the master than they were at the Colosseum. Whatever activity and events that had presented themselves at the hotel had clearly furthered their bitterness toward my master. Something about saving his life, one of them muttered.

The brides reposed on the cold marble floor, Petra in clear discomfort at not having her native Egyptian soil at the ready, as was the usual circumstance in her abandoned coffin, if I am understanding the master's explanations rightly. Regardless, the darkie's feelings were irrelevant to me, the master is all that matters to me now that he has saved me from insanity and given my life a new, glorious purpose...

I went forth to fetch the replacement coffins and was able to procure them for a reasonable price, a hefty tip ensuring no questions would be asked or answered with regard to this matter, with the underlying threat of retribution to insure this. These looked like old coffins, not the well-to-do coffins that they all had before. These were just regular coffins for regular folks, which made me laugh thinking that these royal people had to sleep in them.

Returning to the crypt, I filled the Italian wench's coffin with earth, as I did for the rats as well as the Egyptian tramp. My thoughts briefly went to the notion of creating a funeral pyre of the brides' coffins and setting them ablaze in the middle of the day, but I thought it better to ask my master first. I will write that I heard the Egyptian comment, "I also once had a few loves of my own," to the Italian bird as she slid into her own nest of sin. I know not what to make of that statement, nor do I care. Nor does it surprise me, though the two harpies should show more respect for the master, even though he is vicious with them upon occasion, though I think he does what any master would do with two wild beasts, that is, to beat them before they have a mind to tear him to pieces.

Having loaded all of the coffins onto the wagon, I made for the Italian coast, intent to book passage on the first boat or ship that could escort us around the Italian horn, through the Adriatic and towards the misty mountains and dark forests of the Balkans.

To where I first felt love's kiss.

To my master's home.

---

[243] A cooper is an old profession where a craftsman makes objects like barrels, utensils, drums and coffins out of wood and other materials.

IN THE STREETS OF ROME

Somewhere in the aftermath of the chaos of the balcony, with guests, aristocrats, bankers, politicians and Italian police swarming through the library, examining the shattered doors and demolished suites, Jonathan Harker and his three dear friends numbly made their way out of there and onto the streets, which were also filled with night and with frothing crowds. Since the suites were not theirs, Mina, Jonathan, Quincy and Ian were not held responsible for the damages to the library room, though a few well-placed monetary 'apologies' helped pave their way to freedom from responsibility and more importantly, questions about what they were doing there in the first place.

Hotel staff could be surprisingly patient and understanding if all damages were paid for.

Mina, Quincy and Ian had shouted over the din outside that the first thing they needed to do was to find Abraham's body, and Jonathan found himself agreeing with them with his words while his heart disagreed completely. Yet he said nothing and just held onto Abraham's old bag of tricks as Mina stood outside the hotel while she and Ian anxiously debated the approximate trajectory that the bats had taken when they had flown out over the city and dropped their last living family member. Jonathan patted the bag like it was an old friend, which it was.

By the time Morris had used his Texas frontiersman's nose for tracking to align the search for them all, Jonathan had all but made up his mind as to what he was going to do, and when the policemen's whistles brought what seemed like most of the population of Rome out into the street, they wove their way through the crowds, and he lingered a bit, all the while understanding that when he let go of Mina's hand like he intended to do, it would be for the last time in their lives they would see each other.

They pushed resolutely through the surging crowd, moving to the vague direction of Abraham's descent and fighting the buffeting energy of the people moving around them.

Somewhere in all that, Jonathan Harker let go.

I wish I had married, you, my love, was what Jonathan thought as he released her, and with regret consuming him he watched all of her strength, charm, intellect and beauty run away from him, pointing and leading Ian and Quincy in their pursuit of a dream, her free hand gesturing back toward him, certain that he was right there with her, just behind her, as he had been always, since they were children. They refused to believe that their Uncle Abraham was dead, that their leader lived no more, that the adventurer could never die, but Jonathan had been in a better position than the others, he had seen Van Helsing's fall.

He knew.

Harker stopped, and his eyes filled with tears as he watched her go, away from him for the last time. He knew she would look back his way in seconds, and he had to be gone by then. *Whomever you marry, may he know that he becomes the happiest soul in the world*, and his throat swelled with emotion and his eyes filled with tears, as he watched them melt into the crowd. He stopped, wished them well, and moved away diagonally and in the opposite direction.

Away from his friends, his own love.

Toward Hell.

TRAIN

An hour later, Jonathan sat exhausted and alone in the seat of a train, which was about to depart the Rome station.

He'd wandered through the nighttime streets of the Eternal City, in a daze, still overwhelmed at the suddenness of Abraham's death and his decision to go forward alone, but the man who had been no blood relation to him but loved him like few people had in his life was gone. A million memories of Abraham Van Helsing, professor and adventurer now flowed through Jonathan, from his childhood, appreciating his father, yet enthralled with the two-fisted traveler that would come visit them all from time to time, bearing gifts and stories from all over the world, and Jonathan's eyes flowed with tears more than once as he stumbled along the streets, wide and narrow, as he thought of Abraham's smile, his strength, the way other men admired him and how women swooned over him, yet as much as Lucy's mother had chased him, as did other women around Van Helsing, he never seemed to be content with anything other than telling charming stories of his late wife. He grinned at the memory of a particular Christmas party where Abraham had enthralled all of them with his stories of his previous Christmas in the Holy Land. Now, as a young man, Jonathan reflected on those memories and could now see a sweet loneliness in the late Abraham Van Helsing, a man who, when having so tragically lost his own family, turned to them for comfort when he wasn't out seeing the world, or as Harker had recently discovered, tracking down dark things and ridding the world of them.

Jonathan knew dawn was just a few hours away because every bakery in Rome had the addictive, delicious odor of freshly-baking bread wafting out of their chimneys, a fact not lost on Jonathan's stomach. It growled at him, and he ignored his pang of hunger since the city had come to a crawl in the hours before dawn.

As he moved farther way, the commotion coming from the scene outside the hotel had died, and all there was left were Jonathan's shoes clicking against the cobblestones and sidewalks, alone even in their scattered echoes, his shadow running along the far walls of the streets, lit by gas lamps that in Roman times would have used oil.

At last he found the railway station, alone and dark, just like him. The ticket office was closed and dim. Jonathan Harker curled up on a bench, then fell asleep. The next moment he was shaken awake by a still-sleepy ticket taker. It was nearly dawn, and he got up off the bench and went over to the ticket station, bought his ticket, and staggered onto the train.

Now, at the lowest point of his life, Jonathan sat down in his chair as the engine coupled with the car. As the entire compartment was jolted and swayed, Jonathan thought that until this moment, he'd never felt alone, even through his travels through Europe to find Uncle Peter. Even in his journeys back and forth across the Atlantic with his parents, young Harker had always felt like he had the love of his parents, the love of his friends, the love of their parents and above all, the love of Wilhelmina Murray.

Jonathan rummaged through his own bag as well as Abraham's until he found Uncle Peter's journal and one of Abraham's fountain pens among Van Helsing's small but beloved collection of quills, ink wells and ball points. He flipped to the unused, unwritten pages in the back of the journal and wrote:

Mlle. Wilhelmina Murray
Murray estate
Whitby England

Dearest Mina,

I love you eternally. Leaving you and our friends back in Rome was the most difficult decision I have ever had to make in my life, I do want to explain to you in this letter, in Uncle Peter's Journal, whenever and however it may make its way back to you, that you are my beloved. I have loved you since we were children, and I knew that I loved you when we were eleven years old, and that my heart is yours always and forever. Seeing you for one last time as you moved away from me in the crowd in Rome will haunt me as long as I live, which will surely not be as long as you. I love you so much that I let you go, so that you may yourself live your life fully, not chasing corpses through graveyards at the witching hour. That is no way for a lady such as yourself to lead her life, and as the woman of my dreams I must also understand that you deserve better, you of all people with your class, dignity, and amazing grace, deserve someone better than a rumpled young man like myself who has lost everything, including you. You are the woman I have based my life upon, you are my ideal, you are my one truth. I can always treasure our memories, but your smile, your laughter, the sparkle in your eyes, the way you make me feel like I can conquer the world, that I will carry with me.

I leave you now, with the hope that this journal and this farewell will be found and make its way back to you. I am sorry for all of the times I have failed you. You made me a better man because you were always a better woman. You were always the woman of my dreams. I adore you and we loved a lifetime's worth, and there was only really you for me, always.

Yours forever,
JH

Jonathan, his eyes brimming with tears, closed the journal and placed it and the fountain pen back within Abraham's bag. Now his parents were dead, along with the rest of his family, and he had left everything that mattered to him back among the crowded streets of Rome. He felt more alone the more the engine surged and the train shook forward, swaying the few other passengers on the train moving in the same direction, yet none of them headed in the direction of certain death.

Harker felt drained but satisfied that his friends would have no further involvement in all this. *I'll climb up into his fortress the same way I was thrown out*, he thought, trying not to consider how far he had fallen into the river when Dracula had tossed him out of the castle window, which seemed like a lifetime ago. Harker also set aside the skeletons and rats as well. He'd already lost Lucy, Arthur and Abraham on this journey, to say nothing of their parents, so Jonathan felt good reason to spare anyone else what lay at the end of his pursuit.

He reached over and patted Abraham's bag of tricks again, for more comfort, as he looked out the window. Trees flew by, seeming to be flying of their own accord instead of being planted along a forest hillside adjacent to the railway. Everything he had known in his life, his family, was gone, and now more memories flooded over him, dinners, parties, holidays, and he thought at *least they will live on. I hope she marries a good man.*

Exhausted, Jonathan Harker closed his eyes, slid sideways in his seat and drifted off to sleep.

The train compartment rattled around.

He dreamed of the beauteous Mina Murray and bats that blasphemed in Latin.

EASTERN EUROPE
LATE SUMMER, EARLY FALL 1899

Five thousand years before Jonathan Harker fell asleep on a train headed Northeast through Italy, toward inevitability, the Balkan region had been one of the cradles of civilization.

Somewhere between Venice and the Black sea, the region held a deep, mysterious, cultural mosaic of society, faith and war. Ancient Rome and Ancient Greece had expanded, warred, conquered and died over a span of eight hundred years. Hannibal's elephants thundered over the entire region in its fateful war with Rome and ended up conquering most of the Ancient World. Julius Caesar was born, ruled and was assassinated in Rome's Theatre of Pompey[244], about a hundred years before the city of Pompeii was itself engulfed by the eruption of Mount Vesuvius[245]. It was after Caesar's death that Cleopatra, last Pharaoh of Ancient Egypt, half-Egyptian herself, then aligned with Mark Anthony, despite the fact that she had borne a son to Caesar. She would bear twins to Anthony as well. Ancient Rome and Ancient Greece took turns expanding and contracting their empires over the region through the centuries before the Christ was born, lived and had been crucified. Hun, Mongol, Goth and Lombard roamed the lands. Phoenician became Greek, which then became Cyrillian. The Bible was assembled as a result of the Council of Nicea, held in 325 AD at the behest of the Roman Emperor Constantine. It was written in Aramaic, then translated to Greek, then to Latin. Greece and Ancient Rome took turns in death throes, As the classical era gave way to the Byzantine era, peoples and armies surged and retreated over the region, each leaving their sandal, sword, paint brush or cross behind. With the great schism, The catholic church split in two, with the Vatican and Greek orthodox church deciding that their differences could not be overcome. The Carolingians began to divide western Europe, then Charlemagne decided to give Italy to his son as a gift. Crusaders swarmed to the Holy Land, initially in search of access to the holiest of the holy and reclaiming Jerusalem for Christianity, but with the siege of Jerusalem and the Children's Crusade serving as evidence of many dark, sobering moments that came to pass.

After the Third Crusade, a shadow decided to cast itself over the entire region over the next few centuries. And all of them, soldier, cleric and blasphemer alike knew that in a certain part of the Carpathians, in a very specific castle, there was only death to be found.

---

[244] Gnaeus Pompeius Magnus, or simply Pompey the Great (106 BC- 48 BC) was a political and military leader of the Roman Republic.
[245] Vesuvius erupted August 24th, 79 AD.

ONE

As he slumbered on the train seat, dreams, memories and nightmares mingled in Jonathan Harker's soul:

Of one of his earliest memories was of his parents taking him into London for the first time; he was perhaps five years old, and he recalled how massive and amazing the city felt. He remembered what it felt like to feel his small hand clasped by his mother's, and how he felt swept up into the air when his father picked him up to carry him along.

At sea, back and forth across the Atlantic with his parents, enjoying how the breezes felt in his face.

Then he was thirteen, on a family outing, leaning in toward Mina, seeing the sparkle in her eyes as they both felt the electricity of their first kiss.

He was in the Slaughtered Lamb a few years later, pounding the bar in hysterics at one of Quincy's inane and utterly hilarious expressions, along with Ian and Arthur, who were both crying, they were laughing so hard. Quincy was laughing so hard that *beer was running out of his nose.*

Then about nine months ago, at the offices of Uncle Peter, who was showing him around the firm on the first day. Peter was particularly interested in showing Jonathan a large map of Eastern Europe as he said, "Journeying out to the Orient next week, my boy. Meeting an eccentric nobleman interested in purchasing Carfax Abbey. Money to be made out there, you know."

The smell of Christmas overwhelmed Jonathan Harker, and he stood in front of a massive, decorated tree about ten years ago. The boy he was stood in front of the massive, worldly, impressive Abraham Van Helsing, who handed him a worn box that looked a hundred years old. Mina stood next to him, as did younger versions of Ian and Arthur and Lucy, who only had eyes for young Arthur as Abraham looked at Jonathan and said, "It's for you. If your father or mother disagrees, tell them I gave it to you."

And Abraham Van Helsing beamed as the boy-Harker opened the box and an intricate, ancient object peered up at them from inside.

"It's an astrolabe!" exclaimed Mina in astonishment.

"The Moors used those instruments to chart the world," said Abraham, patting him on the shoulder, "and so will you, my boy."

"I never had any children," continued Abraham, surveying them all with wet eyes, "But if I had, I should have wanted them to be all that you have become."

Bells rang at church on Christmas day, he a mere boy in tight-fitting new clothes, younger versions of his parents and their friends around them at service, Victoria Westenra whispering a rebuke at an extremely unhappy Quincy, cowboy hat upon his head *even back then*, to stop fidgeting. Young Ian and Arthur exchanged a pence, another wager won/lost, Arthur clearly losing a bet on the patience of one Master Quincy Morris. Lucy and Mina, both young girls, giggling at Quincy's misfortune.

Falling through the cold, dark night after being thrown through the castle window by Dracula, Jonathan sees his hands in front of his face as he falls through the unknown, down through leaves blowing through the air, feeling the bitter wind bite and howl at him, then realizing the howl is his own scream just before he hits the bleak, black surge of a river.

Holmwood Hall was filled with garlands and mistletoe, and the table was set with another sumptuous Christmas feast, as boy-Jonathan ran up to the table, holding his mother's hand. Boy-Jonathan was swept up into his mother's arms as she sat down at the opulent table, decorated with a Christmas theme, an extravagant dinner laid out before them. William reached out from his chair to their right and took Jonathan's young hand and squeezed it with warm, fatherly affection, and Jonathan Harker never felt more loved.

The same room, years later, Jonathan burst in, but most of the same people are dead. Abraham Van Helsing was pinned under a coach, Lucy's mother a corpse on top of her, Arthur Holmwood pinned to the floor by the venomous-looking Andromeda, and Mina wailing like a beaten child, a surreal sight that was only furthered by the yawning, jagged window through which both the vehicle and Jonathan had just come. And in the middle of it, a tall corpse, dressed all in black, with a mouth filled with jagged, canine teeth, a leering grin that only took humor in debauchery.

Lucy and Arthur, standing in a rat-infested sewer in Paris, aflame with death and love.

Uncle Peter, crucified upside-down, looking at Jonathan, the spear through his torso dripping blood.

"Run, Jonny," groaned Hawkins, as his tear-filled eyes died.

Abraham Van Helsing, a toy-like silhouette over the Rome night, falling helplessly from the clutches of a gigantic black bat.

In the deep, dark pitch, a leering white face filled with jagged malice, whispering, "Die, Mr. Harker."

The train shuddered Jonathan awake, and the compartment rattled like a tin can with wheels on it.

There were people around him, and Jonathan figured he'd better get up before his pockets were picked when he realized someone held a delicious piece of warm, fresh, delicious Italian bread under his nose.

He sat up and took in Quincy Morris, Ian Seward and Mina Murray miraculously gathered around him. Their leers matched Dracula's but were laced with love and friendship instead of hate and malice. It took Jonathan a moment to realize that his friends were actually there with him.

"You're all *idiots*!" shouted Jonathan, at his wits' end and knowing not what else to say.

All three of his friends, of his remaining family sat there, shaking as the train shook, stupid smiles of warmth splashed all over their faces.

Quincy, dunking his bread in a cup of coffee, was unbowed. "Gimme my bread back then, if I'm an idiot."

"You should not take bread from idiots, my good man," chided Ian, himself partaking in a piece of freshly baked Italian bread that smelled like it had been baked in Heaven. "Good God, that's delicious."

Mina's smile waned, and while her eyes still showed relief at seeing Jonathan, her eyes never left his as she sipped from a cup of coffee. When she was done, Mina said coolly, "If I did not love you more than the sky is blue, I would put a round from my Derringer right through you for running out on us like that. Did you not know we could deduce your destination and method of transportation?"

"We jumped on the last car, as it was pulling out," added Ian with a silly nod.

"Almost split my pants," added Quincy before taking an *enormous* bite of bread.

"Damned fools, all of you," spat Jonathan, reaching for the bread nonetheless.

"Who's more foolish, us fools, or he who follows the fool?" chirped Morris through a mouth full of food, not afraid to have his mouth wide open during a conversation.

"You're— you're literally calling yourself a fool," said Mina as she shook her head in surprise at the Texan.

Quincy looked at Mina like she was the dumbest person in the world as he began, "No, you're dumber than a carved pumpkin— oh wait, yes I am. Strike that last comment, Tiger Lily."

Seward just chortled at Morris past his *pane*, bread.

Jonathan looked out the window. The sun was trying to peer out from behind the mountains of Northern Italy, which were so dark they seemed like cardboard cutouts. Harker sighed and said sadly, "You should have all stayed in Rome, and gone on to lead happy, contented lives."

"Go to Hell, Harker," he heard Morris say, "We're with you all the way."

Jonathan nodded sadly, then turned to Quincy. "Oh, we're going to Hell, mate, more than you know."

He then looked at Mina and Ian. "More than you all know. That's why I attempted to come alone, to spare all of you that mean so much to me what's on the other end of this journey. You all forget, or perhaps more truthfully I have not had time to explain to you, that we go toward the mouth of Hades on Earth, for *his* castle, where Uncle Peter met his end and I almost met mine, is the worst place any sorcerer or necromancer could ever conjure."

Jonathan looked right at Mina and sighed angrily, "We go to our deaths, and I did not want that for you. Any of you."

Harker took a bite of his bread, his gaze finding the darkness and light show outside.

Morris was oblivious. "If that place is so darn awful, how come a chicken-legged City Slicker like you made it out?"

Ian shook his head at Quincy, a combination of empathy and bemusement.

"After murdering Uncle Peter, he threw me through a window and I fell through darkness and into some fierce rapids below. He thought me dead." Jonathan's voice cracked with emotion as he said, "Thought I was dead."

Quincy stopped chewing. The emotion lingered there in the swaying, bumping compartment, they all felt it, and hated Dracula even more for it.

Mina stifled a cry, then reached out and took his hand. "And do you not know by now my love, that I would follow you to the end of this Earth?"

Jonathan looked up at all of them and said, "That's why I'd prefer that you all live out your lives and be merry—"

Ian cuffed Jonathan on the shoulder with a serious look on his face. "Without you? Without our dear friend Jonathan Harker?"

Seward shook his head at Harker. "Hard enough trying to live without our parents, not to mention Lucy and Arthur. And Abraham, my God. Poor Uncle Abraham."

"I'll gut the *nosferatu* like he gutted poor Uncle Peter on that crucifix," nodded Jonathan. "That upside-down crucifix."

"I'll help ya, Jonny," hissed Quincy as he spat bread.

The train rolled on.

Mina knitted her brows as she contemplated their thoughts. "Our purpose then is to exact mere *revenge*?"

Jonathan shook his head. "Yes— no, not for revenge so much as to stop a…vermin from spreading his plague again. From murdering any more innocents—"

"But were our fathers innocents either?" interjected Ian. "They *did* kill his wife."

"That woman was a child murderer," said Quincy flatly. "We read Uncle Pete's journal. She deserved to be strung up higher than a *Piñata*. I'm all right with revenge. An eye for an eye, as Uncle Abraham used to say."

There was a weighty pause at the mention of Abraham Van Helsing.

"I've always agreed with Uncle," nodded Ian. "Though I do take your point."

"I dislike the notion that we operate under the same guise as the vampire," said Mina. "Our goal has not changed, yet in this strange, mad dash across the continent. I'd prefer to think we have a loftier sense of purpose."

"Contradicting myself, remember Seward hall, Mina," said Ian. "Remember what he did to our *parents*. My mother, our mothers, did not deserve that."

"Very well. Revenge it is then," said Mina, now turning to look out the window herself. "So be it. But I do not care for the taste of it. The things I have seen since we began this pursuit, this hunt... they have changed me. I've spent my entire life in worship on Sundays, and perhaps this is a reflection upon me as a person, but the illuminated crucifixes, the absolute fear that these creatures show in the presence of good, the Holy Water, how it causes them to ignite, all that tells me that we are in the right and that we are acting on behalf of a higher power. This is all now not just superstition and myth, it is good against evil. We battle darkness."

Jonathan sighed, reached out and took Mina's hand in his. Her grip tightened around his, and when he looked up at her, Mina was glaring a hole though him.

"If you ever leave me again, I'll kill you," said Mina without the slightest trace of a smile.

"That literally makes no sense," snorted Ian.

"It does if you're from Texas," chuckled Morris.

Jonathan nodded, accepting everything Mina had just stated, yet he said, "I could not sit out my life knowing that Dracula still exists. Our mothers, the servants in our employ that were like family, had nothing to do with this. I could accept, even tolerate that there are more of his kind out there, like lions or wolves, who upon occasion feed upon a human being, because don't we do that to each other as humans? But not for making us all orphans the way he did."

"I understand, Jonathan," replied Mina, "and I accept our task on a personal level and in a broader sense of representing all that is good in this world, despite our flaws and faults."

"I'm nobody's example of a choir boy," Quincy began, "But I hate what he's done to everyone he's encountered. Renfield—"

"'Uncle Monty' was lost to us all long ago," chimed Jonathan. "But I see what Mina is saying. As I reflect now, I see Uncle Abraham garnered his religious fervor when we were younger. Perhaps that is how he dealt with his grief at the loss of his own family. If he was battling these legions of Satan, surely this all gave him comfort as a man who knew there was good on the other side of all this, God Rest His Soul."

"God rest his soul," whispered Mina, and for a moment, they all mourned him as the train rattled along. After that moment passed, Mina added, "Then, if we die during this endeavor, we shall all die as orphans together attempting to represent all that is good in the world."

"And die we will," answered Jonathan wryly, "but not before we take him with us."

"Very well," nodded Seward, "but if we are to indeed undertake this impossibility, tell us more of where this journey is headed."

"And don't leave out the dancin' girls," Quincy quipped with a wink.

Mina was lightning in her response, "Quincy Morris, my Jonathan would never entertain such ideas or frequent such an establishment!"

A lightning-quick but slow-witted series of glances between the men was clumsy, poorly-timed and told a suspicious Wilhelmina Murray everything she needed to know.

"For the sake of our objective we will table this discussion," she slowly told Jonathan with arched eyebrows and a look of utter suspicion at her fiancé, "until after all this is over."

Over Quincy and Ian's giggles, Jonathan gave a small, dry noise to clear his throat, before he said, "My response to your previous question about my previous journey, Ian, is to tell you all a ghost story, and it is no fiction, I experienced it. And it nearly killed me. It has become the stuff of my nightmares. All of it, and it all began on my journey in a coach in the middle of the night, to Borgo Pass…"

FROM THE JOURNAL OF MONTAGUE RHODES RENFIELD

I am weary, but the Master must never know.

The days are long, and I am alone more than ever in my life. Dawn and dusk seem to melt into each other, and my solitude wears upon me. We have left Italy, procuring a boat by the master's usual means: Bribing a scoundrel of a ship's captain with gold coins, which were curiously old when I happened to look upon them as I dealt with the captain, we also purchased the ability to transport our 'boxes' without any documents presented or questions asked. Funny how money moves mountains. Since I grew up poor as a dog, I would never have known save for the master's mercy and decency.

My original plan was to do away with the meager crew of disgusting foreigners that occupied the boat, but the master was most insistent as he whispered to me from inside his coffin, that we retain our relative secrecy on this journey. So instead I had to scour the ship for rats for the master and his miserable concubines to consume, since he held some loyalty to the vermin locked in the fourth coffin. The master ventured that some of them had begun to consume each other inside the coffin, which was a bit of a contradiction to his order not to use said rats as their own food, but I am here but to do the master's bidding. I spend much time alone, since the crew is full of non-Englishmen, so I refuse to speak or endeavor to communicate with the lowly examples from the darker continents of this bleak world. I wonder, does my master pray before he sleeps? And to who? His father? I know not to pray for, I only pray for myself, that my death would be much more glorious than my life.

We were at last let off at the port of Athens, where the ship's captain was given the other half of our agreed sum. It was after midnight when we left the ship, and once out of sight of the ship the master and the brides, as well as the legion of rats emerged from their coffins. At this point the concubines observed the Greek location and commented with sarcasm and irony toward the master that this was the cursed bride Andromeda's ancestral home. They then turned into bats and flew away for the night's hunt. I nearly commented to the master himself that he appeared in need of rest, though he just had left his coffin, but kept my mouth shut as to avoid his wrath. He transformed, and I watched the bat fly into the night skies.

The rats simply poured out onto the streets and disappeared into and among the buildings, and as I drove the wagon with the coffins toward the cemetery which the master had pointed out to me as a rendezvous point, I noted with morbid dread that some of the disgusting vermin were trailing along the wagon, leaving as soon as others arrived, often with bloody, moistened snouts.

I had doused my lantern as to avoid any un-needed encounter with the Greek public, yet in one of the dark, dank streets I was stopped by one of the policemen, who spoke the strange, foreign Greek tongue so hastily that he sounded like a chirping night bird, so in the end, as he began to inspect the coffins and gesture for my travel documents, I simply reached behind him and broke his neck with one stiff blow. Reminded me of my childhood when I'd to the same thing to puppies and kittens. Ha! I took the body and stuffed it into the rat's coffin, and no sooner had I done that when the lethal vermin spread word of the kill to each other and they swarmed back to the wagon as I made my way near to the cemetery, and as I drove I could hear the horses neighing in fear as the rats began to feed on the body of the Greek bobby. The coffin trembled in the back of the wagon, and when I opened the coffin next, there were only bits of clothes left.

Some hours later the master and the concubines returned, and I noted that they did not speak to each other as they retreated to their individual coffins, the evil whores laughing at some personal slight at the Master, I presumed. Strange, but I took the sense that the master had not only been to this part of the world before, but actually seemed to enjoy the crumbling temples that mixed right with buildings that were built in these days.

Before the dawn was whole I had steered the wagon out of Athens and into the surrounding forest roads. I did not stop for fear of the discovery of the murder of the policeman by the rats to spread, or his disappearance, I should state, would be discovered so I wanted to evade any possible road closures that seemed to always follow those circumstances.

I knew not the roads, mountains and forests of the region, but I was guided by the steady whispers of the master in his coffin, who had tread over the region for hundreds of years, he informed me. I did not stop that day, even to feed the horses, until we were deeper and deeper into the mountains of the region, nearer to the fortress and castle that my master calls his residence.

The night the master rose, and at last I stopped to sleep while the others hunted for the foolish villager unfortunate to encounter the likes of which they had ever seen. The master returned from his hunt before the concubines, and I relayed to him my disgust at the behavior of the brides toward him, showing him no regard or respect, and he told me that he had been considering a special punishment for the two wenches awaiting them at the castle, which cheered me greatly.

After days and days, we have entered the Transylvanian region, my master tells me. Though the brides are not speaking to him, he upon occasion slips into one of their coffins, oftentimes against their will, because of the force the master must use to open the coffins to enter, and their deathly hisses of protest as he closes the coffin lid that fill the night's air.

I tend to mind me own business, knowing that the master's wrath will be upon these trollops when we arrive.

Whatever strange passions between them, I do not know, but even stranger for me is the notion that at times, after the master has his way with them, I do hear them sobbing within their caskets. And it does fill me with a bit of a heavy heart, but they had it coming, crossing the master the way they did.

The brides have taken to sleep in the same coffin lately, presumably to take refuge from the master, and I do hear their occasional chuckle of mutual contentment, but as I said, I mean to mind my business.

Whores.

A DRAGON IN BUDAPEST

For Wilhelmina Murray, Jonathan Harker, Ian Seward and Quincy Morris, time continued to melt together as they traveled, their collective experiences blending into one fluid, languid journey. All train stations began to look alike, regardless of their posted language, as time liquified and flowed around them.

The road to Rome begat the road to Vienna, which then begat the journey into Hungary.

Train became horseback.

Their clothes, particularly those of one Jonathan Harker, became more worn and frayed as the days went on.

City became town, and town became road, and road became town once more before another city loomed again.

They stopped somewhere along the line to purchase tools with which to camp and climb.

Time ebbed and flowed through days and weeks the way heated wax oozed down a candlestick.

Then they arrived in Budapest.

The 'Heart of Europe' and 'Pearl of the Danube' was an old city, just as Hungary was an old country, but the city itself was old enough to start off as a settlement for both the Celts and Romans, and to survive the Huns and Mongols. Christianity was introduced to the region by István I, King of Hungary. Budapest grew to become one of the larger cities in Europe if not the world. Sitting precariously yet proudly between Asia and Europe, it reflected the beauty of both continents yet also held featured the Dohány Street Synagogue as well as the Tomb of Gul Baba, the second largest synagogue in the world and the northernmost Islamic place of worship, respectively. The area had been both taken and relinquished by the Habsburgs and the Holy Roman Empire.

Brilliant architecture filled the city, including the massive amazing Széchenyi Chain Bridge, which opened in 1849. The bridge was conceived by politician István Széchenyi, at times referred to as the Greatest Hungarian, after he had been stranded on one side of the Danube during a particularly harsh winter. He had no way to attend his father's funeral in Vienna because at that time only a pontoon bridge spanned the river, so he vowed to have a permanent bridge built. It would be designed by British civil engineer William Tierney, one of the earliest designers of suspension bridges, and built by Scotsman Adam Clark, who oversaw the construction from 1839 to 1849, even during the Hungarian Revolution of 1848.

Enormous stone lions were sculpted and placed on either side of the Széchenyi in 1852. Story has it that the sculptor of the beasts, János Marschalkó, was told by an apprentice shoemaker named Jakab Frik that his sculpted lions lacked tongues. Regardless, the Danube flowed and divided the western and eastern sides of the cities, known separately as Buda and Pest, which had only recently united into one city in 1873. An underground train system had just opened in 1896, as the city celebrated its first thousand years of existence.

The streets of Budapest teemed with people that were busy beginning their lives, living their lives, wasting their lives, and watching their lives begin to dwindle, in some cases savoring those days, in other cases counting the hours until they had to face their maker.

Through all this moved Murray, Harker, Morris and Seward.

As they resupplied, a cherubic, bespectacled merchant gave them general directions. They had learned not to state specifically where they were going, to avoid the usual warnings about 'that fortress in the Carpathians'.

The merchant also told them something very special, that lovers had begun to leave padlocks on the Chain Bridge as a testament to their love, so as they crossed the Széchenyi, after Quincy sized up the lions on the Western side, Mina and Jonathan scratched onto an old case heart padlock they had bought from the merchant and clamped the rusted, strong thing onto one of the lamps.

WM
JH
1899

They then moved to Pest, and to the east.

Leaving bridges and progress, moving closer to myth and legend.

From science to magic.

Yet the city itself was not their objective.

As per Abraham's counsel in Paris, they sought an old monastery.

With a dragon.

Just outside of Pest, up in the hills, after a few townsfolks who could understand Ian's broken Hungarian pointed the way, they found it.

The weathered monastery was a bleary paint swatch on a woodsy hillside that left Pest far behind. The weary, motley building was tilted and hewn out of centuries-old stone and covered with ivy, trees and shade. The structure was asymmetrical, caught somewhere between Occidental and Oriental, between Pagan and Christian. Stonework knuckles and wood slat cobwebs arm-wrestled under a complex, almost indescribable type of roof, which looked like it had withstood a million winters and could survive maybe a hundred more. A chimney in one part of the strange, jutting roofing puffed the smoke of comfort. In front of the edifice, which seemed to want to hide among the tree-filled hillsides around it, stood a broken statue of a knight lancing a dragon that was sculpted during the Dark Ages. Though lanced through the body, the dragon's neck arched forward, about to cleave the knight in half with its ferocious mouth.

A cloud drifted above, and the birds that had been serenading the afternoon now paused.

After the cloud wafted by, the birdsong resumed.

As Mina said that she missed D'Artagnan, who was safely stabled at the rebuilding Seward Manor and grumpily enjoying afternoon oats, they all dismounted in front of the odd building, tied their horses to the dragon's flailing, motionless tail before moving to an ornate front door that was as much medieval as the wood it was made out of.

It was then that they noticed all of the gnarled crucifixes and weathered crosses sticking up from the ground, tiny, small, medium and large.

And nailed to all of the saddened trees.

And hanging from the irregular, lonely branches.

And carved into each of the moldy bricks that made up the decomposing monastery itself.

And above the skewed windowsills of the aged window frames that peppered the building in an odd, asymmetrical alignment.

"Ummmm," said Quincy, pointing at a crucifix that hung above the doorway. It was made of wood, and had a small skull nailed to the intersection of the carved wood.

Animal skull.

Bat.

Morris instinctively felt for his Colts, then checked his horse saddle for the Winchester.

Everyone followed suit, Ian with his Webley, Mina with her Winchester, Arthur's old Webley and her Derringer, as well as Jonathan's own tried-and-true Webley, which Quincy silently rolled his eyes at in provincial disgust.

"Yes, Quincy, we see it," said Jonathan with a nod as he rang the small, skull-shaped bell that hung on the right side of the doorframe. Harker felt the warm hand of Mina slide into his left palm, filling him with comfort.

He heard Mina say to Quincy, "You could always just shoot the bat skull, Quincy."

"I'm sure that would in turn bring us courteous service as a response," laughed Ian, behind them both.

"That'd get me as far as it got you for your 'ringing church bell' incident," chuckled Morris, which gave the others a much-needed laugh.

"It was a Winchester, not a slingshot and I meant to put a hole through the bloody thing," hissed Mina proudly.

"Never seen Uncle William that angry," said Ian, which brought a nostalgic grunt of agreement from Morris, who followed with, "I thought he was gonna pop like a pimple."

"I've never seen Uncle Abraham prouder," chuckled Jonathan, as footsteps on stone neared the door from within. A chuckle and the tightening of Mina's hand around his told Jonathan he'd made Mina very happy.

The door swung open. A priest only a few years older than they were stood there. He wore a traditional catholic cassock. Behind him was pitch black that made his head and hands seem to float in the darkness like in a Singer Sargent painting.

"Jó napot," he said past a warm grin. *Good afternoon.*

When he realized they could not speak Hungarian, the priest smiled and politely said, "Sprichst du Deutsch? Francais?" *Do you speak German? French?*

"Well," interjected Quincy, "I've been known to speak a little Parlez-vous—"

Ian reached out and patted Quincy squarely on the shoulder. "You're going to hurt yourself, mate. Let me give it a try."

Ian cleared his throat and sort of said, "Sárkányt keresünk." *We seek a dragon.*

The priest simply pointed at the dragon behind them as he sported a look that read *Didn't you see that thing right behind you?*

Mina successfully suppressed a giggle.

They collectively gave up and shook their heads, and Jonathan added, "Sorry, do not speak Hungarian."

The young priest recovered nicely and replied in clipped, cultured English, "Good afternoon. Can I be of help to you?"

Mina beamed smartly and said, "We're looking for Father Tibor Kovacs."

The priest shuffled his feet, unsure. "Who shall I say is calling?"

Jonathan started, "We are friends, family rather, of Abraham—"

"—we are in need of his specific counsel," finished Mina.

"I see. One moment, please," said the priest, returning Mina's smart smile as he closed the door. The sound of his stride receded.

Quincy snorted and said, "I spoke French just fine at the Moulin Rouge that one time—"

"What were you doing at the Moulin Rouge?" snapped Mina instantly at Jonathan.

I'm going to murder that Texan thought Jonathan Harker.

What an idiot agreed Ian Seward.

I've gotta fart thought the vast, empty, ingenious chamber that was the mind of Quincy Morris.

Jonathan went wide-eyed and just a little too panicky as he blurted, "We were all trying to pull Quincy out of there, my love! I swear it."

"Then why does Morris have such a stupid grin smeared over his face?" she insisted.

Jonathan turned to the leering Texan, gave him a wearied yet dirty look, and said, "Because he is stupid, my dear."

"Then why was I not made aware of said evening of Texas debauchery at the Moulin Rouge before?" Mina's glare was directed at her Fiancé, who at the moment preferred to look at a bat skull nailed to a crucifix rather than at his beloved.

"Because our childish shenanigans should be beneath such a lady's notice," said Ian in a gallant attempt at a last-second save.

God bless him thought Jonathan.

Mina would have none of it. "I am in the presence of three hooligans!"

Quincy chuckled at the droplets of perspiration that were forming on Jonathan Harker's brow. They were noticed by Mina Murray, and her eyes squinted in suspicion.

"Aw, leave Jonny alone, Tiger Lily!"

Mina hissed like a hundred vipers in a church, "You shut your mouth Quincy Morris before I fire off a telegram to one Consuelo Morera-Lopez of Austin Texas!"

The leer and the mouth on Quincy Morris instantly shriveled.

Countered 180° by the enormous smile that grew out of Jonathan.

Sound of the priest's return stride began.

With one last, wicked look at a relieved Jonathan, Mina composed herself.

The door yawned open to them, the priest gesturing into the darkness. "This way, please. May I take your coats?"

They all shook their heads politely as they walked inside.

It was a strange, wonderous place. The main chamber that they entered was lined with stonework that begat brickwork in places. The oddity began with wooden beams that lined the room. But the strangeness was furthered with all of the tiny, small, medium-sized and large crucifixes that were all nailed to the walls.

The crosses all lined the large, very old room, with a huge centuries-old tiled stove as the centerpiece of the room, nearly unseen in the darkness, yet somehow ample with comfort. A benevolent stone floor was covered with various rugs from the divergent cultures and faiths of the region. It was as if the darkness was a blanket of tranquility, not an enemy. An even darker hallway loomed, lined with unlit candles in candleholders that protruded out of the walls since before Columbus set sail to the west. The young priest led them through it. After he had picked up a worn, bronze candleholder he had left on a dusty bookshelf, they all moved down the narrow hallway, their shoes knocking against an unexpected wood floor, and into a larger room.

Lit by warm but scarce candles, the larger room was lined with crumbling bookshelves crammed with antiquated books. an unsteady coffee table with rickety chairs and a downward-curving sofa, surrounding it. A hearth that looked like it wanted to fall over and die sat in one corner, and a window whose storm shutters had been closed, nailed shut and which had dusty garlic woven around it filled another. Above the bookshelves were piles of manuscripts and scrolls, and above that were more crucifixes nailed into stone walls that led up to a wooden roof that was ripe with origins in the Byzantine era. The lone sofa had stacks of books heaped upon it as well, and amid them sat a worn, kind-looking man who looked to be about Abraham Van Helsing's age, yet he had been worn down by life's struggles and appeared much older. He took them in with bright, intelligent eyes that rippled with gentility and wet candlelit reflections. His Cossack was older, and he wore a comfortable old brown sweater over it.

"Father Tibor," said the younger priest in his clipped, cultured English, "here are the young people who said they needed to speak to you."

Smiling, the older priest looked like a portrait painted by Rembrandt. He beckoned them with a warm smile and said, "Thank you, Father Gábor." Please sit down, *gyermekek*[246]. Please seat yourselves. How can I be of service to you?"

The old priest's English was confident and international, with years of practice and confidence behind the words. The young priest had closed the door on his way out. They all felt somehow comfortable with this old man, perhaps because of their knowledge that Uncle Abraham had approved of him.

As they all sat down, Jonathan said, "My name is Jonathan Harker. This is my fiancée, Wilhelmina Murray, and the gentlemen with us are Mister Quincy Morris and Mister Ian Seward."

Father Kovacs looked at them with deep thought. He blinked, once, twice, then whispered, "Your family names are known to me. From long ago."

"As are you to us, Father," said Mina. "And your experience with our fathers."

Father Tibor searched their faces for what they thought they knew, when they knew it and how much they really knew.

Quincy saw this and stated the obvious. "All is known to us, Father."

"Everything," followed up Ian.

It was not tension or anger that swept over Father Kovac's face, but rather a sense of discomfort. The room somehow felt a little darker. Ian and Quincy shot glances filled with understanding, and they shared them with Mina and Jonathan. Through his concern, the old priest was polite enough to gulp, "It is my pleasure to make your acquaintances, yet I have lived enough life to know that you all would not have traveled this far without a serious purpose."

They sat there, staring at him, and it was Father Tibor's turn to read their faces. "Your faces speak of their passing. Death is but a door, my children. May they rest in peace, with the love of God in their hearts. Your fathers were good men. Not perfect men, but they did what needed to be done. The experience pained them, to say the least."

There was no reason to hide it any longer so Jonathan said, "Abraham Van Helsing is— was, our uncle."

"Not directly," drawled Quincy, "But he loved us more'n our regular blood kin."

"*Was*?" asked Father Tibor, his eyes enlarging with deep, beauteous concern. "Abraham has passed as well?"

"Yes, Father," nodded Mina, with emotion.

"Dear old Abraham Van Helsing," said the old priest with a single shake of his hairy head and a sign of the cross. "He was a dear man, and a force of nature in his own right. I assisted

---

[246] The Hungarian word for children.

him in a few of his nocturnal, eh— errands throughout Europe, when we were younger, and I not so spent. I hope his passing was far more peaceful than his life was. He never recovered from the deaths of his wife and child, you know."

"Before he died, Uncle Abraham told us that you had helped him with the *nosferatu*. And that you could help us now."

The old priest sat there, fear growing in him at the realization of what his next question would have to be.

"The woman from the village. The vampire they killed. We seek her *husband*," said Ian, answering it.

Silence sat with them.

Father Tibor shook his bearded, balding head over one long, breath, then said, "You cannot revenge yourself upon a biblical miracle, a desert mirage, a thing of the night. A beast that wears a crown. And all of that is what Dracula of Transylvania is. He is no mere blood-drinking ghoul or cadaver, he is the son of all that is foul on this earth, children. There are parables, writings, superstitions, songs and fables about Dracula of Satan that date back a thousand years. He crossed swords with Saladin and Sir Richard during the Crusades. He did not sire the *nosferatu*, but when he was able, he brought them all under his rule, and they pay tribute to him in the fashion of a Roman tax collector. Those of his own kind who cannot pay tribute are executed! He inspired some voivodes and royals to form a cult in our region, and some of the royal families took the name of Dracula. Dracul, they called themselves. And do you know what the monster did? He betrayed and devoured them. And those that he did not eat, he posted their corpses on stakes for the carrion eaters to feast upon, and for the world to observe. He craves fear. When Constantinople fell, he was there. When the Jews were persecuted out of Castile, he was there. When the Doge of Venice needed smiting, he was there. Go to any old archive and read through the old, hidden chronicles of the last thousand years, and you will find whispers of a dragon. Markings in old ledgers that spoke of a great shadow with long, powerful claws. China and India shuddered when he moved through their terrains with secret, malicious intent. When the Moors were expelled from Spain[247], when a Cardinal had his daughter married on Vatican ground[248], he was there.

"Dracula mated both myth and reality.

"Once, hundreds of years ago, all of the royals of this continent aligned and sent their armies to face him, to rid the earth of his malice and cruelty. Yet it was *he*, the dragon, that smote them. His symbol, which no one would look upon, was and is a Satanic dragon consuming a Christian lion. All those soldiers, their horses, elephants and siege engines, torn asunder. He has trampled and mocked history for hundreds of generations, yet you seek to finish what entire armies could not accomplish? And you think *him* arrogant? No one ever went to that castle again to defy him. He was left alone to sustain himself on the people of his region, yet far enough away from the rest of humanity. I never knew that when we killed that hellion, that gorgon, that filthy devourer of children, that we had killed his *wife*. Otherwise, that might have stayed my hand."

Father Kovacs looked at them blankly and said, "You seek among the worst to ever walk this earth."

Quincy wiggled in his seat, snapped his fingers with confidence and sniffed, "You know, ya wouldn't have thought that when we damn-near killed him in Rome, did we, fellas?"

Incredulous that Morris would dare profane in front of a woman much less a priest, they all

---

[247] The Alhambra Decree of March 31, 1492, by both Isabella I of Castile and Ferdinand II of Aragon, ordered the expulsion of practicing Jews who would not convert to Catholicism from Spain by July 31st of that same year.
[248] Lucrezia Borgia, daughter of Cardinal Rodrigo Borgia, would marry Giovanni Sfroza on Jne 12th, 1493 in Rome. Rodrigo Borgia would be named Pope Alexander VI in 1493.

gaped at him. Ian almost laughed at him, and Mina merely sizzled like bacon grease.

"What?" said Morris with a Texas-sized shrug. Father Kovacs looked askance at the Texan, and Jonathan made a mental note to tease the Texan of his intrepid feat later.

"Your mouth, my son," said Father Tibor, with a wrinkle of a suppressed grin on his cheek. "It is both your blessing and your curse."

"It is definitely *our* curse," sighed Mina.

"We will kill Dracula," said Jonathan with a confident glint in his eyes, "and we come here asking for your help. Uncle Abraham said you could muster other people to help us, that you would aid us."

"We nearly killed him in Rome, Father," said Ian. "We really did. He escaped and ran like a dog. We know how to do it, we just need help to finish the job."

"I congratulate you on your fortune in Rome. But it is a different matter when the dragon is in his lair."

"Help us, Father," added Mina. It was a plea.

"I think it best that you return, children, to your machine-powered Britain and your collective safety. Leave the shadow undisturbed."

"He is our uncle Abraham's murderer!" Mina nearly shouted. "And our parents' as well. He came to our homeland, *our home* and murdered them all."

"In front of us," added Jonathan, placing his hand over Mina's to calm her, "and left us for dead."

"He burned my home down to the ground," gulped Ian, wrought with emotion, and it was Quincy's turn to pat his friend on the shoulder in comfort.

"Children, there is no fruit in revenge, there is only the tranquility that Abraham and your family are at peace and with God—"

"Father, *we* are not at peace! We know how to get to his castle!"

"Journey there and know you will never return—"

"I journeyed there and survived, father!" Jonathan now shouted.

The old priest looked at Jonathan in a moment of surprise, then flatly as he said, "Then you know better than to ever return there again, my son. After the ordeal in the village, after that foul beast of a woman had kidnapped the child Renfield and taken him into her coffin, and after Abraham had staked her with the holy symbol, it was thereafter that I discovered that she was the wife of unholiness itself! I went back to the village years later and found that it had been *burned to the ground*, and all around the charred remnants of the homes were stakes, with burnt skeletons of men, women and children still hanging from them in every conceivable fashion. He has no mercy, my children. He has faced armies in front of his castle, and you think you can present yourselves and do away with him on your own? Go back to your homes—"

"Help us, Father! Help us speak to the Budapest officials to use soldiers to aid us—"

"They fear him more than I do! They will not hear you, and once they know your destination and whom you hunt, will not aid you. They may in fact arrest you. Everyone knows whom you seek, and *we in turn avoid seeking him*. Dracula is but a dark whisper in Hungary, and a word never spoken in the Carpathians, a name to scare children from wandering into the forests, and youth from venturing at night. He is the unfulfilled wish, the last sin and the ender of dreams. Go back home, young ones, and fulfill your lives, not end them. Master Jonathan and Mistress Wilhelmina, have children, take care of these two fine young men here until they have families of their own. An old saying of ours, here in Hungary, 'There is no medicine against death', and surely, if you go to his castle, you only face death."

Jonathan gave Father Tibor a long, quiet look before he said, "Before we leave I just want you to know that we came to you for help, and you as a man of God who knows who this fiend is, refused to help us.

"Good day, Father."

"I do God's work here, after a lifetime of marrying couples, baptizing babies, burying my friends and chasing ghouls. I have earned my rest. I ran around this world aiding Abraham and his like, and I have spent myself doing so. You are all welcome to stay for the night, or a few nights. Your journey has been long, and you have our humble hospitality. I wish you all well, and you have my blessings."

"If you really wanted to bless us, then you would help us."

Father Tibor said nothing, but guilt and fear raced over his face.

"Thank you for seeing us, Father," said Jonathan before he stood and shook Father Tibor's hand. The old priest had tried to stand as politely as he could, but Jonathan gently and respectfully placed his hand on his shoulder to save him the effort.

"Farewell," said Father Tibor in a sincere way, but the irony was felt in the room. The sounds of their stirring brought Father Gábor back, and he led them back out. "Your faith in Him will serve you."

Outside, they had mounted their horses and were preparing to ride off when Jonathan turned to Mina and said, "We should be married before we leave Budapest, my love."

It was also Jonathan's attempt to mitigate whatever repercussions of the Moulin Rouge conversation, but he meant it.

Mina knew this, grinned that strong grin that had always attracted him to her and said, "I don't need to be wed to you to know you are mine, and that I am yours."

"If I am to die," said Jonathan, "I would rather die as your husband."

"Well it depends on your thinking," replied Mina. "If our cause is indeed just, if we are intended to rid the earth of this hellish creature, then God will see us through this, and we can then be married in a proper way."

"Why is it that the women always say all of the clever stuff?" snorted Quincy, on his horse and ready to go, along with Ian.

"Because we are smarter?"

They all laughed.

Ian added, "I'm never going to get married."

He meant it as an additional joke after Mina's quip, but after he said it, Ian could not help but think of Lucy Westenra, and his lost love for her. They all saw this, and compassion for Ian melted from them, and they simultaneously all thought of Lucy, Arthur, their lost marriage and lives, their entire family, and these passionate, melancholy thoughts led them back to their purpose.

"They'll never know our children," said Mina.

A regret, not a statement.

"Sure they will," said Quincy with a croak that suppressed tears, the smartest thing he'd said all afternoon. "They'll all meet one day. We all will."

"Let's go then," said Jonathan Harker as he pointed to the mountain range in the distance. "Before the winter comes for us."

Mounting their horses, they rode through the hillsides of Hungary and toward their fate in the mountains of Transylvania.

Though I walk through the valley of the shadow of death,
I will fear no evil, for thou art with me
Psalm 23:4

A FEW HAUNTINGS

They journeyed on.

Budapest then became the open road, with less people as they moved from city to town to village to farm. Sharp, tailored coats and flowing Victorian gowns gave way to torn overalls and frayed traditional dresses. The layered smells of the city became the simple scents of the countryside. Autumn had begun to take hold of Europe, and leaves fell with abundance, cascading around them as they rode along the lonely and lonelier roads.

Those roads became narrower, surrounded by forests that grew deeper and deeper by the day. Evergreens began to turn grim, the autumnals started to dry their branches and whither their leaves. Villages became scarce, they encountered farming fields less and less frequently. Nights sleeping in the forest became more frequent than staying at an inn. Directions from farmers and villagers became more and more vague. And fearful. Over the next weeks, meals went from being served at a table to being eaten in front of a campfire. Tree groves also seemed to grow closer together, as if huddling for comfort, forcing the dirt roads to become narrower and narrower. Instinctively, everyone began to ride their horses with one hand on the reins and the other on their weapons.

The road melted and wove and undulated out of Hungary and into the Carpathian Mountains. Cries from wolves during the night went from distant calls of warning to haunting yips and snarls in closer proximity. Sprawling hillsides swept above and below them as they rode, through gargantuan, parched meadows and across creeks that had been surging rivers in the spring but now slowed to an ebb in anticipation of the oncoming winter.

Nights grew colder and colder and when they could not find an inn among the tiny villages, they started to sleep out in the woods, each of them taking turns keeping watch through each night, with Mina vehemently insisting on taking a turn herself. The young men had become too tired to argue. As they moved higher and higher into the mountains, days were cold and nights became frigid, anticipating the oncoming deep frost. Quincy had taught them all how to dig a below-ground campfire with two connecting holes, so there would be no smoke or fire visible.

Everyone conversed less and less, even Morris, whose boisterous demeanor that so often inspired and enlivened everyone had his voice taken away by the arduous, somber journey. Everything became shades of grey or darkness, color exsanguinated. Their horses became more and more agitated, at things they could not see but things they could sense.

When the surroundings had been drenched with morbidity, the supernatural began to dance around them:

They happened upon a decrepit, broken pagan shrine, covered with ivy and dead leaves. The broken, worn statue of Venus was bleeding from its eyes.

At the foot of the statue, rats lapped the blood.

Ian discovered a moss-covered crypt along the road that read, *'Et in arcadia ego*[249]*'* scrawled across its front.

An open area, away from the trees, had three upside-down wooden crosses planted onto the ground. Bird corpses of different species lay everywhere at the bases of the crosses, and they all stayed in their saddles and watched in confusion, until a small bird tried to land on one of them and dropped dead upon its touch.

Another day, the group was riding up along a sliver of a road that headed higher and higher into the depths of the Carpathians, a lone dog ran out onto the dirt before them, in the distance. It stopped

---

[249] *Et in Arcadia ego* is a Latin phrase that translates roughly to 'I am also in Arcadia', taken from two paintings called *Les Bergers d' Arcadie* or the Arcadian Shepherds by Nicolas Poussin (1594-1665). The phrase is also the subject of various alternate history and conspiracy theories.

and looked at them, and at that moment, they all realized that the dog had *the head of a man*.

It snarled at them, ran off and melted into the forest before Quincy could snake out his Winchester to get a shot at it.

That night, Morris was on watch while the others slumbered among a gnarled grove of trees when he saw lights from the road they had come from. He woke the others and they crept forward, guns at the ready, and they saw a line of ghosts, wearing armor from hundreds of years ago, treading dourly down the dirt path and in the direction from which Quincy and the others had just arrived. Many of the soldiers were wounded, more of them had mortal wounds, walking away in a spectral procession after a fierce battle lost so long ago. Jonathan whispered it reminded him of the ghost he'd encountered at Borgo Pass so many months ago.

Another day, they found a shallow grave near the road, filled with the bones of children and dogs. They had all been impaled. Upon each other. Some of the bones had been broken. The breaks had toothmarks upon them.

They spied a very old crypt that was more Roman than Byzantine, and its front door kept swinging open and closed of its own accord.

A few days later, a trio of lit candles sat on a stump under a tree, dripping wax *up* into the dead branches above.

Another night, they came upon a tiny crucifix, aflame as it silently floated in the forest air. It *slowly turned upside down* as they watched it.

Another time they passed by an old graveyard where bones rolled freely from one open grave to another. A tiny, dry giggle belching forth from one of the graves kept them moving.

Despite the fact that it was snowing nearly every night now, they found some roses that had bloomed out of an open-mouthed human skull near one of the roads they traveled.

They heard playful, happy whistling from under a small, rotting bridge they crossed, but when they went underneath the bridge to search for the owner of the whistle, they found only the chilling echoes of a child's laughter.

One night, Ian woke up. He had fallen asleep even though he had been on guard that night. During that night's snowfall, which was becoming more frequent as the days passed, small human tracks were being formed in the drifts around the sleeping Mina, Jonathan and Quincy. The horses neighed nervously. Ian took his pistol out, trembling as he did so, when a voice said, "I'm not here to bother you, just watch," before the tracks headed back out into the depths of the tree line.

Ian kept this to himself.

They came upon a tree-lined crossroads, and in the middle of the intersected paths was a corpse that had been buried up to its neck. As they rode by, it softly creaked, *"Ajutati-mâ." Help me.*

Ian whispered to the corpse, "Will we succeed?"

"Yes," it whispered, "and no."

BOWIE KNIFE AND CAMPFIRE

Somewhere, along one of the many narrow roads of the historical region of Transylvania, the forests became more dense and darker, if that were possible.

They bought some sausages, cheese, tomatoes and wine from one of the villages, which had gone from small to tiny. That feast alone was reason to celebrate, and they ate upon a large rock that overlooked the village, which was itself halfway up a tree-covered mountain.

The sun dropped behind the horizon as they ate, Jonathan, Quincy and Ian bringing kindling to build a campfire as they silently and collectively decided to spend the night at this spot. Jonathan took out Abraham's bag and spread out its contents before them. Aside from their own firearms, camping and climbing equipment, the bag held:

A pair of old dueling pistols.

Rounds for the dueling pistols.

Uncle Abraham's beloved *kukri* knife.

Four small crucifixes.

Four more sharpened crucifixes.

Small bottles of Holy Water.

Uncle Peter's Journal.

A bag of garlic.

Four jagged, sharpened pieces of wood.

A wooden mallet.

Three hunting knives, with crucifixes engraved onto the blades.

Various medallions of different religions, cultures from around the world.

Knives of different sizes and proportions.

A butcher's cleaver.

Quincy gave a slow, long whistle of admiration. "Good gravy, he could have taken on Santa Ana and the entire Mexican Army with all this!"

"And don't forget the climbing equipment!" said Jonathan.

"How could we?" said Ian. "My horse is the one who has to lug it all around."

Mina plucked out a single envelope from among the many pockets of the bag. She opened it and read aloud:

Children,

I write this letter hastily, while you all sit at the other end of the ferry that is taking us to France and read your Uncle Peter's account of our tragedy in the village. You all look so young yet so old, caught in that precious time between childhood innocence and adult responsibility.

If you are reading this, I am at last with my beloved family and the vampyre has defeated me, but more importantly I have failed you. I fear greatly that this circumstance may arise, so I write you all this letter in the happenstance that you are left without me, and after you have lost your parents.

If I know all of you, and I believe I do since I've held you in my arms as infants, I know that you are all resolute and that you would continue to pursue the villain despite my death. If you are in Budapest, feel free to seek the assistance of Father Tibor, who was in the village with me when I impaled the vampyre's wife. He should still be in a monastery east of the city, and should be able to guide you, if not *help place soldiers to aid you. The name of the monastery fails me but there should be a dragon statue somewhere upon the grounds. In closing, I would simply wish you God's protection, and that nothing hard in this life or the next is easily attained.*

Your loving uncle,
Abraham Van Helsing

"Well, that stinks like a hard-boiled egg gone bad," huffed Quincy.

"Yes it does," agreed Ian.

It doesn't change anything," said Jonathan, stirring the fire. "This is still something that must be done; whether Uncle Abraham had died or not, we are the only ones that can stop him, because no one else would even believe that Dracula even exists. He and his kind are seen as myths, ghost stories, fairy tales.

"I remember," said Mina her eyes alight and shining in the campfire's light, "when I was a child and my mother and father gave me a copy of Grimm's Fairy Tales—"

"I remember that!" laughed Jonathan. "You felt you *had* to learn German simply to read the book."

Ian threw a few large logs onto the fire, embers leaping up into the night like terrified stars. "Wasn't there an English edition out by then?"

"Not sure," said Mina, smiling at Seward, "but it helped me to learn German. *Kinder-und Hausmärchen.*"

"You're gonna throw out your back talkin' like that," giggled Morris, using his Bowie knife to skewer the last of the sausages and roast it over the fire.

"It's the German title, Silly," chuckled Mina at Morris.

"Ya drove yer dad crazy until he got ya that damn book, Mina."

"No, Daddy was always very patient," nodded Mina, absorbed by the fire. "As was Mother. They both understood my enthusiasm for the stories."

"Honestly, who learns another language just for one book!" said Ian, stretching out over his saddle and blanket, his usual signal that he was ready to turn in. "And grim indeed, if I remember some of those stories."

"Ian, it's *Grimm* as in Jacob and Wilhelm Grimm, the authors, not grim as in grim—"

"I know that, Jonny," sighed Mina, smacking dust off what used to be a very pretty, very fashionable black dress.

"I dunno," said Quincy as he gulped down two half-cooked sausages, "there's that whole story about the witch tryin' to eat the kids."

"That's *Hansel and Gretel*, Texan," chastised Ian as he tossed his blanket over himself.

The Texan threw his arms out and laughed, "I'm better at faces than names!" he pointed the Bowie with the remaining sausage at Jonathan and said, "You get my point, Harker. Not exactly stories for young 'uns."

Mina raised an 'I know more than you do' eyebrow at Quincy and said, "The later editions were actually changed, Morris. Early on, the mothers in both Hansel and Gretel *and* Snow White were both mothers, not stepmothers."

"Are you sayin' this 'cause we're stuck out in the woods?"

It got very quiet around the campfire for a moment, and the silence filled it conspicuously.

Mina sighed, her eyes finding the fire again as she said, "No. And yes. When I was a child, I believed those stories wholeheartedly, and some of them scared me. Then I grew older and the book seemed full of made-up fantasy to scare children, but I never knew that I would come to understand that there would be a real witch that ate children from a tiny village."

"Good Lord that is quite creepy," said Ian as he rolled over to look at Mina.

They all took in the fire as it crackled, empathizing with them.

"Well hell, Mina, way to put a capper on the evening. And you know tomatoes are my favorite!

"Sorry, everyone," said Mina, Jonathan sliding his hand over hers in a 'not to worry' gesture.

"Aw, it's okay, Mina," snorted Quincy after he down the last of his Bowie sausage. "I'll take the first watch tonight. I hope I don't see any wolves. More and more of them these nights."

They all knew that meant they were getting closer and none of them decided to acknowledge that.

The fire cracked again, a few logs collapsing into the ashes.

Everyone settled into a comfortable silence, the kind reserved for close families or life-long friends. The wood popped from the water still inside of each of the pieces of kindle, crackling into the now-dark mountainside, the hills below now consumed by the gloom and pitch. The horses, just above them in the treeline, neighed softly, trying to stay as close to the fire's heat as possible. Mina snuggled into her blanket, her saddle now a convenient if less-than-comfortable pillow, and Jonathan reached over from his makeshift bed to kiss her.

"Goodnight, my one true love," said Mina after the kiss, to which Ian made a face that simulated the retching after a bout in a pub.

"You know," said Quincy as he turned to Jonathan, "we could get lost for a while if y'all need some space."

"The hell I will," spat Ian with a smirk. "It took me long enough to get comfortable on all these rocks and twigs."

"Quincy Morris and Ian Seward, you are both children," sighed Mina, not aware that Jonathan was making a lurid face right next to her. When she turned to her fiancé for support, she caught the face-making and feigned disgust and pushed him away with a laugh. They all laughed, in the night, in this mountainside, which was closer to a dead king than it was to their dead families.

"Goodnight all," said Ian and he flipped over and fell into near-instant slumber, the cacophony of snoring beginning a few moments later.

"Could you strangle Ian for me, dear?" said Mina, nearly asleep.

"Of course," agreed Jonathan, himself almost dreaming of better days without vampires and blood.

Quincy Morris sat there, alone, the fire crackling again.

He reached into his pockets, searching for something.

One, two, not in his outside coat.

Three, four, inside his outside coat, before he found it, and pulled out a small box.

Morris opened the box, and inside was a small photograph. He took the photograph out, looked at it like it was a pool of water in the searing desert.

The fire crackled.

Horses neighed again.

Quincy sat down on a log, and he put the photo on the log next to him. He looked over at Mina and Jonathan, slumbering as they held hands. Then back to Ian, whose would-be love first betrothed to a now-dead Arthur, then lost to a fiend.

Back to the photograph of a beautiful Mexican woman.

"Don't know if I'm ever gonna see ya again, *Amor*," sighed the Texan, "But if I ever do, ain't nothin' gonna keep us apart again. Even if it means y'all comin' here with me."

"I love ya, Darlin'" he said to the dark," "'cuz I just can't do otherwise."

TRANSYLVANIA
FALL 1899

It is not in the stars to hold our destiny, but in ourselves.
—*William Shakespeare*

Death is nothing, but to live defeated and inglorious is to die daily.
—*Napoleon Bonaparte*

When your turn comes to die,
be not like those whose hearts
are filled with fear of death,
so that when their time comes
they weep and pray for a little
more time to live their lives
over again in a different way.
Sing your death song,
and die like a hero going home.
—Tecumseh

Some people die at 25 and aren't buried until 75.
—*Benjamin Franklin*

The boundaries which divide
life from death are at best
shadowy and vague. Who
shall say where one ends,
and where the other begins?
—*Edgar Allen Poe*

Be calm. God awaits you at the door.
—*Gabriel Garcia Marquez*

BORGO PASS

Two days later, Jonathan Harker, along with Wilhelmina Murray, Quincy Morris and Ian Seward, crested that same hill and arrived at Borgo pass.

Where Harker had met those corpses, the swollen graves, the bleeding virgin statue and that monstrous bat all those months ago.

Their horses neighed, wary as they all were enveloped by banks of drifting mist.

Jonathan circled his horse around at the top of the crest as he felt the strangest sense of déjà vu. He took another deep breath and saw it exhale in the late afternoon's cold as his eyes adjusted to the gloom, which they did after a few seconds. The road still crested at the top of the pass, the elaborate silhouettes of tree lines still lined both sides, and that fateful, smaller road still led off to the right. A bloated, hidden sun ebbed with what light it could and cast it down over a large bank of mist, which snaked toward them faster than a man could run.

Ian Seward's eyes danced around in his sockets like he wanted to turn and bolt in the other direction, as did his horse, but he was able to ignore the strange sights around them and concentrate on their greater objective.

To their left, the remains of the three swollen corpses still hung by rope to several large hanging posts, hands still clawing at their throats, the wind rocking them back and forth, still. Their torsos had been gnawed away from the rib cage down. Bite marks raked at their exposed vertebrae. Five graves lay to his right, all sagged now. The three rune-covered stone monoliths had not moved but had been vomited upon. The generations of dried vomit contained various bits of broken bones, human and animal. The desecrated virgin shrine had been desecrated even further. The crucifix-covered roof was gone, and the top half of the figure had been torn away.

"Well shit this is scary as all hell," gulped Quincy as he reached back and patted his beloved Winchester that sat strapped to the haunches of his horse.

"This is it," said Jonathan to no one in particular but to everyone around him. "This is where I met him."

Harker pointed to the hard-scrabble road that ran perpendicular to the Borgo Pass route, the one that Dracula's carriage had taken back to the fortress. "He took me that way. The carriage had no horses drawing it, and he flew along as a bat. I was terrified."

Everything in that terrible place was perfectly still.

Eerily motionless.

The mist hit them, cleared, then deepened again.

The bloated orb sank more, even it was afraid of this terrible place.

Cold swarmed over them.

Mina's teeth chattered.

The same lone light that came through the mist at Jonathan before now drifted toward them again, and the horses neighed with fright. Out of the swirl came the apparition of the *Cuirassier*[250], his chest and front of his legs still covered in metal, and he held the same lamp and sword.

Jonathan nodded at the apparition, and the ghost nodded back. Harker trembled with both cold and fear as the ghost staggered past him.

The mist began to clear.

"Here you are again, lad," whispered the ghost.

"I told you I would return," smirked Jonathan, proud and unafraid.

---

[250] European armored cavalry, dating from the 15th century through the Napoleonic Wars (1803-1815).

"You looked bloody horrible the last I saw of you," said the ghost. "Crawled out of that river down there and made your way back over to me, babbling on about being on your way home. Forgive this dead soldier for doubting you. You here to take your revenge upon the vampyre?"

"He took everything from me," replied Jonathan, simply.

"Not everything," said the ghost, waving the lamp hand at Mina, Quincy and Ian. "You should have spared them the trouble, and to be honest, their deaths."

"I tried to," shrugged Jonathan. "They have decided to come along."

"We insisted," added Mina, never afraid to speak her mind, even to a ghost.

The spectre looked Mina over and nodded at Jonathan with approval. "You could both turn around, head home, she'd bear some lovely lads and lasses for you."

"I've been put on this earth to do more than bear children," sassed Mina.

"Dracula took our parents as well," said Ian soberly.

"The vampyre has separated man from woman, child from parent, and soldier from sword for a thousand years," sighed the ghost. "Everyone fears him and leaves him be. It be *he* who seeks others out."

"Well, he's been runnin' from us since the get-go!" sniffed Morris.

"You speak strangely," said the ghost to Quincy. "I have heard all the tongues of the continent, but yours rings odd to my dead ears."

Ian said, "Ehhh, he's from Tex—another part of the world."

Excited at even the partial mention of the word 'Texas', Morris bragged, "I can shoot a tick bug off a cow's ass at forty paces!"

"He appears to be an idiot," groused the ghost.

Mina gave out a single, sharp cackle.

Quincy Morris, honored to be insulted by a ghost, gave a kind, sharp nod in reply.

Ian snorted at Quincy's charming silliness.

At this the ghost turned to Mina and said, "Young lady, impose the will and wiles that all women possess and take these three young men away from their deaths."

"I shall not," she hissed. "I am to be without my father at my wedding day, or mother at my bedside during childbirth because of this fiend."

"This is no place for a woman," added the ghost.

Mina responded by pulling out Arthur's Webley, spinning the chamber around inside of the pistol expertly before she pointed the barrel at the ghost. She then holstered the gun and winked back as she said, "I decide what and where this woman's place is. My place is here, killing your so-called conqueror."

"Conquerors are always fiends," said the ghost, though he began to nod in acknowledgement to Mina. "Very well, I have tried to dissuade you, but you have journeyed far and deserve your chance at him. What help may I give to you, young ones?"

Jonathan looked around quizzically. "How do I get back to the base of the cliffs at the rear of the castle? I remember passing through here—"

The ghost sniffed, "You were covered in blood and horror, Boy. Your clothes were in rags, so be kind to yourself if memory does not serve you well."

"Why are you here, Sir?" asked Mina. "At this place, if I may ask."

"I died not at peace, and in battle. I told this to the boy when I first laid eyes upon him, on his way to meet the hellspawn. The entire continent aligned against the vampyre, so we marched against him. He slew us like we were the daemonic dragon and he the pious Saint George. We had not considered his rats. He keeps them ravenous, and they feed upon each other when there are no others to consume. And his skeletal legion has known no match for five hundred years. Since he brought them back from China."

They all stood in silence as the ghost let the thought about the cannibalistic rats and skeletal soldiers sink in.

Then the ghost looked at Jonathan with an expression of acceptance and said, "Take this road down from the pass, then veer to the left when you see a rough pathway. That is the path you took upon your return. After a half-day of riding you will enter a steep canyon and hear the river. Leave your horses above the high-water line you'll see in the canyon walls, and when the cliff on the right turns black and cold, you will see the castle above. That is where you will begin your climb. About halfway up, there will be caves in the cliff face. They will take you through to his dungeons. If you prefer, continue to climb. There is no defense wall to prohibit your entrance to the castle."

Ian wrestled out a large Romanian map of the area, but the *Cuirassier* saw this and said, "You will not find this canyon on any map."

"Thank you," said Mina.

"Are there any guards in the dungeons?" asked Ian.

"There is no need, my boy," chuckled the apparition. "That is Hell on Earth, and who would want to go to Hell?"

"To kill Satan," growled Quincy.

"Satan's son," whispered Jonathan.

The *Cuirassier* reached out to pat Jonathan on the shoulder in sympathy, but his hand drifted through Harker's body. The soldier then remembered he was a ghost and said, "I would warn you, if you cannot ascend to the castle by sunset, lash yourselves to your ropes and wait out the night upon the cliffs, then enter the castle at dawn. Do not engage the conqueror at night in his own fortress. Make no fire or noise in the eve. They would find you. Mind what I told you about his vulnerability during transformation."

"How do ya'll know all this?" asked Quincy with a snort.

"I survived the failed frontal maneuver against the fortress, but not the cliffside ascension. He rained the vermin down upon us, and I died as rats entered my stomach through my mouth."

The ghost pulled open his clothes to reveal a gaping, gnawed hole in his stomach.

After collecting her revulsion, Mina said, "What is your name, sir?

"My mates called me Merry John. I laughed a great deal. They told me I'd die happy.

"I did not."

ENCAMPMENT

The group did as the ghost of Merry John instructed and made their way down into a small valley that was losing its spring and summer verdant luster and preparing for an all-encompassing blanket of winter, if the nearby mountaintops were to be judge or prophet. Their horses took Mina, Jonathan, Quincy and Ian down where they wanted to go, yet they neighed with trepidation and quivered with nervousness as they descended the hills that became canyon walls. Quincy, who fancied himself a sage when it came to horses, was snorted at by Ian's mare when Morris condescendingly reassured the animal once too often. Around one of these canyon walls was a river, nearly bled dry with the fervor of the spring rains and currents far behind it.

Leaving horse prints on the riverbed as they moved upstream, it was with relative ease that they spotted the steep sheer cliff wall where Castle Dracula squatted atop like a malevolent gargoyle. Even during the day, the monstrous countenance of the fortress spread out and into the cliff, foundations staggering and collapsing and melting into the canyon wall like the structure had been built, shored up, rebuilt, then built again over centuries, utilizing whatever piece of conquest that had been ripped from its original place of construction and brought to this place of utter evil. Clouds seemed to avoid the place, and scavenger birds soared higher above, their disdain clear.

"That where Dracula threw you from?" said Quincy, pointing up toward one of the top spires above the many irregular medieval walls, buttresses and towers.

Jonathan simply nodded, and Ian followed up Quincy's lone, impressed whistle with, "Good Lord, Jonny, I have no idea how you survived that plunge."

"Morris, your timing would impress a court jester," sighed an annoyed Mina.

"Why thank ya, Missy," said Quincy, with a tip of the cap that showed he'd completely missed the point.

Ian did not, and said, "Sorry, Jonny," as he turned to Jonathan, who was looking all the way up the cliff face, hundreds of feet up, to where the underside of the spire where he was thrown from could be seen. It looked like a birdhouse.

"It's all right, Ian," replied Jonathan as Mina reached out and took his elbow in a gesture of sympathy. "River was pretty full at that point of the year. If it happened today, I'd have been scavenger bait."

He turned to Mina and flashed the smile she'd fallen for all those years ago. "I'm good, promise. Just glad to be back to finish this."

They neared the side of the cliff, and there was more riverbank than creek at this point. The cliff walls on either side of the river pinched together here, and in looking up, everyone had failed to look down, so when the horses began to neigh and side-step, everyone had the opportunity to look down.

All along the cliff bottom were bones. Human bones mostly, but animal as well, all piled up into fresh, recent, old, decaying, and mud-covered objects that projected from the soil. Femurs, tibias, ribcages and skulls all lay atop each other. Knife lines and bite marks covered the bones, with careful holes placed in the soft part of the skulls for presumably easier removal of the brain. Generations of mud and dust had left many of the older bones looking like a strange cobweb of protrusions from the earth, underneath the more recent specimens.

Above them only the cliff face, and in the heavens, the tower.

On the other side of the cliff face, the sun had begun its downward arc.

"We'll camp here tonight," said Jonathan, "then make our climb at dawn."

The Texan began, "We can make it up—"

"We can't afford to get caught at dusk. We at least need to give ourselves the entire day. No campfire. And tether the horses."

Dusk arrived and drifted among them without incident. Resting under a rocky outcropping along the greenery of the riverbank as it lay among the canyon, they all checked and rechecked their weapons and ammunition. Jonathan paid close attention inspecting the contents of Van Helsing's bag. They ate some barely not-moldy bread and dried fruit, before drinking from the creek that had been a frothing river last spring.

There was not much talk among them, though their thoughts were clear to each other. Mina took out a pen and a notebook and wrote for a while. Ian and Quincy asked her what she was writing, and Mina told them both to mind their manners. After a while, Mina seemed to finish her thoughts and passed the notebook to Jonathan, who spent the last rays of the afternoon sun reading and adding some thoughts of his own. Jonathan finished what he had needed to add to Mina's writings, then handed it back to Mina, who read his words with a sweet expression on her face. She then leaned forward as the night blanketed the canyon and gave Harker a quick kiss laced with gratitude before she closed the notebook and put it away in her knapsack.

Ian took down the blankets and bedding from the horses, who grazed contentedly above them in the green hillside. Quincy begged, cajoled and pleaded Mina and Jonathan to let him dig up another 'South Dakota Fire Hole', but they would have none of it. Morris explained that they might be spied that night by the inhabitants of the castle anyway, and Mina retorted that if they were indeed spotted, then a 'Southern Texas Hell Hole' would be the least of their concerns. Jonathan added that the protrusion of rock made them not visible from above, so with that bit of good fortune, they stood a great chance of lasting the night. Ian, back with the blankets, added that he'd tether the horses at a distance to avoid detection.

Jonathan thought it over and replied, "Let the horses go. At least they will have a chance to make it back."

THE CLIMB

The night's duration was only surpassed by the bitterness of the cold.

The castle/fortress above them was quiet for most of the night, though early in the evening, as they all lay in their beddings under the rocks, the sound of enormous fluttering and flapping wings of bats was heard far above, echoing throughout the canyon. Night deepened, and wolves howled in the distance. That woke up Quincy with a snort. He had fallen asleep during his watch and had to endure his embarrassment at realizing that Mina, Ian and Jonathan all watched him, annoyance splashed over their faces. Mina wondered if the horses, who had galloped away full tilt when they were untethered, were alright. The howls continued longer, giving them no answer.

Ian, rubbing his hands to keep them warm, stepped out from under the outcropping to stretch. He looked up and saw a bank of clouds drift apart to reveal a grove of stars, ready to be harvested.

The witching hour came and went with only one incident. A few ghosts materialized under the pile of bones across the creek, right under the cliff wall that supported the castle. None of them were skeletons, rats or bats. All of them were men-at-arms from different periods of time, all standing and paying Mina, Jonathan, Ian and Quincy no mind, but there they stood, praying for the souls of their lost comrades.

Or their own.

Somehow they all slept after the ghosts decided to leave, and that last stretch of night was quick, their exhaustion overtaking their fear of being overwhelmed as they slept.

A few strands of clarity came over the top of the canyon to announce the dawn. Jonathan woke them all, given that he had taken the last watch. They all rolled up their beddings, collected their possessions and left them under the rocky outcropping before they waded across the knee-deep creek. Without a word among them, Ian passed out a measure of rope, and they tied themselves together, each knotting the rope around their waists[251]. Jonathan wore Abraham's backpack, Mina and Quincy had their sheathed rifles. They all had belts with climbing tools: picks, pitons, extra rope and small hammers.

"Once more," said Jonathan, "unto the breach, dear friends.[252]"

---

[251] The English Alpine Club had been founded in 1857, at the beginning of the age of 'Mountaineering', a time during which many of the highest mountain peaks of Europe were ascended. The Matterhorn, or Mount Cervino, a mountain in the Alps between Switzerland and Italy, was first ascended by Edward Whymper in 1865.
[252] *From Henry V*, Act III, Scene I, by William Shakespeare.

And they all began to climb, hand over foot. Quincy first, he explained that he had the largest hands, therefore in Quincy logic land that meant he was the best climber. Jonathan second, Mina third and poor Ian last, having to conspicuously not look up too much if it meant looking up Mina's dress as she climbed above him. This brought a wicked smirk from Morris, which brought a silent, glaring rebuke from Jonathan.

They wore gloves, which helped a little against the rocks, which were dark as pitch, colder than ice. When the rock wall became too steep, Quincy solemnly yet somehow quietly hammered pitons[253] into cracks in the rock wall, after which he would loop a rope through and climb up. The others would follow, and Ian, as the last climber, would undo the rope.

Higher they went, and the breeze at the bottom of the canyon had become an intermittent gust that blew dust and specks of rock into their faces, eyes and mouths. They were over a hundred feet above the creek in no time, so much so that when Ian happened to look down he gasped. Quincy, pounding a piton into a crack said, "Poor Ian can't look down or up."

Jonathan, just below Morris and clinging to the wall, grinned despite himself. Everyone was careful, and no one slipped, and they reached a point where the bend of the cliff wall below them made it difficult to see the creek at all. The day was still very early, yet they fought a sense of urgency to scale the cliff wall as quickly as possible, remembering that a fall could end their crusade quicker than the vampires they were hunting ever could.

About fifty feet higher, Quincy, clinging to the cliff wall, flailed his left arm out and above him in order to find the next handgrip. His hand found a protrusion from the cliff face. Morris gladly took it, and lifted himself up to it, only to have bewilderment take over. Quincy had lifted himself up with the assistance of a wooden stake, about six inches round and three meters long that had been pounded into the rock wall hundreds upon hundreds of years ago. The stake's circumference was round, but the end that pointed out toward the opposing cliff wall on the other side of the canyon had been shaved and cut into a wicked point. Yet that was not the most intriguing thing about the stake. That would have been the three corpses that hung upon the stake, all impaled generations or centuries ago, with such force that their individual rib cages collapsed and broke upon impact. Yet judging from the apparent agony with which the long-desiccated cadavers were positioned, they had flayed about in a torturous manner until death overcame them. Pieces of armor, and uniform beneath the armor, clung to the three male cadavers, and because of the mummy-like condition of the flesh, it was impossible to tell where the armor ended, and the skin began. The farthest out was a Russian *Streltsy*[254], then a French *Grenadier*[255], then closest to Quincy was a Hungarian *Hajduk*[256].

They fluttered in the breeze like war banners.

As did the other hundreds of stakes and corpses that hung out over the cliff wall, above them as far up as they all could see. The collection of bodies had hung as they had since they had been impaled there, hundreds of years ago. Some of the stakes were wooden, many were metal. British uniforms from different ages wrinkled with the speed of the air around them. And German. As well as Prussian. Ottoman. Even Chinese and Indian. A morbid collection, dead butterflies for a collector of human corpses, pinned to the wall like a museum exhibit, or more likely, as a stout warning against trespass.

"Jesus, Mary and some whiskey," gasped Quincy.

"Just—" grunted Jonathan, right below and behind him, wincing as he drew himself up. "—keep climbing, Texan."

---

[253] A piton is a needle-shaped piece of metal that was/is used in mountain climbing.
[254] Guardsmen from 16th to 18th century Russia.
[255] Assault troops from France (and other countries) that were specialized infantry units, utilizing grenades, and at times riding horseback.
[256] Bands of fighters in the Balkans who would plunder wealthy Ottomans and Muslims, and at times protect Christians from the Ottoman Empire, comparable to the English parable of *Robin Hood*.

"I'm glad I'm here with y'all," said the Texan as he reached for solid rock. "Glad to be here with my family."

It was a sweet thing to say, and they all took it in and loved it.

"Your family in Texas loves you, Quincy," said Mina. Your Uncle Billy—"

"Aw, Uncle Billy was a drunken snake and hated me, called me a good-for-nothing half-breed Mexican Injun Buffalo Soldier. Can't nobody be kin that talks to me like that."

They all took that in with empathy for the Texan as they climbed before Jonathan, as always, said the perfect thing.

"He was just jealous that you could shoot better than him."

They could all feel Quincy beam and tear up. He nodded at Harker and said, "I shot his damn Stetson clean off that time he went for my sweet Momma with a knife."

"Perhaps your most impressive shot ever," added Mina as she leg-lifted herself higher.

"Definitely his most impressive shot while sober," said Ian, down below them, busy reaching for a handhold while trying to avoid looking up and underneath the hem of Mina's dress.

Mina saw this and whispered/hissed, "Ian Seward, you look up my dress one more time and I will gut you like a fish! I expect such behavior from Morris, not a proper English Physician!"

"No," said Ian, I was—"

Then Ian's handhold slipped.

And he fell off the wall.

Mina reached for his sleeve, and found it, mid-air.

Her own hand-hold began to fail.

She could then not hold on herself.

Ian's sleeve ripped from her hand.

Ian resumed his fall.

Jonathan reached for Mina, who herself had begun to fall.

Quincy, straddling the stake post, reached for Harker.

Ian looked up at his friends, falling away, knowing he was the one falling.

Then his rope ran taut.

And viciously yanked them down with the weight of his body.

This ripped Mina Murray from the wall, and she too began to fall.

Jonathan wrapped the nook of his wrist around her neck and held on for his life.

She slipped and fell out of Harker's hand.

Quincy was helpless to do anything but hold onto the desperate, squirming Jonathan.

Mina's rope length found its end, yanking on the waists of both Harker and Morris.

Both Mina and Ian swung with the zephyrs, along with the corpses.

Jonathan tried to rip himself from Quincy to reach Mina, but Quincy clung onto him.

All this in the silence and wind of the lonely canyon, abandoned only to the dead.

Ian took a knife out from the depths of his clothes and gave a long look of love up at his friends.

Ian then slashed at the rope.

Mina, still tied to the wall, swung herself like a pendulum down at Ian's arm as he slashed.

Seward cut the rope.

She floundered for his arm.

Ian fell.

His right wrist, still holding his knife, was caught by Mina.

"Let go," pleaded Ian in a near-whisper.

"Idiot," said Mina, who held firm, her face flush with intensity, her hair falling over her face.

They dangled.

And spun.

Like a backward-moving clock.

Jonathan found Mina's waist.

Quincy, straddling the stake, among the corpses, clung to Harker's trouser leg.

Jonathan, somehow upside-down but with his left hand clinging to the wall again, wrenched his body, turned his right arm toward the wall and swung Mina inexorably toward the wall.

They did not get there.

"Let me go!" begged Ian, in a whisper-yell, trying to squirm out of Mina's grip.

"Go to Hell!" snarl-whispered Wilhelmina Murray.

They all arched out over the yawning, dry canyon.

"Jonny," gasped Morris.

"This time," hushed Jonathan.

They swung back, in a wider, non-direct arc.

And collectively collided with the wall.

They all found handgrips somehow.

And Mina reached down, made sure that Ian was attached to the wall, then found his scalp and gave Seward's hair a single, jagged yank.

Ian suffered it in silence, hugging the wall, knife still in hand, yet thankful to not be bloody pulp against the creek rocks hundreds of feet below.

"I will murder you if you do that again!" spat Mina at a quivering Ian, who clung to the wall like it was his mother's apron.

"Sorry," said Ian, his scalp roots still afire.

"You just saved his life!" said Jonathan, his arm releasing Mina's waist and searching for his own handhold. As Jonathan spoke, Quincy said right over Harker, "Murderin' Sewie after savin' him really don't make sense—"

"All of you shut the hell up!" spat/whispered/scolded Mina, trying to gather herself and regain the feeling of her right arm.

They all clung to the cliff wall as the early morning sifted by them.

"I'm surrounded by stupid men," sighed Mina. "Ian, climb above me and we'll re-tie our ropes—"

"Dearest," started Jonathan, "I don't think we should—"

Harker took in Mina's glare as Ian clumsily clambered over her, so he said, "All right then."

As Jonathan and Ian re-did the ropes, Quincy looked down at Mina and with that familiar sly, stupid grin said, "Tiger Lily, you've put on a little weight—"

"Ian, hand me your knife," laughed Mina, then they all did, and the tension had passed.

Ropes re-tied, they all resumed their ascent, using the stakes above them as leverage to gain height.

The rest of the climb was in silence, weaving their way through the corpse-ridden stakes, which were helpful in the most and an obstacle in the least. Individually they all questioned why the stakes were there at all, then slowly came to the conclusion that Dracula of Transylvania was not one to concern himself with burglars or thieves. Ravens and vultures had made nests among the staked soldiers, and those were avoided as much as possible as they neared a ledge above that appeared to frame a larger opening on the cliff wall. Wilhelmina Murray, Jonathan Harker, Ian Seward and Quincy Morris painfully wrapped their knuckles around the ledge, thankful that they had made it this far.

Other events awaited them.

THE DUNGEONS

UNUM

"I am the way into the city of woe,
I am the way into eternal pain,
I am the way to go among the lost.

Justice caused my high architect to move,
Divine omnipotence created me,
The highest wisdom, and the primal love.

Before me there were no created things
But those that last forever—as do I.
Abandon all hope you who enter here."

—Dante
Inferno

One by one they reached the ledge, and after helping each other up and untying the rope, collapsed in utter exhaustion.

They trembled, both from the effort but also from the unspoken dread at the prospect of a journey that they knew, in their heart of hearts, could only end in their deaths.

One by one, after they had regained their breath, energy and nerve, each looked around the ledge, which was not a ledge at all, but the mouth of a cave. The walls were frigid, slick and yet here was more than one cave opening, or rather, five openings of various size and width that yawned open before them. About fifteen feet high and thirty feet wide, the cave openings all had natural columns that made it look like there were five tunnels, but they all fed into one large tunnel. The walls were solid rock.

Yet not only solid rock.

Above them, along the ceiling, were stories.

Like stars in the sky, but within the mouth of a cave.

Lines, not stars.

Painted lines.

Above and around them.

Stories.

Of horses.

Painted horses.

The painted horses ran, elongated legs and sweeping necks holding up eyeless heads.

Bears, colossal and imposing, reared up on hind legs, or worse, charged with graphic ferocity.

Elk, with expansive, painted antlers that stood regal and respected.

Glyptodonts, massive armadillo-like creatures with tails that ended with maces, fed innocuously from hand-painted grass.

Cave lions, much larger than today's African versions, plotted in watercolor-like washes.

Saber cats, dark, simple and dangerously drawn, prowled and stalked along the edges of the colored herds.

Laden with heavy coats of fur, wooly rhinos watched the cats, daring them to make an animated charge that would never happen.

Mammoths and mastodons, magnificent and majestic, resplendent in their crowning glory, wandered through the frozen veldt, young ones massed in the middle of the herd, daring any of the predators to try and intercede.

Chasing, creeping, plotting, and hunting among all of these amazing examples of prehistoric life were simple shapes of human figures, holding spears and simply trying to survive among the array of megafauna around them.

All of these scenes, tableaus, and parables of the Pleistocene era were stretched along the canvas that were the walls and ceilings of the tunnel entrance.

"That's plenty of huntin' to talk about over a campfire," chuckled Quincy.

They unpacked their weapons, Quincy with his Winchester slung over his shoulder and his Colts on his hips, while the others had their Webleys, save for Mina who also had the prize she had won from the Texan on that idyllic hillside behind Seward Manor so many months ago. They coiled up the ropes and most of the climbing equipment, leaving it all stacked up for the journey back out, taking some with them for the unexpected necessity inside.

In they went.

The tunnel before them went completely dark, and the floor became slick, wet, and lined with large, flat, stones. Jonathan produced the electric torch from his bag, and the others followed suit. Harker then led them into the narrow passageway. An overwhelming stench of bile, death, trash, rot, vomit, excrement, urine and decay blew out at them, the wind from the depths of the tunnel and the dungeons ahead was so strong that Ian threw up on the spot. Everyone else put the crook of their elbows against their mouths until they could manage to tie a handkerchief to cover their faces to partially escape the noxious, nearly toxic combination of odors that bled out at them though the air.

"What—" said Mina, but before she could continue, Jonathan swept the floor with his torch and saw that what floor was visible had sunk on either side of the tunnel, as a result of erosion. Crammed with human bones, dung, ashes, vomit, candle wax and blood. The floor shifted, and the resulting light had revealed white, bloated maggots, all squirming and slipping along the stones and the ground, consuming whatever disgusting remnants they could encounter.

Slivers of light danced off Jonathan's electric torch when he stuck it into the tunnel's darkness, shining and ebbing along with the torch's change of direction or focus. The passageway was so dark the light simply dissipated after a few meters. Fetid water dripped down from everywhere, along gaping holes in the ceiling and walls, which were a combination of rock wall and stone column from antiquity. Protruding out of the walls were the source of the lines of light in the gloom.

Spikes.

Countless.

Long, short, straight, jagged. Wooden, metal, man-made, found, forged and all menacingly pointed down into the center of the tunnel.

Corpses too rotted to be discerned by gender or time period hung lifeless from spike, skewered through their skulls, necks, abdomens, groins, legs; still holding the shackles around their wrists and ankles. Right where they had slipped along the floor and into their impalement. Some of the fresher corpses swelled with feeding maggots. A few human hands, adult, child and infant, also hung upon the spikes, where they had been *amputated or chewed off to the bone.*

In addition to the wooden spikes, there were also multitudes of metal weapons, rusted, broken and corroding, that had been jammed into the walls, lining them with swords.

Blades.

Swords from throughout history.

Hilts crammed solidly into the rock walls.

Blades pointing out to the center of the cave.

Hundreds of them.

Thousands.

A most beautiful of patterns.

Rusted, worn, broken, sharp, new, old.

All of them hungry for a piece of skin.

Or flesh.

Or tissue.

Or bone.

Every type.

All of them.

From every corner of the world.

Khopesh xiphos, asi, makhaira, falcata, kopis, gladius, spartha, paramerion, khmali, arming, long, stoc, curtana, sabina, espada ropera, zweihänder, flammard, broadsword, schiavona mortuary, basket-hilted claymore, backsword, katzbalger, cinquedea, executioner's sword, rapier, cutlass, smallsword, dirk, scian-dubh, spadroon, sabre, pistol sword, shashka.

From Africa there were ida, billao, takoba, kaskara, shotel.

From China were jian, dao, baguadao, butterfly sword, changao, dadao, shanmadao, yanmadao, wodao, miao dao, taijijian, piandao, mazhadao, liuyedao, hudieshuangdao.

Japanese blades were also represented: bokken, chisakatana, chokutö, hachiwara, liatö, wakizashi, tsurugi, shikomizue, shinken, shinai, ökatana, ödachi, nodachi, nagamaki, kodachi and the katana.

Scimitars from the Near East also filled in with the others. Afghanistan's pulwar, Persia's shamshir. The nimcha from Morocco, kilij from Turkey, talwar from India, mameluke from Egypt, kaskara from Sudan, and the shotel from Ethopia.

Amid the swords, spearheads glistened with cold hunger: angon, falarica, assegai, dancea, pilum, djerid, yari, hoko, jaculum, hak, plumbata, lklwa, verutum and spiculum.

Flower metals of forged beauty.

It was as if they were looking into the tooth-lined mouth of some massive undersea creature.

Water dripped like saliva into the caveway, dripping along the rusted sword/teeth of the Leviathan's maw.

"Smells like my old Sunday School boots in there," sniffled Morris.

"Look at the floor," said Ian after a very large gulp.

The middle of the path was smoothed, worn stone that had been purposefully built up in the middle, so that either side of the passageway angled down toward the walls.

Toward the swords.

"Anybody slips in here is going to get a nice how-do-you-do," said Ian.

They cast their torches deeper, light dancing off the blades, rust and cave wall.

"One at a time," said Mina, "And keep yourself low in case you slip."

"Gotcha," said Quincy with a crisp nod.

Mist poured out from the depths and darkness of the mouth and toward them, clinging and cloying along the ground as it moved around them, grey serpent's tongues hissing at their calves.

And into this they all went.

Mina and her Winchester led Jonathan, who in turn were followed by Ian, with the Texan last.

The tunnel was completely dark, yet as they moved through the effervescent mist, waving their torches everywhere, they could see a quiver of light at the end of this fiendish, spiked throat.

Jonathan did as Mina suggested and crouched down, keeping his center of gravity low, and proceeded very slowly. In addition to the incessant blipping of water droplets, dust also started to cascade upon them as they moved through the imbedded blades, a strange garnish from the few dry sections of the tunnel ceiling.

Water continued to pulse all around them, off downward-facing sword edges, along cave walls, adorning their clothes.

Drip.

Drop.

Drip.

"The ole' steersucker's clever, I've give him that," said Quincy, in hushed tones and a begrudging nod. "This tunnel makes it easy for him to get out, but no way an army makes it through here without somebody getting' stuck like a pig."

Glancing at one of the skewered armored corpses along the ground that had clearly slipped and skidded to his death, Jonathan replied, "Makes it easy for him to guard the gate."

"As he waits for us to arrive," chimed in Mina, her sober words silencing them.

"We could always turn around, head back home and lead normal lives, as Father Tibor suggested," said Ian, still half-sneezy with a torch and a crucifix in his left hand, and his Webley in his right.

"And wake up one night in a few decades with a gaunt, ghostly pale vampire face staring down at me through the night?" growled Jonathan. "No thank you."

At that moment Ian inhaled some dust, stopped and quivered from the effort to suppress a sneeze.

Quincy, who was behind Ian, stopped and snapped his fingers at Mina and Jonathan, who turned around and watched for a few terrifying moments as a suppressed sneeze almost backed Seward into a particularly jagged and rusted pike end, but the fit passed and they moved on.

More swords and speartips loomed as the four crept along, and upon closer scrutiny they all noticed bits of rotted, desiccated flesh that clung along the ends of the swords. Scores of rib cages, leg bones, skulls and even dried viscera littered each side of the berm that dared anyone to take a single, wrong step.

Light flickered from the far end of the tunnel, beckoning them as they neared the far end.

Swords, spears and pikes lining the walls became fewer and fewer.

Beyond the cave walls was what could only be described as a grotto-like chamber, still with black natural rock, but rock that had been chipped away into this natural yet unnatural grotto.

No prehistoric animal paintings adorned this room.

The small chamber was hewn round, about twenty feet wide and the floor was lined with more decrepit, armored skeletal remains, these were posed in death throes, their armor either pierced with broken pikes or *gnawed to pieces by millions of tiny, deadly bites*. The floor was not natural, lined with bricks. On each of the hundreds of bricks was the same Isosceles triangle:

VI

VI   VI

Along the edge of the chamber was a dark, gnarled, stone circular staircase that led to another floor above. There was only one light source in the room, from a flame that fluttered from a pile of wood in the middle of the room. A circular wall made of more imprinted bricks contained the fireplace, but instead of smoke rising out of the fire, arcane, obscene, secret, lost, forbidden and heretical symbols fluttered up, bright white to intense yellow to sinister crimson. Like evil butterflies, the symbols fluttered up to the low-hanging ceiling of the chamber, which at first was seen to be lined with wooden supports, but as their eyes adjusted to the light, they all saw that the beams were made of tibias and femurs, end-to-end, one after another, spanning the ceiling. Stranger still were the eerie, humanoid corpses that had been leaned stiffly against the cold, wet walls, covered with cloth and tied with gnarled, thorned rose branches that had been twisted and tied into vile, prickly ropes.

Mina was reminded of the Capuchin Monks from Italy, Franciscan friars who left their dead in repose to dry out, staking their bones along the inside of the burial chambers.

The armored human remains were haphazardly piled *on top of* the clothed corpses, explaining er battle had happened with the humans, the bound corpses were there first.

t was not the strangest thing in the room.

f the shrouded figures, indeed the walls of the very chamber itself were covered with a symbol. The symbol was that of a cross, or rather an inverted cross, and close to the n of the cross, from the top length and each of the sides, was painted or etched the same an numerals. Each set of numerals formed an isosceles triangle of sixes on the transom ection of each of the upside-down crosses.

of the covered figures not only had the body wrapped in the thorn-laden rope and covered with the 666-symbolled cross, they also had the mark of the beast carved onto their foreheads, *because the blood underneath had soaked through the fabric.*

"Holy shit," whispered Ian.

But he was not referring to the bound corpses.

They were not the strangest thing inside the chamber.

That horrific honor belonged to the corpse that floated above the fire, amidst the dancing runes and in the center of the thorn-tied figures of mystery. Twice as large as a human being, its legs and arms were tied together by more of the mysterious thorned rope. It floated in a fetal position, arms tied at the wrists, and legs at the ankles, along with an elongated tail that ended in a multi-tipped, many-barbed, scorpion-like stinger. Huge, membraneous wings, with armature that was reminiscent of a Gothic painting and clearly used to fly were also tied together. More thorn twine wrapped around the neck, which sat above a humanoid torso covered with the same triangular set of Roman numeral sixes, *which had been seared onto the skin.* The chamber reeked with the stench of burnt flesh A large, oblong skull featured six empty, haunting eye sockets, desiccated multiple nasal chambers and a mouth that yawned open in an expression of complete agony, so full of canines that the teeth overlapped each other like bizarre crystals growing in clumps. Topping the head were three sets of barbed horns that grew in and around each other in an eerie fashion. Onto the corpse's forehead had been branded a larger trio of Roman numeral sixes.

They all walked around the bizarre, floating corpse, and then toward the staircase, the only other way out of the chamber. Quincy pulled out his Colt and pointed it at the demonic head as he stalked around it.

"It's dead, Morris," whispered Jonathan.

"Everything we run into these days is dead," hissed the Texan, "But they still keep movin'. I saw a dead chicken come back to life once in west Texas."

Jonathan, Mina and Ian looked at each other while Quincy continued to point at the demon's head, and Mina mouthed, "Don't ask," at them.

Once the Texan was satisfied, he spun the Colt around on his index finger, shooting contest-style, before holstering it.

The demonic body remained inanimate as Mina, Jonathan, Ian and Quincy ascended the staircase, along with the delicate plume of smoke runes, and as they neared the room above, the air then changed.

A cold, hard breeze ran down at them.

It made the smoke runes scatter and brought them the foulest stench yet as they reached the top step and came upon another extraordinary sight.

An enormous, horrific stone altar lay before them, as large as a dining table. On this ornate altar were carved multitudes of demons in panels in the style of medieval woodcuts that depicted them throwing suffering human beings into flames, decapitating them, hacking their arms and legs off, eating their children, violating the women, cooking old men and women, vomiting onto apostles, impaling fleeing boys and girls with 666-crucifix lances. Numerous cuts and lacerations crisscrossed their way over the top of the altar, with a single sentence cut into the rock:

SUPER HANC PETRAM SERVIRE PATRI MEO[257]

Dried blood, delicate washes laid down over centuries filled the multitude of knife marks that had nicked and scratched the altar top. On each corner of the altar were four oblong, misshapen candles that swelled out in irregular shapes, with the bones of human and animal infants mixed together inside the wax. The candles burned slowly, sending the noxious odor of decay up along with the smoke up to the canopy, or *baldacchino*[258] above them.

From each corner of the altar area, four Solomonic columns, made of solid gold and twisted into helical, twisting pillars rose spectacularly into the cold, fetid air and held up the black opulent canopy, which upon first inspection appeared to be a complex expression of Rococo flamboyance, when in fact the baldachin was made entirely of burnt human and animal bones, skin and flesh. The scale of the columns was gigantic, rising high into the multi-storied darkness of the architecture of both the canopy it held and the gargantuan, domed ceiling still further above. Around the edges of the dome was carved, in enormous letters:

---

[257] 'Upon this rock I will serve my father.', a blasphemous perversion of Biblical verse Matthew 16:18, which states, 'Upon this rock I will build my church.'

[258] *Baldacchino*, or Baldachin, is a canopy supported over an altar.

SUM LUCIFER ET SUPER HANC PETRAM
AEDIFICABO ECCLESIAM MEAM. ERITIS MIHI IN REGNUM
CAELORUM ANIMAS

I am Lucifer, and on this rock you will build my church.
You will give me all the souls in the kingdom of Heaven.[259]

Inlaid marble floors spread endlessly and expressed geometrical patterns of the three groups of Roman numeral sixes they had seen below.

To the left and right of the altar and baldachin were corridors, narrow relative to the massive chamber before them, and as tall as the corridor behind them. On each 'corner' of the intersection of the corridors were enormous niches that contained huge statues, each carved out of jagged, razor-sharp obsidian.

The first statue, to their right in front of the altar, was of a human body crucified upside-down, with the head decapitated and nailed to the top of the inverted cross. The body's stomach had been sculpted like it had been cut open, and detailed stone viscera lay splayed out along the base, intertwining with tiny, impish demons that danced rococo-style upon and along the exposed entrails. A ghoulish, skeletal hound urinated upon the exposed, slit throat. Along the ornate obsidian base, and carved onto the base, were the words:

SANCTI ANDREAE.

To the left and across the nave was another enormous niche that contained another blasphemic statue on a base, meters taller than the largest man. A spectacular and massive Roman lance had been thrust down and through the mouth of the dead, sculpted body of a man in Roman armor. The angle of the lance was so steep that it burst out through the ribs on the left side of the torso, and at the end of the lance, tiny, Renaissance era demons danced with glee at the Roman Centurion's complete agony. The figure's torso writhed in classic sculptural emotion, his body flowing with the carving yet expressing its tortured, heart-wrenching pain, which only enhanced the carved glee of the demons.

Upon the massive base was carved:

SANCTI LONGINI.

Realization crept through Mina as she whirled to face the next statue, behind her and to her left.

Set deep into its own niche, this sculpture was that of a female figure. The robed torso had been decapitated, the arms had been sculpted delicately so to explain that the hands had been tied behind the back, as were the legs, at the ankles. The body lay on its side, against a sculpted rock, back arched backwards, reacting to the dozen arrows that had been hewn to appear as if they had pierced into the body. The head lay to the side of the body, still on the base, where obsidian, gnarled ravens pulled at the tongue, poked at the eyes and pecked at the exposed neck flesh. The sculpture was allegorical and as refined as any sculpture in Renaissance Florence or Venice. Upon the base was carved in a perfect typographical manner:

---

[259] 'TV ES PETRVS ET SVPER HANC PETRAM AEDIFICABO ECCLESIAM MEAM. TIBI DABO CLAVES REGNI CAELORVM' This contrasts the exact Biblical quote in Saint Peter's Basilica in Rome, which is 'You are Peter, and on this rock I will build my church' and 'I will give you the keys of the kingdom of Heaven.'

SANCTI HELENA CONTANTINI MATER PRODITOREM[260].

Mina pivoted, anticipating the next, last statue in a similar niche, but before that her eyes fixed upon the back end of this unholy, infernal church, where a domed, multi-storied, semicircular apse soared above an elaborate, opulent and heretical sculpture. Hewn out of gold and obsidian, rays flung out of the centerpiece of the ornamentation, a seven-headed, seven-crowned silver dragon. The rays that projected from the dragon seemed to keep it held in place, imprisoned, both worshipped and condemned. Around the golden rays were obsidian sculptures of scaly, vulgar imps, who writhed around the golden rays of evil in reverence and agony, adoring and blaspheming the eye around them.

Blood supernaturally trickled down from the forged symbol of Satan and onto to the golden rays pointing downward. The blood splattered upon four statues below, all of Gothic daemonic countenance, yet with the two on the left reflecting western garb typical of medieval Europe, while the two on the right were covered with sculpted attire from the near and far east. These four demons gestured in agony and exhilaration both up to the blasphemic symbol of the book of Revelations, and down below, toward a lone chair that sat upon a sculpted stand. The chair itself was made of burnt, blackened wood, with arms and a high backrest. The arms were covered with secret, occult runes, layered with forbidden, arcane knowledge. The seat was an expression of surreality, with nails, spikes, thorns, stakes and lanceheads all thrusting upwards at whomever would dare to sit upon the unholy throne. The backrest was also covered in sharp-edged objects, and atop the chair, floating in the air above the seat was a single plume of crimson, ever-burning flame. All of this sat upon a prodigious, multi-tonned base that flowed with a decorative, almost rococo opulence, the combination of flowing batwings, scarves covered with secret daemonic runes and phrases, mixing with sinning demons in positions of orgiastic blasphemy.

Mina looked quickly to her left, to take in the last niche in the sacrilegious, accursed place, and she saw the statue that she had anticipated seeing, that of a huge shroud, covering in a grotesque fashion, yet in the mastery of the Italian Renaissance, the body of a young woman, and this woman's hands were reaching out in a vain attempt to rip and claw the shroud away *as it attempted to pour into her mouth and suffocate her*. Atop the shroud, ingeniously and blasphemically sculpted with such perverse grace, subtlety and irony, was the image of the body of Jesus the Christ as depicted upon the Shroud of Turin. Upon the stout base that was identical to the other three that created the intersection of the transept was carved:

SANCTI VERONICA

"We're in a place of worship, a church," muttered Mina, her conclusion complete. Her voice echoed in the evil splendor that surrounded them.

Jonathan finished his open-jawed look at the place and nodded in agreement.

"We're what?" said Ian, trying to keep his voice down.

"This is the nave before us, and behind us, the apse!"

Quincy's eyes shot wide open. "Well Godamn—"

"Yes," agreed Ian.

"Not just any church," continued Mina. "Don't you remember our childhood trip to Rome? This is an exact replica of Saint Peter's Basilica. A blasphemous replica."

The basilica's scale was mammoth, farther than a football field before them and a half a field

---

[260] "Saint Helen, mother of the traitor Constantine."

behind them. Each side of the transept disappeared into gloom.

Thousands of candles, shaped in obscene, blasphemous shapes, copulating Virgin Marys, huge candles filled with the skulls of small children, goat heads with open jaws and multiple candles vomiting out of them garnished the steps down from the altar where they stood, where they had come out of the daemonic chamber below. Cat head, rooster leg and goat horn floated in silent sleep as heated wax melted around them.

"Lordy," said Quincy.

"Yes," agreed Jonathan.

"I've never—," began Ian, his torch trembling in his hand. "Good God."

"Saint Peter's Basilica. This is an exact recreation."

"The satanic version."

"Then who's the fella we passed on the way in here, buried down there instead of Saint Peter?" wondered the Texan.

His question lingered among them, unanswered.

They all watched the smoke continue to spiral out of the open pit, twining like a coiling serpent as it mixed with the air above the altar.

"We've got to hurry," said Jonathan as he ran out around the sacrificial altar table. He stopped, agape.

Now that they were out from under the *baldachino*[261], they could see the dome above. Inside the dome was a fresco so sacrilegious that Ian gasped in astonishment. A darkened, blood-soaked sky illuminated a scene upon a cloud where God lay across the cloud, dead to the world while above his decapitated, bloodied body, Satan incarnate held God's severed head high about his, with angels writhing around them in Renaissance fashion, crying out in agony at the tableau. Satan's gargantuan, membraneous wings unfolded all around the interior of the dome, with his body facing out from the apse.

Depicted in a near-identical manner to the monstrous apparition that consumed the demoness Lilith all those years ago in Wallachia, Satan's multiple horns, eyes, and blasphemic mouth raged with evil triumph. Above Satan was a scroll or ribbon that had been painted onto the dying sky above him, and on the ribbon was written:

ISUM FILIUS PERDITONIS[262]

"Let's get the hell outta here," hissed Quincy, after a long look and gulp at the fresco, his pun not intended.

They did, turning and running as quietly as they could down the colossal nave.

They all sprinted down through the massive nave, and as they looked up, Mina, Jonathan, Ian and Quincy were astonished. Soaring high above them, instead of the geometric patterns seen in its counterpart in Italy, was a mural that was dark, majestic and poetic. Hundreds of years of smoke and moisture on the underground rooftop had given the enormous mural a smoky, mysterious countenance.

Sprawled out in a style typical of the Renaissance masters were beauteous figures in various stages of violence, all over roiling storm clouds. A legion of darkened, bat-winged demons of human size and description, all of them holding daggers, swords spears and lances, were impaling, hacking and violating bird-winged angels all the way along the enormous ceiling, clouds swirling along the bottom edges of the piece, with the middle section of the frescoed ceiling darkened with millennia

---

[261] A *Baldochino* is comprised of fabric, metal or stone over a throne or altar, generally for ceremonial purposes.

[262] "I am perdition."

of soot that caressed the cracked brushstrokes into a majestic abomination. Both sides of the battle wore flowing, opulent robes befitting the styles of Michelangelo, DaVinci and Raphael, with the composition frothing with organic composition and volume.

Swirling, rendered scrolls, painted just above each demon identified each of the beasts, who possessed human anatomy, at least from the waist up.

LUCIFER, a very pale, handsome, human male figure, with flowing raven hair, two piercing, all-seeing eyes. His expansive bat wings spread out to nearly twice his size as he held aloft a golden lance, which glowed supernaturally as he prepared to plunge it into the heart of an angel laying on a bank of shadow-covered clouds. On the lance were the words LONGINUS LANCEA.

Next to the body of the angel about to be impaled was a frescoed scroll with one word engraved upon it: HOSTIUM[263] ·

"Let's get out of here and keep moving," said Jonathan.

They ran for the end of the nave, their shoes clattering and reverberating sound throughout the gargantuan chamber. All along were alcoves filled with dark, twisted sculptures of corrupt popes, blasphemous cardinals and hypocritical priests. The expansive dark marble floor reflected them perfectly, mixing Mina, Jonathan, Ian and Quincy among repeated inlaid images of the arcane triangular six pattern that led them to the back of the colossal structure.

There, below a darkened choir balcony and surrounded by dimly burning candles was a door larger than any of them had ever seen in their lives. It was a double door, with stout hinges that could have supported a mountain framing each side. The frame itself was ornate with dancing, squirming, writhing imps and demonesses, but also the remnants of generations of what appeared to be concrete washes that had been broken and sealed and broken again.

Above the door, scrawled into a beaten, bronze plaque, were the words:

PROFANA OSTIO

"The 'unholy' door," whispered Mina, more to herself than the others. "Just like at Saint Peter's."

"What the hell are those things?" said Ian, huffing along with them.

There were sixteen panels on the doors, two rows on each side, with four rows.

The panels were made of gold that had been pounded into bas-reliefs.

The first image along the top row depicted a scene in the Garden of Eden where the serpent mated with Eve while Adam looked upon them with anticipation and lust.

Next to that panel was a depiction was a demon lancing an angel in front of the Garden of Eden, with Adam and a pregnant Eve observing.

On the top row of the opposite door was a scene where one demon hacked at the Archangel Gabriel with a sword while another violated Mary, the mother of Jesus. The inscription above the panels read, "Quod nos effugeret a Eva et Maria et Gabrielis.[264]"

The first panel on the second row was a scene depicting Saint John the Baptist being hacked to pieces by imps, animate skeletons and minor demons in the middle of the River Jordan. Underneath was the inscription "Fatum odio habuit.[265]"

Beside that was a tableau of skeletons chasing a flock of sheep with spears, lances and swords. "Ad interficiendos infirmos maior.[266]"

---

[263] Latin for 'the enemy.'
[264] Latin: "What we took from Eve, Mary and Gabriel."
[265] "The Fate of the hated."
[266] "To slay the weak."

The third image in the second row was that of the prodigal son slitting his father's throat. "Pater omnia quaecumque habes sit pax.[267]"

Next was a depiction of Jesus being attacked by demons while trying to heal the sick. "Legio nomen mihi est. Quia multi sumus.[268]"

The third row of golden, obscene bas-relief began with the Penitent Woman on a throne of human anatomy, with four demons bearing her upon their shoulders. "Nos adorabis ea.[269]"

Beside that was Saint Peter, crucified upside-down. "Eum quem timentibus.[270]"

Next to that was the image of Peter weeping after denying Jesus three times on Holy Thursday evening. "Et infirmitatem nostrae triumphus est.[271]"

Mina quickly recognized it as the only exact copy of its counterpart image at the Holy Door in Saint Peter's Basilica. Beside that was the image of demons dancing between the crucified Christ, with the inscription: "Hodie nostra paradises est.[272]"

The lowest and final row of the Unholy Door began with the image of Jesus being pulled from the cross and down to Hell by imps and minor demons. "Beati qui crediturunt.[273]"

The next three were the depiction of the seventh seal being broken, the seven-headed dragon risen, and Lucifer incarnate upon earth.

Underneath all of that was the inscription, "Nostri triumphi inevitabilis est.[274]"

As they neared them, the Unholy Doors stood before them in evil resolve.

"We've got to figure out a way to open—" said Jonathan, interrupted as the massive doors yawned open on their own, hinges working smoothly and silently.

Beyond the doorframe, some sprawling, dark steps, framed by a massive portico.

Helical columns, covered with evil runes and sculpted, oversized thorns, twisted up to a roof covered with rococo images of mating imps.

Beyond the steps, a yawning underground cavern.

Beyond the cavern, another dark, cold tunnel.

DUO

"Do not be afraid; our fate
Cannot be taken from us; it is our gift."

—Dante
Inferno

As they ran out from the portico, Ian turned back to see the colossal doors closing silently behind them. Framing the doors, and to Ian's wonder, was the opulent, ornate façade of the front of the blasphemous edifice. A spectacle of rococo splendor, details swirled over the church front, making the intricate façade of the University of Salamanca seem simplistic in comparison. Yet within the swirls and currents of sculpted intricacy were bas-reliefs of imps

---

[267] "Father, I take all that is yours."
[268] "My name is Legion: For we are many."
[269] "We worship her."
[270] "He whom we fear."
[271] "His weakness was our triumph."
[272] Latin: "Today is our paradise."
[273] "Happy are those who believed." Also the exact inscription in the same place on the Holy Doors.
[274] "Our triumph is inevitable."

chasing nuns, minor demons staking bishops with wooden poles and major demons spearing and violating angels. Still running, Ian stumbled as he scrutinized the façade, realizing that the sacrilegious façade was in swirling, three-dimensional motion. In this mythological sea of sculpted art, the lizard tails and bat wings of the imps slid from side to side in flickering anticipation, the wooden poles of the minor demons arched back and forth before the strike, and the major demons yanked pieces of sculpted stone eagle wings off of the angels. On each side of the portico were enormous glass pots, each as large as a man and looking like elegant, infernal examples of Venice's finest glass-blown art. Yet inside the pots, mixed in with the hundreds of pounds of burning wax, was a wick as thick as a man's arm, along with the skeletons of mothers and their children. The twin pots cast evil yet beauteous shadows over the sculpted motion, with the darkened silhouettes of the helical columns slicing through the sea of sacrilege on their way up to the roof of the church front, which melded with the dark, twisting rock of the cave ceiling.

The entire structure, apse, nave, transept and façade, the entire structure, within and without, had all been carved *out one piece of solid rock*. It sat there, blinking at them like Leviathan or Behemoth[275], its undulating, writhing façade slithering over itself like snakes in a coffin.

"Ya don't see that every day," gasped Quincy as he ran, as they all ran, away from the unholy of unholies and up the sloping tunnel ahead. Underneath them, tiles became bricks, which then became cave floor once again. Their footsteps echoed ahead of them, and they slowed, fearing to be revealed in this breathtaking and ominous place. Their breathing came in heaves, and the dirt that covered Mina, Jonathan, Ian and Quincy made them feel more and more disheveled. The tunnel was not completely dark, one side rock wall and the other open, with stalactites and stalagmites drooping from the ceiling or rising out of the ground, with other, amorphous and sinister natural chambers in the depths and distance.

The ground went from cave floor to more placed 666-inscribed bricks, yet here and there, amid the dust that had collected upon the bricks over the centuries could be seen footprints.

Animal tracks, running all around.

But not animal.

Not just animal.

Demonic.

Human.

Cloven.

Enormous bird claws.

And reptile feet.

And the imprints of skeletal foot anatomy.

And billions of tiny rat tracks, waves going in either direction.

As he ran, torch in one hand and Webley in the other, Jonathan decided not to give those tracks any more thought.

Mina gave that all one big shudder as she swung her torch in front of them and hoped that nothing moved of its own accord.

But she found something macabre nonetheless.

Ian swung his electric torch over and found the same thing that Mina had discovered, and fought off the urge to turn and bolt back the way they had come in.

"Jerusalem crickets," was all that Quincy could say.

---

[275] Behemoth, like Leviathan, is another enormous biblical monster. Behemoth is mentioned in the book of Job (40:15-24), while Leviathan is mentioned in the Books of Job (3:8, 40:15-41:26), Psalms (74:13-23, 104:26), Isaiah (27:1) and the Book of Amos (9:3).

In the gloom ahead lay eerie mounds of figures piled one upon each other in odd, disturbing fashion. Limbs, arms and torsos were grotesquely intertwined off to one side of the tunnel. For a moment a scene of biblical frenzy depicted in one of Gustave Doré's etchings seemed to be realizing itself in front of them. They all stopped and pointed their Webleys and Winchesters at the heap of anatomy. Darkness shrouded these strange masses, and in the flickering light from the electric torches became not a cabbalistic orgy or a litter of corpses, but dozens of statues of men and women, sculpted demons and angels. Some were complete sculptures, some in the transition from marble block with a torso or head protruding from the mass of stone. They were clothed in marble garments or stone nudity, a wing of an angel reaching out from the pile, reacting— it turned out, to a lance that had never been completed, thrust into its geological flesh. Gothic, baroque, rococo were represented, most of the poses in Renaissance flourish, hands splayed and feet spread in the anatomical flair that Michelangelo or Bernini would have approved of. When Jonathan's paranoia of the whole experience let him realize that the eyes staring back at him were vacant, he lowered his pistol.

Next to the pile of sculpture was another enormous black, bleak iron door, and as with the doors of the infernal copy of Saint Peter's Basilica, these doors again swung inward in utter silence to admit them. A darkened chamber loomed.

Kling-clang, echoed from within.

Clang.

Kling, kling, klang.

Clank.

Metal-on-metal, the sound of chains bouncing against each other echoed out from the dark and cascaded over them.

"Sounds promising," said Jonathan with a sarcastic twist of his head.

In they went, their torches cutting diagonal lines through the gloom.

They found faces.

Or rather, their torches did.

Happy.

Sad.

Faces.

Some feminine, others masculine.

Beautiful, young women.

Older, beauteous queens.

Dashing young men.

Bearded, men of scholarship.

Laughing.

Crying.

Some crying and laughing, faces split in two like the comedy and tragedy mask symbols associated with theater[276].

Some, outrageously, were the faces of Jesus and Mary.

Or the devil himself.

Cast.

Out of iron.

Iron maidens.

All of them.

---

[276] The two symbolic masks are of Melpomene and Thalia, the Greek muses of tragedy and comedy.

A single candle lit the dusky, dust-lined chamber. The candle was on a stand in the middle of the room, a bookstand, ornate and ancient. On the bookstand lay a single object, a dusty, brown mold-encrusted ledger, so old that the stitching of the pages within was visible. The candle was attached to the upper right-hand corner of the bookstand, up on a little wicked candelabra of its own. The candle itself sagged because of the heat, but also because of the tiny human baby's skull that floated inside of the melting wax, the wick intertwined around the neck area. The light from the candle flickered over the room like a wide brush of light, barely illuminating the different array of personal torture chambers that were leaned against each other, one generation against the previous, with the most recent additions closer to the bookstand. In the darker recesses of the room, enormous cobwebs similar to the ones in the castle blanketed the older, broken damsels of torture.

A lone, wooden door on the opposite side of the room, with a demonic cherub carved onto it, led out to more of the complex mysteries of these dungeons.

Mina's torch found the bookstand, and she walked up to it and opened it, waving aside the gentle tide of dust that the movement of the book had caused. A few of the first pages crumbled to dust in her hands. Mina gently flipped through the rest of the pages, her eyebrows raised in surprise. The pages were vellum, and along the edges were illustrations of demons frolicking with the body parts of angels, serpents consuming children along with imps ravishing priests and nuns.

"This ledger," said Mina, "is filled with names and dates that go back for centuries. Each of these torture devices has someone inside of it. Listen to this: Contessa Elizabeta Báthory de Ecsed, born 1560, and according to this, died in lot number 332 sometime in 1631."

"The last entry is—"

"Kill us," hissed a familiar voice in the darkness.

The hiss reverberated throughout the room.

They all pivoted like clockwork, along with their Holy Water-blessed firearms.

One of the nearer, newer maidens, this one with a medieval representation of an angel on its front, had a single eye slit that ran across the face of the angel, who had wings folded neatly alongside her robes as she looked up, clearly on her way to the reward of heaven. Inside the eye slit glowed and blinked two embers filled with sorrow and menace.

"Please," begged the feminine voice, "end my life."

"And mine as well," added another, garbled, nearly unrecognizable hiss from another maiden, this one with another female angel, playing a harp as robes flowed with the sculpted zephyrs created by her wings. Two eye holes held eerie, glowing eyes that blinked back tears.

These iron maidens differed from the others, now it was noticed, because they had small crucifixes tied all over them with string, along with garlands of garlic and roses.

"Who are you?" shouted Jonathan, who had not lowered his Webley.

The maidens remained silent, two sets of incandescent eyes peering out at them from the torture coffins.

Looking up from the ledger, Mina whisper/shouted, "Good Lord! According to this entry, that's Venus!"

Ian lowered his Webley and ran over to peer into the other maiden's slit.

"Careful, Ian," said Jonathan, his own Webley trained right on the lovely, wooden female demon's head.

Quincy was covering the iron angel with his Winchester.

"Bloody hell!" spat Seward, his mouth agape. "And Petra's in this one!"

Quincy stalked over to Venus' maiden, slid the barrel of his Winchester against the lip of the torture chamber's eye slit and hissed. "I've got a mind to take my Holy Water and pour it down through that opening and scald you like a rattlesnake on a tin plate—"

Venus' reply was as shocking as it was swift. Her voice trembled as she gurgled, "I would consider such a gesture to be chivalrous and one of courtesy."

"Like the chivalry you afforded Uncle Abraham in Rome?" snarled Mina. "Like the courtesy you gave my parents in England?"

Then, from Petra's maiden, the soft sounds of a woman weeping.

"Anything," moaned Petra, "rather than to stand in here hour after hour as our legs to give out and collapse against these inner walls."

Venus' voice had regained a measure of calm. "He lined these coffins of torture with crucifixes and garlic-laced spikes, such was his compassion."

"We stay here to rot," finished Venus. "Such is his wrath."

Quincy's hold on his Winchester's trigger waned, but he said, "Good."

"You have no sympathy from me" snarled Mina. "You slaughtered our families! In front of our eyes!"

"We ask for death, not sympathy," said Venus from the depths of her tomb, "Yet with respect, does an owl deserve scorn for hunting mice? Or lionesses for stalking a zebra?"

"We were beheld to our master like servants," continued Petra, before any of them could respond, "No! Servants held a share of dignity! We were his—"

Silence.

Petra could not continue.

More silence.

Then, Venus de' Medici finished Petra's thought for her.

"Whores," moaned Venus, the pain from the depths of her soul. "We were beheld as concubines in a brothel, never wives and mothers to his children."

Ian lowered his Webley a bit.

Just a little.

"You had no children like our parents did, you could never know—"

"Nor were we ever allowed to bear any heirs for him! He denied us our titles of countesses, wives and mothers. Despite all the loyalty we gave him, of our minds, hearts and bodies, and in the end our fate is like all the others, banishment, imprisonment and execution. Our reward for loyalty to his 'royal' hand."

Jonathan, who did not lower his Webley, would have none of it. "Our parents were *butchered* like livestock-"

"So then take your pound of flesh[277], boy!" demanded Venus from her prison, proud to the end. "Use your Holy Water, pour it into our coffins, turn away, smell our burning dead flesh, knowing you have had your vengeance!"

"I'm all right with takin' mine," nodded Morris to Jonathan, and they both began to search for their bottles of Holy Water.

"I am not," said Ian, who took a step back and lowered his pistol.

Mina, Jonathan and Quincy all looked at him, incredulous.

"Ian, after what they did to your parents?"

"I will mourn them in my own time," said Ian, and his eyes blazed with determination, "or join them in the Hereafter shortly. In the meantime, we have something to bargain with."

---

[277] The phrase 'pound of flesh' originated from he play *The Merchant of Venice*, written in 1596 by William Shakespeare.

"Are you mad?" asked Mina, shaking her head at him as she closed the ledger and raised her Winchester at Venus's eye slit.

Ian turned to the maidens and said, "Here is my bargain: Tell us where Dracula sleeps in this castle, and after we kill him, we will set you both free on our way out."

"You *are* mad," gasped Jonathan with a vigorous shake of his head.

"We have no choice!" shot back Seward. "We know not what lies ahead, how far this impossible journey will take before we even leave these dungeons—"

"There are four more dungeons on your journey into the fortress," came a rumble from within Petra's maiden.

"After the dungeons, you must then find him within the castle," added Venus. "Not an easy task."

Quincy gave Ian a wide-eyed look of incredulity. "Sewie, I love ya but this is Longhorn bullshit."

"Every moment we argue wastes time!" Ian nearly shouted at his friends. "They will tell us where he rests during the day, with specific instructions, and when we dispatch him," he continued, parrying to the maidens, "I will stay behind and release both of you as we make our way back down through these dungeons."

There was silence between them all, and deep thought. Finally, Ian said what they were all thinking. "You all know that whether we kill Dracula or not, we're going to die here, tonight. If they can give us any information to help us accomplish our goal, which is to rid the earth of this shadow of evil, we must take it!"

"And it is the right thing to do," finished Seward.

"They killed yer mom right in fronta' ya, pal," said Quincy, still half-arguing with Ian, but he had lowered his rifle, as had the others.

Ian's eyes filled with tears at the memory of Henry and Lilian Seward, but he shrugged at Morris. "Our only objective is to kill the fiend. The greater good."

Mina took a long look at Venus' glowing, squinted, thinking eyes in the iron maiden and made up her mind. "Where is he now and how do we get there the fastest?"

"Will you honor our bargain?" said Petra in a half-moaned sigh filled with pain and bad memories.

"Madame, I give you my word as an Englishman and a doctor," said Ian, stepping forward, standing straight and clicking his heels together with such sincerity and dignity that whatever quip that the Texan had on his lips stayed there.

Quincy's silence did not last long. "How do we know that this isn't some kind of trick or double-cross?"

Venus hissed impatiently through her eye slit and snapped, "Because we would have screamed out already and brought his unholy legions down upon you all."

"Incantations upon these openings keep us from transforming into mist and escaping," said Petra, talking over Venus, "but he derives amusement from any cry of pain from these parts of his fortress."

"Leave us each with a bottle of your Holy Water," added Venus. "If you fail, we will hear of it regardless of the commotion, then we will at least have the ability to be mistresses of our fate. We would be grateful for that opportunity."

"More than our parents had," grumbled Jonathan, but bowed his head to Ian's and Mina's annoyed expressions, making clear to them that he understood the greater objective. Morris was not happy either, but he also saw reason.

"Well, if we survive this barnburner," said the Texan, thinking out loud, "I'm leavin' through the front door, not the back."

"Listen, mate," said Jonathan, "you are by far the candidate for eternal optimist if I've ever seen one, but you heard them. This has always been a suicide mission."

"Okay, hey, I get it, but there might be a chance."

"There won't be, Quincy," said Mina with a deep gulp.

"The Englishwoman is correct," Venus' rasp of a voice interrupted them.

"The lady is my wife, Wilhelmina Murray— eh Harker!"

"We are not yet married, my foolish love," giggled Mina with a grimy smile at Jonathan.

"Such a deep love," gasped Petra, as her voice quivered with relish. "We envy it.

"The Holy Water please," gasped the voice of Venus from within her maiden. "You must accept our perspective, that the odds of chance are against you. We at least would have our own demise and dignity left."

"Fair enough," said Mina.

Jonathan fumbled through Uncle Abraham's bag and pulled out two small bottles that had *Aqua Sanctus* written on them, as well as the symbol of a tiny cross beneath it. As he passed the bottles through the eye slits of the iron maidens, the pale, feminine fingertips of both Venus and Petra reached out to accept them, then retreated into the darkness. Slight hisses emanated from the torture boxes until their twin glowing eyes returned to the openings.

"I consider this a bargain of circumstance," said Jonathan, fishing through his bag for a bottle. "If we see you after all this, no quarter shall be given, nor allowed—"

"No. If we free you, you stay away from us, our children, and their children," said Mina. She gave Jonathan a hard look until he nodded in reluctant agreement, then glared at Venus. "Your word."

"As well as yours, Petra," Mina's glare swept over to the Egyptian. "If we all survive, our direct descendants are not to be hunted. Neither by you or any of your brethren."

Mina's eyebrows arched as she reiterated, "Your word."

After a moment, "My word," and "As well," slithered out from the eye slits.

"And your oath as well, in return," hissed Venus.

Mina nodded. "Our word."

"Yer not speakin' for me, Tiger Lily!" growled one Quincy Morris.

"Yes I am. Shut up, Morris!" snipped Mina. She looked to the vampiresses again. "We will leave you alone, and in turn you and any of your people will leave us and anyone in our bloodlines be."

"Agreed," came from the recesses of both Venus' and Petra's prisons.

"I will return to free you both," said Ian. "My word."

"It is only fair to warn you," said Venus, "because we now have an accord. Our former master and husband has anticipated and planned for your attempt, since he is no stranger to assassination attempts. Indeed, there was one such attempt upon his unearthly life when we reached the English coastline on our way to hunt you. He knows not the hour, day, month or even year of your arrival, but he knows you would have tracked him from Rome to here. He means to do cruel and horrific things to you all. Dracula of Transylvania is no fool, he knows you are not capable of a frontal attack. He has always left the dungeons open for everyone as a courtesy, *an invitation* for those foolish enough to make the attempt that you are undertaking."

"I'm that foolish," said Quincy with a sniff, a leer and a twirl of his Winchester.

"Quincy Morris of Texas, you are as stupid as you are handsome," said Petra with a half-giggle.

All three women giggled at Petra's statement, to the bewilderment of the men around them. Somehow, a brief pact of unity fell among them because of that moment.

"And Dracula waits for you, in anticipation of your arrival," continued Venus. "In short, you walk into a trap, Wilhelmina Murray. I respect you enough to explain this to you."

"How can we make our way through these dungeons before nightfall and still find him?" asked Jonathan.

Venus' eyes became two slits as she whispered, "He has emptied the dungeons to entice you into the castle, where the rats and skeletons await to devour or cut you to pieces. Dracula rests in the chamber next to the altar of his birthplace, yet he has *multiple chambers of rest on the first floor*. If you can make your way to the floor *above* him, then rappel down onto his casket before the skeletons discover you, then you may have a chance of removing his coffin lid to deal him a killing blow before you yourselves are murdered by his guardians. Either way you go to your deaths. You will be overwhelmed the moment you strike, successful or not."

The silence in the dungeon let Venus' statement sink in.

Ian nodded and accepted it.

Mina and Jonathan held hands.

Quincy shrugged, the vote against him.

"You would have no chance at an attack from the first floor," added Petra. "You would be discovered and devoured."

"What of Primus and Adso?" asked Jonathan. "Do they rest beside their master?"

They heard Venus inhale deeply, a long hiss from a contemplative, captive serpent. At last she said, "The skeletons would be on the first floor, awaiting anyone to make the climb up through the dungeons. The majority of the skeletons keep watch in front of the castle. When you arrive at the mouth of the first dungeon, it holds one of his libraries, with the bookcase of his Cabinet of Curiosities. Do not open that trap door, or you will be set upon. There is a strange column in that library which has been used to shore up that part of the castle. It is Chinese in origin, from one of his ancient conquests, before our time, in his youth. It has a dragon carved onto it. Ascend the back of the column with the handholds that have been carved into the pillar, up through to the ground floor. The column is covered with rock wall on the ground floor so you will not be revealed. This will take you up to the second floor, where you can plan your attack upon him."

Petra hissed an additional response. "The hallway leads to two chambers, those are his main chambers of repose. He has many throughout the castle, but those are his primary places of rest. He does that to avoid the assassination you are about to attempt. There will be a coffin in each chamber. Whichever coffin is covered in pieces of bone, Dracula is *not* within. Those are the skeletons, eager to protect him and loyal to their master, but merely a ruse. Dracula resents being protected, thinks it a weakness on his part, and his pride, his *vanity* has created your opportunity."

"The closed casket, with no bones, is where you will find him."

"Free us!" interrupted Venus' voice, perhaps with too much eagerness. "We can assist—"

"No," was all Jonathan would say, yet grateful for the interjection.

"You murdered our parents!" hissed Mina at the maidens. "This is as far as our trust could ever go with you both."

"When you reach the first dungeon, extinguish your lanterns before ascending the Chinese pillar. Or they will see you coming, and in turn descend upon you."

Ian took out a knife and cut off the crucifixes, garlic and roses from the maidens. The crucifixes hissed when they hit the ground, burning holes where they touched the blasphemous earth, but remained intact. Jonathan helped, while Quincy and Mina stood with the Winchesters at the ready.

"To facilitate your escapes in whatever circumstance arrives," said Ian when it was done. "You have both earned that much, from my perspective."

"Did they earn it when they killed my Aunt Lillian and Uncle Henry?" groused Quincy. Ian raised his arms in a pointed shrug to Morris as if to say *what would you like me to do about it?*

"Let's go," said Jonathan.

All four then turned and moved to the other door of the dungeon, a dilapidated wooden door that opened of its own accord as they neared. Behind them, Venus' voice purred, "I say this with utmost respect, you are worthy foes fit for a glorious death."

The others ran ahead, as Ian said over his shoulder, "I shall return for you, God willing."

"I find the irony to be horrific," Mina dead-panned at the glowing, blinking, undead eyes of Venus de' Medici. "We have an understanding, but there can never be peace between us."

"You are valiant, Wilhelmina Murray," added Petra. "I would not have done as you have."

"It is Ian you should thank," replied Mina. "It is he who helped us all in this regard."

"We thank you, sweet Ian," whispered Venus, the echoes from her iron maiden rasping her gratitude.

Ian said nothing, merely bowing in courtesy.

"Farewell," said Mina as she turned away.

"And you, fair Quincy," whispered Petra.

"Go to Hell," growled Morris as he tightened his Stetson around his head.

They moved to the broken wooden door with the demonic cherub carving.

After Mina, Jonathan, Quincy and Ian had closed the dungeon door behind them, a soft, haunting chuckle followed.

Within her prison, Venus giggled wickedly to herself as she whispered, "'Behold, I stand at the door, and knock. If any man hear my voice, and open the door, I will come in to him, and will sup with him, and he with me[278].'"

TRIBUS

"Hope not ever to see heaven.
I have come to lead you to the other shore;
Into eternal darkness;
Into fire and into ice."

—Dante
Inferno

Another set of ominous, massive dungeon doors loomed before them, twenty feet wide on each side, and nearly that high. Pounded into relief onto the doors was an enormous, expansive dragon reminiscent of the grand depictions from China, with touches of Byzantine and Christianity, a peculiar, particular design in this horrific underground realm. The dragon had wide, demonic wings that spread out malevolently, and trapped within the canine-laden jaws was an agonizing lion, clearly Christian by the halo over its feline head. Among the twining serpentine body were the same three sets of roman numerals:

---

[278] Revelations 3:20.

VI

VI   VI

Behind them was the roughly hewn underground road that connected the dungeons, to one side, an ornately sculpted baroque archway that not only framed the blasphemic cherub-adorned wooden doorway that they had just passed through, but also featured its own group of writhing demons artistically intertwined amongst each other. The dungeon wall itself was made out of a strange combination of rock wall, clay, cement and human bones, almost spackled together amid and in between the natural wall of the vast cave formations.

Single, flickering candles on either side of the wooden doorway basked the tunnel in intermittent, erratic incandescence.

In front of them loomed the dragon doors.

Not knowing what else to do, Quincy took a few steps forward to figure out if there was a lock of some sort.

After the Texan's third step, the doors swung silently open, spreading and pulling apart enormous, canopy-sized cobwebs in the process. Bloated, bulbous spiders the size of a human hand scampered to hide in recesses within the dragon and lion.

"Lovely," gulped Ian.

A further invitation into the macabre.

Ian held his electric torch out in front of him, at the dragon that consumed Christian lions, the beam trembling and wavering in his nervous hands. Everyone else brandished their weapons as they reacted to the opening of the doors. A fetid, dry blast of hot air hit them from inside the pitch-black chamber, laced with the scent of death.

In they plunged, the doors closing behind them *without making a sound,* like hands of an enormous ancient deity, sealing them in like the fronds of a Venus flytrap the unwary insect. Ian waved his torch around, and so did Jonathan, both of them understanding silently that Mina and the Texan were the better shots by far.

Before them, nothing but blackness, and unexpected cold, cobbled flooring. More scent of death filled their nostrils, pouring out from the depths of the pitch, obscene zephyrs filled with ancient evil.

"At the ready," whispered Jonathan, reduced to an illuminated sliver in the darkness, with his Webley out before him.

No kidding, thought Quincy.

Without even a creak, the doors sealed behind them, complex metal latches and gears locking into place with oiled precision. Ian's beam followed the dank, irregular cobblestone floor until it hit more large medieval bricks with the Roman numeral 666 stamped onto them, placed unevenly and leading upwards, a slight incline. The beam then reached further and found a worn stone staircase. Next to the bottom of the staircase was a single copper post that protruded from the wall. The corroded post had been hewn into the shape of a snake. The snake struck out, open-mouthed and vicious from the angelic cherub that had been carved into the face of the wall.

On the snake post hung a single key.

It appeared to be a simple skeleton key[279], but closer inspection revealed the engraved portrait

---

[279] A key that opens all locks in a particular house, building, or in this case, a dungeon.

of the dragon on the doors, the dragon with the angelic lion in its maw, and with the same three numbers cast among the intertwining serpentine body:

VI

VI   VI

"Perhaps this might also unlock the iron maidens that hold the brides," said Ian as he reached for the key.

When his fingers touched the key, it gave off a single, audible and violent *hiss*.

Seward recoiled his hand as if bitten.

The key rattled in violence for a second, then remained hanging, alone and resolute.

"Well, pants me and call me crazy," woofed Quincy.

"Leave it be," said Mina with a wary look on her face.

"Not if we can use it to free the brides later," said Ian, reaching into his trouser pockets and fishing out a handkerchief."

"I dunno Ian," said Jonathan.

Ian held the handkerchief in his hand as he reached out, but when the cloth made contact with the skeleton key, the handkerchief burst into flames. Seward yanked his hand back in surprise and let the remnant embers flutter to the ground.

The key gave out a chilling giggle and stayed still.

Save for their torches, blackness once again embraced them.

"Good Lord," whispered Ian.

"You'd need a spell to pick it up I guess," said Harker. His torch beam swung away from Ian's and the key, then ran up along the stone floor, until it encountered motion.

The electric torch panned back.

A hand.

A human hand.

Lying upon the cold ground.

Inert, the tips of the fingers bore torn skin, exposing bone.

Behind the hand, a forearm, and beyond that, an elbow, which turned downward and into a prison-cell-like opening on the floor, complete with curved, aged bars that upon inspection in Jonathan's electric torch, bore other elbows, forearms and hands, of different sizes, ages and pigments, all splayed out like some absurd spider. All the fingertips were also worn to bone. Scratch marks on the stones surrounded the prison hole.

"Bloody hell!" shout/whispered Jonathan, and Ian's beam found his again. Jonathan could smell the Winchesters on either side of him before he could see them, and he could hear Mina gasp as Ian's beam found another spider cell.

Then Jonathan's torch found another cell.

And another.

Yet another.

"He would simply lock people up down here and never come back for 'em," sighed Quincy. "Sounds like ole' Steersucker."

Then the electric torches found a beam, a wooden support beam, thicker than a tree, which rose up from the arms-lined stone floor.

Move the torches away," said Mina. "Let our eyes adjust. There may be enough light to see the rest of the chamber."

"She's right, move the lights, Jonny and Sewie," said Quincy. "We might be able to see better."

Ian and Jonathan swept the beams of the torches away, behind them.

After a few seconds of complete darkness, their eyes adjusted and the chamber revealed itself in the gloom.

Stretched out before them was another real-life version of a rendering by Piranesi. Colossal would be the only way to describe the complex chamber that sprawled out before and above them. Everywhere were enormous wooden timbers, supporting a complex inner structure that rose asymmetrically into the darkened heights of the vast chamber. A complex system of wood braces lined the multiple chambers, enormous, large, small and tiny, with stairs sculpted and built out of stone and wood along the way.

Creeeeeak, whispered something above them.

Rifles and pistols jerked upwards at the sound.

They found themselves looking up at the bottom of a hanging prison cell, which swayed in the stagnant gloom, suspended by a chain that rose up into the heights of the chambers' shadows and mysteries. The dancing, jittery electric torch lights found more of the suspended prisons, mixed amid countless chains of various sizes and beings in various stages of decomposition hanging from that section of the ceiling, which was made of stone, wood and pillars of both.

"We need to keep going," insisted Jonathan in a half-whisper, and they moved to the right and began to ascend the staircase. He led them, with one beam of his torch above and ahead of them. The stone steps were partly carved out of the rock wall, and partly built out by brickwork that sagged, worn by countless feet and covered in generational washes of urine and blood, centuries old.

"Light in front of us and eyes behind us," whispered Jonathan, but his whisper echoed over the staircase, the wall and the dungeon itself. They climbed about three stories, Jonathan in the front with Mina behind him, Ian and Quincy taking up the rear and Seward's own torch and Webley pointed behind them.

Mina gasped and said, "The staircase ahead of us is collapsed."

When their collective torches swung upward, a little farther ahead of the steps above, an entire section about thirty feet wide had collapsed. Below was the reason: one of the timbers, four feet thick and wide, had slipped from its place and slammed into the staircase during its fall, either last night or a hundred years ago.

"Aw hell," hissed the Texan. Quincy slipped through the group and pushed up one of the large splinters of wood until it precariously spanned the small chasm.

"I don't know," said Mina as she frowned at the beam with doubt.

"Precarious is the word I would use," agreed Jonathan.

"Look here," burst out Ian, behind them still, and when they turned Ian was casting his torch's angle down along the floor of the dungeon, among the corroding floor prison cells.

"Well," said Mina, "that is interesting."

"Let's see if it works," sighed Ian, with a quick nod in reference to Quincy's efforts. The Texan nodded back in appreciation.

Below them, in an open section of the dungeon floor, covering a few prison cells, was a large, wooden platform, about twenty feet square. Held together by steep straps and rivets that looked like they had been forged during the Dark Ages, chains and ropes rose from each corner and melted into the still, dank air above. Above and among the chains were a complex series of pulleys[280], and above that an enormous series of wooden platforms, all supported and held in place by the pulleys of various sizes and textures. Jonathan and Mina descended back down the stone stairs, behind Ian and ahead of Quincy, who continued to sweep the floor below with his own torch, looking for any sign of movement, supernatural or otherwise.

As they stepped onto the platform, the wood cracked slightly, easily able to hold their weight. The wood that made up the platform was sturdy and thick and seemed capable of handling much greater challenges than four young people. Chains rustled and clinked with their movements. As Mina reached for one of the circular chains that hung from above, Ian said, "What if this whole device creaks and groans like a bunch of old women at tea and biscuits[281] on a weekday afternoon?"

"Then," said Mina as she took the chain in both hands with the intent to turn it, "We are dead."

On the other side of the platform, Jonathan had already grasped another chain, and they, in sync as always, pulled on one end of their respective chains. In Harker's hands, the chains felt strangely cold, but well-oiled. Their torches were set on the ground, along with their weapons. At ground level, the torches gave them all a ghostly, underlit pallor.

Without a sound, the entire platform lifted up off the ground and started to rise. They continued to pull down on the chains, the entire system lubricated so well and engineered so cleverly that the chain systems at the other two corners almost ran without being touched. Clouds of dust blossomed around the edges of the platform as it lifted up off the ground, drifting up through the creaking, hanging prison cells.

They continued to pull down on the chains as they rose, the complex pulley system whirring almost silently above the platform. Jonathan thought to say, "Mina and Quincy, alternate holding your rifles out so we are not without defense."

"Though the second we discharge any weapon, we're all dead," reminded Mina. "Try to use our other weapons first. Pistols and rifles as a final resort."

As Harker continued to pull down on his own chain, which then whirled back up to the darkness above them, he bent over and picked up his torch and held it above them to make sure that nothing supernatural awaited them. There was only gloom and chains above, so then Harker's beam swept downward and danced along the dungeon walls. The staircase that had broken apart below them wound upwards and around the gargantuan chamber, with groined stone 'bridges' built into the spaces that could not have stairs carved out of them. Prison level was stacked upon prison level, and the main staircase gave way to stone pathways that led along each cell level. Some cells were much more ornate than others, with even some sculpture carved into some of the stonework around each cell, from dancing imps to evil goats to demonic cats to vomiting demons. Renaissance collided with medieval haphazardly. Even some occasional wired filigree in the shapes of cockatrice claws or horned tails protruded from the sculptures. But those were the more recent cells. Alongside and juxtaposed with them were much older cells, lacking any of the grace of the more complexly built, the simple, brutal, cold and old prison cells, iron bars that were bordered by simple stonework. Some of the older cells did not have even cell doors, simply bars without any shape or form of lock.

As the platform swayed under their weight, Jonathan added to what Mina had previously stated. "If we are attacked by an individual, we fight with knives, stakes and Holy Water. If a swarm of anything supernatural comes upon us, then shoot all you like, since we'll be dead in moments anyway. Surprise is our only real weapon."

---

[280] A pulley is a wheel with an inward groove made of stone, metal or wood, through which a rope passes, which is used to lift substantial weights by redirecting the force applied to the rope.

[281] Tea and Biscuits is a British expression for afternoon tea.

Still rising, they neared a colossal, wooden cross-beam, and Mina's corner of the platform gently cuffed and scraped the beam, which had been worn at that spot from decades if not centuries of such collisions.

Quincy pointed below to the collapsed section of the staircase, and the splinted beam he had pushed into place. "Well, at least if we're in a hurry we can always use that to get across, in case there's a bunch of critters chasing us back out of this miserable place."

"The last thing I am going to do is trust my life to that twig," said Mina. "I would just leap and trust my angle of descent to make it across."

"Quincy smiled at Jonathan, who laughed at Mina with respect and said, "Of course you would, Darling. And you'd make it."

Jonathan held up his electric torch above them. The beam revealed a craggy, old, wooden trap door, surrounded by a steel frame. Around the trap door was the granite ceiling of the dungeon, and along the ceiling were millions upon millions of bats. Quivering, crawling, sleeping or chirping, some of them were hanging from the door, and they clambered away upside down toward the comfort of darkness when Jonathan's beam found them.

Quincy's eyes became glass orbs of horror. He dove for his Winchester and cocked it. "They're gonna god-damned bite us all over and I'm gonna soil my britches![282]"

"You mean 'wet your britches', Old Man," said Ian, nervous as well. His Webley quivered like it was about to fall out of the young doctor's hand.

"No," said Morris with a disgusted shake of his head at the waves of bats crawling and writhing in hairy masses over the ceiling. "I mean soil."

Her Winchester also drawn, Mina watched the bats, watched them crawl over each other upside-down along the granite, away from the door and away from them as their platform neared the door. She shook her head and said, "They're just ordinary cave bats. Nothing supernatural or sinister about them."

"So far," muttered the Texan.

As they drew nearer to the ceiling, the chains, ropes and pulleys whirled almost silently, and the door above them opened upward, floor doors that were in fact trap doors to another level above. They all raised their weapons at the opening, anticipating a hellish creature to burst down at them from the darkness above, so it was to their collective surprise to hear nothing but the unexpected and desperate sound of a crying baby.

QUATTOR

"Here pity lives only when it is dead."

—Dante
Inferno

The platform elevated the foursome into another atrophied, darkened room. The air was so thick with dust that Ian had to muffle a cough. A locking mechanism on the pulley system clicked into place, and the platform shook, then settled. Several long, silent moments allowed them to adjust to this new dungeon. Four candles burned delicately at each corner of the lift, which allowed their

---

[282] Britches, or *Breeches*, were antiquated versions of pants. Breeches usually ended just after the knees and could be tied at the end of each pant leg, though some breeches did go down to the ankle. Some breeches had buckles or buttons at the waist and some were specific to riding or fencing. Quincy's reference is to his underpants.

eyes to adjust. The entire floor was covered in beautiful, countless and complex tiles. Byzantine but not Latin. Latin but not Arabic. Arabic but not Chinese. Chinese but not Byzantine. No isosceles triangles of Roman numeral sixes, but the tiles all had the same dragon symbol gracing the center. Many hues and textures had been fired into the tiles, and they created patterns and shapes on the floor, but the gloom and dust around them let the tiles melt into the distant recesses of the circular chamber. The candles illuminated the area around the trap door, but little else.

Mina, Ian, Quincy and Jonathan's hands extended their torches and tried to cut through the dust and the pitch with little success. They held their weapons out in their other hands, a little cumbersome for both Mina and Morris, who held their Winchesters out, while Ian and Jonathan did quite well with the familiar Webleys in their shooting hands.

The cries of an infant continued.

Mina felt them coming from the direction her lantern was pointing in.

"This way," she said, and plunged into the dust-ridden pitch without fear, her Winchester leading the way.

"Careful, everyone," whispered Quincy as they followed.

Their collective lantern lights formed four pools of light on the dirty, cold floor, and they instinctively drew together, though Jonathan said, "Quincy watch the rear."

They moved as one, kicking up clouds of accumulated dust, soot and memories in silence.

Tension mixed with the clouds.

In front of them, on the floor, an old Roman shield lay within the mosaic.

As did a Sumerian spear

The crying ahead of them stopped.

Mina tried to rush forward, more concerned about an unknown waif than her own life, but Jonathan found her wrist, and held it fast.

"Let go of me," she snapped.

"We don't know what's ahead," replied Harker. "They could be waiting for us."

The child's cries resumed.

"If so, they should fear *me*!" hiss/whispered/spat an impatient Wilhelmina Murray, shaking loose of Jonathan's grip and bounding forward with her torch and rifle.

Seward, Morris and Harker raced behind her.

The torches danced along the dragon tiles until they found an old, wood-hewn rocking crib in the chasm of the surrounding darkness.

It rocked on its own accord, not out of movement from inside, but from supernatural means.

A waif cried from within.

Carved onto the wood were artisan versions of cherubs, roosters, cows, dogs, cats, playful all under the hewn wooden sun.

Very beautiful, innocent and completely out of place in this haven of horrors.

An infant's place of comfort and rest.

"Oh, my good Lord," cried Mina, staggering to a halt in front of the crib.

Her eyes became liquid lights filled with both tears and horror.

Her eyes went wide and Mina threw the crook of her left arm, holding the electric torch, over her mouth so as to not scream out.

Wilhelmina Murray did scream out, but not before she stuck her head into the cloth of her elbow to absorb the sound.

The others caught up, and after looking in, Ian nearly vomited. For there, inside the crib, covered and warm in quilts and blankets, lay *two* infants.

One was pink and dying, the other pallid, *and lapping blood from the other child's arm.*

The vampiric infant supped while the human baby cried out, slowly being drained of blood and life. The undead infant was covered with an embroidered lace shawl. The human boy was unclothed yet covered with welts in the shape of inverted crucifixes. Blood trickled from a few of them.

"Christ almighty!" spat Quincy, who pocketed his torch and reached out for the babies. Jonathan's right arm shot out and blocked the Texan, who scowled and tried to knock Harker aside, only to be further restrained by Ian and Mina.

"Don't touch it!" hissed Ian, "Don't touch *them*!"

"We can save 'em," gasped Quincy, almost begging, his eyes riveted on the tableau on the bed.

They watched as the vampiric infant opened its mouth, exposing a mouthful of infant-sizes canines, before re-positioning its bite on the arm of the human baby, which tried to recoil its arm but could not.

"No we can't!" said Mina, also pushing Quincy away, "We cannot help them."

"They are both dead already," said Jonathan, his face stone-cold.

After another moment of struggle, Quincy came to his senses and relaxed, as did their collective grip upon him. He waved an arm at the infants in a gesture of futility. "What do we do?"

Without a word or a glance, Jonathan reached into his bag and had pulled out two small crucifixes, sharpened at the base, as well as a wooden mallet.

Quincy's eyes went wild, "We can't do that! They're—

"—already dead, Morris!" said Jonathan matter-of-factly. "One is Undead. The other is about to be."

Ian said, "We have to— do away with them both!" as he struggled once again to restrain Quincy. Seward had to constrain himself from using the word 'kill'.

"—and we must do it quickly and move on!" hissed Jonathan, readying the first crucifix "There are more important matters to attend to in this castle!"

"We can't leave these infants in this state," said Mina, who began to move to the other side of the crib. "I can help you."

As she maneuvered, Mina bumped into a dark, hunched-over shape that her shifting torchlight had revealed. She whirled, spooked by the shadow of the bound figure and thrust out her Winchester.

It was a cadaver, and it was knelt over, yet restrained in its kneeling position by a metal collar that had a metal spine that led to a wrought-iron base. The woman wore the garb of a peasant, old, frayed cloth. The metal collar clasped around her neck, the cadaver had died reaching out in vain to the crib, the left arm stretched out in agony toward the crib, with the right arm still locked in a set of handcuffs attached to a copper corset around her waist. The victim's neck was swollen with welts from the collar, her ankles bound by rope.

"Good God," wailed Mina, lowering her rifle. "That was this child's mother!"

"Whatever this poor mother did," added Jonathan, "Dracula had her positioned like this so she could watch her son have his blood drained from his body *while she was forced to watch.*"

The mother's dead eyes stared at her still-struggling baby, her son. Food for the undead.

Jonathan turned to Ian and Quincy and said, "Make sure we are alone here, and find the exit. Time is precious."

Harker nodded to Morris, "Don't look back here until we are done, Texan."

They both nodded, Quincy visibly shaken, then he turned to the rest of the dungeon as they raised their torches to get a good look around. After a few seconds their eyes had once again adjusted enough to take in the rest of the dungeon, which they realized was an enormous dome, like the Pantheon in Rome, but without the segmented side walls. Along the walls of the dome was the most spectacular fresco, another spectacular, elaborate depiction of the great dragon consuming the Christian lion. Interwoven throughout the scene were the triple Roman VI symbols, as well as the following, running continuous along the bottom edge of the dome:

MORTEM DRACO MAGNUS DILECTUS[283]

"Look at those welts! He was beaten in front of his mother," said Mina as Jonathan came and placed a sympathetic arm around her.

Jonathan rubbed Mina's back in sympathy as she continued, "She was left here to watch her infant's life be drained by this infant *nosferatu*."

They watched the baby feed, and the human infant begin to writhe in what were death throes.

"Think he left this for us?" wondered Mina. "To tease us, to let us know we have no chance?"

"Perhaps," nodded Jonathan solemnly. "To dishearten us. He thinks like that."

"Does his disgusting malice and bloodlust ever end?" Mina whispered.

"Today it does," nodded Harker. "I'll kill these two, you all have no need to have their blood on your hands—"

"No," interjected Mina. "I'll do it."

"You don't have to be strong in front of me," said Jonathan, looking at Mina. She held a wooden stake over the heart of the human infant. He had a similar stake, which he had produced from the depths of his bag, over the back of the female, vampiric infant, who was still sipping from the arm of the human baby. Jonathan also held a worn, wooden mallet.

"This is a horrible thing we are doing," said Mina as she sobbed a little.

"I agree. It has even managed to frighten Morris. But the world has seen and lived many horrible things, and we are trying to make it a better place."

Jonathan added after a beat, "For our children."

Mina's face crinkled with emotion as she cradled the face of the male baby. She looked up at Jonathan with tears lining her eyes. "Oh, you foolish, loving man. We won't live to see the end of this day."

Jonathan said nothing, but gave her an understanding, pained grin.

Mina took the stake and placed it over the baby's heart. "I wish we could somehow scoop them both up at take them home and give them love."

"We must kill the human child before it dies and becomes undead," interjected Jonathan. "I can do this."

"No, I'll go first," said Mina. She took the mallet from Jonathan's hand.

"Make it one blow, so it doesn't suffer," said Jonathan, "Then hand me the mallet."

"I've found the way out," said Ian from the other side of the dungeon. He and Quincy had keenly followed some sandal-and-wheel tracks along the dragon-symbolled, mosaic-lined floor to another vast, metal door, with its own depiction of Satan sitting on a throne of human sinners in Hell. Inscribed below the throne were the words:

PATRIS NOSTRI DEI[284]

The shape of the door itself was huge, rounded to a half-circle, with two sides, and enormous hinges on either side as well. Below that was the mosaic floor, an ornate, opulent depiction of the

[283] Latin: 'The death of the beloved by the Great Dragon.'
[284] Latin: 'Our most divine father.'

rape of an angel by three demons. Tiles were not the only things lining the floor. Maces, shields, lances, catapults and battering rams. Lastly, a collection of towering siege engines[285] stood stout amid the shadows and the other weaponry.

Quincy, trying to snap out of his shock at the sight of the infants in the crib, ran over to the door and began to pull on one of the door handles that seemed fit for a colossus.

Behind them:

Shkat!

The sound of a mallet striking flesh.

A tiny gasp.

"Don't look back, Texan," said Ian, as he gently pushed Morris' shoulder so he faced the doors. Quincy had tears streaming down his face. He pulled at the door handle like he wanted to rip the entire thing right off.

Shk-kat!

Another strike upon flesh.

Quincy squinted with wrenched agony, pretending to look over the doors while agonizing over what was happening behind him.

"Those ol' babies," he sobbed.

Ian joined Quincy, helping him pull on the enormous door handle, which slowly began to move back with their efforts, in silence, as if the hinges had been oiled every day for a hundred years.

"The deed is done," said Jonathan as he and Mina ran up from the middle of the chamber to join them.

They all pulled the huge door open. To their surprise, shafts of light knifed through the gloom to engulf them.

Still pulling, Quincy snarled. "Gonna put a Holy Water round in that sewer rat's eye if it's the last thing I do."

"I know you're in pain, Morris," said Mina, "but lower your voice. We're entering the last dungeon."

QUINQUE

"Here pity lives only when it is dead."

—Dante
Inferno

The door yawned wide to blinking, tepid, fearful light.

Lit by a few ebbing candles that dripped wax and bones of children, the library was expansive and enormous. Stone slabs lined the floor in a somehow more organized and coherent way than the rest of the floors in the dungeons they had been through. There was a step down into a center area lined with ornate old sofas, settees and benches from different time periods, places in the world and styles. Byzantine, Chinese, French, English, Russian, Japanese, German, Persian and even American Colonial made up the furniture that offered comfortable concentration, in direct opposite of the seats offered a few floors below. Gigantic rugs from Persia covered the floor. This

---

[285] Siege engines were multi-story weapons used in the Ancient World to destroy walls of cities and fortresses during siege warfare. These mobile towers were made of wood and could attack either from a distance, by flinging stones or large pots filled with combustible or flaming materials, or at close quarters using a battering ram to rip open city gates.

all was framed by six walls in a loosely hexagonal shape, two stories high, with another, square room in the distance. After the square room came a set of stairs that led up to two huge, ornate trap doors. A second story offered railings and a circular staircase between the hexagonal and square rooms.

Venus' words of advice hissed in their minds: *When you arrive at the mouth of the first dungeon, it holds one of his libraries...*

All of the walls, both stories, were lined with shelf upon shelf of books, portfolios, ledgers and journals. Hanging from the ceiling, which was hewn from the cave rock, was an unlit, wrought-iron chandelier. Generations of candlewax dripped wet, drying or built up-for-generations wax from the chandelier's candleholders and upon the furniture, rugs and stonework below.

The pillars at each end of the hexagonal room were gigantic: Egyptian antiquity, Sumerian might, Byzantine opulence, Roman Corinthian splendor, Greek and somehow, in the oddest way possible a pillar whose rightful place was among the ruins of Stonehenge.

Wrapping around the pillar of Chinese origin was the tail of an enormous dragon. Despite its origin and influence of the period in Chinese history, the dragon was unmistakably the lion-eating symbol of Dracula. The pillar protruded out from the wall just slightly more than the other pillars.

Venus' voice flicked like a serpent's tongue in their minds: *There is a strange column in that library which has been used to shore up that part of the castle. It is Chinese in origin, from one of his ancient conquests, before our time, in his youth.*

The Greek pillar was in sections that jutted out toward the middle of the library, like an octogenarian's aged limb.

All around the chamber, a collection of macabre candles flickered in unison, as if serenading themselves with their own chorus.

Into this chamber crept Mina, Jonathan, Quincy and Ian, knives unsheathed. This time Ian and Quincy led the way, with Mina and Jonathan covering them from behind. Their eyes remained fixed on the trap doors beyond the distant, square room, all that remained between themselves and the actual castle.

Do not open that trap door, or you will be set upon.

They moved toward the Chinese pillar, whose dragon tail seemed to move in the dim, dancing candlelight. Behind them stood massive bookcases, teeming with works published hundreds of years ago. The bookshelves themselves were stout, ornate, yet they sagged with the weight of both the information they held and the place that they had ended up in.

The pillar has a dragon carved onto it.

Many books, old, worn and caked with dust.

And knowledge.

They moved past *Los cuatro libros de Amadís de Gaula*[286], originally published in 1508.

Then past another book of chivalry, *Tirant lo Blanc,* published in 1490.

Beside both of them was *Las hazañas de Esplandián*, from 1521, which told of the exploits of the son of the knight Amadis.

Then came *Don Olivante de Laura*, published by Antonio de Torquemada in 1564, and his next work, *El Jardin de Flores*, from 1600.

Félix Marte de Hicrania, from Lenchor Ortega de Ubeda in 1556 followed.

El Caballero Platir was next, and anonymous, from 1533, about the fictional knight Palmerín.

Then came the two-part *El Caballero de la Cruz*, published also anonymously, in 1521 and 1526.

---

[286] The Four Books of Amadis of Gaul, a series of stories about a chivarlric knight.

Next to that was *El Espejo de la Caballeria*, from 1533, which was next to Jerómino Fernández' *Don Belianís* in 1547.

Then, on the warped and buckling shelf was *Historia del Famoso Caballero Tirant lo Blanc*, both in Catalan and Castilian[287].

Beside it, and looking as if it had been read, re-read and placed back partially into its space between *Tirant lo Blanch* and *Diana la Segunda* by Alonzo Pérez, was *Los Siete Libros de la Diana* by Jorge de Montemayor[288].

Next to them both was *Diana Enamorada* by Gil Polo, published the same year as Pérez' Diana story, in 1564.

After that came *Engaños de los Celos* in 1586, *Nifas de Henares* by Bernarrdo Gonzales de Bobadilla in 1587 and 5*El Pastor de Iberia* by Bernardo de la Vega in 1591.

After that was *El Pastor de Fílida* by Luis Gálvez de Montalvo in 1582.

Tesoro de Diversos Poemas by Pedro de Padilla in 1580.

And *Divina Comedia* by Dante Alighieri.

Then came *Libro de Canciones* in 1586 by Gabriel Lopez Maldonado.

And *La Galatea*, by Miguel de Cervantes, in 1585.

Followed by 1569's *La Aruacana* by Don Alonso de Ercilla.

La Austraíada in 1584 by Juan Rufo.

And *El Monserrate* in 1588 by Cristóbal de Virués.

Lagrimas de Angelica was next, in 1586 by Luis Barahona de Soto.

Then *La Caraolea* by Jerónimo Sempere in 1560.

El León de Espana by Pedro de la Vecilla Castellanos in 1586.

And *Hechos del Emperador* by Don Luis de Avila.

The books of chivalry looked like they had been left untouched and unread for many many years, while the pastoral romances were covered with fingerprints as well as dust.

Still the youths moved, as a group, in silence, toward the pillar, toward the dragon.

The shelves around them, in this horrible, horrible place, however, held wonders of scholarship and mystery.

Treviso Arithmetic[289], or *Arte dell'Abbaco*, from an anonymous author in 1478.

Liber Abaci[290], by Leonardo Fibonaci, from 1202.

Summa de Arithmetica, Geometria. Proportioni et Proportionalita[291], by Luca Pacioli in 1487.

Secretum Secretorum, a book also also known as the *Secret of Secrets*, a work of Aristotle on a broad range of subjects, such as astrology, magic, alchemy and medicine, written toward the end of the first millenium in Arabic, then translated into Latin and spread throughout Europe.

Or the forty or fifty volume set of *Corpus Scriptorum Historiae Byzaninae*, as well as its previous twenty-four-volume French edition *Corpus Scriptorum Historiae Byzaninae du Louvre*, published first in Paris between 1648 and 1711, and subsequently in Bonn between 1849 and 1897.

Written on vellum and translated into Latin in the 10th century, was *Liber de Orbe*, written three hundred years earlier by Arabic astrologer Mashallah ibn Athari.

---

[287] Castillian Spanish is known as the oldest form of the language, whereas Catalan, though sounding much like Spanish, is directly taken from the Latin.

[288] *The Seven Books of Diana* was the first pastoral novel in Spanish and one of the major works of the Rennaissance.

[289] *Treviso Arithmetic* was one of the first European books that dealt with science and mathematics, explaining to people in commercial trades the basics of addition, subtraction, multiplication, division and how to calculate interest.

[290] *Liber Abaci* is a book on the history of arithmetic and responsible for introducing the Hindu-Arabic numerical system (1,2,3 etc) to Europe. The title literally means "Book of Calculation."

[291] Pacioli's work furthered arithmetic and wove it into the double-entry bookepping system that is prevalent today, yet back then made it possible for merchants to bookkeep without a university degree.

Beside *Liber de Orbe* was a book of astrology and magic entitled *Picatrix*, or *Ghãyat al-Hakìm*, which was repsesented on the shelf by having all three translations, Arabic, Spanish and Latin, in order and next to each other. In a strange occurance, *The Hermetica*, which were texts of wisdom from Egypt and Greece from the second and third centuries, stood beside *The Picatrix*, ironically, so many years later after having inspired their combination of wisdom and ancient magic.

Kitãb al Kîmyâh, an 8th century work on Alchemy, written in Arabic by Jâbir ibn Hayyân, aslongside its translation three hundred years later by Englishman Robert of Chester and retitled *The Book of the Composition of Alchemy*.

The Book of Fixed Stars, or *Kitab Suwar al-Kawakibi*, was a scrolled text on astronomy written around 930 AD by Persian astronomer Abd al-Rahman al-Sufi, who would later have the lunar crater Azophi named after him.

After that was *Kitãb al Masãlik wa'l Mamãlik*, or the *Book of Roads and Kingdoms*, an 11th century scrolled text written in Córdoba, al-Andalus[292].

Principles of Hindu Reckoning, or *Kitab fi usul hisab al-hind* was a book on Mathematics written by Persian Mathematician Kushyar ibn Labban seven hundred years before Mina, Jonathan, Ian and Quincy Morris made their way into the world. *Kitab fi Usul Hisab al-Hind* was about Hindu Arithmatic and used Hindu numerals, yet were written in Arabic.

A series of books entitled *Naturalis Historia* followed, an early encyclopedia from the Roman Empire written in Latin by Pliny the Elder.

The last object on that shelf was not a book but a large, square jar, with the fetus of an unborn demon inside. Floating in embalming liquid was a head with four goat and deer horns, three pairs of reptilian-textured and clawed arms, satyr legs of a pig, and twin serpentine tails. Entry and exit wounds of a spearhead were on opposing sides of the torso.

The next shelf held a small book, about eight hundred years old, written in Latin, with the title *Antidotarium Nicolai* on its spine. The tiny book held recipes, ingredients and formulas from which medicines could be made of minerals and plants.

Next to it was an even smaller book, *Antidotarium*, by Constantinius Africanus, an 11th century monk who converted from Islam to Christianity.

A taller red book, with vellum pages torn at the edges, was *De Ceremoniis Aulae Byzantinae*, a book of ceremonial protocol in the Byzantine court of Constantinople. The title of the book in Greek is *Explanation of the Order of the Palace*, or Επεξήγηση της τάξης των Ανακτόρων. This book was written or commisioned nearly a thousand years before by Enperor Constinine VII, who also wrote the next book on the shelf, *De Administrando Imperio,* or *On the Governance of the Empire*.

Between Mina, Jonathan, Ian and Quincy and the dragon pillar was an ornate bookshelf with opulent glass doors.

As they passed by, Mina peered into the cabinet and past the glass, which had engravings of demons emasculating angels. She gasped in disgust.

...the library with the bookcase of his Cabinet of Curiosities...

Inside the bookcase, inside this curious cabinet, were the following:

The head of a human child, drifting in crude embalming fluids, with scars in the shape of arcane, evil symbols covering the victim's face. Clearly beheaded, the nerves, blood vessels and spine were visible, even through the preservation fluids.

Διαθήκη του Σολομώντα[293], or *Testament of Solomon*, a strange, little book, sewn-together

---

[292] Present-day Spain.

[293] *The Testament of Solomon* was written sometime in the early part of the first millennium by an unknown author. The writings describe how King Sol-

vellum with delicate Greek writing on the cover, as well as a depiction of a king commanding a demon.

Le Veritable Dragon Rouge was comprised of two books that were strapped together, *Sanctum Regnum* and *Secrets de L'Art Magique du Grand Grimore.*[294]

An odd, worn book was next to it with words Περίπλους τῆς Ἐρυθράς Θαλάσσης, and *Periplus Maris Erythraei*[295] written along the spine in both Greek and Latin.

An ornate wooden board leaned up against the back wall of the glass bookcase. Upon it was the pelt of a black cat, streched out over the board, with nails and pins to keep the skin in place. Yet the final oddity, the final horror was that the face of the cat was not that of a cat, but rather *that of a human being*.

MALLEVUS MALEFICARVM, MALEFICAS, & EARUM HÆREFIM, VTPHRAMEA POTENTILSIMA CONTERENS had been carved on the leather cover of a large, brown, worn book.[296]

Another glass jar held ashes, and a skull that looked like it had been burnt to smoky blackness. Engraved on the outside of the jar were the words:

Pope Alexander VI
Rodrigo Borgia
Omnipotentia sua sancta
Vicarius Christi
1431-1503

Ian shuddered.

Each step became lighter, each footfall more deliberate, with the dread and knowledge that their quarry lay one floor above them.

They reached the dragon column, which had a circumference that was easily wider than anything in ancient Byzantium or biblical, solemn Egypt. Around the tail of the dragon were carved tiny human figures, adorned with clothes from along the Silk Road, all screaming in terror while cascading off the mighty reptilian tail and down toward the base, which featured bas-relief mountain villages, wrapped around the enormous base.

Stars also fell with the bas-relief villagers.

At least that's what Quincy saw as he passed his torch over the base.

But not stars.

Holy hell, thought Morris.

The stars were not falling stars.

Not stars but tiny, sculpted rats.

Consuming the villagers.

Rapaciously.

Mina, Jonathan, Quincy and Ian all stared open-mouthed at the column.

---

omon, a biblical figure from before the time of Christ, used a magical ring to command demons to build his temple.

[294] This *Grimoire*, or book of incantations, written by Antonio Venitiana del Rabina, make up what is known as *The Grand Grimoire*, a book of black magic. The title above is what the books are referred to in Haiti, where the books are used for occult purposes.

[295] The *Periplus of the Erythaean Sea* is a mid-first century book that describes navigation and trading along the coast of the Red Sea, Northeast Africa and as far as India. Author unknown. In gerneral, a Periplus is a document that explains ports and geographical distances to aid a ship's captain in navigation.

[296] The Malleus Maleficarum was known throughout the world as the 'Hammer of Witches'. Written by German clergyman Heinrich Krämer and published in 1487, this book explains how to identify and exterminate witches, and was responsible for the countless persecutions and deaths of women throughout history.

"He's been conquering for a long time," said Jonathan.

Twin tapestries, covered with triumphant, rapacious demons and invaded, violated angels hung on either side of the pillar of the dragon.

They fluttered slightly at cold, angry zephyrs that came from behind, like a curtain at the mouth of a cave.

Mina looked back at them, nervous but resolute, and Jonathan, Quincy and Ian gave her the same steely-eyed look of resolve and support.

With the business end of her Winchester, Wilhelmina Murray found the edge of the nearest tapestry, where an imp was crucifying a cherub, and pushed it aside.

Behind the blasphemic curtains lay blackness and frigid cold.

In they went, one after the other, and once they were behind the tapestry, Mina joined them, careful not to make any noise as she folded the defiling imp cloth behind her. In front of them was the dragon pillar, reaching up into the darkness above. To their left was the cold, black rock wall that the castle sat upon. To their right was the blanketing tapestry. Above them a hole in the library ceiling between the wall and dragon pillar, which was rife with chips and scars from pickaxes from the time of the construction of the fortress.

And divots.

All chipped into the column, along the dragon's body as it snaked up toward the very foundation of the fortress.

Ascend the back of the column with the handholds that have been carved into the pillar, up through to the ground floor.

Quincy, whose inability at times to grasp the obvious came into play, and he swung his electric torch upward with the intention of lighting it, but Mina instantly and silently smacked Morris along the back of his neck. The Texan shrugged at Mina questioningly until the logic of the moment took hold, and he turned off his torch and slid it back into the depths of his coat.

They all did.

Without a further glance, Jonathan Harker, who had arrived at Castle Dracula as a solicitor of a simple land lease to Carfax Abbey all those months ago, reached up, found a handhold and began to climb.

Hand over foot, they all began to scale the pillar in silence, the cold not bothering them as much as the need for complete silence. The higher they went, the darker it became, lit only through the fluttering horrific tapestries by the flickering candleabras below. In a few places the space between them and the rock wall behind them was nearly too tight for them to get through, with Ian once grimacing in pain but maintaining his silence when his rib cage came on the losing end of an encounter with a protrusion of dark, cold rock. Their eyes adjusted. About mid-torso along the dragon's body, or about a third of the way up the pillar, Jonathan had to squeeze tightly around a single, massive stone, a corner of the foundation.

The column is covered with rock wall on the ground floor so you will not be revealed.

The foundation block itself was poured cement, but within the cement, much to the astonishment and revulsion of the group, were broken crucifixes, shattered statues of saints, and human bones of all shapes and sizes. Harker reached up and found the next handgrip along the cold, mammoth pillar, but then his right foot lost its hold, slipped and for a moment he hung there, in silence, the others below him helpless to do anything but watch, for they were so high now along the column that any fall would kill them, or reveal them and bring death in many forms down upon them.

What saved Jonathan Harker and the rest from disaster was a broken piece of crucifix, carved of wood and hammered metal, that protruded from the foundation block opposite him. Harker held onto the protruding arm of a copper beheaded Jesus until he could gather himself enough to recover his foot grips.

Just below, Mina aged a few months in those few precious seconds, both at her fiancé's peril but at the idea that his fall would end not only their objective, but their lives shortly therafter. She could accept death, but not failure before any attempt that they could have upon Dracula. The gusts blew cold and wet around them, flying around them from top to bottom and back up past them again, and Ian had to somehow button up his coat while hanging on to the chipped hand and footholds of the dragon pillar.

They climbed upward, understanding their fortune and knowing they had reached the first floor of the fortress.

This will take you up to the second floor, where you can plan your attack upon him.

On either side of them were the two stone walls that made up the walls of the first floor.

Just above them, through that shaft of darkness they were climbing through, they could see more flickering light and hear the quiet flutter of more tapestries. Jonathan continued to climb the pillar, the brick walls of the castle surrounding him. Each of those bricks had the isosceles triple sixes stamped onto them. Wooden support beams criss-crossed around them. They had reached the second floor. Jonathan wrestled with his bag, then Abraham's, and took out a wooden stake, took a deeep breath and stepped out through the tapestries.

There will be a coffin in each chamber. The closed casket, with no bones, is where you will find him.

Jonathan had to squint to adjust to the comparative difference in light. A lone open hallway stood before him, stonework on one side that bordered on Neolithic, with oddly-shaped stones stacked to fit one on top of the other, and the other side from somewhere early in the Renaissance, elegantly cut and fit. A single, flickering torch stuck into a protruding brick along the wall illuminated the hall. The one aspect the hallway did have in symmetry were the wooden stakes that protruded from either side, many of them still holding up the rotted corpses of victims who were slammed into the jagged, broken ends generations ago and had been left to rot, and Jonathan once again noted the scratches from rat inscisors left on the exposed bones. The oppressive stench of rotted flesh and rat urine was overwhelming. Harker felt Mina behind him, and the rustle of Quincy and Ian as well, followed by the additional sound of them each drawing their weapons again. A quick glance back by Jonthan confirmed that the Texan was somehow cradling his Winchester while simultaneously cradling the handle of his Bowie knife. The hallways' ceiling was also stone, with support beams stretched haphazardly, spanning the Middle Ages in a few feet, some with details and ornamental carving in the wood that mixed Central Europe and Han Dynasty China from beam to beam, as if an aggregate of materials and artisanry from all over the world had been used to assemble not just the hallways but the fortress itself. They made their way collectively down the hallway. And did any of the impaled skeletons they had just passed turn their rotting skulls at them? Did any crimson-eyed rats scamper between two fetid, decomposing corpses?

No.

Silence was also their enemy, since every scrape of their shoes, every sigh or throat-clearing was amplified down along the forboding hallway, which seemed bloated with dread. They walked over large, square slabs of stonework, all of which had the same series of words carved onto each piece:

"Et adoraverunt draconem, qui dedit potestatem bestiæ.[297]"

Sweat drenched them, and poor Ian, exhausted and terrified, began to quiver again, his Webley shaking in his hand so much that Quincy, who had taken to glancing behind them as the defacto

---

[297] Revelation 13:4. "And they worshipped the dragon which gave power unto the beast:"

rear guard, had to reach over and place a comforting hand on Seward's shoulder. Somehow the Texan was hungry, even though they were in the most horrible of circumstances, and his ravenous appetite was of some strange comfort to him in all this.

I'll have some butter pecan flapjacks next to Uncle Peter, Lucy and Artie in a few minutes, if they let me in through the Pearly Gates, that is. Lord, I'm sorry about stealing the Sunday School lunch money as a kid and that whole business with the dancing girls show in Austin, and I hope you take into consideration that Consuelo took it out of my hide anyway, Amen.

Up ahead, Jonathan tried to wriggle his way past Mina into the lead, only to sense that she deliberatly wanted to stay in front and was consiously counter-blocking him so she could stay ahead, and protect them all. *God, what an amazing woman*, he smirked, even as they neared the mouth of the hallway.

The hallway leads to two chambers.

Filled with silence and veiled light, the intersection before them was a strange, surreal scene. Vaulted Corinthian pillars from a stone ceiling cascaded down to the brick-lined floor. Portions of the pillars were carved, other sections, particularly the areas that connected with the ceiling, were left untouched and covered with strange fungi-like protrusions that somehow grew out of infected stone, stone that had been bloated and sickened, swelling into orbs of odd, sinister proportions. The infected stones incredibly oozed puss and ichor from horrific orifices that had begun to overwhelm the compromised stonework. Closer to the ground, the uninfected pillars formed into an odd form of Gothic architecture, with wandering drifts of accumulated dirt along the edges, which met with the brick-laden walls. And strange bricks they were, some larger, smaller, rectangular, square, oblong and even triangular in some places. Many bricks had the horrific isosceles triangle of roman numeral sixes stamped upon them, and Ian shuddered at the thought of how the bricks were actually created with the number of the beast marked upon them. More wooden stakes protruding from the brick walls held a few more corpses and skeletons, all of them in agonized positions from dying horrible deaths, some of them reaching out futilely to each other, in one last act of love in a castle that was dedicated to the eradication of the emotion. Expansive cobwebs also blanketed the pillars and walls, some of them collapsing under their own weight into their own eerie tapestries.

Each of them knew they moved toward their deaths, knowing that they would be overwhelmed by this trap that Dracula of Transylvania had set for them, this irresistible, macabre jar of honey laced with the miniscule and implausible opportunity for vengeance, and yet they moved as one through this intersection, past the fungi stone, the Satanic brickwork, the blankets of cobwebs, the desiccated testaments to love and warfare all around them.

Banks of mist swirled around them, playing tricks and havoc with their electric torches.

They focused.

And squinted.

Through the mist, two groined archways on either side of the large intersection could be seen.

To the left was a short hallway that led to the second floor of the vast hall into which Jonathan Harker had been dragged by Dracula so many months ago. The obsidian stone slab where Dracula had first turned himself into a storm of bats could be seen.

Jonathan had to force himself to stay calm and not react as he could see the spot where Dracula had once placed his lantern back then, and in the distance, the crumbling hallway into which he had been led en route to meet the brides and to begin his horrific encounter with evil.

Harker looked to the right.

That arch led to a short, midnight-black hallway.

Beyond the hallway, was a stone landing.

And steps on the right.

Leading downward.

This is it, raced through their minds faster than adrenaline through their hearts.

Ian, overwhelmed with terror, could not control his shaking, which intensified.

Quincy saw this and again reached out to his dear friend, patting Seward on the back. "Steady, ol' pal," he whispered.

Though his eyes never left the recesses of the hallway before them, Quincy kept patting until the young doctor half-turned his head and nodded his appreciation to the Texan.

Mina's eyes were fire as she moved forward, slowly and silently cocking her Winchester, which she held in front of her like a cobra ready to strike. Jonathan followed her into the dark maw, his Webley and sharpened crucifix at the ready in one hand, his electric torch in the other. He wanted to point out to Mina that if she fired at anything at this point, the thunder of the rifle would break the seal of silence over the castle and bring the collective forces of darkness that resided within the horrible walls upon them, but he decided that she had to know this herself, and that she might turn around and fire at him simply for reminding her, so Wilhelmina Murray was in the end best left alone.

As they came out of the dark hallway, their eyes readjusted.

Littered around the tunnel mouth were bits of bone, animal and human, protruding from around the mouth of the tunnel, mixed into the original stone and cement work. No brickwork was visible around the rim, just a haphazard combination of carved rock and cement.

To their left was another tunnel in the brick and rock wall, leading to more darkness.

The first crypt.

To their right was a decrepid set of wooden stairs that looked like they had been there for centuries.

To the tunnel they moved.

They had to wait for a moment at the mouth of the tunnel for their eyes to adjust to the greater darkness. Frigid gales began race along the walls, buffeting their faces, hair and clothes. One by one they stepped inside, led by Mina, holding her Winchester out like a talisman. She knew the risks of discharging her rifle and alerting the rest of the unearthly inhabitants of the castle, but Wilhelmina Murray meant her blow to be for their intended prey. Mina and Jonathan looked and moved forward while Quincy, holding up the rear, somehow kept his Bowie knife pointed behind him and his Winchester in front of him.

As they moved toward their goal, toward their deaths, the tunnel slanted downwards at an angle, and the curved ceiling was lower, just over their heads. Jonathan could see the end of the tunnel, their objective, but his thoughts moved to his friends and their lives, and how he should have found a way to do this alone, to kill Dracula alone, or at least die trying, so that Mina, Quincy, Ian, and even Arthur and Lucy did not have to suffer the same fate is their parents had. Jonathan's thoughts then turned to his parents, all their parents, slaughtered mercilessly like the fallen of a besieged castle. As his hand reached out and took in the oblong bricks that lines the tunnel, Harker reflected that he would either never see his parents again, or he would see them again very, very shortly. He then shook his head, accepting that the supernatural events that had filled their lives recently pointed to the latter, that this battle of good and evil was eternal, and if he and his friends were to die here today, that all of their experiences had taught him he would, at his death, find himself with his family once more. This warm thought flooded his heart, filled him with cheer to face this ancient evil once more, and he stepped out out the tunnel behind a fiercely intense Mina, in front of a terrified Ian and foolishly arrogant Quincy Morris, all to face their fate.

The only source of light was a single blapshemic candle that dripped age-old wax out from the recess where it had been crammed. The candle glowed with rat guts and bones of infants inside, just another macabre detail from this horrific place.

More mist drifted, conjealing above the tunnel's floor, wrapping around their ankles like efferverscent shackles, drifting past them and toward the end of the passage, then finally conjealing around the first crypt. Carved completely out of obsidian, the sarcophagus sat in the middle of the large chamber that lay below them, which itself sat upon a three-step platform of granite and porphyry. Square at the head and rounded at the feet, an enormous, complex bas-relief over its lid of a fiery, resplendent dragon consuming a roaring, opulent lion with a Judeo-Christian cross glowing, which was securely placed, no signs of recent disturbance. Running along the base of the sarcophagus was the following:

> "CUM CONSUMMATI FUERINT MILLE ANNI,
> SOLVETUR SATANAS DE CARCERE SUO.[298]"

The crypt was covered with a pile of rotting human bones. Ian shuddered. His breathing was coming in heaves and sweat had drenched him.

Quincy gulped, his grip on his Winchester tightening.

Jonathan scanned around them, still anticipating some kind of attack.

Mina clenched her teeth with determination.

Whichever coffin is covered in pieces of bone, Dracula is not within. Those are the skeletons, eager to protect him and loyal to their master, a ruse.

Not here.

They slowly backed away.

Back to the landing.

And toward the wooden staircase.

Leading to the large chamber below.

Still cradling her Winchester, Mina slid her right shoe onto one of the crossbeams of the stairs and started to ever-so-slightly press her weight onto the wood. A small creak began, then ceased instantly as Mina withdrew her foot.

She moved to the outer spiral of the stairs, the steps imbedded into the crumbling brick wall, and put her weight onto the first step.

No sound.

She took another step, her rifle still pointed at the crypt, and her shoe found the second step.

It did not creak either.

Wilhelmina Murray found the third step as Jonathan Harker's shoe set itself upon the uppermost step.

Jonathan waved his arm in a broad way at Quincy and Ian, telling them to get in line as he realized they were going to try and cross the landing from the inner edge.

They made their way down the craggy, broken stairs.

They looked at Mina's brandished Winchester, which Jonathan noticed and gave them a nod and reached out to Mina, giving her a 'ssh' sign before gesturing to his own knife and stake. Mina nodded at them all but did not lower her rifle as she began to put her right foot out to test the right end of the landing's crossmember, near the wall stud that supported it. Jonathan gave Ian and Quincy a 'told you' gesture with his face as Mina pressed.

---

[298] Revelation 20:7. "When the thousand years are over, Satan will be released from his prison."

Nothing.

Not a sound.

The tension was overwhelming, and they were all now bleeding sweat.

Their collective chests were heaving from tension and effort, trying to catch an elusive breath that refused to be captured.

Jonathan decided to attempt to step ahead of Mina once again, but she beat him to it and cut off his angle, absolutely resolute and fearless. She looked back to make sure the jittery Ian and rear-guarding Quincy followed, and her expression told Jonathan everything he needed to know.

She was here to kill Dracula and she had no fear of death.

The second crypt was larger than the first, simple, and to the point. Carved cave walls formed one side, with the other end of the chamber lined with old, worn bricks that sagged under their own weight. The bottom section was much larger than the bricks above, as if this particular corner of the castle was part of the foundation. The ceiling was rounded rock, with a small corner comprised of a combination of crumbling brickwork and a portion of decaying Byzantine wood roofing and tiles. Somehow through all that makeshift roofing came a singular shaft of light, which creased its way diagonally across the chamber and onto the carved rock wall, where a simple stone altar protruded. The light illuminated the objects above the altar, which were human skulls, all without lower jaws, planted against the wall, forming an inverted cross. Inside each skull were flickering candles, placed haphazardly inside. Blood mixed with the hot wax dripping from the eyes and nostrils of the skulls, onto which were carved phrases like *Jesus ardebit in inferno*[299], *Virgo enim non est virgo*[300], and *Omnes angeli ad mortem!*[301] On the altar was a bowl filled with blood and human flesh, which drew the attention of Mina and Jonathan, who locked eyes as soon as they saw the bowl. *He's bloody here*, they both thought, before their eyes slid over to the second sarcophagus.

Covered.

With a lid, and nothing else.

The closed casket, with no bones, is where you will find him.

Hewn of granite, the sarcophagus was simple, comparatively, to its obsidian counterpart in the other crypt. Around the base was carved *hic iacet filius diaboli*[302], and below the carved insription were the familiar sets of roman numerals:

VI

VI   VI

Carved onto the sarcophagus lid was an inverted cross, with a Gothic-style representation of the inversely-crucified Saint Peter. At the 'top' and at the arms of the cross were small demons, impaling Peter's feet and hands to the crucifix. Also atop the lid was the fresh skin of a small human being, stretched out to approximate and mimic and mock the depicted crucifiction.

Blood from the skinned child was spattered across the lid.

Twin stone stairways curved along the walls of the crypt and down around the sarcophagus. Gathered at the threshold of the tunnel now, Mina gestured to Jonathan to lead Quincy down to the

---

[299] "Jesus burn in Hell."
[300] "The virgin is no virgin."
[301] "Death to all angels!"
[302] "Here lies the son of Satan."

left staircase, and she yanked Ian down to the right before he could react. They all gathered around the crypt and noticed that the sarcophagus lid was ajar.

Feverish now to deal the killing blow, Jonathan gestured in silence to Quincy and Ian to push the lid simultaneously, then he and Mina would stab violently with their wooden stakes. Everyone nodded in agreement and Mina raised her stake over her head in anticipation, standing over the 'head' of the sarcophagus, her arms shivering with anger, fear and adrenaline. His own heart pumping, Jonathan watched Morris and Seward leave their stakes at the base of the sarcophagus and readied themselves to push aside the lid. Sweat ran over all of them like river water. They nodded back, then Jonathan nodded his affirmation.

They all exchanged looks that meant:

Good luck.

You will always be my friend.

I love you all,

This is for our family.

And between Jonthan and Mina:

You are my forever love.

Jonathan then silently mouthed:

Three.

Two.

One.

With a collective heave, Quincy and Ian shoved aside the sarcophagus lid.

Then, many things happened very quickly.

Inside of the hewn-stone sarcophagus sat the black, shiny coffin of Dracula of Transylvania, glinting like a crouched scorpion.

Ian feverishly tossed aside the obsidian coffin lid, which clattered into the gap between the coffin and the sarcophagus.

Jonathan and Mina then both began to stab violently into the coffin, Harker with Abraham's *kukri* knife, and Mina with her sharpened cross.

Mina clenched the carved Jesus that sat in her cross like she was trying to wring any and all good fortune and luck out of it.

Harker merely wanted to do in the vampire with his uncle's most trusted weapon.

Quincy lashed down with his Bowie knife, as did Ian with his own crucifix stake.

Blades glistened and sang as they sliced air.

Mina's blows fell first, with slits of red fury.

Fury, fear, dread, horror, and ferocity were unleashed.

They wept as they cleaved the air, and their blades ripped deep.

Ian Seward wept for everything, for his mother and father, for whom he'd never really had a chance to mourn.

Mina was so livid that she unknowingly bruised her forearm against the side of the coffin with her blows.

Into the wooden bottom of the coffin.

Slashing through the Transylvanian soil that lined the box.

And through a conjealed black mist that swirled around on top of the soil.

The mist churned violently.

Effervescent black rage.

A bolt of black lightning exploded out of the mist; it was not light, but rather Dracula's powerful right arm, still with the texture of mist.

The obscene, obsidian arm shot up and out out of the coffin.

Then it savagely clamped around Jonathan Harker's neck.

An iron vice around his throat, Jonathan flailed with the *kukri*, leaving boiling but self-healing sears along the arm.

Her body flush with adrenaline, Mina panicked and began to stab at the arm, along with Quincy and Ian as the mist arm began to raise itself out of the coffin, out of the sarcophagus, and out into the crypt.

While still strangling Harker in its grip.

Mina reached into Jonathan's bag, which rose to her eye level, and took out a vial of Holy Water. Ripping the top off the bottle, she turned and splashed the water down into the coffin and over the mist, which responded by writhing like an impaled serpent and roaring in pain.

Jonathan choked, fought against Dracula's stranglehold, and he could hear the Transylvanian rumble from the depths of the coffin, "I prefer to take the form of mist when I repose so as to prevent assassinations, Master Harker!"

Dracula's wicked, disembodied chuckle rumbled all around the crypt.

Though he was still in mist form, Dracula snarled like a lion as a panicked Quincy and Ian threw their own Holy Water onto the mist, which began to swell grotesquely and surge out from the sarcophagus.

As Jonathan swung with his *kukri*, the others continued to stab at the *nosferatu* with their sharpened crucifixes, and while they did make slashes in the mist that bled red blood-like ichor before healing itself nearly instantly.

Quincy frantically dealt a few vicious blows with his Bowie knife as he turned his attention to the mist's elbow in an attempt to separate Dracula's arm from his body.

"Godammit!" roared the Texan in frustration, his voice echoing around the crypt.

Mina hacked at the mist's arm over and over, leaving red incision lines over the mist as she shook with pain and rage.

The realization that they had failed began to dawn upon her.

Upon all of them.

Jonathan tried to scream for Mina to look out for the skeletons that were racing down the frigid wooden steps behind her.

Then a bony hand clamped around Harker's scalp and Primus' voice filled his ear.

"Welcome back, Master Harker."

Then, after a blow to the back of his head, Jonathan Harker heard no more.

Revelations 13

*The dragon stood on the shore of the sea. And I
saw a beast coming out of the sea. It had ten
horns and seven heads, with ten crowns on its
horns, and on each head a blasphemous name.
The beast I saw resembled a leopard but had
feet like those of a bear and a mouth like that of
a lion. The dragon gave the beast his power
and his throne and great authority. One of the
heads of the beast seemed to have had a fatal
wound, but the fatal wound had been healed.
The whole world was filled with wonder and
followed the beast. People worshiped the
dragon because he had given authority to the
beast, and they also worshiped the beast and
asked, "Who is like the beast? Who can wage
war against it?"*

CASTLE DRACULA
ONE

Once again, utter blackness.

Then pain.

Like a knife.

Out of the blackness, Jonathan's neck was ablaze with searing pain.

Harker realized that he was being dragged along the wet, cold ground. The familiar, ominous stench of rot, mold and death overwhelmed his senses, so Jonathan instantly knew he was back outside of Castle Dracula. With a groan he opened his eyes and saw two skeletons staring down at him with gloomy, open eye sockets as they pulled him along by his feet. High above the skeletons loomed the blackest of night skies, boiling with dark clouds and menace. Harker was grabbed by his disintegrating lapels, yanked off the ground and laid lengthwise across a large wooden beam while more skeletal hands ran rope past his eyes, lashing him to the beam, now a full-sized cross.

Grunts, scuffling and macabre chitters around Jonathan told him he was at an epicenter of activity. He coughed, his throat bruised and sore from Primus' stranglehold upon him.

Above them all, soaring out of one of the towers that overlooked the gorge and river below was the great bat. It banked around the top of the castle towers and battlements while hundreds of the skeletons cheered him on with a roar from the collective hellspawn.

His head clearer, Jonathan looked around wildly for his friends.

And found them.

Mina, Ian and Quincy were all lashed to their own crosses with ropes looped under and over their arms and chests, their feet tied together, right-side up, unlike Uncle Peter. It felt odd for Harker to see the crossbars so low to the ground, from the crosses to be turned one hundred and eighty degrees like that but surely the most distressing part of what Jonathan was observing were his friends bound like they were criminals at a hanging or an execution.

More like an execution, thought Harker.

They were out in front of the keep, the building where Dracula's coach had brought Jonathan so many months ago. Mina was stolid in the face of the situation they were in, a look of strength over her face while tears silently streamed down her face. She glanced back at Jonathan with concern, realized he'd wakened, then love and terror intermingled in her stare as they locked eyes. Though he was already up on his cross and in the air, Ian's ankles were still being tied together by a few of the moldy skeletons. Ian spat at them in anger and disgust, but they simply ignored him and finished the job.

Quincy twitched awake, and the first thing he said when he took in their predicament was, "Well, we're all pretty much screwed three ways to Sunday."

"Our plan was always a suicide mission," sighed Jonathan, straining for comfort as bony hands tied his arms and legs.

"Agreed," nodded Ian, now secured. The skeletons neglected to bind his ankles to the beam, so Ian kicked a particularly rickety skeleton in the head as it retreated.

The walking anatomy lesson adjusted his skull back into place and paid Seward no mind.

"It was the only option," said Mina, herself kicking away a few ogling skeletal soldiers.

His body now lashed to his cross, Jonathan Harker was hoisted up next to his friends, all with their backs to the keep, just in front of the strange, dark slab of rock that Jonathan instantly recognized, the same slab that had witnessed the birth of the child-sized Dracula bat nearly a millennia ago. Still covered with the same mysterious, indecipherable runes, hieroglyphics and petroglyphs. Still covered with the isosceles triangle set of Roman numeral sixes.

Next to them on the ashy ground of the castle court yard area stood the twin iron maidens from the dungeon, ornate and beauteous. The eye slits on both were crammed with garlic and crucifixes.

Whimpers could be detected emanating from within.

On the blasphemous rock lay all their bags and weapons.

On that same boulder that had helped birth the Son of Satan landed the great beast, its twin ember eyes blazing scarlet.

Huge wings folded up like they held all of the evil secrets of the world.

The Dracula bat looked up at them with a cold glare, cocking its huge black head as it then checked the bindings on the crosses. It turned around and faced the unholy gathering, as the rat hordes surged over the rocks and toward the four.

With a gesture of one massive black wing Dracula stopped them from ripping Jonathan, Mina, Quincy and Ian to shreds.

The winged arms stayed high in the air, maintaining silence over his domain.

Then, slowly, a chant began among Dracula's infernal legion.

The wing lowered.

"Ave!" began some.

"Satanus!" answered the others.

"Ave!"

"Satanus!"

"Ave!"

"Satanus!"

"Ave!"

"Satanus!"

"Ave Satanus!" roared the skeletal crowd.

Many of them held swords and pikes, and those who wielded the pikes began to pound the ground with the blunt ends of their weapons, a gargantuan drumbeat that led to a skeletal chant, over and over.

"Ave Dracula!" bellowed the skeletons.

"Ave Dracula!"

"Ave Dracula!"

The wavering, wavering wind made the torches twitch with mystical resonance, ashes from hundreds of soldiers past, victims and sacrifices wafting through the air, past the hollow orbital sockets of the skeletons, whose petrified faces all looked to the four figures lashed to the crosses before them. The great bat then turned to the crowd, which was roaring with a religious fervor. As the bat raised both its wings, the vampire metamorphosized back into human form.

Adso, the grotesque, fungi-laden caretaker of the castle, stepped forward out of the crowd and knelt before the vampire.

"Ceea ce este dorința ta, stăpânul meu?" rumbled Adso, the broken teeth in his skull clicking as he spoke. *What is your wish, my Master?*

Dracula pointed at the iron maidens and growled, "Volo concubinarum largitus mihi testes in cruce homines ad prius vivi demissi autem sunt." *I want my concubines to witness the crucifixion of the humans before they are buried alive.*

The vampire turned to the metal torture devices and snarled at the brides in disgust. "Cooperculaillis nunc sunt, numquam aperietur, ad iterum. Sit ex medio eis putrescet!" *Those are now coffins, never to be opened again. Let them rot from within!*

Screams and wails of agony from the imprisoned Venus and Petra gave chills to Mina, Jonathan, Quincy and Ian. The screams and wails then turned to serpent hisses and wolf snarls as the women vented their unfurled hate at Dracula of Transylvania.

"Lordy, he's pissed at them," said Quincy.

"And they're bloody pissed right back at him," added Mina.

"I'm a little more worried about us at the moment," said Ian. Seward then saw Renfield wade in through the macabre crowd, the massive man standing out from the skeletons as he leered at Mina without blinking, saliva seeping from his chin and onto his soiled wool coat.

"Hello Lass," he drooled at Mina with unblinking, lascivious eyes.

"Is she to be mine?" he asked of Dracula.

The *nosferatu* turned his head to Renfield in that peculiar, predatory bird kind of way and shook his head at the massive man. "You are filth compared to her. She will die with a measure of dignity."

Renfield began to sob uncontrollably, a wicked leer of lust still running over Mina, who did not give Monatague the satisfaction of even meeting his gaze.

"Renfield's gone bloody mad!" gasped Ian.

"He's *been* bloody mad, Sewie," retorted Quincy.

Dracula raised his arms to the crowd of skeletons and chanted, "Protege nos, Domine Satanus, Tuis mysteriis servientes." *Protect us, Lord Satan, servants of your mysteries.*

The unholy son's right hand extended over the perverse celebrants as he rumbled, "Ego vos benedictio in Nomine Magni Dei Nostri Satanus!" *I bless you all in the name of our great god, Satan!*

The dark skies above them rumbled, clouds rippling like angry denizens of Olympus.

An insane roar bellowed from the skeletons. The chanting grew in its depth and chorus.

"Ave Satanus! Ave Satanus! Ave Dracula!" screamed the skeletons, and poor Montague Rhodes Renfield, berserk with perverse satisfaction that he had found, at last, his rightful place in the world.

Adso, caretaker of the fortress, raised his infected, bloated skeletal arms and bellowed, "Ave Dracula!"

The night reeked of evil.

"Ave Satanus!" roared Dracula like a lion who had found his prey.

"Ave Dracula!" shrieked the bones of the night.

After a moment engorged with a pulsating stillness, the son of all evil then raised his arms again and shouted, "Rupere Pater tui quia liberasti mihi inimici mei!" *Unholy Father, you have delivered mine enemies unto me!*

Dracula then turned to Jonathan and the others and grinned salaciously as he hissed, "O pater profanum, hanc accipere humana sacrificiumest in ordine ad praestas." *Oh most unholy father, accept this human sacrifice in order to bestow upon us your presence.*

"Accipe humanam sacrificium pro munere a unigenito propter." *Accept this human sacrifice as a gift from your only son.*

"Aaaawwwww, so's your mom!" grumbled Quincy as he uselessly fought his bindings. As if breaking free would have been any use; he'd have been skewered by a dozen pikes if he managed to do so. Morris and Ian exchanged a look that said *this is it for us*.

The skeletons kneeled in silent, blasphemous unison.

A few of the torches illuminating the scene wept tears of blood.

Dracula then signaled to Primus, who stalked out of the crowd in his ungainly manner, holding an ancient clay jar, careful not to spill the contents.

"Accipite haec sacra, pater," said Dracula as he pointed to the base of Ian's cross. *Accept this sacrifice, Father.* The skeleton made its way toward Seward, who was between Quincy and Mina, all of them struggling in vain against their bindings.

Primus stopped solemnly in front of Ian's cross. Dracula snarled, "Ut invenias cruciatus in inferno." *May you find agony in Hell.*

Poor Ian was so scared that he began to tremble in absolute terror.

Primus then flung the jar against the base of the cross, where it crashed and spilled oil all over the base and Ian's feet and ankles. Realization dawned upon the four, as Dracula ripped one of the torches from a skeleton and tossed it onto the base of Ian's cross. It burst into wicked flames, Ian screaming in pain as his lower limbs were instantly engulfed in fire. Jonathan, Mina and Quincy screamed in anguish at the sight of their friend's agony, to the glee of Dracula, whose eyes danced in liquid joy at Ian's pain.

"At least let Mina live, you filthy coward!" shouted a defiant Ian past his agony, and the vampire's features darkened.

Dracula reached out with an open palm and summoned one of the rusted, decrepit Roman swords from one of the skeletons. It flew through the air into the vampire's hand, and in one serpentine, evil motion, Dracula threw the sword blade-first right through the heart of Ian Seward, cleaving the cross that held him.

Mina, Jonathan and Quincy screamed with horror and pain, wailing like children as they watched their friend writhe in abject agony, his feet aflame and his heart punctured.

Ian Seward coughed blood, his torso convulsing in pain, and he looked over at his friends with a tearful, warm smile.

"Be well, my dear loving friends."

Ian Seward then dropped his head and whispered, "Lucy," before giving up his spirit.

Dracula gestured to the skeletons to get their attention, then pointed at the limp form of Ian Seward.

They all lowered their pikes.

And stomped forward.

A hundred pikes pounded and skewered the body of Ian Seward simultaneously, and repeatedly.

"Stop it you bastard!" shrieked Mina.

"Leave him be!" raged Jonathan.

"God damnit, ya already killed him!" bawled Quincy Morris at Dracula, "He was my dear friend, ya damned monster! You don't know what the hell a friend is!"

At last Dracula, with the satisfied grin of a despot, waved his hand and the skeletons retreated, pikes in hand, back to their sword-bearing brethren.

Ian and his cross burnt like kindling.

Jonathan, Mina and Quincy openly wept over the loss of their lifelong friend, sagging in defeat on their crosses while Dracula sucked in their sorrow and mourning with more relish than when he drank blood from an innocent.

"Ya goddamned dog!" roared Quincy through his tears at Dracula, who simply glared at the Texan as if to say *you are next.*

Then, as if the night could not become darker, the darkness sharpened.

A sharp *crack* from the wood.

A spark, a flicker.

Then flames.

The wood around the rock burst into abrupt, violent flames, and out of the flames grew the massive, darkened wing of a demon.

Gigantic.

Monstrous.

Another grew and twitched outward to the stars.

A titanic shadow spread out from the wood and the slab and the fire and the night.

The hate-filled entity snarled like a thousand lions.

Jonathan's jaw dropped open as he watched the gargantuan, bleak shadow of Satan grow out of the flames.

Dracula stepped forward and knelt in front of Satan, as did all of the skeletons, the rats pulsing in from the recesses of the fortress and the darkness and writhing all around the rock.

"Holy Jesus," said Jonathan, gasping in awe at the sight of Satan's great shadow.

"Holy shit, more like," said Quincy, shaking his head in amazement and disgust.

"He exists," said Mina simply. "Dracula has at the very least proven that to me."

"This is proof that Hell exists," continued Jonathan, "so then must Heaven."

"Amen," said Quincy.

Thunder rumbled above.

Wood cracked at the base of the cross.

Wrath slithered about.

Fully formed, Satan's three eyes blinked malice, injustice and evil.

"Patrem meum," said Dracula, his head reverentially bowed to his father. *My Father.*

"Meus profana filius," rumbled the dark shadow like a hundred lions, wings stretched like they could touch each horizon. *My profane son.*

"Vindicta est completum," said Dracula to his father. *My vengeance is complete.*

"Non, non tamen," replied the shadow, and he pointed at the three on the crosses. *No, not yet.*

"God bless you, Ian," said Jonathan, his lips quivering from sadness and exhaustion as he looked at his friend's slumping body as it continued to burn.

"Fight me like a man!" growled/sobbed Quincy at Dracula, "Face me in a fair fight!"

Dracula turned from his bow and looked at Quincy and laughed like a boy who had gotten all he had wanted for Christmas. "Like your fathers did when they murdered my wife?"

"Your wife," hissed Mina, "is now the wealthiest whore in all Hell because of our fathers, and I shall die most happy for it!"

God, I love you, Mina beamed Jonathan.

Quincy saved the happiest laugh of his life for now, and he let it loose for the world of evil around him to hear. "Haaahahahahahahahahaha! She made your lady sound like the two-dollar pigsticker that she is! God bless ya, Tiger Lily!"

Morris's taunt flushed Dracula with unbridled fury.

Mina and Jonathan just laughed at Morris' joke and Dracula's rage.

Dracula of Transylvania turned with his owl eyes to look right at Mina, who stopped laughing, took this all in as she gave Dracula a dirty smirk filled with satisfaction.

Before she spat at the vampire.

"Yer bow-legged goat daddy ain't nuthin' but a flea-bitten turd!" continued Morris as he watched Dracula's eyes lock on Mina, "And yer mamma swims with—"

Dracula stood straight, a beacon of fury, then in a tempest of rage threw his hand out for a second sword.

"You fight for the honor of a *whore*!" raged Mina with an evil leer.

Another flew to his hand from the scabbard of another skeleton.

Hilt in his palm, Dracula roared as he threw his arm back to skewer Mina.

Jonathan whispered to Mina, "'—and if God choose, I shall but love thee better after death.'[303]"

Mina beamed at Jonathan as if she were the sun and he the moon.

"Coward!" bellowed Mina at Dracula, from the depths of her soul.

With all the hate and bile inside him, Dracula threw the sword.

Wilhelmina Murray and Jonathan Harker locked eyes, resolute that their love would withstand all of this, with the satisfaction and knowledge that they would be reunited once more in a few mere moments.

Mina grimaced, bracing for impact.

As did Jonathan.

It never came.

The sword soared by Mina, having missed completely.

Then they all looked at Dracula and knew why the vampire had missed his mark.

Mina, Jonathan and Quincy were astonished.

As was everyone else.

For protruding out of Dracula of Transylvania's neck were five wood-tipped arrows, without arrowheads yet with sharpened ends.

Dracula's raptor eyes went wide, incredulous.

In shock.

And then, Dracula of Transylvania experienced something he had not felt in a long, long time.

Bright, burning agony.

It rippled though him.

Blood pooled inside of his left eye, and it popped out into the air, like a pimple.

"Holy shit!" spat Quincy.

Mina and Jonathan were agape, agog with shock.

Dracula tried to speak but only gurgled.

He tried to force speech out of his mouth, but he vomited blood instead.

Thunder rumbled above.

"Again!" came a voice in the darkness.

Dracula could barely stand, he staggered, reaching for the arrows in his neck, when another *fifty* arrows flew out of the night and embedded themselves all along the vampire's arm, neck and torso. One pierced Dracula's cheek. Three entered under the *nosferatu's* jaw. Blood poured and burst out of the wounds and the vampire found his voice and bellowed at the moon, and the entire world seemed to shake.

A brazen, strong figure raced and staggered out of the night and into the firelight.

"God bless us all," said Jonathan when he recognized the figure.

"Holy shit in a barrel!" bawled one Quincy Morris.

Mina merely beamed with joy and tears.

The grizzled, bruised, cut, wounded but resilient form belonged to Professor Abraham Van Helsing.

---

[303] Elizabeth Barrett Browning- Sonnet 43, "How do I love thee? Let me count the ways."

TWO

From behind Abraham and out of the darkness charged not hundreds but *thousands* of soldiers from the Austro-Hungarian Army[304], their collective roar thunderous enough to frighten Alexander the Great's elephants.

"Father," supplicated the badly-wounded Dracula as another wave of sharpened arrows peppered his body.

Without another word, and in a wisp of smoke, Satan, the First Liar, was gone.

Out of the night and the shadows, through the open castle gates and down from her walls poured the troops, firing rifles or swinging swords at the stunned skeleton army. Hundreds of villagers from the region, emboldened by the army's march to the castle, followed with pickaxes and scythes. The troops surged forward, shooting at the skulls of the skeletons, which exploded into dry brain dust and hollow gourds while the rest of their bodies stayed upright. Other soldiers blazed to the fore with swords and hacked at the disoriented, beheaded skeletal forms where they stood. Bits of bone flew everywhere as the Austro-Hungarian army overwhelmed the skeletal legion. Following behind the soldiers were priests of Catholic, Greek Orthodox, Jewish and Muslim faiths, including Father Tibor, shouting encouragement while holding talismans of their faiths out in front of them, displays of purity in the face of evil.

As if on cue, the vicious, omnipotent rat hordes surged out from the keep, bent on ripping Abraham Van Helsing, the Austro-Hungarian army, the villagers, the holy men and anyone else to pieces. The human army, terrified by the forward swell of vermin, surged backward, and the tide of the battle turned. The blasphemous, serpentine, disease-filled tide of rats burst forward along the ground with murderous intent in their unholy, crimson-filled eyes.

But Abraham Van Helsing, who was no fool, was ready.

"Now!" he shouted.

Soldiers, villagers and priests all dove to one side.

Four teams of Hungarian soldiers stepped forward into the space between the rifles of the soldiers. They each wielded the same, strange contraption.

One of the most closely guarded secrets of the Ancient World were the ingredients that made up the incendiary weapon referred to as 'Greek Fire', though weapons utilizing fire had been in use for centuries before, like flaming arrows and clay pots filled with combustible materials. But in this case, the Western Roman Empire, the Byzantines, used these arcane, mysterious devices not to soak weapons to make them flammable or to light a wick on a clay pot before flinging it at the enemies, but rather as siphons to violently project a highly combustible fluid that burned anything it touched, and could even *burn underwater*. In fact, the Byzantine ships were able to wield their weapon from

---

[304] The Austro-Hungarian army was formed in 1867 by the constitutional union of Austria and Hungary. The ground force was comprised of many ethnicities and while having limited resources because Austria and Hungary chose to equip their own soldiers instead of the entire forces. The army lasted through World War I until the disbanding of the Austro-Hungarian agreement and monarchy.

their boats, spewing flame directly onto an enemy's vessel. With this weapon, and an impregnable three-layered wall, Constantinople was nearly impervious to attack until the Sultan Mehmet was able to topple the city in 1453 AD.

When, where and how the Austro-Hungarian Army could have replicated the strange contraptions was uncertain. The siphons, and there were four of them, looked like the front end of a firehose screwed onto an oddly assembled clay pipe, which led to a simple metal container containing the mysterious fuel. Behind that was a strange set of bellows.

A wave of rats as wide as a football pitch burst forward, and Abraham Van Helsing shouted, "Fire!"

Ignited, the descendent of the ancient secret known as Greek Fire bellowed waves of liquid Hell, all over the wave of crimson-eyed rat hellions.

The Ancient World, renewed.

Bellows-propelled fuel surged all over the rat legions, and they all were consumed by the same flame that kept the Arabs out of Constantinople nearly fifteen hundred years ago[305]. Waves of fire bloomed, blossomed in the night.

Beauteous fire engulfing vicious animalistic fury.

A million screams of agony, extinguished by an enormous inferno of humankind's cruelty.

The pendulum of the battle had swung violently and suddenly back into the hands of the Modern World.

That first blow of the Greek Fire incinerated eighty percent of the rat horde.

Dracula, staggered from his wounds, who had experienced the Fall of Jerusalem and Constantinople, had seen soldier and citizen slaughtered, was taken completely by surprise.

Into the aftermath of the first blow waded the men of faith, to intercept the charge of the remaining rat horde, which swarmed over the charred, still-flaming corpses of their rodent brethren. The holy men held large bottles of water.

Holy Water.

In Christianity, Holy Water is also referred to as *agua santa* or *sanctus aqua* in Spanish or Latin. In the Muslim culture there is *ãb-I shifã*, or 'healing water', and in the Jewish faith there is *Mikveh*, a water of ritual immersion. The holy men opened their bottles and violently threw water at the wave of oncoming rats; the blessed liquid hit the remaining, accursed vermin like a million whips covered with acid, and the rats recoiled and writhed and screeched in agony.

The priests then stepped backward just in time to avoid the next blast of Greek Fire.

From all four cannons.

The blasts were devastating.

Any rats that remained withered like grass under a summer glare.

Father Tibor threw Holy Water at a charging Primus, and half of the massive skeleton melted instantly like a wax figure.

"At last," gasped Primus before he withered away. "Thank you."

A Rabbi held out a menorah and pressed it against the forehead of a charging Adso, and the grotesque skeleton's forehead crumbled into dust.

A group of Imams holding out Tuareg crosses ran at the skeletons, which disintegrated with the mere touch of the sacred objects. Some of the skeletons nearest the slab recovered and where able to charge in response, but most of them by that point had already been disabled or turned to ash.

In moments, the skeletal army that had conquered legions and kingdoms for centuries was felled by soldiers, villagers and farmers from the threshold of the twentieth century.

---

[305] During the Siege of Constantinople (674-678 AD)

Gone.

Jonathan, still bound to his cross as were Quincy and Mina, shook his head to clear his eyesight and saw hundreds of Austro-Hungarian soldiers holding quivers along the inner wall of the castle, and above the great gates of Castle Dracula. They continued to fire volley after volley into the body of Dracula of Transylvania, who had begun to transform as he staggered in agony, hundreds of arrows pin-cushioning his body. His anatomy warped and pulsated the anatomy of a bat, a rat, a wolf as the vampire roared in agony. A wailing Renfield was overwhelmed by infantrymen and pinned to the ground.

Abraham had reached the altar, and he shouted, "Shoot him again!" as he leaped onto the blasphemous slab, slammed a dagger into Dracula's torso and dove aside to avoid the waves of arrows hailing down upon the nosferatu. Van Helsing used another knife to begin to free Mina.

Bristling with arrows, the vampire threw his head back and bellowed like a wounded bull, blood spurting out of his throat and mouth. He clawed vainly at Abraham, who was far too nimble and had already rolled away. When Van Helsing was clear, the unrelenting waves of arrows began again. The Austro-Hungarian archers were vicious and focused as they emptied their quills into the great beast, just as were villagers bent on crushing with their farming tools any skeleton that had evaded the army's advancement. It was as if an entire region had decided that the time of being preyed upon for centuries by a blood-sucking entity was over.

"He is weakest when he is transforming!" shouted a joyous Jonathan Harker as arrows whistled by him, in search of the being who had experienced the decimation of Constantinople and the Inquisition in medieval Spain.

"Give 'em hell in a cookie jar!" spat Quincy amid a maniacal cackle.

Abraham shot the strangest, amused look at Morris and laughed as he finished cutting Mina loose.

Quincy then sheepishly looked at Van Helsing and chuckled, "Well, you know what I mean, Uncle Abe."

"You're a sight for sore eyes," said Jonathan to Abraham, who playfully slapped Harker's check with affection.

"I'll explain after we have rid the world of this plague upon humanity," said Abraham as he watched Dracula collapse down to all fours, one arm a bloated rat's claw trying to pull himself bodily off the rock, while a dozen more arrows sunk themselves into his back. Wave after wave overwhelmed the vampire, the monster completely under siege, as was his castle.

The arrow-riddled thing that was Dracula slid off the rock and onto the cold, grey earth like a wounded, dying dog. The Hungarian soldiers pursued him past the upside-down crosses where he had bound Mina, Jonathan and Quincy, the vampire's body melting from one horrific form to another.

Bat to wolf.

Wolf to bat.

Bat to mist.

Mist to man.

Then the forms began to melt and meld together, horrifyingly.

The wounded thing what was Dracula reached out with a melting bat wing and pulled his body along as the *nosferatu* bellowed with pain, his body bristling with arrows. A quivering rat's tail that was part of a left arm reached out and pulled him agonizingly along. Dracula's wolf and rat legs, trembling with pain while shapeshifting from human to rat to bat to wolf, moved the quagmire of a body along even as the soldiers took turns stabbing Dracula with pikes, swords and daggers. A few of the soldiers with rifles opened fire as the shapeshifting monstrosity that was Dracula of Transylvania slid and slogged toward the castle's keep, and in a sudden burst of energy, the creature avoided getting pinned by the pikes and swords and sprang up to cling to the side of the castle wall like a perverse spider with multiple, differing limbs, a strange zoological specimen out of a Darwinian nightmare. The thing screamed, moaned and roared in anguish, blows from weapons raining down upon his body from pursuing infantrymen. A few pike blows to the head left temporary holes in Dracula's scalp and went out below his jawline while the vampire squealed like a wounded dog before the misshapen head reshaped itself. Into a malformed tumor of a wolf's head.

A dying wolf.

For in a stunning reversal, Dracula of Transylvania, the shadow that made the Old and New Worlds tremble for a thousand years, was mortally wounded.

Everyone was agape at the realization.

The great bat was dying.

The son of Satan, the undead, was at death's door.

Mina was free and she was helping Abraham liberate both Quincy and Jonathan. Abraham took in the lifeless form of Ian Seward and burst into tears as he cut Morris' binding.

"I failed you, King Arthur and Lucy," Abraham sobbed, and Quincy gave Van Helsing a huge hug of both love and sympathy when he was free.

Quincy and Jonathan both wept as they pulled the burnt, dead body down off the perversion that was the inverted crucifix, and Abraham cradled the body in his arms and continued to sob. "Held you as a baby, loved you as a boy, never thought I would see myself holding you like this, my little, dear, dear boy."

"You dirty whore!" roared Renfield at Mina as a dozen soldiers continued to pin him to the ground while battering him with their rifle butts.

Montague ranted, "You did this to the master! God help your soul, vile woman of no moral worth! And the rest of you, bloody filthy rats! To Hell with all of you! Van Helsing! Help me! You betrayed the master but you were always kind to me even when my family hated me!"

"I feel sorry for ya," said Quincy, instinctively stepping in front of Mina to shield her from the great brute. Not needing his shield, Mina nevertheless appreciated Morris' great gesture and patted him on the shoulder with affection.

Quincy half-turned to Mina and winked, "I gotcha covered Tiger Lily."

One of the soldiers grew tired of the wrestling with Renfield, stood and swung his rifle around to shoot the enormous, raving man in the head, but Abraham shouted, "Place him under arrest! He needs a trial and an asylum, not an execution."

Overwhelmed at last by the soldiers, Renfield went still, and rope was brought to tie him up.

Other soldiers ran over to the iron maidens and managed to unlock them. When Venus and Petra staggered out, filthy and exhausted, they fell to their hands and knees, trembling and crying from the effort it took not to lean against the spikes that lined their prisons. Around them, the infantrymen all raised rifles and swords, preparing to attack them. Both of the brides looked disheveled and terrified, and far too helpless to do anything to protect themselves.

The holy men stepped forward holding bottles of Holy Water, ready to drench and burn the *nosferatu* like unholy rats.

"Leave them be!" shouted Mina at the soldiers, and when Abraham shot her an incredulous look, Wilhelmina Murray softened, "We have an arrangement, Uncle Abraham. You have to trust me."

"She's right," added Jonathan, nodding at Abraham.

"We made a deal with 'em, Uncle Abe," added Quincy to Abraham, while nodding at the brides. "Mostly Ian, rest his soul, and I feel like we need to honor it."

"We would not be here without their guidance," said Mina with finality.

Van Helsing looked at Mina and thought for another moment of simply giving the order to cut the vampires to pieces. The *nosferatu* were on their knees before them, spent and vulnerable, yet Mina's continued pleading look convinced Abraham, so he shook his head at the soldiers and they backed away. Venus and Mina exchanged long looks mixed with hate and understanding before Venus and Petra both nodded to Mina in gratitude, still weak from their imprisonment.

"Our debts are paid, we hope you honor your word," said Mina. She stepped forward and reached her hand out to help Venus to her feet, resisting the urge to strike the vampire.

Jonathan did the same for Petra, who gave Harker a polite nod of regard as she resisted the urge to rip his head clean off.

"A noblewoman's word is her bond," replied Venus.

"Ain't never gonna forget what you did to my kin though," snarled Quincy, who nevertheless took his cowboy hat off in the presence of ladies.

"Nor us what you did to our sister," hissed Petra, and there was an animalistic growl mixed in with the last of her words.

A monstrous, inhuman howl of agony from the Dracula thing that combined wolf, lion, bear and tiger shook the castle to its foundation and ended their conversation.

Friend and foe alike all looked over to the wall, where the soldiers and priests were firing arrows, bullets and Holy Water at the shapeshifting form of Dracula as he continued to clamber over battlements and ruins.

"After all this time," said Venus, and she placed her hand over her breast in emotion, "He is dying, and I do not know why I am not sad. He was my husband for a few summers, then many winters."

"Because he never honored us the way we honored him.," said Petra, clasping Venus' free hand in sympathy. "We were never truly his wives."

The soldiers continued to pelt Dracula with arrows and bullets, the strange creature mewling like an injured rat one moment, screeching like a wounded bat and howling an unholy howl like a wolf near death. Its human head poured bat over wolf features, and rat over wolf, new arrows digging into the body as old ones either broke or fell off.

Renfield, wrestled to his feet, wrenched himself free from the soldiers and ran to Dracula with his arms up in a protective gesture, screaming, "Leave him be! Leave my master be!"

"Poor fella," gulped Quincy, meaning Renfield.

In the next instant, the liquid, shapeshifting monstrosity that was Dracula reached down with its mouth full of bat, wolf, and human teeth and bit deeply into Renfield's neck the way a fox overpowers a rabbit.

Everyone gasped.

Renfield's eyes spasmed, then closed. The vampire, with Renfield's body hanging limply from his jaws, raced higher up along the battlements.

The soldiers kept firing while trying not to hit the massive form of Montague Rhodes Renfield, whose powerful arms and legs swayed limply with the vampire's movements.

Dracula's howls had attracted the scant remains of the legion of rats, and some of them scurried along the wall in an attempt to reach their wounded master when one of the catholic priests threw Holy Water bodily onto the creatures, like throwing washtub water out of the window, and to everyone's surprise the entire legion of vermin was engulfed in white-hot holy fire. The rats cascaded off the wall like falling candles in the night. A new, sudden wind began to pick up, sending gusts all around them, and Dracula slithered toward the back of the castle, still clinging to the ancient battlements, sliding over gothic arches and around antiquated minarets, remnants of the vampire's conquests throughout time, all the while twisting his head out to hold Renfield bodily out as a human shield. The enormous man came to consciousness, and despite his predicament, threw his hands out at the crowd below them.

"Don't kill him!" shouted Renfield pathetically. "He is my master!"

As he neared the back end of the castle, the soldiers moving laterally with him, ready to fire, Dracula twisted his wolf/bat/rat/human head and threw the wretched, sick man violently to the crowd below, then continued to sprint along the wall like an enormous, grotesque spider as the rain of arrows began to pursue him again.

Venus smiled in sadness as she watched Renfleid fall, knowing Dracula the way she knew him. "He could never accept assistance from anyone. Ever."

The soldiers and priests parted.

Renfield's body crunched savagely when it slammed into the ground.

Montague Rhodes Renfield moved no more.

His face riddled with arrows, Dracula clung to an elaborate mosaic from ancient Greece that had been placed in the castle wall, a depiction of a wealthy Greek family and their resplendent, content household, no doubt ripped away from its *in situ*[306] location and brought here as more spoils of war. More arrows punched into Dracula's neck and back, making the mighty vampire look like an absurd porcupine. He attempted to change into mist, but even as the mist shape took form, the wounds and slashes sizzled to life, and brief flames flickered over the wounds and the vampire was unable to altar his form, remaining a constant mixture of animal physiology.

His clawed hands trembled with effort as he clung to the fresco.

Dracula of Transylvania began to taste his end.

Another wave of arrows just pummeled the vampire, a sharpened list of sins and judgements. He screamed in absolute agony and rage, then looked to the brides, who walked behind the thousands of soldiers, lingering near Mina, Jonathan, Quincy and Abraham as they followed Dracula along the wall of the castle. The noblewomen's faces were masks of sadness, the others were bloated with a strange combination of rage and satisfaction.

Then another amazing thing happened.

For the first time in his existence, Dracula of Transylvania shrieked, "Adiuva me!" *Help me!*

He was roaring at the brides, who began to silently weep as they watched him, tears of hate, relief and joy, for they knew they were about to be freed. Within the roar was a plea, a plea to be spared. A plea to be helped. His face, melting from wolf to bat to human, was laced with agony, as well as a growing fear. Dracula extended his right hand, a few fingers shaped like a bat and the other three like that of toe pad of a wolf. With a single glance the vampire begged for help.

And with a responding glance.

The brides turned their heads away.

Heads held high.

Noblewomen once again.

Dignity restored.

Petra burst into tears, and Venus held and steadied her.

---

[306] *In situ*, an artistic term to mean 'in its original place'. Some artwork is created to to be viewed in a location, like a fresco or mosaic painted or created as part of a specific wall.

They both then turned away completely.

And began to change.

Becoming bats.

Things of the night.

The humans around the nosferatu looked at each other as if to say *Are we really letting them leave freely?*

Abraham felt for his bag.

Quincy's right trigger finger flickered over his Winchester.

Mina stepped between them and placed her hands over theirs.

Jonathan nodded to both of them.

We may not like it, but we have an understanding, was Harker's look.

Petra and Venus stepped out between villagers, who gasped at realizing that two nosferatu were among them.

"Remember our pact," said Mina firmly.

The Petra bat nodded, the Venus bat snarled, resenting the need to remind a royal.

The two giant she-bats then flapped their great wings and soared over the battlements.

And away.

To the west.

Into the night.

Chasing the night.

Two brown bats.

Two women, two carnivores, two noblewomen, at last in search of what they had not had in a long, long time.

Mina, Jonathan, Quincy and Abraham and everyone else watched them drift into the gloom.

Mina, hair nearly undone from the mayhem of the night and pushed by the wind over her face, watched them go.

Dracula watched his wives go and bellowed one last primal plea for help.

Petra Ali and Venus de' Medici became one with the night.

Everyone turned their attention away from the bats and back to the Dracula thing.

Atop the castle, a lance flung by one of the soldiers pounded into the base of the vampire's neck, and the Dracula bat thing nearly fell into the crowd, where he would have been surely torn to pieces and burnt. The dozens, if not hundreds of spears and lances hanging from the Dracula thing weighed so much that they began to drag the inhuman beast down, down to the ground, where Dracula of Transylvania would have certainly been hacked to pieces. The Dracula thing vomited blood and green bile and girded himself into one last great effort as it crawled along the wall, even growing another limb, a misshapen bat/rat/wolf limb as it gathered speed and sprinted along the wall. Dracula began to change, to metamorphosize, yet again, and it was not a bat or a wolf or a rat or even mist that desperately tried to make an escape, but rather a serpentine, winged dragon.

Jonathan used his Webley, and Quincy emptied his Winchester into the dragon, yet despite the Holy Water-laced rounds, the great evil continued to bound toward the back of the castle.

Toward a broken, battered battlement.

With a misshapen, atrophied, winding staircase at the far end.

That led to the east.

To the open air.

Abraham walked along the back of the crowd of soldiers and priests, and when he saw the vampire's objective, he shouted, "Ő próbál elérjük a hátsó fal és a menekülési" *He is trying to reach the back wall and escape!*

Immediately dozens of archers bolted to a broken staircase attached to the back wall of the castle and continued to fire arrows at the dragon, who shook the ground with his pained roar. Quincy whipped his Colts out of their holsters and emptied his pistols into Dracula with no effect, and with a great, majestic effort, the dragon leaped from the back of the castle, over the heads of the archers, and onto the steps, and began to slide/crawl/slither and lunge toward the top of the stairs, the back wall, and the night.

Cut him off!" shouted Abraham as he rushed forward.

The soldiers raced up toward the Dracula bat, who had turned, took a deep, ragged breath, and swung his right wing out and slapped the wave of onrushing soldiers away with a tremendous blow.

"No!" screamed Mina.

And with a proud roar, the Dracula dragon dove forward, reaching for the top of the stairs and freedom.

Everyone fired everything they had.

Even as he left a trail of blood that would have bled ten others to death, even as arrows, spears, and bullets pelted him and the stonework around him, the Dracula dragon snarled with satisfaction. He knew he had survived *yet again.*

The Dracula dragon arched itself to leap, to free-fall to safety.

The dungeons, he thought. *I can fall from here and catch myself upon the rocks of the dungeon entrance. I will survive, even with these wounds. I will rest and heal and then I will hunt them all down, crush them. Like the INSECTS and SPIDERS that they are. Thank you, Father for this test of faith—*

Dawn broke over the distant mountain ranges of Transylvania.

The sky pulsed with crimson, and everyone was bathed in sunlight.

Bathed in daylight, the Dracula dragon, conqueror of continents, destroyer of kingdoms, warrior of unholy faith, bellowed in sheer agony as he burst into unholy flame.

Mina sobbed, as did Jonathan.

The gentle caress of dawn hit Dracula like an atomic explosion, tearing into his skin and muscle and igniting him aflame in an instant. He raised his winged arms to block his face from the blast that everyone else took as the sublime coming of the day, and the rays tore at his flesh, and as he caught fire, the vampire metamorphosized into humanoid form again, his clothes catching fire, his face igniting in the holy light that the new day brought.

Dracula roared in absolute anguish and turned away from the sun and into the oncoming Abraham Van Helsing, who bolted up the last few steps, brandishing a large, sharpened, wooden crucifix, and he raised the cross over his head. His intent was to plant it *through* Dracula's torso.

"When you are in Hell, think of who put you there!" screamed Abraham Van Helsing, who then swung back the cross even further, for the death blow… and stopped.

The vampire known as Dracula the Transylvanian was completely alight with holy flame, and the undead royal was dying, and Van Helsing knew it. Abraham looked into the eyes of Dracula, who in turn saw the soul of Van Helsing, and even for one who was alight with fire, the incandescence of Abraham's soul was too bright for the vampire to take in.

Dawn made the Carpathian Mountains sing with hues of purple, the color of royalty, and for the first time in a thousand years, the mountains, hills, meadows and streams awoke in peace.

The Hungarian soldiers, the priests, Mina, Quincy and Jonathan all gathered around the vampire, and Dracula's soul, so filed with hate, rage and so empty of the simple, beauteous thing called love, reached out a taloned hand, and in response Abraham Van Helsing held out his crucifix, and the vampire recoiled at the sight of the cross, and fell off the altar.

Fell, like Jonathan Harker had fallen all those months ago, from Castle Dracula.

Like a fallen angel.

A star fell from the morning sky.

Icarus fell from the sun.

A devil was given his due.

They all stepped forward, all of them, and watched the moth fall from the candle.

Dracula the Transylvanian; foe of pasha, pope, crusader knight, emperors of China, kings and queens of Europe, and all that was good that had stood in his way for the past thousand years fell like a struck match.

They all took it in, and there was a moment of silence before Dracula plunged past the dungeon entrance and collided with the rocky part of the river bed far below, and from the still-dark trench of the river came a howling blast of wind that threw everyone back, a dark, cold, evil zephyr that ran through them all like a winter's blasting gale, and after everyone was nearly thrown to the ground by the force, the wind subsided from one moment to the next.

A single, dying hiss escaped Renfield's mouth as his broken soul left his broken body. "Love me, Master."

And the behemoth who had been kissed by a *nosferatu* was gone.

"May god rest his wretched soul," said Abraham to his childhood friend, long lost.

A few remaining infernal rats that were still alive caught flame and dissipated.

Any broken skeleton still waving an arm with a sword in it crumbled to dust, even Adso, who said as he lay with an empty, broken skull, "Many thanks to you all," as he became cinder.

All of them looking down, soldier, priest, prisoner, nephew, son, daughter and uncle, all of them knew Dracula was dead, and only a madman mourned him.

"*Ad mortem tyranni*," said Abraham.

"God damn, that was a hell of a thing," added Quincy with sweet satisfaction.

THREE

Dawn bloomed over castle Dracula.

The imams, rabbis and priests conferred. They then asked a few of the villagers that had accompanied them to return to their villages to spread the word of Dracula's demise and to request food and supplies to feed the soldiers.

They then held prayer services for all of the faiths, right there on the grounds that had held and created so much evil for so many centuries. The ceremony was a beauteous moment where all devotions celebrated their triumph over evil, together, in a respectful, dignified, tranquil way. A few of the soldiers even wept during their prayers, countless disappeared relatives now avenged and at peace. Father Tibor and all the other holy men read simultaneously from a document they had all helped to write:

"Evil can never triumph. It can never be allowed to take root or fester like a sickness in our bodies and must be fought in the heart, the soul and the mind, at all times, and at all costs. Good will continue to pave the way for us, for future generations, so that all mankind may not see the likes of Dracula of Transylvania again. We live in a time of miracles in machinery and science, but we must never stop looking into the human soul for compassion. Empathy is our sword and shield, but we must use the sword carefully. Help those others who may not believe what you believe, appear as you appear. We all need to live together below the Kingdom of God."

Mina, Quincy and Jonathan were grieving for the soul of Ian, and honestly for all of their family, so they stayed with Ian's shrouded body while they prayed with the Catholic priests and soldiers. Abraham took it upon himself to spend time praying with the representatives of each of the faiths.

All this seemed to have a calming effect on the castle grounds, and during the prayers the castle began to rumble, then began collapsing upon itself, taking some of the its secrets with it.

Ian Seward was buried in a quiet spot on the castle grounds.

Renfield was buried near the castle and the master he had held so dear.

Jonathan found Renfield's journal among his possessions and handed it to Abraham, who stuffed it into his returned bag.

After the prayers, the rabbis, imams and priests then blessed the grounds, and as they did, more beauty transpired as flowers began to blossom throughout the grounds. Though winter fast approached, the cold of the time of year somehow did not stop the grounds from becoming a vast meadow of color, fields outside the castle sprung grass and flowers and became vast meadows that engulfed the dead armies that had laid unburied for hundreds of years outside the castle's massive gate. Birds of all kinds and sizes then began to sweep over the grasses, their chirping and singing yet another sign that all was right now. All were stunned by the beauty of the gentle, supernatural but natural events, but none more amazing than the roses that sprang up around Ian's resting place.

Around mid-day a gaggle of villagers arrived, with food and good cheer for the soldiers, and they all feasted as children climbed and played on the battlements.

"I— we were a day behind you the entire journey," said Van Helsing as he took a long slug of beer to wash down some bread. "I landed on a bed in Rome. You should have seen the look on the faces of the honeymooners when I plunged through their skylight."

"Glad their bed cushioned your fall, Uncle Abraham," chuckled Quincy, who had just gulped down a big piece of chicken. The villagers had cooked and served a veritable banquet to everyone, soldier and priest alike, respectful of all faiths, in appreciation for the deeds of the night before.

"Naturally," laughed Abraham with a wicked grin. "I've never heard Italian spoken both so quickly and quite so very profanely."

"I'm sure the groom was quite upset," stated Jonathan to much laughter.

"The bride was actually the profane one," giggled Abraham to even greater laughter.

"Well, here's to the bride," said Mina as she raised her cup of country wine in a toast, and they all joined her, laughing.

"We approached Father Tibor and he declined to help us," said Jonathan, lapping up what was a delicious broth with vegetables. The menu was vast and varied, such was the gratitude involved.

"Something that had agonized him when I arrived," said Abraham with a nod to Father Tibor, who was dining with the other holy men. "In fact, he was packing up to follow you, and he was most helpful in rallying the soldiers. They had had enough of Dracula and brought along that magnificent Greek Fire. We would not have made it here without Old Tibor."

"Well, he can make it up by marrying us," said Jonathan.

"You should be best man, Uncle Abraham," said Quincy. "A finer man I have never met."

"I don't agree—" began Abraham. He clapped Quincy on the shoulder, and now he knew what everyone else was thinking.

"—You're bloody thick, mate—," laughed Jonathan when realization swept over the Texan like a herd of Longhorns over West Texas.

"And that is why," said Mina with tears in her eyes, "you are."

Jonathan could only beam in agreement.

And that afternoon, as the gentle sun caressed the mountain range, amid the floral splendor of the blessed castle ruins and also next to the grave of Ian Seward, all of the holy men helped join Wilhelmina Murray and Jonathan Harker in holy matrimony.

EPILOGUES

ROME
SPRING 1900

Late one evening of the following spring, under a bulbous, fungoid moon, a very resplendent Venus de' Medici stood with dignity and nobility upon one of the floor pillars of the Colosseum. Below her were the dungeons of Ancient Rome, around her the stone seats of the crumbling, spectacular amphitheater. Venus wore a sumptuous gown of silk, black pearls and human skin. Her hair was made up in a formal updo, with black roses, indigo ribbons and charred human finger bones woven into the cascading locks in an elegant manner befitting the turn of the century, because loath were vampires to admit it, at times they enjoyed imitating the contemporary styles of the very beings they hunted. She stood in royal magnificence in front of a rococo-styled throne made of burnt human limbs somehow torqued, sewn and nailed into the form of the chair, complete with armrests made of femurs and skulls of small children.

Beside her stood Petra, in the decadent fashion splendor of her Italian love, wrapped in a silken black Victorian era gown, and her curly tresses also pinned up atop her head in a bun, with dead black baby snakes interwoven into her hair like perverse bows. She wore a spectacular ebony shawl of black silk and desiccated scarabs. Both of the vampiresses had recovered from their torture in Transylvania. The cuts and nicks along their skin had healed, and a winter of sipping blood from jewel-encrusted goblets had, ironically, brought color back into their pallor.

The throne sat in the Emperor's box in the Colosseum.

Above the throne floated three symbols, aflame and dancing in the night:

VI

VI   VI

Below the flame, and seated on the throne was the massive, black silhouette of Satan. Leaning to the right side, Satan's clawed right hand held up his massive, grotesque head. Lucifer's six crimson eyes remained fixed, unblinking, upon Venus.

Behind Satan, and scattered among the seats of the Colosseum, were hundreds of pairs of emerald, glowing eyes. Vampires all of them, from all over the world.

Watching Venus and Petra.

A black-robed shadow separated itself from the darkness that was Lucifer.

A bleak, gaunt figure that grew out of the bleakest shadow there ever was.

As tall as a man or woman, yet neither.

Nor human.

The acolyte's skin was wrinkled obsidian, and blood flowed out of its mouth as it leered menacingly at Venus and Petra. The strange, robed shadow with the bleeding mouth reached into of the many crinkled folds within its robe and pulled out a gnarled, worn, book.

Spitting blood out between needle-like teeth, it began to read, and the others in the crowd began to chant along with the unholy acolyte, "Volumus puros dempta stella Bethlehem. Volumus lacerandos sigillum septimum. Et volumus habet capita septem et cornua decem et septem diademata draconem opprimere Michaelis Angeli damnati. Speramus magnum exitium Agno pugnabunt, et in iudiciis corrumpendis exercitati, omnia bona et alterum." *We wish for the dimming of the Star of Bethlehem. We desire that the Seventh Seal to be torn asunder. And we wish for the seven-headed dragon with ten horns and seven crowns to crush Michael and his accursed angels. We hope for the destruction of the Great Lamb, and the corruption of all that is good in this and any other world.*

The arcane book disappeared into the bleak folds of the unholy acolyte, and the clawed, decaying, obsidian hand turned over, palm up, and a crown of black gold, opal and the bones of fetuses materialized. The harrowing apparition strode over the open ground, defying gravity, and neared Venus, who bowed gracefully, royally. Petra smiled, happy for Venus. They had been through so much together.

"In nomine pater et rupere, in nomine sui mortui rupere filius, et in nomine omne malum ego Coronas coronabit te regina lamia." *In the name of the Unholy Father, in the name of his dead Unholy Son, and in the name of all that is evil, 1 crown thee queen of vampires.*

The crown was placed gracefully onto Venus de' Medici's head.

"Corona tibi et regina nostra," snarled the unholy acolyte. *I crown thee our queen.*

There was silence, other than a few scattered hisses of resentment, from the crowd.

The King of Lies leaned forward in his throne. Everyone gasped.

"Mea voluntas tuum esse voluntatem, vel vos patietur, et patimini, et pati adhuc," snarled Satan. *My will be thy will, or you will suffer, and suffer, and suffer still.*

"Ita, pater et sponsum," replied Venus with a noticeable gulp in her throat. *Yes, father and husband.*

"Sic fiat," rumbled Satan. "Nostris fatum intertexti." So *be it. Our fates, intertwined.*

The flame flickered out.

Out of the crowd flew six large bats, and after they all had landed on the floor pillars around Venus and Petra, the bats all became six young vampiresses, each from a different part of the world. All of the young carnivores were dignified, elegant and ferocious.

African.

Mexican.

Persian.

Japanese.

French.

Indian.

Presenting themselves to to the newly-crowned queen, they all bowed formally to Venus, then two of them turned to Petra, bowed with grace and class to her before they moved over beside the Egyptian. Venus and Petra had their ladies-in-waiting, their palace women.

Venus ascended to her throne, and another beautiful, macabre chair was brought forth for Petra, who was seated in resplendent grace beside her queen.

"Et de Harkers?" asked Petra. *And of the Harkers?*

"Nos non autem treugam frangere," said Venus. *No. We will not break the truce.*

And with a cool glance at the city lights of the Eternal City that danced outside of the Colosseum, Venus said, "Est hic saturare sanguinem et Romae." *There is enough food here in Rome.*

"يتكلم معن," said Petra with a supple, aristocratic nod of her head. *Yes, my queen.*

The vampires in the stands had glided out among the broken pillars of the collapsed Colosseum floor, where so much blood had been spilt since the Roman Empire had stretched from Britannia to Byzantium. They all had begun to form a line in front of Venus, and a courtly Spanish *nosferatu* strode forward from the head of the line, he bowed and purred, "Mi Reina." *My Queen.*

Venus extended her right hand, ever graceful, and as the Spaniard took her hand and kissed it, the rest of the vampires in line began to chant, "Volumus puros dempta stella Bethlehem. Volumus lacerandos sigillum septimum. Et volumus habet capita septem et cornua decem et septem diademata draconem opprimere Michaelis Angeli damnati. Speramus magnum exitium Agno pugnabunt, et in iudiciis corrumpendis exercitati, omnia bona et alterum…" *We wish for the dimming of the Star of Bethlehem. We desire that the Seventh Seal to be torn asunder. And we wish for the seven-headed dragon with ten horns and seven crowns to crush Michael and his accursed angels. We hope for the destruction of the Great Lamb, and the corruption of all that is good in this and any other world…*

ENGLAND
SUMMER 1905

The warm afternoon was filled with dandelions, seeds, birds and happiness.

A supple breeze blew through three rocks that had been thrown into the air, soaring across an idyllic creek that stretched lazily across the back end of the Harker Estate, like a sleeping garden snake sunning itself and basking away the long, warm time before the sun began to set. The rocks landed in the bushes on the other side of the creek, landing among the flora of the green, inviting grove of forest that was bordered by the creek.

Three children, two darling, brilliant girls and a charming, happy boy, each picked up more rocks and continued to aim and throw, all missing their target, which was the sculpture of Pan[307], which held his flute to his mouth upon a short, marble Roman column, Ionic in the style its base. The column had sagged to its left, and some of the ferns and vine and grass had begun to envelop it.

Nevertheless, Pan played his silent tune as the children continued their bombardment. Farther behind the children/bombardiers, on another spacious back lawn, this time behind the Harker Estate, sat Mina and Jonathan. Harker was still in his work attire, though he had loosened his tie and starched collar. He sat on a two-seater lawn chair with his arm draped around Mina, who wore a sky-blue dress. They were comfortable with each other like the happily married couple they were, still in love.

Next to them, in their own wide lawn chair, sprawled one Quincy Morris and his wife, Consuelo, a beautiful Mexican woman. Quincy was his languid self, poured out over the lawn chair like a pancake, while Consuelo was regal, composed and dignified. They sat close to each other, with Consuelo's left hand, sporting an impressive diamond ring, idly tapping Quincy's knee.

Quincy wore a cowboy hat nearly as large as his ego.

To their collective left sat Abraham Van Helsing, his hair longer and greyer, looking more like one of Rembrandt's self-portraits by the day. He held a palette filled with different hues of oil in his left hand, and a paintbrush in his right. He slid brushstrokes over a canvas, smiling as he painted away. The Pan was his subject, and not a bad attempt in the Impressionist style.

"How's everything at work, Jonny?" said Quincy as he lay in some shadow behind the statue.

"Alright, but at times, I get to thinking that being a solicitor is not necessarily the most life-affecting thing to do with one's time."

Abraham stopped painting, looked at them all with a smile and said, "You mean like stopping the Son of Satan from fulfilling the prophecies of the book of Revelations?"

It was the first time they'd talked about the events of 1899, and when they all smiled they all truly knew it was over.

A precocious four-year old, Lucy Morris stood stout and hit the statue with a rock.

---

[307] In Ancient Greece Pan was the god of nature, shepards and the wild. Often depicted as having the legs and horns of a goat.

"Excellent, Lucy!" said the little boy.

"Thank you, Ian!"

"Daddy, I did it!" she shouted, full of the joy of a happy child.

"Your turn, Judith!" said Lucy to her sister, who eagerly scooped up some more rocks and began to fire away.

"Lucy's got an eye like her Pa!" roared Morris, which elicited eyerolls from both Mina and Consuelo. "Judy as well!"

"I actually cannot wait until they are old enough to target practice with me," conceded Consuelo, looking over her daughters with pride.

"Whoa, hold on, no daughter o' mine's gonna shoot!" wailed Morris, nearly jumping to his feet, "They're gonna be ladies!"

Mina knitted her brows while Jonathan rolled his eyes.

"What the hell is *that* supposed to mean, Morris?" snipped Mrs. Harker.

"Yes, *Querido*," said Consuelo, her own brows furrowed. "What exactly does that mean?"

"It means exactly what it means!" shouted Quincy, perhaps an octave too high. "My li'l darlin' daughters aren't gonna touch any pistols, or rifles, or any of that nonsense."

"That might be the stupidest thing you've ever said," marveled Mina with a nod. "And there is an extensive catalog on that subject."

"You yourself were taught to shoot by your own mother!" gasped Consuelo, who looked like she was about to slap her husband.

"Don't matter!" sniffed Quincy, oblivious to the warming water he'd put himself into. "No guns for my sweet li'l girls. Back me up, here, Harker."

"This is your battlefield, my friend," laughed Jonathan, safely staying out of it.

"Uncle Abe—" sought Quincy.

"I'm retired and am battling oil on canvas these days, Quincy, such was the Frenchman's lily paintings' affect upon me. You'll have to parry for yourself, I'm afraid."

Consuelo gave Quincy a semi-cross look and said, "And you met me at a shooting contest in Texas, my Husband! An event I won, if I remember correctly!"

"After I adjusted your right arm a l'il bit," said Quincy, "sort of" under his breath.

Sort of.

Mina and Consuelo fumed.

"I've never considered divorce," said Consuelo, "But murder fills my thoughts at the moment."

"You have an accomplice at your service," scowled Mina.

"Sticks and stones, Love," sniffed Morris, once again resuming his pancake posture.

"I will teach Lucy and Judy myself then," chirped Consuelo, to Mina's blossoming grin.

"No yer not," said Morris, who then followed that up with a sarcastic *puff*.

"Or I will have her *marina* teach them," beamed Consuelo, looking at a beaming Mina.

"It would be my pleasure," leered Mina.

"Godmothers don't get a vote, Mrs. Murray."

"Steady, Quincy, her last name is Harker now."

"Or Murray-Harker," smiled Consuelo at Mina, who grinned in turn and said, "I like the sound of that!"

"Mind your bees wax, honey," said Quincy.

Consuelo's glare told him otherwise.

"Would y'all like some tea, honey?"

"That," said Consuelo with a sweet smile at her husband, "is more like it."

"No guns for my babies," insisted Quincy nearly under his breath.

Nearly.

"We shall see," nodded the indomitable Consuelo as she blew a kiss to her daughter.

"Uncle Abe," said an exasperated Quincy, "A little help representing' our gender."

Abraham Van Helsing then gave the laugh of his life, because he knew what subsequent events would ensure with his response, yet he went ahead and said, "You should all have a shooting contest to decide."

And, as everyone roared with laughter aplenty and challenges renewed, Jonathan Harker, Wilhelmina Murray-Harker, even Quincy Morris all gave warm grins of both happiness and tranquility.

TRANSYLVANIA
FALL 1907

As the years went on and the seasons melted into one another, the castle remained empty and cold. During one of the winters, the back end of the vast, dark structure had collapsed down into the frigid, icy waters. Columns that had been harvested in China and Constantinople centuries before tumbled down through the icy rock and into the sandy, rock-laden riverbed. Books that had been illuminated seven hundred years ago on parchment that was created during the end of the Dark Ages fell into the water, and everything was slowly dissolved and decomposed into the sometimes steady, sometimes ebbing river or stream, depending on what time of year it was.

One brilliant summer night, when the stars were gigantic in the sky and one could almost stir the milky way with a soup spoon, a bright, holy fire consumed the ruins of the inner castle, and the walls that had cherished evil also fell upon the holy fire, and the villagers in the distance commented on the bright plume of light from between the jagged, dark mountains that used to house a very dark shadow with a legion of skeletons and an army of rats at his beck and call.

Another season later, another year later, on a clear spring morning full of blue and white in the skies, the entire castle tumbled into the river, a felled dinosaur, dragging its walls, dungeons, battlements and remains of armies long conquered along with it with a loud mournful roar, and for a few days and weeks in the following spring, the water gathered and coagulated, but eventually went under and around the remains of darkened days of the past. Slowly the remains began to be covered with mud, disintegrate or tumble downstream.

On what remained of the fields that used to lay before Castle Dracula, shepherds began to take their sheep to graze on the lush, fertile grass, and birds returned and began to nest in the fields, sing in the skies and twirl in the air after insects and each other, when nesting time came. Rats returned, along with mice, but the rats were meek animals, not witch crafted legions of Hell-spawned vermin, and they began to nest and gather.

Young people dared once again to fall in love amid the fields and under the skies.

And all through this time, on the opposite bank of the river, under a protruding rock that overshadowed that bend in the river, lay the burnt, dead remains of a gargantuan bat, arrows still protruding from the remains.

Bright, beautiful flowers were growing on the bones.

FINIS

CODA

AMSTERDAM
OCTOBER 1, 1669

Two hundred and thirty years before the death of Dracula of Transylvania, an old, worn man sat in a darkened studio in Northern Europe, hunched over his painting. The workshop itself was comfortable, enriched by the warmth of the hearth to the left of the painter. A lifetime full of painting, drawing and etching had taken their toll and the man, the artist, the painter and the etcher seemed near his end.

Oil paint of differing hues, values and saturations coagulated beautifully and fell in love with each other over the canvas, with the aid and insistence of the experienced brush. The artist painted confidently, with bold strokes, his brush overloaded with the lighter valued paint he was using the perfectly place the final details of his piece.

His subject sat before him, watching intently, with the unblinking, piercing gaze of an owl or eagle. He was posed reclining in a chair, with a candle burning brightly to one side and the crackle of the hearth flickering to the other. In front and behind the subject was the painter's most fascinating subject: the infinite darkness.

The *nosferatu* sat regally, with both hands clasped together in front of him, and staring straight back at the artist, who knew he was almost finished and would not have to endure the malevolent presence before him much longer.

He was certainly not being compensated enough for the portrait, but the painter needed the money. So experienced was the painter that he mixed different chemicals into his paints, both to speed up the drying of the oil-based paints as well as to brighten the brights and embolden the darks.

He painted in silence, completely comfortable in it.

The vampire was not.

He was accustomed to affecting the people around him, and this painter was different.

So, the vampire spoke and broke the silence.

"Je gaat dood," said Dracula. *You are dying.*

"Ja," agreed the artist as he reached for another dab of paint. *Yes.*

Dracula saw how much the old man was laboring. The vampire was so familiar with death, he could see when it approached, and it satisfied him. He smiled.

"Mijn hoop is dat je zal sterven als een varken in de straten," said Dracula plainly, staying in his pose while the paint continued to be guided over the canvas by an expert hand. *My hope is that you will die as a pig in the streets.*

"U hebt waarschijnlijk gelijk, maar hoe ik sterf is mijn zaak, niet waar?" shrugged the artist. *You are probably right, but how I die is my affair, it is not?*

It never ceased to impress the vampire that however many times he'd come to pose for this piece, the old man never seemed to be phased by the presence of a royal, of a vampire in his studio. The old painter painted on, and Dracula could see the canvas bulge inward from his point of view from behind the easel on which the painting was being created.

"Niet als ik besluit om van je dood mijn affaire te maken," nodded Dracula, deciding to see if he could test the nerve of the steady hand before him. *Not if I decide to make your death my affair.*

It did not work.

The steady hand painted on.

"Dat is altijd jouw manier geweest, de weg van alle tirannen," said the artist after a shrug of his shoulders. *That has always been your way, the way of all tyrants.*

"Je spreekt tegen me alsof we gelijk zijn—" hissed Dracula, insulted somewhat, but entertained by the honesty. *You speak to me as if we were equals—*

The old painter laughed as he took a much wider brush, dabbed it over the the portion of his pallete that held a large glob of dark-value paint, a black mixed with raw umber. He leaned over to his right in front of his easel and looked Dracula square in the eye and said, "Toch zijn we dat niet. Ik walg van je, en kon nooit mijn gelijk zijn. Ik heb empathie, jij niet." *Yet we are not. You disgust me and could never be my equal. I have empathy, you do not.*

Dracula, who had once demolished the army of Imperial China, had trampled the militia of the collective European city states in front of his castle, was impressed by the valiant if foolish honesty. The vampire was no stranger to debate or conflict, so he easily rebutted, "Dat zegt de man die zijn huishoudster verleidde." *Says the man who seduced his housekeeper.*

Bold strokes of dark paint slid over the canvas. The piece was nearly done and the yet the darkness, the pools of light and therefore the depth were being expertly laid in by one of the great masters of light and dark, of mood, of controlled atmosphere. He giggled like a large, old child as he retorted, "Toon me een man zonder fouten en zonden en ik zal je de man laten zien die nog nooit heeft geleefd." *Show me a man without failures and sins and I will show you the man who has never lived.*

"De Christus van Nazareth," said Dracula the next instant and without hesitation. *The Christ of Nazareth.*

The old man took a smaller brush and began to boldly carve darkness into the paint, much like he was carving into the subject of portriature before him. "Hoe ironisch dat je hem als voorbeeld gebruikt. Er was de kwestie in de tempel met de handelaren. Hij verloor zijn geduld. Heb je de jouwe nooit verloren?" *How ironic that you use him for your example. There was the matter in the temple with the merchants[308]. He lost his temper. Have you ever not lost yours?*

"Ik beschouw dat niet als een zonde," chuckled Dracula, intrigued with the conversation despite himself. *I do not consider that a sin.*

Then the battered old artist laughed, and it was an enormous belly laugh, even as he painted, carved and created with his brush, the brush which would be just a brush in anyone else's hands. He was still laughing when he said, "Dat is een kwestie van mening. En u zou weten wat een zonde is, niet waar?" *That is a matter of opinion. And you would know what is a sin, would you not?*

Not accustomed to being laughed at, espeically by a disheveled painter, Dracula snipped, "Ben je bijna klaar?" *Are you almost finished?*

"Je bent als een ongeduldig kind op een korte reis. Een bloeddorstig kind," sighed the old man, sculpting the underside of an arm in dark brown detail and glory. *You are like an impatient child on a short journey. A bloodthirsty child.*

A silence lapsed over them, and the painter continued to paint.

Outside, a dog barked in the depths of the Amsterdam night.

---

[308] Mathew 21:12 "And Jesus went into the temple of God, and cast out all them that sold and bought in the temple, and overthrew the tables of the moneychangers, and the seats of them that sold doves,"

It bothered Dracula that somehow this man was comfortable in his presence. The vampire had grown accustomed to seeing the courts of Europe throught history recoil at the realization that he was in the room. This intimidation had helped in business, in war, in peace and this one man was impervious.

Flexing one of his hands, which had grown tired of staying in the same pose for the last hour, Dracula decided to probe in another direction, and said, "Ik heb je vrouw gezien. Ze is een koe. Zoals alle vrouwen in je leven. Vet, vruchtbaar en lelijk." *I have seen your wife. She is a cow. As are all the women in your life. Fat, fertile and ugly.*

The painter, who had seen his fair share of life as well, was not fooled and would not take the bait. He giggled again and replied, "Mijn koeien hebben me gelukkig gemaakt. Hebben je demonen en verleidsters je vreugde gegeven? Natuurlijk niet. Hoeveel dolken heb je uit je rug getrokken?" *My cows made me happy. Did your demonesses and seductresses give you any joy? Of course not. How many daggers have you pulled from your spine?*

"Oude, doorleefde dwaas," hissed Dracula more annoyed with not being to annoy the painter than anything else. *Old, spent fool.*

"Plaag op mensheid," shot the artist right back, with an impish grin. *Plague upon humanity.*

"Voor een keer, we het eens," said Dracula with a smile. *For once, we agree.*

They both laughed, men who have lived enough to be able to enjoy such moments of multiple meanings.

"Alsjeblieft niet grijnzen, het zal het schilderij verpesten." *Please do not grin, it will ruin the painting.*

The vampire was amused. He laughed, repressed the smile and sat up straight, back in his pose. After the artist continued to add darkness to his piece, Dracula said, "Ik ben vorig jaar een van de Medici tegengekomen. Hij sprak heel slecht over je." *I came upon one of the Medici[309] last year. He spoke very poorly of you.*

"Ik kon niet minder zorg," *I could not care less.*

And he proved it by continuing to work and idly humming a soft melody as he did so.

The painter confounded Dracula, who sat there in his regal majesty, the being who knew all the answers to all of the political and religious secrets of the past millennia. He could not understand how this otherwise simple man could not be more interested in him, he who had brought popes and kings to their knees.

"Ik ben bijna klaar," announced the painter. *I am nearly finished.*

"Wie beslist wanneer het werk voltooid is?" *Who decides when your work is complete?*

"Ik doe." *I do.*

"Misschien zal ik iets te zeggen hebben." *Perhaps I will have a say in the matter.*

"Je doet niet, snipped the artist. *You do not.*

"Als het werk klaar is, is het klaar. Je betaalt me dan." *When the work is done, it is done. You will then pay me.*

With raised eyebrows and an expression that conveyed menace, Dracula said, "Ik kan je gewoon vermoorden en het schilderij nemen. Ik heb niet gevoed vanavond, en de nacht ebt." *I may simply kill you and take the painting. I have not fed tonight, and the night ebbs.*

"Dan zou je een dief te zijn, evenals een tiran," scoffed the painter with a laugh. *Then you would be a thief as well as a tyrant.*

He picked up a smaller brush, this one also filled with a large amout of the dark brown/black that made up the beautiful ambience of the master's past works.

---

[309] Cosimo III de'Medici, Grand Duke of Tuscany (1642-1723).

He pointedly ignored the *nosferatu* in front of him, too absorbed in his work to realize how close he was to death.

"Ik neem er nota van dat je de pigmentatie van blauw of groen in je werk niet gebruikt," said Dracula, *I take note that you do not use the pigmentation of blue or green in your work.*

It was a rare statement from the vampire, a rarity.

A compliment.

The painter did not care.

"Je zult me niet vertellen hoe je moet schilderen, en ik zal je niet vertellen hoe je moet verkrachten, plunderen en corrumperen," he said as he took a step back to see how the piece would look, how it would come together from afar. *You will not tell me how to paint, and I will not tell you how to rape, pillage and corrupt.*

"Je gebrek aan angst verbaast me," snapped Dracula. *Your lack of fear surprises me.*

The painter moved to one side of the piece, observed it, then to the other side, concentrating on the overall effect, mesmerized in his own work. "Uw aanwezigheid walgen me, maar elke schilder moet zijn opdrachtgevers." *Your very presence revolts me, but every painter needs his patrons.*

"Ik zal je schilderij ophangen in mijn kasteel, tussen alle andere vergeetbare kunstwerken van anonieme kunstenaars die ik in de loop van de tijd heb verzameld," said Dracula, trying to goad the man into insult. *I will hang your painting in my castle, among all of the other forgettable works of art from anonymous artists that I have collected over time.*

Shaking his head and seeing Dracula's attempt coming from far away, the old man looked at Dracula with a glint in his eyes and said, "Je zult op een dag opscheppen over mijn schilderij aan vreemden die voor altijd mijn naam zullen kennen." *You will one day boast of my painting to strangers who will forever know my name.*

Reaching for the stool that he had used, the artist moved it out of the way as Dracula wondered, "Ik kon bloeden je droog het moment dat je klaar bent." *I could bleed you dry the moment you finish.*

The old man then reached to his easel and found his favorite cloth rag. He took the canvas, which was framed with wood, out from the easel and ran the rag around the outer edge of the painting to pick up any stray remnants of paint. He looked at Dracula as he did so, almost amused as he said, "Oude mannen hebben niets te vrezen, omdat ze weten dat de dood is bijna op hen." *Old men do not fear anything, since they know death is nearly upon them.*

Dracula stood, knowing the portrait was now finished, the moment of their arrangement at hand.

He glared at the old man, pointed a taloned finger and snarled, "Rembrandt Harmenszoon van Rijn, zul je sterven als een varken, en u zal worden begraven in een onschadelijke gemeenschappelijk graf samen met alle van de unmemorable boeren waarmee je verwant zijn." *Rembrandt Harmenszoon van Rijn, you will die as a pig[310], and you will be buried in an innocuous communal grave along with all of the unmemorable peasants with which you are kin.*

Rembrandt shrugged, looked Dracula square in the eye and said, "Eén ding is verzekerd. Als je sterft, Dracula van de Karpaten, sterf je als een hond zoals alle tirannen. Ik zal sterven als een varken en als een arme man, maar met alle vreugde die je nooit hebt of ooit zult beleven. Wanneer je op het punt staat om je laatste adem te halen, doe me dan de hoffelijkheid om te onthouden dat deze dwaze handwerksman je dit heeft uitgelegd." *One thing is assured. When you die, Dracula of the Carpathians, you will die as a dog like all tyrants. I will die as a pig and as a poor man, but with all of the joy that you have never nor will ever know. When you are about to breathe your last, do me the courtesy of remembering that this foolish artisan explained this to you.*

---

[310] Rembrandt would indeed die a few days later, on October 4, 1669, and would be buried in a communal grave for the poor. His bones would be disinterred and lost in time.

Rembrandt stood, a gnarled man in his dying days, unafraid of the monster before him. For a moment he was in his magnificent youth in one of his earliest self-portraits, the toast of the artistic world and the entirety of Europe. In a few bold steps, he walked over to the vampire and handed him the canvas. "Hier is je portret. Let op dat de olie een paar dagen nat zal zijn. Ik heb nog maar een paar dagen te leven en ik nodig je uit om op mijn lijk te dansen als ik eenmaal ben geslaagd. Nu laat dan of wees er snel bij met mijn dood." *Here is your portrait. Mind that the oil will be wet for a few days. I have but a few days more to live, and I invite you to dance upon my corpse once I have passed. Now please leave or be quick with my death.*

Dracula looked at Rembrandt, worn, spent and broken, contemplated ripping the old man's head from his body in one blow, then took his painting and held it the way a mother holds her newborn.

"Mijn betaling alstublieft," said Rembrandt. *My payment please.*

The men looked at each other.

Artist at tyrant.

Son of Satan at biblical painter.

The moment was fertile with tension.

"Je hebt een van mijn betere werken. Ik verdien een woord van dank voor mijn inzet," said Rembrandt at last. *You hold one of my better works. I deserve a word of thanks for my effort.*

Careful not to disturb the oil paint, Dracula took a step back into the shadows, he became one with the pitch, still there, only a set of glowing crimson eyes in the dark.

Out of the dark was tossed a small cloth bag. It landed on the workbench nearest to one of the greatest portraiture artists who has ever lived.

"Parels voor de zwijnen[311]," rumbled the vampire. *Pearls before swine.*

One moment the animal eyes glowed in the darkness.

And in the next, they were gone.

Melted into the night.

---

[311] Biblical quotation, Matthew 7:6. "Do not give what is holy to the dogs; nor cast your **pearls before swine**, lest they trample them under their feet, and turn and tear you in pieces." Given during Jesus' Sermon on the Mount.

A NOTE FROM THE AUTHOR

It was my sincere effort to tell this story utilizing as many languages as possible within the context of the story's setting. For the older languages, specifically Latin, I arranged the syntax to match the English translation word for word instead of the entire phrase. Most of the other sentences were as translated using internet search and translation engines. I firmly believe in globalization and the inherent beauty of all of the world's cultures and hope that, while I have tried to depict the languages in the story as accurately as possible, those who are easily more familiar with the language of their ancestors would forgive any mistakes on my part in exchange for my eagerness to show that this world is full of one people, not many separate tribes. It is my hope that a young person in one corner of the world would read my fragile attempts at other languages and find interest enough to perhaps even explore that other place in the world one day. If so, then my silly ghost story, based on an amazing work of literature, which I recommend far more than the feeble book you hold in your hands, will have served its purpose.

ABOUT THE AUTHOR

Ricardo Delgado is an American artist/writer of Costa Rican descent. He was born in Los Angeles, California and is a graduate of the prestigious Art Center College of Design in Pasadena, where he presently teaches..

As a film Illustrator, Ricardo has helped design such live-action films as *Apollo 13, Men in Black, Star Trek: First Contact, Jurassic Park 3, The Matrix Reloaded* and *Revolution*. In Animation, Ricardo has designed for animated features like Disney's *Atlantis-The Lost Empire, Emperor's New Groove*, Pixar's *The Incredibles, Wall-e*, Dreamworks' *How to Train your Pet Dragon* as well as TV shows like Nickelodeon's *Avatar-The Last Airbender* and Disney's *Tron-Uprising*.

Ricardo has worked with directors such as Steven Spielberg, Ron Howard, James Cameron, John Landis, Ron Clements and John Musker as well as the Wachowski siblings. Among Ricardo's career titles are Comic Book Creator, Novelist, Director, Production Designer, Art Director, Concept Artist, Background Designer, Prop designer, Character Designer and Storyboard Artist.

Ricardo's dinosaur comic book series, *Age of Reptiles*, for Dark Horse Comics, has been published all over the world for a quarter of a century. His first two novels are the children's novella *Sam Specter and the Book of Spells* and the hard-boiled science fiction noir *Warhead*. He is a family man who enjoys a quiet life, the outdoors, ancient architecture, old libraries, monster movies, sports, people who speak other languages and a well-done cheeseburger.

THE GREAT BAT
DRAWLA
@RDELGADO
08.18

THE DRACULA WOLF
DRAWLA
@RDELGADO
08.18

THE DRACULA
DRAGON
TXAWA
©RDELGADO
05.20

THE DRAGUA RAT
DRAGUA
@RDELGADO
08.18

THE
UNHOLY
MOTHER
TXAWN
@RDELGADO
10.19

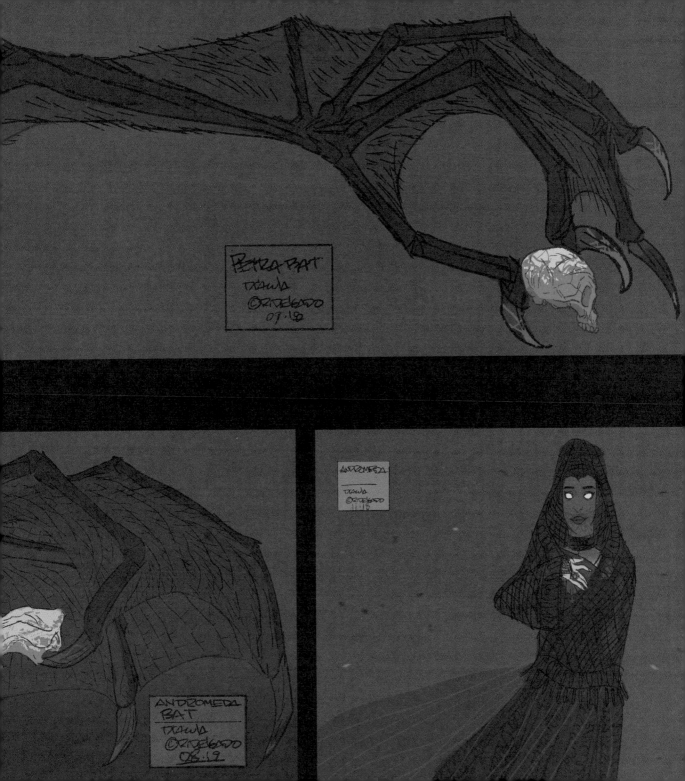

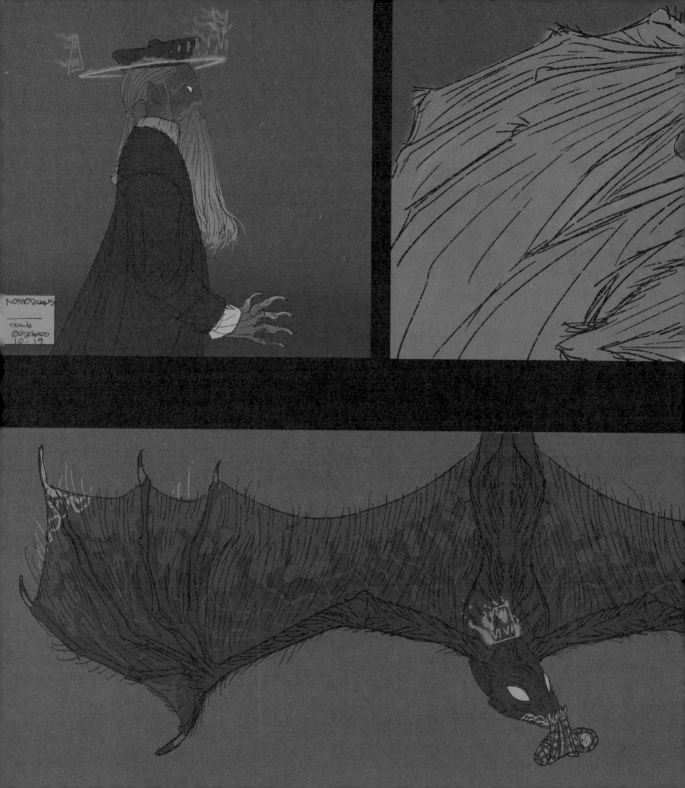

THE
NOSTRADAMUS
BAT
TXAWA
@RXDELGADO
01.19

THE VENUS
BAT
TXAWA
@RXDELGADO
09.18

VENUS
TXAWA
@RXDELGADO
11.18

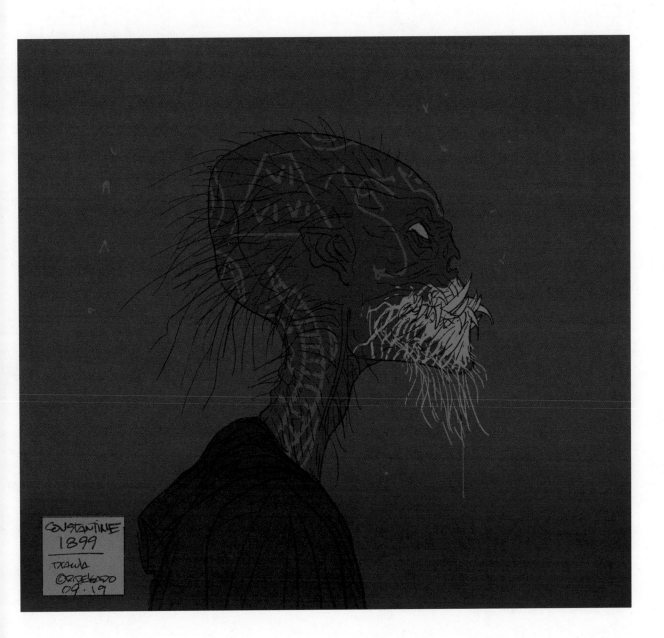